Rory Clements

Rory Clements lives in a seventeenth-century farmhouse in
Norfolk and is married to the artist Naomi Clements-Wright.
As well as writing, he enjoys village life and a game of tennis
with friends. There are five books in the *John Shakespeare* series
of Elizabethan mysteries, all available from
Hodder & Stoughton.

Praise for the John Shakespeare novels

'Enjoyable, bloody and brutish' *Guardian*

'Sixteenth-century London comes alive in all its tawdriness'
Daily Mail

'A world spiced with delicious characters . . . The novel wears its
historical learning lightly, and Clements seasons it with romance
and humour' *Mail on Sunday*

'Beautifully done . . . alive and tremendously engrossing'
Daily Telegraph *****

'A cracking plot full of twists right up to the last minute. I look
forward to the next' *Sunday Express*

'Colourful . . . exciting . . . vivid' *Sunday Telegraph*

'Sharp and challenging, this book is missed at one's peril'
Oxford Times

D0259695

Also by Rory Clements

Martyr
Revenger
Prince
Traitor

The Heretics

RORY CLEMENTS

HODDER

First published in Great Britain in 2013 by John Murray (Publishers)
An Hachette UK company

First published in paperback in 2014

1

Copyright © Rory Clements 2013

Maps drawn by Rosie Collins

A CIP catalogue record for this title is available from the British Library

ISBN: 978 1 848 54436 9

Printed and bound by Clays Ltd, St Ives plc

Hodder & Stoughton policy is to use papers that are natural, renewable and recyclable products
and made from wood grown in sustainable forests. The logging and manufacturing processes are
expected to conform to the environmental regulations of the country of origin.

Hodder & Stoughton Ltd
338 Euston Road
London NW1 3BH

www.hodder.co.uk

For Brian,
everyone needs a brother

Wisbech

London

Penzance

Port-Louis/Blavet

Bay
of
Biscay

S p a i n

Portugal

Salamanca

Escorial Palace
Madrid

Toledo

Guadalquivir River

Seville
Sanlúcar de Barrameda
Cadiz

N

Miles
0   100   200   300

Chapter 1

THE KNOCK AT the door came as John Shakespeare unhooked his sword belt from a nail in the wall. 'Come in,' he said.

His assistant Boltfoot Cooper limped into the comfortable library of his master's house in Dowgate, close by the river in the city of London, and bowed. 'You have a visitor, master.'

'Not now. I am expected elsewhere.' He began buckling his belt. 'Pass me my cloak, Boltfoot.'

Boltfoot picked up the old black bear fur from the coffer where it had been flung and held it up for Shakespeare to pull about his shoulders.

'It is a man named Garrick Loake, sir. He begs you to spare him two minutes. He says he has most urgent business, of great import to the safety of the realm.'

'Who is he?'

Boltfoot's coarse seafarer's brow twisted in a frown. 'I know not, but from the varied colours of his attire, I might guess him to be a player or a poet. He did mention that your brother William recommended him to come to you.'

Shakespeare sighed. 'Send him in. Tell him he has two minutes, no more.'

*

Loake did indeed wear colourful clothes. They were in the Italian style, including a hat with an enormous feather. Boltfoot was right: he could not be anything but a player.

'Mr Loake? Is it true that my brother sent you?'

Loake bowed with a dramatic flourish. 'He did, Mr Shakespeare. And I am most honoured to make your acquaintance for I have heard a great deal of your bold exploits.'

'*Why* did Will send you here?'

'I took the liberty of confiding in him that I had concerns about a certain matter and he said straightway that you were the man to talk with.'

'Mr Loake, I have little time to spare you. Perhaps you would return tomorrow when I am less pressed.'

'I beg you to listen for a brief moment. I know what a busy man you are.'

Shakespeare remained standing. The library fire was blazing away and soon he would overheat in this fur. But he kept the cloak on. He did not wish to give this man the impression that he would stay and talk with him.

'I know your distinguished brother from the Theatre, Mr Burbage's fine playhouse in Shoreditch,' Loake continued. 'If you are as straight dealing as he is, then I am certain I can trust you.'

Shakespeare, a tall man with long hair, waited, merely smiling. His presence alone was often enough to lure men into revealing their secrets.

'I sometimes play there myself,' Loake went on. 'I am not a member of the company, but there is usually work for me as a hired man in one capacity or another. Yesterday, I was working with the costumes.' He twirled to display his brilliant outfit. 'I borrowed this, Mr Shakespeare. It is Capulet's apparel. Do you not think it becoming? Am I not a noble Veronese gentleman?'

'The certain matter, Mr Loake—'

'Forgive me, I shall come to that straightway. I have a secret to impart, you see. A secret involving papist intrigue. I believe young Cecil will pay very well for such intelligence.'

'You mean Sir Robert Cecil.' Shakespeare was not about to let his chief man be referred to as 'Young Cecil' by a stranger.

'Indeed, not old Burghley. It is the young Caesar who runs the Privy Council these days, is it not? His father holds the purse-strings, but the boy spends the gold. Your brother mentioned that you might have a pathway to that purse.'

Shakespeare was losing patience. He could not imagine that Will had said anything of the sort. 'Tell me the matter, Mr Loake. And do not refer to Sir Robert Cecil as *the boy*.'

'My information is worth twenty sovereigns, I am certain of it. Twenty gold sovereigns.'

'I fear you are ill informed.' The figure was laughable. There were too many snouts in the trough already. 'Very little is worth even twenty shillings. Twenty sovereigns is out of the question.'

'Well, that is my price. I have great need of gold, and I need it in haste, which is why I have come to you. I cannot go a penny below my asking price.'

Shakespeare stepped away from the oppressive heat of the fire and moved towards the door. 'Tell me what you know. And be quick about it.'

'What I know,' Loake said, 'is that there is a most foul conspiracy unfolding. It wafts from the papist fastness of eastern England, gathers force in the seminaries of Spain, but it will blow into a tempest here.' He lowered his voice for dramatic effect. 'A conspiracy the like of which England has never seen.'

'How do you know this?'

'It is my business to listen well, for I sometimes hold the book and prompt the players.'

'Names,' said Shakespeare wearily. 'Give me names. What manner of plot is this? Tell me the circumstance.'

'I will, Mr Shakespeare, when you give me twenty sovereigns. For the present, I must hold my peace, for if I say more, then you will know as much as I do, and I will have no power to bargain.'

Shakespeare suddenly caught a whiff of sweat. This man was scared and desperate. 'You are wasting my time. Say what you know.'

Loake put up his right hand, which had a ring on each finger. It shook. 'I will tell you one thing, one thing only. The seminary involved is the College of St Gregory in Seville.'

'The English college of Jesuits?'

'The very same. So you will tell young Cecil to give me a purse of twenty gold sovereigns, as agreed?'

Shakespeare laughed. 'Mr Loake, I have agreed nothing. Now I must go. If you have something to tell me, then return in the morning.' He waved a hand in dismissal.

Many men came to Shakespeare's door, scratching like curs for coins in return for information; at times of want it was a daily occurrence. Most of the intelligence was worthless, scraps of tittle-tattle overheard in taverns and gaols. But it all had to be listened to and some of it, no more than a tiny portion, had to be investigated. There was something in the demeanour of this man that interested Shakespeare. He would like to see him again, to delve more deeply. But not now.

'Twenty, I must have twenty. Sovereigns.'

Despite himself, Shakespeare stayed. It was plain to him that Loake had no concept of how to conduct a negotiation; no idea that you must demand a high price so you can meet somewhere in the middle.

'Even if we could agree a figure, I would need to seek authorisation for the payment, and that would be impossible without first knowing the details of your intelligence. Trust is required on both sides in such a transaction. I promise you this: if you tell me a secret as valuable as you claim, then I shall obtain up to five pounds on your behalf. Is that not fair dealing, Mr Loake?'

'I cannot go so low.'

Shakespeare rested his hand on the hilt of his sword as if to underline who held the power here.

'You must bear in mind, Mr Loake, that you have now informed me that you have knowledge of some treachery directed at this realm. If you do not tell me all you know, then you will be laying yourself open to a charge that you are an accessory to that treason.'

Loake drew himself up to his full height, which was not great, and wiped a sleeve of gold and blue across his sweat-glistening brow and prominent nose. 'Did your brother then lie when he said you were to be trusted?'

Shakespeare shook his head. 'I will not listen to insults, Mr Loake.'

Should he have Boltfoot take the man to Bridewell or the Fleet prison for the night? He rejected the notion; it would be a betrayal of his brother.

'Come back when you have collected your wits. I may have an offer for you if you tell me enough of interest. Be here half an hour after first light and I will see you.'

Chapter 2

It was dusk by the time Shakespeare got to Newgate prison. He came in secret, wearing his hat low over his forehead, his body swathed in black fur, concealing his identity from the long lines of curious onlookers already gathering for the next day's entertainment. The gloom was lit by a dozen bonfires and blazing cressets. Makeshift stalls had been put up to sell food and ale to those who would camp out here in this long, cold night to ensure the best view in the morning. Some among the waiting crowds stared at Shakespeare, but he ignored their insolent gaze and walked on with purpose.

He stopped at the main entrance beside the gate in the city wall. The road beneath his feet was cobbled and slippery; the gaol, towering above him, rose five storeys high into the darkening London sky. The last of the day's carts and drays clattered through the archway into the city. A flock of geese, driven by a man in a smock, waddled in to meet their fate. Shakespeare hammered with the pommel of his dagger on the gaol's heavy oak door. The head keeper, who had been waiting, opened it to him, welcoming his visitor with a bow and a sweep of the arm. The ring of keys that hung from his broad oxhide belt jangled as he ushered Shakespeare inside.

'How is he faring, Mr Keeper?'

'He does well, master. Never have I met so rare a man.'

Shakespeare turned and pushed back his hat to look into the keeper's eyes, gratified by what he saw there: honesty and genuine affection. He was not surprised; the condemned prisoner had that effect on many people. Shakespeare held the keeper's gaze. 'Where is he? In Limbo?'

The keeper nodded, a pained expression curling his lips. Limbo was a dark pit in the lower reaches of the ancient gaol, lacking light and air, where the condemned prepared themselves for the hangman. Its meagre bedding of straw was clogged with the ordure of frightened men.

'But at least he is alone there, master. No other felons await death.'

'Bring him to an upper cell. Let him breathe before he dies.'

'Mr Topcliffe commanded me, master—'

'Damn, Mr Topcliffe. I am here under orders from Sir Robert Cecil. Bring the prisoner up.'

The keeper hesitated, but then uttered some sort of grunt and shuffled off into the rank depths of the gaol. Shakespeare pulled his hat back over his brow and waited.

Within a minute, the keeper returned. 'I have ordered him brought to a cell on the second floor. I will take you there now. You will not be disturbed.'

The single window was barred by a grating of iron rods, embedded into the stone walls. It was a small aperture, scarcely big enough to admit the last of the day's light. The cell was clean and the cold air as fresh as could be hoped for in such a dungeon.

Shakespeare had not seen Father Robert Southwell in eight years and the passage of time had not treated him well. The years of solitary confinement in the Tower and episodes of torture at the hands of Richard Topcliffe had broken his body. His once serene face was now gaunt and his slender back bent, yet his eyes shone in the grey light. It seemed to Shakespeare that he had the exquisite fragility of church glass.

Southwell, his palms together in prayer, sank to his knees at the sight of his visitor, but Shakespeare raised him to his feet and clasped his hands. He turned to the gaoler, still hovering by the iron-strapped door. 'Bring us a flagon of good wine, Mr Keeper.' He dug fingers in his purse and pulled out a coin. 'That will pay for it.'

The keeper bowed and departed, leaving the door open.

'I could overpower you, Mr Shakespeare, and make my escape.'

Shakespeare smiled at the sad jest. Southwell would be hard pressed to do battle with a kitten.

'Shall we sit down, Father?'

There was a table and three stools, but the condemned Jesuit shook his head and continued to stand. His breathing was fast. Thin trails of vapour shot from his mouth and nose and vanished in the cold air. 'There is time enough for these bones to rest.'

'Are you being treated well?'

'I count the keeper as my friend. Many good people have sent in offerings of food and he has brought it to me, along with their messages of support. I never ate so well in the Tower as I do here.'

'Well, that is something at least.'

'Their generosity of spirit gladdens my heart, Mr Shakespeare. And on the matter of kindness, will you not tell me of your beloved wife, Catherine? You have a child, I believe.'

Shakespeare stiffened. Long before he had met Catherine in the year of eighty-seven, she had been a friend of Southwell and had received the sacraments from him. But now Catherine lay in her grave.

Southwell saw his pain. 'I am sorry. I see I intrude on some grief. Is she with God?'

'I must pray that she is.'

'Forgive me, I had not heard of your great loss, Mr Shakespeare. In the Tower, I heard nothing of the world beyond my four walls. I loved Catherine as a daughter or sister. I will pray for you both . . . and the child.'

'The child is well. She is called Mary. Catherine did not suffer . . .'

Shakespeare's voice broke and he shuddered, for the word resonated icily in this room. *Suffer.* He knew what agonies Southwell would have to suffer on the morrow. Convicted of treason at the court of Queen's Bench this day, he would be collected from his cell at dawn and dragged on a hurdle along the jarring road to Tyburn. There he would be hanged in front of a crowd of thousands, then cut down while he lived so that the butchers could tear his belly open and rip out his entrails to burn before his eyes. And at last, he would be quartered and beheaded.

Southwell noticed his visitor's unease. 'I think you are right, Mr Shakespeare. I will sit down. Come, sit with me. There are things I must tell you, though I am sure you are a busy man. Does Mr Cecil know you are here?'

'Yes, Sir Robert knows.'

'Ah – so he has been knighted. You see, I hear nothing. Well, I am sure it is deserved. He is my cousin, you know.'

'Yes, I know that. And I know that he admires your courage, if not your religion. And I can tell you, in confidence, that the Queen also knows I am here. She wishes to be told the contents of your heart. She wishes to know why one so holy and poetical should strive to bring about the destruction of her estate.'

Southwell frowned, as if he did not comprehend the question. 'I fear she has been fed falsehoods. I never meant the destruction of Her Majesty, nor any harm to England. I sought nothing but the eternal good of souls, including hers. Even now I call on the Lord God to enlighten her, and her Council, and not to hold them guilty for my death.'

'But your Church excommunicated her. The Jesuits support invasion by Spain—'

'Many errors have been made on all sides, Mr Shakespeare. You may tell Her Royal Majesty that I honour her as my sovereign lady. I have prayed for her daily.'

'I will tell her. Is that why you asked me to come here, Father?'

The keeper arrived with the wine and two goblets. Setting a tallow rushlight on the table between Shakespeare and the condemned man, he bowed and backed away to the door, without a word. Again, he left the door open. Shakespeare poured the wine.

'He watches and listens, Mr Shakespeare,' Southwell said quietly. 'He fears I will take my own life. He has been ordered to keep me alive so that my death is witnessed as a warning to others.' Southwell reached out and grasped Shakespeare's arm in his thin fingers. 'Did you ever hear of a Catholic priest that hurt himself so? Why should we add the destruction of our souls to the demise of our bodies?'

Shakespeare understood. He sipped his wine and waited.

'And so to your question. I asked for you, Mr Shakespeare, because there is something I must beg of you. One favour. If you will do this one thing for me, then I may go to my death in peace in the hope that I will be saved by the Passion of our Lord, Jesus Christ.'

'Then you had better tell me what it is, Father.'

The priest sighed, closed his eyes for a moment, then spoke, little more than a whisper. 'There is a girl, Mr Shakespeare. A girl named Thomasyn Jade. I want you to find her.'

Shakespeare got up and walked to the door. A figure shrank

back into the passageway beyond. Shakespeare shut the door, then returned to sit at the table.

'This harks back nine years to the dangerous days of summer in eighty-six,' Southwell said, his voice still low. 'It can be no secret to you that I was newly arrived in England, for I know that you were then working for Mr Secretary Walsingham, and his spies had told him of my coming.'

Shakespeare nodded. He recalled all too well those feverish, fearful days and weeks. It was the time of the Babington plot that had led to the downfall of Mary, Queen of Scots, and brought so many foolish young Catholic men to the scaffold, condemned for plotting to assassinate Elizabeth and put Mary on her throne.

'Within a month of my arrival the so-called plotters and others had been rounded up. Some were racked, many were executed. Among those held was Father William Weston of the Society of Jesus.'

'I know all this.'

London had been a cacophonous circle of the inferno. The bells of the city churches pealed all day long and into the night; the streets were ablaze with fires celebrating that the plot had been uncovered and foiled. And on the river, an endless procession of captured conspirators and priests was carried upstream, bound hand and foot, from the baleful Tower to the courts at Westminster, and then drawn to the place of execution. It had seemed as though the slaughter would never abate.

'Indeed, Mr Shakespeare. And I am sure, too, that you will know of the other dark events that occurred in those months, when certain Catholic priests carried out exorcisms on unfortunate souls possessed by demons.'

Shakespeare's mouth turned down in distaste. It had been a disgusting affair. Young women and men had been held for days and weeks on end, being subjected to the most repulsive treatment by a group of priests and their acolytes, all in the name of ridding them of supposed demons. Many who had been sympathetic to the popish cause had been turned against it by the whole foul story.

'Yes, I remember it, Father Robert, for I spoke with Weston himself, but I believe the practice stopped at about the time of your arrival in England.'

The priest's eyes were downcast. His fine features brought to mind the name he had been given by the townsfolk of Douai in Flanders when he had attended the English College there as a young man: *the beautiful English youth*. That youth was now long gone, worn away by pain and deprivation, yet Shakespeare could still see the strange, troubling beauty in his soul.

'Yes, the exorcisms were halted. But much damage had already been done, and not just to the Catholic cause. The real victims, I fear, were some of those whom the priests were trying to help.'

'Was Thomasyn Jade one of them?'

'She was. It is no secret now that I met my Jesuit brother William Weston soon after my arrival and not long before his arrest. I did not know it at first, but it seems he was the prime mover of these exorcism rites. We travelled together to a house in Buckinghamshire – I will not tell you more than that – to confer and rest. We stayed there a week. During that time, a girl of seventeen or eighteen – Thomasyn – was brought to us by certain priests to be rid of devils. She had already undergone many more such ordeals at Denham House, near by, which, as you must know, was the centre of these goings-on.

'I watched in horror as the ritual was played out. She was stuck with pins to catch the devils beneath her skin and she was made to drink concoctions of herbs. The holy thumb of the martyr Campion was thrust in her mouth. Brimstone was burnt beneath her nose so that I believed she would choke to death. I was affronted, Mr Shakespeare, for I saw that those who did these things were in mortal error. Those who witnessed the events were struck with such fear that they quaked and trembled and wept most bitterly. Within a short while, I brought the ceremony to a halt and, though Father Weston was my superior, I advised him that he would do well never to partake in such things again.'

Shakespeare was surprised to hear Southwell voice such open criticism of a fellow of the same order.

The priest waved his hand. 'Do not misunderstand me. I have nothing but admiration for the work and ministry of Father Weston. He is a saintly man. Perhaps too saintly sometimes, too unworldly. He did what he did out of fine motives, trying to save souls. But he was misguided in subscribing to the rite of exorcism, nor am I alone among the Catholic fraternity in thinking this way. I have sometimes wondered since whether the simple fact of his failing eyesight might have made him easily deluded by others less honest. I do not believe he saw evil spirits under the girl's skin, nor do I believe he truly saw them coming from her mouth and . . .' He hesitated, scarce able to say the shameful words. 'And from her privy parts. But *he* believed he did.'

'Why do you want me to find the girl?'

'Because she was ill used by us. When she came to the house, she was shaking with fear; she was halfway mad with frenzy and weeping. I should never have allowed the exorcism to proceed as far as it did.'

'And what became of her at the end of the day's torments?'

'She was given cordials and food, and I spoke soothing words to her. I tried to discover more about her, but she could not speak. I tried to pray with her, but she became yet more distressed. I was at a loss. I did not know what to do for her. With five sisters of my own, I understand women's ways, but I am aware that the years among men at the Society colleges have made me less easy in their company. Thomasyn could not stay at that house and I could not take her with me. Instead she was taken away by the priests who had brought her, back to the house near by whence she had come.'

'Denham House?'

'Indeed.'

Shakespeare gave a wry smile. He had heard much about Denham House, a putrid place, a dark hole of corruption and wickedness.

'I fear I did not do well by her, Mr Shakespeare. Three weeks later the priests who housed her were themselves arrested, as was Father Weston. Thomasyn Jade was taken away by the pursuivants, but her story reached certain courtiers and she was soon freed into the care of a great Protestant lady, the Countess of Kent. It was hoped that she would undo the priests' efforts to reconcile the wretched girl to the Church of Rome, and take her back to Protestantism. But within a few days I heard that she had disappeared. I prayed for her every day and worried for her, for she was an afflicted young woman and in need of proper care and spiritual nourishment. I sought her as best I could, but in the year of ninety-two, as you know, I was myself arrested. I have heard nothing of her since. Her memory haunts me, and I cannot go easily to my death.'

'And if I find her?'

'My family and friends have set aside money on her behalf. They will be as godparents to her and she will be well cared for. There is nothing sinister, no more exorcisms. Nor will they seek to influence her choice of faith. I ask only that you find her . . . if she is alive.'

'Why should I do this for you, Father Southwell? You came to England as a traitor. Since then you have longed for martyrdom. You must see that you are my enemy.'

Robert Southwell crossed himself. 'You know that is not so, Mr Shakespeare.'

It was true. They were not enemies. And while Shakespeare could never comprehend Southwell's quest for death, nor like the way he held to the superstitions of Rome, he admired his courage, his piety and his poetry. If it was true, as the English state insisted, that some Jesuits contrived the death of princes, then Southwell was not one of them. Either way, though, he was about to have his martyrdom.

Shakespeare nodded slowly. This man had once risked life and liberty to help him; he could not refuse him now. 'I will do what I can, Father. You had better tell me every detail you know.'

Just over a mile north-east of Newgate, near Bishopsgate, Garrick Loake sat alone in an alehouse booth. He had downed four pints of strong beer and was beginning to feel hazy. Yet he was not drunk, not enough to ignore the uncomfortable feeling that his meeting with John Shakespeare had gone badly. Would it go any better on the morrow? A fresh tankard was slopped down in front of him. He paid the maid a penny, then picked up the vessel and drank deeply.

The problem was there was no going back now. He had told Shakespeare too much to shirk their next meeting, and so he would be at his house in the morning. What about tonight, though? He couldn't go home; it wasn't safe there. Not now. He looked around at the other drinkers in the taproom. Every man seemed a threat.

He fished out his purse and saw that his hand was shaking. Counting the meagre contents, he gauged that if he drank no more, there might just be enough for a room for the night at one of the cheaper inns. And he would say a prayer that Mr Shakespeare would save his skin.

Chapter 3

IT WAS ALMOST eleven o'clock when Shakespeare reined in at the brick-built gatehouse facing the green on the north side of Richmond Palace. In the distance, way beyond the outer wall, lights flickered behind a multitude of windows in the fourteen towers of the royal lodgings, clustered around the inner quad. Shakespeare patted the horse's neck. It had been a hard ride from Newgate along eleven miles of treacherous roads.

A squad of six halberdiers approached and barred his way. He showed them his papers and one of them disappeared beneath the archway into the echoing spaces of the outer courtyard.

Soon, an elegant, white-bearded man appeared, attired in black except for a crisp white falling band about his neck, and carrying a lantern. Shakespeare nodded in recognition; it was Clarkson, most trusted retainer to Sir Robert Cecil.

'Mr Shakespeare, sir, you are expected straightway.'

Clarkson held the lantern forward and studied the new-comer's mud-and-sweat-stained fur cloak, hesitating, as though worried that such poor clothes would not be acceptable in the royal chambers. Finally he dismissed his concerns. 'Please dismount and follow me. The guard will take your horse to the stables.'

Cecil, who was waiting in his apartments, did not bother with pleasantries. 'Well, John, what did Mr Southwell have to say for himself?' His voice was brisk and businesslike. 'I take it he did not offer to recant and plead for his life?'

'No, he desires martyrdom.'

'Then we shall not disappoint him. Will he make a good death?'

'I believe he will. He shows no fear.'

Cecil seemed disappointed. 'Why did he wish to see you?'

'He asked me to tell Her Majesty that he is, and always has been, a loyal subject.'

Cecil emitted a dry laugh. 'Yet like all his order he condemns her as a heretic. And we well know what the Inquisition does to those they accuse of heresy. Anyway, how can we believe a single word he says, now we know of this Jesuit policy of equivocation? He might be saying out loud, "I am loyal to the Queen," while in his heart are the words, "*though my first loyalty is to the Pope and King Philip, and therefore I will conspire to kill her*".' Cecil almost spat the words. 'Is that all he said?'

'No. He wants me to find a girl. She is on his conscience. I think he fears he will not be saved if I do not do this.'

'What girl? I had thought him Christ's fellow.'

'Thomasyn Jade, one of those ill used by the exorcists back in the year of eighty-six.'

'Who is she?'

'I know nothing more than her name – and that she was brought to a house in Buckinghamshire to be exorcised by Weston in the few days that he was with Southwell. When Weston and others were arrested, she was taken by pursuivants. By then she was insane, which is why Southwell feels such guilt. He fears their rites helped destroy her mind. Lady Susan Bertie, the Countess of Kent, took the poor girl under her wing, but then she vanished.'

'God's wounds, Southwell and his like will have much to answer for at the day of judgment.'

Shakespeare did not point out that it was Southwell who had brought the girl's torments to a halt. He was aware that Cecil did not wish to hear a good word said about his condemned Jesuit cousin – not this night. Tonight Cecil had a heavy conscience of his own to contend with.

Southwell had become a forgotten man during his thirty months of isolation in the Tower and Gatehouse prisons, and he might have seen out his days in squalid obscurity, had he not drawn attention to himself by writing to Cecil's father, Lord Burghley, begging either to be allowed visits from friends or, failing that, to be brought to trial to answer charges. Old Burghley's response had been brutal and terse: *if Southwell is in such haste to be hanged, he shall quickly have his desire.*

It had been an uncharacteristically impatient and ill-judged response, but perhaps the Lord Treasurer's chronic gout had been the true irritant. Once the decision had been made, however, the younger Cecil had no choice but to issue the order for Southwell to be transferred from the Tower to Newgate to meet his fate.

The trial in the court of Queen's Bench, before Chief Justice Sir John Popham, had been swift and vicious. Attorney-General Edward Coke had led the prosecution, but it was the torturer Richard Topcliffe whose voice had been loudest. His ranting and raving had been such that Popham had had to silence him.

The worst part was the unexpected arrival of the one witness for the prosecution: Anne Bellamy, a young woman whom Southwell had once called friend and whose betrayal had led to his arrest. Now she was married to Topcliffe's young apprentice, Nicholas Jones. As she stepped up to the witness stand and testified how she had been taught to equivocate – to lie – by Southwell, he hung his head, crushed. How, shouted

Topcliffe, could any man or woman believe a word a priest said if he spread a doctrine of deliberate falsehood? The jury took fifteen minutes to find him guilty and sentence was pronounced.

Shakespeare knew, however, that the Queen and her Council were rattled. A week ago, Father Southwell had languished unremarked in his Tower cell. Now his name was on everyone's lips and the whole of London would be there to see him brought to his doom. It would be a huge spectacle and one that would not show the Queen or her government in a good light.

'Well, John, what was your reply to the Jesuit's request?'

'I said I would seek her, Sir Robert.'

'Did you so?'

Cecil stretched his aching neck. He was a man of small stature, with a slight hunch to his shoulder that he tried in vain to disguise by altering his posture. These days, he was increasingly exhausted by the burdens of state. His bed called out to him, but as long as the Queen was awake, so must he be.

'And do you think you have the time for such trifles? Do you not think we have rather more important matters to contend with?'

Shakespeare knew that he did. Listening to informants such as Garrick Loake, for instance. But he said nothing. He and Cecil both knew that his work as chief intelligencer left him little enough time to hunt for a maddened girl who could be anywhere, or dead. How could he find room for such a quest when the threats from the Escorial Palace of Spain and the Vatican increased day by day, when plots to kill the Queen were a constant threat, and when King Philip had made no secret of his plan to avenge the Armada defeat of the year eighty-eight by sending a yet greater war fleet against England?

'Well,' Cecil said, the curtness of his tone beginning to dissipate, 'Her Majesty awaits you, so let us hasten to the Privy

Chamber. The sooner this is done, the sooner I shall slumber. Come.'

With Clarkson and another retainer following them, the two men walked out into the inner quad. Shakespeare glanced up at the vast turreted confection that enclosed the night sky. They mounted a flight of steps to the hall, then traversed an ante-room, past the guards and into the Presence Chamber. A group of courtiers and petitioners watched them with tired, drunken eyes and, spotting Cecil, bowed low.

Cecil did not acknowledge them. He knew them well; they all had suits to press on him and he did not wish to hear them. He and Shakespeare marched on towards the Privy Chamber. Two liveried Lifeguards with raised swordpoints stood at the door but moved aside at the sight of Cecil.

Inside, the Queen was playing at cards with three of her gentlewomen beside a hearth of fragrant, slow-burning ash logs. She waved her companions away and they vanished like prodded ants into adjoining chambers.

Shakespeare and Cecil dropped to their knees, hung their heads low and waited. Without haste, Elizabeth approached them, holding out her white-gloved hand to Cecil. He kissed it. 'You are not a nighthawk, cousin,' she said, then touched his shoulder to raise him up.

'Indeed I am not, Your Majesty.'

She held her hand out to her other visitor. 'And you, Mr Shakespeare, we bid you welcome.'

Shakespeare, likewise, kissed her hand and then was raised up by her touch. He bowed again. 'Your memory is as faultless as your beauty, ma'am.'

They had not met in many years, but he knew well enough how she liked to be flattered, even by her most lowly subjects.

She recoiled slightly at the sight of his unkempt appearance. 'You look like a farmer, Mr Shakespeare.'

He bowed yet again. 'Yes, Your Majesty.'

'The hour is late and Sir Robert yearns for his bed, so tell me straightway about Mr Southwell. Is he still set on his course of self-destruction?'

'Yes, ma'am. But he wishes you to know that he honours you and considers himself a true and loyal subject. I believe he intends saying as much at Tyburn in the morning.'

'If he is my loyal subject, why did he come into England secretly, as a traitor?'

'He says he wished to bring comfort to those of his faith and meant no harm to you or your estate.'

Elizabeth tilted her head back, then looked at Cecil. 'What do you say to this, cousin?'

'He calls us heretics, ma'am. He would not defend you against the armies of the Pope. He is a traitor.'

'And yet . . .' She sighed, then looked again at Shakespeare. 'Please continue. I am sure you have more to tell me.'

He had half expected to find her in her nightgown and cap. But though it was late at night, the Queen was immaculate in a gown of gold threads and pearls. Her red wig was fixed as evenly as possible and her face was thick-coated with white powders. She would not let her guard down before any man, be it distinguished statesman or mere intelligencer. He had been expected.

Although he towered over her, he felt stiff and awkward under her falcon gaze. He repeated all that Southwell had told him about Thomasyn Jade. The Queen listened in silence until Shakespeare had ended his tale, then turned once more to Cecil.

'I believe I recall the story of this young woman. Cousin Susan was most distressed when she disappeared. I think we must find the girl. Is that asking too much?'

'No, ma'am. If she is there to be found, we will find her.

Mr Shakespeare will set one of his intelligencers on to the matter.'

'I had thought Mr Southwell had particularly asked for Mr Shakespeare. Should *he* not do the searching rather than some underling?'

'Mr Shakespeare is mighty occupied protecting the realm, ma'am. We have reason to fear conspiracies in the offing.'

A spark of irritation flickered in Elizabeth's bloodshot eye. 'Little man, we have retained the love of our people these thirty-six years of our reign by caring for the smallest and most humble as well as the great. If the people did not rest assured of our special love towards them, they would not readily yield such good obedience. There is none in the realm of greater importance to us at this time than this Thomasyn Jade. Is that plain?'

'It is, ma'am. And we shall keep you informed, as always, of Mr Shakespeare's progress in the matter.'

'And you, Mr Shakespeare. You will go to Tyburn on the morrow and ensure that Mr Southwell does not suffer unduly. You know what that means?'

Shakespeare bowed low. He knew what the Queen meant.

Chapter 4

SHAKESPEARE WAS EXHAUSTED. After leaving the Queen's presence, he rode back to London and slumped into his bed at Dowgate. But, unable to sleep, within two hours he was up and riding out to Tyburn with his assistant, Boltfoot Cooper, to ensure a position close to the scaffold.

The green at the execution site was already crowded long before dawn, which was the time that Robert Southwell would be taken from his cell at Newgate. Outside in the cold air, the horse would be waiting, harnessed to a hurdle of wood, on which the Jesuit would be tied, his head sloping down to the rear so that every jolt of the journey to death would bring agony to his back, neck and head.

And so the procession would begin, watched by crowds all along the way: across the dirty floodwaters of the Fleet, then uphill towards Holborn, through the fields of St Giles and on to the long, muddy highway that travellers took to Oxford. Southwell's journey would stop here, at Paddington Green.

A bellman rang out the hour. Six o'clock. Shakespeare knew that Southwell would not have slept.

'You know what to do, Boltfoot?'

'Yes, master.'

Shakespeare looked at his squat assistant and wondered about his terse, grunted reply. He was uncommonly abrupt this day, but perhaps he had reason to be; he was being asked to perform a task that no man could enjoy. Shakespeare considered explaining himself to Boltfoot, telling him why it would not be politic to do the deed himself, but he held his tongue. Boltfoot understood such things without need of explanation.

Shakespeare put a sixpence in his hand. 'Fetch us possets, Boltfoot. I saw a seller a little way off to the west.'

Boltfoot took the coin and limped off into the crowd to fetch the warming spiced drink of curdled milk and liquor. Anything to keep the chill at bay. Soon, he returned with the possets and they drank in silence. The morning was crisp and fresh. By now, the procession would be on its way.

The wait seemed interminable until, at last, a murmur arose in the crowd. The throng surged forward. Shakespeare sensed danger. There were screams and moans as men and women struggled to maintain their footing in the deadly crush. In the distance, Shakespeare saw the horse dragging Robert Southwell on the hurdle. It halted, unable to pass through the crowds. The sheriff ordered in a squadron of pikemen to clear a path, and the procession of death moved on.

Shakespeare was in the front rank, within a few yards of the scaffold, among the noblemen and city aldermen who had come to witness the traitor's execution. A few yards away, he recognised Lord Mountjoy. The Earl of Southampton was there, too. Shakespeare knew his open secret: like several other nobles, he was a crypto-Catholic. The whole court knew it, but nothing would ever be done about it. Common men and women might die for harbouring priests, but the earl could keep a dozen of them at Southampton House and never once have his peace disturbed by the dread knock of Topcliffe and his pursuivants.

The buzz and roar of the crowd grew louder. Someone

called out a paternoster. Shakespeare knew there would be seminary priests and Jesuits here in this press of bodies, all praying for Southwell's soul and, all the while, hoping to catch a thrown cap or a shred of clothing from the condemned man. The merest drop of spittle or blood could change a man's life. Henry Walpole had told his questioners that he had decided to become a Jesuit missionary after watching the execution in 1581 of Edmund Campion and being splashed with his blood. Now Walpole awaited his fate in the Tower, broken by Topcliffe's torture.

The hangman untied Southwell from the hurdle and hauled him up into the back of a cart. The Jesuit looked around at the ocean of expectant faces. His eyes met Shakespeare's, but then Southwell looked away. Was he searching for some face he knew, perhaps his father or a sister, or a fellow Jesuit?

Without ado, the hangman turned his attention to the condemned man's clothing and began to loosen the ties of his doublet.

'May I speak to the people?' Southwell said in a clear voice.

The hangman stopped his work and stepped back. 'Yes, speak if you will.'

The huge mass of people hushed. A baby cried and a dog barked, but no one said a word. Every eye with a view was trained on Robert Southwell.

A man shouted out: 'Hang him and to hell with him. The devil awaits the foul traitor.'

Shakespeare recognised the voice. It was Richard Topcliffe, standing at the far side of the scaffold by the cauldron into which the condemned man's bowels and heart would be tossed. Beside him stood several of his black-clad pursuivants. When the crowd hushed him, he spat into the ground.

Southwell ignored the interruption and began his speech. He had had many years to prepare these words. He told the crowd that he never intended harm to the Queen and that he had always prayed for her. But his message was not untrammelled, for he made clear that he prayed for her to be brought to the righteous path – the path of the Roman Church.

'And lastly, I commend into the hands of Almighty God my own poor soul. This is my death, my last farewell to this unfortunate life, and yet to me most happy and fortunate . . . I hope that in time to come it will be to my eternal glory.'

Topcliffe's voice raged out again. 'He has not begged pardon of the Queen! He has not begged pardon for his treasonous crimes!'

Southwell rocked back and forth. For a moment, Shakespeare thought he would crumple and faint, but he held firm. In a voice that seemed to say, *I am tired of this life, it is time to go*, he spoke yet again: 'If I have offended the Queen with my coming to England, I humbly desire her to forget it, and I accept this punishment for it most thankfully.'

And then he called on any Catholics present to pray with him, so that he might live and die a Catholic in the presence of members of his faith.

Topcliffe jumped up on to the scaffold and scowled out into the crowd. His hair was as white as the frost, but his eyes were hot with fury, daring any Catholic to defy him. He tapped his silver-tipped blackthorn cane on the wooden deck of the death place, looking for dissenters.

The hangman moved forward and removed Southwell's doublet, then pulled back the collar of his shirt. Without bidding, Southwell put his head into the noose. He called on the Mother of God.

'Blessed Mary, ever a virgin, and all you angels and saints assist me. *In manus tuas, Domine commendo spiritum meum . . .*'

There was no hood. Shakespeare saw no pain in his eyes, only an insistent love and a longing for death.

Topcliffe slapped his stick against the side of the cart and the butchers dragged it forward, leaving Southwell swinging and kicking at air. The only sound was the creaking of the rope and the breeze. Southwell hung there, choking, his neck unbroken. Topcliffe moved towards him, knife in hand to cut the rope and bring him, still alive, to the butchers' platform so that he might be forced to watch his own evisceration. But Boltfoot Cooper and Shakespeare were already there. Boltfoot clasped the dying man's body and clung to it, dragging it down to shorten his suffering by hastening death. Shakespeare stood in Topcliffe's path.

'Get out of my way, God damn you, Shakespeare, or I will slit you with this dagger.'

Now Lord Mountjoy was at Shakespeare's side, then they were joined by more noblemen, all standing firm against Topcliffe. A man from the crowd stepped forward and assisted Boltfoot in his act of mercy, choking the life out of Father Southwell until he hung lifeless in their arms. They let him go and he swung, unresisting, in the cold breeze. Quite dead.

Shakespeare stood back. 'He's all yours now, Topcliffe. He is gone way beyond your cruelty, I pray to a better place.'

He looked at the frothing torturer with incredulity. He knew he was cruel and brutal. What he had not understood was quite how deranged Topcliffe had become by the gallons of blood that had washed through his fingers. *This man should be locked away among the mad and the dangerous.*

Topcliffe cut the dead body from the hanging tree and brought it to the platform, where he attacked it with insane ferocity, slavering as he dragged out the entrails. He snatched the axe from the headsman and began chopping the flesh into quarters.

At last he held up the once-beautiful head and shouted, 'Here is the head of a traitor!'

The crowd was supposed to shout back, 'Traitor! Traitor!' But they remained silent. Only the wondering Lord Mountjoy had anything to say, bringing his mouth close to Shakespeare's ear so that no one else should hear.

'I cannot answer for the Jesuit's religion, Mr Shakespeare, but I wish to God that my soul may be with his.'

Jane Cooper held little John in her arms outside the old stone house in Fylpot Street. The boy was two now, and could walk, but he was sickly and weak. She looked down at him, listless in her arms, and mouthed some words of prayer.

Summoning up all her courage, she banged on the door. Boltfoot had forbidden her to come here, calling it a place of magic and necromancy, and declaring they should have none of it. Well, that was fine for him to say, but he had no ideas of his own how to help their son. Anyway, her friend Ellen Fowler had sworn that Dr Forman, who lived in this house, could cure any ill known to man.

'I don't know how he does it, Jane, honest I don't, but I promise you that he makes things right. *Whatever* ails you. I'd go to him with the pestilence if I had it, and I'd hope to be saved.'

Jane banged on the door again. A boy of about thirteen answered it and glared at her. 'He's busy. You'll have to come back.'

'When? When can he see me?'

The boy ran his nail-bitten fingers through his straggled hair, and then scratched the front of his grubby hose. 'When he's free.' He went to close the door, but Jane pushed forward.

'No. I've come this far. I want you to tell him I'm here. Then *he* can tell me to go away if he wishes.'

The apprentice spat into his hands and slicked the hair back from his forehead. 'Wait here. Don't come in. He don't like to be disturbed when he's about his business.'

Was there something lascivious about the way the boy studied her? She never even considered her looks these days. All her thoughts were for others: little John, of course; getting food to the table for the master and his children; keeping an eye out for the new girl, Ursula Dancer. Anyway, she had no looking glass. Boltfoot Cooper loved her but he would never tell her she was pretty or any such thing.

The apprentice wandered off upstairs, taking his time, glancing back. After a few minutes, he returned.

'He says he'll see you in a quarter-hour, when he's finished with Janey. He says you can come in, wait here in the hall.'

'Thank you.'

'I'm John Braddedge. You can tip me a farthing for my trouble.' He held out his hand.

'Maybe after I've seen Dr Forman. Not before.'

He nodded to a table by the window. 'Go over there then.'

She went and sat down. Baby John began to cry and she rocked him gently.

The Braddedge boy stood and watched. 'Shall I get him a beaker of milk?'

Jane shook her head. 'No, thank you.'

She heard footsteps on the stairs and looked up. A woman about her age was coming down, clutching the railing. Her head was bowed and Jane thought she might be crying. She stood up and went to her and asked if she could help.

The woman looked up; she wasn't crying, but nor did she look happy.

'Jane Cooper, meet Janey,' the apprentice said. He laughed, as though he had made some sort of jest.

Janey glared at him. 'Go and geld yourself with a blunt knife, Braddedge.'

From upstairs, there was a call. 'Boy! Come here!'

Braddedge slunk off up the stairs.

'Never mind him,' said Janey. 'He's as daft as a dawcock. Been with Dr Forman these six months and won't last another six.' She looked at the bundle in Jane's arms. 'You here about the child?'

'Yes . . . and other things.'

'What ails the mite?'

Jane shook her head and felt the prick of tears. She couldn't bear it if anything happened to him. The way things were going, she'd never have another baby.

Janey put an arm around her. She wasn't pretty and she had wary eyes, but Jane saw kindness there.

'I'm frightened, that's all. He won't eat, nor drink more than a thimble-full. He's wasting away. Just lies there, day by day. Boltfoot – that's my husband – says all will be well, but I know that he don't really think that. Dr Forman's my only hope . . .'

Janey peered into little John's face. 'He's a fair little thing, isn't he? Does he take after you or your man?'

Jane laughed. 'Me, God willing. His father looks like the stump of a tree. But, pray tell me, will Dr Forman help us?'

'Most like. He's a good man in his own way, but you be careful with him, Jane Cooper, because you're still a pretty enough lass and if you let him, he'll have his hand up your skirts and his prick out before he's asked you your name.'

Jane was shocked. But then she recalled the curious glint in Ellen Fowler's eye and remembered that what ailed Ellen most was the lack of a man in her bed.

'Mistress Cooper, he'll see you now.' The boy had reappeared on silent feet. He handed a package to Janey. 'And this is your philtre. He says you know all about it.'

Janey ignored the boy's begging palm and smiled at Jane. 'Just tell him to keep his dirty hands to himself and he'll leave you alone. Good fortune with the babe. I'm sure all will be well.'

Simon Forman sat at a table and wrote down the names of Jane, her husband and son, then began to ask her questions. How long had the child languished? Could she still produce milk of her own? When did she last have marital relations with her husband? Did either of them have the pox? Then he wrote down the date and hour of the babe's birth and her own, as far as she knew it.

Jane's hands were shaking. Dr Forman was a thickset, hairy man with a wiry beard that went from yellow to red. She was alarmed to discover that they were in his bedchamber. The canopied four-poster had rumpled sheets as though it had recently been occupied. Her eyes flicked from the strange man to the bed and back again.

And yet despite his alarming appearance, she gradually found herself at ease with him. Soon she was answering the most intimate questions about her monthly flowers and her bedtime activities, with and without Boltfoot, with complete honesty. These were not normally subjects she would discuss with her own mother or sisters, nor any other woman on earth – and certainly not with a man.

'Now hand me the boy.'

John was still whimpering. Jane put him in Simon Forman's hairy arms. He was very gentle, stroking the hair back from the boy's forehead with the tips of his fingers. John's crying subsided a little and he opened his eyes wide, fixing them on the stranger's face.

'Don't fret about the boy, Mistress Cooper. You have come here about another matter, have you not?'

Jane's face reddened. How did he *know* that? She nodded.

'Why not tell me? I may be able to help.'

She hesitated. He waited. At last she nodded and spoke what was on her mind. 'I want another baby, Dr Forman. I am scared I'll lose little John and never have another.'

'You won't lose little John, I promise you. I have often seen children in this poor way and I have never lost one. I shall give you a tincture of herbs for the boy. But it's *you* that I'm most worried for, Jane Cooper. Have you had many shifts?'

She closed her eyes and looked down. 'I have miscarried six,' she said quietly. 'Maybe seven. The last one just three months past.'

'Does your husband know?'

'He knows of the shifts, though not all of them. I cannot truly tell him all my fears. We lost our first at birth and I thought Boltfoot would die of torment. He blames himself, you see, because he is lame with a club-foot. He believes it is his bad blood that damages the unborn babes.'

'So you want me to help you bring a babe to term.' Forman spoke slowly. 'And are you presently with child?'

'No.'

'Well, the first thing I must do is cast your chart. It would help, too, if I could have the date and time and place of your husband's birth so that I may cast his, too.'

Forman smiled and handed the child back to his mother. He walked through to an adjoining room. Through the open door, Jane could see strange objects on shelves. Large glass jars and small vials, like those to be seen at the apothecary's shop. There were other curious things: rolled papers and parchments, books, something that looked like a dead animal or a demon. She averted her eyes. Her heart was rushing like the conduit.

Forman returned and handed her a twist of paper. 'Take this in the evening and again tomorrow morning, then return to me in four days. All will be well, Jane Cooper.'

Chapter 5

JOHN SHAKESPEARE SURPRISED himself. He was hungry. On the way back to London from Tyburn, he and Boltfoot stopped at a busy post inn, sat in a booth and tucked into sirloins of beef that overlapped their trenchers, with half a loaf each of manchet bread. They ate it all and downed quart tankards of strong beer.

They did not talk. What was there to say? Instead, they just ate, drank, pissed in the gutter outside, then remounted and rode for Dowgate. Their morning's work was done. As commanded by the Queen, they had ensured that Robert Southwell had not suffered unduly.

Back at Dowgate, Shakespeare asked whether he had had any visitors, but no one had called. He tried to shrug it off. So Garrick Loake was a time-waster. And yet there had been a quiet desperation about Mr Loake that worried him and he resolved to seek him out when time permitted. For now, he ordered a fresh horse saddled up, then went to his chamber to wash the grime and dust from his face and hands. Perhaps, too, he was trying to wash away the memory of the brutal, unnecessary death of a poet.

He found his daughter, Mary, and his adopted daughter, Grace, in the schoolroom with their tutor. Grace was growing into a fine girl. She was twelve years of age, tall like her brother,

Andrew, but slender. She held little Mary's hand and stroked her hair, as if she were the smaller girl's mother.

Shakespeare gazed on them for a few moments and said a silent prayer of thanks to God for this calm sanity and kindness at the centre of his life. Then he kissed them and left for his meeting with Cecil.

Cecil's mood had not improved. The Queen had kept him with her until the early hours and when, at last, he had been freed to go to bed, he had plainly not slept well. This morning he had risen with the dawn to ride for London.

'You will make the obvious inquiries, John,' he said to Shakespeare, waving him irritably to a chair. They were in the high-ceilinged meeting room of Sir Robert's small mansion in the Strand. 'Talk to the Countess of Kent, find the others who were subjected to these exorcism rituals, find any priests who were at Denham House. Go through it by rote. Take two days, no more. If you have not discovered the fate or where-abouts of this Thomasyn Jade within forty-eight hours, then you will say she is believed dead and the investigation will be forgotten. Dropped like a stone into a well, never to be seen or heard of again. Is that understood?'

Shakespeare nodded.

'And you, Frank.' Cecil turned to Francis Mills, the other senior member of his intelligence staff. 'Take a close look at this.' He slid a paper across the table. 'I do not pretend to understand what this is about, but, in John's absence, you will put your mind to it. Is that understood?'

Mills took the paper. Shakespeare watched the tall, hunched figure as he read the document. Preoccupied by his wife's infidelity, Mills seemed thinner and more haunted than ever. Word had it that his neighbours had taken to jeering at him. Cuckold's horns had been nailed up above his front door; Mills had not even had the energy to tear them down.

'That letter was seized by a searcher at Gravesend,' Cecil said. 'It was among the belongings of a mariner who died of the bloody flux aboard a carrack named *The Ruth*, returned from Bordeaux. No one knows for whom it was intended. The letter was concealed and would not have been found, had the courier not died. You look at it, too, John.'

Shakespeare took the paper from Mills. It was written in English.

'*Be strong in faith, Father. The plan is advanced, and you must only be patient. We will come to you, that between us we may rid England of Satan's seed for ever. With the love and righteous vengeance of God, the demons will be cast down with raging tempests and torrents of rain. Like the flood of old, we shall sweep away the rotten House of Tudor and all that dwell there. Be ready to play your part. Yours, in the love of Christ our only saviour and Gregory, great England's truest friend, this twenty-third day.*'

'It is the hand of Robert Persons,' Shakespeare said without hesitation. 'I have seen enough of *his* letters and writings.'

Suddenly, Cecil was alert. 'Persons? You are certain?'

'Never more so. And the reference to Gregory might suggest Seville, the Jesuit college of St Gregory.' As he spoke, a hot shiver seared into Shakespeare's blood. Garrick Loake had mentioned the College of St Gregory.

'And from what we know, Persons has been in Seville much in recent months,' Cecil continued.

Mills took the paper back and cast his eyes over it again, but Shakespeare was not sure he took in what he saw. The man appeared to have little enough mind left to don doublet and hose of a morning, let alone inquire into important matters of state. This letter should be Shakespeare's task. The Thomasyn Jade affair had arrived at a most inopportune time.

'Frank, are you with us?' Cecil said sharply. 'It is as if you were in another county!'

Mills closed his eyes, then opened them and nodded to his master.

'You understand what the missive is saying?'

'Yes . . . I agree with John that this is the hand of Persons. But the implication is not clear. Perhaps it is encoded.'

'That is possible, of course, but even without encryption, we can see murderous intent: "sweep away the House of Tudor". There is no ambiguity there. Are they talking about another Armada? Is this a call to the Catholic faithful to be ready to rise up when the invasion starts? We know King Philip is preparing a new war fleet. Or is this something else, something more specific and yet more sinister?'

'What could be worse than invasion, Sir Robert?'

'I don't know, Frank. That is for you to discover.'

'We can see that it is intended for a priest,' Shakespeare said. 'It is addressed *Father*.'

'There is Jesuit conspiracy here,' Cecil said abruptly.

Shakespeare grimaced. Cecil's surmise seemed not only possible, but highly probable. 'The number twenty-three, at the end, is interesting. That *could* be code. Why would Persons mark down the date of writing? I think he is revealing a date when something will happen. But which month? As for the mention of Gregory, that is exceedingly interesting. A man came to me last night, one Garrick Loake. He spoke of a plot emanating from the seminaries of Spain and mentioned the Gregory college. This is no coincidence. I will seek him out today.'

'Seek him out? Why is he not in custody?'

'On what charge? He was bringing me information, Sir Robert. He wants money – a great deal of money.'

Cecil rubbed his neck to ease the stiffness of his hunch.

'Well, we must hope and pray that he returns with the information. Promise him what he wants, then when he has told what he knows, give him its worth.'

'Very well.'

'And remember, the Jesuit college in Seville is a very hornets' nest of intrigue. The whole of that coast east of Cadiz is awash with traitors . . . The English trading community in Jerez and Sanlúcar, those men who stayed behind when the war began. Catholics to a man, many married to Spanish women.'

Shakespeare was thinking hard. 'One thing is clear, both from the hints Garrick Loake gave – if we are to believe him – and from the letter: the plan, whatever it is, is already known to somebody in England. This letter is merely to say that it is now confirmed and imminent, and that those involved should be prepared. Perhaps it was intended for Henry Garnett. He is the Jesuit superior in England – and he is still at large.'

'Keep an open mind.' Cecil scowled with exasperation. 'But are we getting ahead of ourselves?' He stabbed the paper with his right index finger. 'Perhaps there *is* some hidden code there. In God's name, John, I wish you had never mentioned the Jade girl to Her Royal Majesty. You must talk with this Garrick Loake before all else.'

Shakespeare said nothing. He had given his word to a condemned man. He would not break such an oath.

Cecil read his thoughts. 'As for giving your word to a Jesuit traitor . . . sometimes, I do wonder whether you are seduced by the devilish nature of these hellhounds. They call themselves the Society of Jesus, clothing themselves in Jesus's name, and yet they carry beneath their cloaks most unholy weapons of murder and treachery. They are all traitors, every one.'

Shakespeare said nothing.

Cecil did not press the point. 'The matter with Southwell is done and, soon, so will be the affair of Thomasyn Jade. In two days' time, John, you will take over the inquiry into *this* letter and follow up any leads that Garrick Loake gives you. Two days. That is the limit I will allow you. In the meantime, Frank, I desire you to make rapid progress. Examine the letter in great detail. Is there secret writing there? A code we cannot see? Do this, but also find out all you can about the dead sailor in whose box the letter was found. Is he linked in any way to Loake? Someone must know who he was. The captain of *The Ruth* is here in my hall, awaiting you. He will escort you downriver to his vessel. The crew has been held aboard. Get someone to help you, if necessary. Robert Poley perhaps – no, Anthony Friday would be better. He knows everyone. Get him into the Catholic cells and houses. Have him listen for whisperings. But no more than two marks a week. Is that understood? And you, John.'

'Yes, Sir Robert.'

Shakespeare hoped Cecil did not hear the wry note in his voice. Poley was untrustworthy and Friday was unreliable. How, he wondered, was it possible for Cecil to have hundreds of informants around the world, as well as two score or more here in London, and yet be unable to find sound assistance when he needed it? The service required more gold to train recruits in the art of intelligencing, as he had been taught by Walsingham.

'I would talk to you privately.' Cecil dismissed Mills with a curt nod.

Head hanging on his long, uneasy frame, Mills shuffled from the room, clutching the intercepted letter. To Shakespeare, he looked a broken man. Cecil closed the door and returned to the table.

'Who do we have in Seville, John?'

'One man inside St Gregory's. Real name Robert Warner. I do not know what name he is using there. Two merchants at Seville, one at Jerez.'

'Nothing from them?'

'Nothing unusual from the merchants. We hear of war preparations, the fitting of fleets for the Indies and a new Armada, but you have all those details. Nothing on this specific threat.'

'What of this Robert Warner?'

Shakespeare winced. 'I have not heard from him. In truth, Sir Robert, I have fears for him.'

'You think him turned?'

'I fear the worst.'

'I'm sorry.' Cecil paced to the window and back. 'And Frank Mills . . . what are we to do about him?'

'You know about his wife?'

'Indeed. But the slattern has been spreading her legs for years. What has changed?'

'His neighbours. They know all about it now and have been taunting him most grievously. Even the children in the street call him cuckold and make lewd gestures at him. He is not thinking aright.'

'No, and if it were not for this Thomasyn Jade, I would have him relieved of his duties. Yet for the present I cannot. I had dared hope that the welcome death of Cardinal Allen would give us some respite from these turbulent priests, yet this letter proves otherwise.' The young statesman shook his head in weary frustration. 'John, I have great fears for this year. We have left Brittany to the enemy, for our armies are needed in Ireland, which bubbles up. Tyrone is raging for a fight. Meanwhile our greatest captains-general are either dead or engaged on other matters. Ralegh has set sail on his errand to find the gold of Guiana, though unkind enemies at court whisper that he is hidden away, terrified, in a Devon cove. Drake and Hawkins have been given royal let to fit their fleets for some secret expedition. God's blood, is this a time for such ventures? I would have them confined to home waters, but I suspect Her Majesty sniffs Spanish gold. And she needs it, for I have here the figures spent in these last two years: two hundred thousand crowns on Essex's vain expedition to help Henri of France; forty-seven thousand, two hundred and forty-three on last autumn's foray into Brittany. The coffers are full of nothing but air, John.'

Shakespeare nodded. The only good news was that the King of Scotland had finally ceased vacillating and was levying armies to bolster England's defences against Spain. But when England seemed so vulnerable, it did seem a mighty curious time for Drake and Hawkins to be embarking on foreign ventures.

'I will send messages to all the ports, Sir Robert. We will double and redouble our efforts against the possibility of assassins or others sliding into England. The port searchers will hold anyone about whom they have the slightest doubt.'

'Good. And John, more than ever, I will rely on you and your war of secrets. Deal with this Thomasyn Jade gibberish in short order. We have not a moment to spare on such trivial matters.'

Chapter 6

Shakespeare returned to Dowgate and remained there several hours, but Garrick Loake did not arrive. He told Boltfoot that if Loake came, he was to detain him, by force if necessary.

Furious with himself for ever letting the man go, he rode hard to the Theatre in Shoreditch, where Loake had claimed to be working. He spoke to his brother, but Will had not seen him, nor knew where he was lodged, and neither did anyone else.

'But fear not, brother, he is reliable enough,' Will said. 'He will come to you.'

'If he arrives here today, hold him at gunpoint and bring him to me.'

Will laughed. 'I do believe you are confusing me with one of your intelligencers.'

Shakespeare smiled. 'Forgive me. These are trying times.'

'For all of us.'

'Will, Garrick Loake told me you suggested he should come to me. What precisely did he say to you?'

'He said he had some intelligence of great importance to the realm. He seemed to believe it would be worth a lot of money.'

'Did he tell what that information was?'

'No. He told me nothing, only that he had it. I thought of you straightway.'

Shakespeare cursed. 'If you hear anything – anything at all – I beg you send word to me.'

'You know I will, brother.'

From Shoreditch, Shakespeare rode back south to London, seeking a once-great house just north of the city wall, in Barbican Street. He found what he was looking for, reined in and gazed up at the old stone mansion. None would have marked the place; it was ugly and neglected. He was not surprised by this, for the house belonged to the ancient Willoughby family and its air of austerity reflected the character of the present Lord Willoughby. Peregrine Bertie was known far and wide as a stern, fearless soldier and a severe Protestant with little time for material show.

Not that the earl was here at present. He was off on his travels, the way he had spent much of his life. Instead, his sister, Susan, the Countess of Kent, lived here and made do as best she could. Widowed by the age of nineteen, she was now married to Peregrine's impoverished brother officer, the equally heroic Sir John Wingfield. It suited her very well to use this great house, even though the hangings were threadbare and repairs remained undone.

A servant asked Shakespeare to wait in an ante-room and soon summoned him to the library, a homely room with tall shelves of books and a warm fire. Lady Susan was with four friends, all women, all close to the hearth. One sat on a settle with cushions, one on the floor, her arms about her knees, drawing on a pipe of tobacco. The other three stood. Shakespeare bowed to them, and then addressed Lady Susan.

'My lady.'

'Mr Shakespeare, what a pleasure to see you.'

'Forgive me for intruding. The footman did not tell me you had company.'

'Oh, take no note of these gossips, Mr Shakespeare. They are all worthless creatures with whom I idle away the hours in inconsequential chatter.'

'Might I have a word alone?'

'Do you have state secrets to impart to me?'

'Not exactly.'

'Then you may discuss whatever you wish in front of these ladies. We have no secrets between us. Husbands, children, affairs of state, philosophy and religion, all are as one in our little debates.'

Shakespeare looked around the gathering. He recognised three of the four women. One was the exquisite black-haired musician Emilia Lanier, the former courtesan of Lord Hunsdon. She was standing close to a yet more striking woman whom Shakespeare knew to be Lady Lucia Trevail, lady-in-waiting to the Queen. The dark-haired and matronly woman on the settle was familiar to him from court as the eminently sensible and witty Countess of Cumberland. The woman on the floor was the only one he did not know. She was younger than the others, probably in her mid-twenties, and sat gazing into the fire from beneath a mass of hair that tumbled across her forehead, all the while smoking her pipe. She seemed quite oblivious to their conversation.

'Come now, Mr Shakespeare. Anything spoken within these four walls is safe with us.' It was Emilia Lanier who spoke. 'Do we look the sort of ladies to spread tittle-tattle?'

Indeed, they did. Shakespeare smiled.

'You know, Mr Shakespeare, you need spare us nothing. We will not swoon at some horror you tell us, nor will our little minds be befuddled by matters of high politics, the sciences or exploration.' Lady Susan looked to her friends for approval.

'Do indulge us, Mr Shakespeare,' Lady Trevail said. 'We gather here to discuss matters of great weight ... and mutterings of no import whatsoever. It would be such a diversion to hear a little of the world of intelligencing.'

'But you must know I am sworn to secrecy, madam.'

The Countess of Cumberland, on the settle, put a hand to her mouth and made a noise like a chicken clucking, which was evidently laughter. 'Oh, Mr Shakespeare, please,' she said. 'It amuses us to call ourselves the School of Day. Is that not droll?'

Lady Susan took Shakespeare's arm. 'Come, sir, you need have no fear of us. We are as able as any man on the Queen's Council to discuss great matters of state. Why, we were just talking of the succession. Who do *you* think should succeed to the throne when Her Royal Majesty finally succumbs to time's fell hand, as, certain, one day she must?'

'I have no opinion on such matters.'

'Oh, come, come, Mr Shakespeare. No one talks of anything else these days. You must know that this book late out of the Low Countries, Father Persons's *Conference about the Next Succession to the Crown of England*, is spoken of in every great house in London. It is said he favours the Spanish infanta.'

'Well, *I* would favour almost any man or woman above the wormlike little Scotch king,' Lady Trevail said. 'Even the monstrous Arbella Stuart who thinks herself a queen already would be preferable, for she must at least be pliable. Such a shame poor Ferdinando of Derby was not more careful about his venomous diet. He would have made a magnificent king of England, if a little proud.'

'And a little too Romish, perhaps?' Lady Susan said. 'Or what of my lord of Essex? Now *there* is a man with the stomach and bearing of a monarch. Nor must we forget the charming infanta. Father Persons assures us that young Isabella is of John of Gaunt's lineage.'

'And she keeps a dwarf,' the Countess of Cumberland said, adding with mischief, 'just as our own beloved Elizabeth does.'

Shakespeare looked at her sharply and saw the glint in her eye. He was well aware that 'Elizabeth's dwarf' was meant to be Sir Robert Cecil. This was dangerous talk. If it was intended to provoke him to discomfort, they were succeeding in their aim. So he was providing the ladies with their day's mirth, but they would do well to be more circumspect; there were many ears in England. The Queen had never been amused by discussions about her throne and crown, and she especially disliked to hear of the merits of *Spanish* claimants.

'Do you think it wise to talk of such things?' he asked politely.

'Are you afraid of losing your head, Mr Shakespeare?' Lady Trevail said. 'I had heard you were a brave man.'

Their eyes met and held. 'I do believe that courage without caution is foolhardiness.'

Lady Trevail clapped her delicately gloved hands.

'Mr Shakespeare,' Lady Susan said. 'I have no idea why you are here, but you are very welcome. At least take a sip of sack with us, for we would love to prise some secrets from you. Do you know all my friends?'

'Indeed, I have met Mistress Lanier and I recognise the ladies Trevail and Cumberland from court.'

'The young lady by the fire, who seems to be in a tobacco-induced dream, is Miss Beatrice Eastley, my young companion and protégée. Now then, Mr Shakespeare, be good enough to tell us why you are here.'

Shakespeare had little time. If Lady Susan would not see him alone, then so be it.

'Very well, my lady, let me be direct with you. I believe that some years ago, the year 1586 to be precise, you took into your household a young woman named Thomasyn Jade.'

The woman on the floor looked up and removed the pipe as though she would say something. Meanwhile, a frown of puzzlement crossed Lady Susan's brow, then her lips parted in surprise. 'Thomasyn?'

'You recall her?'

'Of course, Mr Shakespeare, how could I not? Do you know where she is?'

Shakespeare shook his head. All eyes were fixed on him as though he were a bear in the ring. 'I am afraid not, my lady. But I am looking for her. I had hoped you might be able to help me in this quest.'

'Thomasyn Jade,' Lady Trevail said, emphasising every syllable. 'Wasn't she the—'

'Yes, Lucia, she was the poor young girl who was subjected to such horrible torments by those egregious priests. The things they did to her were beyond hideous.' Lady Susan turned to Shakespeare. 'But pray tell me, why are you looking for her now? Do you believe her alive? To speak true, I feared that, in her insanity, she had run away with intent to destroy herself.'

'I regret I have no idea whether she is alive or dead.'

'But *why* are you looking for her, Mr Shakespeare?' Lady Trevail said. 'What interest can Sir Robert's chief intelligencer have in her?'

'I cannot say. Did you meet the girl, Lady Trevail?'

'Indeed, I did. And felt deeply for the poor thing.'

His eyes scanned the assembled ladies. 'Do any of you know where she might have gone?'

'I had believed her to come from Buckinghamshire, Sir George Peckham's seat,' Lady Susan said. 'For that was where these rituals took place. But, Mr Shakespeare, this is most unusual and mysterious. Can you not give us a little notion of the reason for this strange visit?'

'No, my lady.'

'But it is clearly important to you and Sir Robert.'

'Indeed, it is.'

The countess sighed. 'I have thought about her often and would dearly love to discover what became of her. Mr Shakespeare, I shall do all I can to help.'

'We will *all* do what we can,' Lady Trevail said, to approving glances and nods from the Countess of Cumberland and Emilia Lanier. Only the girl by the fire, Beatrice, did not respond, nor even seem interested.

Shakespeare bowed again. 'Thank you. In which case, Lady Susan, I would be grateful to hear all that you remember of her. Whom she met, whom she talked with.'

'She was not well, physically or in the mind. I offered her sanctuary, for she needed a safe and loving home to recover from her torments.'

A maidservant came in with a tray bearing wine and a goblet for Shakespeare. He took it with gratitude and sipped the wine, which was sweet and smooth.

'She was with us a week,' Lady Susan continued. 'I did not have her brought here as a servant, but as a pupil, just as I educated my friend Mistress Lanier here in her youth.' She nodded towards Emilia. 'It is the correct way, Mr Shakespeare. Girls need education as much as boys. Is not Elizabeth herself among the greatest scholars in the land?'

'Indeed, my lady, I do not need convincing. My own daughters are taught to a high degree.'

'Thomasyn had endured a great ordeal. But after four or five days, I truly believed that she was settling here and becoming more tranquil and serene. I thought she would fit very well into our household and that we would make a fine young lady of her, for she had wit enough.'

'But something happened?'

The countess gave a sad smile. She was remarkably well kept for her forty years and there was kindness in her eyes.

Shakespeare wondered why Thomasyn Jade had wanted to leave such a welcoming home.

'No, nothing happened. Not that I know of, anyway.'

'She disappeared on a day very like today, Mr Shakespeare,' Lady Trevail said. 'We were all here as usual, talking of poetry and music. Of course most of the talk in those days was of the Babington horrors and the exorcisms. Also the likely fate of Mary Stuart and the possibility of invasion. On any other day, that would have been our bill of fare, but we had too much sensibility to discuss treason and horror in front of the girl. The last thing she wished to hear was talk of executions and conspiracy.'

'How did she seem?'

'Agitated,' Lady Susan said. 'Greatly agitated. She asked to be excused from our presence, hurried from this very room and was gone. That was the last anyone saw of her. No one witnessed her leaving the house. She did not even go to her room to collect her few belongings.'

'None of the servants saw her leave?'

'No.'

'And what belongings did she leave behind?'

'We found her purse with two pennies and a farthing in it, a comb, and the night garments I had given her. That is all. She took nothing but the clothes she wore.'

'Can you describe her to me? Was she tall? Fair? Plump?'

'Mousy red, I would say,' Lady Susan said. 'Not especially pretty, but fair enough. She was thin, but I don't think she had eaten properly for weeks on end. She did not like to meet your eye.'

'She might look very different now,' Shakespeare said, musing aloud.

'Indeed she might, if she has recovered from her madness.'

The woman on the floor said something too. Her voice was

low and rough with smoke, and he could not make out the words. He leant forward. 'Miss Eastley?' he asked, hoping she would repeat her observation, but she did not.

He would have asked them more, might well have enjoyed passing the day with them, but he was learning very little and there was too much to be done elsewhere. He bowed. 'My ladies, I will take up no more of your time, for the present.'

Francis Mills accompanied Captain Roberts in the barge downstream to Gravesend. He asked little and heard almost nothing; his head was filled with crashing waves of noise, like an incoming tide on a pebble beach.

'Who was this dead mariner, Captain?' Mills asked, like a child repeating its numbers by rote.

'His name was Franklin Smith. He was an ordinary seaman. The ship's master, who you will meet on board *The Ruth*, says Smith approached him when we were in Bordeaux. He was looking to work his passage home. From what the master tells me, he was no more than a bilge monkey, useful for loading of goods or hauling of cables but nothing more. Lower than the rats in the scuppers.'

'And what is your cargo?'

'From Bordeaux? Wine, of course, Mr Mills. Well, here we are, sir.' The barge pulled into the quayside near the smoking chimneys and massed masts of Gravesend. Captain Roberts lifted his chin in the direction of a large carrack, at anchor with its sails furled, a little way from shore. 'And there she is, *The Ruth*. The sooner this is all over, the better. The men are becoming restive, penned in like livestock, and we must discharge our cargo. The investors will not allow another day's delay. Mr Mills? Mr Mills . . .'

Francis Mills did not move at first, but then rose from his bench seat and disembarked with Roberts, who hailed a ship's boat. Through the surging roar of his mind, it occurred to Mills that he really should have heeded Sir Robert Cecil's instructions and brought someone with him to help interview the crew of this vessel. Alone, it was a daunting prospect. No, it was impossible. He could not do it this day. He was not thinking aright. Not thinking right at all. He wasn't really here. He was in a bedroom, dank with lust and sweat and skin. There was a blade in his hand and he was wondering how it would slip through flesh.

Suddenly he was caught short of breath. He closed his eyes and grasped the captain's arm.

'Mr Mills, you do not look well, sir.'

He couldn't move. He felt his knees would give way and that he would fall. The rushing in his head was a storm. His breathing was fast and shallow. A pain assailed his heart. He bent forward and clutched at his chest. He was going to die; he knew he was going to die.

'Mr Mills . . .'

Mills turned and stumbled back towards the barge, still holding his chest, fearing his heart would burst from his body. He had to get home; he had to get back to London.

Chapter 7

'HE LOOKS A little better, Jane,' Boltfoot said, staring at his two-year-old son who lay in the small wooden cot he had made for the boy. 'Do you not think he looks more lively?'

'I do so think, Boltfoot. I pray it is so, leastwise.'

'And is he taking more food?'

Jane nodded. 'A little more.'

'Did I not tell you it would be so? We have no need for physicians and apothecaries with their unholy magic and conjuring of spirits.'

He might say such things, but Jane knew her husband worried even more than she did about the boy.

'Boltfoot Cooper, I do sometimes think the years you spent at sea turned your brain to pease pudding.'

Boltfoot smiled at his wife then leant into the cot and kissed the boy. He patted Jane on the small of her back and was about to take his leave of her and go in search of Mr Shakespeare, when she stayed him.

'Why is it that we never celebrate your birthday, Boltfoot? What day were you born?'

'You say my brain is turned to pease pudding, Jane. What of yours, to be asking such daft questions? I don't even know the year I was born, let alone the day.'

Jane let him go. How was she to discover the information Dr Forman needed to cast a chart if Boltfoot did not know it himself?

They were all living in cramped quarters, in the part of the house that had survived the fire of last year. There were still smoke-black marks on timbers, but the structure, close to the Thames at Dowgate, was sound enough. The part of the building that had been utterly destroyed had been cleared away and was already being rebuilt, from the ground up. This time the house would be smaller, with a larger garden and improved stabling.

Shakespeare looked up from his table, where he had been scribbling a note to Cecil, telling him of the meeting with the Countess of Kent and her circle. He would need to speak with Lady Susan again, and preferably without the distractions of her companions. He wished to learn more about her ward, the sullen Beatrice Eastley, too. Something seemed not quite right there. He would also welcome another meeting with Lady Trevail; but that was another matter.

'You summoned me, master?'

'Ah yes, Boltfoot. I take it there is still no word of Mr Garrick Loake?'

'No, master.'

Shakespeare cursed. The man had disappeared like smoke in air. Well, Loake would have to wait. He would add word of this in the letter to Cecil, and urge him to engage Anthony Friday to find the would-be informant. Friday was unreliable, but no one knew the world of players and playhouses better than he did.

Shakespeare turned back to Boltfoot. 'We are riding for Buckinghamshire. Have horses saddled.'

'Yes, master.'

'And Boltfoot . . .'

Boltfoot stopped. It seemed to Shakespeare that he had aged five years in the past few months since the fire. This latest sickness afflicting their child had only made matters worse.

'How does little John fare?'

'Better, master. Better.'

'Good. Well, if he requires remedies or if you wish him to be seen by a physician, I will bear the cost.'

'Thank you, Mr Shakespeare. I am sure we won't need that.'

'As you will, but the offer is there. And send Andrew to me, if you would.'

Shakespeare continued to write his note to Cecil. Within a minute his adopted son, Andrew Woode, appeared in the doorway.

'Andrew.'

'You wanted me, Father?'

'I had meant to talk with you at length this day, Andrew. But I must be away on Queen's business. For the present, I desire you to know that I have been considering your suggestion with great care and I have concluded that you are truly set on a seafaring life. So, yes, you may go with Drake and Hawkins with my blessing, if they will accept you. Mr Hakluyt's book *Principal Navigations* has much to answer for, I fear.'

Andrew beamed. 'Thank you, Father.'

'You should talk with Boltfoot. No man knows the hazards and joys of the sea better than he does.'

Andrew laughed. 'I have already spoken with Boltfoot. He thinks I am mad to even consider going with Drake on his voyage. He says he will rob me and treat me like a dog. Also, that I will die of scurvy if I have not first drowned or been killed by a Spaniard.'

'And you are not deterred? You may have the size and strength of a man, Andrew, and I know how brave you are, but you are still only fourteen years.'

Andrew walked forward and knelt before Shakespeare. He kissed his hand. 'The world is out there, beyond the western sea, and it holds my future. I am more certain of this than anything in my life.'

Shakespeare gazed down fondly at the boy he regarded as his own son. Andrew's short life had not been easy, and Shakespeare knew that he had considered his decision to go to sea with great thoroughness.

'Then God speed you, boy. And learn well. Master the astrolabe and quadrant, the hourglass, the compass and the chart, for then you will be a true mariner and indispensable to your captain. But that is for tomorrow. For today, I have an errand for you.' He folded the letter he had been writing and sealed it, then handed it to Andrew. 'Take this to Sir Robert Cecil for me.'

Regis Roag slid from the saddle in the noisy Plaza de la Magdalena. He had been riding since dawn, but he was still cool and his long, oak-brown hair was unruffled. With sharp, experienced eyes, he glanced around at the bustle of traders, the working men, the women scrubbing stone steps and the promenading señoras in their mantillas. All the time, he looked for the face that might seem out of place. As a hunter of men, he knew how to spot a predator.

There was warmth and the scent of orange in the evening air. Roag breathed deeply. Seville was a fine place. The magnificent buildings, the wide-open squares, the perfume of strange plants and incense, the many religious houses, the workers in gold: all spoke of a town created by God. This was the wealthiest city in the greatest empire in history – a world away from the mud, stench and squalor of lowly London, the city that had spat him out like a stone, and its dirty neighbour Southwark, the place of his birth.

Tethering his horse to the base of a palm tree, he composed a smile and pushed open the door of the four-storey, anonymous house that held the grand title of the College of St Gregory. It was an inadequate building for its purpose, a poor tenement wedged between a bakery with intoxicating aromas and a leather shop that exuded animal stench.

He recoiled at the noxious blend of stinks. This was no place for the training of young men in the disciplines of faith. The boys who came here from England needed to pray and meditate in quiet solitude if they were to return to their homeland as God's soldiers and to die as martyrs. Here, they were closeted together like sheep in a pen. In the high summer, they sweltered, with no relief from the cloying heat and the stale sweat of each other's unwashed bodies.

Even as he stepped inside, he sensed panic in the air. A boy, no more than eleven years of age, was scurrying past. Roag grabbed him by the shoulder. 'Where is Father Persons?'

The boy was wide-eyed. 'He is with Thomas Eaglet.'

'Where?'

'In the sickroom, at the back.'

'Take me there.'

A group of robed men stood around a bed. Roag instantly spotted Father Robert Persons among them. He was standing beside his assistant, Father Joseph Creswell.

Roag touched Persons on the shoulder. Slowly, he turned around and Roag saw that the priest's once-handsome eyes were deep and haggard.

Persons made the sign of the cross. '*Dominus vobiscum*, my son.'

Roag bowed, his mane of hair falling about his glowing face. '*Et cum spiritu tuo*, Father.'

'You have arrived at a most sad time, Mr Roag.'

'So it seems.'

'Thomas Eaglet is close to death.'

Roag looked beyond Persons to the shrunken figure curled up on the cot, laid on his side to minimise the pain. But it seemed Eaglet was already past such worldly cares. His shallow breathing was only just audible.

To Roag, the dying man's body looked like raw flesh on a butcher's counter. He gazed on the loathsome mess of meat with interest, nothing more. No skin was visible save on Eaglet's face and hands.

'How has he come to this state, Father?'

'He scourged himself with a flail. It is *white martyrdom*. That is what we will call it, but it is a waste. It is not true martyrdom. It will be the second such death at St Gregory's this year. Such things unsettle our other young men and boys.'

Roag nodded. More than the unsettling of the boys here, he realised that if news of the event reached England it would not reflect well upon the Society of Jesus. 'I will end his misery.' His hand went to his dagger.

Shock registered on Persons's face. He reached out and restrained Roag's hand. 'Indeed, you will not. God will decide the time.'

Roag removed his slender fingers from the dagger and said nothing more.

Persons shook his head. 'I am told young Eaglet and others have risen every midnight these two weeks past, to scourge themselves with the discipline in front of the Blessed Sacrament. They must be commended for such diligence in the mortification of the flesh, but Eaglet did not know when to stop. *Why* would he not stop? He has lost so much blood.' Persons suddenly steeled himself and touched the dying man's hand, one of the few parts of the body that still looked human. He turned to Father Chamberlain, who was acting as nurse. 'Has extreme unction been given?'

'Yes, Father.'

Persons walked across the room and picked up a heavy iron brace, studded with short spikes designed to dig into the flesh and keep wounds open, however rotten they became.

'He wore this, Mr Roag. The Lord only knows where he obtained it. We must all pray for his soul. He is a very brave young man. You know, when he first came here I doubted his faith, but he has proved me wrong.' Persons made the sign of the cross over the forehead and face of the young man in the cot, then turned away. 'Come, Mr Roag, let us go to my office.'

The room was austere. Nothing but a table, chairs and papers. Its only ornament was a gilded cross on the wall. A shaft of late sunlight lit the thin arm muscles of the crucified Christ.

'Is everything ready?' Persons asked. 'The ships arranged, the money all in place, your men trained?'

Roag had a youthful smile that would win over maidens and emperors with its easy charm. In his forty-third year, he could pass for a man of thirty, exuding warmth and confidence. 'All is in place.' He held up a scroll. 'I have the authorisation of the *casa*.'

The document bore the seal of the *casa de contratación* – the house of trade – whose absolute seat of power rested within the Alcázar royal palace and whose word was law in all matters of shipping and without whose authority no vessel might leave Spain.

Persons nodded. 'Good. Which just leaves the matter of the traitor. He is in the hands of the Holy Office. I shudder to think that we ever trusted him. I fear he will burn in this world and the next.'

A lazy tic fluttered in the parchment-thin skin around Persons's left eye. There was a softness about the priest, but he had a certain aura. His beard was short and neat, his eye clever and wary. He had an intimate manner that turned those he met into either devoted friends or dedicated enemies. Roag knew he was not given to squeamish women's ways, nor subject to doubts in matters of faith. Yet he could see that the prospect of burning live human flesh disturbed him, as though the stench would remain in his nostrils, like bitter wormwood, for all eternity.

'Men such as Warner make life difficult for us here,' Persons continued. 'And yet it were better it did not come to the fire.'

'Then we must make do,' Roag said evenly. 'I will go to the Castillo de Triana from here. I am sure I will have a hearing.'

Joseph Creswell, Persons' loyal assistant, sensed his superior's discomfort. 'Remember, Father, the holy doctor Thomas Aquinas himself concluded that execution by the secular authorities was the proper way to deal with heretics who refuse to be reconciled. First, excommunication from the Church and if, stubbornly, they refuse to recant, then by His law they should be excluded from life itself. The fire is God's hand.'

Persons nodded, but without conviction.

There was silence in the room. From outside came the shouts of Spanish traders and the thump of drums.

'Would you be a king, Mr Roag?' Persons said suddenly.

'Would you have me be a king?'

Father Persons smiled and folded his arms. 'Come, I will hear your confession now, before you embark on your great enterprise.'

Roag did not move. 'No, Father. I will confess when I return to you, for I know I must commit mortal sins in this holy war. I cannot yet cast off my coat of steel.'

'Do not imperil your immortal soul, Mr Roag.'

'No, Father.'

Creswell watched from a first-floor window as Roag unteth-ered his horse and trotted eastwards towards the fish market and the bridge over the Guadalquivir. 'He is cold and mad,' he said, half to himself, half to Robert Persons who sat at the table behind him. 'He has no religion, only resentment.'

'He will carry out the task we wish, in the way we desire it.'

'Will he? Can we trust him that much?'

'Have faith, Joseph, have faith. After all, it is said he is the son of a king.'

'And do you truly believe he has royal blood in his veins?'

Persons shrugged his shoulders but did not reply.

Chapter 8

REGIS ROAG GAZED up at the Castillo de Triana. The stone walls were sand-coloured and warm, yet the overall impression was of dark foreboding. The fortress had been built on a massive scale to dominate the old Moorish town of Seville and to many people it was hell on earth, a huge cavern of pain and horror. Roag was not a sentimental man, but even he was struck by its grim power.

The castle stood on the western bank of the Guadalquivir river in the poorer quarter, where the old mariners and prostitutes, the manumitted slaves and beggars, scraped a living. It was the first sight of Seville to greet ships navigating up the olive-green waters of the river and it never failed to cast a gloom over the mariners' mood. For a hundred and fourteen years now, the building had served as the prison of the city's Inquisition. Countless men and women – mostly Jews, Moors and Lutherans, but also Catholics – had been brought here, accused of heresy and other crimes. Thousands had been tortured and hundreds had been handed over to the civil authorities – *relaxed to the secular arm*, as they called it piously – to be burnt at the stake. Those who repented, the fortunate ones, would be strangled by garrotte before the fire was lit.

Roag glanced back across the river to the fish market and, a little further south, to the splendid Torre del Oro. The tower of gold shimmered with warmth in the evening light, amid a tangle of shipyard masts and rigging. Turning back to the Castillo de Triana, the contrast was palpable. He entered through a great arch, next to the pontoon bridge, then dismounted and led his horse on foot. Roag was well known here and faced only peremptory questions from the guard. Striding across the outer courtyard, he passed a queue of black-clad and cowled men and women. He knew, from their furtive glances and the hiding of their faces, why they were there: they were informers, come to denounce enemies, neighbours, mothers or brothers, for gain or spite.

'She is a fornicator,' one would say in a shameless whisper; 'I have heard him lauding the Luther sect,' another would rasp, venom in her voice; 'I saw her place a crucifix on the ground, then spread her skirts, squat down and piss on it,' a scorned suitor would say, 'what is worse, she is a Jew.' And so those accused would be hauled before the Inquisitor, while the accusers slunk back into the shadows.

The malice here, amid the immense walls and embattled turrets, was almost tangible.

Roag was recognised by the gatekeeper, who showed him where to tether his horse, then admitted him through the heavy iron door. The would-be informers surged forward, but the gatekeeper pushed them back at the point of a pike and told them to wait for the prosecutor or his secretary. They were in Carmona with the Inquisitor-General, he said with a sneer. He did not know whether they would be here this week or the next. If the informers didn't want to wait, they could take their chances with the civil authorities and have their testimony passed on to the assessors.

Roag had enough Spanish to ask to be taken to the gaoler, a magistrate named Enrique Jorge whose serious face betrayed no laughter lines; it did not do to laugh. One woman had found herself incarcerated simply for smiling when the name of the Virgin Mary was mentioned during a sermon. The witness who denounced her called the smile a *sonrisita* – a smirk.

But though he dared not smile, Enrique Jorge was a likeable, well-fed man who clearly enjoyed his mutton, bread and wine. He also enjoyed Roag's company.

'It is pleasant to see you again, Señor Roag,' Jorge said. 'But it always surprises me when you come here. I know of no other man who enters these walls unpaid and of his own volition.'

Roag bowed his head. 'I am here to see Mr Warner. If you would take me to him, Señor Jorge, I would be happy to make a donation of gold to the Holy Office.'

Enrique Jorge shook his head and refused the money. 'That will not be necessary. First drink a little *chocolatl* with me, then we will go to Warner. He is chained and has the *mordaza* about his face, for he is like a brute beast without it, cursing the Inquisitor, the Jesuit college and even you. He uses words that no Christian could repeat.'

Roag and the keeper drank their exquisite beverage, sweetened with sugar and spiced with vanilla, then walked through the echoing halls of the prison.

Enrique Jorge threw open the door to the cell. Roag gazed in with distaste. It was cold, gloomy and damp. Water streamed down the walls and settled in puddles.

Warner, the only prisoner, lay curled on his mattress, a clamp across his mouth. His hands were manacled in front of him, and he was chained to the wall.

Roag turned to the gaoler. 'Would you remove the *mordaza* for me, señor. I must speak with the prisoner.'

'I cannot do that, Mr Roag, for it has been ordered by Don Juan de Saavedra, the Chief Constable of the Inquisition. We require tranquillity within these walls and Mr Warner has been a disturbance to the peace.'

Roag bowed. It would make no difference to him whether the gag stayed or not. He had all the information he needed: under torture, they had extracted his real name – Robert Warner – and he had confessed that he was a spy, sent by the office of Sir Robert Cecil to report back on the College of St Gregory. His fate was sealed.

'I understand. Perhaps, though, you would leave us a little while, for I must try this one last time to reconcile him. If I fail, then nothing is left but to pray for his soul and relax him to the secular arm.'

The gaoler bowed his grave, tonsured head, handed a candle to Roag and left the cell. Roag closed the door, put down the candlestick and went to sit on the mattress beside the prisoner, 'Are you afraid, Mr Warner?' he whispered. 'Do you have demons? Do not be afraid. You will not die in the fire. I will rid you of your demons.'

Warner's eyes were wide open. He struggled to speak, but the iron clamp prevented anything emerging but guttural, animal sounds from the back of his throat. In terror, he scrambled backwards, into the corner, away from Roag.

A needle glinted in the candlelight. Roag held it between the thumb and forefinger of his left hand. It was a long needle, three or four inches, sharp but strong. The sort of needle sail-makers used in their craft, the sort he had used as a child working in his mother's sail-loft in Southwark. Strong enough to pierce the heaviest canvas.

Roag smacked his right hand hard up into Warner's throat, just beneath the iron brace that encased his mouth and lower face. His hand caressed the throat.

'There is a demon in here, Mr Warner. I feel it moving, just beneath the skin. Its claws are fixed tight. It is inside your throat, hooked to you like a bat on a beam.' His voice was quiet, ice in the prisoner's ear.

In a frenzy, Warner tried to push Roag away, but the manacle and chains sapped his strength and he did not have the force to protect himself.

'It is this demon, Mr Warner, that has made you a tool of the heretics. It is this demon that endangers me.' Now Roag had the bright tip of the needle at the side of Warner's throat. 'Here, here is the devil, dug deep into your gullet. I think it is Beelzebub himself. Feel his sharp little claws and his ugly snout. He is here and I will do for him.'

A bead of white saliva flecked the edges of Roag's lips. His right hand smoothed Warner's lank hair. He smiled at him, kissed his forehead. His left hand stroked Warner's throat, at the side, just below the arc of the jawline, identifying and singling out the great vein that throbbed there. He slid the needle in, jerking downward to cause a jagged wound. Warner went rigid with the shock. His blood spurted out, across the mattress and the stone floor.

'Hush, Mr Warner, all is well. I am the seed of a monarch and I will protect you from Lucifer's sting. I have dealt the demon a mortal blow. He will die soon, and then you will be free of him for ever. Be still.'

In his mind, unspoken, words reverberated: *I can smile, and murder while I smile. I can smile, and murder . . .*

Roag went to the cell door and hailed the keeper, ordering him to fetch the gaoler.

The floor was sticky with a deep pool of blood. Roag had blood all over his hands but he had been careful to avoid it spoiling his expensive gold and black doublet. He held up his hands. 'I tried to stem the flow of blood, but the wound he made was too great.'

'Where did he get the needle?'

'You must ask the constable that, or one of your guards.

They should have searched him with greater care. One moment I was talking with him, attempting to reconcile him, the next he had the needle in his manacled hands. Before I could move, he was stabbing at his throat. He knew what he did.'

The gaoler looked at Roag with suspicion. 'What did you say to him? What happened in that cell?'

'I told him he was a disgrace.'

'Why should I believe this story?'

'Why should you not, señor? It is no difficult thing to conceal a needle. Who would not prefer the sudden stab of a needle to the lingering pain of the fire?'

For a few moments, the gaoler's gaze held Roag's, then he gave a brusque nod. 'Well, such things happen from time to time, and the inquisitors have a great deal too much work as it is. These Jews, these *conversos*, these Moriscos. I suppose it is one less for the fire. They can burn Mr Warner in effigy if they so wish.'

'Indeed, señor. Indeed they can.'

Chapter 9

Riding hard, Shakespeare and Boltfoot arrived at Denham House, near Uxbridge, in a little under three hours. The house was down a long track through overgrown woods. It was bleak and shuttered. So this, thought Shakespeare, was where the priests had wrought their evil. A dozen or more of them had found refuge here and had done unspeakable things for months on end in the name of their religion. It was no surprise that Father Southwell had trouble going easy to his death. But what had happened to the Peckhams, the owners of the house? And what had become of the unfortunate souls subjected to the exorcisms? Surely the local people must have known what was going on.

Shakespeare dismounted and approached the front door of the brick-built building. He hammered at it, more in hope than in expectation of a reply. The sound echoed, but no one came. 'Break open the door, Boltfoot.'

Boltfoot slid from his horse and unpacked an iron crowbar from his saddlebag, forced it into a gap near the lock and wrenched. The lock gave and the door flew open.

'The lantern.'

Boltfoot returned the crow to his saddle and unhooked the lantern, struck a light with his tinderbox and handed the lamp to Shakespeare. He pulled out his pipe, tamped in a wedge of tobacco, lit it and drew deeply, then waited by the horses as his master entered the house.

Shakespeare stepped in through the doorway and held the lantern aloft. The hall was large and empty of furnishings. No table, no settles, no hangings. He tried to imagine the exorcism services held there: a table in the centre of the room, with just one girl sitting there, bound, while priests and acolytes swarmed around, chanting their Latin gibberish, describing the demons in detail as they were cast out. Behind them, all the Catholics from the district would be gathered, to watch and wonder. It would have been some display; his own brother, Will, might have been pleased with such powerful theatre.

He walked through the echoing rooms of the shuttered house. There was nothing here but emptiness and a pervasive whiff of damp and rot. Certainly, there was nothing to give a clue to the whereabouts of Thomasyn Jade.

Back in the main hall, he spotted some writing on a wall and held the lantern up to read it. The strange words sounded like the names of demons. Hobberdidance, Modu, Succubus, Mahu and many more. Some scratched in ink, some scrawled in paint. He returned to the front door.

'Come, Boltfoot.'

They mounted up again. 'Did you note the gatehouse, master?' Boltfoot said.

'I did. It seemed as empty as this place.'

'There was a thin spiral of smoke behind it, as though a bonfire had been lit.'

Shakespeare nodded, recalling the scent of burning wood. 'Let us go there.' He handed the lantern to Boltfoot. 'Keep that lit; we may need it.'

They rode back along the track. Night was closing in and soon they would have to find an inn. The gatehouse seemed to be unoccupied but Boltfoot had been right: there was a bonfire, still alight. Shakespeare went to the back of the little house and lifted the latch on the door. It was unlocked and he entered. The gloom was pervasive, but the lantern showed him all he needed to know. There was a home-made coffer containing threadbare linen from another age, a single palliasse instead of a bed. Some bread, dried oats and a leather jug with a meagre mouthful or two of spirit at the bottom; a tallow rushlight, extinguished.

'Someone doesn't wish to be found, master,' said Boltfoot. 'Must have seen us coming and fled into the woods. Perhaps a vagabond or an outlaw.'

'Or a priest.'

Boltfoot stood at the doorway, surveying the woods for movement. They were vulnerable here, especially with the lantern illuminating them. A silent arrow from the trees, a musket-shot . . . they wouldn't even see their killer. Boltfoot unslung his caliver from his back and loaded it.

Shakespeare turned over the palliasse but there was nothing underneath, then he tipped the old linen from the coffer. He was about to put it all back in when he spotted a scrap of paper in the fold of a sheet. He picked it up and held it close to the lantern. It appeared to be a map, showing southern and eastern England. Certain towns were marked with dots: Norwich, Yarmouth, Lincoln, Wisbech, Bury St Edmunds, Canterbury, Sandwich, Winchester, Portsmouth, Weymouth. Beside each town there was a set of initials. He stuffed the paper in his doublet, then returned to the palliasse and felt carefully along its seams, but found nothing.

He looked up at the walls. A small recess caught his eye. On his toes, he could just reach into it. At first he felt nothing but dust, but when he stretched a little higher, his hand went further and touched something else, some sort of small jar or jug, set back deep into the wall. He could not get a grip on it.

'Come here, Boltfoot.'

Reluctantly, Boltfoot left his guard post. Shakespeare locked his fingers into a mounting stirrup to hoist him up. 'There is some kind of jar in there, Boltfoot. Bring it down.'

Boltfoot used his master's hands as a step-up and quickly retrieved the jar.

'There is something in it, master.'

Shakespeare smiled. He had a good idea what it would be. He was correct. It was money – a great deal of money.

'Come, Boltfoot, I think I know what all this is about. Let us take this jar. We will return here soon enough. First, we will go to the village.'

They found a room at the Honest Brew, near the square-towered church in Denham. The inn seemed to be the only place in the village with any warmth, yet there were few drinkers. Shakespeare and Boltfoot settled into a booth near the taproom's well-tended hearth. They would eat and drink and make some inquiries before taking to their beds.

The landlord brought tankards of beer to their table, soon followed by beef puddings and peas.

Shakespeare gestured the landlord to stay and talk, which he seemed happy to do for he was clearly not busy.

'Strangers are always welcome in my house. Times are hard.'

'I am sorry to hear that.' Shakespeare took out a sixpence and put it on the table. 'You might be able to help us,' he said. 'We wish to know of the Denham manor house. Does no one live there these days?'

The landlord stiffened. 'Who are you?'

'My name is John Shakespeare. I am on Queen's business. Does that worry you?'

The landlord laughed, but it seemed to Shakespeare that he was uneasy. With greasy fingers, he took the coin, thrusting it into his apron pocket. 'No, that don't worry me. What would worry me is if you were one of those demon-hunting priests come back to haunt us.'

'So you are not a Catholic?'

'No, that I am not.'

'I am from the office of Sir Robert Cecil and I would like you to tell me all you know of the house and what went on there.'

'Back in eighty-six, you mean? Those were ugly days. But, of course, it all came out at the time. Topcliffe, Justice Young and all the pursuivants moved in and cleared out the vermin. All been told before.'

'But I wasn't here, so tell *me*. Did the people of the village know what was going on at the house?'

The landlord pulled at his wiry beard. At last he nodded. 'I'm not saying I knew what was going on, but most folks knew all right, Protestants as well as Catholics. You understand that I never went to one of the exorcisms. But even if I had known – and, of course, I didn't – who would I have told? It was Sir George Peckham's estate, and he was sheriff of the county!'

'But he isn't there any more?'

'Crown property now, they do say. Lost all his money on one of those New World ventures. Seems he had ideas of setting up a colony for English Catholics there. I think he fell foul of the recusancy laws, too. Twenty pounds a time for non-attendance at the parish church. That'll ruin any man in short order. Peckham went deep into debt and the Queen's lawyers took the house from him. It's been shut up these five years.'

'And the gatehouse?'

'What of it?'

'Who lives there?'

'No one.'

'We have just come from there and found food. Bread no more than two or three days old, and a fire outside.'

'Someone passing through then, a vagabond.'

Shakespeare cut a wedge of pudding with his knife and pushed it into his mouth, all the time looking hard at the landlord. There was no reason to disbelieve him, and yet he did.

'Have I told you all you wish to know, master? I have work to do.'

Shakespeare shook his head and gulped down his mouthful. 'A few more questions, that is all. Did you ever know or hear tell of a girl named Thomasyn Jade?'

The landlord hesitated, averted his gaze, then stared into Shakespeare's eyes a little too long. 'Yes, I knew of Thomasyn. How could I not?'

'So you heard her story?'

'Yes.'

'But did you know her yourself?'

'Mr Shakespeare, this is all a long, long time ago. Should it not all be laid to rest? Must we plough it up like last year's topsoil?'

'What is your name, landlord?'

'Do you need my name?'

'If I am to write my report for the Queen and her Council, yes, I need your name. I need to be certain, too, that what you tell me is the truth, for it would not sit well with you to be discovered in a lie.'

Shakespeare caught Boltfoot's eye as he spoke. Boltfoot had his caliver on the bench at his side; now his hand went to it and stroked the ornate Spanish stock. The landlord saw the movement.

'My name is Swinehead, Augustus Swinehead.' The landlord glanced around the room. A customer was waiting to be served. 'Might we talk of this a little later, Mr Shakespeare? I pledge I will tell you all I know, for I have nothing to hide.'

'No, we will talk now. Sit down, Mr Swinehead.'

Reluctantly, the landlord sat down. Sweat was dripping from his brow. He brushed his hands down his beer-stained apron. Shakespeare noted that they were shaking.

Boltfoot lit his pipe from a candle and passed it to the man. 'Try that, Mr Swinehead. That's fine tobacco. That will soothe you.'

The landlord shook his head. 'I'll tell you who to talk with.' He looked across the room to a large man standing close to the kegs, as though he could not bear to be too far from the source of his ale. 'That's Goliath. He's Thomasyn's brother-in-law. His wife was Thomasyn's elder sister.'

'Thank you, Mr Swinehead.'

With Boltfoot limping behind him, Shakespeare strode across the taproom. The drinkers watched them with a mixture of hostility and fear.

'Mr Goliath?'

The man rose to his full height, his thick stack of hair scraping the beams. 'Who wants me?'

'John Shakespeare. I am from the office of Sir Robert Cecil. I am seeking Thomasyn Jade.'

Goliath was well named. Shakespeare was six feet, but this man was two inches taller, and brawny. He eyed Shakespeare and Boltfoot with disdain and spat into the sawdust. 'And what is *this thing*?' he demanded, indicating Boltfoot.

'Boltfoot Cooper, my assistant. And he does not take kindly to being called a *thing*.'

'Is that so? I could kill both of you before he got off one shot from his little musket.'

The big man looked for support from the other drinkers, but

got none. Despite Goliath's great size, Shakespeare had already reckoned him as all bluster.

'It will go easier with you if you cooperate.'

Goliath wavered, then nodded. 'Buy me a gage of beer, Mr Shakespeare, and I'll tell you what I know.'

'Let us sit down then.'

They went back to their booth. Boltfoot ordered the landlord to bring beer.

'Talk,' Shakespeare said. 'Tell me about Thomasyn Jade. I believe she was your wife's sister.'

'Yes, that is so.' Goliath rocked back and forth. His mouth was turned down at the edges and he seemed a long way away. 'That is so, indeed. My late wife Agatha was the best a man could have, but Thomasyn was always trouble. Got with child unwed and no one knew the name of the father.' He gazed around the taproom. 'Could have been any one of this lot.'

'Where is this child?'

'Thomasyn lost the babe in the sixth month, which was a mercy from God.'

'How did she become involved with the priests?'

'That was her mother's idea. When she heard what was going on up at the manor, she decided Thomasyn must be possessed of demons, too. I heard there were thirteen or fourteen priests up there, and they were doing their demon-chasing through night and day. Like harvest time for the saving of souls, it was. Mother Jade marched the girl to the manor and left her there, prisoner of the popish fiends.'

'What happened?'

'You must have heard it all. They pricked her with needles all over and put relics inside her, God knows where, and gave her herb broths and burning brimstone that made her yet madder than she already was. Tied her to the chair and stuck her like a pig and burnt her with holy water and bones till she cried out in pain. I saw her spit out needles and pins, and I saw devils come crawling from her belly, clasping at her with their talons, like horned cats with no fur.'

The landlord brought the beer, avoiding Goliath as best he could. He was drenched with sweat.

Shakespeare tried to stop him. 'Mr Swinehead?' But the landlord scurried away. Shakespeare let him go. There must be a good few men in these parts who would rather not be reminded of Thomasyn Jade. He turned back to Goliath. 'So you saw these exorcisms?'

'I saw one. The priests let local people attend, mostly relatives of those to be exorcised, for they were after the catching of souls and they wished them to see their kin being saved. They were careful at first because they were worried that spies would come and report back to the Council, but it all came out of their control as more and more people from hereabouts went to gape and gasp. Great Catholic nobles and gentlemen from London and elsewhere, too. Many men – and goodwives – liked the exorcisms better than a hanging. It is to my eternal shame that I went even that once.'

'Why shame, Mr Goliath?'

The man drank half his beer and sat for a few moments, lost in his memories again. Shakespeare waited.

At last Goliath spoke, carefully, in measured tones. 'Though I am a big man, I must tell you that I was scared almost to the point of death by what I saw. You may doubt what I say, but I saw the demon run up her leg, under her skirts, and I saw her shiver with pleasure as it entered her. I tell you, Mr Shakespeare, I never went there again and nor have I missed a Sunday service at St Mary's ever since.'

Shakespeare lowered his voice so that no one beyond the booth could possibly hear him. 'Take me to the house where she lived.'

'There is no point. It's been empty since her mother died. No one will live there, for they believe it haunted.'

'Take me. Finish your beer and we will go.'

'Very well, if I must.'

They rose from the table, Boltfoot, too, but Shakespeare restrained him. 'Stay here, Boltfoot. Get sleep. I will go alone with Mr Goliath.'

Boltfoot nodded. He knew what to do.

Goliath picked up his beer and downed it in one long gulp. Stooping beneath the low ceiling, he trudged to the doorway. Shakespeare demanded a lantern from the landlord and went out on to the street. The track was slippery, making it difficult for them to keep their footing as he and Goliath walked warily past the church.

'Was it *you*, Mr Goliath? Was it you who went to the pursuivants to put an end to the exorcisms?'

Goliath's whole body shook. 'No,' he said. 'But I wish I had done so. It went on for many months. I should have done something sooner while there was still hope for the girl. But I didn't. I was a coward, you see, and a poor Christian.' He stopped before a bank of hovels set against the muddy road. Piles of horse dung clogged the path. 'There it is,' he said.

It was a tiny house, no more than twelve feet wide, and windowless. There was no front door, just a hole. Holding the lantern in front of him, Shakespeare stepped over the threshold. The yellow light threw strange shadows around the single ground-floor room There was nothing except rubble and dirt. It seemed to him that this whole village was composed of lightless empty houses, like a town after the plague had swept through – the echoing emptiness of the Denham manor, the eerie presence of the gatehouse and now this wreck of a hovel.

'What of the father?'

'Tom Jade? Died when Thomasyn was ten. Trampled to death by cattle.'

'They must have other relatives in the village.'

'No more. Look around you, Mr Shakespeare. The very heart has been ripped out of the place by what happened.'

'Someone must know where she is. She must have made contact with someone from Denham.'

'Not to my knowledge. I do not know where she is, which I will promise on the Holy Bible. I believe she has not been seen in Denham since the pursuivants took her away. If you were to ask me my opinion, I must tell you I believe her dead. Most likely by her own hand.'

Shakespeare would not let it go. 'On the way to Denham House, there is a gatehouse. Someone is living there. Could that be Thomasyn? Could she have come back here?'

Goliath creased his mouth down firmly. 'No. If there's anyone there, it must be a vagabond passing through.'

'That's what Mr Swinehead said.'

'Well, it's probably true, that is why.' There was an edge of frustration or anger in his voice.

'And yet I am surprised that the people in such a small village should not notice a new inhabitant with a fire and bread. Has bread been stolen – or has the baker been selling loaves to strangers?'

Goliath said nothing, just stood there, arms wrapped around his chest against the cold.

'So where, then? If Thomasyn is not dead, and she is not in the village, where might she be?'

Goliath sighed heavily. 'Who knows? Not me. But if you asked me to make a guess, then I would say she is probably in a stinking whorehouse, somewhere . . . or in Bedlam Hospital.'

*

Boltfoot bade the landlord goodnight and went to the allotted chamber. He closed the latch, listened a moment, then opened the casement window and clambered out as soundlessly as he could.

Dragging his left foot, he limped halfway around the building to the stableyard, where he hid behind a puncheon cask. He did not have long to wait. Augustus Swinehead emerged from the inn, ordering his customers out into the cold night air and home. A minute or two later, after they had all gone, Swinehead went back inside before re-emerging swathed in a heavy cloak. He looked around furtively before setting off at a brisk walk into farmland at the back of the building.

With no more than a sliver of moon to light his way, Boltfoot followed at a distance, just enough to muffle the sound of his soft-shod feet. But the task was simple enough, for he knew exactly where the landlord was going; ten minutes later, they arrived at the gatehouse to Denham House.

Boltfoot unslung his caliver and crouched in the undergrowth. Quickly, he primed and loaded the weapon. He had a clear view of the open doorway, thanks to the guttering glow of tallow indoors. Swinehead was in the house and there was someone else with him; he could not make out features, only shadows and yellow light. He heard a murmur of voices, though he could not discern words. He rose from his hiding place and walked forward, the butt of his caliver wedged firmly into his chest, the muzzle moving from side to side. Without hesitation, he pushed into the house.

Two pairs of eyes turned on him in shock and alarm.

'Be still, Mr Swinehead.'

Boltfoot's caliver swivelled from one to the other as he assessed the situation. Swinehead was unarmed; he was no threat. His companion was even less dangerous: a small, bent old woman, scarcely as big as a child of eight. Boltfoot lowered his gun.

'Who are you?' he demanded.

'No,' the old woman replied, her voice high but surprisingly firm. 'Who are *you* to come marching into my home?'

'Boltfoot Cooper. My master John Shakespeare has questions for you. And you, Mr Swinehead . . .'

Swinehead's shoulders slumped.

'Come with me,' Boltfoot said. 'Both of you.'

'And if I don't?' The old woman raised her chin in a way that spoke defiance.

She wore a plain black gown and it seemed probable to Boltfoot that she was a member of some religious order. He shrugged. 'Then I shall bind you and leave you here until I return with my master.' He turned to Swinehead. 'You, however, *will* come with me, or I shall shoot you dead.'

'Very well,' the woman said. 'I will come with you, too, though I have nothing to say to you or your master. Nothing at all.'

Chapter 10

SHAKESPEARE WAS SITTING on the bench in the booth, leaning against the wall with his feet on the table. He looked up as Boltfoot ushered Augustus Swinehead and the old woman into the taproom, then rose and walked over to them. He placed a hand on his assistant's shoulder. 'Well, what have you brought me, Boltfoot?'

'She was in the gatehouse. Won't tell me her name. Looks like a nun to me.'

'He is a man of great wit, your little fellow,' the woman said.

'Indeed he is.' Shakespeare stared at her. She was undoubtedly a nun and, from the tuneful timbre of her voice, he imagined that she might be Irish.

'She insists she will say nothing to you, but it occurred to me, master, that she could have been sent here by Rome and that she has entered the country illegally, which is counted high treason.'

'You may well be correct, Boltfoot. *Is* he correct, mistress?'

'I have never entered any country illegally in my life. I was here before this usurper came to the throne and I shall still be here after she has died and gone to hell, God willing.'

'What is your name?'

'And why should I answer your questions? Who are *you* to be inquiring of such things?'

Shakespeare turned to the landlord. The man was terrified. He knew what could become of those who harboured priests or those deemed traitors. 'What is this woman's name, Mr Swinehead?'

'Michael . . . Sister Michael.'

'Tell him nothing, Augustus. There is no crime committed so he has no power over you.'

Augustus Swinehead put his hands to his head and dug his cracked fingernails into his scalp. He could not decide whether to look to the woman or to his interrogator. 'Mr Shakespeare, please—'

'Now I ask you again, Mr Swinehead. Who is this woman and what was she doing in the gatehouse? If you answer honestly, it may go well with you. If you do not . . .' He left the other possibility hanging in the air.

The woman stepped forward and pushed Swinehead away. 'You are a poor sort of man, Swinehead. Will you lack courage like this at the judgment? If so, then I know which way you will be sent. Fetch me brandy and be done with you.' She turned to Shakespeare with a face of stone-hard loathing. 'Very well, I will tell you what you want. Swinehead says you want to know about Thomasyn Jade.'

The landlord produced a small cup of brandy, which the woman took from his quaking hand. She threw the contents down her throat. Shakespeare studied her more closely. Her black habit was crusted in dirt. She wore a common coif that had become as grey as the strands of knotted hair that protruded around her forehead and temples. He estimated her age in the region of sixty but realised he could be ten years out either way.

'Oh, I know all about Thomasyn Jade. When first I saw her there were more dirty, wicked devils in her than a hive has bees. But she was not a fool; she knew she needed our help and came to us willingly to have the demons cast out. Nor did she run away, even when her trials were hard and full of great pain. Six months she was with us and we worked day and night to free her with our prayers and supplications. Father Weston prayed on his knees all night every night. He was racked to the limits of endurance with the agony and his eyesight was failing, yet never did he cease to pray. Those months almost brought the father to his death from pain and exhaustion.'

Shakespeare was having none of it. 'She was brought to you against her will and you held her prisoner, just as you did with all the others. It was all a trick to convert those who witnessed or were subjected to your trickery and foul super-stitious rites.'

'Think what you like, Mr Shakespeare. I know the truth, for I was there. She could have gone at any time, but then she would never have been rid of the evil. She ran from *your* fine friends, though, didn't she? Lady Susan and her damnable coven. She ran from them as soon as she could.'

'How do you know of Lady Susan?'

The old woman laughed with scorn. 'We know everything that goes on in this realm of sin and heresy. We have friends everywhere, in the palaces and the courts of law. Do you think we don't? Do you think this pseudo-religion can survive? It will be cast out as surely as the demons were expelled from Thomasyn Jade.'

'Where is she?'

Sister Michael looked Shakespeare directly in the eye. He saw no fear there, only reproach.

'Perhaps Father Weston will tell you. Why do you not ask him? You must know where he is for you keep him in your dungeons, even though he is frail and sick. As for myself, I have told you all I will say. You have no power over me for I took my vows in the reign of Queen Mary, so I was here in the days before the accession of the usurper and contravene none of your heretical laws.'

At this, she dropped to her knees and began to pray silently. Shakespeare removed the paper he had found from his doublet and held it up. 'You know what this is. I found it in your coffer. This paper could hang you, mistress.'

The nun kept her eyes shut.

'It is a map of routes and safe houses. You are organising the secret transport of young men and women to the seminaries and convents of Europe. This is so, is it not?'

She did not move nor acknowledge his presence.

'These initials are your contacts in these towns. They provide safe lodging for the would-be priests and nuns as they make their way to the coast. And the ones in the coastal ports organise berths upon vessels to France or the Spanish Low Countries. Answer me or face yet greater consequences!'

At this, a quiet smirk seemed to cross the old woman's lips.

'And then there is the matter of the money. Funds from Rome to pay travel expenses, yes?'

At last he got a reaction. Her eyes opened and he detected a glow of such cold revulsion that it almost seemed *she* was the one possessed. Shakespeare tried hard to contain his own fury. He held up the jar of money, which he had counted out to forty-two pounds and a few shillings. 'This will remain as crown property until you can prove ownership. As for questioning, I will not press you further this night. Boltfoot, you will hold this woman under armed guard until morning, when you will escort her to London and have her held in Bridewell.'

Boltfoot lifted his caliver.

'And you, Mr Swinehead, will think very carefully what else you might wish to tell me, unless you, too, desire a journey to the treadmill and whipping post.'

*

Shakespeare slept lightly. In the morning, he found Boltfoot and the nun in the taproom, where he had left them. She was still on her knees, in prayer, her eyes closed. He ignored her, spoke briefly to Boltfoot and gave him money to buy food for himself and the woman, and to hire a horse.

'I will see you in Dowgate this evening.'

Shakespeare rode alone. The road was pitted, but he made good progress and was at Dowgate by late morning. He found Jane still out of sorts and reassured her that Boltfoot would soon be home.

'This came for you last night, master,' Jane said, handing him a letter. He recognised the seal as Cecil's and sliced it open with his dagger.

Mr Mills is sick and frenzied. I can no longer spare you on the matter of Thomasyn Jade. Go to The Ruth *at Gravesend without delay.*

Shakespeare uttered a low curse and threw the letter into the hearth. He wrote a brief reply with news of Denham, then walked at a brisk pace to the Old Swan waterstairs.

'Queen's business!' he called, striding to the front of the mass of people awaiting tilt-boats. A pair of young men dressed in black like lawyers were clambering into a four-oarsmen barge, but Shakespeare ordered them out.

'Damn you, sir, we have business at Greenwich Palace.'

Shakespeare thrust his letters patent from Robert Cecil before their eyes. 'Argue with that if you will.'

Grudgingly, they made way for him and he commanded the oarsmen to row him to Gravesend with all haste. The journey was long and tiresome and when he arrived, he saw that he was too late. *The Ruth* was already being unloaded.

'The investors would not wait another day,' Captain Roberts said, as they sipped wine from Bordeaux in his cabin. 'I had no option in the matter but to let her be discharged and lay off most of the crew.'

'You could have said Sir Robert Cecil ordered the cargo impounded.'

The captain smiled. 'Indeed, I might, but the investors included Sir Robert's own father, Lord Burghley, as well as the Earl of Essex and the Mayor of London. Since this war started, French wine sells at a fine price. Investors want their money in their coffers, not wallowing in casks aboard ship. And after Mr Topcliffe's visit, I had no more cause to delay.'

'Topcliffe was here?'

'Why, yes, not twenty hours since. Sent by Sir Robert Cecil like your good self, sir. And I hope I do not speak out of turn in saying it was a most uncomfortable experience for all concerned.'

'God's wounds, Mr Roberts! Tell me what happened.'

'He lined up the crew, called them papist dogs and threatened them with the rack if they did not speak out and denounce the traitors among them. We were all mighty bewildered.'

'What did he discover?'

'Nothing. He scared all the men into utter silence.'

So with Shakespeare away and Mills incapacitated, Cecil had panicked and brought in Topcliffe. He was the last person to extract information by subtle means.

'However,' Roberts continued, 'all may not be lost. When things had calmed down, I made some inquiries of my own among the crew, and I did find one man who knew the dead mariner, though not as a friend. He begged me not to reveal this information to Topcliffe.'

'Don't worry. His name will not be revealed to Topcliffe by me. Where is this man now?'

'Still with us, grumbling at being kept from the bawdy

houses and drinking dens. His name is Jed Yorke. He is an ordinary seaman. Wait here and I will have him brought to you.'

'And I would like to see the dead man's box, where the letter was found.'

'Of course. I have it here.'

Roberts called in a midshipman and sent him to get Yorke, then fished under his bed, which was short and narrow, seeming scarce big enough for a child of twelve. He fetched out scraps of wood that had once been the box, a cup, a tin eating vessel and a knife.

'That's it, Mr Shakespeare – or all that remains of it after the the searchers broke it apart.'

Shakespeare examined the objects. They were cheap, everyday things, without markings on them. The box was no more than firewood.

The midshipman returned with Jed Yorke, an unremarkable man with long whiskers and a brow lined by a great many sea-winds. He bowed in deference to the captain and then to Shakespeare, clutching a felt cap tightly.

'Mr Yorke,' Shakespeare said, 'I believe you knew the dead mariner.'

'Yes, master. He called himself Franklin Smith.'

'Did you doubt that was his real name?'

'I doubt it of *all* mariners, sir. Many seafarers have reason to go under aliases. Wives they never wish to see again, justices they wish to escape . . .'

'I understand. Tell me, what did you make of Mr Smith?'

'He was not a seasoned mariner, sir. He did not know the ways of a ship. I would say he could not tell a capstan from a keel.'

'Indeed.' Shakespeare turned to the captain. 'Where is the corpse, Mr Roberts?'

'Fifty fathoms deep, Mr Shakespeare. Stitched in canvas and buried at sea.'

'And his clothes?'

'Dispersed among his crewmates.'

'And his crewmates are all gone. Mr Yorke, did *you* have any of his apparel?'

'Only his cap, master.' He held out the cap. 'This.'

'What is it worth?'

'It is a poor thing, in truth. No more than a groat.'

Shakespeare took the cap and examined it. He slit it open and felt inside the lining for secret messages, but there was nothing. 'Now tell me more. I want to know of all your conversations.'

'He did not talk much, but there was one thing I recall, master.'

'Yes?'

'He asked me where he could get a berth to work his passage from the Thames to the east of England. He wanted to go to Wisbech.'

Wisbech. *A papist fastness in the east.* The words of Garrick Loake came gusting back. He had said the plot 'wafts from the papist fastness of the east, gathers force in the seminaries of Spain, but it will blow into a tempest here. A conspiracy the like of which England has never seen.' Wisbech was certainly a papist fastness, for it was in the castle of that eastern port that the most aggressive of the country's renegade Catholic priests were interned.

'Did he say why, Mr Yorke?'

'He said his home was near there.'

'And what did you tell him?'

'I told him I had no idea, master, for it is the truth. I do not even know quite where Wisbech is, though I believe it to be near the Wash.'

✝ 87 ✝

'Did he talk with anyone else about this matter?'

'I do not know.'

'Very well.' He gave the man the remains of the cap, and sixpence compensation for its destruction. 'Thank you, Mr Yorke. That will be all.'

Chapter 11

O N THE RIVER barge back to London, it became clear
to Shakespeare that he must go to Wisbech in
Cambridgeshire. The thought of travelling to that remote outpost of England did not fill him with joy, but Cecil would
demand it of him, and he would be right to do so. It was
almost certain that the letter from Father Persons had been
destined for the castle prison there. One name above all came
to mind as the intended recipient: the zealous Father William
Weston, who sometimes went by the name Edmunds, former
superior of the Jesuit mission to England and still highly influential among England's Catholics, even though he had been
incarcerated these nine years.

Shakespeare had met him once before and did not like him
much. He would have no qualms about interrogating him hard
to discover the truth about this letter. And while he did so, he
could question him concerning Thomasyn Jade's whereabouts.

Ursula Dancer was pushing her handbarrow across the
courtyard when he arrived at Dowgate. He hailed her. 'A good
day at market, Ursula?'

'Surviving, Mr Shakespeare. Just surviving.'

He laughed out loud. Ursula was eighteen years of age and
though she had been at Dowgate only since the autumn, she was
already part of the family. The children loved her and Jane valued

her assistance. Recently, Shakespeare had given her funds to set up a market stall among the booksellers of St Paul's. He knew some printers and publishers, and had contacts at Stationers' Hall who had agreed, against their better judgment, to help her make a start. Boltfoot had accompanied her on her earliest outings to ensure she did not suffer violence at the hands of her competitors, but it soon became clear she could look after herself very well in the sharp world of street-selling. And she quickly realised that there were more profitable commodities than books.

'How much have you sold today?'

'Every ounce of tobacco I could scour from the ports. And all my pipes.' She swept her arm across the barrow, which was, indeed, almost empty, save for a few books and some curious artefacts from the Indies. 'It's the sotweed that sells, not the books. The lawyers want it and so do the churchmen. I could do the same business twice pigging over, Mr Shakespeare, if only I could find the sotweed to sell!'

'Well done. But you must also attend to your lessons, Ursula, for if you learn to read and write I do believe you will be a great London merchant one day.'

She screwed her pinched, yet strangely beautiful, face into a smile. 'Yes, sir.'

He laughed again, for he knew her well enough. When she said, *Yes, sir*, she really meant, *Lessons? Only after I have gone down to the pigging dockyard taverns and ships to see what I can buy from the homecoming mariners to sell at a great profit at St Paul's.*

'I do believe you will soon be the wealthiest member of this household,' he said. More importantly to both of them, she no longer had to steal for a living. Her days of vagabondage were, he hoped, at an end. He was about to walk on when she stayed him.

'It seems you have a visitor, Mr Shakespeare.'

'Garrick Loake?'

'I don't think so. I have no idea who or what Garrick Loake is, but, I promise you, it's better than that.'

'Indeed?'

'A beautiful lady, looks like a princess. A very goddess to steal away your heart.'

'Thank you, Ursula. I am too busy for this.'

'But you *do* have a pigging visitor. Jane put her in your solar and took her sweetmeats and wine, not half an hour since. And there's another one, too, out by the horses. A dismal pigging cow that one, won't say a word.'

Shakespeare strode on and found Jane in the kitchen with baby John. 'Is Boltfoot back yet?'

'He is, master. But I have put him to bed. It seems he had no sleep last night.'

'Let him sleep a while longer. Ursula tells me I have visitors.'

'A lady named Trevail. I told her I did not know when you would return, but she said she was happy to wait.'

'Thank you, Jane. Please inform her that I will be with her presently.'

So, Lucia Trevail was here. Why, he wondered, did that seem to brighten this grey day?

'And there was another young lady with her, but she has stayed at the stables with their horses. And good luck to her with her sullen way and her sotweed smoke.'

He bowed to Lucia Trevail. 'My lady, this is a most delightful surprise. You are well served with refreshment, I hope?'

'Your servant has treated me most hospitably. And I must say that the pleasure is all mine, Mr Shakespeare. We were all most intrigued by your visit to Susan's house. None of us could quite understand why the whereabouts of poor Thomasyn Jade should suddenly be of such interest to an esteemed government officer.'

'I can understand your puzzlement and I would tell you more. But I am not at liberty—'

She put up a hand, encased in a delicate white-kid glove. 'Please,' she said, 'I am not here to question you on the matter. Rather, it occurred to me that I might be of some little assistance to you. You asked what Thomasyn looked like. Well, I now recall that she had a distinguishing mark – a faint red blemish above her right eyebrow, in the shape of a crescent moon. I found it quite intriguing and beautiful.'

'Thank you. That may well be of use to me.'

'It is not much, I know. But I wish to help. We all feel some guilt in the matter. Perhaps we were too beguiled by her story, which made us seem a little unkind, though that was not our intent. We peppered her with all manner of questions . . .'

Shakespeare nodded. Thomasyn had been an object of wonder during the exorcisms. She must have wished for a quiet life and, instead, found herself stared at all the more.

He found himself wondering why Lucia Trevail was here. She could as easily have told him of the crescent mark in a letter. He wondered, too, why she was not at court, for the Queen did not like her ladies-in-waiting to take leave of absence, especially not a Gentlewoman of the Privy Chamber.

She answered his unspoken question. 'Mr Shakespeare, I have been given time away from court to attend my properties in Cornwall, where I must go to deal with some legal matters. On my return, I would dearly like to help you in your quest to find Thomasyn, if you have not already discovered her fate.'

She had a crisp tongue that did justice to her sharp mind. He could well understand why Elizabeth valued her company. Her attire was well cut from the finest cloths, neither modest nor brazen in the manner of most court ladies. Nor did she wear powder or paint on her clear-skinned face. She was beautiful, but he guessed that she was too clever to try to outshine the sun queen by donning glittering apparel and great pearls as others did, often to their cost.

What else did he know of her? Only that, like Lady Susan, she had been widowed before her twentieth birthday and left wealthy. He guessed her age now at late twenties or thirty.

'Mr Shakespeare, you are looking at me most intently.'

He averted his gaze quickly and thanked her for her offer. He had been looking in her eyes, where the fire was reflected.

'Mr Shakespeare?'

'Forgive me. My thoughts drifted.' *To the fire, where many a man had followed and fallen.*

'Well, I just hope that in helping poor Thomasyn, we might right a wrong – and discomfit the papist traitors who treated her so ill.'

'I am told you have a companion here with you.'

'That is Miss Eastley, whom you met at Susan's house. She is to accompany me to Cornwall where she has distant relatives. Susan asked if I would take her.'

Shakespeare nodded. 'Does she ever talk?'

'Very little, particularly not with men.' Lucia lowered her voice. 'In truth I think her a little mad. However, I am delighted to have her with me, and to help her with her studies, as Susan has done. She is young, Mr Shakespeare, and we both hope to set her on the correct path of life. I am afraid she is not always easy with others. As I said, it is the company of men she avoids. She has reason enough, I think.'

Shakespeare dared look closely again at Lady Trevail's exquisite face, not quite sure what he hoped to divine. Humour, certainly, and more besides. He was about to travel one hundred miles to the north and she was heading two hundred or three hundred miles south and west. It was bad timing.

*

Shakespeare's meeting with Sir Robert Cecil was curt and direct. 'You must indeed go to Wisbech, John. I can hardly spare you here, but I have no one else to send.'

There was someone, but Shakespeare would not say his name: Topcliffe. He would be delighted to go and wreak torment among the Catholic priests.

'I know what you are thinking, John,' Cecil continued. 'And no, I shall not be sending Mr Topcliffe, delighted as both you and my lord Puckering would doubtless be to have him out of the way.'

Shakespeare smiled at the reference to the Lord Keeper, Sir John Puckering. He was at present trying a long-winded Chancery case involving Topcliffe, and word had it that he was not enjoying the experience.

'I have no desire for yet more martyr priests,' Cecil went on. 'I desire no torture, no executions. I am sure I do not need to impress that upon you.'

'Indeed not.'

'Then go, discover what you can – and return in haste. In the meantime, I shall set Mr Anthony Friday to work.'

'He will not like it.'

'Fear not. I have a hold over Mr Friday. A stranglehold.'

When Boltfoot awoke, Shakespeare summoned him and asked about the old nun, Sister Michael. 'Did she maintain her silence all the way to Bridewell?'

His assistant looked uneasy. 'She did, master . . .'

'Boltfoot?'

'Master, it is not my place to say such things, but I believe I must speak plain. I could not but be troubled by the woman, sir. I wondered what she had done to merit confinement in Bridewell, for I would not put a dead cat in that place.'

Shakespeare nodded. It had been preying on his own mind

and he wondered about his motives for sending her there. He did not like locking people away simply for the supposed crime of helping others to seek religious freedom in another country. Perhaps he wanted her imprisoned simply for refusing to answer his questions. Or was there more to it than that? Had it been purely because he disliked her? He felt uncomfortable at the thought.

'You are right, Boltfoot,' he said finally. 'Go to the keeper and authorise her release. Bring her to the Swan Inn, give the landlord money for her keep, and tell her she must stay there or be damned as an outlaw. I will speak with her on our return.'

Chapter 12

The going was easy enough until Cambridge, but Shakespeare knew it could not last. Soon they would be entering the strange, boggy flatlands of the fens and the rain was coming hard. They stayed the night at the Dolphin Inn, hoping the rain would stop, but in the morning he looked from the leaded window of their chamber and saw that it was worse. The downpour was cold and relentless. Instinct told him to wait here in comfort until it let up, but duty told him they must press on regardless. Duty won.

Progress became desperately slow. Six hours later, at two o'clock, they had managed only a little over five miles along a drenched causeway that, at times, became completely submerged beneath the flood. They found themselves crossing between islands of mud until they made landfall at the village of Waterbeach. They stopped at a tavern, ate and drank without talking, then travelled on. Two hours later, Shakespeare's worst fears were confirmed as they reined in their horses, up to the fetlocks in thick, peaty earth, and surveyed the way ahead.

'Should have come by sea, master,' Boltfoot grunted testily.

The causeway sloped down at a gentle gradient and simply disappeared into water. They were looking across the desolate spectacle of a lake that seemed to stretch for ever in front of them until black water melded into sky in a dismal haze. A few hundred yards offshore they could see a small island with a few trees, no more than a spinney. There was no other sign of land. Somewhere in the distance, the lonely clang of a church bell revealed that there was life.

'Is that so, Boltfoot?' Shakespeare replied, his tone as tart and impatient as his assistant's. 'Well, it seems we have a sea to cross now, so let us find a way.'

Shakespeare hunched into his bear cloak. Though the fur was soaked flat, the skin should have kept him dry. Except that the cold rain slid from his hat down inside the back of his collar.

'Over there,' Boltfoot said with a nod of his head. 'I do believe I make out a church spire. That's the only way across the fens when they flood. Follow the line of churches, for they are all on higher ground. That is why they ring their bells.'

Shakespeare sighed. They were hopelessly equipped for a journey across such a waterscape. If they could not see the line of the causeway, horses would be useless. Even if the water was only a couple of feet deep in most places, they would never know when they came to a river or other decline until they were on it and the horses lost their footing in the black depths.

Beneath his breath, he cursed Sir Robert Cecil for insisting they ride to Wisbech rather than go by ship. 'If the winds are against you in the North Sea, you could take weeks over such a journey. God's blood, John, the land route might be hard, but you should be there within three days, or four at the outside.'

Well, they had come *the land route* and now they were faced with what looked like a vast inland sea.

During the ride here he had been thinking of Lucia Trevail. She stirred him mightily, but he was enough the man of the world to be aware that something was not right. There had been matters unspoken when they met in his solar; questions unasked and unanswered. He had mentioned her visit to Cecil.

The young statesman had uttered an uncharacteristically lewd laugh.

'Beware, John. Your prick has led you to trouble before, like a bull pulled by the nose to slaughter. There can be no greater peril for a man than to lure away a lady of the Privy Chamber. Mark the fate of Ralegh when he married Bess Throckmorton! You would do better to meet a thousand furies in combat than cross Her Majesty by bedding one of her favourites.'

Shakespeare became defensive, shocked by Cecil's bawdiness. Very rarely did he engage in such low tittle-tattle. 'Sir Robert, I merely mentioned that Lady Trevail had come to Dowgate with information, that is all.'

'Indeed, John. Well, I shall take your word for it. Mind you, Lucia is a fine woman, one of us.'

By which he meant, Shakespeare deduced, that she was a hard Protestant in the Cecilian mould. He would find out more about her when he returned from this mission. Whenever that might be.

'We'll have to stable the horses and find a boatman to carry us. Come, Boltfoot, let us return to that tavern in Waterbeach.'

Even as he said the words, he recalled the repast they had taken there. It had been cheery enough with good ale and a blazing hearth, but the laughter of the other drinkers and the landlord had made him uneasy. Now he realised why they were so merry: they were laughing at the two horsemen who thought they could ride to Wisbech . . .

'They will cheat us there, master. I wouldn't trust one of the villains to take us across the Thames in a tilt-boat, let alone carry us across this ocean.'

Boltfoot was right. Shakespeare wheeled his horse's head and shook the reins. Slowly, they began to retrace their steps while he contemplated their position. Ahead of them, a lone rider was approaching. Shakespeare hailed him.

The rider halted. Shakespeare recognised him from the night before at the Dolphin in Cambridge. He was a traveller, like them.

'There is no way ahead,' Shakespeare said.

The man grinned beneath his rain-sodden hat. 'Not for a horseman, no. But I have other means. Where are you headed?'

'Wisbech.'

'Then travel with me. My name is Paul Hooft.'

Shakespeare noted that he had a very slight Dutch accent; his name obviously emanated from the Low Countries.

'John Shakespeare. I am on Queen's business. This is my assistant, Mr Cooper.'

'Then you are well met, sir.' Hooft reached back and took a chart from his packsaddle. The map was on vellum and waxed against the weather. He held it out to Shakespeare and stabbed his finger at an inked cross on the word *Abbey*. 'This is my property, Mr Shakespeare, it is a little way east along the high banking. We can stay the night there, then travel on in the morning, for I have business in Wisbech myself.' He stowed the map.

Shakespeare hesitated. 'What is your business in Wisbech, Mr Hooft?'

'I export farm produce to the Low Countries, for they have much need of food and wool during these endless wars. That is where my family hails from.'

'We saw you at the Dolphin in Cambridge. Do you have business there, too?'

'Indeed, sir, yes. And I believe I saw you there also.'

They rode a mile along the raised gravel bank at the edge of the flood. A little way off, on slightly higher ground, Shakespeare made out the buildings of what had clearly been one of the great religious houses of the fens. From the preponderance of livestock and agricultural implements in the vicinity, it now looked very much like a farm – if a rather grand farm.

A dairymaid carrying pails on a yoke across her shoulders bowed her soaking head to Hooft as they rode past. He nodded back to her and they continued on to the flint priory, which seemed to have survived the Dissolution almost intact. They reined in to a halt before the front porch.

'This is my home,' Hooft said with a sweep of his arm. 'You are most welcome. Please, a groom will see to your horses. Come inside. This is no weather for travel.'

Paul Hooft was a fair-haired young man with a short, neat beard but no moustache. With his heavy riding cape removed, Shakespeare saw that he wore the plain broadcloth and falling band of a Puritan.

'You are on Queen's business? Then I am doubly bound to help you, sir,' Hooft said. 'Over meat and drink we will discuss how to get you to Wisbech from here.' He summoned a servant and ordered beds to be prepared, then turned back to his guest.

'Thank you, Mr Hooft.'

'It is my pleasure as well as my duty, sir, for your country has given my family refuge from the wars. I am delighted to have the opportunity to help.'

'That is good to hear, Mr Hooft.' Shakespeare was polite but circumspect. Hooft seemed genuine, but it did not mean, however, that he was to be trusted without question.

Their host was warming to his subject, his blue eyes shining in the firelight. 'I am a man of many parts, Mr Shakespeare. I am a trader, a farmer and an engineer, and I do all this work for the furtherance of God's glory. It is honest toil that reaps rewards. Man must not simply wait for the Lord to provide. He has given us this world to cultivate and cherish so that we may bring forth riches.'

'It is a point of view,' Shakespeare said. *A rather Calvinist point of view, perhaps.* Mr Hooft was a most curious young man.

'In northern Holland, I believe the land under cultivation has increased by a third in just fifty years. Once the fens here are drained, this land will have the richest soil in all England. I tell you, the pasture here will put beef on the table of every family in your country.'

Shakespeare nodded, indulging his host. 'That would be most welcome.'

'Forgive me if I press my case hard, but the evidence is there for all to see. I go to many markets in this country and nowhere do I find a cow that weighs above a thousand pounds, yet in Holland and Friesland you may commonly find cattle of sixteen hundred pounds. God helps those who help themselves, which is something the papists will never understand.'

As Hooft spoke, Shakespeare could see the glow of visionary zeal. But he saw, too, that he was a hard and practical man who might well have his way.

'I would be most grateful, Mr Shakespeare, for your assistance in this. I must have the patronage of wealthy men for my notions to be transformed into great works. I have sent letters to members of the Council before, but received no reply. Would you carry word from me to Sir Robert Cecil? Truly, he could enrich himself and the crown with this work.'

'I will carry letters for you, Mr Hooft, but I can promise nothing on Sir Robert's behalf.'

'Thank you, sir.'

It was becoming clear to Shakespeare why Hooft was so helpful and welcoming to two rain-sodden strangers. Their arrival had been like a piece of driftwood to a drowning man. He saw them as the pathway to men of influence.

The Dutchman told them that his great-uncle had bought

the old abbey and lands in the 1560s; on his death in the late 1570s it had passed to Paul Hooft's father, Cornelius.

'My great-uncle saved this house and farm from ruin, but my father had little taste for it. He was more interested in making war on the Spanish tyrants and died fighting. He had already sent my mother here to run the farm for him and I came with her.'

'Is she here?'

'She went to God last year.'

Shakespeare studied Paul Hooft closely. There was something unsettling about the man. Was it the casual denunciation of papists, or merely the gleam in his eye that seemed slightly unwholesome?

Hooft brought out a chart and showed Shakespeare the route they would take on the morrow.

'We will go by boat across to the Isle of Ely, and from there onwards to the isles of Chatteris and March before the final crossing to Wisbech.'

'What of the causeways? My own map shows a path from Cottenham to Rampton, then Haven Drove, Belsars Hill and Aldreth Bridge.'

'All under water save the bridge itself. We must go by boat. The bargemen who are certain of their paths might trust the heavy horses to wade along the courses, but I am not so certain. I will not take my horses into that flood. We must move you stage by stage, but I cannot promise you that it will be an easy journey.'

Shakespeare thought wryly of the decision to imprison the priests in Wisbech Castle. That had been the work of the late Mr Secretary, Sir Francis Walsingham, back in the 1580s. The wily old fox had chosen well, for it would surely be easier to escape from the Tower of London than get away from such a remote and desolate place.

The guests ate well in ill-fitting attire lent them by Hooft while their own clothes dried at the hearth. Shakespeare dismissed his initial doubts about his host's zealotry and began to see that his ambition could, indeed, bring great wealth to this part of England. There might be something barnacle-like in the way he had fixed himself upon his guests, but then the truth struck Shakespeare: the man was simply lonely. Shakespeare found himself speaking his mind.

'Do you not think you might be a little happier here if you were to take a wife?'

The sadness in Hooft's eyes told the story. 'There was someone, Mr Shakespeare, but it did not end well. I do not like to talk about it . . .'

'Forgive me, Mr Hooft. I should not talk in such a way on first acquaintance.'

Hooft tried to laugh. 'Well, I am sure we will be better acquainted by the time we reach Wisbech. But you are right, it will never be easy for me living here. Though I speak English as a native and have lived here most of my life, yet I am still a stranger. People are not welcoming, unless they are one in religion. And many of those here have little or no faith. You did well to find me, for they will not help *you* either. They are a breed apart, living mostly by fowling, fishing of eels and common thievery. They think no more of traversing the floodwaters than you or I would think of walking along a city road. They resent all strangers and see them but as prey to be robbed.'

Shakespeare turned to Boltfoot, who had remained silent. 'I think Mr Hooft is telling you to keep your cutlass honed and your powder dry.'

Boltfoot grunted dismissively. When had he *not* been prepared for a fight?

After supper, they sat before the fire with cups of wine while Hooft read them some verses he had composed; Shakespeare thought them rustic but fair and thanked him, then they retired to their beds.

Before sleep took him, he wondered again about Lucia Trevail, but her face vanished and was replaced by the grim visage of the old Marian nun, Sister Michael. He had worried that he was wrong to imprison her; now he was concerned that he might have made a worse error of judgment in having her freed. He had made a similar mistake in letting Loake go away instead of extracting his secret first. Two errors, both of them bad. Was he losing his way?

At last, he descended into a dreamless sleep.

The morning was crisp and chilly. On the bank of the Thames at Richmond, Annis Farrier was walking her dog. This morning, like every other, she threw sticks for the mongrel. It was the time of day she liked above all others, for she would slip out of the house and let the children fend for themselves; they were old enough now and she needed a little peace for herself. The remainder of her day would be given over to backbreaking work in the palace laundry.

One of the sticks landed in the river. The dog jumped in to fetch it, but instead of bringing it ashore, he began tugging at something caught in the roots of a tree. Annis called the animal to come out, but it would not. Edging carefully down the muddy incline she saw that the dog was pulling at something pink with blue, spidery veins. She recoiled in horror. It was flesh that she saw, something very much like a hand, with rings on all the fingers. She gasped. It *was* a hand, and it was attached to a body . . .

Chapter 13

JANE COOPER WALKED to the Stone House in Fylpot Street with hope and fear in her heart. Her son John was already over the worst of the sickness and was up and about again. She had left him with Ursula so that she could come here alone.

The serving boy John Braddedge opened the door, looked at her and said, 'Oh it's you.' He held out his hand for money.

'You had a farthing before. I'll tell Dr Forman you have been demanding money.'

Braddedge snorted. 'Why should I care what old Hairy Balls thinks? He can't sack me – I know enough of his little secrets. He was up the skirts of a bishop's wife yesterday, and you won't be the first one he's swived *this* day, mistress.'

Jane wanted to slap the boy for his lewd impertinence, but simply pushed past him into the hallway. Braddedge shrugged indifferently and closed the door. With ill grace, he trudged up the stairway to his master's rooms, then reappeared a minute later.

'You can go up. He's waiting for you.'

Jane was relieved to find Forman looking businesslike. He was fully dressed and the bed was unruffled.

'Good morrow, Mistress Cooper,' he said cheerily. 'Have

you not brought the little one? How does he fare? Sit down, sit down.'

Jane took a seat. 'He is a great deal better, thank you, Dr Forman. He has his vitality back.'

Forman smiled. 'I knew all would be well with the boy. It is good. But, pray tell me, what of you and your husband? Have you increased the frequency of your congress?'

She shook her head hurriedly. 'He is away at the moment.'

In truth, she was pleased he was absent, for she had dreaded making some excuse to come out today to see Dr Forman. Above all else, she could not bear to think of betraying Boltfoot by deceitful dealings, even in a good cause.

'Well, when he returns, mistress, make sure he couples with you each day, for it is certain that the more a man occupies his wife, the more potent is his seed. Wait here if you will, for I have cast your horoscope and that of little John.'

He went through to the next room and returned with charts, full of circles, lines and astrological symbols that Jane did not understand. He laid them out carefully on the floorboards.

'You see here,' he prodded an area of the paper with his stained yellow finger. 'This tells me that you will experience new life, which I believe to mean a healthy baby.' He smiled at her briefly, then pointed again at the chart and his eyes betrayed concern. 'But there is death also, someone close to you.'

'A death?'

'Not a child. More than that I cannot say. I am certain of this because I have your son's chart here.' He indicated the second paper. 'It shows a healthy line and prosperity. The heavens say he will live to a good age and bring you great pride.'

'Who then?'

'I cannot say, Mistress Cooper. I am sorry.' He hesitated a

moment too long. 'Did you bring me Mr Cooper's time and place of birth?'

'He does not know it. Do you think *he* is the one in danger?'

'No, no, mistress, I did not say that. Now tell me, did your month arrive?'

'Yes, two days since.'

'Then you must engage in congress four days from the last day of flux. Do not fail in this.'

'But I do not know if Mr Cooper will be returned by then.'

He jabbed his finger once more at the chart. 'It is not my rule; this is merely what the stars tell me, Mistress Cooper.' He shrugged. 'Next Tuesday at noon. It must be done if you would get great with child and come to term.'

Jane averted her eyes. She could not bear the way he looked at her, nor the unwanted churning she felt inside as he spoke. She rose from her seat. 'I must pay you,' she said, still looking away. 'How much do I owe you, Dr Forman?'

'We will talk of that anon.' He handed her a ring, a twist of metal in which were trapped fragments of coral. 'This is a sigil that I have made for you, with symbols of fecundity from the warmer regions of the earth. Wear it close to your wedding band. Return to me next week and we will discuss money then. I can see that you are not wealthy, mistress, so I shall ask a pittance from you, nothing more.'

Jane hunched her head into her shoulders and scuttled to the door, clutching the ring tight in her fist. She hurried down the stairs, horribly aware that the boy Braddedge was leering at her. She did not wait for him to open the front door, but bolted past him into the street, as though she were escaping from the abyss.

Simon Forman watched the woman go, with interest. He closed the door after her, then picked up the charts, rolled them neatly and took them into the adjoining room, where he kept his immense collection of books and cures. Here was his life's work. It was here that he had divined his cure for the plague and it was here that he wrote the encoded diary of his work. He knew that men derided him, particularly those fools from the College of Physicians, but he knew, too, that he was in the right. He was the true man of science and none of them understood the significance of the stars as well as he did.

He put down the charts on a bench with dozens of others. They told men whether or not to propose marriage, whether to invest in a voyage and whether they would live to old age. They told women how to find love, what name to give their new-born son for good fortune, and whether they would be found out if they went to bed with a handsome servant.

Beside the charts, there were many more papers and books. There were, too, glass vials small and large, and earthenware pots, copper pans for heating substances and glass jars for examining them, and the curious dead bodies and foetuses of animals from the Africas, the Indies and the Russias.

There was, too, a woman in the room. He gazed at her thoughtfully and scratched his beard.

'Well?' she said.

'I say she is genuine.'

'But you say, too, that she is a servant at Shakespeare's house.'

'That is by the by. You have nothing to worry about.'

'I am not so certain. Indeed, I am not certain at all.'

At the front of Ovid Sloth's ancient farmhouse, his grooms assisted the two moneylenders to mount their horses. They were sober-looking, dressed in black and dark brown, with no evidence on display of their vast wealth. Their retinue of twenty-two armed men waited motionless on their mounts. Sloth stood before the great door and watched them. Their meeting had not been easy, but he was relieved that he had bought some time.

The quieter of the two creditors settled himself into the saddle, clutched the reins of his steed and leant towards Sloth. 'Remember, Señor Sloth,' he said, without anger or any other emotion in his voice, 'if you do not repay at least half of the twenty thousand ducats by summer's end, all your goods and properties will be seized. Everything you possess in Spain.' He nodded towards his expensive attire. 'Even the clothes you wear.'

Sloth nodded in acquiescence and his immense bulk shook. 'You will have your gold.'

'If we do not, then there will be yet worse,' the other moneylender said. 'We will have not only your vineyards and houses, but your eyes.'

Sloth smiled at them. They gazed back at him for a moment, without expression, then wheeled their horses' heads and kicked the animals into a trot with their retinue around them. He watched them go, along the dusty path to the nearby port town of Sanlúcar de Barrameda, from whence they would take the river ferry to Seville. At last, his shoulders slumped.

The meeting had been deeply unpleasant. He had promised them everything they asked, and more. He had boasted of his new ventures with expansive optimism, but they had not been mollified.

Their words were spoken in soft voices, but Sloth knew that the moneylenders meant what they said. They would, indeed, pluck out his eyes. Now, like a top-heavy galleon, he turned away and waddled on splayed feet through the courtyard of his palatial farmhouse. It was built in the Moorish style, with light walls, a large square patio with cool cloisters on three sides. All this and more would be lost to him if trade did not improve, and soon.

He stopped beneath a mature olive tree and supported himself against the trunk while he caught his breath. He had a thirst that ate at his soul. A breeze blew the leaves above him; nearby, a fig and an oleander swayed. A central fountain sparkled in the sunlight.

The crack of a musket-shot broke the still air. A vein in Sloth's neck bulged, but with an effort he moved on across the courtyard and out through the arched entranceway. Before him stood a large outhouse with white walls, thick and strong to keep the interior temperature as constant as possible throughout the year. Through the dark doorway he could just see the immense barrels of manzanilla ranged before him, comfortingly dark, rich and timeless.

Sloth shambled into the bodega with a ponderous, awkward gait. The cellarman stiffened and bowed low at his approach, but Sloth ignored him. He ran his white bulbous fingers along the staves of a fine oak cask. This, above all, was his love. He breathed deep, separating the scents he knew so well into their constituent parts, imbibing the intoxicating aromas of fermented grape and salt from the sea. It was said he could tell the quality of wine by sniffing the air in the cellar, while the wine was still in the cask. He signalled to the servant with a curt tilt of the chin. The servant knew what was required of him and instantly produced a long-handled ladle, dipping it through the bunghole of one of the casks. With a flourish, he proffered the cup to his master. Sloth gulped down the wine, then gasped and wiped his sleeve across his dribbling lip and his beardless chin. He ran his hand across his glistening bald head.

The conversation with the creditors spun through his mind. 'Go and live in England with your own kind, señor,' the smaller of the two had said with a sneer. 'Leave all this for us.'

'I am Spanish, damn you.'

'Your mother may have been Spanish, but you are English, like your father before you.'

'You will be paid. In full.'

'Time is running out.'

He could not believe that England had not fallen yet. When it did, his coffers would fill again like the incoming tide. It should have fallen in eighty-eight, the year he had borrowed so much, certain that Medina-Sidonia's Armada would triumph. He could not possibly go to live in England; his debts there were, if anything, deeper even than they were here and his business interests, such as his investment in the playhouses, were simply inadequate to cope.

Like a dripping tap, every day that passed without resolution emptied his coffers a little more, brought his affairs closer to ruin. His family had been trading wines from Sanlúcar to England for more than a century. These last eight years of open warfare had brought an embargo and put an end to legal trading. Sloth needed this war to end. He needed Spain and Catholicism to gain power over England. He needed the trade routes to London and the west country to reopen – and fast.

A second musket-shot split the peace of the morning. Sloth swore, then threw the long-stemmed cup to the floor. He waddled out of the bodega and stood in the cool air. The last miles of the Guadalquivir river stretched before him, flowing from right to left to spew into the Atlantic. They were just east of Bonanza, the riverside docks from which both Magellan and Columbus had once departed on momentous voyages.

Sloth glared into the bright morning light. Hugh Fitzgerald, one of the pretty brothers he had found at the Irish College in Salamanca, was engaged in swordplay with three Spanish soldiers in armour. He was working with his short sword, cutting at the left side of the neck of the first man, then back into the right side of the neck for the second, before bringing the blade forward again for a thrust into the belly of the third. His skill was impressive. The clang of metal blade on metal armour rang across the plain. The whole sequence – step forward, cut, cut again, thrust – took less than four seconds. Had the three Spaniards not been heavily protected by chain mail and steel, they would be dead by now.

Hugh Fitzgerald's brother, Seamus, was working with knives. He stood, arms outstretched, a knife in each hand. Opposing him was a Spanish soldier with a short sword. Seamus was weaving and thrusting, evading the Spanish sword and jabbing with his own blade, like a prizefighter. Nearby, the diminutive Dick Winnow was powdering his wheel-lock, preparing to take another shot at the waterfowl that lived on the river and in the wetlands beyond.

'No more, God damn you!' Sloth shouted. 'It is like a circle of hell! You disturb my morning peace.'

The Irishmen stopped their training and looked across at him, then made a face at each other. Seeing this, Winnow approached them with his pistol and, though they were a head taller than he was, pushed them hard in their chests with the butt. 'Move away,' he said, an edge to his voice. 'If he says stop, then do so. Do not rile him for he is a boiling kettle.'

The Spanish soldiers retreated towards their encampment. But the Irish brothers and Dick Winnow stayed. Winnow was no more than five feet tall, yet he was afraid of no man, least of all these two callow Irish gentlemen with their jewelled swords and knives, their gentry airs and their tutored swordplay. He gazed at Ovid Sloth and wished to God that Roag would return soon. Surely they could wait no longer.

'Come on, move away,' Winnow repeated, pushing Hugh and Seamus Fitzgerald out of Sloth's line of vision.

'Why should we pay heed to the slimy fat sodomite?' Hugh said. 'What can he do to us?'

Winnow grasped Hugh Fitzgerald's balls in his left hand and with his right thrust the muzzle of his gun up into his jaw. 'Because without him, none of this will work, Mr Fitzgerald. Make it easy. Come away.' He squeezed the balls. Hard. 'He is indispensable. You may not be.'

Hugh Fitzgerald let out a small howl. His brother pulled him away, laughing.

Winnow released his grip. 'Go to the other side of the farm-house and rehearse your moves there. You will need them, sure enough. Just as you may need your balls one day.'

Just then, Seamus Fitzgerald held up his hand. In the distance they heard the sound of horse's hoofs on the hard, dusty earth. Dick Winnow and Hugh looked towards the east and there was a palpable easing of tension. Roag had returned.

Roag reined in to a walk. He did not dismount, but rode right up to Ovid Sloth. Leaning from the high-pommelled saddle, he clasped Sloth's naked head between his dusty hands and kissed his brow.

'*Pax vobiscum*,' Roag said. 'I just saw some friends of yours on the road.'

'Those dirty moneylenders are no friends of mine, Mr Roag.'

'Well, I bring fair news. We sail.' He brought out the *casa de contratación* authorisation document, waved it in the air and then replaced it in his doublet. 'Let us load up our weapons. We will have a mass said, then sail on the tide.'

Sloth heaved a great sigh that seemed to shake his whole body in ripples. He took Roag's hands and clasped them between his own. 'Thanks be to God,' he said.

Roag removed his hands from Sloth's and gazed around the vineyard. 'Where are Ratbane and Paget?'

'Drinking, whoring . . . who knows?' Sloth said. 'Can they even read?'

Roag laughed. 'Well enough for our needs.'

'And the spy?' Winnow said quietly.

'He is no longer a threat, Dick. No word will ever pass his lips again.'

Roag put his head on one side and regarded Winnow. Warner may have been caught, but there would be others. Could one of *these* men be a spy, too?

Chapter 14

RAIN AND WIND swept across the inland sea. Paul Hooft pushed the large punt away from the muddy shore with his quant – a long, heavy pole with a prong at the end to prevent it sticking in the mud. They were watched by a sullen crowd of fishers, preparing their osier eel hives and sharp, three-tined glaives. Within a few moments they had disappeared into the rain. Paul Hooft stood at the back of the punt, poling, while Shakespeare and Boltfoot sat on the benches, gazing into an endless vista of grey sky and black floodwaters.

'Would a rowing boat not get us across faster, Mr Hooft?' Shakespeare demanded, worried by the prospect of a long, tortuous journey. 'Perhaps a sailing skiff would make more haste.'

'This will suffice, sir. Its bottom is flat and will skim over areas of reed, sedge and thatch. You will see.'

A narrow barge, heavy laden with corn or grain and six sodden sheep, emerged from the north and drifted past them going south. She was being drawn by two heavy horses, up to their withers as they waded through the shallows. The two men steering her gazed across at the punt without a word or even nod of greeting and were gone as suddenly as they had appeared.

Within minutes, three men carrying rods and nets strode

past them through the flood, as though walking on the water. Shakespeare and Boltfoot looked at them in astonishment.

'Stilts,' Hooft said. 'They are walking on stilts, like the clowns you must have seen at Bartholomew Fair. Many men use these in the fens.'

Occasionally, they passed islands of higher ground where they saw men with eel hives. Sometimes they spied men with muskets for fowling and Boltfoot fingered the trigger of his caliver, which lay in his lap, wondering whether any of his powder was still dry in this world of eternal damp.

The minutes wore on into hours, and it was impossible for Shakespeare to tell what progress they were making, though Hooft continually insisted they would be in Ely by dark, and would find an inn there. A church steeple loomed out of the grey. The water lapped at its very base. As they glided past, they made out old gravestones protruding from the flood, ghostly and ominous.

Then, at last, long into the afternoon as the sky was darkening, they saw the immense tower of Ely Cathedral emerge into view, as welcome a sight as any sailor ever saw when spying land.

The taproom was thick with a heady blend of woodsmoke and the aroma of beer. Over a supper of roasted eels, they considered their situation. Shakespeare was grateful to Hooft for bringing them thus far in safety, but he was anxious to get to Wisbech and felt certain there must be a faster way to travel. When they landed on the isle, he had noted the various ferrymen and bargees shouting prices for their services.

Now, as they wiped up the last of the fish juices with dense slabs of bread, Shakespeare announced that he intended talking to the ferrymen to discover their opinion of the best way ahead.

'They will rob you, Mr Shakespeare.'

Hooft paused as a serving girl came over. Her hair was long and uncovered and her dress was low-cut, showing off her inviting breasts.

Hooft stood up from his stool. 'Cover yourself, mistress!'

The girl looked shocked and put a hand to her chest. Shakespeare smiled at her. 'Ask the landlord or one of his men to come over and serve us,' he said softly. He touched the Dutchman's sleeve. 'Sit down, Mr Hooft. It has been a long day.'

Hooft watched the girl back away, then sat down slowly. 'Why do they employ whores to serve us? Is there no modesty here?'

Shakespeare tried to calm him. 'It was ever thus in England, Mr Hooft. You are not the first newcomer to be surprised by the freedoms enjoyed by our womenfolk.'

Hooft bowed his head. 'Forgive me, Mr Shakespeare. I do indeed sometimes feel a stranger to this country, even though I have spent a great deal of my life here. I was brought up by my mother to expect modesty and domesticity from women and girls. But you are right, I spoke out of place.'

'We are all tired. Let us retire to sleep and be on our way at dawn.'

When they awoke, Paul Hooft had gone.

He had left a few coins – his portion of the reckoning – but the promised letter for Cecil was not there. After breaking their fast with bread and eggs, they walked in the shadow of the great cathedral down to the water's edge. The rain had stopped, but the sky was still grey and lowering. They discovered that Hooft's punt was also gone.

'I think we offended him, Boltfoot.'

'Well, master, that is his choice.'

There were two ferries. One already had two passengers but there was room for two more.

'Where are you headed?' Shakespeare demanded.

'Where are you going?' retorted the ferryman, a slight man of fifty years or so.

'Wisbech.'

The ferryman looked them up and down. 'Clamber in. It'll be three shillings for both of you.'

Shakespeare gazed at the man, who looked like a water-rat, slick-haired and pinched about the mouth. He glanced at Boltfoot, who shrugged.

'You'll find none quicker, master,' the ferryman continued. 'We'll be there in six hours, which will include an hour's stop for our midday repast at Chatteris.'

The ferry was a large rowing skiff with four oarsmen. Soon they were out on the broad flooded plain, with Ely Cathedral receding behind them.

It was then that Shakespeare really took note of the rowers and the other two passengers. They *all* looked like water-rats. A whole family of them, throwing sly glances at each other. Shakespeare sighed and looked sideways at Boltfoot. He, too, had seen the connection between the men. And they were out-numbered seven to two. They would be robbed; it was simply a matter of when.

'Well, Boltfoot, this is going to be an interesting journey.'

'Indeed, master.'

Visibility was better than the previous day. Now they really did feel as if they were on an ocean. Save for a few spots of land and distant pinpricks, which they knew to be church spires, all they could see was black water, in all directions.

'Where you from, stranger?' the ferryman asked Shakespeare.

'London.'

'That's like Fenland only different, so I'm told.'

The ferryman was clearly the father of the family. He stood at the rear of the boat, directing the course and urging the rowers on.

The attack came with terrifying suddenness. They were half an hour out, near a small island, and there were no other boats in the vicinity, no witnesses, and no help.

Shakespeare noticed that the rowers were slowing. His hand went to the poniard in his belt. Boltfoot drew his cutlass.

'Now,' said the ferryman.

The four rowers dropped their oars and the two fake passengers were up in an instant. The boat rocked violently and Shakespeare was nearly thrown into the water. He dropped his poniard and gripped the side to steady himself, only to find three men surrounding him, all with weapons out and ready to kill. The sharp edge of a blade hovered at his throat. Daggers prodded at his belly. He was utterly at the mercy of the assailants.

Boltfoot had somehow edged himself into a better position. He was at bay, cutlass held out before him as he crouched at the side of the boat. Three heavily armed men were closing on him.

'No need for unpleasantness, masters,' the ferryman said in a quiet, well-mannered voice. He was still standing at the rear of the skiff, hands on hips and unconcerned, as though this were his daily business to be attended to. 'It is time for the collection of fares. Hand over your purses and your weapons and we will set you down safely upon that island there. If you resist, you will discover that my sons are as adept at filleting a man as they are at drawing the entrails from plover, swan or bittern.'

Shakespeare brushed the blade away from his throat with the back of his hand. 'I must tell you that I am on Queen's business. If you rob me or harm me, you will all hang.'

The ferryman smiled. 'You are mistaken, Mr Traveller, for if we decide to slit your throats, then you will sink into these waters as food for pike, and none will ever know that you are there.'

Boltfoot reached out with his left hand and gripped Shakespeare's arm. 'Give him your purse, master. It is not worth dying for.'

Shakespeare looked at his assistant with surprise. Boltfoot never shied away from a fight.

'Listen to your serving man, Mr Traveller. He is a man of wisdom.'

The ferryman nodded to his accomplices, who all stood back in the boat to give their victims room to hand over their possessions. Again, the shallow-keeled vessel swayed alarmingly, but this was home territory for the attackers and they kept their footing with ease.

Shakespeare pulled open his bear cloak and removed his kidskin purse from his belt. He also picked up his poniard and handed it over, hilt first, although it hurt him greatly to do so.

'And your sword, master.'

Shakespeare shook his head. 'I keep the sword, and it will stay sheathed until you are gone.'

The ferryman ignored him and turned to Boltfoot.

Boltfoot did not loosen the grip on his cutlass. 'No, I will *not* give up my weapons.' His voice was hard, stubborn, unbending. 'I travelled the world to take this cutlass and this caliver from Spaniards, and I will not surrender them to an English rogue.'

'Then it is simple. You will die.'

'And you will, too, Mr Ferryman. For whatever else happens, I will make certain of your death, even as I go to mine.'

The ferryman hesitated. The eyes of his men were on him, waiting to see which way he would turn, waiting to plunge their blades into Boltfoot at their master's word. 'Travelled the world, you say?'

'Aye, with Drake. Across all the oceans. And this –' he indicated the floods – 'is naught but a puddle of piss to me.'

The ferryman laughed. 'Very well,' he said. 'I like your spirit. That gun across your back would not do for fowling anyway. But hand me your powder, shot and purse – and I will consider the bargain struck.'

Boltfoot took his purse from his thick hide jerkin; there was little enough money in it. He tossed it to the ferryman, followed by his powder horn and bag of balls.

The ferryman poured the contents of the two purses into his slender hand. His eyes widened at the gold coins Shakespeare had given him. 'Well, indeed,' he said. 'This is a good day. This will pay for your lives and you may even keep your weapons.'

'Put us on the island,' Shakespeare demanded.

'Take yourselves there, masters. If you will step from my craft, you will find the water no more than three feet deep. And so I bid you God speed – and I will thank you to pay my respects to the Queen, and inform her that she will always be welcome in the fens.'

Chapter 15

Behind closed doors at the upper end of Westminster Hall, the court of Chancery was in session. No members of the public were admitted. The Queen and Council had commanded that this case be heard in secret.

The case of Richard Topcliffe, Queen's servant, priest-hunter and official torturer, against Thomas Fitzherbert, commonly known as Tom, had been a long, drawn-out affair with constant adjournments, but it was about to take a dramatic turn.

Topcliffe was suing Fitzherbert for non-payment of a contract for five thousand pounds. The money had supposedly been promised to Topcliffe if he would persecute to death Tom Fitzherbert's papist father John Fitzherbert, so that Tom could inherit his estates.

The case was dragging on because no one, least of all the Queen of England, wanted to be on record as allowing a contract to murder to be sanctioned. It would be a gift to her many enemies at home and abroad.

Lord Keeper Sir John Puckering, resplendent in his ermine and scarlet robe, lounged back in his great throne of a chair as Topcliffe, incoherent in his rage, repeatedly berated Tom Fitzherbert and his advisers for their bad faith.

'Do you think you can agree this sum, to be paid on John

Fitzherbert's death, and then, when he dies, not pay?' Topcliffe's voice was a mastiff growl.

Puckering yawned and his eyes turned upwards to the heavens. This had been told and retold a hundred times. He just wanted them all to give up and go back to their wives and whores.

Fitzherbert rose to his feet. 'But, I repeat, your honour, my father died of natural causes, so why should I pay?'

Topcliffe slammed his fist on to the table in fury. 'Yes, but he was in the Tower – where *I* put him and tormented him! He died of natural causes because *my* racking weakened him to the point of death!'

Puckering had had enough. His gout ailed him and he had other matters on his mind, particularly the forthcoming visit of Her Majesty to his home in Kew. He knew that he must entertain her lavishly if he was to be sure of her continuing favour, so every detail must be attended to. He had a good mind to call another adjournment to this never-ending case. Hopefully by summer's end either Topcliffe or Fitzherbert or both of them might be dead, and then the case could be shuffled away. Quietly.

Topcliffe stormed towards Fitzherbert, brandishing his silver-tipped blackthorn stick.

Puckering was suddenly alarmed. He wanted no blood spilt here. 'Mr Topcliffe, you will halt where you are! Sit down, sir, sit down. This is a court of law, not an alehouse or your foul dungeon.'

The old white-haired torturer looked at Puckering with loathing. His stick hovered with menace. 'He is a dog, Mr Puckering, and he must be beaten like one. You must order him to give me my money!'

'Sit down, Mr Topcliffe.'

Grudgingly, Topcliffe lowered his heavy cane and slunk back towards his seat.

Puckering sighed. He had felt it prudent not to make comment on the merits or otherwise of the case. But he was mightily tired of this pair.

'Thank you, Mr Topcliffe, and in future you will address me as your honour or as Lord Keeper Puckering. You will not call me *mister* in this court. Is that clear?'

Topcliffe looked away sullenly.

'It is incumbent upon me to say a few words at this juncture,' Puckering said. 'I have listened to your plea with restraint these many months, but it is time now for me to speak. And I must tell you that whatever the claim you have in law, you have no *moral* right to make such a contract, nor demand it be honoured.'

Topcliffe turned back and glared. 'So the law means nothing in this court. A contract is to be torn up because of your finer feelings, *Mr* Puckering.'

'It cannot be right to accept five thousand pounds for murder, Topcliffe.'

Topcliffe smirked, looked around the assembled lawyers in their black robes, then pointed his blackthorn at the judge. 'And is it right, therefore, for Judge Puckering to accept ten thousand pounds in a bribe? For I know he has done so. Why should I not accept five thousand, when he takes ten?'

Puckering blanched, then the blood rose to his face. He turned to his fellow judge, Sir Thomas Egerton, Master of the Rolls and sometime friend of Topcliffe. Even he had had his fill and he shook his head slowly. Puckering brought his fist down on the table with a resounding thud.

'Enough. Topcliffe, you have gone too far.' He leant over the table to his side. 'Mr Clerk, you will have the guards take Topcliffe into custody for contempt of court. Have him taken in manacles to the Marshalsea to await our pleasure.' He hammered his fist again. 'Court adjourned!'

*

Frank Mills shuffled into the office of Sir Robert Cecil. His head was low and, though he had made some effort to brush his hair, he did not look well.

Cecil recoiled. His assistant secretary was unwashed and stank. 'Sit down, Frank,' he said, indicating the far side of the table; as far away as possible.

'Thank you, Sir Robert.' He took the seat.

Cecil remained standing. In front of him, on the table, were a book and a sheet of paper. He squared the edges so that they were both aligned and neat, like his own immaculate black attire and his trimmed little beard.

'Anthony Friday will be here shortly. First, I must talk with you, Frank. In truth, I can no longer do without your services. You must stiffen your resolve and return to your duties. Do you understand?'

'Yes, Sir Robert.'

'For, by God's faith, you seem absent even when you are with us. However, I shall allow you to stay at your desk. You will deal with the intercepts and reports from abroad. I am hoping that Mr Friday will agree to be at your service, for while John is away in the east, you will need assistance.'

'Thank you.'

'Good man.' Cecil produced a paper. 'For instance, there is this report. It tells us that four companies of General del Águila's most effective Spanish troops are engaged in intense training at Port-Louis, in Brittany. You have a mind for such things, Frank. What does it signify?'

Mills read the letter quickly. 'It might suggest that they intend returning to the Crozon peninsula, to rebuild the fortress.'

Cecil shook his small head. 'I don't think so. Henri of France will not allow it. Since Norreys and Frobisher took the fortress in November, the Spanish have looked vulnerable. It suits

Henri that they stay down. He will fight such a move, and Águila knows it.'

'Ireland then?'

'My thoughts, too. So put your mind to it, Frank. And call in reports from Brittany and elsewhere to discover what they are about. I do not like such unexplained manoeuvres.'

There was a knock at the door. Clarkson appeared.

'Mr Friday is here, Sir Robert.'

'Show him in.'

Anthony Friday strode into the room. With a sweep of his right arm, he bowed so low that his long fair hair almost brushed the wooden floorboards. He then drew himself up to his full height, which was not great, and bowed again to Cecil, though it might have been taken as merely an exaggerated nod of the head.

'Good morrow, Mr Friday. Be seated beside Mr Mills, whom I believe you know.'

'Indeed, Sir Robert, and good morrow to you.' He smiled at Mills in acknowledgment, took the seat reserved for him and reeled at the waft of bodily odours.

Cecil clapped his hands. 'Well, gentlemen, this must be like old times with Mr Secretary Walsingham. You worked together then, I believe, and I am sure it will be well for you to work side by side once again, for Queen and country.'

Friday shifted uneasily, but said nothing.

'We have a problem,' Cecil continued. 'A shortage of man-power, to be precise. Mr Topcliffe, as I am sure the whole of London knows, is sweating in the Marshalsea, scratching pleading letters to Her Majesty, so he is of no use to us. Mr Shakespeare, meanwhile, is away, engaged on other matters. To be plain, Mr Friday, I would have you return to service for me, if only for a short while.'

Friday spread his palms extravagantly. 'You know, of course, that I would do anything for you and for Her Majesty, but I am exceeding busy. The playhouse owners are impatient and I must produce plays for them. I also have a private commission of great value to me.'

This was about money. If Friday was going to work for him, he expected a good deal of gold. Cecil was having none of it.

'I recall when you were busy priest-hunting with Topcliffe, Mr Friday. I recall the days when you put your quill to use to denounce the Pope, the Jesuits and all their diabolical works. And while you did so, you were given leeway for your less salubrious writing. A translation of the lewd works of Aretino . . . that was yours, was it not? Now, if that had been brought to the attention of the Master of the Revels or Stationers' Hall, how would you have fared? Why, you would have been a guest of Mr Topcliffe's dungeon, not his comrade-at-arms. Has so much changed now? Do you think *all* your present writings would pass muster?'

If he was worried, Friday strove not to show it. He was a player as well as a playmaker. 'I have a wife; I have children. A man has needs, and so I must write. I am contracted to the Rose and have commissions from the Theatre. My playhouse masters are hard men and will allow me no respite. And, as you may know, the world of the intelligencer is fraught with dangers and erratic rewards.'

'And this?' Cecil pushed the book across the table to him. 'Why, only this week this work crossed my desk. *The Pleasures of the Flesh*, it is called. Do you recognise it, Mr Friday?'

He shook his head. 'Sir Robert, I have never seen this book.'

'Here, let me show you.' Cecil leant over the table and opened the pages. There were drawings of men and women engaged in all manner of couplings, with erotic verses to accompany the pictures. 'What do you think, Mr Friday? How would Stationers' Hall react to this?'

'This is a calumny, Sir Robert! This is not my work. Look, my name is nowhere to be seen. I am not the coter. By no means, no, sir.'

Cecil smiled. '*The Pleasures of the Flesh*. The printer Christopher Bynneman tells me it has sold well and made a fine purse. I believe he is not as circumspect as his late father was in the books he chooses to publish. He tells me *you* wrote it, Mr Friday. Now, who am I to believe?'

Friday shifted uneasily. 'Why would you believe that flea-arsed dog Bynneman?'

'Because he has shown me the contract between you.'

'I'll geld him, God shrivel his balls!'

'I think it fair to say that he was under some duress when he admitted as much to me. I think it also must be said that a word of this, from me to Stationers' Hall, and you will likely lose fingers, if not a hand or two.'

'How much will you pay me?'

'Two marks a week, Mr Friday. But I expect results. The main problem I have is the death of a man named Garrick Loake, fished out of the Thames at Richmond. Does the name mean anything to you?'

Friday suddenly showed interest. 'Garrick Loake dead? How?'

'We are still trying to determine that. It was only the etching of his name on all his rings – and it seems he had a lot of them – that enabled him to be identified at all.'

'I am sorry to hear of this, but Garrick is – *was* – of no importance to any man other than his creditors. Why is the government interested in his death?'

'Because he came to Mr Shakespeare offering secrets for sale and then disappeared. A tale of a plot fomented in Spain, which we might not have taken seriously, except that we have corroboration. I rather suspect he was murdered because the plotters feared they were about to be betrayed.'

'Plenty of men might have wished him dead. He owed money to usurers. Debts he could not pay. That is reason enough to hurl a man to his doom in this town.'

'Find out which usurers, then. Talk to anyone who might know anything. His body is now with the Searcher of the Dead, Mr Peace.'

Anthony Friday, visibly disconsolate, stood up as if to go.

'Sit down, Mr Friday. I have not finished with you yet. I want you to do more. I want you to revisit your old haunts. In the past, you have posed as a papist. I wish you to do so again, and listen carefully to all that is said. There is a plot out there and I want it uncovered, and fast. You will go to every mass and meeting of priests in London, and you will discover what is going on. And you, Mr Mills, you will decode every scrap of paper that comes our way at double speed. You will bring every sliver of information to my attention. Something is happening; a snake of insurrection is rearing its head, and its sting is deadly. It comes from Seville and it may involve the army of General Águila. Someone in England, some traitor, knows what it is about. I am as certain of this as anything in my life. It may be that Mr Shakespeare will cut this serpent off at the head, but we cannot take that for granted. Until he returns, gentlemen, I am relying on you.'

The two men looked at their master with reluctant obedience. There was no doubt who held the power in this room.

'And Frank,' Cecil continued, 'in God's name, bathe. Whatever troubles afflict you in your home life, you must deal with them like a man. Go bravely, sir, go bravely.'

Shakespeare gazed out across the bleak landscape. His nether-stocks, hose and half his cloak were soaked through. He and Boltfoot stood by the reeds at the water's edge on an island of no more than acre.

'By God's faith, Boltfoot, we are in the middle of a sub-merged field! This is nowhere near the route to any town. No passing boats will see us. Should we try to wade through the flood? If so, which direction should we take? There are not even any church bells to show us the way.'

Boltfoot shook his head. 'We'd stumble and drown walking any great distance through that.'

Whereas if we stay here, Shakespeare thought wryly, we could just starve.

Boltfoot suddenly laughed and pointed into the distance. 'Look, master.'

A quarter of a mile to the south, there was the clear outline of a craft in the water, coming in their direction.

'I do believe Mr Hooft is coming to fetch us to safety.'

Chapter 16

T HEY STOPPED AT the town of March for the night. Paul Hooft paid for the inn and their food, and refrained from excessive gloating.

'I knew they were thieves, Mr Shakespeare, so I followed at a distance. Mostly, they like to rob the Catholics who flock like crows to Wisbech to receive blessings from Father Weston and others. But they are not always as precise as they might be in their choice of victim.'

'So you know about Weston?'

'He is famous in these parts. The papist idolaters come from great distances to see him.'

In the morning, they inspected the Fen Causeway, but it had vanished into the floods, so they continued by punt. By midday, Hooft's little vessel drew up at the long coastal bank on which the port of Wisbech stood. It was a strange town, looking one way to the Wash of the North Sea, the other across an inland sea of floodwater.

'Even in long spells of dry summer weather, it is stranded between the river Nene to the west and the marshy estuary of the Ouse to the east,' Hooft told them.

Behind the town stood the castle. The old fortress had long since been destroyed and replaced with this building, commissioned by Archbishop Morton when he was Bishop of Ely a hundred years ago or more. He was, said Hooft, an enlightened man for a papist and he applauded his early efforts to drain part of the fens.

Shakespeare examined the building. It had a high outer wall, but it had obviously been built as a comfortable bishop's palace rather than a fort and it still held much of the lustre of past glory, a pleasant surprise in this bleak waterland. He was, however, alarmed by its vulnerability; it was practically defenceless. Its crenellated towers were constructed for show rather than effect. Anyway, how could a brick-built structure with no cannon be defended? It could not even keep out the water, for the waves lapped against the lower portions of the outer walls and washed over the drawbridge.

The keeper, William Medley, greeted Shakespeare warmly, but when he turned to Hooft and Boltfoot his body stiffened and he frowned, as if in recognition of something he disliked. He did not acknowledge them and addressed Shakespeare alone.

'In truth, sir, I am mighty amazed you have made it here, for no one recalls worse floods than these. Our cellars are flooded and we have lost much from our victual stores.'

Shakespeare was brisk. 'Mr Medley, I am here on urgent business from the office of Sir Robert Cecil. I would be grateful if we could confer privately. In the meantime, perhaps you could find lodgings and food for my assistant, Mr Cooper. And you, Mr Hooft?'

'I usually lodge at the inn, Mr Shakespeare.'

'Well, this time stay here at the castle. I am sure there will be a berth somewhere.'

Shakespeare stood in front of a blazing hearth in the keeper's office, which was sumptuously appointed.

Medley apologised for the lack of wine. 'It is all under water and ruined, I fear. But we have ale or beer.'

'English ale will suit me well enough.' Shakespeare removed the letter he carried from inside his doublet, where he had kept it protected in a waxed packet. 'Look at this, Mr Medley. It was discovered in the box of a mariner who died of some sickness aboard a vessel named *The Ruth*, out of Bordeaux. We have no exact knowledge of its intended recipient, but we do know that the courier had asked about a ship to carry him to Wisbech, claiming it was his home. That is an obvious lie. He was ordered to bring the letter here. I am certain the intended recipient was a priest.'

Medley laughed. 'There is no shortage of those. Take your pick: we have thirty-two of them.'

Shakespeare studied Medley. On the surface, the prison governor was smooth, confident and urbane. But underneath the bluff exterior he seemed nervous. Was he worried by the intelligencer's presence?

'Indeed, I know you have a veritable snake pit of priests,' Shakespeare replied, 'yet I think it most likely the priest is no ordinary seminary man, but a Jesuit—'

'Then it must be William Weston, though some say that Thomas Pound has taken Jesuit orders in secret.'

'My instinct and all I know tells me it is Weston.'

What Shakespeare knew was that Weston had always been a stern, unbending enemy of Elizabeth and her government, and a close friend of Robert Persons, the Jesuit author of the letter. There were many who believed Weston should have gone to the scaffold as a conspirator in the Babington plot, but nothing had ever been proved. For some reason, Lord Burghley and Walsingham had seen fit to let him live and rot in gaol.

'What do *you* make of the man, Mr Medley?'

'William Weston? He divides people. The stricter priests – eighteen of them at last count – revere him as though he were a martyr and a saint. He organises their studies and devotional practices, distributes the alms sent them and generally keeps order. The other thirteen cannot abide him. They are led by one Christopher Bagshawe, who nurtures a deep loathing of all Jesuits and Weston in particular. I honestly believe that he would happily see him cast into eternal hellfire. Things are so bad between the two factions that they eat apart and barrack each other across the halls. One of Bagshawe's men was put in solitary confinement after trying to club a Weston follower to death with a stone mug. None of this is pleasant to see, even for one not of their faith.'

'Well, I shall need to talk with Weston as soon as possible. I will see Bagshawe, too, and perhaps others if I deem it necessary. Please ensure that I have access to them as and when I desire.'

'Very well. But I can tell you that they are not locked away. Conditions have been relaxed considerably since the unfortunate death of my predecessor, Mr Gray. Those were my express orders from the Privy Council.'

'Is that so? Well, not too lax, I trust.'

'No, indeed not . . .' The prison keeper paused, looking even more ill at ease.

'Mr Medley, was there something else I should know?'

'It is nothing.'

'No? Well, be so good as to tell me what this *nothing* is.'

'It is merely . . . well, I could not help notice that you arrived with Hooft, the Dutchman.'

'Do you know him?'

Medley nodded. 'I hope I do not speak out of order, for he seemed to be a companion of yours.'

'He helped us make our way here, that is all. Say what you wish about the man.'

Medley drew a deep breath, then exhaled. 'Very well, I must confess that I find him an irritant. A *great* irritant, and not just to me but to the peace and well-being of my prison.'

'I know nothing of him, except that he has been of assistance. A little zealous in his enthusiasms, perhaps, but that need not be a bad thing. Tell me more.'

'He is a Calvinist hedge-priest. He comes here all the time. Every Sunday, he gathers all of the more righteous Puritans of the county and leads them in prayer, either on a patch of land inside the castle, or sometimes, when the land is dry, on the roadway and green outside. I must tell you, Mr Shakespeare, that even in this time of flooding, the numbers he summons are growing. I do believe there were a thousand or more men and women here last Sunday. He foments Bedlam, sir.'

'How long has this been going on?'

'Since before I arrived just over two years ago. You must know that my predecessor, Gray, was a most upright Puritan who welcomed these hordes. The Puritans hold their services in loud voices so that the Catholic priests might see and hear them from their cells. It is done to provoke them, for the Puritans know how despised they are by the priests, and the feeling is mutual. There is much disputation and odium within the ranks of the Puritans, too. They even strike each other with fists over the meaning of certain passages in the scriptures.'

This was preposterous. Shakespeare's voice sharpened. 'Well, why do you not get your guards to clear them away? Pull up the drawbridge, call in the constable and townsmen?'

'It is not so easy. The Puritans evoke much sympathy among the townspeople, and among my watchers. Four local justices are meant to maintain discipline, but they, too, are of a Puritan bent. I feel outnumbered and powerless, Mr Shakespeare.'

Shakespeare suddenly realised that the keeper, for all his airs, was out of his depth. He was not fit to run a Southwark stew, let alone a prison of such importance to the realm.

'God's blood, Mr Medley, this is intolerable!' He clenched his fist, hard.

So Hooft was a hedge-priest as well as a would-be engineer. He wondered, briefly, about their meeting at Waterbeach. He could not quite shake off a vision of a spider in its web, waiting for flies to buzz into its net unawares. He wondered, too, about the security of this castle. Why, if things got out of hand, there could be a massacre. He would have to bring order to this place, and quickly. The most pressing matter, however, was the Jesuit.

Suddenly, from somewhere within the castle, they heard a cacophony of shouts and banging.

'What is that noise, Mr Medley?'

'I fear it is disputatious priests.'

'Take me to them.'

They found the clerics in the dining hall. A short, box-shaped man with red hair and beard was being restrained by two of his friends. He was struggling to free himself and yelling.

'You are a foul corruption and a fraud, Weston! You steal from us by the day. I say you are more wicked than the devils you purport to expel!'

Shakespeare saw that the priest was not fighting hard against the restraint of his fellows. He had no desire to enjoin physical battle.

At the other end of the room, four or five men were making their exit. At their centre, Shakespeare noted the unmistakable, short-cropped grey hair of William Weston. He did not look back but allowed himself to be smuggled away to safety.

'What is this, Dr Bagshawe?' Medley demanded of the man being restrained.

'God forgive me, I wish to kill him. He is a viper. He has been trying to bring his unspeakable ways into this place. He insists young Master Potter has been infected by a succubus and has told him he will exorcise the devil from his loins. It is heresy.'

Medley shook his head. 'You know, Dr Bagshawe, I cannot tolerate this behaviour. If you wish to have the freedom of the castle, you must live in harmony.'

'Tell that to Weston.'

Shakespeare had heard enough. 'Take this man to his cell,' he ordered the two guards restraining Bagshawe. 'Lock him there until I come.' As the guards removed Bagshawe, Shakespeare turned again to Medley. 'Is this true that there are exorcisms here?'

Medley's face reddened, betraying his dismay and pain at being spoken to in such sharp terms by his guest. 'Not to my knowledge, Mr Shakespeare. Indeed not.'

'Nor will there be. Come, sir, take me to Weston.'

William Weston was in his forty-fifth year, but looked to Shakespeare like an old man of sixty. It was still possible to see how his features had once been remarkably handsome and admired by women, but his hair was dry and brittle, his skin sallow and tired. His robe was a rag, held together by much darning. He knelt, motionless, praying at the side of his rolled blanket, for he would have no bed.

'Get up, Father, you have questions to answer.'

Slowly, Weston turned his body, the movement clearly causing him pain in the joints. Shakespeare bent forward and offered his hand to raise him to his feet. The priest's eyes were dull and distant.

'My name is John Shakespeare. You may recall that we met in the year eighty-six, shortly after you were arrested. I was with the clerk of the Privy Council at your interrogation. Do you remember?'

Weston reached out and took Shakespeare's hand. The Jesuit's own was shaking, but there was strength left in it and he was able to pull himself to his feet.

'You may sit if you wish.'

'I will stand.' The priest moved his face closer to Shakespeare's, trying to make out his features. 'I cannot see you clearly, but I recollect your name and your voice. Why are you here? Are you to take me to the scaffold for my martyrdom?'

'No. You will stay alive for the present. But you will answer my questions.'

'Ask your questions. But I may decline to answer.'

'Why was Dr Bagshawe angry? What did you do to him?'

'I do nothing to Bagshawe. He does it all himself – drunkenness, womanising, thieving. Ask him about Mistress Wentworth who visits him behind his bolted cell door, if you will. Worse, though, he is a traitor to God and his faith, as you must know, Mr Shakespeare, for is he not one of *your* spies?'

Shakespeare ignored the question; it was more than likely that Bagshawe had once worked for Walsingham. Instead, he held up the letter, too far away for Weston's half-blind eyes to read.

'This is a letter, sent by Robert Persons at St Gregory's in Seville. I believe it is intended for you.'

A glimmer of light brightened the priest's eyes. 'Father Robert has written to me?'

'I believe so.'

'Give me the letter, please.' He reached out to take it, but Shakespeare held it away from his clutching hand.

'He urges you to be strong in your faith.'

'If it is for me, then place it in my hands. My spectacle-glasses are lost and I cannot see, save close to my eyes.'

'No, it is evidence. I will hold on to it.'

'What else, then, does Father Robert say? You cannot imagine the joy, Mr Shakespeare. This letter is like water at the lips of a dying man.'

'There is no joy in this letter. He threatens England and the

Queen in most violent language. What do you know of this? And think well before you reply, for I will not be taken for a fool by you.'

Shakespeare looked around the room. The cell was austere. All Weston had was a picture of saints on the wall, his blanket, a three-legged stool, and a table that seemed to serve as an altar, for it held a Latin Bible, two candles and a crucifix. There was, too, a reliquary, which Shakespeare opened, to reveal a small golden cross, a bone and a string of ivory beads.

'Campion's finger?' Shakespeare demanded, holding up the bone.

Weston's face was a mask of ice. 'I will have you know that certain of Blessed Father Campion's bones burn the devil most wonderfully. But I would not expect a heretic to understand such things.'

'Or a chicken bone, perhaps . . .'

Weston looked to the door. A serving boy of about eleven years stood there. He moved towards his master, but Weston shook his head and the boy held back.

Shakespeare returned the bone to its box and turned once more to the matter of the letter. 'Persons says you must be ready to play your part. He says the plan is advanced and will bring down the House of Tudor. This is prima facie evidence. You are party to treason, Father Weston.'

'What can you do to me? How can you frighten me with threats of sending my body to its tomb when this cell is already sepulchre to my soul? You think you can scare me with your talk?'

'This is not just you. It is all the other priests here. You will not be executed, but others will, and you will be responsible for it. Would you have that mortal sin on your conscience?'

Shakespeare was lying, for there was nothing in this letter to say who the intended recipient might be and nothing that might convict any man.

'Mortal sin? How little you heretics understand us! Every martyrdom is but a rung on the ladder to God's kingdom.'

Shakespeare pulled back his fist. Weston did not flinch. Shakespeare's hand quivered in fury, then fell. The secret was here, in this prison; he was certain of it. But he was equally sure that giving Weston a bloody nose was not the way to discover it.

He thrust the letter back into his doublet. He remembered now why he had so disliked Weston at that first meeting. It was the lack of doubt, the utter certainty that he was right and that anyone who disagreed with him was wrong and was destined for damnation. It was, too, the man's utter contempt for human life, his own and everyone else's, that riled him. He and the clerk had got nowhere with their questioning nine years ago; the chances now seemed equally slender. This priest had grown old in austerity and defiance.

For the moment, Shakespeare would take another tack. He calmed himself, tried to soften the ire in his voice.

'We will move on then,' he said. 'There is another matter. Among the many young men and women you tormented with your exorcisms, there was one named Thomasyn Jade. Do you recall her?'

If Weston was surprised by the question, he did not show it. 'Yes, I recall her well. She imbibed the light of Divine grace. We saved her for Christ.'

'You left her broken, in spirit and body. She has been missing ever since then. Is she alive or dead? Mad or sane? I want to know where she is.'

'I cannot help you.'

'It was Father Southwell's dying wish that she be found and cared for.'

The priest's palsied shaking suddenly intensified. His knees seemed to be giving way. Shakespeare put a hand to his elbow and helped him to sit down on the stool.

'Father Southwell is dead?'

'Executed at Tyburn a few days since. He died well. The crowd refused to denounce him.'

'And you spoke with him before his death?'

'In his last hours. He called me to his cell and asked me this favour, to find Thomasyn, for he was sore troubled by her fate. He did not agree with you that she had been saved. Quite the opposite, I would say.'

Weston closed his dull, opaque eyes. 'It is true. We did not concur on the best way to rid the body of demons ...' Suddenly, he clutched Shakespeare's hand. 'Please, I beg you, tell me more of Father Southwell and his martyrdom.'

'No one who saw him die was unmoved. I am not of your faith, Father Weston, but I would say he died in holiness.'

The Jesuit crossed himself. 'We must sing mass for him, this very day. This day, and every day hereafter. I must proclaim the news—'

Shakespeare pulled his hand free. 'You will have time enough for that. First, I ask again: do you know where Thomasyn Jade is? If you do, then you owe it to your brother in Christ to tell me.'

The priest shook his head. 'I know little about her, Mr Shakespeare. All I recall is that she was haunted by lustful thoughts and imaginings and would have gone to hell without us. I recall that many demons were in her. We cast them all out with Campion's bone, holy pins and vapour of brimstone. They fled with great screaming and beating of wings into the dark night.'

'Did she come with friends, family? Who else might know where she is?'

'I cannot help you. I am sorry, for if this is Father Southwell's wish, then I would indeed give my assistance.'

'There must be something you recall.'

The priest hesitated.

'Yes?'

'There was one to whom she seemed close. An old nun . . . one who is beyond your reach, for she was here at the time of good Queen Mary. I am sure she must be with God by now.'

'Sister Michael?'

'Yes, yes. How did you know?'

Shakespeare cursed silently. He should have let the old hag rot in Bridewell. Now, she would be long gone.

Chapter 17

CHRISTOPHER BAGSHAWE WAS a very different man to Weston, but Shakespeare was drawn to him no more than he had been to the Jesuit.

'I believe you and Father Weston do not agree on much, Dr Bagshawe.'

'He would corrupt our faith. Weston and Persons – all of them from the so-called Society of Jesus. They design their morals to suit their needs. They bring man's politicking into a world of heavenly spirituality. He thinks to rule us here, but I will not have it.'

'Did you strike him?'

'No, I have never done that. *Would* never do that . . .'

'And yet you had to be restrained.'

'They could not have held me back had I wished to attack the man.'

'He accuses you of licentiousness.'

'I accuse him of tyranny, like all Jesuits. He would rule here like a very king.'

They were in Bagshawe's cell, which stood in remarkable contrast to the plainness of Weston's, for it was cluttered with books, half-burnt candles, a comfortable but tangled bed, boxes with clothing. There were more boxes with food spilling out. Two wine flagons, one on its side and empty, the other stoppered. Bagshawe's countenance oozed cunning.

'You hear a great deal, Dr Bagshawe. I need you to help me, for I am trying to solve a puzzle.'

'The only puzzle is why you do not hang the egregious worm. Why does the Council send the saintly Campion to the gallows and leave Weston alive? We had morris dancers, card-playing, feasting and hobby-horses at Christmas in times gone by, but he forbids them with his rules and insists, instead, on solemn high mass and spiritual exercises. I cannot abide him. What gives him the right to rule over ordained priests who are not of his order?'

Shakespeare had no interest in the dispute between Bagshawe and Weston. He went straight to the point. 'In times past, too, I know you supplied intelligence to Walsingham and my associate Mr Mills. What is the price these days for information about conspiracies?'

'There are conspiracies here by the cartload. How much will you pay? When they instituted the daily recitation of the lit-anies after dinner, it was nothing but a device to cover the hatching of plots. They beg God's mercy on England, all the while planning schemes to bring her under the Spanish king's sword.'

'I am interested in one specific plot. It involves your old friend Robert Persons.' Shakespeare paused and smiled.

'That treacherous earwig is no friend of mine.'

'No, I know your history. You are old enemies from Balliol College, Oxford, I believe.'

'I have nothing but contempt for the man. So he and Weston have a conspiracy? Well, that does not surprise me. They both make me wish to puke up my bread and meat, for they do Catholicism more harm than ever Topcliffe did. Catholic and Protestant could live side by side peacefully in

England were it not for Persons, Weston and their ilk. Every day is a plot for them. Weston was in with Babington and the others, right up to the collar of his fetid hairshirt. He should have been hanged and bowelled.'

'So tell me what you know.'

Bagshawe's mouth creased as though he had broken open a rotten egg. 'Do you think they would tell *me* of their dirty dealings? If you want to know anything, talk to that whimpering catamite of his.'

'His servant boy?'

'No. Caldor. Gavin Caldor. He is no Jesuit yet, but he fervently wishes to be one. He's always around Weston, like a flesh-fly around an ulcer. See how he cringes and wrings his sinful hands.'

'I shall talk to him.'

'Ask him about the many visitors Weston has received these past two years since we were allowed the freedom of the castle.'

'Do you know these visitors?'

Bagshawe laughed without mirth. 'They are too sly for that. None of them come under their own names. I have seen one or two and have been suspicious of their fervent eyes, but I could not tell you their true names. And then there are the boys who come as servants, as though they were Wisbech lads looking to earn a penny. In truth, they are the sons of great families sent in to study under Weston, as though this place were a seminary, not a gaol.'

'Is that how Caldor came here?'

'No, but he will tell you all you wish to know. Show him the rack: that will open his mouth wide enough to satisfy any effeminate boy-priest.'

'That is not the way I work, Dr Bagshawe.'

'No, indeed, I know it is not. We may be almost at the

other end of the world here, but we hear enough. I know a little about you, Mr Shakespeare. There are those who call you a crypto-Catholic.'

'You should not listen to gossip, Dr Bagshawe. You should work for me. There will be gold for you, perhaps freedom. Bring me true intelligence as you once did for Mr Secretary Walsingham.'

'We shall see. In the meantime, I wish you well in your quest. I shall sing high mass myself if you can bring Weston to the noose.'

Shakespeare ordered the keeper, Medley, to have Gavin Caldor brought to the office. Caldor was to come in chains, his hands manacled, guarded by two men.

Medley looked slightly bewildered. 'Caldor is a lamb, no threat to anyone and the least likely of all the prisoners to try to escape. Why, I think he would jump from his skin if I clapped my hands behind his back. There is no need for such stern measures.'

'I will decide what is necessary, Mr Medley.'

Medley bowed without conviction. 'As you will.'

'And, Mr Medley, when was the last search of all the cells carried out?'

'As I recall, it was Michaelmas.'

'That is half a year and more! Have all the cells examined this day. The prisoners will be removed to the dining hall and held there under guard while the search is carried out. And make it thorough. I want all writings and letters brought to me, bundled up and unread by you or the guards. All, Mr Medley. None are to be discounted as unimportant. Every scrap of paper. Do you understand?'

'Yes, Mr Shakespeare.'

'Now leave me.'

Medley bowed nervously. 'There is also the matter of Mr Hooft . . .'

'We will discuss that later.'

'Yes, sir.' Medley bowed again, even lower, then backed from the room, all swagger gone.

When Caldor arrived, flanked by guards, Shakespeare was lounging on a settle, his feet up and his hands behind his head. He watched the prisoner out of the corner of his eye without moving. He let him wait a few minutes, then languidly rose to his feet and walked over to the prisoner so that their faces were little more than a foot apart.

'So you are Mr Caldor. What are you: priest? Jesuit? Conspirator?'

Caldor's eyes were wide and grew even larger in horror at the accusation. 'I am a lay brother, sir,' he stuttered. 'I have served the Society of Jesus and others in certain ways.'

Shakespeare saw that the young man was drenched in sweat. He walked across to the fire and turned his back on him. Moments passed. A faint aroma of urine wafted across the room from the prisoner. Shakespeare shook his head as though in despair, then turned back to him.

'Helping to build hiding holes, I do believe. You are fortunate to have your head. Have you been brought to trial?'

'No, sir.'

Shakespeare tried to estimate Caldor's age. He could not be much over twenty and looked younger.

'Well, that can be arranged, if I deem it necessary.'

The young man shook uncontrollably. His slender body slumped and had to be held up by the guards at either side of him.

'I have a few questions for you, Mr Caldor. Direct, honest answers will serve you well.'

A dark stain of urine had spread down across the front of the young man's hose. Shakespeare suddenly felt a stab of shame for using him thus. But better to be questioned in this way than have his body crippled for ever by Topcliffe's rack.

'Tell me more about yourself, Mr Caldor. Are you carpenter or stonemason?'

'I was a carpenter, of sorts.'

'And where did you learn this skill?'

'In the playhouses, sir. I built props and scenery.'

'And then you turned your hand to hidey-holes. Did you work alone on them?'

'Please, sir, do not ask that of me.'

'Where did you work?'

'Great houses. I beg you, do not ask me which ones. You must know the one where I was caught.'

'You do not answer my questions, Mr Caldor. Do you have no care for your life? I tell you what I will do for you: I will put those matters aside for the moment. Whether or not I return to them depends very much on how you answer my next questions. It has been suggested to me that you are Father Weston's catamite. Is this true?'

Caldor's sweating brow knitted in confusion. 'Catamite?'

'His partner in sodomy.'

The horror on the young man's face was evidence enough. 'In God's name, no, sir.'

'Why should I believe you?'

'Because I speak the truth. I am a chaste man, sir. I would never engage in such things, nor, I am certain, would Father Weston.'

'You are close to him, though. Does he confide in you?'

'We talk much. We pray a great deal together and meditate on the holy scriptures. He instructs me in my studies and teaches me Hebrew. Sir, I consider Father Weston my best teacher and mentor. I revere him.'

'What are his secrets?'

'He has none. He is what he seems, a man of God.'

'Your cell is about to be searched, Mr Caldor. Tell me precisely what will be found there. Letters? Secret codes? Correspondence from Father Persons in Seville?'

The prisoner shook his head with vigour. Beads of sweat splashed on to the rush-matted floor.

Shakespeare fished the Seville letter from his doublet. He handed it to the young man and watched his eyes as he read it, looking for a reaction. All he saw was fear.

'What does that letter mean to you?'

'Nothing, sir. It seems like treason, but I have no knowledge of it, neither who wrote it, nor for whom it is intended.'

Shakespeare took back the letter and tilted his head to the guards. 'Remove the manacles and chains.'

One of the men, surly and heavy-set, unlocked the heavy iron bands.

'You may sit down, Mr Caldor. Take the stool by the table.'

'Thank you, sir.' Caldor sat down, leaning forward in the vain hope of concealing his pissed-upon hose.

'Now, I repeat, what will be found in your cell?'

'A cross, sir, a Latin Bible, a rosary, letters from my mother in Ripon, a mattress and blanket, some conserved greengage. That is all. No, forgive me, there is also my comb, some quills, an inkhorn—'

'The letters from your mother, what do they say?'

'She asks after my health, gives me news of home and prays that I may stay strong in the love of God.'

'And with whom is she in contact? Does she receive letters from Seville? Should I, perhaps, send pursuivants to search her house?'

'Please, sir, no. My mother is very sick with a canker. I confess she is true to the Roman faith, but surely that is no crime. I promise you, there are no secrets there.'

'What does the name Loake mean to you?'

'Loake?'

'Garrick Loake.'

'Nothing, sir, I do not know the name.'

Did he hesitate? Was his voice a note higher as he gave his answer? He was so nervous, his sweating so profuse, that it was difficult to discern a reaction.

'Let us return to Father Weston. I believe he has had a number of visitors during the past two years since the prison regime was relaxed. Which of those would interest me most, Mr Caldor?'

'I cannot think that any of them would interest you—'

'Have there been any Jesuit priests?'

Caldor averted his eyes.

Shakespeare seized on this. 'Well?'

'Father Walley has been here.'

'Walley?' The name struck home like an arrow. 'You mean Henry Garnett?'

This was serious news, if true. Henry Garnett was superior of the Jesuit mission to England. He had held the position since the incarceration of Weston and Southwell. He was the most wanted man in the country.

The young Catholic prisoner closed his eyes with shame at having revealed such important information. 'I did not know he was Father Garnett.' His voice was a whisper. 'I knew him only as Walley.'

'When was this?'

'Fifteen months since.'

Shakespeare felt his stomach tighten. Yes, that fitted. Garnett had been using the name Walley at that time. He had probably changed it again since then. But his alias was not the important thing here; the vital matter was what had transpired between Garnett and Weston when they were alone together. What had they plotted here in the supposedly secure confines of this castle while Keeper Medley looked the other way? What plans did they hatch and what messages did they agree to send to Seville?

Shakespeare drew his sword from its scabbard and brought the shining tip to rest on the prisoner's bare throat.

'So tell me, Mr Caldor, what did they discuss? Did they plan to kill the Queen with poison, blade, powder, pistol?'

Caldor could scarce breathe for fear. He put his hands to his throat and tried to fend off the sword, drawing blood from his fingers along the edge of the unmoving blade.

'I am running short of patience.'

'Please, sir, nothing,' he gasped. 'I heard nothing. They sang solemn high mass and they spoke of the imprisoned men's studies, nothing more.'

'Were you with them all the time, then?'

'No, sir. They spent time together alone, but I am certain it was a meeting of joy. It was not a secret meeting of conspiracy. That is not Father Weston's way. In the name of God, I beg you to believe me.'

One thing was certain: Garnett and Weston would not have had a meeting without conspiring to further the cause of Rome and the Society of Jesus by whatever means they considered effective, either criminal or otherwise. It would not have been in the nature of either man to pass up such an opportunity.

Shakespeare withdrew his sword-tip from the prisoner's throat, but did not replace it in its scabbard. 'Very well,' he said at last. 'But let us return to your background. You said you learnt your trade in the playhouses. Which ones?'

'The Theatre and the Curtain in Shoreditch.'

Garrick Loake had worked at the Theatre. Did he have any link to Wisbech? To Caldor? Shakespeare thought back to Loake's warning: *There is a most foul conspiracy unfolding. It wafts from the papist fastness of eastern England* . . .

'I ask again, did you have dealings with a man called Garrick Loake?'

'No, sir, I do not think I know him. Is he a player?'

'You understand the consequences if you lie to me?'

'Yes, sir. Every word I have said to you is true, though it has caused me great distress. I feel as though I have betrayed Father Weston.'

Shakespeare looked at Caldor, trying to see beyond the man's fear. He could not make up his mind about him. His terror might suggest guilt, but equally he could just be afraid. Shakespeare had come across enough innocent men and women who quaked with fear at the name Topcliffe. He would have to find other ways to discover the truth.

'There is something else. I believe there have been converts while the priests have been here. Men and women who have gone over to your faith, yes?'

'There have been many.'

'And have any gone away to the seminaries? In particular, have any spoken of becoming Jesuits? Have you heard of any going to the seminaries of Spain?'

'It is possible . . . I do not know for certain.'

'Some young man, perhaps, so inspired by Father Weston's teachings that he enrolled in the College of St Gregory at Seville?'

'I cannot say, sir. If that happened, then I was not party to it. Yet I can tell you that many have come here heretics and been reconciled to the true Church.'

One of the guards cleared his throat. Not the sullen one

with the keys but his companion. Shakespeare had almost forgotten they were there, but now he turned his attention to the man.

'Did you wish to say something, turnkey?'

'Forgive me for speaking out of order, master, but there was the Gray girl. She had her head turned by Weston and went away. There are those that said she went to Rome or France, sir, perhaps to become a nun.'

'Gray?'

'The daughter of Thomas Gray, the former keeper of Wisbech. Mr Gray is no longer with us sadly, drowned in the Nene. He was a strict Puritan gentleman, much respected in these parts for his stern dealings with the prisoners. The coroner found that he took his own life, distraught at the loss of his daughter to the papists. At one time, it is said, he ran at her with a knife as though he would kill her. Her name was Sorrow. Sorrow Gray. She is long gone from here. It was a scandalous event at the time. I hope that I am not doing anyone a disservice, master, but I am sure Mr Medley could give you the complete tale, if you wished to hear it.'

'Thank you, guard. It is something I shall look into.' Shakespeare turned back to Gavin Caldor. He had one last question. 'Did you know this woman, this Sorrow Gray?'

'To say good day to, yes, sir. But I could not say I knew her well.'

'What sort of young woman was she?'

'I cannot say. She was a Puritan and then a Catholic. That is all I know.'

Shakespeare looked at him long and hard. Gavin Caldor was close to collapse. 'If I find you have kept information from me, I shall return to this place and take you to the Tower. You know what that means?'

Caldor nodded frantically.

'Go now.' Shakespeare dismissed him with a flick of the hand. 'Take the prisoner to clean himself up,' he ordered the guards, 'then put him in the dining room where the others are to be mustered. Keep him apart from Weston. I do not want them talking. And have Mr Medley sent to me.'

Shakespeare watched the departing back of Gavin Caldor. He had had his fill of papist priests and their acolytes this day.

Chapter 18

MEDLEY NODDED HIS head gravely 'So you have heard some of the tale of Sorrow Gray,' he said. 'Tell me what you know and I shall endeavour to fill in the spaces.'

'All I know is that she was converted by Weston and has gone to be a nun.'

'Converted? I would say *perverted*. As to whether she became a nun, no one knows, but it is certainly possible.'

'Start at the beginning.'

Medley was trying to regain his composure having felt the sting of humiliation, but it was all too clear that, while he was here, Shakespeare was the master of the castle.

'Indeed, from the beginning,' Medley said. 'As you must know, my predecessor as keeper, Thomas Gray, had no truck with the ways of the papists. He kept them locked in their cells save for an hour a day of exercise. And when they dined, he would sit at the table with his deputy and with his wife to monitor all that was said.'

'He had a daughter, Sorrow, yes?'

'He had three daughters – Sorrow, Comfort and Endurance. They were raised in the Puritan way and went modestly at all times. From what I have heard, I would say they were as devout as their father, particularly Sorrow, who was considered a prophetess in these parts, for she had visions. She begged her father to allow her to dispute with the priests, that she might through argument and sermonising demonstrate to them that they were in error.'

Shakespeare laughed grimly. 'But the old serpent Weston lured her to *his* way instead.'

'Yes. At first, she kept her conversion secret. She found excuses not to join the Puritan meetings and Bible readings. But she could not keep living this lie and confessed all. Her father was aflame with rage. He tried everything to turn her away from her foolishness, but she would not listen. He tried locking her away, depriving her of food. In the end he ran at her with a knife, but she managed to escape.'

'There must have been a hue and cry.'

'Indeed. But there was no sign of her and she has not been seen since. Most men assume that she had learnt of some safe Catholic house in the neighbourhood and that she went from there to the Carthusian nunnery at Louvain. Some say her father found her and killed her, sinking her body into the mere. Whatever her fate, her father was a broken man. I think the shame was too great for him. He drank a great deal of brandy and threw himself into the torrent.'

Shakespeare was thinking hard. There could be many possibilities other than those suggested by Medley. Perhaps she had travelled to Seville, not Louvain. It was not impossible that she had taken messages from Weston to Garnett and then onwards to Robert Persons. She would not be the first woman involved in subversion.

'And then, there is the matter of Paul Hooft,' Medley continued.

'What has he to do with all this?'

'That is what I have been trying to tell you, Mr Shakespeare. He was to have married Sorrow. Their wedding day was settled. It would have been the grandest event of the year in Wisbech.'

'Hooft was engaged to this woman?' What in God's name had been going on in this outpost?

'He was left at the altar, so to speak. But his reaction was very different from that of her father. He did not sink into melancholia, nor did he rage against her. What he did do was to become yet more zealous in his Calvinist faith. He spent all his time preaching, winning converts as though it were a contest between him and Weston as to who could gain the most souls. Nor was that enough for him. He brought more and more of his Puritan followers here to the prison, to taunt and threaten the priests with hellfire.'

'You do not like him.' It was a statement, not a question.

'I fear there is darkness in so firm a faith. Hooft and Weston are two halves of the same form, cast from the same mould. They may seem like opposites yet they share much in common. Neither will allow any doubt that they are right, and neither would balk at the killing of a man they see as a heretic or idolater. I do believe they would each take pleasure in the other's death. That is why I was concerned when you gave Mr Hooft access to the inner castle, sir.'

The smell of baking bread in the kitchens was balm to Shakespeare's senses. He found Boltfoot sitting at a small table, with a trencher laden with half a loaf of steaming manchet and a rapidly disappearing roasted waterfowl.

'Where is Mr Hooft, Boltfoot?'

'He said he had some business, master.'

'Inside the castle, or without?'

'He did not say.'

Suddenly there was a din of shouting from elsewhere. Shakespeare felt a chill. 'Come with me, Boltfoot.'

*

The dining hall was in uproar. Paul Hooft was standing on a square table in the centre of the room, clutching his Bible in both hands, facing down the two groups of priests: Weston and his cohort at one end of the room; Bagshawe and his followers at the other.

'You are all steeped in venery, superstition and wickedness!' Hooft bellowed. 'Before God, you stand condemned. Your way is total depravity!'

One of the priests from Weston's crowd pushed forward, like a bull daring to advance from the herd. '*You* are the sinner, Hooft. *You* are the heretic!'

Hooft pointed past the priest at Weston. 'You, Weston, are the Antichrist, the archdemon, the lewd acolyte of Satan! I say you are an abomination in the sight of God.'

Weston crossed himself but did not respond. Shakespeare watched the scene, aghast at the image of chaos and disorder, then clapped his hands for silence.

The hubbub died down to a murmur as the priests and Hooft turned towards the two newcomers. The three guards, who had been enjoying the spectacle of traded insults and rhetoric, looked sheepish at the sight of Shakespeare and began trying to shepherd the priests back into lines.

'Get down, Mr Hooft,' Shakespeare commanded. 'Guards, make the prisoners sit on the floor. They are to observe absolute silence until they are free to return to their cells. Any spoken word is to be recorded and will be punished by a week's solitary confinement with short commons.'

Hooft did not move. Shakespeare nodded to Boltfoot, who stepped forward and dragged the man down from the table.

'Take him to Mr Medley's room, Boltfoot.'

Boltfoot thrust his powerful arms under Hooft's shoulders and began to haul him across the floor.

*

Hooft showed no repentance for his action and met Shakespeare's fury with a defiant glare.

'Any more interventions like that and you will be clapped in irons, Mr Hooft.'

'Why should I not talk to them thus? They are all traitors and idolaters, every man of them. You know this yourself.'

'Indeed, there are traitors among them, but I am on Queen's business here and I will be impeded by no man. Now, a matter has come to my attention. The affair of you and Sorrow Gray. Why did you not mention her?'

'Why do you think? Would you wish to tell the world of the bride who betrayed you?'

'But you knew of my interest in the events at this place. Tell me your story, Mr Hooft.'

'Very well. We were betrothed before witnesses; she had no right in law to turn aside from me. I would sue for breach of contract if she could be found. As for her apostasy, she has ruined many lives.'

'I wish to know more about her. Could she be involved in conspiracy?'

There is no man, nor woman, more intense and dangerous than a convert, Walsingham had once told him.

'Sorrow Gray is capable of any deceit or evil. Beyond that, I cannot help you for I can scarce utter the words. If you wish to know more of her, speak to her mother or sisters. They live within half a furlong of here, by the market square.'

'Take me there.'

'As you wish.'

'It must have been hard for you, Mr Hooft.'

Hooft laughed without humour. 'I had thought that we would conquer the world for God, Sorrow and I. Truly, I did believe we would transform this landscape, both physically and spiritually, draining the fens and spreading the word.

But Satan proved too strong for her. I never knew she was so frail . . .'

'Thank you, Mr Hooft.' Shakespeare's voice softened. Hooft was a man scorned in the most brutal fashion. 'And, please, write your letters to Sir Robert Cecil on the Fenland drainage. I will happily convey your message to him.'

The house in Wisbech was constructed of knapped Norfolk flint and was well kept. Thorny rose briers neatly enveloped the front.

Hooft knocked at the door, then pushed it open. 'Mistress Gray,' he called out. 'It is I, Paul Hooft.'

A woman bustled through into the hallway, brushing her flour-dusty hands on her apron, and then adjusting her plain white coif. She was slender, of middle years and good-looking. She smiled at Hooft. 'It is good to see you, Paul. Are you well?'

'Yes, I am well.'

'Then you should come to see us more often. You are still as welcome here as you always were.'

'Thank you, mistress. Perhaps I will come more when the land is dry again.'

The woman's gaze turned to the newcomer.

'This is Mr Shakespeare,' Hooft said. 'He wishes to speak with you.'

'I am Mary Gray. How may I help you, sir?'

Where had he seen that face before? No, not that face, but one a little like it. Something in the eyes . . .

'He wishes to hear about Sorrow. He is here at the castle on Queen's business.'

The woman's eyes flicked from Hooft to Shakespeare, unsure of herself.

'You have nothing to fear from me. This may not have any

bearing on your daughter,' he said, 'but at the risk of opening old wounds, I would ask for your cooperation.'

'Very well, sir. We have naught to hide in this house. You know a little of the story, do you? Well, when we called her Sorrow, I fear we did not know how well named she would turn out to be. My husband insisted on the name, for he said we must always remember that this world is not given to us solely to experience joy. At the end, he rued his choice.'

There was a movement behind Mistress Gray and another, younger, woman entered the room. Shakespeare gazed on her face with utter astonishment.

Beatrice Eastley stood before him. Beatrice Eastley, the brooding, pipe-smoking companion of Lady Susan Bertie, Countess of Kent.

'This is my daughter, Mistress Adamson,' Mary Gray said by way of introduction. 'She is twin sister to Sorrow, but unlike her in all but looks, thank the Lord.'

'Your name is Adamson?' Shakespeare asked, the incredulity clear in his voice. 'What is your first name?'

'Comfort, sir. Comfort Adamson. I am wife to Shipwright Adamson, an alderman of this town.'

'Your name is not Beatrice Eastley?'

She laughed. 'No, sir.'

'Does the name mean anything to you?'

'Indeed it does not, sir.'

'And would I be correct in thinking that you are identical to your sister Sorrow?'

'In looks, she may be,' Hooft put in. 'But not in other ways. Sorrow has a hollow heart.'

So Beatrice Eastley was none other than Sorrow Gray. It had to be thus. There was no other explanation. Sorrow Gray had not gone off to be a nun, but instead had become a lady's companion in one of the great Protestant houses of England.

For a few moments, he gathered his thoughts. *A strange move for a devout Catholic convert.* That was the first thought, and then, *What plot is hatching here – and what is Lady Susan Bertie's role in it? Is she an innocent dupe, or what?*

A sudden fear struck him: Beatrice Eastley was now with Lucia Trevail on her journey to Cornwall. A dozen questions spun through his mind, all at once. He sensed terrible danger.

He turned again to Mary Gray. 'Have you heard anything of your daughter? Has she written or contacted you in any way?'

'No, sir. I know not whether she be alive or dead. When she left, she cursed us and swore that God would unleash raging tempests upon the land. She died for us on the day my husband took his life in the flood.'

Raging tempests. The words were familiar. Had not the letter found aboard *The Ruth* vowed to bring down raging tempests and torrents upon the House of Tudor?

'I must ask you again, for this is mighty important: you are certain that you know of no woman named Beatrice Eastley? You have no close cousin of that name?'

Mother and daughter both looked blank. 'No, indeed not, sir.'

'Or Lady Susan Bertie, Countess of Kent? Do you know of her? Has she had any contact with this family?'

Mother and daughter shook their heads. 'No, sir.'

Hooft put up his hand like a schoolboy in class. 'If I may be permitted to say something, Mr Shakespeare?'

'Go on.'

'It is none of my business, you might think. But I believe that William Weston turned her mind with his rites of exorcism. He told her she had demons within and she believed him. I saw the pinpricks where he stuck her with needles. I believe she was sent mad by the Catholic slurry that he heaped on her . . .'

'What are you suggesting?'

'Would it not be the correct thing to do to take Weston back to London for questioning in the Tower? There is a rack there, I believe. That will make him talk. If there is some conspiracy, he will know it all.'

Shakespeare stared at Hooft. 'You are right,' he said at last. 'It *is* none of your business.'

Apart from his own distaste for torture, Shakespeare had not forgotten Cecil's command: there was to be no more martyrdom. The other thought in his mind was the strange coincidence that he was now looking for *two* young women who had undergone exorcism: Thomasyn Jade and Sorrow Gray. Mere coincidence? Mr Secretary Walsingham would not have believed it so, and neither did he.

He turned back towards the mother. 'If you ever hear word of your daughter, you are to send messages to me. Is that understood? Mr Medley at the castle will know how to contact me.'

He returned to the Dutchman, with some reluctance. 'Mr Hooft, I will have to make haste from this place. I would be grateful to have your assistance once again in crossing the flood. Please be ready at dawn to escort me back to Waterbeach.'

He bowed to the two women. 'Good day to you both.'

Chapter 19

WILLIAM WESTON WAS brought to Shakespeare in Medley's office. The old Jesuit's face was set hard.

'I believe you entertained a visitor in recent months, one Henry Garnett, Jesuit superior in the England mission.'

'Garnett? Is he in England? I recall him from Rome, of course, Mr Shakespeare. A Christian with saintly virtues.'

'So you are talking. That is a start. Garnett, as you well know, has been in England since the year eighty-six. He came over that summer with Father Southwell, and you met them both shortly before your capture. When he came here to Wisbech, he went by the name of Walley. You spoke to him alone and conspiratorially.'

'Ah yes, I remember Mr Walley. Another fine gentleman who wished to be reconciled to the Sacraments of Rome. But I thought you mentioned Father Garnett? Do you have news of him?'

'Is this your damnable practice of equivocation? We know all about it now, thanks to Father Southwell's trial. You may think yourself full of wit with such clever answers, but they are lies, and you are guilty of mortal sin by uttering them.'

The priest's face remained blank. Neither amused nor angry.

'This will end badly, Weston. You must know it. Some of

you Jesuits think you can meddle in affairs of state, but the Bible tells us what happens when a man sows the wind.'

'You have had your say, Mr Shakespeare, and I have listened. It is late. If that is all, then I would like to return to my cell, which is my oratory. It is time for compline.'

'No, that is not all. You mentioned to me that Sister Michael was close to Thomasyn Jade. Write me a letter to take to her, instructing her to assist me, for so far she is of no help. I promise you that no harm will come to the girl, or to Sister Michael. Do this for your friend Father Southwell.'

Who was a better man than you, Weston, or any of the stubborn, disputatious priests in this forsaken castle of despair.

'Very well.'

'Here.' Shakespeare handed him a quill, inkhorn and paper. 'Do it now.'

Weston took the writing implements and wrote a brief letter in Latin, greeting Sister Michael in Christ, and telling her to trust and assist Shakespeare in any matter concerning Thomasyn Jade, but in no other way. He signed the paper, sliced off the edges with the quill-knife so that no extra words could be added by forgery, then folded it and handed it back to Shakespeare.

'Thank you. Now let us talk of Sorrow Gray.'

At last Weston showed some emotion. He smiled. 'Sorrow? Was ever a child so ill named. I tell you, Mr Shakespeare, the casting out of her demons and her conversion to the true faith brought me more happiness than any other event in my life.'

'So you *did* practise your foul rite of exorcism on her?'

'I saved her from the devil and baptised her anew.'

'And so you learnt nothing from your disgraceful treatment of Thomasyn Jade. You bring one girl to madness, then another. Is this your true religion, Father? Is this what God desires of you?'

'You know nothing of it, Mr Shakespeare. You live in error, ignorance and heresy, and you will burn in the fire with no hope of salvation.'

Hellfire. Shakespeare understood. Weston had given the girl her new name: Beatrice, the woman who guided Dante out of purgatory to heaven.

'Beatrice Eastley,' he said, and looked for a reaction. He saw it, a mere flicker of shock in Weston's eyes, then back to the face of stone. 'I know exactly where she is, Father Weston. Whatever is plotted by you, it is in your power to end it here and now, with a few words to me, for I would not wish the alternative on any man or woman. Help me, otherwise I fear Sorrow Gray will reap the whirlwind you have sown.'

'I have nothing more to say. Do your heretic worst. Take me to the Tower and give my bones to Topcliffe. I will do what I must.'

By the light of a solitary candle, Francis Mills gazed down at the two bodies with a curious lack of passion. He had longed for the day when he would see his wife and her lover lying naked, bespattered with blood, their throats torn open. But this was not how he had imagined it in his tortured dreams.

Anne Mills no longer looked pretty, no longer looked like his wife. Her fair hair was thick with gore; her eyes were open, staring in horror. Her hands were bound before her with twine and so were her ankles. Blood was spread in jagged smears across her pale pink neck and breasts. Her lover, the grocer, was also naked, also tied up. His eyes were closed, but his mouth was open in an endless scream.

It was their fault. They should not have been here, together, naked like this, for this was Mills's marriage bed. How could they expect to survive when they indulged in their glistening obscenities in another man's marriage bed?

Mills had a knife in his hand. It was clean and shiny and hung loose from his fingers. Suddenly he dropped it. He looked around the bedchamber he knew so well. The candle stood on a coffer by the window, guttering in the draught and throwing strange shadows across the walls and ceilings. He walked over to the coffer, put the candle on the floor, then opened the lid of the ancient box. Inside were blankets and linen. Stooping down, he took out a large woollen blanket. It had come to them from Anne's father, with the marriage bond. Now it would make a shroud for the harlot. He grimaced at the word. No man should speak ill of the dead, however much their death was merited.

With exquisite gentleness, he spread the blanket over her and turned away, his tall thin body hunched into his black doublet and hose like a pecking crow. Even in death, he loved her. He averted his eyes from the grocer's screaming mouth. It disturbed him. For some reason he picked up the knife again. He wasn't thinking clearly. He walked to the chamber doorway and just stood there for a few moments. The stairway in front of him led down to the hall. His neighbour, Barnaby, was there, at the foot of the stairs, holding a lantern.

'We heard the screams, Mr Mills. What is it?'

Mills held up the knife, as if by way of explanation. 'They are dead, Barnaby. Anne and the grocer. They are in here.'

'You had better come downstairs, Frank. The constable is with me. Come on, drop the knife and come down.'

Mills placed the knife on the flat-topped newel post, then nodded his head in silent acquiescence and began walking down the stairs, slowly, as though they were his last steps to the gallows.

Shakespeare prepared to set off from Wisbech Castle with Paul Hooft in the grey chill of dawn.

'Is it too late to persuade you to bring Weston with us? I do believe most powerfully that he should be brought away from this place and be held in the Tower. This castle is not safe—'

'Mr Hooft, you have suffered greatly by the loss of the woman you were to have married, but I do not wish to hear another word on this subject of William Weston.' He looked the Dutchman in the eye and saw sullen resentment. 'Come, load the boat. I want all the castle inmates' correspondence kept safe and dry.'

Shakespeare turned away and bade farewell to Boltfoot.

'I have told Mr Medley that you will be overseeing the security of the prison. He tells me Wisbech has a trainband of townsmen, smiths and traders. They are mostly Puritans. Bring them in, explain that I fear some trouble and have them mount watches, day and night. At least six men, in addition to the guards. Is that clear?'

'Yes, master,' Botfoot said without enthusiasm.

'From what I understand, some of the priests have even been allowed to make visits to the market. That will cease unless the Privy Council orders otherwise. If there are any visitors, you will sit in on the meetings with a clerk supplied by Medley, who will take a note of all that is said. These notes, as well as all letters going in or out, will be retained and brought to me. You may let the priests know that this is intended as a temporary measure until I am certain that all threat has passed. Is that clear?'

Boltfoot nodded. His face told the whole story: he was mighty disconsolate.

'It should not be for long,' Shakespeare reassured him. 'A squadron of soldiers will be despatched here as soon as that can be organised. All being well, you will be able to follow me home in a week. If I am not there, I will leave instructions with Jane.'

He did not like leaving Boltfoot here like this, but Cecil and the Privy Council had to know about the way things were at this prison. The priests' letters and papers had to be gone through in fine detail, for there could be clues in them. Most importantly of all, he needed to track down Lucia Trevail and her new companion, Beatrice Eastley. The young woman had many questions to answer.

Shakespeare clasped Boltfoot's hand in his, then turned away and stepped into the punt, where Hooft was stowing a large pack of letters, all bundled up in waxed cloth. Hooft stood up from his task and took his position in the back of the craft, holding his long wooden quant. With a smooth practised movement, he pushed away and the punt slid off into the flood.

The day was fair. Progress should be swift, God willing. Shakespeare's heart quickened. The thought of meeting Lucia Trevail again stirred him with pleasant apprehension.

John Shakespeare retrieved his horse and took his leave of Paul Hooft at his farm near Waterbeach. After that, he rode hard, sleeping at the roadside when necessary, and eating and drinking only while his horse was being fed and watered. By the time he reached London and was ushered into Sir Robert Cecil's office at his mansion on the Strand, his clothes were ragged and his face haggard with exhaustion.

He bowed to the Privy Councillor and placed his bundle of papers on the table. 'Sir Robert.'

Cecil was brisk and to the point. 'Before you say anything, I must acquaint you with grave news. Frank Mills has been arrested on a charge of murdering his wife and her paramour, a grocer named Heartsease. Frank is now held at Newgate.'

Shakespeare was about to take a seat at the table, but he remained upright, his body stiffened with shock, all aches suddenly forgotten. 'Christ's blood! Is this certain?'

'Their throats were slit and he had the knife in his hand when a neighbour and the constable went to the house. They had heard a scream.'

'Has he said anything?'

'Nothing of sense. He has been taken by madness.'

Shakespeare drew a deep breath. This was the worst news. There had been an occasion when he had had cause to despise Frank Mills, but in recent times they had worked together well enough. He should not be surprised by the crime; Frank had been threatening to do for his wife and her lover for the best part of two years now. And yet Shakespeare had never really believed he would do it.

'It seems he found them in the marital bed,' Cecil continued. 'I have ordered the bodies removed to the Searcher of the Dead at St Paul's, though I cannot think he will discover anything of interest. The sheriff says it is a clear case of murder by a cuckold. A story as old as human life itself. The fact that Mills holds a position as assistant secretary in this office will not save him from the noose.'

'I must go to him.'

'Indeed, do that. And go to the Searcher, too, for I have other news. Garrick Loake has been found dead. You may visit the corpses together. Now then, John, let me hear your report.'

Loake dead? Shakespeare slumped into the chair. How had he let him slip through his fingers? There would be time enough to reproach himself later; for now he had to reveal all he had discovered at Wisbech Castle. Cecil listened carefully.

'The stink of conspiracy emanating from that foul dungeon is as high as a jakes in summer,' Shakespeare concluded. 'I suspect Weston knows the truth of it. Perhaps this woman Sorrow Gray, too. There is another I'm not certain of, a young carpenter named Caldor. He is close to Weston, and afraid.'

'You haven't brought Weston with you, please God.'

'No. I think I understood your instructions quite well, Sir Robert.'

Cecil smiled. 'He would never have broken under torture anyway.'

'Indeed not, Sir Robert. He relishes pain. He has a hairshirt, he kneels most of the night at prayer and, when he sleeps, he reclines on the hard stone. Pain is very ecstasy to him. He would happily embrace martyrdom, and still you would not get a word from him.'

'Then he is better consigned to obscurity. That is why Wisbech is so useful. If only . . .' Cecil trailed off.

Shakespeare knew what words he withheld: *if only Father Southwell had been sent there rather than to Tyburn, where he had won an undoubted victory for the Pope.*

'But you are sure there is a plot?' Cecil continued. 'In God's faith, it is like chasing air.'

'The letter is real enough. So is the death of Garrick Loake. And so is the strange departure of Sorrow Gray, a Catholic convert, and her reappearance as Beatrice Eastley, posing as a loyal member of the English Church.'

'Indeed. But what are they up to? Every sinew in my body tells me that we are under attack. But what is the nature of the assault? Where will it come?'

'The history of these past few years tells us they will try to assassinate Her Majesty. It has been tried often enough.'

'I agree, John. But let us not discount the alternatives.'

'As I see it, there are four other possibilities. Firstly, it could be an attempt to assassinate someone else of importance. They tried to kill Drake before. Whom might they target this time?' Shakespeare looked at Cecil; he would certainly be a prize for Spain and Rome. 'Secondly, it could be yet another invasion plan, but that would not involve priests at Wisbech. Thirdly, it might involve the smuggling of books or the setting up of an illegal press. Fourthly, there is the possibility of an attack on some vital target. Something that requires the assistance of spies and traitors already in England: shipping comes to mind.'

'Plymouth? Drake and Hawkins are fitting their fleets there . . .' Cecil produced a paper from his shelf. 'I have this flimsy report from Trott. He says there is an unconfirmed report of Spanish shipping around the western coasts. Like most reports from Trott, I treat it with scepticism. I am sure, however, that Drake will have his own preparations against attack.'

'Again, if that is the target, then what is the link to Wisbech?'

Cecil looked at the bundle that Shakespeare had deposited on the table. 'Perhaps the secret lies there. Those papers and letters must be gone through in fine detail.'

'In other days, it would have been a task for Frank.'

'Well, that is not an option. I shall have to call in favours. I want Thomas Phelippes to look through them.'

Phelippes? Shakespeare frowned. Phelippes was England's greatest codebreaker. In the old days, working for Sir Francis Walsingham, he had deciphered the letters that had brought Mary, Queen of Scots to the headsman's axe. But now he worked for the Earl of Essex, most bitter rival of the Cecil faction.

'I know what you are thinking, John, but I know enough of the earl's dirty secrets to hang him ten times over.' Cecil's thin lips turned down with distaste. 'I think I can secure the services of Mr Phelippes. Leave that to me. Turn *your* thoughts to Susan Bertie's companion. I know Susan well enough and I find it hard – nay, impossible – to believe that she would do anything against England. Do you agree?'

'I scarcely know her. Anyway, the girl is now with Lady Trevail and gone to her Cornish estates.'

'Then you will have to go to her. Something of a holiday

after Wisbech, I imagine,' Cecil continued drily. 'I cannot accept that any of the women in Susan Bertie's circle would be involved in popish plots, but we cannot take that for granted – nor can we assume that there is no danger to them from this renegade companion of theirs. Find this she-serpent Sorrow Gray, bring her in. See if she is party to conspiracy.'

Shakespeare nodded.

'Before you go, I want you to talk with Anthony Friday. I have employed him to insinuate himself into the Catholic circles he knows so well, to see what he can discover. I have been expecting him to report to me, but there has been no word. See what is going on. He knew Garrick Loake and those of his circle. If anyone can discover the truth about Loake's secret – and his death – I am certain it is Friday.'

Shakespeare kept to himself his feelings about Anthony Friday; the man was a ferocious anti-Catholic attack dog who had often ridden with Topcliffe in pursuit of priests and those harbouring them. Would any Catholic now trust him?

Cecil continued his theme. 'In the meantime, I shall send a squadron of eight men to Wisbech to ensure the prisoners are held secure and that the castle is properly defended.'

'It would help to send a clerk, too. Someone to read and censor all incoming and outgoing letters.'

'A good thought. Weston and company can pay for it themselves. They have been living too high, so their diet will be reduced.' Cecil sat back in his seat. 'And, John, let me just add that all is not bad with the world. You will likely be pleased to know that Richard Topcliffe languishes in Marshalsea gaol, condemned for contempt of court. He is reduced to writing anguished letters to the Queen, begging her to intercede. But for the present, she will not.'

Shakespeare wanted to laugh out loud, but there was nothing remotely amusing about the murder, rape and torture that had been committed unchecked for so long by Richard Topcliffe.

Cecil held up a paper. 'The man has the wit of a flea-infested mongrel. This is one of his letters to Her Majesty. He writes, "I have helped more traitors to Tyburn than all the noblemen and gentlemen of the court, your counsellors excepted. In all prisons rejoicings; it is like that the fresh dead bones of Father Southwell at Tyburn and Father Walpole at York, executed both since Shrovetide, will dance for joy."'

'What make of man would brag of hunting other men to their deaths? He is where he belongs.'

'However,' Cecil said, 'whatever we think of Mr Topcliffe, he did work for us. Now that he is in gaol, we are another man down. So it is imperative that you stoke the fires of the idle Anthony Friday and make him earn his two marks!'

Chapter 20

F ROM THE STRAND, Shakespeare repaired straightway to his home in Dowgate, where a letter awaited him. He shook his head in dismay at the writing, which was the scrawl of an idiot infant: Topcliffe. His inclination was to hurl it into the fire unread, but he cut it open nonetheless.

'You may think yourself free of me, but do not. I am your master in the Marshalsea as ever I was on the outer side, for you must know I have men everywhere, men who love God and England. Have you brought the traitor Weston to London for godly racking? If not, then send for him now, for the Queen Her Majesty will not abide any man that lets the dirty Jesuit go untormented and his secrets so undiscovered. Do this or I will wreak such storms on your head that you will wish yourself dead, and your spawn likewise.'

Shakespeare crumpled the letter into a ball and lit it from a candle. It burned bright and fell in black ashes to the ground, where he stamped on its embers.

Jane served him rabbit and capon pie with a goblet of good wine. After that, he bathed, then slept.

In the morning, he ate breakfast with his family. The table was busy and noisy. Andrew was talking enthusiastically about his new-found knowledge of navigation and sailing.

'Are you still set on this course?'

'More than ever, Father. I wish to join Drake at the soonest opportunity.'

'But you do not even know where he is planning to sail! No one does except Drake himself, Hawkins and the Privy Council. Even I have not been made party to this secret.'

In truth, though he would not say it, Shakespeare did know that the intended destination was Panama, where the Spanish treasure fleets gathered. But that was not to be spoken, either in this room or anywhere else.

'I would not care if the voyage was to the moon. I know this to be my destiny.'

Shakespeare smiled at the boy; Andrew had seen enough in his fourteen years not to have a romantic notion of what he faced. 'Very well. I am going westward and will escort you to Plymouth, where we can talk with Drake himself.'

Shakespeare had no doubt the admiral would take him. It was difficult enough to find crew for such a voyage at the best of times. A lad like Andrew would be a godsend.

'Thank you, Father.'

Shakespeare clasped Andrew to his breast. The sea brought perils but also the potential for adventure and riches. It was the boy's own choice.

Their discussion was interrupted by a fit of girlish giggling. Mary and Grace were deep in some secret conversation that was causing them enormous mirth.

'What is it, Mary?' Shakespeare asked his daughter.

'Ursula's got a swain,' Mary said without hesitation.

'She told us not to tell anyone!' Grace looked at her younger sister with mock fury.

'Well, she has. Ask her yourself.'

'Mary, if Ursula has a swain, then that is her business. And if she asked you to keep it a secret, then you should abide by her wishes. Do you understand?'

'But he is very handsome. He walked her home from the market last night and we saw him kiss her. She said he has a stall selling salad vegetables from the Dutch gardens in Islington.'

Ursula could not hear this betrayal of her new romance for she was already out buying produce for her stall. Shakespeare felt content. It was, he reflected, the way life should be: a family laughing, being indiscreet and squabbling as they planned their day; a welcome refuge from the unwholesome tribulations of Wisbech and conspiracy.

His only worry was Jane. She had seemed miserable as she served fresh bread and eggs for them all. Clearly, she was unhappy that Boltfoot was still away, but Shakespeare had known her long enough to see that something else was wrong. She could barely meet his eyes when he greeted her with news of her husband.

After breakfast, he took her aside. 'Jane, if you are anxious about something, you must know that you can always confide in me, whatever it is. You are family to me.'

'I know that, master.' She looked down at her feet as she spoke.

Shakespeare saw that she had lost weight. Her normally ample bosom was shrunken and there was a gauntness in her cheeks. He saw, too, that she had a new ring on a finger of her left hand and could not stop twisting it.

'I do not mean to pry, you understand. But neither can I stand by and say nothing when I see you in such anguish, especially with Boltfoot away. Can I ask you, Jane, is this something to do with the sickness that lately afflicted little John? I had thought him better than he was. He eats well and seems full of life.'

'Oh, master, if I were to speak to you, would you really not go to Boltfoot with what I say?'

Shakespeare had no intention of coming between a wife and husband, but neither could he fail to help Jane if she needed him. He nodded. She seemed on the edge of tears. 'You can trust me, Jane.'

There was silence between them, then Jane spoke so quietly that he could only just hear her. 'I have disobeyed my husband.'

Shakespeare frowned. Had she been unfaithful to Boltfoot? He could not believe it of her. 'Tell me more.'

'I went to Dr Forman. Boltfoot had said he was a conjuror and forbade me to go, but other wives told me he really could cure ills. I went to him secretly and he told me little John would be well, and he was.'

'Did he give you that ring to wear?'

She reddened furiously and hid her hand.

'Then all is well. Say nothing to Boltfoot and think no more of it. But do not let him see the ring.'

'I am racked with guilt for my disobedience, for there is another matter . . .'

'Yes?'

'I cannot speak of it.'

'Are you worried that Dr Forman will reveal your secret?'

'I – I don't know. He is a most strange man. I talk to him in a way I could not talk with my own mother or sisters. And then when I am gone from him I worry about the things I have revealed. Private things: things that no wife should say to any man other than her husband.'

Shakespeare knew Forman well enough, having had cause to deal with him on official matters in the past. He was a lewd, bawdy man, but clever and honest. He doubted that he would betray one of those who came to see him. But that opinion of his character was not going to put Jane's mind at rest.

'I will go to him, Jane. I have power over him, for I know

certain secrets about him. I will extract a promise from him that he will never speak of your visit. Would that help?'

Jane looked frightened. 'There was something else, master.' Her voice was barely audible. 'He asked for details of my birth and John's and Boltfoot's to make charts for us. I fear he is a necromancer and I might be hanged for consorting with him.'

Shakespeare put an arm around the terrified woman's shoulders. 'No one is going to be hanged, Jane, least of all you. Simon Forman's practices might earn him a few weeks in the Clink, but nothing more. You are safe, believe me.'

The tears were streaming down her cheeks now. A sob escaped from deep within her. She nodded, and buried her head in his chest.

'I will see him before I leave London, Jane. Consider it done.'

As Shakespeare reined in close by the Theatre in Shoreditch, three boys raced forward, offering to hold his horse for a farthing. He slid from the saddle and handed the lead rein to the fastest of the three. The boy tipped his hat and offered to have the nag fed and watered for a farthing more.

Shakespeare agreed to the deal and said he would pay him when he departed, not before.

It was a few minutes before three o'clock in the afternoon. The pennant was raised atop the playhouse mast and a trumpet blared to show that the play was about to begin. Shakespeare glanced at the bills posted on all available spaces. *Romeo and Juliet*, they pronounced in bold letters. If he had the time to spare, he would view it, for the play was already the talk of London. But first he had work to do.

He strode up to the entrance. Four whores pushed their wares in his direction, offering use of their bodies in exchange for admission to the play and a bottle of ale. He declined their soliciting politely.

At the door, a large woman with the muscles of a man barred his way. 'It's full. Every inch of space is taken.'

'I am here on Queen's business. I must go to the back of the stage to speak with a member of this company.'

'Who do you want?'

'Mr Shakespeare. Will Shakespeare.'

'He's a very busy man,' the woman said, thrusting her grimy hand forward for a bribe. 'A very important man. The whole world wishes to speak with him.'

'He is my brother.'

The woman's begging hand shot back. 'That's different.' She stood aside. 'Go on through. Do you know the way?'

'Indeed.'

The noise inside the playhouse was deafening. Shakespeare could see that the ground space, where the poorer sort stood for a penny, was packed as tight as the doorkeeper had said. Men, women and children were crowded together in an unwashed mass, stinking of ale and sweat. The galleries in the upper two tiers, where the wealthier patrons sat for tuppence with a cushion for an extra penny, were equally full. Sellers jostled and pushed their way through the noisy, excited throngs, shouting out their offerings.

'Filberts and oranges here.'

'Saffron cakes! Four for a halfpenny.'

'Strong beer!'

He found his brother behind the scenes in the tiring-house, making last-minute adjustments to the costume of a fresh-faced boy who was about to play the part of Juliet.

'Good day to you, Will.'

Will tugged at the stays on the boy's elaborate gown, gave them a last twist to tighten them, then pushed him away with a pat on the shoulder and turned to greet his brother. 'John, well met.'

The brothers embraced. Will pulled back apologetically.

'I am afraid the play is about to begin. You have caught me at the worst of times.'

'Forgive me, I had no option.' Shakespeare looked his younger brother up and down and noted his rich costume.

'Is anything amiss?'

'No, you look splendid. Like a king.'

Will laughed. 'Not a king, a noble gentleman of Verona. Montague. And I am Chorus, too, so I must make haste, for I am first on. Briefly, John, how may I help you?'

'I am looking into the death of Garrick Loake. I need to go over the same questions I asked you before. There must be some clue here. Whom was he close to among your company?'

'He was good with needles and threads and worked mostly in the wardrobe. In truth I would happily murder him myself, were he not already killed, for he took a mighty expensive costume with him to his death. But I cannot say that he was especially close to anyone. Not to my knowledge, leastwise.'

'It was at this playhouse that he learnt the secret that probably led to his death. What I need to know is from whom he learnt it. Was it overheard – or did someone confide in him?'

'As you say, I have told you all I know. And these are the selfsame matters that Anthony Friday put to me. He is working for you now, is he not?'

'Is he here?'

'Why, yes. He is in the sharers' room. You will find him there with the company manager. Together, they are making amendments to some works that we are thinking of putting on this summer.'

'Then I had better go to him.'

'Can you not watch the play first?'

'Another day.'

The trumpet blared again. 'That's it,' Will said. 'I must go into the lions' den and play my part.'

The sharers' room did not offer much respite from the audience's roars, cheers, shouts and gasps. The company manager was not in evidence. Only Anthony Friday was there, sitting at a table chewing at the end of a quill, staring down at a much scrawled-upon sheet of paper. His hands were covered in ink stains, as was the table and the floor around him. He did not look up as the door opened.

Shakespeare walked over to him and grasped his long fair hair in his fist, dragging him to his feet.

Friday recoiled from the assault, and then recognised his assailant. 'Mr Shakespeare!'

'Is this what Sir Robert Cecil pays you two marks a week for?'

Friday tried to twist free, but Shakespeare's grip was too strong, and he was six inches taller. Suddenly, he released him and pushed him back down on to the stool.

'What in God's name is going on, Friday? You know better than this.'

'I must finish this work, whatever Cecil says. One play is too long, another is too short. Both are horse-shit. Besides, I have reached a stone wall in my questions regarding Garrick Loake.'

'You have spoken to everyone here who worked with him?'

'Yes, and I have been to his lodgings. There is nothing. And before you ask, he lived alone. No wife, no mistress, no boy. None in evidence, leastwise.'

'You told Sir Robert that Loake owed money. Why did he borrow the money – and who was the moneylender? How much was due?'

'Cutting Ball lent him the money. A hundred and fifty

pounds, I am told, at usurer's rates. Loake was behind with his payments and was told to produce twenty sovereigns or he would be gelded like a pig.'

'Have you found Ball?'

'No, nor would I wish to. Anyway, Shakespeare, you know Ball did not kill Loake. What use is a dead man to a money-lender?'

Shakespeare nodded. The only relevance of the debt to this inquiry was that it explained why Loake had his heart set on the specific sum of twenty sovereigns. This death was linked to a conspiracy stretching from Wisbech Castle to the College of St Gregory in Seville. But why would a lowly playhouse factotum hear about such a plot?

'What of a young man named Caldor? Gavin Caldor? Have you heard of him?'

Friday thought a moment, then shook his head. 'No.'

'He used to work here building sets and props.'

'What of him?'

'He is in Wisbech Castle now.'

'Well, I'll ask around for you. Your brother should know him if he worked here.'

'What of your orders to infiltrate the Catholic netherworld?'

Friday ran a hand through his hair where it had been tugged and tousled. 'God knows, I told Sir Robert I had work to do, but he insisted. A man must make a living. I am also writing a play for Henslowe at the the Rose. Am I supposed to let these people down? This is my livelihood.' He sighed. 'I have been trying to fit in some inquiries for Cecil, though.'

'You are trying to *fit in* some inquiries?' Shakespeare was incredulous. 'Would you like to go now to Cecil and tell him that?'

For the first time, Friday looked ill at ease. He shook his head.

'You will leave this work and go about the business to which Sir Robert Cecil has contracted you. I shall square it with my brother and Mr Burbage. Do you understand? You will go to the gaols and to the inns where the known Catholic agitators gather. You will bring every titbit you hear to me.'

Friday shook his head more violently, so that his long fair locks swung like barleycorn in the wind. 'They know me too well, Mr Shakespeare! I have had occasion to search many of their pox-ridden houses when riding with Mr Topcliffe. Now, they slam their cell doors in my face when I go to the gaols. The lackeys will not let me past the gateways to the great Catholic houses. And when I try to overhear them in their drinking dens, they shy away and vanish.'

'Then you had better get yourself a new costume here in this playhouse and find yourself a fine disguise. That is daily bread for players like you, is it not? And when you have done that, you will prepare a report of everything you have told me and all other details you have not said, and bring it to my house at Dowgate by nightfall. Get you gone, Mr Friday. Do what you are best at – or I will have you whipped at the cart's arse!'

Chapter 21

SHAKESPEARE LOOKED ACROSS at the players. He was standing close to the Theatre exit. His brother was on stage, declaiming about an *envious worm*. He needed to talk with him again.

His gaze wandered around the assembled throng and his eyes lifted to the second and third galleries. Did anyone here know the secret of Garrick Loake and his death? Suddenly his eyes alighted upon a booth on the third tier. There were two faces he recognised, peering intently at the stage: Lady Susan Bertie, the Countess of Kent, and one of the young gentlewomen he had met at her house in Barbican Street, Emilia Lanier. Shakespeare smiled to himself. Very convenient.

Lady Susan caught his eye and nudged her companion. They both waved to him.

He tilted his chin in acknowledgment, then ducked down into the outer passage and found the wooden steps that led up to the gallery where they were seated. In the gallery, the crowd was so dense it had spilt beyond the seating into the aisles, and he had to elbow his way to the front to reach the women. He bowed to them.

A voice boomed from behind. 'Get out of the way, you outsized maggot!'

Shakespeare turned and apologised to the irate spectator, then sank to his knees at Lady Susan's side.

'Forgive me for interrupting the performance, my lady,' he said as quietly as possible. 'I had wished to talk with you.'

'It is quite perfect to see you, Mr Shakespeare. But why should I be surprised? Of course you are here; it is your brother's play. We are great admirers of Will Shakespeare.' She turned to her companion. 'Are we not, Emilia?'

'Hush, for pity's sake!' Another angry voice from the row behind.

'I think now might not be a good time to talk.' Lady Susan's voice lowered to a discreet whisper. 'Why do we not meet directly afterwards, if we can find each other in the throng?'

'Thank you, my lady. I shall be behind the scenes.'

Two hours later, Shakespeare found Will in the tiring-house and complimented him on his play, then apologised as he explained that Anthony Friday would have to be removed from work on the other dramas.

'In truth, I am not worried,' Will said. 'The plays he was working on are poor things that have been submitted to us by members of the company. We merely wondered whether Friday could salvage something from them, for he is a fair writer. There is no hurry.'

'There was another thing I meant to ask you. Do you recall a scene-builder named Gavin Caldor?'

'Yes, I do. Why?'

'Did he have any connection to Garrick Loake?'

'Not to my knowledge.' He shook his head. 'No, he could not have done. Loake did not work here in those days. Again, I ask, why do you wish to know? What happened to young Caldor? Always rather indiscreet in his papism, I recall.'

'It's led him to gaol.'

Lady Susan, Countess of Kent, and her companion swept regally into the tiring-house and seemed not at all alarmed to find themselves in the company of a dozen or more men in various stages of undress. The brothers turned at their approach.

Lady Susan beamed a beguiling smile and proffered her hand to be kissed. Will obliged with a flourish.

'Well, well, Emilia, *two* Mr Shakespeares. What more could any lady ask? You amuse yourself with one, while I talk to the other.'

Shakespeare did not like this public place. 'My lady, perhaps we might go to the sharers' room to talk in private.'

'As you wish, Mr Shakespeare. This is all exceeding mysterious.'

'I hope your brother is safe with Emilia, Mr Shakespeare. She is a very naughty girl, you know.'

'I am sure Will can look after himself, my lady. However, I am here to ask you about Beatrice Eastley. How did you meet her?'

The countess was wandering around the room, picking up papers and examining them in an idle fashion. She cast a glance over her shoulder. 'Very naughty indeed. You must know that Hunsdon, the Lord Chamberlain, is father to her whelp.'

'It is generally known. But back to the point—'

'Why would you wish to know how I met Beatrice?'

'Because she is not the person she seems to be.'

'Is that so? Tell me more and perhaps I will tell you what I know.'

'Her real name is not Beatrice Eastley, but Sorrow Gray. She is the daughter of the late keeper of Wisbech Castle gaol.'

'How very interesting. But then, are *any* of us what we seem?'

'She was an evangelist Puritan, and she was converted to Catholicism by William Weston, the notorious Jesuit. From what I am told she has become a very devout, unyielding Catholic. Those who knew her rather imagined that she had gone off to Louvain to be a nun.'

Lady Susan stopped her perambulation. 'Now that *does* surprise me. I think her a little too worldly to be cloistered away in a nunnery. But nuns are all mad, are they not, and Beatrice has always struck me as not quite of this world.'

'Before her change of heart, she was to have been married to a most correct Calvinist gentleman named Paul Hooft, but she ran away from him and from her family, so successful was Weston in seducing the young woman from her original faith. So you must see, my lady, why I am intrigued to know how she came to be in the company of a group such as yours.'

'Yes, I do see that.'

'I cannot speak for your other friends, but I am given to believe that you and Lady Lucia Trevail conform powerfully to the established English Church.'

'That is true, but I am not so precise in religion. For all I care, Beatrice could be a pagan or a Mussulman, so long as she is amusing company. You see, I took her in because I believed that with education and guidance she might become someone of note. It is what happened with Emilia, who had her education in my household and is now a most remarkable poet. We must give young women a chance, Mr Shakespeare . . .'

'I must tell you that I fear this is a matter of conspiracy against Queen and country.'

'Mr Shakespeare, what are you saying?'

He weighed his words delicately. How much could he trust this charming, beautiful, good-humoured and very aristocratic woman? He decided there was nothing to be lost by being direct and honest with her.

'What I say to you must not go beyond these walls. We fear a great conspiracy coming out of Wisbech. I have no evidence against Miss Gray, or Miss Eastley if you prefer, but we must pursue every possibility. That is why I wish to know how she came to be in your company. Nothing about her makes sense to me.'

The countess stood facing Shakespeare. She hesitated a moment, then sighed. 'You seem worthy of trust, so I shall tell you all I know, which is little enough. It may surprise you to discover that it was through this very playhouse that I came to know of Beatrice, as I must still call her. We are all great devotees of the players' art. It is through this closeness to the playhouses, and your brother's poetic works in particular, that we came to know Beatrice. At one time she was living with a player, who treated her ill, beat her without mercy and then simply disappeared, taking all her few possessions and what little money she had. When I met her, she was destitute, and so I took her in.'

'Who told you of her?'

'Why, your own dear brother did, Mr Shakespeare. Well, in truth, he first mentioned her plight to Emilia Lanier, who is a good friend to both of us. Emilia came to me with the tale and my heart was touched. How could I resist such a challenge? I consider the schooling of women my life's work, you see. Emilia was my first. I tried to do the same for Thomasyn Jade, as you well know. There have been others, too, and I am proud of every one of them. I do not ask them their religion, nor do I ask for thanks. My only failure has been poor Thomasyn. Does that answer your question, sir?'

'Who was the man, the player who mistreated Beatrice?'

'You will have to ask Will.'

Shakespeare pressed Lady Susan for all she knew of Beatrice, but the answers did not help him.

'I fear I did not interrogate her before taking her in, Mr Shakespeare. How terribly remiss of me.'

He saw that she was mocking him and bowed to her curtly before going off to seek out his brother again.

Will recalled the girl instantly. 'Why, yes, John, of course I recall Beatrice. A strange beauty. Intense and troubling. The sort that any man should learn to avoid before they have reached manhood.'

'In what way?'

'Nothing obvious, but those who know to look for the signs might see the touch of madness. An inability to meet the eye, a strange sweetness of tongue for some, long silences with others, and then, on occasion, ferocity in argument, particularly in matters of religion, which I took to be most unwholesome.'

'Papist?'

'Probably. It was difficult to discern. A puritanical papism if that makes any sense. And beneath the surface, something crawls, not quite visible. It is the unspoken threat of violence that jars with the softness of the skin and the paleness of the breast.'

'You seem to know her well.'

'She came to this place frequently and would watch as we rehearsed. That was how she met Emilia, who was here directing the musicians for me.'

'And so Emilia and Beatrice became close.'

'Too close. I thought it unwise of Emilia to befriend such a woman, but I could say nothing. It was none of my business.'

'And the man who beat her? Lady Susan says he was a player and that he attacked her with great force, then disappeared.'

Will shook his head slowly. 'I know nothing of such matters, John. That is the story Beatrice told Emilia, but I do not have any knowledge of such a man, and she has given no name to him. Players come and go, for in some plays we need a great cast and our company is small, but I have no idea who this man might be. If he existed at all.'

'You doubt even that?'

'I doubt *everything* about Beatrice Eastley. In truth, I was delighted when the countess took her in, for that meant she stopped coming here.'

'What of the beating she had? Was she badly injured?'

'Cuts and bruises about the face. She could have walked into a wall for all I know. Emilia might have more to say on the matter. Perhaps she even knows the name of the player who supposedly loved her and left her.'

Shakespeare drew a deep breath. 'Then let us talk with Emilia,' he said.

He found Emilia with some of the players, all of whom clearly knew and liked her. It was with some difficulty that he prised her away from them and managed to ask about Beatrice.

'I wish I could help you,' she said. 'But I fear I know no more than Lady Susan. I became quite friendly with Beatrice, but she never confided in me. Then one day she came to me in a bad state, saying she had been beaten by her lover, who was one of the players. She did not tell me his name and I did not ask. All I know is that he treated her badly and we rescued her. Is she in some sort of trouble?'

Shakespeare did not answer the question, but pressed on with his own. 'What is her character? Do you trust her?'

'I would not say a word against her. You have not seen the best of her; perhaps none of us has, for I believe her to have hidden qualities.'

A large spider crawled up Francis Mills's leg. By the thin light of a small barred hatch set high in the ceiling of the pit, he watched it without moving. It crawled on up his hose to his doublet, which was stained with his own vomit and his wife's blood. At another time, he might have squashed the creature in his hand, but he had neither the inclination nor the energy to kill it.

The cell walls dripped. One of the other prisoners suddenly screamed and rattled his chains against the stone flags, then fell silent as quickly as he had erupted.

Shakespeare stood and gazed on the scene with pity but no astonishment. He had been inside gaols often enough to know how low the prisoners could be brought. Some pissed themselves and eased their bowels without moving from where they sat, for they did not have the strength nor the care to drag their chains and their skeletal bodies to the corner where the stinking, ordure-thick straw was banked up.

Shakespeare carried a blackjack of ale and a box of bread and meats. He crouched down at Mills's side and showed him the box, then held the leather jug of ale to his lips. Mills sipped at it without enthusiasm, then looked up and his dead eyes met Shakespeare's.

'I am sorry it has come to this, Frank.'

'She is dead, isn't she? I must have killed her.'

'Do you not recall it?'

'No. All I remember is looking at their bodies, the dagger in my hand. I have dreams . . .'

Shakespeare put down the blackjack, broke a piece of bread and spread it with butter. He applied a slice of cold beef to it and handed it to Mills, who shook his head. 'I cannot eat in this place.'

'You have to.'

Mills laughed. 'So that I am alive for the hangman?'

'So that you can plead intolerable provocation. There must be hope of a pardon for you have done much service on behalf of the crown.'

'I care not for my life.'

Mills's back was bent and the notches of his spine at his bare neck were like stepping stones. He was a carrion crow on an icy midwinter day, sitting alone, waiting for whatever fate might bring him.

'Tell me about your dreams, Frank.'

'I have dreamt of this for two years, slitting both their throats in a great cataract of blood. Now, in this place, I have a new dream. I dream that the house was deathly silent and I was scared. I drew my dagger, mounted the stairs and stepped into that room, and found the bodies there. But that cannot be so . . .'

Another man might have held a kerchief or pomander to his nose in this place, but Shakespeare merely endured the stench. The prisoners had no option in the matter, so he would join them in their discomfort.

'No,' he said, 'that cannot be so, Frank.'

'And yet I cannot recall killing them.'

'You were found with knife in hand and blood on your apparel. It must have been you.'

'She was ugly, lying there, naked and covered in gore. I had to cover her.'

'You must write letters. One to Her Majesty, one to old Burghley and another to Cecil. I will send a lawyer to you to help compose them. They are your best hope.'

'And if I am pardoned, will I not just die here in depravity? A hanging is a quick end to all misery.'

'I will send a lawyer anyway. Tell him everything. Mention your dreams. I will send you a churchman, too, if you wish.'

'No.'

'Frank, much has happened since you have been in this place. Were you aware that the letter found in the box aboard *The Ruth* was bound for Wisbech Castle, to the Jesuit Weston?'

Mills's long, crooked frame quaked with what Shakespeare took to be laughter. 'So the old fraud is at his tricks again. He should have gone to the gallows long before Southwell ever did.'

'What could they be plotting? Garrick Loake is dead, too. His fate and the letter to Weston both lead back to Seville and the College of St Gregory. And yet my man there sends no word. Is he alive – or is he dead? I admit, I fear the worst.'

'Perhaps it is nothing. Loake knew dangerous men. Cutting Ball is not a man to borrow money from if you care for your health.'

'It wasn't him. Loake died for the secret he offered to sell to me.'

In a quiet voice, Shakespeare then disclosed all he had uncovered at Wisbech and the truth about Beatrice Eastley.

Mills appeared to listen, drank a little more ale and picked at some of the food.

'John,' he said at last, 'I cannot help. My hours here are spent weeping and dreaming. I would put my mind to your puzzle, but I cannot. All I can do is wait until the day I dance my jig at Tyburn.'

Chapter 22

SHAKESPEARE LEFT MONEY with the Newgate keeper in return for a promise to ensure fresh food and ale for Mills, then walked the few yards to St Paul's. He found Joshua Peace in the crypt where he carried out his duties as Searcher of the Dead. Peace immediately wiped his hands on his apron and shook his visitor by the hand.

'Welcome, old friend.'

'It is good to see you looking so hale, Joshua.'

'Do not mock me, John. I know I look like one of my corpses.'

Shakespeare held on to Peace's hand. 'Let me look at you then.' He affected to study him in minute detail. 'Yes, the hair is a little thinner. Completely bald on top, but a few strands decorate the edges, like a monk. There is an extra wrinkle at the side of each eye, a touch of pallor about the cheeks. And from the chill of your hand, I would estimate you had been dead for two days at least.'

Peace roared with laughter. 'Any man's hand would be cold here in this crypt! Just don't examine me any further, you might not like what you find.'

'You know why I am here.'

'You wish to know what I have discovered about three bodies that were entrusted to my care.'

Here in the old crypt it was, indeed, as cold as the grave. In the middle of the room stood a pair of trestle tables with small wheels at the end of their legs to make them movable. Two bodies were stretched out on them on their backs, staring up at the stone ceiling with lifeless eyes.

'Yes, that's Mills's wife,' Peace said. 'And I am told the other one is called Heartsease and made his living as a grocer.'

'What have you discovered?'

'That the time of death was about an hour before the constable arrived. Certainly no more than that. Cause of death was massive blood loss due to throat wounds. They had copulated a short while before their deaths. When they were found, they were both naked and bound, so it is possible to imagine that they were surprised in the act and threatened in some way to submit to their bindings. A pistol comes to mind; otherwise why would a strong, healthy man like Heartsease allow himself to be tied up? But that is merely my speculation.'

'I do not think any pistol was found.'

'Then it is up to you to discover how they were subdued, John. But don't get me involved in your investigations, please. They are too dangerous.'

Shakespeare walked over to take a closer look at the bodies. He was well aware why Joshua Peace would wish to avoid further involvement. He had been involved once before, a few months since, and had got in so deep that his very life had been imperilled. Such ventures were not in Peace's nature.

Gazing down at the still, bloodied corpses, it was hard for Shakespeare to imagine them ever having been imbued with life and passion. He had met Anne Mills only twice and had thought her unremarkable, mousy even, but he was aware how much she had meant to Mills. It was almost as though she had possessed him, like some evil spirit. What a thing was the human heart, that one man should give his life and soul for a woman that another man would not even grace with a second glance. Shakespeare touched the woman's face gently, with his knuckles.

'The interesting thing for me is that Mills remembers being in the room with the bodies, but does not remember the killing itself.'

'Are you saying you have doubts about his guilt?'

Shakespeare shrugged. 'I would merely like to be certain that he has a fair trial. His brain has become addled and I have worked with him too long to see him go to his death if there is any chance that he is innocent.'

'Well, I have already looked at the bodies closely, but I will examine them again. I do not expect to find anything of note, though.'

'Thank you, Joshua. I would ask you to get word to the lawyer Cornelius Bligh at Lincoln's Inn. He is a good man. Ask him to visit Mr Mills and represent him as best he can. I shall pay his fees.'

'I will do that today.'

'And what of the remains of Garrick Loake, the body from the river?'

Peace nodded towards the doorway into the other room. 'He's in there. Would you like to see him?'

Shakespeare had no desire to see or smell the putrid carcass; he knew what a few days in the Thames could do to a dead body. But he had to show willing. 'Very well.'

The corpse was every bit as repulsive as he had expected, so bloated and mutilated that only the distinctive, over-large nose could tell you that the man was Loake. The skin was slimy and mottled, like a dead goose that had been hung far too long before roasting. There were cuts in many places, particularly on the head and face.

'It was tangled in branches, pulled this way and that by the currents. What was left of his clothing, part of a doublet and his breeches, were in tatters. What I cannot establish yet is whether the skin tears and the deeper wounds were the result of buffeting against logs and banks, and feeding by predators, or whether the injuries were caused before immersion.'

'So you do not know the cause of death?'

'I am as certain as I can be that it was not drowning. No water emerged when I pressed down hard on his ribs, which suggests to me that he was dead when he entered the river. He could have been murdered elsewhere and thrown in. He was found upstream of the tideway close to Richmond, therefore he could not have entered the water anywhere downstream of there. The body is washed clean of blood, so I am still trying to determine the location of the death wound. It is not obvious, I am afraid, but I will not give up.'

'Do you not even have any possibilities?'

'There are wounds of different shapes and sizes. I need to look at them all individually to see if any are likely to have been caused by a dagger. The head injuries are more difficult. Cracks in the skull would indicate battering by a heavy object. This is not a simple task, John.'

He picked up a basin from a shelf. From it he took a number of rings and a thin chain with a cross at the end.

'The rings were on his fingers. You will see his name carved on each of them. The cross was in the pocket of his breeches. It is possible it means something to you.'

Shakespeare turned the silver chain and cross in his hands. The only thing it meant to him was that, perhaps, Garrick Loake had been a Catholic. There were plenty of such men and women in England: people who clung to the old faith in secret but found it made their life more tenable to pretend otherwise. Perhaps the most interesting thing about Garrick Loake was his connection to the Theatre – a connection he shared in common with Beatrice Eastley, late of Wisbech. If both were Catholic, then the circle seemed complete. Had Loake perhaps heard his lethal secret from Beatrice, or someone close to her? Had she, in fact, tried to recruit him to conspiracy?

He handed the object back to Peace. 'Keep it safe.'

'As always.'

'And keep me informed, Joshua. Will you share a flagon of Gascon wine at the Three Tuns before I leave you? I am certain I promised you as much.'

Peace shook Shakespeare by the hand again. 'Another day, John. For the present, I must force some more work out of my decrepit limbs and brain.'

Shakespeare found Ursula at her market stall among the booksellers. Three books lay on her table, but they were there for show. It was the leaves of tobacco that caught the attention.

'Another good day, Ursula?'

'Like stealing from babies. The pigging lawyers are the best. They'll pay anything to get their hands on an ounce or two of verinshe sotweed. Brown gold, they call it, and they're not far wrong.'

'Well, I was merely passing, visiting an old friend, and I thought I would see how you were faring.'

He looked at her fondly. She was well fed now, but her pinched mouth and cheeks would always betray the truth: that she had been ill nourished as a child.

Ursula's transformation was amazing. She had been born to the wild, staying alive by cheating and thieving as part of one of the feared vagabond bands. She had done a good deed for Shakespeare and his family, and in return he had taken her in, promising her an education and a home if she would help with the younger children, Grace and Mary.

'Got something for you, Mr Shakespeare. Here.' She handed him a paper, folded over like a letter.

He took it. His name was written in bold lettering on the front. 'Where did this come from?'

'A little brat brought it, said it was for you, then ran away, so I couldn't question him. Read it and see.'

Shakespeare cut open the letter, read the words and recoiled. The letter was unsigned and was written in a brownish-red ink. It said, *Exorcise your own demons, lest they claw away all you hold dear.* There were two names, in capital letters: GRACE at the top; MARY at the foot of the page. The whole effect was of a cross. And then Shakespeare realised what the ink was: it was blood. He shuddered.

'What does it say, Mr Shakespeare?'

It was a warning. *Cease your delving or your family will pay a terrible price. A blood price.* But whilst he might discount threats from Topcliffe while he remained in gaol, this one could not be ignored.

'I must go.' He looked at the girl and knew that she could see the fear in his eyes. 'You must take care, Ursula. Come home before dark. Have your young man accompany you, for the sake of safety.'

'You're pigging worrying me now.'

'There is nothing for you to fear. I just want you to be safe. Do you understand?'

She nodded. She wasn't going to argue with him about this; she had seen enough misery and death to know terror when she saw it.

Shakespeare ran the half-mile home through crowded streets thick with horse-dung and piles of waste, pushing carters and apprentices out of his way. At the house in Dowgate, out of breath, he shouted for Jane, who came hurrying and tried to hush him as he demanded to know where the girls were. She took him to the schoolroom and pointed to them.

'There, master, see. They are safe.'

They were sitting at a table, working very seriously together. Without thinking, he swept them both up in his arms and hugged them.

'What is it, master?' Jane said. She stood in the doorway, her face creased with confusion and anxiety.

He shook his head, unable to express what he knew and feared. All he could do was try to think how he could protect the girls. He had to go away soon, that was set, but first he had to find somewhere safe for his family.

Of a sudden it came to him. If Sir Robert Cecil wished him to do this work, he could protect his family. There was space enough at his mansion on the Strand, and guards aplenty.

'Jane, we are all leaving this place. This very hour. The girls can collect their most favoured possessions and clothes, and then we go.'

When Cecil read the blood letter, he nodded. 'Yes, John, of course they must stay here. The girls can join classes with our own tutors. They will be well cared for. Your servant, Jane Cooper, is welcome, too, with her son.'

'Thank you, Sir Robert. My mind is greatly eased. Someone does not wish me to continue my inquiries.'

'But from the death of Loake, we can assume the conspirators are utterly ruthless and relentless. Would such people send threats, or go straight for the kill?'

Shakespeare shrugged. 'I do not know. But the threat seems serious enough.'

'Indeed. And now you must go westward at speed. Find Beatrice Eastley and bring her in. Logic tells me that she is the key to everything and instinct tells me that she is dangerous. I do not like the thought of her being in company with Lucia Trevail, for Lucia has access to the Queen.'

Jane, the two girls and little John Cooper were waiting in an ante-room with their bags of possessions. Other clothes and belongings had been packed up at home, waiting to be fetched by Cecil's servants. But where was Ursula Dancer? She could not stay at Dowgate alone. Shakespeare decided to send a message to her with money; she might be safer at an inn, or perhaps her swain's parents might find room for her.

Cecil held up the blood letter again. He seemed as troubled by it as Shakespeare himself. 'Who wrote this foul missive, John?'

'I wish I knew.'

'And you think it written in blood?'

'I do.'

'John, something very bad is happening. Take your leave of your daughters and go. You can rest at ease knowing that they will be safe here. An assassin would need a company of arquebusiers to get past my guards.'

The next morning, Shakespeare rode out from Dowgate with Andrew at his side. He had left messages with the stablehands for Boltfoot, informing him of the whereabouts of Jane and the children. He had also left orders for Boltfoot with Cecil's servant Clarkson; Boltfoot was to follow Shakespeare and Andrew down to the west country.

'I have one last task before we leave London,' Shakespeare told Andrew. 'Come, we must take a detour to Fylpot Street.'

He kicked on into a trot and they rode a little way northwards, up through the early morning streets.

Shakespeare reined in outside the old stone house. It was a place he knew well. Dr Simon Forman had had cause to regret crossing Shakespeare's path before.

The door was unlocked and he pushed his way in. A surly youth stepped forward, but Shakespeare ignored him and strode up the staircase to Forman's chamber.

The doctor was in bed, but not alone. There was not much bedding in evidence. His heavy testicles and notorious prick hung flaccidly along his hairy leg. A woman was snoring softly at his side, her ripe breasts uncovered and pointing in opposite directions. Her hair was a mess. She was not pretty but she was endowed with an air of raw lust.

Shakespeare stood and looked at them for a moment, then jabbed Forman in the ribs with his index finger. 'Get up and put on some clothes.'

Forman stirred. His eyes opened, bleary and full of sleep. He saw his uninvited guest and suddenly he was wide awake. He scrabbled to pull some bedclothes about his person.

'Don't bother about that, get up, Forman.'

The doctor jumped from the bed, then shook the arm of the sleeping woman. 'Wake up, Janey. We have a visitor.'

As she stirred, he scuttled around the floor, picking up his shirt and hose, putting them on as best he could. The woman, meanwhile, sat up in bed, not in the least shamed by her nakedness.

'Who's this then?' she said.

'This is Mr Shakespeare, Janey.'

She looked at him with inquiring eyes. 'Is it now? And who's he?'

Shakespeare looked back at her. Her expression had changed; his name meant something to her. He was sure of it.

'Mr Shakespeare, Janey. Sir Robert Cecil's officer . . .'

'I don't know the name. Have you mentioned him to me?' She smiled with warm lasciviousness. 'Nice looking, isn't he?'

'I don't have time for this. Forman, come downstairs with me. I want to talk with you alone.'

Shakespeare led the way from the chamber down the stairs to the hall. He pushed the protesting servant boy from the room, out of the back of the house into the yard, and slammed the door after him.

Forman was still adjusting his attire when Shakespeare returned. 'Now, Dr Forman, my servant Jane Cooper has been here to consult you in recent days.'

'Yes, I do recall Mistress Cooper. A very pleasant young lady.'

'Never mind that. You have worried her with your charts and potions, and I do not like her to be worried. She is terrified that her husband will discover she has been here.'

Forman stopped shaking. 'Yes, Mr Shakespeare, I know she was worried about that. But tell her she must fear nothing. I would not tell a soul that she has been here under my roof, though I believe I could help her.'

'Good, Dr Forman.' Shakespeare's stern tones mellowed. 'That is exactly what I wanted to hear. And I wished to remind you that I know enough about you to have you consigned to Newgate for the rest of your life, which would not be very long. I know that you have devised a life chart for a certain great lady, a crime that would be construed as treason.'

'You do not need to remind me, sir.'

'Very well. Then we are as one on this matter. Jane Cooper's husband will never hear of her visit.'

'No.'

Shakespeare believed him. He put out his hand and Forman took it tentatively, and they shook on the deal. Shakespeare tilted his head towards the stairway. 'Who is the young lady?'

'Janey? She is no one, a trull of no importance.'

'Does she live here with you?'

'No, she is a drab at a clergyman's house.'

'Which clergyman would that be?'

'Mr Shakespeare, please, is the young lady not to be allowed a little courtesy? She has been found by you in most unfortunate circumstances. She has her reputation . . .'

Shakespeare laughed. 'Reputation? A moment ago you called her trull and drab! And as for being found in unfortunate circumstances, she showed not the slightest degree of modesty.'

Forman sighed. 'Very well.' He lowered his voice. 'She is lady's maid to Alice Blague, the wife of the Dean of Rochester over at Lambeth. She is supposed to be visiting her sister. She would be thrown out of her job and home if Mistress Blague or her husband were to hear of her assignation with me.'

'Why did she affect not to have heard of me when it was clear that she had?'

'Perhaps she was scared of you, Mr Shakespeare. Many people are, you know.'

Chapter 23

THEY STOOD ON the shore at Plymouth, gazing out at the jagged horizon of masts and rigging. Dozens of great ships blotted the skyline with their tangle of spars and sheets. Some rode high in the water, waiting to be loaded with provisions; others wallowed under the weight of guns and balls, ballast and enormous kegs of victuals.

The ride here from London had been long and arduous. Shakespeare clapped an arm around Andrew's shoulder as they took in the magnitude of the great fleet.

'Your new life lies there. No change of heart?'

'None, Father. I cannot wait to board and set sail.'

'Come on, let us seek out Drake.'

They found him aboard the *Defiance*, a royal ship of five hundred tons, heavily armoured with forty-six guns and bearing a lion as its figurehead. Drake was in his cabin, directing operations and complaining loudly about the lack of money and provisions.

'In God's faith, I shall go and find ale and salt pork myself!' he thundered. He turned and recognised Shakespeare. 'Ah, Mr Shakespeare, do you bring word from Sir Robert of beef, munitions and ale?'

Shakespeare bowed, and then looked up at the old mariner. Drake was beginning to show his age. His barrelled chest seemed to have shrunk and his bold head was hunched lower, so that his once-proud beard resembled the tail of a cowed dog.

'I fear not, Sir Francis, but it is a pleasure and an honour to find you in good health.'

Drake sighed deeply. 'Not so good, Mr Shakespeare. But nothing that will not be healed by taking Spanish gold and silver. And what is this?' He nodded towards Andrew.

'My son by adoption, Andrew Woode. He has been studying navigation and wishes now to learn how to use these skills at sea under your command that one day he may aspire to be a ship's master.'

'He looks strong enough. Do you have the stomach to kill Spaniards, boy?'

Andrew met his father's eye. Shakespeare nodded. 'There can be no doubt about that, Sir Francis.'

Drake examined the boy more closely. Realisation dawned, some memory of news heard some months ago. 'Ah yes, now I recall something of the tale. Was he not at the taking of the Spanish fort at Brest, alongside that pirate Frobisher, whom no man mourns?'

'He was indeed.'

'Good. But that does not make him a seafarer. We shall find space for him here on the *Defiance*, starting at the bottom as page to one of the officers. He will turn the hourglass and have an education, but there will be no pay and he will have no favours from me.' Drake looked about, as if searching for a face. 'I am pleased to see you have not brought that misbegotten cripple Mr Cooper with you.'

'Indeed not, Admiral, but I am hoping he will follow soon.'

'Then keep him out of my sight.' Drake poured brandy from a flask into silver goblets and handed them to Shakespeare and Andrew. 'Now then, sir, you have arrived at an opportune time. Spanish shipping has been spotted around these coasts. A fishing boat was seized off St Keverne and the men taken over to Brittany. I suspect they wished to discover the plans of my fleet, but they must think us fools if they imagine we would entrust such intelligence to fishers. I suspect, too, that they might have hopes to attack us here and destroy our fleet in harbour as I did to them in Cadiz. I have ordered five vessels out to sea to stay to windward and watch our backs. I know that Trott has already sent word to Cecil, but I will supply you with all the details as we have them, and you can go to the Council and demand more money for our cause.'

Shakespeare sipped the brandy. 'Forgive me, I am here on other matters. I must visit the Lady Trevail, who has estates in Cornwall.'

'Lucia Trevail? Then your journey is far from done. Trevail Hall is a good deal west of here, abutting Francis Godolphin's estates. I saw her recently. She broke her journey, staying with Lady Drake and myself at Buckland.'

'Who was with her?'

'A retinue of servants, I think. I paid them no heed.'

'Was there one called Beatrice Eastley?'

'Not that I met.'

'Are you certain, Sir Francis? Forgive me for pressing you, but this is mighty important.'

'I was there the whole time. Lucia was at Buckland Abbey only one night and she dined with us alone. There was no one else. Why? What is this about?'

'Nothing that I can reveal.'

Drake laughed loud. 'You were always one for dark dealings, Mr Shakespeare. As I recall, you are an admirer of beauty, too. Lucia is a perfect delicate example of her sex, I think. A gentle summer flower . . .'

Shakespeare did not need Sir Francis Drake to remind him.

'As for this boy of yours, he shall stay aboard ship with me and start his work this very day.'

The Shakespeare house in Dowgate was dark when Boltfoot Cooper reined in at the courtyard close to midnight. That was no surprise to him at such an ungodly hour, but something about the place chilled him.

He lifted the latch on the door and tried to push it open, but it was locked. He was instantly alert, for this door was never locked when people were at home. Suddenly he felt the touch of a crab-like hand on his arm and he pulled back, his own hand going to his dagger with the speed of an adder's jaws.

'They're not here. They are hiding.'

It was the old woman, the nun from Denham. But even as he realised this, the point of Boltfoot's dagger was at her chest and his other hand was clutching her throat. He immediately relaxed his grip and drew back the dagger.

'Why are you here?'

'I am staying just along the road at the Swan Inn as you ordered, Mr Cooper. I gave my word, did I not? And just now, I saw you passing.'

'You say my family is not here?'

'Gone to young Cecil's great house on the Strand. I watched them go. Gone to hide themselves away like molewarps in a tunnel.'

'And my master, John Shakespeare? Is he with them?'

'You had best go and see.'

'I ask again: why are *you* here?'

'Because I may have some matter for your master. I have heard something of the reason for his questioning, and I now believe the Lord God would wish me to help him.'

*

Shakespeare walked through the back streets of Plymouth searching for a house. He had been here once before, in 1587, soon after Sir Francis Walsingham, the late principal secretary, commanded the place to be set up to watch the movements of foreign spies in this most vital of ports.

As the man with complete responsibility for the security of the realm, Walsingham had considered it prudent to have a permanent intelligence outpost in the town. He had spies and correspondents of varying degrees in all the major cities of Europe and beyond, and in all the great houses of England. But he valued this man in Plymouth above all, for it was infested with spies from Spain and the Low Countries. And with the threat of an Armada invasion looming, as it had been then, he knew how dearly King Philip of Spain would love to cripple Drake and his fleets before they ever set sail.

Shakespeare banged at the door with his knuckles. Three times, a pause, and then once. No one came. He tried again, louder, to no effect.

An old fishwife with a basket shuffled down the street past him, then stopped and turned. 'You'll find no one there today, master.'

'Where is he?'

'Haven't seen him in a week.'

'Do you know who he is?'

'Agent of the Queen, it is said. I know he has dealings with Drake and the sea captains, and also with the mayor and merchants. I do not know his name, but he is friendly enough and touches his cap. Many messengers come and go, as does the man himself. It is no strangeness for him to be away in such days.'

Shakespeare tried the door. It was locked solid. The woman was waddling away.

'Wait,' Shakespeare said. 'What do you mean?'

'I mean with the fleets being fitted. Drake and Hawkins off on another great venture, and now the news from Cornwall that the pestilential Spaniards are circling like sharks around a fishnet.'

Shakespeare walked around to the rear of the house, which stood at the centre of a terrace. There was a high wall but the gate in it was open. He walked through the backyard to a door. It was locked, but it was not strong, and he broke it open with his shoulder. Inside, he came across a pantry, which was no more than a store cupboard with plate and jug and a keg of ale.

He pushed on through into the main room. It contained a table and a straight-backed chair, some books, quills, ink, unused papers, a belt and a threadbare hat. No dead bodies, no scene of mayhem. Only a fireplace with the blackened ashes of burnt papers. Good: that meant he was diligent about destroying all messages sent him from London.

A ladder led up from the room to a hatch, which gave way to a loft. Shakespeare climbed up. The upper room was dark and at first glance he thought it empty, but then he heard a sound, like a pig at its feed. He peered more closely into the gloom and spied the mound of a body beneath blankets. Shakespeare prodded it with his foot. It groaned and turned.

'Wake up, Mr Trott.'

The man emitted a long, drawn-out snore and turned again. Shakespeare bent down and pulled the man up by his shirt, noting the overpowering stench of liquor. He slapped him hard across the face.

Trott grunted with shock and recoiled, scrabbling against the wall.

Shakespeare withdrew his poniard and thrust it against the man's throat. 'If I were your enemy, Mr Trott, you would be dead now. Is this what we pay you for?'

Trott went rigid at the touch of the poniard's point against his skin. Shakespeare pulled the weapon away and thrust it back in his belt. 'Get up, man. You are a disgrace.'

Trott stumbled to his feet, shivering and shaking. Shakespeare estimated his age as fifty. He had been in the service of Walsingham throughout the eighties and had passed into Sir Robert Cecil's employ on the principal secretary's death in 1590. Shakespeare had met him only once before, eight years ago, when he had looked a great deal sharper. He would have to be replaced. But for the moment, Trott was needed.

'Forgive me . . . the ague.'

'The ague be damned. You have been drinking too much strong beer.'

The man could not stop his shaking. He bowed his head.

'Now, Mr Trott, collect your thoughts. There is work to be done. First, I need you to collate detailed and to-the-minute reports of these Spanish shipping manoeuvres and send them post to Sir Robert Cecil before day's end. Go to Drake and local captains for this. Then you are to inquire into the whereabouts of a woman named Beatrice Eastley, also known as Sorrow Gray. I believe her to be in the train of Lady Lucia Trevail of Cornwall and I will be continuing westward in search of her. But there is a possibility the young woman has not made it that far. Lady Trevail stayed at Buckland Abbey and Sir Francis Drake does not recall meeting Miss Eastley there. So perhaps she has broken away from the retinue near here, for it is said she has relatives in the west country. And, though I doubt this, I cannot ignore the possibility that it is true. I can tell you that she affects to smoke a pipe and has a curious, rasping voice. If you find her, detain her in the town gaol until I return. If you fall down on this, if I find you drunk, I shall have you arraigned on a felony charge of misuse of crown monies and you will be hanged. Is this clear?'

'Yes, Mr Shakespeare. Please do not tell Sir Robert.'

'That is in your hands. Find the woman and you may be given another chance.'

Chapter 24

TWO DAYS LATER, Shakespeare arrived at Trevail Hall. He found the old building bathed in late evening sunshine. Its grey stone walls nestled into warm folds of woodland as though it had always been there, placed by God rather than man. It seemed to Shakespeare the most perfectly proportioned house he had ever set eyes on.

He trotted his horse up to an arched gateway, which led into a pleasant courtyard. A groom appeared and took the reins while he dismounted. The groom summoned a serving man, who informed Shakespeare that Lady Trevail was visiting the Godolphins for a few days. It was only a short ride away, or there was an inn close by if he so desired. The hour was late and it would be dark soon, but Shakespeare accepted directions from the footman and rode on.

Godolphin House was only two miles further on and the sun had just dipped below the horizon as Shakespeare made his entrance. It was built around a courtyard, with stables near by. Like Trevail Hall, it was made of granite, but it was larger and more splendid, as befitted the deputy Lord Lieutenant of the county, Sir Francis Godolphin.

He heard music. The leaded windows were lit by the flames of many candles. Shakespeare handed his horse into the care of the stableman and went in search of a servant. A pair of pikemen barred his way and made him wait outside while one of them went to fetch a more senior officer. After a few minutes a grey-haired man appeared in black clothes and a crisp white ruff, inquired after the nature of Shakespeare's business, then asked him to wait in an ante-room.

'Sir Francis might be a few minutes. He is entertaining guests.'

Shakespeare turned away and examined his surroundings. The room was richly appointed with linenfold panelling. Indeed, the whole house reeked of the great wealth that the Godolphin family had accrued from the mining of copper and tin. He swung round at the sound of footsteps. A man of military bearing with a ruddy face and a good-humoured aspect stood before him.

'May I inquire who you are, sir?'

Shakespeare gathered that this must be Sir Francis Godolphin and bowed to him. 'John Shakespeare. I am from the office of Sir Robert Cecil.'

'Good evening to you, Mr Shakespeare. You are welcome.' He took his guest by the hand. 'And you will be pleased to know that you are arrived in good time for the dancing. Come, sir, join the revels for you have come a damnable long way and must need stretch your legs and take wine and food.'

'If I might just explain why I am here.'

'Well, I *hope* you are here because of the hostile Spanish shipping in these waters. I would like it all the more if you could tell me that you have brought a company of fighting men with you, but I fear from your face that you have not.'

'Have there been more sightings?'

'Spanish ships-of-war have taken an English merchantman in the Channel and it is possible they have captured more fishers, six men of Newlyn, whose craft has not returned to safe harbour. The Spanish galleys have also been spotted off the north shore of Cornwall, past St Ives and close by St Eval. That was three days ago. I am informed that Grenville raised a militia, armed them with calivers and manned the beach; the Spanish did not attempt to land. Of course I have sent messengers with all this to my lord of Essex and to Cecil, but it would be well if a voice such as yours were to press our case to the Council, Mr Shakespeare.'

'I will take back your reports and recommendations to Sir Robert. But I am also here to talk with a guest of yours, Lady Trevail. A private matter, Sir Francis, but one of most potent concern to the realm.'

'Sir, it is not my way to inquire into other men's secrets, so I will not ask you to explain yourself. All I will say is that Lucia is among my oldest friends, and I would wish you to treat her with courtesy and respect, whatever your business with her. Do I make myself clear?'

Shakespeare bowed again. 'Indeed.'

'Good man, then come and join the merry-making. We will talk more of hostile Spaniards on the morrow.'

Lucia Trevail had shrugged off her modest court attire and replaced it with a dazzling gown of gold and silver threads that caught the light and made her the centre of attention for every man and woman in the room. In the light of the candle flames, Shakespeare thought her sublime.

There were about fifty guests in the hall, talking and drinking in little groups to the sound of viols and lutes. Shakespeare stood at the entrance as Godolphin clapped his hands for silence. The music ceased, and all eyes turned to him.

'Lords, ladies and gentlemen, we have an unexpected guest, Mr John Shakespeare. Please do me the courtesy of extending him a warm Cornish welcome.'

The guests all nodded their heads in acknowledgment, but

Shakespeare's own eyes were fixed on Lucia. She smiled and left her group to step towards him.

'Mr Shakespeare, what a marvellous surprise.'

He took her small gloved hand and kissed her fingers. 'My lady . . .'

'Am I so irresistible that you travelled this far to see me?'

He laughed. 'I would, of course, traverse the Straits of Magellan and swim the Pacific Ocean for the honour of kissing your hand.'

'I should hope you would, for such bounty is bestowed on few and is as precious as nutmeg. Now then, sir, why are you here? Yet again, you are most mysterious.'

He scanned the room. There was no sign of Beatrice Eastley.

'Are you looking for something, Mr Shakespeare?'

'Could we repair elsewhere to talk? I have questions to ask.'

'Why, yes. Let us take the night air. And I should be pleased to have a few answers myself.'

Outside in the gardens, the air was warm. With their way lit by burning cressets of pitch, they wandered through arbours, across a lawn to a bank of yew, where they were well away from eyes and ears.

'It is about Lady Susan's companion, Beatrice Eastley,' Shakespeare said. 'Is she still with you?'

'No, indeed she is not. Why?'

'I had expected her to be here with you.'

'So had I, Mr Shakespeare, so had I, for we left London together. Along the way, she decided she did not like me or my company, though I am still puzzled as to what exactly happened. I do not lie when I tell you that I have never been spoken to in my life the way that hussy addressed me.'

'What happened?'

She began walking again, slowly, into the darkness where only the moon and stars lit her path.

'We were at an inn, just before the leg of the journey towards Buckland Abbey. I was expecting to go to see Elizabeth Drake and from there we would take a little detour to the relatives of whom Beatrice spoke. At the inn, we were in our room and somehow the talk came around to matters of religion. I do not know why, but I had always assumed she was of the same persuasion as me, but it appears I was wrong. In my bags, I had a small copy of sections from Foxe's *Book of Martyrs*, telling the horrific yet chastening tales of our brave English men and women who died in the fires of Bloody Mary's inquisition. Have you read it, Mr Shakespeare?'

'Indeed.'

'Well, Beatrice suddenly turned into a wildcat. She snatched the book from my travelling bag and tore out the pages, one by one, and threw them on the fire. "Let their memory turn to ashes," she said, "for they were all heretics and will burn in hell for all time." I was shocked to my soul and perhaps did not react as quickly as I might. She picked up a cup, threw it at me and called me a heretic whore and worse. Despicable words that I cannot repeat. I shied away from her, for I suddenly wondered whether she might have a dagger, but she merely stood her ground and laughed at me. My fear turned to anger and I told her to get out. She made an obscene gesture, Mr Shakespeare, then spat at the ground by my feet and was gone. I have not seen her since, and I thank God for it.'

'I need to find her. Exactly where did you part?'

'A village called Bickleigh, by the bridge over the Exe. Mr Shakespeare, I cannot tell you how distraught I was. Though I did not count Beatrice a friend, yet I had always thought she must have the makings of a gentlewoman, otherwise why would Susan have taken her on as she had? And, certainly,

Emilia always thought well of her.' Lucia Trevail stopped beneath the spreading branches of a cedar. The music from the hall had faded to a distant hum. 'I find myself agitated to think of it still.'

Shakespeare touched her arm and his fingers lingered a moment.

Her hand clutched his and held it. They were a quarter-mile from the house and the light cressets.

'Now *you* must talk to me, Mr Shakespeare. What exactly is your interest in Beatrice and why have you come so far in quest of her? The last time we met you were engaged on a hunt for Thomasyn Jade. Now it seems you have switched your attention to my erstwhile companion. I believe you owe me some explanation.'

'Very well. Beatrice Eastley is not her real name. She is Sorrow Gray, the daughter of the late keeper of Wisbech Castle.'

Shakespeare told her all he knew about her conversion and the suspicions now raised against her.

'Sir Robert Cecil and I had great fears for *you*, Lady Trevail, for you are close to the Queen.'

'Are you suggesting you suspected *me* of something?'

'I did not say that, but you were in the company of an impostor. We need to be certain: did she insinuate her way into your acquaintance, or was she welcomed?'

She removed her hand from his, sharply. 'You seem to be calling me a traitor.'

'You have access to Her Royal Majesty. It is my job to be suspicious.'

'What exactly do you suspect me of doing?'

'I am simply being cautious. I must find out what Beatrice Eastley is scheming.'

'I feel rather insulted, sir.'

'My intention is merely to clear your name from this difficult inquiry.'

For a moment there was silence. Then Lucia Trevail shivered and smiled. 'Come, you are right to have suspicions. It is indeed your job, sir.'

The night air was cooling. He moved towards her, but she stepped lightly aside.

'Mr Shakespeare, we are in danger of straying too far.' She took his hand in hers once again. 'Take me back to the hall and let us join the dance.'

Chapter 25

H E DRANK A good deal too much brandy and danced late into the night. The dancing, which had started sedately with the pavane, progressed to a vigorous volta and a riotous galliard. Lucia was like a feather in his arms when he lifted her and held her. They danced with abandon.

He had not drunk this much in many years. It was the headiness of the night, the long ride here – and his desire for her. He could not go to his chamber while she still danced, and so he stayed. Yet each time that he felt he could carry her away, she kissed his cheek and fluttered off like a butterfly, to the company of others. Then, as he consoled himself with one more silver goblet of brandy or wine, she was there again.

At last, some time in the early hours, the music stopped. Sir Francis Godolphin clapped his arm across Shakespeare's back.

'You, sir, will be the worse for drink, come morning. But, damn me, I say you hold it well, for you have downed enough to drown a horse.'

Shakespeare couldn't speak.

Godolphin laughed. 'Come, I will have a bluecoat show you to your chamber and fling you on to the bed.'

Shakespeare looked around through a fog of liquor. Where was Lucia? He groaned as he tried to find her in the crowd of dispersing guests.

Godolphin was at his side again. 'She has gone to her chamber, Mr Shakespeare,' he said quietly. 'Alone.'

He woke late in the morning. Sun streamed through open shutters. He rose from the bed and wondered what had come over him. He could not recall a time when he had been so drunk. It was not his way. Now his head hurt and he felt in great need of a bath to cleanse the dust of the road from his face and body. There was a knock at the chamber door.

'Enter.'

A servant came in and bowed. 'Sir Francis's compliments, sir. He has urgent business at Penzance and would like you to accompany him. He leaves within the hour.'

'What business?'

The footman hesitated, but then decided it was safe enough to talk. 'It is said that Spanish men-at-arms have landed in Mount's Bay, Mr Shakespeare. The whole house is in turmoil.'

Shakespeare looked at the man as though he had not quite heard him properly. 'What did you just say?'

'The Armada has come, master. We are being invaded.'

'Bring me water to wash, and some milk, bread and meats to wake me. Quickly, man. And tell Sir Francis I will be down very soon.'

'Yes, sir.' The servant bowed and backed out of the room.

Shakespeare sat down on the bed and held his head in his hands and, through the cup-shotten stupor that passed for a brain, tried to make some sense of what he had just been told.

Two dozen men were already mounted in the stableyard when Shakespeare arrived. He had scrubbed himself in haste, and had thrown food and milk down his throat.

Sir Francis Godolphin was just mounting up. 'Ah, good man,' he said. 'Have you been told what has happened?'

'A servant suggested Spanish soldiers had landed. Is this true?'

'It seems so. That is what I intend to find out.'

Shakespeare looked around the motley group Godolphin had thrown together. Some were faces he recognised from the dancing; others, from their rather more lowly manner of dress, were retainers. Three of them had white hair and, though they sat bravely, they did not look as though they would be of great help in a fight. All were armed in one way or another. He made out three old matchlock arquebuses, and a pair of ornate pistols thrust into Godolphin's belt. Swords and daggers, of course, and crossbows. A horse-drawn wagon was loaded up with bills, pikes, halberds and half a dozen muskets; also some powder, shot and various pieces of armour, shields and helmets.

Shakespeare gripped the saddle of his own horse and a groom made a cup of his hands for his boot, to help him up.

'Now, gentlemen,' Godolphin said in a firm voice, 'we will ride from here to Penzance. I have sent a pair of scouts ahead to order the trainband, and all fishers and townsmen, to gather arms and to meet on the western green. I have also sent messengers to Drake and Hawkins at Plymouth to consider what is to be done for their own safety and our defence. Orders have gone to Captain Hannibal Vyvyan at St Mawes fort to send all available men.' He pulled his shoulders back and lifted his chin. 'Only the Lord knows what this day holds for us, but let us acquit ourselves with dignity and courage, as Cornishmen and true subjects of Her Royal Majesty. God be with you all.'

Towards the south, plumes of dense black smoke were visible for many miles around. Sir Francis Godolphin raised his hand to call a halt to his troop. They looked down from the higher ground above Penzance, and saw four galleys at anchor, close to the shoreline on the south-western coast of Mount's Bay.

'In God's name, that's the village of Mousehole ablaze,' the deputy Lord Lieutenant said, horror in his voice. 'So it is true.'

At his side, Shakespeare's hand went to his sword hilt. All along the coastal path, he could see streams of people hurrying away from the fires, northwards in the direction of Penzance. He could see no Spanish soldiers, but he could hear explosions as they mined houses with gunpowder.

Suddenly he realised the date. It was the twenty-third day of July. The letter found aboard *The Ruth* had mentioned the twenty-third, though there had been no month. *Yours, in the love of Christ our only saviour and Gregory, great England's truest friend, this twenty-third day.* Was this the start? Was the long-feared invasion to start this day?

The commander summoned his two closest lieutenants. 'Ride ahead, ensure that men are gathering at the green. There must be no panic, no retreating. Tell them there are only four galleys. There cannot be that many enemy soldiers; surely no more than seventy or eighty. Instil courage in our men. Tell them they will be reinforced soon, by sea and by land.'

The lieutenants kicked on.

Shakespeare had doubts. His main fear was that there could be many more troops than Godolphin estimated. Large galleys, such as the ones in the bay, equipped with both sails and oars – galleasses – could hold a hundred soldiers each with room to spare.

Worse than that was the knowledge that the Spanish already had a beachhead. The only point at which this ragtag force of Godolphin's could have stopped seasoned fighting men in their tracks was when they were wading ashore, burdened with armour and arms. Now, it was too late. And who knew how many other ships were stood out to sea, protecting the galleys should Drake's fleet arrive. Indeed, the horrible thought struck home that this could all be a trap, a means to lure the ships at Plymouth out of their safe harbour.

The scene on the greensward to the west of Penzance was one of utter chaos. Men in fishermen's smocks and hats were clutching any weapon that came to hand. Some had mooring rods from their boats; others had old billhooks and bows and arrows.

They surged forward as Godolphin's wagon of weapons and armour arrived. His men tried to bring order to the throng. 'What skill have you? Have you used pike or halberd? Are you well trained in bowmanship?' Each man was handed a weapon dependent upon his answer.

Women and children milled around among their menfolk. Some carried packs of hastily snatched belongings and food. Godolphin drew one of his pistols from his belt and fired it in the air. Some people began to scatter, thinking they were under attack, but their din of clattering arms and wild talking died down enough for Godolphin's booming voice to be heard.

'I will have order! Line up in ranks, from west to east. The chief man of each village is to come to me.' He nodded to the men who had accompanied him from Godolphin Hall. 'Line them into squadrons of a dozen men. Anyone between the ages of twelve and sixty. None are to move away on pain of death. Women and younger children to carry on without their men and seek refuge where they may, in Penzance or beyond.'

Two men trudged towards him.

'Who are you?' Godolphin demanded of the older of the two, a thickset fisher with little hair and hands like frying pans.

'Jacob Keigwin of Mousehole.'

'Tell me what happened.'

'They came out of the morning mist. We did not see them until they were upon us. They drove ashore in shallops, which are still on the beach. Three hundred or more soldiers, mostly with hagbuts and pikes, all in heavy armour. They strode into Mousehole as if they owned the place. Turned us out of our houses and began to fire them with pitch and powder.'

'Did they kill villagers?'

'My brother Jenken. He would not let them take his house, so they shot him dead where he stood. We had nothing to fight them with and came away, thinking to raise the trainband at Penzance.'

Shakespeare listened with dismay. If this was happening here, were there simultaneous attacks elsewhere along the coast? And where did this group of raiders plan to go next? Would they march eastwards towards the heart of England?

'I am sorry to hear about your brother,' Shakespeare said, 'but I must ask you, where are the Spaniards now?'

Another man stepped forward. 'Some of them marched up to Paul village and set fire to the church, which is the most ungodly act I ever heard of.'

'How many of them? What are their arms?' Godolphin pressed.

'I would say a thousand. They are like men built of steel with guns the manner of which I have not seen.'

'Well, return to your squadrons and help keep them in good order. I am relying on men such as you. Stout men with hearts of Cornwall and England.'

Godolphin looked at Shakespeare. They were not going to get an accurate view of the Spanish invaders from these villagers. The two men shuffled off, back to their friends.

'We need sound intelligence,' said Shakespeare. 'A scout to bring back definite numbers, movements and armaments of the enemy. I will go.'

Chapter 26

H<small>E TOOK TWO</small> wheel-lock pistols, both primed with powder and loaded with shot, and a map drawn by Godolphin, and rode towards the little fishing village of Newlyn. There he tethered the horse and began the long steep climb inland on foot.

A black dog loped past him downhill. Otherwise the dusty path was deserted and the fishers' houses were empty. Acrid fumes from the burning dwellings in the nearby villages of Mousehole and Paul blew across the sky in a black cloud. At the top of the hill, he stopped in the shade of a windblown tree and consulted his sketchy chart. He could see Paul less than half a mile away, ablaze, the flames leaping and roaring. As he got closer, the smoke thinned and he ducked down behind a grass-covered knoll. He could see Spanish soldiers on the northern fringe of the village. Some were lined up in order, defensively. Others sat and smoked pipes or drank from clay jugs, refreshing themselves from the hot work of destroying other men's homes and possessions. None looked in his direction.

Shakespeare moved in short bursts, from cover to cover, behind hedgerows and trees, going around the village's western margins. Finally, as he came closer to open ground, he dropped to his belly and crawled. He spotted a sentry, some two hundred yards from the village, standing nonchalantly, his pike resting over his shoulder. Shakespeare pulled out his dagger and wondered about taking him, but he was too close to the village. He let him live, and skirted around him.

On the south-western edge of the village, he came across two men, standing by a cottage some distance from the rest of the troops. One wore the clothes of a workman: hide jerkin and hose. The other looked like a senior Spanish officer. Shakespeare moved on through the woods, keeping them in view. When he was close enough, he dashed at a crouch to the shelter of a wagon, laden with crates of fish, not more than twenty yards from the two men. Above them, the roof of the house crackled and burnt, but they paid it no heed.

Looking out from between the wheels of the heavy oak cart, Shakespeare strained to hear what the two men were saying. Suddenly, they both laughed, and the officer slapped the workman on the back. As the man turned, Shakespeare got a good view of his features. The jerkin might be that of a labourer or a blacksmith, but the smooth, tanned skin, the handsome face and the long, well-kept brown hair were those of a gentleman. The officer said something in Spanish, which Shakespeare could not quite catch, and his companion drew his sword from its scabbard. He ran his finger along the razor-sharp edge and drew blood.

'See how my sword weeps . . .'

Shakespeare froze. He had spoken in perfect English.

The man licked the blood from his finger and grinned at the Spanish officer, then they turned and walked back into the village.

For the next hour, Shakespeare hid in undergrowth and in whatever cover he could find, watching the soldiers' movements, counting their strength and assessing their armaments. Finally, when he had learnt as much as he could, he began to descend the hill towards Mousehole, keeping to the woods that shrouded the steep, narrow pathway.

From a vantage point just above the little fishing port, he saw that thirty shallops – longboats for transporting men ashore from large vessels – were beached, just as Jacob Keigwin had indicated. He concealed himself in undergrowth where he could watch and wait. Spanish soldiers were everywhere – above and below him – destroying everything they found.

In the middle of the afternoon, the soldiers in Paul suddenly began to move. They were lined up by their officers and marched downhill to Mousehole. They passed within twenty yards of his hiding place, their arms shouldered. He counted them: three hundred in all. And he reckoned a hundred more had stayed at Mousehole to protect the boats. That meant a total strength of four hundred.

Within half an hour, they had embarked on the shallops. And then they were gone, leaving only fire and ashes in their wake.

As the longboat rowers hauled across the still seas of Mount's Bay to the galleys, Shakespeare watched them from the shade of a tree on the hillside. In the distance, across the bay, stood the fortress of St Michael's Mount, its heavy cannon too far away to attack the vessels. He could not see the green where Godolphin was attempting to raise a defence force. Would it be needed, though? Had the Spaniards gone for good, or was this return to their vessel merely the prelude to another attack, somewhere further along the coast? Was this all a test of defences? Or was it, as he had already wondered, something more: a ruse to lure Drake's ships from safe harbour at Plymouth, or even the first shots in an invasion?

He turned and strode downhill between the burning,

blackened ruins of family homes and outhouses. At the harbour shore all the fishing boats had been coated in pitch and set ablaze. In a scene of desolation, only one house remained unburnt. A man's body was sprawled, half in, half out of the doorway, surrounded by a dark stain of blood in the dust. Shakespeare turned him over. This must be Jenken Keigwin, who had refused to leave his house to the fire. Shakespeare felt sick; if he had ever doubted the rightness of the war of secrets that he and Sir Robert Cecil fought, those qualms had gone for ever.

Shakespeare looked out to sea once more and realised with dismay that the longboats were not returning to the galleasses after all, but were heading north towards Newlyn and Penzance. And in their wake came the main ships, their ranks of slave oarsmen rowing hard, their big guns already rolled out. For Godolphin's band of defenders it would be a deadly onslaught.

Encumbered by his sword and pistols, Shakespeare ran along the cliff path until his lungs burnt from exertion and the choking smoke.

He reached Newlyn in about ten minutes, to find his horse still there. He pulled himself up into the saddle just as the first of the longboats reached the shore. The galleasses, meanwhile, had moved on north towards the green where the defenders were preparing to make their stand. As he kicked on, he saw that the four vessels were stopping, ready to stand off, no more than a hundred yards from the English militia.

The first bombardment came as he rode towards the green. A shattering blast of powder, the guns belching fire and smoke as they hurled their iron balls and stones at human flesh.

And then he spotted Lucia Trevail. She sat astride her horse like a man, at the side of Sir Francis Godolphin. She had a pistol in her hand. It was pointing out to sea, towards the galleys. She pulled the trigger, the steel wheel spun, the spark lit the touchpowder. Smoke and fire spewed forth and the shot was hurled harmlessly into the water.

She looked across at him with a curious smile. 'Ah, Mr Shakespeare, I thought you had run away.'

He rode forward and came alongside her. 'What in the name of God are you doing here, my lady?'

'Shooting at Spaniards. What else should I be doing? How many would you like me to kill to prove that I am no traitor to England?'

'You must return to the safety of Trevail Hall.' He turned to Godolphin. 'Sir Francis—'

Godolphin shrugged his shoulders helplessly. 'She is beyond my reckoning, Mr Shakespeare. Always has been.'

'My lady, this is no place for you. Hundreds of heavily armed enemy soldiers are presently coming ashore no more than half a mile from here. They are in murderous mood.'

'Mr Shakespeare, did you learn nothing when you came to our little gathering at Susan's house in Barbican Street? Do you think the ladies you met there are fainthearts who would be ruled by men or would miss the spectacle of a Spanish invasion? Anyway, I have brought three of my retainers. They will soon learn to be fighting men if they wish to remain in my employ.'

She tilted her head in the direction of three serving men standing beside packhorses. They bowed at her gaze and, thought Shakespeare, looked mighty disconsolate.

'You are not practised in the art of war. Look around you at the damage being wrought. At least one man has already been killed. Others are fleeing for their lives.'

'I know how to shoot a pistol as well as any man. And you must know that when I return to court, the first thing Her Royal Majesty will demand of me is a full account of this day's events. How, I beseech you, will I provide her with the detail she requires, unless I witness whatever befalls? I would not miss it, sir. Come, allow me some courage. Does not Elizabeth herself have the heart of a king?'

Shakespeare sighed. He looked to Godolphin for support, but he was preoccupied with sending messengers to collect arms and men. Well, so be it. For the moment, he had other things to do, the first of which was to move the English militia to a better defensive position. He rode to Godolphin's side and interrupted him.

'We have little time, Sir Francis. The Spanish army will soon be upon us and we will be overwhelmed. We must make a tactical retreat, for we have no hope of defending this flat green against insuperable odds.'

'How many men do they have?'

'Four hundred, as Mr Keigwin suggested. Possibly more than that, and they are true soldiers whereas your men—'

'—are a rabble. Yes, I know that, Mr Shakespeare.'

'I merely meant to say that they are untried in battle.'

A cannonball ripped into the earth just a few feet from them. Shakespeare's horse reared up and nearly threw him. Godolphin reached over and grabbed the reins to steady him. 'Be careful, Mr Shakespeare. We need you alive.'

Shakespeare patted the spooked animal down the neck to soothe it.

'Come, let us head for the market square in Penzance,' Godolphin said. 'It is higher ground and we will have cover among the houses. Give the order, sir.'

As Shakespeare looked around the green, it became clear that an orderly retreat was already out of the question; the men were deserting eastwards like a stampede of terrified cattle. And then he realised why: Newlyn was on fire and the Spanish troops were advancing from the west.

*

By the time they reached the market square, Godolphin's force was reduced to twenty men – mostly his own retainers and colleagues – and Lady Lucia Trevail. For half an hour, they fought a battle of musketfire. Shakespeare's arquebus became so hot with firing that he feared it would explode.

A Spaniard raced forward, a pistol in hand, his head encased in a steel morion. Shakespeare took aim and shot him in the apex of the collarbone. The man crumpled, blood shooting before him into the dusty road.

It was a small victory, for there were hundreds of Spaniards behind him, all heavily armed and advancing steadily.

'This is hopeless, Mr Shakespeare,' Godolphin said. 'We cannot defend this position. We must retreat to Marazion and the fortress of St Michael's Mount.'

Shakespeare well understood why the commander's expression was so grim. 'We must hope reinforcements arrive very soon or I fear the worst.'

He knew that if the enemy was not thrown back from the beaches in short order, they would entrench and set up defensive works of their own. If that happened, they could use Mount's Bay as a haven for their fleets, while landing troops at will for a full-scale invasion.

Godolphin gave the order. 'Collect up your arms and follow me. I want a fighting retreat.'

The trek to Marazion was dogged every step by the Spanish advance guard. At the causeway to St Michael's Mount, the tide was encroaching, but they managed to cross before the path was lost to the waves. Exhausted, they climbed the steep, rocky footpath to the ramparts of the fort that topped the Mount.

Godolphin shook his head in something akin to despair. 'Cowardly dogs,' he muttered to no one in particular, though

Shakespeare understood that it was not the Spaniards he was talking about, but his own countrymen.

Across the bay, Penzance had been taken and was in flames. The evening was darkening and the fires lit the sky with a hellish red glow all around the shoreline. The boom and crack of cannon fire and gunshot filled the air over the fishing town.

Godolphin summoned a castle servant and ordered brandy. The only thing that gave him any hope was that small boats had begun pulling into the harbour at the base of the Mount, discharging men from villages and towns throughout the south-west. Many were armed with ancient weapons; all were volunteering to fight.

There was news, too, from a messenger who had arrived after a gruelling ride from St Mawes fort, at the entrance to Falmouth Harbour. He blurted out his message before catching his breath.

'I bring word from Captain Hannibal Vyvyan, sir. He has sent a company of men. He believes they will be here by morning.'

'Good man. But be pleased to tell Mr Vyvyan that one company is not likely to be enough.'

'Word has gone post to Drake and Hawkins at Plymouth. They have been asked to send ships-of-war, sir, and soldiers by land.'

Shakespeare stood at Lucia Trevail's side. Night had almost come, but her face and eyes were alive with the reflected light of the fires.

'Have you seen enough of war now, my lady?'

'Why, it is like a display of fireworks, Mr Shakespeare.'

'It is not so pretty for those who have lost their homes, livelihoods or lives.'

'Indeed not. I had not meant to make light of their misery.'

She moved closer to him, so that he could smell her soft scent, mingled strangely with the smoke of gunpowder.

'Sir Francis tells me you were quite the hero today. That you scouted the enemy positions on your own. Will you not tell me about it?'

'There is little to tell. I managed to make an estimate of their numbers and armaments, and I saw the body of a man who had had the temerity to resist them.'

'And that is all?'

Yes, except that I also saw an Englishman among their number; but I will keep that information to myself until I see Sir Robert Cecil.

'That is all, my lady.'

She looked deeper into his eyes, as though searching for something. 'You are a strange, mysterious man, Mr Shakespeare. I think you keep much to yourself. Do you trust *anyone*?'

'Experience has taught me caution.'

She kissed him quickly. It was a chaste kiss, the sort of kiss that men and women at court gave to each other in greeting. And yet it wasn't chaste at all.

'War and death, Mr Shakespeare. Whatever your misgivings, you must own that they stir the passions. They do something to a man, do they not?'

He looked out at the distant flames. He knew that what she said was true. He knew, too, that the same effect could be wrought in a woman at war.

'Do you think me forward, sir? I seek no pardon for that, for I do not have time to wait on wooing. I tell you, the Queen's Privy Chamber is a very nunnery of virgins, so I have not time enough nor do I care for the good opinion of the world when I am away from her presence. Come to me tonight, Mr Shakespeare.'

Lucia looped her arm into Shakespeare's. Her fingers touched his side like a feather.

Inside the fortress hall, more than a hundred candles blazed on the orders of Godolphin.

'We shall light up the night as well as they,' he said, as they entered.

This island, rising so dramatically from the sea, had once housed a Benedictine monastery. Now it was home to a Cornish family called Morston and, though ill defended, it dominated the bay. Shakespeare hoped its presence would make the Spaniards think hard about the wisdom of moving against it.

A castle servant approached and bowed low. 'There is a man to see you, sir.'

'Indeed. And who is he?'

The servant grimaced as though he had put something foul-tasting in his mouth. 'He says he is Boltfoot Cooper and that he is known to you.'

Shakespeare smiled. 'Thank God.' He turned to Lucia. 'My lady, Mr Cooper is my manservant. Forgive me. I must go to him.'

Lucia released her grip on his arm. 'Mr Shakespeare, you do not escape from me that easily. I shall reserve a place for you, next to mine.'

Chapter 27

Shakespeare clasped Boltfoot to his breast, then stood back and looked him up and down. He looked like some nameless creature that had crawled out of the Fenland mud and slime.

'Good God, Boltfoot. It is a fine thing to see you. Is Wisbech secured?'

'I believe so, master. The squadron arrived and straightway set about bringing military order to the prison. I was less happy about leaving London, though, sir.'

'You found Jane at Sir Robert Cecil's residence?'

'Yes. But I am most fearful about this threat that has been laid against your girls. I wished to protect them myself, but Sir Robert said that all would be well in his house and that I was to follow you.'

'You did the correct thing. We need every man we can lay hands on. But first, have you eaten? You must need sleep.'

Boltfoot took out his pipe from his mud-encrusted jerkin pocket. 'This will do me for the present, master.' He knocked it against the wall and dirt and ashes fell to the floor. He tamped in the last few strands of his tobacco and lit it from a candle, sucked deeply, then exhaled smoke. 'But I do bring other news. You recall the old nun, Sister Michael?'

'I could not forget the hag.'

'She came to Dowgate, looking for you.'

'Now that *is* interesting. What did she have to say for herself?'

'She said she had information for you, that word had reached her that you should be trusted in the matter of Thomasyn Jade.'

And how did she learn that, when he had not yet managed to pass on to her Father Weston's letter? He recalled what the old nun had said when they were at Denham: *We know everything that goes on in this realm of sin and heresy. We have friends everywhere, in the palaces and the courts of law.* It was a disturbing thought, but maybe she spoke true; she had clearly learnt somehow of his meeting with Weston.

'Did she tell you what the intelligence was?'

'No, master.'

'Is she in safe keeping for me on my return?'

'She is still at the Swan Inn. I think she will stay there and come to you. She asked me to thank you for ordering her release from Bridewell, which she said had surprised her greatly.'

Shakespeare sighed. The whole matter of Thomasyn Jade and the exorcisms seemed unimportant in present circumstances.

'Master,' Boltfoot said tentatively, 'there is something we might do this night. It was something Drake planned once, when we were off the coast of Peru back in the days of our voyage around the world.'

'Yes?'

'There are many boats hereabouts, and many fishers. They must know all the shoals and rocks in this bay as though it were their own backyard, and so are able to traverse the waters by night, unseen. I do believe that sometime between midnight and dawn, on the middle watch when most aboard the galleys sleep, we might approach them in silence, by cockboat or skiff, and shoot arrows of fire into them.'

'Did this work for Drake?'

Boltfoot's mouth creased. 'I had hoped you would not ask me that, master, for in the end he decided not to attempt it. And yet he did lay plans of this nature and I could see no reason then why it would not have worked. Nor can I see any reason not to try it now.'

Shakespeare computed the possible gains and risks. Everything would depend on utter silence and surprise. The fishing boats would be vulnerable to counter-attack, for it would not take long for the galleasses to turn their guns on them. Oar-driven vessels could lift anchor and mount an attack very quickly. For the plan to work and the men to survive, they would have to launch dozens of fire arrows in a minute or so and then row like the devil for shore.

Finally, he nodded. 'Come, Boltfoot, let us put your scheme to Sir Francis Godolphin. I will speak for it.'

For the first time that day, Godolphin's florid face lightened a shade. 'Yes, let us do it. I shall order it organised straightway. Thank you, Mr Shakespeare, and please convey my gratitude to your man for devising the plan.'

'Let us pray something comes of it.'

Godolphin waved his finger like a stern minister in the pulpit. 'Nothing can be worse than has already occurred, sir. I tell you, this has been the most shameful day in the proud history of Cornwall. Never did I expect to see Cornishmen turn tail in the face of an enemy, however great their numbers. All honour is lost. We can but hope that this attack upon their ships will enable us to atone in some small way for the disgrace of our men's cowardice.'

'Sir Francis, I shall go on this foray.'

Godolphin shook his head. 'No, sir. You are no seafarer and you have done quite enough with your scouting. I will not allow you to hazard your life. I need men with your experience at my side. You are a vital member of my council of war.'

'Sir Francis—'

'I say again, no. This mission requires seamen and archers, not intelligencers. You would be a hindrance, not a help, sir. I would, however, desire your Mr Cooper to command the expedition. As a former Drake man, he has experienced sea warfare, has he not.'

'He has.'

'Good. Then he is the man.'

Two boats slipped their moorings and slid away on the still water, each containing six men. Two per boat would row on the way out; all would row on the way back. As the boats had to remain silent, the oars were dipped in the water with exquisite care to avoid splashing. They had to remain invisible, too, so there were no lanterns.

The only light was a burning match, held beneath a canvas so its glow could not be seen. The light of the moon came and went with the swirls of the mist.

'God go with you.'

Shakespeare mouthed the words rather than spoke them, watching from the rocky shore on St Michael's Mount. After a few minutes the boats had vanished into the sea fret. He could see nothing, hear nothing. Just as it should be. The mist had come as a blessing. There was no light from shore, for the blazing houses of Penzance and the other villages had been reduced to blackened, lightless husks.

Somehow, the boats carrying the archers had to get almost within touching distance of the enemy ships. Though the killing range of a longbow might be two hundred yards or more, these arrows would be shot from an insecure platform, the rocking belly of a small rowing boat, at the mercy of the sea's swell and the archers' own unsteadiness. They would have to be as close as fifty yards if they were to hit their targets. But was fifty yards also far enough away for them to have a chance of escape?

Every sinew in Shakespeare's body was stretched taut and his teeth were clenched so tightly he feared they could crack. He turned and made his way back up the long climb of rocky steps to the fortress at the top of the Mount; there would be no rest this night until Boltfoot and his eleven companions were back safe.

Boltfoot was gratified by the skill of the oarsmen, but their care meant that the going was extremely slow, especially as they were moving against the incoming tide. They had timed the assault thus, so that the currents would add speed to their escape.

The galleass lights glimmered in the distance, through the thin mist. The vessels were far out where the bay met the open sea and where the water would not be so calm. At this rate, Boltfoot reckoned it would take them half an hour to get there. The question was: how quickly would they able to return to shore afterwards?

Lucia Trevail was garbed in a long gown of white silk that shimmered in the whispery breeze at the top of the Mount. 'I thought I might find you here, Mr Shakespeare.'

Shakespeare was gazing into the shifting fog. He had lost track of how long he had spent here, on the battlements, waiting. Sometimes the mist lifted and then he could see the Spanish vessels clearly, sparkling with a mass of lanterns like four golden carriages. And then the mist came down again, as a theatre curtain closes, shutting out all but the faintest glow. How close were the fishers with their puny boats and their arrows of wood?

He turned and gazed at her.

'You are shivering, my lady.'

'I could not sleep. A strange bed. And I was thinking of you. Our paths have crossed in a rare fashion, sir. War and death . . .'

Shakespeare was unsettled by her in more ways than he cared to admit. He pulled her to him. She was slender and warm against him. He kissed her and she responded with soft, sweet lips. He held her closer, and his fingers slid through her tumbling hair.

In her eye, he saw a sudden reflected light. Gently, he pulled back from her and held her in his arm as, together, they looked across the sea into a rain of fire.

Boltfoot was manning the flaming taper and the half-keg of pitch. The archers dipped their arrowheads into the black tar, touched them to the flame, then drew back their longbows of yew and shot. One every ten seconds. Ten archers in all – five per boat with one man holding the fire and pitch.

They were attacking just one of the four Spanish vessels. Some of the arrows hit their target, but more fell woefully short, hissing into the waves. They weren't close enough and there was too much movement in the boats. Within a few seconds, there was shouting aboard the galleass. Then came the first retaliatory musketfire.

'Two more arrows each!' Boltfoot shouted. 'Then we go.'

Half a dozen fires had started aboard the galleass, but it was already clear to him that they would easily be put out.

More arrows flew through the night, but more fire was now coming back their way. And then Boltfoot saw the saker cannon being rolled out. He gave the order to man the oars. 'Row for your lives, boys! Row for your lives!'

Shot from muskets peppered the water around them. The man beside Boltfoot gasped in pain and shock, and fell back into the water. Boltfoot leant over the side and grasped the shoulder of his woollen smock. 'Help me, lads.'

Two of the other men dropped their oars and assisted Boltfoot to drag the wounded man aboard while the remaining two continued to row. The injured fisher clutched his shattered left arm but did not groan. Boltfoot tossed the pitch keg overboard, extinguished the flame and laid the injured man down as gently as he could in the floor of the boat. He cursed beneath his breath; one man less to row.

Without a word, he returned to his own oar and joined the other six in heaving and hauling with all his considerable strength.

Time was running short. Boltfoot saw that men were already clambering down ropes at the side of the galley to get into the longboats. The saker boomed, and a ball crashed into the water fifteen feet to starboard and a little way ahead.

'Speed men, speed. They'll be on us.'

He dropped his own oar and picked up his caliver, which was already primed and loaded. Resting it carefully in his arms, the stock wedged against his heart, he squinted along the barrel and pulled the trigger. The gun recoiled against him like a rock. There was a scream and one of those climbing from the galleass clutched helplessly at the rope before plummeting into the dark water. *That should slow your enthusiasm for a few moments.* Boltfoot reloaded, fired again without hitting anything, then put down his weapon and returned to the rowing.

Their only hope of escape lay in the darkness of the sea and their superior knowledge of these waters, for the longboats from the galleys were better manned, faster and more powerfully armed. The cannon boomed again. Its shot fell just six feet from the stern, throwing a tower of water into the air and down on the fishers' boat. It rocked violently.

And then it drifted back. The merciful mist . . .

In the candlelight, Shakespeare looked at Lucia's perfect skin without emotion, only hunger. What was she? Whore or lover? Why did he not trust her?

When their lust was sated, he slept without dream and without shame.

He awoke alone in Lucia Trevail's bed. By the light streaming in through the leaded window, he estimated the time at about eight o'clock. There was a note for him. It said simply, *Until we meet again, Mr Shakespeare*. He smiled. Quickly, he dressed and walked out into the hall.

He spotted one of her servants. 'Where is your mistress?' he demanded.

'She is riding for Trevail Hall, master, and then straightway on to London. I am to collect the last of her accoutrements when you have vacated the chamber, and offer my services to Sir Francis Godolphin.'

If the man was at all embarrassed by the knowledge that his mistress had shared her bed with a man, he did not show it. Perhaps this was not such an unusual occurrence in the life of Lady Lucia Trevail.

'You may collect her things.'

'Thank you, sir.'

He found Godolphin on the battlements. The mist had gone and it was a clear morning. 'What news, Sir Francis?'

'You see those specks on the horizon? Those are the Spanish ships-of-war, Mr Shakespeare. They have departed in this last half-hour.'

'Well, that must be good. Perhaps the fire arrows proved some deterrent to them.'

'Perhaps. But where will they land next? From their direction, I confess I fear they might head for the Scilly Isles.'

'How strong is the garrison there?'

'A hundred and fifty men. Strong enough, I pray.'

Shakespeare gazed towards Penzance. It was a desolate mass of charred wood, ash, fallen stones and spiralling black smoke. A line of ants, as it seemed, marched forth from the ruins in the direction of Marazion and this fortress.

'Before you ask, Mr Shakespeare, those are Englishmen released by the Spanish. Some are fishermen taken in the Channel; others are captives from a merchantman or various other prisoners of the wars in Brittany. They were found there this morning, cowering together. I have ordered them brought here for questioning.'

Well, well. That was most interesting. Perhaps they might reveal something about the Englishman he saw talking with the Spanish officer in the village of Paul.

'With your permission, Sir Francis, I will interrogate them. I think we might discover some secrets.'

Chapter 28

SHAKESPEARE WALKED UP and down the great hall like a muster master, inspecting the freed captives. There were more than a hundred of them and they were a bedraggled lot, though pleased to be home with their lives. They knew all too well the fate of other prisoners of Spanish troops. Summary execution was commonplace.

Calling them to order, Shakespeare told them they would be fed and given ale from the castle store-rooms, after which they would be required to answer some straightforward questions. The clearer their answers, the sooner they would be allowed to find passage home to their families.

'Is this all of them?' he asked Godolphin's adjutant, Thomas Chiverton.

'All but one, who ails and is being seen by a physician.'

'Was he wounded?'

'I do not know, Mr Shakespeare. All I can tell you is that the physician is attending to him.'

He left the prisoners in the hall to await their victuals and went to find Boltfoot, who was just waking. Shakespeare had bought some tobacco from one of Godolphin's junior officers and now handed it to his assistant.

'Well done,' he said.

'It amounted to nothing, master.' Boltfoot took the few

ounces of tobacco and thrust them in his jerkin pocket. 'The Spaniards doused the fires as fast as we could start them.'

'Perhaps it meant nothing in military terms, but it was good for English morale. You let the Spaniards know we were here and that we were not to be played with at will. More than that, you showed the Cornishmen that they could fight back.'

Shakespeare had requisitioned an office from the castle steward. After they had eaten, the freed captives began trooping into his presence one by one. He took down each man's name, his port of origin, where he was captured and what experiences he had endured. Many of them spoke of a renegade English pilot aboard the lead galleass, and one man, Barnaby Loe of Ipswich, knew him of old.

'Aye, it was Captain Burley. Richard Burley, most treacherous papist that ever sailed the narrow sea. I saw him close-coupled with the Spaniards, showing them the way through English rock shoals and currents.'

'How do you know him?'

'I sailed with him ten or twelve years ago before he turned coat. He sailed out of Falmouth, but other ports, too. Mostly carrying tin and copper. It pains me to say it, master, but he was a fine pilot. He knew all the waters well, from the Germanies and Low Countries all the way to Spain and beyond. But these were the waters he knew best of all.'

'Describe him.'

'Strong man. Long hair. Bull chest. What more do you want?'

Could this be the Englishman at Paul? It made sense.

'I can tell you, too, that he hails from Weymouth originally. He had a wife and some children, whom he took away when he threw in his lot with Spain. He has a beard down to his breeches.'

Well, that did *not* sound like the man Shakespeare had seen, for he had no more than a short, well-trimmed beard.

'Would you call him handsome or plain-featured?'

'Handsome? The man looks like a pig's arsehole, which you might think mighty disrespectful to pigs' arseholes. When I caught his eye, he summoned me over and did sneer most menacingly, saying that the King of Spain was so rich that he would lay waste to this whole coast, this summer and the next, and every year thereafter.'

'Did he say anything more about their plans?'

'No. I cursed him and he told me to watch my mouth or he would have me put to the oars as a galley slave. By God's faith, master, I did believe him and shut my mouth, for that is a fate I would not wish on any man save a traitor such as Burley himself.'

'Thank you, Mr Loe. And to your knowledge were there any other Englishmen aboard?'

'Only us captives. But we were split between two of the galleys, so I can account only for the one I was in.'

By evening, Shakespeare had not interrogated more than a third of the men. He was becoming tired and realised that he might miss something if he continued his questioning too late into the night. He ordered a platter of meats and some wine to ease him through the last two hours, then found himself a mattress and slept.

At daylight, the questioning began again. The first man brought in said his name was Ambrose Rowse, fisher from Fowey.

Shakespeare went through the questions by rote. 'And were there any Englishmen apart from the prisoners?' he asked finally.

'I recall one Englishman,' Rowse said. 'Never heard his name, though. Saw him deep in conversation with a Spaniard and some other men. That was soon before the attack upon Mousehole.'

'How do you know he was English?'

'I heard him speak, didn't I? He was talking Spanish, I think, but then he said something in English. And from the manner of his speaking, he sounded like a native-born Englishman, not a Spaniard. I recall what he said, too, for I did think it a mighty odd thing for an Englishman to be saying. *The gates are open. Let us enter.* That's what he said, then laughed. I took it to mean that he was in on the attack by enemies of his own country. A traitor, no less.'

'What was his appearance?'

'That's easy. He was a fine-looking man. Looks of a king, I would say. The sort of gentleman a common man would bow to.'

'His beard?'

'Short, well kept.'

The Englishman at Paul. This was not Burley.

'How did you come to see him and hear him?'

'I had been sent to fetch water for the other prisoners. That was the way the guard made me go . . . the devil take his dirty soul.' He pulled open his shirt and turned his bare back to Shakespeare. It was striped with lash-marks. 'That's what he did to me, for nothing. As to the Englishman, it was purest chance that I saw and heard him.'

'What else did he say?'

'Nothing in English, only Spanish. I used to speak a little in the old days, but it's all gone now, so I did not understand it.'

'And did you see the man again?'

'No, sir.'

'Did you mention this man to any of your fellow prisoners?'

'No, sir.'

'Then do not. On the pain of your life you are to say nothing to anyone. This is Queen's business.'

The man shifted uneasily, seemingly fearful of what he had got himself into. 'I will not say a word, sir. I will pledge it on the Holy Bible, if you so desire. May I go now, back to Fowey? I have a wife and six children would wish to see me.'

Shakespeare smiled grimly. 'I fear I must keep you here a while longer, Mr Rowse, but I shall recompense you for your time, and I am sure one of your shipmates will take messages to say you are safe.'

The questioning ran on into a third day. Shakespeare questioned Ambrose Rowse once more about the Englishman, and he spoke with Barnaby Loe about his recollections of Burley, but learnt nothing new of value. He was just about to give up when he recalled the man who had been taken ill. Wearily, he picked up his sword belt from the table where he had laid it, buckled it to his waist and stepped out into the castle hall.

There were many soldiers about now; they had arrived from St Mawes and from towns and villages all around. Although too late for the fight, they would form a basis for Godolphin to shore up his defences. From the battlements, Shakespeare could see six ships, the flotilla that had been asked of Drake. They were at anchor, and bristled with gunports. A comforting sight after the experience of seeing Spanish galleys in control of the bay.

He found Godolphin's officer, Chiverton, and asked him to take him to the sick man who was being housed near the kitchens.

The room contained a bed and the personal possessions of the cook. A large man was on the bed, snoring. He looked nothing like the other captives who were, to a man, lean and wiry seafarers of one sort or another. This man was flabby and looked as though he had not done a day's manual labour in his life.

Shakespeare touched his shoulder. The man grunted and turned over. He shook his shoulder a little more firmly. 'Sir, I must speak with you.'

Suddenly the man was awake. He glared at Shakespeare as he struggled to adjust his immense bulk so that he sat upright against the wall.

'I am John Shakespeare, an officer of Sir Robert Cecil. I am questioning all those set free from the Spanish galleys. I am told you have some ailment, but I must ask you to identify yourself.'

The man stared at Shakespeare for a few moments, as though weighing up his options, then emitted a gurgling noise from somewhere in his gullet. His chins and his chest quivered and his breathing was laboured. 'I am sick. Bring me brandy . . .'

Shakespeare nodded to Chiverton.

'Can you at least tell me your name?'

'Sloth. Ovid Sloth of London. Is that what you wish of me? The brandy, if you please, lest you want a corpse on your hands.'

'I have heard of you.'

The brandy arrived and Shakespeare put the goblet to Sloth's lips. He drank greedily, then coughed, and at last sank back against the cushions.

'Is that better, Mr Sloth?'

'Indeed, yes. Indeed. Now, what is it you require of me?'

'You are a merchant, are you not?'

'Yes, yes.'

'Where were you captured?'

'Brittany. And I would thank you to find me passage to London as soon as possible. I am a busy man. I have wasted enough of my precious time in a Spanish gaol and upon their stinking galleass. I cannot spend yet more time in this foul dungeon.'

'This is not a dungeon, Mr Sloth. This is a perfectly good bedchamber, which has been vacated for you at the expense of its regular incumbent. Why were you in Brittany?'

Sloth struggled to rise. 'First help me up from this filthy midden of a bed. There is a miasma of contagion here, I know it.'

Shakespeare grasped him under the arms and helped raise his enormous bulk from the bed. 'Now then, Mr Sloth, I asked why you were in Brittany.'

Sloth breathed deeply, his chest heaving and juddering. 'Use your wit. Why do you think I was in Brittany?'

'You tell me. And talk to me in a civil manner or you will find me a most unpleasant interrogator.'

'To buy wine. What else would I get from that benighted, war-torn finger of land? Talk to the master at Vintners' Hall if you wish to know more, for you will discover I am an assistant of the vintners' court.'

Shakespeare ignored his bluster. 'And did it not occur to you that you might fall foul of the Spanish armies there?'

'Mr Shakespeare, do you enjoy a goblet a wine? How do you think it is come by? Do you think merchants cease trading simply because there is a war on? Anyway, I had not heard of any embargo on French goods. Is Henri of France not our friend? Indeed, I had thought Brittany liberated from the Spanish yoke last autumn when Frobisher and Norreys took the fort of El Léon. It seems I was mistaken for Norreys has now abandoned Brittany and gone to Ireland. What I demand of you is this: how is a man to make an honest guinea if he cannot trade in safety? Ask this of young Cecil, if you would, for it is the brave English merchants that supply the treasury.

Why does he abandon us to the dirty Spaniard? We must be protected!'

'Did you travel to Brittany alone, Mr Sloth?'

'No, I did not. But they kept my clerks and servants. I am to send them gold if I want them returned, which will not happen. Why should I pay gold for them when I can find men aplenty in London?'

'I am told you are sick.'

'It is true I am not in good health. I am not a young man and these weeks of privation have done me much harm. I must get home to recoup my strength. I am exhausted.'

Shakespeare, too, was tired. He would have liked to postpone further questioning until morning when he might think more clearly, but he pressed on. 'Tell me about the ship you were on. Did you communicate with other Englishmen?'

'Those fish-stinking peasants taken prisoner from their boats? What might I have to say to them, do you think?'

'I was thinking of the English pilot.'

'You mean the damnable traitor Richard Burley. Yes I encountered him, and I spat on his shoes.'

'Did you talk with him?'

'No, Mr Shakespeare, though he tried to engage me in conversation.' Suddenly Sloth slumped on to the bed, clutching at his chest.

'Shall I send for the physician?'

Sloth shook his head as he panted. Finally he spoke, his words coming out in short, harsh bursts.

'In God's name . . . find me a ship . . . out of here . . . to London . . . I will pay you well . . . ten pounds in English gold, sir. If I do not get home, I know I shall die . . .'

Oh I will get you home, Shakespeare thought. *Though you may not like the mode of transport I have planned for you, nor your travelling companion.*

'Answer me one more question, then you may sleep and so may I. Was there another Englishman aboard the galley, a man close-coupled with the Spanish officers? Not Burley, in whom I have little interest, but one with long hair and a short beard and the bearing of a man of breeding?'

Sloth's brow creased and it seemed to Shakespeare that he seemed a little alarmed.

'Does the question disturb you? Do you know of such a man?'

'No . . . I know nothing of such a man.' Sloth fell back into the cushions. 'Get me that physician, sir . . . before my heart gives out . . .'

Regis Roag held Beatrice in his arms. They were spread naked across the covers of a bed, a large, ornately carved oak bed with four posts and an embroidered canopy above and all around them, enclosing them. Beatrice drew slowly on her pipe, opened her lips and watched the smoke rise, and dissipate into the canopy. She was used to the name Beatrice now; could no longer bear to think of the heretic name her father and mother had given her. *Sorrow Gray*. Was that a name or a sentence of despair?

She sighed, rolled over and laid the pipe under the bed-curtain on the floor. With the sinuous movement of a cat, she crawled across to Regis and stroked his chest with kisses.

'Beatrice?'

'Yes?'

'I prayed for this every day.'

'As did I.'

He looked in her eyes and saw the madness there. He knew well that she was insane, as crazed as a fox bitch on heat. He had always known it; he could not resist it. But that was because he could control her demons and bend them to *his* will.

'Do you harbour doubts?'

Her fingers tightened like little talons on his skin. 'Do you?'

He laughed. 'Even Christ had doubts. And yet I am here, am I not, back from fair Seville? And I have the men. In all, six of us. Enough. Good men, perfectly fitted for the task, as long as all else is in place. Do *you* have doubts?'

She sat astride him and held his arms down, her short, boyish hair flopping about her face as she gazed down at him intently.

'No. Never. Not one. A tidal surge of blood would not sway me from my purpose. I will rejoice when the blessed Mary's holy Inquisition is returned to these shores and when the ungodly are consigned to the fires of hell in the market squares, to cleanse our land. This is His word. How could I doubt it, when we have sold our souls to God?'

His hands ranged down her slender frame, his fingers playing from her small breasts to her delicate ribs. He kissed a nipple, then held her face between his well-tended hands and admired his handsome reflection in her eyes.

'But what of Sloth?' she said.

'We *had* to leave him. There was no other way. The journey from Spain to Brittany and onward to England has left him sick and exhausted. We had to move from Mount's Bay at great speed. He could not ride, nor could we carry him here. He would have threatened us all if we had tried to bring him.'

'Will they not torture him and discover all he knows? He will betray us—'

'Fear not, sweet serpent, he knows his part and we will retrieve him. As soon as word comes through.'

'And do the other men all know their parts? The little one, the Irish ones, the two hard-bitten ones? In truth I would not trust those last two to tether a horse.'

'I will take them and Winnow. You take the Irish boys,

Seamus and Hugh. Do what you have to do and then we will meet again at the appointed place.'

'Are they strong enough in will as well as arm? Will they really help us rid England of the beast for ever?'

'Trust me, Beatrice. I can smile—'

'—and murder while you smile?' She bit his neck and felt him rise beneath her thighs. 'I will trust your sail-needle and your God-given prick, my king of men, for I know what they both can do.'

Chapter 29

SHAKESPEARE WENT TO Ovid Sloth again and woke him roughly.

'Lucifer take you, can a man not rest!'

'I am here to offer you passage to London, Mr Sloth. My man Cooper will accompany you on one of Drake's ships. You will disembark at Falmouth and, from there, Mr Cooper will find a vessel bound for Gravesend or elsewhere in the Thames.'

'I do not wish to go with your serving man.'

'This is not an option for you, Mr Sloth. It is what you will do whether you desire it or not. And in London, you will be detained in your house until I have asked you more questions, possibly in the presence of Sir Robert Cecil. I am not happy with the story of your venture to Brittany, nor the manner in which you have returned. Do you understand?'

'No, sir, I do not! I am a free-born Englishman, a freeman of the City of London and an assistant of one the greatest of livery companies. I have endured monstrous privations at the hand of the Spaniard. Am I now to be ill treated by my own countrymen? I will *not* be escorted like a common felon!'

Shakespeare looked at him coldly. 'I am afraid you will, at the point of sword and pistol if necessary. Good day, Mr Sloth. Be ready at noon, for that is when your ship sails, and you will be on it. I wish you a pleasant voyage.'

He left Sloth and found Boltfoot, who was not happy at the prospect of taking Ovid Sloth to London, and even less so at the thought of making even part of the journey on one of Drake's galleons.

'You will have assistance, Boltfoot. I am sending another of the freed prisoners with you, a Mr Ambrose Rowse. Require of him what help you need, for I will recompense him.'

Shakespeare wanted Rowse in London, for he was the only other man who had seen and heard the unidentified Englishman.

As he strode through the castle, seeking Godolphin, he thought over the events of these past days. Was it mere coincidence that Beatrice Eastley had been heading west when the Spanish attack came? Instinctively he felt there was a link and that it somehow connected back to events in London and Wisbech: the death of Garrick Loake; the letter to the Jesuit William Weston in Wisbech Castle. Could this Spanish strike, like a bolt of lightning, be the true meaning of the letter found aboard *The Ruth*?

The possibilities remained jumbled in his mind like the stones of a fallen house. Somehow, he knew, they all made a whole, but for the moment they looked like nothing but rubble. The thing that made the least sense was this attack on Cornwall. Why would Spain authorise such a raid and then vanish into the haze? Yes, it had been a blow to English morale, yet was it worth risking ships and fighting men just for that? England had suffered no material loss to its military machine, And it was likely to serve as an alarm to the Privy Council that defences along the south coast must be strengthened. How would that help Spain?

Shakespeare put these points to Godolphin, who agreed that he too was puzzled by the Spanish action.

'Do they have more ships? Is there still a full Armada waiting to strike? Or do they plan to attack Drake and Hawkins in Plymouth Sound? I have had reports of sixty vessels in the Manacles off the Lizard. Another speaks of forty vessels to seaward of Mount's Bay. And yet I have not seen them. Did you discover anything from your interrogations, Mr Shakespeare?'

'Only that there were four hundred fighting men aboard, from the ranks of General del Águila's regiments, and that their pilot was an English renegade named Richard Burley.'

'I know of him. He is notorious along this coast for his treachery. We cannot take chances, so I will build our defences here, and send word to St Mawes and to the Scillies to prepare likewise. If the Spanish do attack again, however, we may still be found wanting. We need new levies and more powerful shot and armour. It would be best if you return to Cecil straightway and request assistance.'

Shakespeare nodded. That was his plan. What he did not mention to Godolphin was the presence of the unknown Englishman; that intelligence was for Sir Robert Cecil's ears alone. First, however, he had business to attend to, here in the west.

Shakespeare tethered his horse deep in the woods and moved slowly towards his goal. Every few steps, he stopped and listened. His searching gaze swept the rich, ancient woodland of oak and ash and chestnut. He moved on until he could see Trevail Hall, then he stopped and nestled into a bed of leaves to wait until nightfall.

He could hear the yelping of a pack of hounds in their kennels and the whinnying of horses. From his hide, he saw men in workman's attire going about their business. One man in the dark apparel of a steward or a lawyer walked to the stables where a groom waited with his grey mare, saddled up. He mounted and rode away along the tree-lined drive.

A little later he saw the serving man who had given him directions to the Godolphin estate a few days earlier. He was deep in conversation with another man, who patted him on the back before departing into the house.

Trevail Hall had the look of a house that was being shut up for the winter, leaving only a few members of staff to care for it. What had he expected to find here? Lucia Trevail with Beatrice Eastley and the mysterious Englishman, perhaps? He had come here like a dog; a sleuth-hound with the scent of gore in its nose, following a trail without ever asking why.

Had it been pure coincidence that Lucia had come to the west country with Beatrice Eastley, and at the same time as a Spanish landing? John Shakespeare did not like coincidences.

When darkness fell, he moved from his hide and came close to the house, skirted the stable-block and sought rooms with light coming through windows. He found the kitchen, where a matronly woman and a young drudge sat and talked, then the dining hall, where a serving man polished silver. He came too close to the kennels and set the hounds about their infernal barking. Men came from the house and looked about. He shrank back into the woods and watched as discussion sparked among them: had there been an intruder? Should they send out the hounds? Eventually, the dogs fell silent and the men returned to their quarters.

Shakespeare continued to watch until the early hours, then made his way back into the forest to find his horse. He had not seen Lucia, nor Beatrice, nor the Englishman. All he had got for his pains was a night without sleep and a painful neck.

The next day, he rode on eastward, up the great foot of land that encompasses Cornwall and Devon. At Plymouth, he went straight to the intelligencer's house. Once more it was locked.

As before, he went to the back and pushed his way in. He knew immediately that something was wrong; he could smell it.

In the pantry, he stopped.

'Trott?' he called.

There was no reply. He went on through into the front room. Trott was sitting at the table, with his head slumped forward. Dead. Flies buzzed around him, lazily; others settled in his eyes and on his throat, feeding on his blood and laying their spawn.

Shakespeare examined the corpse dispassionately. Trott's arms were bound behind his back and a loop secured him to the straight back of the chair. In front of him was a small dish of some yellow substance, half charred and blackened. Shakespeare sniffed at it and recoiled. Sulphur, otherwise known as brimstone.

Trott was naked from the waist up. His body was stuck with pins, dozens of them, making him seem as prickled as a hedge-hog. His chest, abdomen and breeches were drenched in his blood. Shakespeare grasped him by the hair and pulled back his head. The flies buzzed away but quickly resettled.

He gazed with distaste at Trott's throat. There were several holes, and he could see the weapon that had inflicted the wounds, for it was still there, thrust into the side, through the man's jugular. Some sort of heavy needle, perhaps one used for sewing leather or hide. He pulled out the needle, wiped it on his fingers, then secreted it in his own doublet.

So Trott had not found Beatrice Eastley; someone had found him instead.

Shakespeare rode harder than he had ever ridden before, switching horses at every inn he came to, grabbing bread and meats on the run, not sleeping more than two hours at a time and then, at the roadside, using his pack as a pillow.

He reached London within forty hours and went straight to Cecil's mansion on the Strand. Although the secretary was not there, Jane and the children were safely ensconced in the house. Shakespeare was able to reassure them that all was well with Boltfoot, before leaving immediately to take the tilt-boat downstream to the court at Greenwich.

Sir Robert Cecil was in his apartment, sifting through a pile of letters.

'Never, John, has one event generated so much paper as this little invasion in Cornwall. I believe I have had fifty differing accounts of the tale. Some say there were a hundred Spanish ships and ten thousand troops landed. Others put it at fifty men and three galleys. What in God's name is the truth?'

Shakespeare told him all he knew of the attack, then put the sailmaker on the young statesman's table.

'A needle?'

'It was used to kill Trott, our man in Plymouth. That needle was pushed through his jugular several times. The rest of his body was a pincushion and he had been forced to inhale brimstone. It had the flavour of exorcism.'

'Who did it?'

'I cannot rule out Beatrice Eastley. We know she somehow insinuated herself into the company of ladies close to the Queen. We know that she, herself, had undergone exorcism. What is more, I had set Trott the task of finding her, for she had broken away from Lady Trevail. There is some diabolical madness here.'

'Another man down . . .'

'But if it was her, I find it hard to believe she could have acted alone. Trott was a drunk, but he was strong enough in the arm.'

Cecil turned the needle in his hands and studied it closely, then he rubbed three fingers across his throat as though he could feel the point thrusting in. 'You must find out, and quickly. There is more. One of my lord of Essex's intelligencers, the codebreaker Phelippes, has been the subject of an attempted abduction close by Essex House. And all since I gave him the Wisbech letter to study. But perhaps we no longer need his services; the letter's meaning is surely clear now. This attack came on the twenty-third day of the month, as the letter pledged.'

'But is that the sum of their plans, Sir Robert? I think it was but the beginning. They wish to break our intelligencing networks. But to what end?'

Cecil nodded. 'Because we have stopped every plot conceived against the realm by King Philip and his hirelings and, even before that, by Mary of Scots. There have been conspiracies aplenty, but all have failed because *we* discovered them. I sometimes wonder whether Her Royal Majesty ever understood the debt she owed to Mr Secretary Walsingham for his diligence in this regard.'

Shakespeare thought probably not, for Walsingham had died so poor that he had to be buried in secret, at night. And yet this memory of Mr Secretary made him think yet deeper about the meaning of the letter. Walsingham would never have allowed complacency to set in. He recalled his words: *Look for the plot behind the plot, John. And when you have discovered that, look yet again.*

Cecil went to the door and summoned a servant, then stepped back into the room. 'John, when did you last sleep?'

Shakespeare shook his head dismissively. He was beyond the need for sleep.

'If you do not sleep, you will not think straight. You will make errors and miss the obvious. Take an hour to eat and refresh yourself. I will have a lodging set aside for you here in the palace. In the morning, get about your business with urgency. Talk to Anthony Friday. Surely he must have discovered something of value. But first do as I say – and sleep!'

Shakespeare knew that Cecil was right: he was not thinking straight. He was working on instinct, not logic.

'Very well, but I must tell you this: in addition to the prisoners freed by the Spanish, there was an Englishman with their soldiers. I went behind their lines and saw him at the village of Paul.'

'Was he this pilot I have heard of, the renegade Burley?'

'No. This man was nothing like him. He wore workman's attire but affected the air of an officer or a gentleman. Apart from that I know nothing save what I heard him say, which was little enough, a mere jest, something about his sword weeping.'

'Do you think he returned to the galleys?'

Shakespeare shrugged. 'I have no way of knowing, but it would be unsafe to assume that he did.'

'We will talk later. I think we must have a meeting with Essex and his men. Her Royal Majesty insists we work together on this. And she will desire a full and true report from you on everything that has happened in Cornwall. It will not be an easy encounter for you, I fear. She is in a rage that any Spaniard dared set foot on her soil, and in a greater fury yet that any man of her subjects allowed it to happen.'

'There was one more thing. Among the freed prisoners was a man named Ovid Sloth, a merchant vintner trading in wines in Brittany. I have ordered him brought here by ship, escorted by my man Cooper. He is, in effect, under arrest, for I am not certain about him.'

Cecil laughed. 'I know of fat Sloth. Men call him Cardinal Quick, for he is not at all quick, but he is very Romish in his ways. Yes, he is a vintner. His father was English, his mother a well-born Spanish lady and he owns manzanilla vineyards at

Sanlúcar de Barrameda. He produces very fine wines, though they are exceeding hard to come by since the embargo. I can understand why you might be suspicious, but I would be amazed if he were a threat to anyone but himself.'

'He did not mention his Spanish connection to me. That in itself arouses my interest. And, as you know, Sanlúcar is very close to Seville and the College of St Gregory.'

'It is hardly surprising that he did not mention any connection to Spain. These days, a man is likely to be hanged by the mob for admitting as much. Nor does it surprise me that he was seeking wines in France, for his Spanish trade is at a standstill. But there is more to him than this . . .'

Shakespeare waited.

'He has worked for me and my father in the past. Anthony Standen recommended him to my father, for he can travel in Spain at will, as easily as in England or France. He feeds us information. Nothing of great import, but he keeps his eye on the likes of Persons. I am told Sloth was once ordained but discovered the life of a priest unsuitable. In truth, I think it was his superiors who found some of his more venal habits unsuitable.'

'I did not trust him, Sir Robert.'

'You are not alone in that. In Spain, Sloth complains that he is suspected of heresy and spying for England, while in England he is mistrusted for his continued dealings with Spain. He cannot win! But you have my authority to find out more. You know how dearly I value your judgment in these matters. Perhaps you should talk with your brother about Cardinal Quick, for he must know him; when not producing and importing wines, he invests in the playhouses. In the meantime, sleep. That is an order.'

Chapter 30

For the first three days after arriving at Falmouth by ship, Boltfoot could not get passage for London.

'No one's leaving port,' one skipper explained. 'They think there's a Spanish fleet out there, just waiting to attack them and plunder their cargoes.'

It was a fair enough point, but deeply frustrating for Boltfoot. He was holed up in a dockside inn with a complaining invalid named Sloth and a fisherman named Ambrose Rowse who seemed to have no idea why he was being taken on this journey and why he could not simply travel home to his family in Fowey.

This day had started in equally despondent fashion. By evening, Sloth had lost all hope.

'Still no ship, Cooper?' he said, a dribble of wine slipping from his lips as Boltfoot came back from the dockside, dripping wet from the constant rain. 'You are a worthless cripple.'

'And you are as fat and ugly as a tithe-pig, Mr Sloth. But we are stuck with what we are and with each other, so there it is.' Boltfoot shook the water from his felt hat.

'Your master shall pay for this imposition!'

'He is most probably enduring sleepless nights over your plight even now. In the meantime, I am pleased to tell you that, after searching all day, I have at last found us a berth. A tin carrier is on its way to Amsterdam by way of Gravesend. You may be required to scrub the decks and hoist the mainsail, however.' Boltfoot turned to the third member of their party and grinned. 'That would be a fine thing to behold, would it not, Mr Rowse?'

Rowse smiled.

Sloth scowled and looked away. These men had no idea with whom they dealt.

'So if you will move your great arse, Mr Sloth, it is time to be on our way. For the tide is right and the skipper will not wait. You know what these Dutchmen are like.'

'You expect me to go now? Good God, Cooper, it is evening and I want my supper and my bed.'

'Tonight, you will dine on ship's biscuit and sleep on a rolling wave. Now move before Mr Rowse and I move you.'

Sloth looked from one man to the other and saw no sympathy, only humour at his discomfort; it would be a pleasure to see them done for. Painfully, he pushed down on to the table, struggled to his feet and began waddling towards the door.

The inn was five hundred yards from the dock where the cargo ships were moored. Despite the rain, the evening was still light. Slowly, they made their way along the muddy path, through streams of stinking ordure and fish offal. Whores clustered miserably in doorways, holding guttering lanterns to light their soggy offerings.

Boltfoot allowed Ambrose Rowse to take the lead, while he stayed a few paces behind Ovid Sloth. All the while he watched the crowds of mariners, fish traders and drunks, keeping an eye open for possible assailants. When they came, he saw them well enough, but his cutlass was only half out of his belt by the time they bludgeoned him to the ground.

He slithered and slipped in the mud and waste, desperately trying to get a foothold or a handhold to raise him back to his feet. How many attackers were there? Three? No, four. A kick to the face sent him sprawling backwards. A gunshot cracked the air. For a moment, Boltfoot wondered if he had been shot, but then found himself on his hands and knees, crawling, trying to see in the rain and confusion. Where was Sloth, in God's name? In the gloom ahead, he made out a cart. Sloth was being hauled on to the back of it. He turned and sneered at Boltfoot.

To his side, he saw Ambrose Rowse. He was lying on the ground. His hands moved in circular motions, as though he were paddling or swimming. The rain washed down his back, diluting the blood that poured from his dying body.

Boltfoot turned the other way and realised a man was standing over him, sword in hand. Suddenly the man's boot was on his back, pushing him into the stinking filth. He tried to twist away, but could not. The man bent down, grabbed Boltfoot by the hair and rasped in his ear, 'Down, down to hell; and say I sent thee thither.'

His hair was released and his head fell back, his jaw thudding with teeth-fracturing force. He sensed rather than saw the short killing sword being raised above him, like a windmill's sail at its zenith, ready to plunge back down. One thrust would do it. Through hide jerkin, skin, flesh and bone, into his vital organs, with a cut that would tear the very life from his body.

Thomasyn Jane Jade closed the door and walked down the Lambeth road towards the Thames. On her right was the great Lambeth Palace, official home to archbishops, but she did not look at it. She kept her head straight ahead, and wore a close-fitting pynner about her hair and ears so that much of her face was shielded from view. She always walked out this way, and yet it did not suit her to go unremarked. She enjoyed the attention of men too much for that; and much pain and distress it had caused her.

The house she had left was the home of the Dean of Rochester, Thomas Blague. Thomasyn worked there as maid to the dean's young wife, Alice. It was a pleasant enough life for she was not worked hard. Lambeth was an agreeable village. The dean's house was large and brick-built and, though dominated by the nearby palace of the Archbishop of Canterbury, was more than adequate for their needs.

Dean Blague still harboured hopes that he might one day inhabit Lambeth Palace himself and, as chaplain-in-ordinary to the Queen with the patronage of Lord Treasurer Burghley, his optimism was not entirely without reason. But at the age of fifty, events were already conspiring against him. Even his chances of becoming a bishop seemed to be ebbing away. The problem was his wife, who was fifteen years his junior and gaining an unfortunate reputation for licentiousness, taking lovers wherever she could find them, including her husband's clerical colleagues. Others in the church and at court disapproved and spoke of Dean Blague behind his back, averring that he should deal with his wife more firmly. A good beating with a birch-rod was generally agreed to be the correct remedy for an errant wife.

Alice's dalliances placed Thomasyn in a difficult position, for she liked both husband and wife each in their own way. Dean Blague was much too kindly for his own good and as for Alice, she reminded Thomasyn of herself: young in spirit and happily abandoned to temporal pleasures.

The situation between Alice and her husband sometimes amused Thomasyn and sometimes worried her; she did not like anything that drew attention to her own person or to those near her. She had succeeded in living this quiet life for nine years and she wished to continue, undisturbed and unmolested. But she was worried that the edifice of safety she had built for herself was about to crumble. For the truth was that she lived every day in terror of exposure. She knew too much, and there were those who would not hesitate to kill her. These inquiries by this John Shakespeare were deeply disturbing.

By the river, she turned right at the horse ferry and walked along the bank road to the stile before the Stangate waterstairs. There she hailed a tilt-boat, then stood patiently and waited. Across the river, the city of Westminster rose up in majesty. On a day when she was less preoccupied, she might have looked across and picked out the towers and spires of the great abbey, of parliament, of Westminster Hall, and of St Margaret's church, then, slightly further afield, the chaotic mass of buildings that made up the Palace of Whitehall. The houses at this point came right down to the water's edge so that the river lapped at the very stonework. She wondered whether a man might dive from his bedchamber window into the churning depths.

Lambeth was very different to the scene across the river. Here it was still rural, with fields and farmyards just beyond the village boundary; here, away from the teeming streets of the twin cities, she felt as safe as it was possible for her to feel.

The tilt-boat drew up at the waterstairs where two black-clad clerics paid and disembarked. Thomasyn stepped into the boat, which rocked gently, and asked to be taken downriver to the Old Swan stairs, just before the bridge.

The oarsmen gazed at her appreciatively. 'Shouldn't cover your hair like that, mistress,' said one of them. 'Don't want to go hiding your bushel.'

She smiled at him. He was handsome and cheerful, a combination she could never resist in a man. 'Very well,' she said. She untied the straps of her crisp white pynner and pulled it off, then shook out her hair. 'Is that better?'

The talkative oarsman grinned. 'A great deal so, mistress.'

'And was there anything else you would like me to remove?'

'Take it all off, my lady, every last thread of it.'

She laughed out loud. 'You will be desiring me to take control of your oar soon. Is it as hard as some say to pull at it?'

She began to replace her pynner with great care. She felt warm, all the way through. *You still have the devil in you. That old familiar devil.*

'My oar is, indeed, a hard and magnificent instrument. It can get any lady to the place she desires quicker than any other waterman's oar. Is that not so, Josiah?'

The quieter of the two merely maintained his inane grin, staring at Thomasyn with a boyish leer, but saying nothing.

The journey to London continued in this vein. They were travelling with the tide, so made good speed and Thomasyn finally prepared to disembark at the Old Swan.

'How much is that, Mr waterman?'

'Pay me in kind, next time you see me, Your Highness. It has been my pleasure to convey a lady of such breeding and bosom.'

She kissed both men on the cheek, then stepped out into the throng and waved them goodbye as they took on a trio of stern-looking courtiers for the trip to Greenwich. Thomasyn walked northwards through the busy streets of London until she came to Simon Forman's stone house in the narrow lane of Fylpot Street.

The boy Braddedge answered the door, but she pushed past him and climbed the stairs.

'He's not alone, mistress,' Braddedge called after her. Thomasyn continued upwards. 'It's your own fine lady, the grubby Alice Blague, if you want to know.'

At the top of the stairs, Thomasyn pushed open the door to Forman's chamber and walked in. Forman was alone.

'Your boy said you had company, Dr Forman.'

'He thinks himself a jester. I shall put him in a stall at St Bartholomew's Fair and see how much merriment he can rouse when pelted with rotten eggs. We might make a penny or two from him.'

'Even better, put him in the pillory.'

'Indeed, Janey, and how do you fare this fine day?'

Thomasyn proffered her cheek to be kissed, then walked over to the bed and sat on the edge, looking about the room. 'Your boy said my lady Alice was here.'

Forman was rolling up a chart. 'Not today.'

'But she comes other days?'

'You know she does.'

'Have you tupped my lady Blague?'

Forman stopped what he was doing. 'I had not thought you one given over to jealousy, Janey. But as you ask, no, I haven't.' He lied effortlessly, as always.

'How do I know you're telling the truth?'

'Have I ever given you reason not to trust me? But you can rest assured of this: even if I were swiving your mistress, Janey, I would never tell a soul. And no more would I tell the world your secrets. All ladies' secrets are safe with Simon Forman.'

Thomasyn was not sure why she had even asked, for she knew exactly what Forman was like – and she knew as much about Mistress Blague. There was, however, another matter on her mind.

'No more sign of that Cooper woman, I hope? The one that works for John Shakespeare?'

'No, Janey, there hasn't been. Not likely to come here either, is she?'

'I pray not.'

'I think you have done rather more than pray, have you not? And much to your discredit, may I add.'

Thomasyn feigned puzzlement.

'Don't give me that look, mistress. You know very well what I mean. She's scared witless. So's the whole family. I think you have something to confess to me, Janey. Something that could get both of us into a great deal of trouble . . .'

On his way to St Paul's, Shakespeare began to sense that he was being followed. He looked around constantly at the milling crowds, but could not pick out his pursuer. It was an unnerving experience, because he was well trained in the business of spotting the man or woman who would rather not be seen.

As soon as he arrived at the crypt, he handed the needle to Joshua Peace.

'Where did you get this, John?' Peace turned it over in his hand. 'I would guess it is a sailmaker – a needle used by sail seamsters. It is a little like a leather needle, but the triangular point is more tapered. I have seen such things before.'

'That makes sense. It is also a nasty weapon. I found it in Plymouth, thrust through a man's jugular.'

'Now that *is* interesting. Come with me.'

They went through to the room adjoining the crypt, where Peace kept his implements and the bodies awaiting examination.

Shakespeare reeled from the stench.

'Forgive me, John. The odour is not good. I am afraid I have not sent your Mr Loake away for burial as yet.'

He pulled back the winding sheet from Garrick Loake's bloated remains, then held the sail-needle to the side of the corpse's throat. It went into a hole the size of a pinprick and passed straight through, like the pin of a brooch.

'There. I do believe we have discovered the cause of Mr Loake's death.'

'So two men, two hundred miles apart, are killed in exactly the same fashion.'

'Possibly with the same needle.' Peace withdrew the instrument and dropped it into the basin where Loake's cross and chain were held. 'Shall I look after this for you?'

'Thank you.'

'And does this bring you any closer to identifying the killer?'

'No, though I have suspicions. Very grave suspicions. My problem is that I have no idea where she is, nor who her confederates are . . .'

'Well, good fortune to you, John.'

Chapter 31

'MIGHT I ASK, Mr Roag,' Hugh Fitzgerald said, an edge of uncertainty in his voice, 'about the mission?'

Regis Roag smiled. This was why they were so tense. They had been blooded like soldiers but now they wanted to know what more was expected of them. How would they react when the cascade of death was laid out before them?

The band had set up an encampment by the road a little way west of London. They had been here for several days, following their rendezvous and the long trek from the west. Eschewing inns, they had pitched camps in the woods and on the heaths, like any travelling company of players, scarcely noted as they passed. Roag had not been with them all the time, for he had business ahead, in London.

Now that they were settled and rested, it was time for them to learn what they must do and the parts each must play.

He studied them closely.

Hugh and Seamus Fitzgerald were the most easygoing of the band, yet even they were feeling the strain. Ovid Sloth had found them in the Irish College at Salamanca, where they were training for the priesthood. They had absolute belief in the rightness of the Catholic cause against Elizabeth and would do Roag's bidding to the death. Their father, a cousin of the Earl of Desmond and of a rebellious nature, was a wealthy trader in good horses. After his death, the boys' mother sent them to England for an education in the house of a northern gentleman, hoping to wean them off their father's ways. But they had already inherited too much of his untamed spirit. In desperation, she ordered them to Spain for the priesthood. Sloth noted their potential the moment he saw them. Not only did they speak with English accents, they wanted nothing more than to fight and kill.

The deadliest ones were Ratbane and Paget. They were lower than dogs, dredged up by the Spanish from the barrel of the renegade English regiment of the Low Countries. They had gone with Roag on his little forays into London, as lethal as foxes in a covey of partridges. Two of a kind, they could kill to order without compunction. They would do what they were told and would not blink in the face of enemy fire.

And then there was Winnow. The cleverest of the lot, and the one that worried him the most.

Roag clapped his hands and summoned them to him. 'Hugh has asked me the mission,' he said. 'Very well. I will tell you.'

Later, Dick Winnow sat apart, watching the others talk quietly around the campfire, seeing their tension. He put a quart pot of strong ale to his lips and drank it dry, then rose. The liquor gave him courage but did not dull his senses. He went over to Roag.

'What is it, Dick?'

'You know what it is, Mr Roag.'

'Tell me anyway.'

'This plan. It cannot work.'

Roag put his arm around Winnow's shoulder. Winnow stiffened at the touch, but did not move away.

'It will work, Dick. You have my word.'

'But we will not survive—'

Roag hesitated. 'Fear not. All will be well.'

But Winnow knew. 'You remember I told you how my father died?'

'I understand, Dick. We have *all* suffered grievously for our faith. That is why we are here and why we must be prepared to hazard our lives for God.'

Sacrifice our lives for God. That was what he meant.

Winnow had no wish to die. He wanted to kill.

'Trust me.'

He did not look at Roag. He could not bear to see the lie in his eyes. 'If I am to die for God, I want to prepare myself properly. All I require is the truth, Mr Roag.'

The truth? That, Roag knew, was the one thing none of them needed to hear, even though they might suspect it.

'I have told you the truth, Dick. It is all carefully planned. God willing, we will all survive.'

Winnow turned at last to stare at Roag through the ale-gauze of his eyes. The liquor brought steadiness and revealed all. 'Thank you, Mr Roag.' He nodded with deference. 'You have set my mind at rest.'

Except that he hadn't, and they both knew it.

Roag might smile, but inside was only the icy darkness of hell. Winnow realised he had two choices: he must either kill, or escape. It was the only way to stay alive. Neither option would be easily accomplished.

A letter awaited Shakespeare when he awoke from a long sleep at Cecil's mansion in the Strand. He recognised the hand immediately as that of his brother Will.

Come to me as soon as you may, brother. I have intelligence for you concerning Mr Friday. Written in haste, the Theatre, Shoreditch.

As he was pulling on his boots, the door opened, and a footman entered and bowed. 'Mr Cooper is here for you, sir.'

Boltfoot back? Thank the Lord for that. 'Please show him through to the hall, and tell Mistress Cooper that he has arrived.'

'Yes, sir.'

Boltfoot presented a grim sight. He stood in the hall, seemingly more dead than alive. His shoulders were slumped, his face blue and yellow with bruising. He had rough, dirty bandages about his head. A long scab coated his cheek. His clothes were filthy, and not just from the journey back to London. Jane appeared from the interior of the house, and immediately gasped and put a hand to her mouth in horror.

'Jane . . .'

He limped over to her and they embraced awkwardly.

Shakespeare left them a few moments and then intervened. 'I have seen you in a bad way before, Boltfoot Cooper,' he said, ushering him through into a smaller, more comfortable room. 'But never have I witnessed a more dismal spectre than you present this day.'

Boltfoot could barely meet Shakespeare's eye. 'I have lost Ovid Sloth, master,' he said quietly.

'Well, for the moment I care more about *you*. Come in, refresh yourself and we shall talk of this anon. Jane, if you would clean your husband's wounds, I shall meet him in an hour's time.'

Will would have to wait a while. Shakespeare went in search of his girls, who were having lessons from one of the Cecil tutors. He watched them so intently that they began to giggle. He was encouraged by how quickly they had settled here in this safe place, and hoped that Ursula Dancer was equally secure. He did not worry for her; she had had a lifetime of looking out for herself.

When Boltfoot returned, cleaned up, Shakespeare took him through to Cecil's library.

'What happened, Boltfoot?'

'I was hammered to the ground, kicked in the face and trodden on, master. But I fear Mr Rowse fared worse.'

'Sit down. You had better tell me everything.'

Boltfoot lowered himself gently on to a settle. Shakespeare thought him horribly shrunken.

'We were in Falmouth three days before I could secure a berth. At last I found a ship carrying tin and we all walked down to embark. That was when the attack came. I saw them, but we were overpowered. There were four of them, I think. They killed Mr Rowse with a pistol shot and clubbed me to the ground. I was about to be despatched myself when two seamen coming from an ordinary pushed my assailant away from me. I thought he would come back to finish me off, but a mob was gathering and he made good his getaway instead.'

'What of Ovid Sloth?'

'He was carried away on a cart.'

'Do you believe him abducted or rescued by these men?'

'From his smirk, I would say he was complicit, master.'

Shakespeare nodded. It had been his immediate thought. He wondered how these men had known that Boltfoot would be in Falmouth with Sloth. It was a troubling question, which made Shakespeare worry that there was a traitor inside Godolphin's camp.

'What manner of man was your assailant?'

'He had a cowl against the weather, which was as stinking wet as a bilge, but I saw his face and eyes. He had a short beard. A woman might call him a handsome man. Perhaps my age, though he may have been a little younger.'

'Did he say anything?'

'Aye, he told me to go to hell. *Down, down to hell*, he said. *And tell them I sent you there.* That's what he said.'

The words jangled somewhere in Shakespeare's brain, as if

he had somehow heard them before. But where could he have heard such a thing said?

'Was there anything more? Did he say anything else?'

'No, master. And nor did I wait around, for I knew I had to come to you straightway. I did not even wait for the constable or his men, I just picked myself off the ground, saw that Rowse was dead and ran from that place as fast as my foot would carry me. I took passage on the vessel that awaited me. The mariners dressed my wounds after a fashion.'

'You look a great deal more presentable, thanks to Jane's efforts.'

Boltfoot nodded. 'Fortunately, we had a fair wind. Did I do wrong? Should I have searched Falmouth to find Sloth and the killers? I confess I have not thought clearly these past hours and days and I have worried greatly that I have failed you in everything I have done.'

Shakespeare put his arm around his servant. 'You have failed me in nothing, Boltfoot. I suspect Mr Sloth did not wait in Falmouth. Indeed, I would not be surprised if he were not already here in London.'

Chapter 32

SHAKESPEARE TOOK TWO wheel-lock pistols with him to the Theatre. The attack on Boltfoot and the deaths of Trott and Loake could not be ignored. He pulled his brother out of the rehearsal and came straight to the point. 'What is this about Anthony Friday?'

'He came here to see me. Said he had to get word to you.'

'Why did he not bring a message direct to me?'

'Is this the Inquisition, brother? What is going on here?' Will eyed the two pistol butts protruding from Shakespeare's belt. 'Perhaps you would like to take me to the rack-room at the Tower—'

'Forgive me. It is just that my man Boltfoot has suffered grievously, another man has been killed – and Anthony Friday is proving as worthless as a capon in a hen-coop.'

'Come, I understand your impatience, but at least let us take wine together.'

They went to the sharers' room, where Will fetched a flagon of wine hidden behind some old books, poured out two cups and handed one to his brother.

'Anthony Friday tried to find you at Dowgate, but was directed from there to Sir Robert Cecil's home on the Strand. At that he panicked for he had no intention of going anywhere near the Cecils.'

That was understandable enough, given the pressure Cecil had applied to the man.

'Anyway, that is why he came to me and asked me to bring you to him. He's in hiding and he's scared. I believe he was working on a play and has gone to finish it. But before you curse and threaten me with your pistols, he's not far from here, at an old farmhouse in the market gardens to the east of Shoreditch.'

'But why is he in hiding? Why is he scared?'

'I don't know, John. But somebody or something has put him in terror, which I suspect is what he wishes to see you about. I will take you to him once you have finished your drink.'

Shakespeare sipped the sweetened Gascon wine and thought of the fat vintner at St Michael's Mount. 'Sir Robert Cecil suggested you might have had dealings with a man named Ovid Sloth.'

'Cardinal Quick? Of course I know him. Everyone does in my world. He likes to think himself a patron, but I haven't seen him in months. What is your interest in him?'

Shakespeare had no intention of talking about Ovid Sloth within the confines of a playhouse, where there were too many ears and too many loose lips. Had that not been Garrick Loake's downfall?

'For the moment, nothing. I will tell you later. But I would ask you one more thing. Do the words *down, down to hell* mean anything to you?'

'Why, yes, possibly. Is there more?'

'*And tell the devil I sent you there* – or some such.'

'*And say I sent thee thither*.' Will chuckled. 'Richard of Gloucester in the third part of my *Henry VI*. Crookback Richard is killing King Henry. Let me find the lines for you.'

He went over to a shelf and rifled through a pile of papers

bound in string, then pulled out one bundle, cut the string and thumbed through the pages.

'Here we are, Act V. Gloucester is doing his dirty work.'

He put the page in front of his brother and pointed out the lines with his inky forefinger.

See how my sword weeps for the poor king's death!
O! may such purple tears be always shed
From those that wish the downfall of our house.
If any spark of life be yet remaining,
Down, down to hell; and say I sent thee thither.

Shakespeare clutched his brother's wrist. '*See how my sword weeps.* Those are *your* words? I heard another man speak them amid the fires of Cornwall.'

'John, what is this about? You are scaring *me*.'

'Who played the part for you?'

'Richard of Gloucester? Well, it has shown on various occasions, first with my late Lord Strange's Men at the Rose three years since. But the most recent player was Regis Roag when we staged it here at the Theatre. He was well cast.'

'In what way?'

'Beneath the charm, there is a touch of darkness in him, a shimmering of violence under the skin that threatens to erupt at any moment. The cold violence of Gloucester . . . *I can smile and murder while I smile.*'

'Was he the player involved with Beatrice Eastley?'

'What a curious thing to ask. I do not see the connection.'

'Just tell me, is it possible? Were they associated with the Theatre at the same time?'

Will stroked his beard and thought. 'I suppose they were,' he said at last. 'It was certainly about the time he played Gloucester. If there was something between them, however, I didn't know about it. I could ask some of the players, if you wish.'

'No, say nothing. I am not sure that it would be good for your health or theirs to ask questions. Come now, take me to Anthony Friday. Let us hear what he has to say.'

The path was nothing but a farm track between rows of salad vegetables: lettuces one side, radishes the other. Men were at work, harvesting the crop for sale in the London markets. They paid the Shakespeare brothers no heed. Half a mile away stood a low cottage with thatching almost to the ground.

'That's the place, John.'

'Whose is it?'

'I have no idea. But Friday told me it was safe and begged me to tell no one else but you that he would be there. He seemed to think me trustworthy.'

As they came upon the house, Shakespeare took out his pistols. He felt the same dread he had sensed at Plymouth just before discovering Trott bound and dead.

This was different. Friday's body was not in the house. The main room was a scene of utter chaos, a battlefield of blood splashes and debris. The trail of chaos and blood led them out through a back door.

Shakespeare had his pistols clasped in his hands, pointing ahead like a galleon with twin prows. 'You may wish to go now, brother. Fetch the constable.'

'I will stay with you, John.'

'Then draw your dagger.'

Chickens dispersed, clucking, at their approach. They found Friday at the far side of the backyard. His half-naked body was slumped forward over the low wall of a sty. Two pigs sniffed at the corpse with interest.

Will Shakespeare turned away, his hand to his mouth in horror.

His elder brother felt the body. It was still warm. He did not have to be the Searcher of the Dead to know that this killing had taken place within the past hour, perhaps a great deal more recently than that. Nor did he have any doubts about the cause of his death; he had been shot in the back.

He touched his brother's arm. 'Be wary, Will. We may yet have company.'

The playwright nodded and took his hand away from his mouth as he fought to regain his composure.

'This is your Richard of Gloucester at work, Will. Help me move the body.'

'Death and murder are not so squalid on stage.'

'No.'

Together, they pulled the corpse away from the wall and laid it on the ground. There was a single hole in Friday's back where the ball had entered. One of his wrists was bound with rope, the other was raw where he had clearly fought to free himself. There were marks on his face.

'John, I really do not like the world you inhabit.'

'It cannot always be contained. It has a habit of intruding into real lives. Yet this is the threat our sovereign has faced every day of her reign, and faces still today. Imagine *her* fortitude if you will. Come, I must look around. Do you have the stomach for this?'

Will nodded and followed his brother back towards the house. Something shone in the mud. He bent down and picked it up. 'Look at this,' he said, holding it between his fingers.

Shakespeare recognised it instantly. 'A sailmaker.'

'Does this mean something to you?'

'It does. It has been used as a weapon in two murders, one of them Garrick Loake's. It seems Mr Friday did not afford his killers the pleasure of using their ungodly implement.'

The house amounted to one room and a pantry. In one corner of the room lay a mattress with ruffled blankets. A table was on its side, surrounded by pieces of paper. Shakespeare picked them up. They were all blank. An inkhorn had spilt its contents across the sawdust floor and there were several quills scattered about, as well as a book. A chair with upright back had been smashed. Pieces of rope were tied to it, similar to the fragment knotted to Anthony Friday's wrist.

'He had much talent, brother,' Will said. 'But like others of our profession before him – Marlowe, Kyd, Munday – he could not resist the lure of danger.'

'What was he writing? You mentioned he was working on a play – was it for you?'

'No. Probably Henslowe. He has worked for him before now. All he told me was that it was a paean to Her Royal Majesty. *This golden ray, this English goddess, this nonsuch of our hearts* . . . or some such flummery. A good idea if he could pull it off without incurring the censorial wrath of the Master of Revels. That is as much as I know on that score. Do you think it has some relevance?'

'I must go down all roads, however narrow.' He held up one of the blank papers. 'Friday did not seem to be progressing well in his work.'

'He would have delivered it sheet by sheet. Have a word with Henslowe.'

Shakespeare knew Philip Henslowe well enough. The money man behind the Rose playhouse in Southwark was his brother's great rival. He examined the blood on the floor. Idly, he picked up a blood-stained sheet of paper that he had missed. Three words were written there, scratched in what looked like a hurried hand.

They are cousins.

That was all it said. What did that mean? Who were cousins? Half of London were cousins with the other half. Certainly everyone at court was cousin to everyone else.

He thrust the paper into his doublet and ground his teeth together irritably. Whenever he made any move towards solving this puzzle, his way was immediately blocked.

'Is Regis Roag behind this? What more do you know of him, Will?'

'I know that he was much given to bragging and considered himself above the common herd of man. One of his claims was that he was once in the employ of the Earl of Essex, but perhaps his greatest boast was his preposterous conceit that he was born to be a king.'

'What do you mean?'

'He believed he was the son of King Edward VI. He tells this to everyone and anyone who will listen, and to plenty of others who won't. No one took Roag seriously, which made him yet more resentful. That was why he fitted the part of Gloucester so well: that sense of rage that others had what he considered rightfully his. I would say his whole life is a play, a drama.'

The great door of the Marshalsea gaol in Southwark creaked open. Richard Topcliffe shook hands with the keeper, thanked him for the excellent food and comfort of his cell, and stepped out into the fresh air. In his hand he had his silver-tipped blackthorn stick, which he twirled.

A pair of goodwives with their children spotted his shock of white hair and crossed the road to avoid him. He was well known in these parts, and feared. Two men were waiting for him, one of them his assistant Nicholas Jones, the other a man well known to John Shakespeare. A man named Paul Hooft.

'Good day, gentlemen,' Topcliffe said, smacking his stick into the palm of his left hand. 'Has Shakespeare found the papist bitch yet?'

Both men shook their heads.

'Are you certain?'

Both men nodded.

'Then we must find her ourselves. We have work to do: a conspiracy to foil and Romish blood to spill, so that I may be raised once more to the intimate affection of my beloved sovereign lady. Let us make haste to Westminster.'

Behind Topcliffe, the keeper closed the door, glad at last to be rid of his celebrated inmate.

These had been fraught days in the Marshalsea. The keeper had striven to walk a thin line between gaoler and tavern host, for he knew it wise to treat Mr Topcliffe more as a guest than a prisoner. With his back to the heavy oak door, he let out a long sigh of relief, then bent forward and picked up a great handful of sawdust from the floor. He rubbed it hard between his fingers, as though somehow he might scour away the evil infection of Topcliffe's touch.

Chapter 33

SHAKESPEARE ESCORTED HIS brother back to the Theatre and told him to stay among friends. There was no reason to believe him in danger, but no one seemed safe at the moment; it was better not to take unnecessary risks.

He summoned the Shoreditch constable and the watch, and ordered them to inform the sheriff and convey the body of Anthony Friday from the farmyard to the crypt of St Paul's for the attention of Joshua Peace. There was a great deal of grumbling from the constable.

'St Paul's is in London. We don't have no jurisdiction there, and they've got none over us.'

Shakespeare did not have the time or the patience to argue. 'Do it or suffer the consequences, Constable. This is Queen's business. And while you are about it, raise a hue and cry. Search the area around the farm without delay. Anything you find out of the ordinary – anything – is to be brought to me at Sir Robert Cecil's house in the Strand, just west of the city wall.'

On the ride back south from Shoreditch towards Bishopsgate and the city, Shakespeare felt the same sensation he had had when walking from the Strand to the Searcher of the Dead in St Paul's. He was being followed. The road was busy with carts and riders heading in both directions. He looked around with great care, seeking the rider who stopped or slowed when he did, on the lookout for the horseman who wore a cowl despite the warmth of the day. But he could not spot the watcher. Was it the killer of Anthony Friday? He clenched a hand around one of the pistol stocks.

At Cecil's mansion, he had a visitor.

'A ragged old woman, Mr Shakespeare,' the footman said, ill concealing his distaste.

He had her brought to him in one of Cecil's quieter rooms, a small office towards the rear of the house where the Privy Councillor did much of his work when he was not at court.

The old nun walked in slowly with short steps.

'Sister Michael,' Shakespeare said, offering her his hand. 'Thank you for coming. I apologise if I did not treat you well before.'

She did not take his hand, nor did she accept the seat that he proffered. 'I am not here to converse with you, Mr Shakespeare, but to tell you that I now understand that I should trust you in the matter of Thomasyn Jade.'

'I have a letter from Father Weston in this house if you would like to see it.'

'I am not interested in letters. Letters can be forged as blessed Mary of Scots found to the cost of her sainted head. I am here only to try to bring Thomasyn to you. Is that not what you want?'

'Where is she?'

'If I bring her to you, what will you do with her?'

'I just wish to make sure she is well and that she is safe. If she needs any assistance, she will be well looked after. You need have no fear. There will be no religious pressure put upon her and she will be well cared for all her life. I have the names of friends and relatives of Father Southwell who made this pledge to him before he died at Tyburn. I know they have monies set aside that will be hers to achieve a degree of comfort and tranquillity.'

'Perhaps she does not need their assistance. Perhaps she is already happy in her life.'

'I pray that it is so, but the essence of the matter is that I promised Father Southwell I would do my utmost to find her, to set all minds at ease, most particularly his. He worried greatly for her.'

Sister Michael clasped her knuckles together at her breast and closed her sharp eyes, as though in pain. 'It is true, we did not treat her well . . . There were errors. I must beg God's forgiveness in this.'

Shakespeare looked at her in surprise. How much effort must it have taken for the old nun to say that the exorcism was misguided – and to a Protestant, too?

'Sister,' he said, 'will you not sit down? Might I have some refreshment brought to you?'

She uncurled her bony fingers and looked at him with utter disdain. 'Do you think I need heretic victuals to survive? Do you have no idea how many of the true faith there still are in this land? Your pseudo-bishops may have the churches, but we still have the hearts, Mr Shakespeare. Forget that at your peril.'

He smiled, bemused by the sudden squalls of her temperament. 'I merely offered you food and drink, in the same spirit as the Samaritan in the scriptures, one human reaching out to another across the divide.'

'I will never take your victuals, sir. But I find it in my heart to trust you, so I will do what I can to bring Thomasyn forth, if that is her desire. She already knows you are looking for her and is in great fear. I will now go to her and tell her you can be relied upon. The rest is up to her.'

*

'It seems I am to die in the morning, John.'

Shakespeare stepped forward and clasped the broken, manacled frame of Francis Mills. They were in Limbo, the lowest hole of Newgate, where the Jesuit priest Father Robert Southwell had spent his last night not long since. Shakespeare stood back, still holding Mills by his bone-thin arms.

'I wish there were something I could say.'

'That you are sorry? Why should you be sorry? The evidence against me could not be denied. I must have killed them.'

'I have my doubts.'

Mills picked grubs from his hair, one by one, and crushed them between his fingers. 'Please, John, do not make it worse for me. Unless you bring a royal pardon, you can have no words to ease my night.'

'Has the lawyer Cornelius Bligh been to see you?'

'Yes. He thinks my case hopeless but said he would do his best. It seems his best was not good enough.'

'What of Cecil? Has he been here?'

Mills smiled with unutterable sadness. 'No.'

'He should have done so.'

Shakespeare could not help sniffing the putrid air, nor could he ignore the scuttling of the rats that sometimes lunged and bit at Mills's sores. Was this noisome hellishness the reason Cecil refrained from coming?

'I hoped he would. I gave him fair service for little reward.'

Holding up the tallow candle, which he had bought from the keeper and which was the only source of light in this evil place, Shakespeare looked around at their surroundings. The cell stank of ordure. Mills was not alone; he shared the dungeon with three other condemned men. It would be a merry morning on the morrow.

'Do you want a priest?'

'No. What I want is to know why you have come here. You

did not come to say farewell, because you did not know I was to die this soon.'

Shakespeare managed a smile. 'As sharp as ever. You will be missed.'

'What is it? Something to do with the letter from *The Ruth*?'

'Yes.'

Shakespeare told him of the trail to Wisbech Castle and Cornwall, and of the quest for Beatrice Eastley.

'And so we come to a man named Regis Roag.'

'Roag, did you say?'

'Do you know him? It seems he claimed to have worked for the Earl of Essex, which is why I have come to you.'

'Yes, we used him when I was at Essex House. Have nothing to do with him, John. He is strange and evil. Oh, yes, I know Regis Roag. He is a killer.'

'Then how has he escaped hanging?'

'Because he was the earl's private assassin.'

Shakespeare took a few seconds to let this information soak in. If Roag was Essex's man, what was going on? Was Essex trying to destroy Cecil's intelligence operation? It was possible, for the earl harboured great loathing for the Cecils and all who took their side. But if that was the case, what role did Ovid Sloth and Beatrice Eastley play in the conspiracy? And how did such a road lead back to St Gregory's College in Seville or to the Spanish raid on Cornwall? Nothing made sense. It was like trying to snatch eels from the river with your bare hands.

'Frank, forgive me. I must ask you more questions. Do you believe Roag is still working for Essex?'

'God's blood, no. They had a bad falling-out over money. That was two years ago, about the time I left Essex House. I thought Roag had been making a living in the playhouses.'

'I was told he has a bee in his head that he is the son of King Edward.'

Mills laughed and immediately began to choke.

'That was always his story, with various embellishments. It seems his mother worked as a seamstress in the royal household and was thrown out when she came great with child. She must have told Roag that the boy king was his father, which seems preposterous enough, given Edward's tender years, his puritanical leanings and fragile health. But the story gave Roag the feeling that he was destined for greatness – and my lord of Essex played on that. He promised him that he would be raised up and that his birthright would be recognised, if only he did certain tasks for him. It afforded my lord much mirth.'

'So he used Roag for his dark deeds, promising him nobility in return.'

'Yes, but what difference would it make even if the boy king *was* his father? He would still be a bastard with no claim to the throne, any more than the bastard sons of Henry VIII had a claim. Roag was vain, but not stupid, however. When he realised how ill he was being used, he walked away from us.'

'Is Roag's mother alive? Where does she live?'

'I have no knowledge. All I know is that she married a sail seamster and that they ran a sail-loft in Southwark, downriver of the bridge. But remember this as you go after him: Roag is a man with a grievance.'

Shakespeare had taken Boltfoot with him to Newgate. Now, as he left Mills to his fate and emerged from the depths of the gaol, he found his assistant waiting for him just inside the forbidding entranceway. He had his caliver, unslung from his back. It rested across his arms, primed with powder and loaded.

'We are being watched, Boltfoot. Why have we not *seen* him?'

'Because he – or she – is mighty good at their work.'

Shakespeare nodded. This was a pursuer as skilled in the art as any of Walsingham's agents. Such men were rare.

'Well, we must take care. You wanted a mission, Boltfoot. I have two for you: find me Ovid Sloth and find me the home of a man named Regis Roag. You may discover them both by going to your dockland haunts.'

'Master?'

'Sloth is a wine merchant. Go to his house by Aldersgate to see if there is any sign of him. If you find Sloth, apprehend him. If he is not there, go to the Vintry by Three Cranes Wharf. He has a counting house there. Ask about. They will know him and he may have been seen. Offer them a few shillings. I must go to Greenwich.'

'And the other mission, Mr Shakespeare?'

'Regis Roag is a most dangerous killer. He is most likely the man who tried to do for you in Falmouth. All I know of his possible whereabouts is that his mother was married to a sail seamster in Southwark; they have a loft there. I do not know her name nor even if she is alive, so I am not expecting a great deal. But we can but try. And Boltfoot . . .'

'Yes, master?'

'Do not let your guard drop for a moment.'

Chapter 34

THE PALACE OF Placentia at Greenwich was abuzz with activity. The royal progress would be under way the following day and there was a huge amount of work to be done. Few understood quite what Her Majesty's annual tour of the great houses of southern England involved. The organisation was terrifying, enough to break any man. More than two thousand men and women on the move, by river barge and horse. Four hundred wagons, two and a half thousand horses. And though the Vice-Chamberlain had effective day-to-day responsibility for the minute detail of the great movement, no one doubted that it was Sir Robert Cecil who carried the burden of overall control, along with his other mass of duties.

Shakespeare was escorted straight to Cecil's apartments, where he found him handing out orders to half a dozen administrative clerks. Cecil shooed them away with a wave, then summoned his man Clarkson.

'Have the Lord Chamberlain and the Lord Steward meet me here in an hour.'

Clarkson bowed and departed. Cecil at last turned to Shakespeare.

'Good, you're here, John.'

'I have a great deal to report.'

'We are going to see Her Majesty. Say your piece then. Be

prepared, for it will not be pleasant. She desires to know every-thing. Do not try to spare her feelings; hold nothing back or she will know and you will feel the tempest of her fury.'

'Very well.'

'At least you look presentable today. Come, leave your pistols here. She will not have them in her presence.'

Shakespeare removed the pistols from his belt and placed them on Cecil's table. The two men walked briskly through the rooms of the palace until they came to the oak-panelled presence chamber where Sir Thomas Heneage greeted them with a weak nod. Shakespeare was struck by how gaunt and ill the Queen's oldest friend appeared. He bowed to Heneage graciously, though he would never take his hand; he was a man he admired in many ways, but could never respect.

'Sir Robert, Mr Shakespeare, it is a pleasure to see you both, even in such fraught circumstances.'

To his left, Shakespeare noted another small group: the Earl of Essex with three of his senior men – the brothers Francis and Anthony Bacon, and the renowned codebreaker Thomas Phelippes.

Cecil bowed to Essex and the earl raised his hand in dismissive acknowledgment. This was the way the hierarchy worked. Cecil might have the political power as de facto Principal Secretary, but Essex was the nobleman. It was no secret that they loathed each other and were engaged in a life-and-death struggle for influence.

Cecil turned to Shakespeare. 'Wait here, I will see if she is ready for us.'

Shakespeare felt a touch on his shoulder and turned around. Lucia Trevail stood before him in her modest court clothes. She proffered her gloved hand. He took it and kissed it.

'It seems I cannot get away from you, Mr Shakespeare. You really do follow me everywhere.'

He laughed. 'You departed very suddenly. I did not have a chance to say farewell.'

'And now as soon as we meet again, *you* are going to desert *me* for Her Majesty's royal charms, are you not?'

'I have an audience with the Queen . . . but I would see you again.'

She moved closer to him and looked up into his eyes. 'When you have done with your meeting, do not run away. I have information for you.'

'Indeed? Tell me now.'

She fluttered her fingers towards the entrance to the Privy Chamber. 'Go, go, you are being summoned.' Briefly she held his hand and squeezed a small scrap of paper into his palm.

Cecil was at the doorway, signalling Shakespeare and Essex's group to approach. Shakespeare hesitated, but Lucia Trevail was already disappearing through a side door.

Essex immediately pushed forward. He towered over Cecil and elbowed him aside so that he might enter the royal presence first. Cecil deferred to him without complaint, and to Heneage, but to no one else.

The Queen was already in the small, intimate room, seated on a tall-backed throne with bright-red cushions and a red footstool supporting her exquisite silver shoes. She wore a gown of white silk, bordered with giant pearls. A heavy necklace of rubies and diamonds hung down her breast. Armed Lifeguards stood either side of her. Cecil and the other courtiers and intelligencers immediately dropped to their knees and bowed their heads low. All except Essex; he merely bowed his head momentarily and did not kneel. Instead, he stood with an insolent air at the front, in the centre, with Heneage to his right and Cecil to his left. Behind them were the Bacon brothers, along with Phelippes and Shakespeare.

The Queen did not like the smell of sweat, so all save

Shakespeare had doused themselves with perfumes. The air was heavy with the ill-matched combination of their scents, from marjoram to lavender, from rosewater to musk and civet. Shakespeare thought he might gag from the fumes; together they were no more fragrant than a hog's fart.

Her Majesty looked at Essex with displeasure and waited. Essex did not move. Suddenly, she rose from her cushions, stepped forward, fist raised, and hit out towards the side of his head. He raised his own hand as if to fend her off. Her Lifeguards, resplendent in their coats of red, faced in black velvet and the Queen's silver gilt escutcheon on the back, moved forward, swords drawn. Essex managed to avert his head from her blow without touching her, then slowly and with great reluctance, sank to one knee. The Lifeguards did not back off.

'We greet you, cousins,' the Queen said, studiously addressing all but Essex.

She stepped towards Heneage, and raised him up with a touch of her hand to his shoulder. He struggled to his feet, obviously in great pain. She moved on to Cecil, then the Bacons, Shakespeare and Phelippes, raising each of them up with a gentle word of recognition and the lightest of touches. Finally she stood before Essex, who looked as if he would explode with anger. She touched his shoulder and he rose to his full and considerable height.

'There, cousin,' she said. 'That was not so difficult, was it?'

Essex scowled and turned his head away.

The Queen was old and fragile. She moved back to her throne and slumped on to her cushions. Above her extravagant starched ruff, her face was coated in white paint of ceruse that clung to her age-lines like marl in the furrows of a field. Her nose was hooked like a hawk's beak, her lips thin. Shakespeare could not but note that her red wig was the slightest margin askew. And yet her black eyes had lost none of their vigour or perspicacity. When she spoke, her voice was not as firm as once it had been, perhaps afflicted by her reluctance to open wide her mouth and reveal the blackness of her teeth. And yet she demanded attention and even the proud and scornful Essex could not escape the force of her words.

'We do not recall such days as these,' she said. 'Even when Parma and Medina Sidonia threatened our very existence, we suffered no Spaniard on our beaches.'

Her courtiers remained silent. There was nothing to say.

'Were I a man, I would not have moved from that Cornish beach though I were alone, standing against an army one hundred thousand strong that had sailed in from the sea with all the world's cannon and shot. And yet, we are told, our Cornishmen fled before a mere four galleys and four hundred soldiers. It is a stain on their county for all eternity, and shames England. What men were these to surrender our realm without laying down their lives? Call them not men, but craven pups who roll over and expose their soft underbellies to their Spanish masters.'

Her voice had risen in the intensity of its fury, but it was not loud, which somehow made it the more terrifying.

'Mr Shakespeare.' Suddenly she turned to him. 'You were there. Why did *you* not give your life for your sovereign and your country on that beach?'

Shakespeare caught Cecil's eye and the barely discernible shake of the head. *Don't try to defend yourself,* he was saying, *ride the storm.*

'I humbly beg your forgiveness, Your Majesty.'

'Have you nothing to say in your defence?'

'No, ma'am. All I can tell you is what happened. I cannot say we were right. We fought, but we were greatly outnumbered and outgunned. Sir Francis Godolphin believed a tactical retreat would serve England the better and I agreed with him, for we were a dozen and they were four hundred. We battled our way back to St Michael's Mount. If Your Majesty believes we were in the wrong, then I cannot disagree.'

'God's blood! Now they know what mettle our men are made of – and it is base, sir, base! What now will deter them from launching waves of invasion along our southern coasts, safe in the knowledge that the defenders will flee at the sight of them? This was cowardice, Mr Shakespeare. My father would have had your head for this.'

Shakespeare felt the breath of fury and rather wished he was back on the beach at Penzance, being shot at. He hung his head.

'Your Majesty—' Cecil began.

'Do you interrupt me, little man?'

'Forgive me, ma'am, but I would speak in Mr Shakespeare's defence, for I know he will not do so himself.'

'Defence! What defence is there for cowardice?'

'I know that Mr Shakespeare hazarded his life in a most perilous mission that may yet prove invaluable to the safety of your realm.'

'Mr Shakespeare, what was this mission?'

Shakespeare looked at Cecil, who nodded. He drew a breath and began his tale.

'I scouted the enemy positions, ma'am. I counted their strength and spied out their armaments and formations. Perhaps most vitally, I saw an Englishman with the Spanish commander.'

'Is this the pilot Burley, the traitor I have heard of in letters from Godolphin and others?'

'No, this was another man and, from descriptions I have, I believe I know his name. I believe, also, that he is still in the country and that he is among a group of enemy mercenaries and assassins who have been wreaking havoc and death among our own. I fear they threaten your secret networks, ma'am, and perhaps the very future of England.'

'Who is this man?'

'I believe his name is Regis Roag.'

As he spoke, he saw the Earl of Essex stiffen.

'Continue.'

'Mr Mills, who is presently in Newgate awaiting sentence of death to be carried out, tells me he has been known to certain intelligencing circles for some years. Until now, however, he has worked on our side. It seems he is a turncoat and a cold, ruthless killer. He is also a man who feels deeply aggrieved, believing himself of the blood royal.'

The Queen, for a moment, seemed lost for words.

'Let me explain, ma'am,' Shakespeare continued. 'Mr Roag is so deluded that he thinks himself the son of your late brother, King Edward. He believes he was begotten by him of a young serving maid. No one takes these claims seriously, of course, but it is said he clings to them as a terrier holds a fox in its lair. It is possible he seeks revenge on England for a perceived slight. I think he or his confederates killed a man of ours in Plymouth, one Trott, and tried to kill my man Mr Cooper. It is possible, too, that he is responsible for the murder of Anthony Friday, the playmaker and intelligencer.'

Elizabeth turned to Essex. 'Have you heard of this man Roag, cousin?'

'No.'

Shakespeare looked at Essex in astonishment. Why was he lying? He read, too, the subtle smile of Robert Cecil. *Go for the kill, Mr Shakespeare. Do your worst, for you have nothing to lose.* Indeed, he did have nothing to lose. He had crossed the Earl of Essex before and knew that he would be an enemy to death. Nothing he could say would make matters worse between them.

'Forgive me for speaking out of turn, ma'am, but it does seem strange to me that Regis Roag is unknown to his lordship, for Mr Mills told me he was for a time in the earl's service at Essex House. I understand that the earl is an exceeding busy man and has many retainers, so perhaps he was not acquainted with Mr Roag. Perhaps Mr Phelippes knows more than I do.'

Thomas Phelippes pushed nervously at the nosepiece of his metal-framed glasses. He was as brutishly ugly as ever, yet Shakespeare knew that his pock-marked face and lank yellow hair were but the external trappings of the man, and that his head housed a brain as fine as a pearl concealed within the rough husk of an oyster.

The codebreaker nodded hurriedly, avoiding his master's merciless gaze, then spoke with extreme caution.

'There was such a man, ma'am – for a while. I took it upon myself to employ him and there was no reason for the earl ever to have met him or to have known of his existence. He seemed useful, for he inhabited the world of the playhouses where treacherous men such as Marlowe and Kyd plied their trade. But I dispensed with his services when it became obvious that he was insane and dangerous.'

'Did he tell you this story of being our brother's son?'

'Constantly, ma'am. I believed it my duty to make some inquiries. What I discovered was that his mother had, indeed, been a drab in the household of the late king, but she had been dismissed for incontinent lewdness with one of the guards. This tale of your brother being Roag's father is egregious nonsense. But there are many such claims made, as I am sure you are aware. If such tittle-tattle were to be believed, you would have a hundred or more half-brothers and -sisters. But these stories are scurrilous, ma'am, all of them – and no one believes them.'

The Queen turned to Anthony Bacon. 'Cousin, you are in

command of the earl's intelligence network. Do you have knowledge of Roag?'

Bacon shifted uneasily. He was unhealthy-looking, his face pasty and wan. Finally he nodded, so suddenly and sharply that it might have been a tic rather than a signal of affirmation. 'I agree with everything Mr Phelippes has said, Your Majesty.'

It seemed to Shakespeare that these men were like children before a stern parent. The Queen surveyed them with her all-seeing eye, then turned to the most difficult son, Essex, the sullen, defiant one whom she loved but could not control.

'And you say you knew nothing of this man, cousin? We are surprised that you were kept in the dark so. Do you not require reports from Mr Phelippes and Mr Bacon?'

'I have more important matters than the wild imaginings of some lowly intelligencer. That is why I employ Messrs Bacon and Phelippes. And if our men are dying, I think we should look where our enemies are gaining their knowledge.' He pointed with menace at Shakespeare, then Cecil. 'I say there is a traitor in *their* midst, ma'am. Look there to find the enemy within, I say. Ask Mr Shakespeare why he let Garrick Loake die. Ask him why he did not bring the treacherous Jesuit Weston to the Tower for questioning under torture.'

It was a common tactic to deflect criticism. Simply move the attack on to someone else. It mattered not that the attack was unjustified; for men such as Robert Devereux, second Earl of Essex, all was fair in court politics. Shakespeare understood this, and yet the words stung, for there was an element of truth in them; he should not have let Garrick Loake die without learning his secret.

Cecil stepped in again, showing no anger. 'Your Majesty, this is all getting away from the true matter, which is that England is under attack from within.'

'What say you, Thomas?' Elizabeth addressed Heneage.

'Your Majesty, it seems to me that Sir Robert is correct. We are under attack. To defend ourselves, we must join forces, not bicker like children.'

'Our thoughts, too,' the Queen said. 'Mr Bacon, what do you say?' She gazed at Francis Bacon, brother of Anthony and a failed contender for high office.

Bacon looked slightly taken aback, as though unprepared for such a question. 'I would agree, Your Majesty, that we are under most grievous attack.'

'But what do they hope to gain?'

'The destruction of our secret army. Like the late Sir Francis Walsingham, they are learning that knowledge is power, so they wish to do away with our intelligence-gathering capability.'

'Good. You speak well, cousin. So now that we know the enemy, you can all slay him together. Spare us the detail of your investigations but work out between you your strategy to protect our realm, for we believe you must have brains enough.' She turned to Essex. 'And we tell you this, cousin, you will cooperate fully with Sir Robert Cecil and Sir Thomas Heneage. Your men will all work with one another and share intelligence. I will tolerate no politicking among you.'

The men all bowed. The Queen rose.

Shakespeare found himself stepping forward. 'Your Majesty—' he began.

'Mr Shakespeare, sir, do not try our patience. We have heard what you have said and we accept that you have shown some valour, but this audience is now over.'

'Forgive me, but I would crave your indulgence on one other matter.'

'Very well. Are you going to tell us that you have found Thomasyn Jade as we commanded?'

'No, ma'am, I am afraid not.'

'Then why do you think we would be interested in what you have to say? You are a man of remarkable contradictions, Mr Shakespeare. One moment, you seem a fine defender of our realm, the next you are running from the beach or failing in a simple mission.'

Shakespeare refused to be daunted. 'It is the case of my colleague Mr Mills, ma'am. He faces the hangman in a matter of hours, and yet he has done great service to the realm and, more to the point, I have grave doubts as to his guilt.'

'What was his crime?'

'He was convicted of killing his wife and her lover.'

'And was there evidence enough to hang him?'

'I fear there was, ma'am.'

'Then he must hang.' And with those words, she swept from the chamber.

Six men sat around a table in the Earl of Essex's sumptuous apartment. On one side, stiff and serious, Sir Robert Cecil held his position beside his chief intelligencer, John Shakespeare. Ranged against them were the Bacon brothers and Phelippes. The Earl of Essex took the head of the table, as if by right of seniority, his tall figure dominant even though sitting. Heneage had remained behind with the Queen.

'Well, gentlemen, it seems you are to work with me,' Essex said, looking at Cecil pointedly, then at Shakespeare with distaste.

From the way he said 'work with me', it was clear to Shakespeare that he meant 'work *for* me'. It was clear, too, that Cecil would have none of it.

'We know who they are,' Essex continued. 'This man Roag, the slithery fat serpent Ovid Sloth, the woman Sorrow Gray or whatever she calls herself, and various others unknown, conveniently allowed into England by Mr Shakespeare and the craven trainbands of Cornwall. What we do not know is their plan. What say you, Francis?'

It was clear to Shakespeare that Essex's intelligence team had not been sleeping. When he had called in Phelippes to help with the documents and letters seized from the priests, Cecil had told them about the Wisbech situation and Sorrow Gray. Essex would certainly have had letters from Godolphin concerning Ovid Sloth; but had Cecil told him about his disappearance?

He wondered, too, about Topcliffe. The white dog was out of gaol now. He would most certainly wish to help Essex if it could do Shakespeare damage.

'It must be an attack on the Queen's person. It is what Spain and that scarlet whore the Pope have attempted time upon time these past thirty-seven years.'

Essex slammed his fist on the table. 'God's wounds, Shakespeare, you bear responsibility for this. You saw Roag when he landed. Why did you not kill him then? You let him go, sir! Thanks to your negligence, they will now have a small army of assassins landed in England. Nay, a *large* army! They did their utmost to abduct and kill Mr Phelippes here.'

Shakespeare looked across at Phelippes. 'You seem remarkably healthy for one who escaped narrowly from such a heinous foe. What did they do, Mr Phelippes, hit you with their toy rattles?'

'I was saved by the quickness of my lord's guards. Do you doubt my word?'

Shakespeare smiled and raised a sly eyebrow. 'Indeed not. Never have I met a less devious man than you, Mr Phelippes.'

'Enough!' Essex ordered. 'Anthony, have your say.'

Anthony Bacon, more sickly and more studious than his brother, sipped at a cordial of herbs prescribed by his apothecary for one or other of the dozen chronic complaints that assailed him. 'What I would like to know, my lord, is the true nature of all this nonsense from Wisbech. Why were we not kept informed while Mr Shakespeare delved there? And why did he not bring the stinking Jesuit Weston to the Tower for more stringent questioning?'

Shakespeare was not listening. He had much to do this night. He still had in his hand the note from Lucia Trevail. It told him the position of a room in the depths of the palace. She would meet him there.

'Have you found the Gray girl yet?'

'I may be about to make some progress,' Shakespeare said. 'When I have found her, she will be presented to you and the Council for questioning.'

Essex was not satisfied. 'What is this *progress*?'

'That I cannot say as yet.'

'God in heaven, Shakespeare, you always were a treacherous cur, but this is beyond treason. You heard Her Royal Majesty. We must *share* information. Would you disobey your sovereign?'

'When I have the intelligence, I will share it. As yet, I do not have it . . . my lord.' He loaded the words *my lord* with as much scorn as he could muster.

'Sir Robert, take your man in hand if you will. We must know everything if we are to fight and destroy this diabolical conspiracy. Is this man up to the task? Why, he has even managed to let Ovid Sloth slip from his grasp!'

Cecil smiled and nodded and listened. Occasionally he contributed a platitude. Shakespeare watched him with admiration, for he knew that inside he seethed. He knew, too, that Essex had shared no secrets of his own, and would not do so, whatever the Queen commanded.

At last Essex had had enough. He stood up from the table. 'We will convene tomorrow evening at Nonsuch Palace. One thing is certain: we must protect Her Majesty at all costs. Double the guard along the route and double it again at Nonsuch. No weapons, particularly pistols, will be allowed anywhere near the Presence Chamber or within a hundred yards of Her Majesty when she is out walking or at the hunt. No one but her innermost circle of courtiers must be admitted to the palace without my written authority as Master of the Horse, countersigned by the Lord Chamberlain. Ensure that all relevant officers understand that, Sir Robert. I will discuss the matter with Lord Hunsdon. And so I bid you goodnight, gentlemen.'

Essex nodded to Cecil then turned to Francis Bacon. 'Francis, come with me. I have a small task for you.'

Chapter 35

THE CRANES OF Vintry Wharf stood stark against the darkening sky. The aroma of wine and aged oak hung like an intoxicating pall over the river bank where the great barrels were unloaded from the carracks to be taken into storage.

Boltfoot Cooper watched the men leaving work for the evening. He stood idly by in the shadow of a doorway like a crippled beggar hoping for alms. The dockers avoided him; they earned a shilling a day and had no intention of parting with a single farthing of their wages, however heart-rending a beggar's story might be.

One of the men was about to walk past when he looked again at the ragged beggar. He stopped, grinned and put out his hand.

'Well, well,' he said cheerfully, 'of all the ungodly creatures of the deep, if it ain't Boltfoot Cooper. Put it there, Mr Cooper.'

Boltfoot smiled from his battered face and shook the proffered hand. 'The pleasure is all mine, Mr Sands. I was hoping to find you alive and well.'

'Never been better, Mr Cooper. Can I buy you a gage of ale?'

'No, sir, you cannot, for I wish to buy you one. And see if I might pick some information from your brain.'

'To the tavern then, you old pirate. Handling casks of

Frenchie wine all day has given me a great thirst for honest English ale.'

They found a private booth in the King Hal and, after ten minutes' talking about old times and old friends from the days when they had sailed the western sea together, Boltfoot got down to business.

'I'm looking for a fellow named Ovid Sloth, a wine merchant who, I am told, has a counting house at Vintry Wharf.'

'Aye, true enough. But I don't believe I have seen him in three months.'

'Do you know where he might be?'

'Cardinal Quick? Up some apprentice wharfman's arse, I wouldn't be surprised. All the lads have to look lively to watch their backs when he's around. Mind you, he could be away. Travels a lot to his vineyards and on his other affairs. Even has interests in Spain, so I am told. When he is here, though, he has a house by Aldersgate.'

'No one there,' Boltfoot said. He had found Sloth's grand house closed and shuttered.

'Well, if he's in town, he'll not be able to stay away from the Bilge for long. Word has it that that's the stew he visits for his fresh meat.'

Shakespeare had no idea what function the room performed. She pulled him by the hand and closed the door behind her. There was no light, only utter darkness. He kissed her mouth and he felt her hand on him, tearing at his breeches. Now they were on the floor, which was strewn with rushes. She was pulling up her skirts and he was kissing the soft skin on the inside of her thigh. She clenched his hair in her hands and pulled him in closer.

'War and death, Mr Shakespeare.' Her whispered words were like a last soft breath; her fingers scraped at him with the ferocity of a cat. 'War and death . . .'

He wrenched his head away from her vice-like fingers and slid up along her thigh. Then he was inside her. Their gasps mingled into a muffled cry of pleasure.

Shakespeare was lost in the darkness. All thoughts of Frank Mills and his sordid end, of the intelligence Lucia had promised, of the gruesome death of Anthony Friday, were obliterated. The only thing that existed in this forgotten palace room was the electric touch of this woman's body. Shakespeare had never felt such heightened sensation. Even with his wife, there had never been a moment of more intensity. When it had finished, they moved apart, panting. He put his hand out and found the curve of her belly, but she pushed him away and began smoothing down her skirts.

'It builds up in you so you think you will go mad,' she said, as though thinking aloud. 'The weeks and months enclosed with her and the other women. The reek of their scented, unwashed bodies, their lewd whispered desires, the closeness of them all.'

'Can you not get out of here and come to me?'

'If she knew we were here, she would have us in the Tower. She cannot abide the pleasure of others.' She entwined her fingers with his. 'I will feign a common cold and come to you tomorrow before the court departs for Nonsuch.'

The word *Nonsuch* finally brought Shakespeare to his senses. He should not be here. The hour was late and he had much to do. And then there was the other matter.

He sat up. 'You have some intelligence.'

'It may be nothing. But Margaret of Cumberland said she believed Beatrice Eastley had been spotted near Susan Bertie's house at the Barbican, as brazen as a halfpenny whore.'

'Near?'

'Around the stables, I believe.'

'Is she still there?'

'Mr Shakespeare, have you not noted that I am cloistered here like a nun? I do not know whether she is still there or ever was there. Go and discover for yourself. And when you find her, you may tell her my mind. Now, we must leave this room without being seen. I shall go first. I pray she does not smell you on me.'

Shakespeare organised a five-man squadron to go to the Barbican and look for the woman known as Beatrice Eastley. If she was discovered, she was to be confined in the Counter prison in Wood Street.

'Use discretion,' he told the captain of the guards. 'We do not wish the Countess of Kent to suffer unwarranted alarm. Yet neither must we assume that she has nothing to hide in the affair of this woman.'

Another matter commanded his own attention: the matter of a man's life. Before midnight, he was at Knightrider Street in the city of London, a little way south of St Paul's, looking up at the tall, dark tenement building that was the home of Joshua Peace, the Searcher of the Dead. Shakespeare opened the door to the side of the six-storey lodging house and climbed the stone steps to Peace's rooms. The door was bolted, as he knew it would be, so he hammered at it with the haft of his poniard.

His other hand clutched the stock of one of the pistols in his belt. He had picked them up from Cecil's apartments before leaving Greenwich Palace for the short boat ride upriver.

'Who is it?' A wary voice from inside the locked door.

'Joshua, it is John Shakespeare. Let me in.'

There was a pause; then he heard the sound of bolts being drawn back. The door opened slowly. Peace clutched his chest in relief when he saw that it really was his old friend.

'Forgive me, John, I am mighty cautious these dark days.'

'With good reason, Joshua. Now in the name of God, give me wine and talk to me.'

Peace wore a long linen nightgown and cap. He was thinner than ever and there was something ghostly about his appearance. He poured two goblets of hippocras, sprinkling a little sugar in each one, and handed the larger vessel to Shakespeare.

'Thank you, Joshua.'

'Is this about Anthony Friday?'

'In a way, yes.'

'Shot dead. Ball through the back, straight to the heart.'

'But I believe he was probably killed by one or more of the same people who did for Garrick Loake, and it is the death of Mr Loake that interests me most.'

'I told you, it was the sailmaker needle through the jugular.'

'Yes, but what I want to know is whether Frank Mills's wife and the grocer, her lover, could have been killed in the same way.'

'Well, they died from wounds to the throat, and it was unusual. They were not slashed, but torn.'

'Could it have been a sailmaker that inflicted the wounds? If the needle had been pulled and manipulated with great violence, could it have been the murder weapon?'

Joshua Peace took off his cap, revealing the thin rim of his hair and bony bald pate. He frowned as he tried to recall the bodies of Anne Mills and Heartsease, the grocer. At last he shook his head.

'I could not say, John. That is the truth. And I am afraid they are both long since buried.'

'But it is possible?'

'Yes, it is possible, but that is all. But why do you think the murderer of Garrick Loake also killed Mistress Mills and her grocer?'

'Mistaken identity. I think the killers found them in Frank's bed and assumed Mr Heartsease was Frank. They are trying to kill every last one of this country's intelligencers.'

'But why hasn't Mr Mills defended himself?'

'Because he was already half deranged and he did not know whether he had killed them or not. He has desired to do for them for so long, he thinks he most probably did it. It is like a dream to him. As for the killers, it meant nothing to them; with Mills in Newgate awaiting the hangman's rope, he is where they wanted him – out of commission. My question to you, Joshua, is to beg you this one indulgence: express your doubts more firmly. Write a letter now that I can take to court to try to gain a stay of execution.'

'This is most improper.'

'It is a man's life.'

Peace exhaled slowly, then nodded. 'Very well. But you know that I would do this for no one but you.' He picked up a quill from his table and rifled through his papers for a blank sheet. 'John, you must realise that if someone wishes to kill all the intelligencers, that must include you.' He looked down at the two pistols in Shakespeare's belt. 'Forgive me, I see you already understood that.'

Shakespeare grimaced. He did not worry for himself, but the threatening note that menaced the lives of his daughters scared him. And yet, the threat seemed out of character for this enemy. These murderers did not bother to issue threats; they merely killed, as casually as a slaughterman at the shambles.

A slender young man with a smooth, naked chest leant against the wall by the entrance to the Bilge in Southwark. To his side there was a low doorway with stone steps that led down into a dimly lit cellar. The strains of a stringed instrument and a soft singing voice wafted up. The doorman spotted Boltfoot from fifty yards away, dragging his left foot behind him as he limped along. As Boltfoot came near, he tilted his chin.

'Help you, sailor?'

Boltfoot stopped and looked the young man up and down. 'Depends what you got to offer.'

'You look like you been home too long from the sea. Need a little company, do you . . . a little mariners' comfort?'

'I don't need a woman, if that's what you mean.'

The man chuckled. 'No women in this hole, master mariner. What exactly did you want?'

'You know what I want.'

The doorkeeper laughed again. 'But I want to hear you say it, don't I? Say the words without shame and you'll be welcome here.'

'I'll go elsewhere.'

'No you won't, because there ain't nowhere else betwixt here and Deptford.'

'Very well, I desire some male company this night.'

'Better come in then, master mariner. A sixpence for me and you can cheapen as you will when you're inside.'

Boltfoot handed over a silver coin and the doorkeeper stepped aside to let him enter. Downstairs, the room was warm and lit by beeswax candles. There was an exotic scent that Boltfoot recognised as the smoke of hashish. Boys and young men lounged around on cushions. A minstrel in red velvet was playing a soft ballad on his lute.

Boltfoot recalled the words Shakespeare had said to him more than once: *It is men's appetites that give them away. When a man has a hunger or a raging thirst, it must be satisfied, though his reason tells him there is a risk of poison.*

Another bare-chested young man, wearing only tight stock-ings that accentuated his manhood, sauntered across to Boltfoot and cocked his head inquiringly. 'I am Ariel. How may I help you, handsome stranger?'

'I am looking for a young man.'

'Now that *is* a surprise.' He smiled engagingly.

Boltfoot thought the young man looked kind, but you do not travel the world without discovering that the tiger's face can be beautiful until its teeth are bared.

'A particular young man, for my master. I am required to bring the young man to my master and I am authorised to offer a sovereign in gold.'

'Well, well, a sovereign! At that price, you may take your pick. What is the name of the lad you require?'

Boltfoot shifted awkwardly and scratched his tangled hair. 'That's the problem, you see. I fell among friends on my way here and drank too much strong ale. I have forgot the name. But I can tell you my master's name, for this young man is a favourite of his. His name is Ovid Sloth, though most of us call him Cardinal Quick. He is a fine gentleman of wealth.'

The youth did not lose his smile. 'Well, we all know the cardinal, but pray, why did he not come here himself?'

'He ails. His great weight drags him down. I think he has a wolf in the leg and the gout, too.'

'Indeed, he has looked slow.'

'Then I have at least found the right place . . . You have seen him recently?'

The youth called Ariel studied Boltfoot. 'Come, stranger, to another room with me. I have fine Italian brandy. Let us drink together a while and we can solve your puzzle to your satisfaction. In truth, I did not know the cardinal favoured any one of us. Perhaps it is me. Would you sample the wares on your master's behalf?'

Boltfoot shook his head hurriedly. 'Women only, me. Just doing my master's bidding.'

'Dear handsome sir, what is a woman and what is a man? I pledge you will not know the difference in the dark. Come, sir.' His soft, smooth fingers curled around Boltfoot's arm.

Boltfoot recoiled. His hand went to the hilt of his cutlass. 'I told you, this is not for me. It is for my master.'

The young man looked at Boltfoot's cutlass, still in his belt. He gave a nonchalant shrug. 'Then pick whichever you will. Take me, if you wish, but I'll need a mark before I go. I promise you he will be happy. Many is the time the cardinal has left my company with a smile upon his lips.'

'No. I will go to him and find the name he requires. He will have me beaten, but it is better this way.'

'Go then, stranger. But you have no notion of what pleasures you have forgone this night.'

Chapter 36

Sir Robert Cecil was not happy at being awoken in the early hours of the morning. 'Christ's blood, what is it, John?'

'Forgive me. I had to do this.'

Shakespeare held out the letter that Joshua Peace had written for him.

Cecil read it quickly. 'This proves nothing,' he said. 'It is one man's opinion that something might be possible. Any judge in the land would crumple it in his hand and throw it at you.'

'It is a man's life. I believe it is likely he is innocent. A man who has given much service to Walsingham, to you, and to his sovereign lady.'

Cecil paced around his bedchamber. From time to time he looked at the letter again, then at Shakespeare. He sat down on the edge of his bed and sighed.

'John, I have *heard* Frank Mills say that he would cut their throats. You have heard him say it. Even when he was apprehended, he did not deny it. He had the knife in his hand. How can there be more evidence than that to prove a man's guilt?'

'Does this letter not put doubt in your mind? Trott is dead by the sailmaker needle. So is Garrick Loake. Anthony Friday is shot dead – and there was a sailmaker at that scene, too. There is a pattern here, Sir Robert. Can there be no slender doubt in your mind that the death of grocer Heartsease and Anne Mills was a matter of mistaken identity? If they wished to kill all those others, why not Mills, too?'

And the rest of us.

Shakespeare had come back to the Palace of Greenwich as he had gone to Joshua Peace's lodging in Knightrider Street, with extreme caution: pistols loaded, eyes alert, sword ready. And all the time certain he was being watched. Even on the river he believed he could feel eyes upon him.

At last Cecil folded the paper and put it down, then walked over to his chamberpot and lifted his nightgown to piss in it. When he had finished, he smoothed down the gown and turned to his chief intelligencer.

'Yes, John, I can see why you harbour doubts. But I am sorry; it is not enough for a royal reprieve. I cannot wake her over this.'

'Could you not take it into your own hands to order a stay of execution? A reprieve until the matter is investigated further? There cannot be more than five or six hours left of Frank's life. A man who might just be innocent. A man who has given much service to this realm.'

Cecil laughed. 'You catch a man in his sleep and wheedle your way into his conscience like a worm. Go on. Tell my footman to fetch Clarkson. I will have the paper prepared for you.'

'Thank you, Sir Robert.'

Shakespeare bowed lower than he had ever felt the need to before.

Boltfoot waited in Mill Lane, just by Bartle Bridge. The youth named Ariel came out of the Bilge soon enough. He was no longer half naked, but attired in shirt, breeches and doublet. He looked about him briefly.

Boltfoot followed the young man as he sauntered through

the quiet streets. There was not far to go, for Ariel turned north into the maze of tenements that fronted the river to the east of the bridge, looking across towards the Bloody Tower. The young man entered the building and soon candlelight showed through a window-pane on the first floor. As Boltfoot had no way of seeing in, he settled down to wait once more and pray that this was the place where Ovid Sloth was hiding.

Had Boltfoot looked out on to the Thames, he might have seen the palace wherry carrying his master, John Shakespeare, as it was rowed slowly against the tide back from Greenwich. Shakespeare carried a leather bag over his shoulder, containing the precious parchment ordering a reprieve for Francis Mills, an assistant secretary to Sir Robert Cecil.

He urged the oarsmen on, glancing constantly back to the east, silently beseeching the morning sun to remain hidden behind the skyline. In his mind, he saw the malign black wood of the gallows and the coarse hempen rope that dangled so that men should dance and die. He knew that Mills would be awake, that there would be no sleep. Had the St Sepulchre's bellman started his mournful tolling yet? Would Mills be at prayer? Somehow Shakespeare doubted it. He would be waiting to be taken from his cell as soon as the sun was on the horizon. From there, he would be carried in a cart the long three miles to Tyburn, where he would ascend the ladder to the noose and a slow, choking death.

The rowers were strong men, but their arms began to tire and the wherry became so slow it hardly seemed to be making progress, so Shakespeare ordered them into land at Haywharf, just before the Steelyard. He jumped ashore before the boat was moored at the stairs and ran along the muddy river bank for Dowgate.

'Hold fast there!'

Shakespeare glanced sideways. It was a nightwatchman with lantern, staff and mastiff. He did not stop.

'Hold, or I unleash the dog!'

Shakespeare stopped. 'Queen's business! I am on urgent Queen's business, Mr Watchman.'

The watchman drew closer, his dog straining at the rope. Suddenly he stopped and tipped his cap with the top of his wooden staff. 'Ah, Mr Shakespeare, sir, I did not recognise you.'

Shakespeare raised his hand in acknowledgment. He was about to run on, but hesitated, to ask, 'How long until dawn?'

'Ninety minutes at most, Mr Shakespeare. Soon you will see the sky lighten to the east.'

He reasoned it would be quicker to fetch a horse from his stables at Dowgate, saddle up and ride for Newgate. He should be in time to save Mills before the cart clattered out from the prison yard on to the dusty road.

The house at Dowgate was in darkness, as were the stables. But there was a glow of moonshine to light his way – enough to saddle up his best grey mare and ride out into the waking London streets. He unlocked the tackroom, laid his leather bag to one side and pulled a harness from the hook. His foot struck something soft. He bent down. Even before his hands felt the whole form, he knew it was a body. A small, warm body. In the darkness he could not tell for certain of its sex, but instinct told him it was female and that she was dead. His mind went to all those he loved; Grace, Mary . . . Ursula.

He needed light. There was always a tinderbox here. He felt about on a shelf beside the harnesses. Without fumbling, he managed to strike a light and lit a stub of tallow candle. It was Sister Michael, the old nun from Denham, lying in a mess of blood. As he straightened up, he heard a sound and turned, but he was too slow, too late. He felt a sharp jab at the back of his head as he swivelled, and caught a glimpse of the face of Regis Roag, his hand on the stock of a gold-engraved pistol.

'Think'st thou I am your executioner? I will blow you to dust, Shakespeare.'

'Roag—'

The muzzle was pushed harder against his head. 'You know my name?'

'I know all about you, your grudge and your designs. I had expected to meet you.'

Roag's hand wavered. Another hand, from somewhere else in the flickering gloom, pressed against Shakespeare's throat with the razor-honed edge of a long blade. Roag pulled it away. 'Wait.'

The knife disappeared.

'You saw me in Cornwall. Mr Sloth said you described me to him. But how do you know my name?'

Shakespeare said nothing.

'It was Warner. Your spy Warner. Was that it? He sent messages, yes? What else did he tell you?'

'Warner? The name means nothing to me.'

'Disarm him.'

He felt hands pulling his weapons from him: his two pistols, his sword, his poniard. There seemed to be three of them, one very short, all with pistols and swords, and one with a butcher's knife. Shakespeare cursed himself for letting down his guard on this of all nights: if he was to die here, then he would never deliver the reprieve for Frank Mills.

The blow came like a smith's hammer, into his temple, and knocked him senseless. The last thing he knew was the crumpling of his knees as he pitched forward to the flagstones and darkness.

Boltfoot watched until late morning. It was a gruelling wait, but finally the youth named Ariel emerged from the tenement building and wandered off into the streets of Southwark. Boltfoot followed him. Ariel went into an ordinary where he ate a breakfast of manchet bread, ale and beef pottage, then came out once more into the sunlight and ambled back towards the Bilge. His way of life may have been profitable, but it was a dangerous one: the penalty for sodomy was death.

Grinding his teeth in frustration, Boltfoot returned to the tenement where the young man had slept. He walked in without knocking at the door and mounted the steps to the first floor. The lodging room consisted of a mattress, a coffer with clothes and some books. Nothing more – and, again, no indication that Ovid Sloth had been here.

It had been a wasted night. The young man clearly had no idea where Sloth was hiding, nor any interest in finding him. Boltfoot realised that watching him had been a long shot, but sometimes such ventures paid off.

He walked back through the streets to a tavern named the Hope, where seafarers gathered. The landlord was as surly as ever, but managed to tilt his chin at him in recognition.

'Not seen you in a year or two, Mr Cooper.'

'Bit far south for me, landlord.'

'Well, if you see any of your poxy old mariner friends, send them along and they'll have a free pint of ale from me. None of them come round here any more and, to tell you the truth, I could do with their custom, mangy company of rats though they be.'

Boltfoot was dejected. Nothing was going his way. It was the old seafarers he wanted, the sort of men who knew about sail-lofts, and they weren't here. He ordered a pint of small ale and some bacon and eggs and sat by the window that looked out on to the river. The landlord came over with his food.

'So what brings you across the bridge this day, Mr Cooper?

Want a fair view of Her Majesty's barge on its way to Nonsuch, do you? Stay here and you'll have no finer view.'

'I'm looking for sail-lofts. One in particular.'

'There's one or two, but they are a little way downriver from here, towards Deptford and Blackwall. You after work, then?'

'No, I'm looking for someone. A man named Regis Roag. I'm told he came from these parts; his mother was a seamstress, and she and her old man, the stepfather, ran a sail-loft here in Southwark some years ago. Want to know if they're still here.'

'Regis Roag, king of Southwark? He used to be well known in these parts. We'd watch him strut down to Paris Garden with his nose in the air like he was a nobleman. That afforded us all a few laughs. Now he's gone on to better things. I saw him playing the crookback Richard of Gloucester at the Theatre.'

'What of his mother?'

'Yes, she had a sail-loft, a little way east of Horsey Down, behind the Shad Thames Wharf. Not heard a word of her in recent years, but why would I?'

Boltfoot drank up and ate his food, then paid and left the Hope. As he wandered along the bank downriver, he heard the sound of ceremonial gunfire and the shooting of fireworks. The great spectacle of Her Majesty's journey from Placentia Palace at Greenwich to Nonsuch in Surrey had begun. Soon the river would be a mass of royal vessels, the most magnificent of all being the Queen's own barge, in which she would sit in state on cushions of gold, pulled by another barge with the finest rowers in all England. Behind her would come the vessels filled with courtiers, clerics, ladies and hundreds of other members of her retinue. Boltfoot paid it no heed; he was mighty tired and he had seen the great event more times than he cared to think on. It made him feel old.

There were a couple of sail-lofts behind Shad Thames Wharf.

'Aye,' the chief seamster at the first one said. 'This used to be Amy Roag's place. The plague took her to her maker two years ago. Her husband went some years before that.'

Boltfoot looked around the loft. It was a light, airy place with an expanse of floorboards laid across the top of the wooden frames of three houses. A large canvas sail was laid out flat, having the finishing touches applied to the hems.

'Does her son ever come here?'

'No. Why would he?'

'To buy needles. Sailmakers.'

The seamster gave Boltfoot an odd look. 'Now that *is* a strange suggestion, friend. Last I heard, Regis Roag was a player. What would he be wanting with sailmakers?'

'To kill people with.' Even as he spoke the words, Boltfoot realised he had made an error.

The seamster had a pair of shears in his hand. His grip on them tightened as he eyed up Boltfoot's weapons, estimating his chances against him. Other men in the sail-loft began to gather round.

The seamster turned to a boy. 'Go fetch the constable, Humphrey. I think we might have a felon here.'

Boltfoot backed off, unslinging his caliver. It wasn't loaded, but would these men know that?

He pointed the muzzle at the chief man. 'You got me wrong. I'm not after killing anyone.'

'We'll let the justice decide on that.'

'I mean you no harm, nor am I a felon. This is Queen's business.'

'If you're on Queen's business, then I'm a baked hedgehog. Now put down your fancy weapon.'

Boltfoot realised he had nothing to gain by staying here.

'Stand back easy and no one will be harmed . . .'

He turned and almost fell into the hatchway. He grabbed at

the rope handrail and stumbled down the steps in a clatter of weapons. Then he ran, as fast as his club-foot would allow.

He limped and tripped into the woodland of Horsey Down, and found cover behind a clump of trees. With as much calm as he could muster, he loaded his caliver with powder and shot, and waited. The moments stretched into minutes. No one was following. He leant against the main tree trunk of an ash grove and allowed his knees to collapse as he slumped into its folds. He was exhausted.

This was the way it had been on watches without number across the great oceans of the world. If a man slept on one of Drake's watches, he would have a dozen lashes. That was for the first offence. Caught a second time, he would face death. Boltfoot had never slept on a watch; he would not sleep now.

Painfully, he dragged himself to his feet. He left the caliver loaded and slung it across his back, its muzzle pointing at the sky, then limped slowly back into the streets of Southwark into a flood of people. They were all going in one direction – to the river bank to cheer their Queen as she was rowed past with glittering pomp.

Boltfoot was not far from the Great Stone Gate at the southern end of the bridge when he saw Ovid Sloth. He knew him instantly from his great bulk and his waddling gait as he shuffled westwards in the direction of St Mary Overy, the parish church of Southwark.

Sloth was with another man, who pushed a handcart. They were walking very slowly, away from the crowds, and were easy to follow. Boltfoot stayed fifty yards behind. Sloth did not turn, nor look about him. The cart-man, slender and lean, glanced around constantly. Was that one of the attackers from Falmouth? Boltfoot could not be sure. After the parish church, they turned south into the pleasure gardens around the Rose playhouse.

There were few people about. Almost all had gone to the river bank. It was less easy for Boltfoot to conceal himself here. His instinct was to walk up to the men, hold the muzzle of his caliver to Sloth's chest and order him to do as he was told. He could either take him across the river to Newgate, as Mr Shakespeare had instructed, or to the nearby Clink; they knew Boltfoot there and would incarcerate Sloth for him until he could be transferred under armed guard. But Boltfoot knew his master too well; he would wish to know where Sloth was heading, whom he was meeting. It was too good an opportunity to pass up. Also, there was the small matter of the man with the handcart; he might be armed.

The two men went into the Rose through the players' entrance, a double-width doorway that allowed carts to be taken straight in for deliveries. Boltfoot moved forward again, his caliver in his arms, his finger on the trigger. All tiredness was forgotten.

The Rose was a compact, timber-framed building, three storeys high, with a multitude of sides so that it was almost egg shaped. Boltfoot waited two minutes, then lifted the latch of the door by which Sloth had entered.

He walked in slowly, taking care to make no sound as he stepped on the boards, all strewn with fresh sawdust. He heard voices somewhere ahead and there, on the stage, stood Ovid Sloth, gasping for breath and leaning against a pillar. He was with three other men, one of whom Boltfoot recognised as Philip Henslowe, patron of this playhouse and attired in his court finery of gold and green. The cart-man and another man, in a wool jerkin, were holding up neatly hung costumes for Sloth's approbation. If he nodded, the article of clothing was put into the cart; if he shook his head, it was put aside.

'And you have not forgot the gilded vizards . . .'

Henslowe's assistant produced a wooden box and lifted the

lid. Sloth looked in, pulled out a golden face mask, then nodded and replaced it.

'They will do well.'

The box was added to the costumes in the cart.

Boltfoot watched in astonishment. What in God's name was going on here?

He looked at the cart-man again. It was no man, but a boyish young woman. Boltfoot tensed. A thought occurred to him: could that be the woman Master Shakespeare sought?

He watched and waited. When half a dozen costumes – men's rich doublets, hats, hose, robes and some armour – had been placed in the cart, Sloth pulled out a large drawstring purse from beneath his capacious doublet. He poured some gold coins into his hand, then held them out and let Henslowe count them. Henslowe seemed satisfied and took the money.

Boltfoot marched forward, dragging his left foot through the sawdust, the stock of his caliver held square into his chest. 'Hold fast. One move, Mr Sloth, and you will die.'

The four people on stage looked at him in shock. Then, like participants in an intricate dance, they began moving apart. The woman trundled the cart sideways. Henslowe and his assistant went wide, then moved forward as though they would encircle Boltfoot. Sloth backed away, towards the shadows beneath the canopy. He was pulling open one of the stage doors used for the players' dramatic exits and entrances.

Boltfoot recalled his master's words: *If you find Sloth, apprehend him. Haul him to Newgate, preferably alive.* Preferably alive. The implication of that was *Bring him in dead if all else fails.*

Boltfoot pulled the trigger.

Chapter 37

THE TOUCHPOWDER FIZZED and smoked, then burnt away. No explosion, no shot. Boltfoot looked at his weapon in dismay and uttered a low oath. This had never happened to him before. It was the poxy tiredness that had caused the error in loading and priming the caliver. He did not have time to reload before they were on him. He slung the gun over his shoulder and drew his cutlass.

Henslowe, unafraid and proud, strode up to him, chest thrust out. 'I know you. You're John Shakespeare's man. What do you think you are doing?'

Boltfoot tried pushing Henslowe aside. He had to catch Sloth. He lurched forward but Henslowe's hand shot out and grabbed his shoulder.

'You were trying to shoot the cardinal! Your gun misfired!'

'I must get him, Mr Henslowe. I beseech you, help me. And that woman—'

'No, God's death, I will not help you! You will not pass. Lend me assistance, Fontley! Bring him down.'

Fontley, who had the litheness and lean muscular body of a tumbler, thrust out a long, well-formed leg behind Boltfoot's knees. With the side of his arm, he pushed backwards against Boltfoot's chest. Boltfoot's lost his balance and his legs buckled. He crumpled backwards to the floor of the stage, his weapons clattering beneath him on the oak boards. Fontley leapt on him and pinioned his arms. Although Boltfoot was a strong, experienced fighter, he was encumbered by his caliver and cutlass. Fontley drew a dagger from his belt and held the tip to Boltfoot's throat. Henslowe stepped forward and eased Boltfoot's caliver from his shoulder.

'I think you have a great deal of explaining to do.'

'Let me up. I must catch Sloth—'

'You are going nowhere. Talk.'

'First hold Sloth, then I will explain all.'

'The cardinal has gone. What is this about?'

Boltfoot groaned in desperation. 'I am Boltfoot Cooper, here on behalf of Mr Shakespeare. This is Queen's business, Mr Henslowe. Ovid Sloth is a wanted man. I have been hunting him and followed him here. I beg of you, hold him.'

'The cardinal wanted? Wanted for what, may I ask?'

'He escaped. I was escorting him to be examined by Sir Robert Cecil and the Council. He escaped at Falmouth.'

'But what has he done? Why were you holding him?'

'He was freed by the Spaniards.' Boltfoot was struggling to think how to explain this. He realised he was making little sense.

'Well, Mr Cooper, you will have to be a great deal more convincing than that. Cardinal Quick is an old acquaintance of mine and has invested a great deal of money in the Rose and various other playhouse ventures. You cannot just go shooting at unarmed men, especially not respectable merchants like Mr Sloth. I fear you will have to answer for your actions in a court of law.'

Boltfoot fought to raise his head. There was no sign of Ovid Sloth, nor of his female companion with the cart. In the distance, he could hear the sound of trumpets blaring and guns being fired as the royal river procession passed through the dangerous narrows of London Bridge. A great cheer rose up.

Boltfoot was shut away in a dark props cupboard, which gave him little room to move and no hope of escape. He found what he took to be a pennant, which he rolled into a pillow. Like a cat, he curled up on the floor, placed his head on the flag and fell asleep. He was woken in the late afternoon by the opening of the door.

Henslowe was there, with the constable. Boltfoot began to repeat his plea that he was on the side of the law and that he was no threat. More than that, he had been grievously injured by those who had assisted in Sloth's escape.

Henslowe listened with interest and some amusement.

'If you cheat the rope, I might ask Mr Alleyn to find you a part in our next play, Mr Cooper, for you have something of the clown about you. The world would love a new Tarleton. He was a short-arsed wreck of a man like you, but he could make princes and paupers weep for mirth. I do believe you would be his equal, for you make *me* laugh.'

'Mr Henslowe, there is no amusement here. Only murder and treason. I must find Ovid Sloth! Mr Shakespeare ordered me to fetch him to Newgate. Why did he take those costumes? If you have doubts, come with me—'

'No, I will not go anywhere with you. As for the costumes, you will have to ask Mr Sloth. He asked for them some few weeks ago, named me a fair price, and so a deal was struck. Such things happen all the time. Great ladies and gentlemen stage entertainments for their great friends. And so I am happy to oblige. No one can afford to keep costumes unused if there is money to be made from them. As for detaining Mr Sloth and taking him to Newgate, I would say that trying to shoot a man is a strange way to arrest him.'

'I feared he was fleeing again, as he has done before.'

Henslowe laughed out loud. 'Cardinal Quick is the slowest creature on earth. He could not escape an earthworm, Mr Cooper. How could he possibly flee from anyone, even one as lame as you?' Henslowe shook his head and turned to the constable. 'He is yours to question, Mr Godfrey. Do with him as you think fit. I will happily testify against him, as will Mr Fontley.'

The constable had a squint eye and a mouth that turned down. His watery eyes looked at Boltfoot in turn, first the left, then the right. 'Are you a good man and true?' he demanded at last.

'Yes, Constable. I am in service to Mr John Shakespeare, an assistant secretary to Sir Robert Cecil. I work for him on behalf of Her Royal Majesty.'

'Then if you are a good man and true, why are you held here under guard?'

'It is an error.'

'In my experience, thieves, vagabonds and murderers are apprehended because they are guilty of crimes. Therefore a man apprehended must be a thief, vagabond or murderer. Which, then, are you – for *you* have been apprehended?'

'I am none of those, I pledge it.'

'Then you have committed some other felony. The chiefest of these are rape, rustling of cattle and treason. Choose your felony, Mr Cooper. The neck will stretch when the noose is about it, whichever you do decide on.'

'I have committed no crime!'

The constable rubbed his neck and stretched it this way and that as though he could feel the rope tightening.

'Why, I do believe there was one went to the Tyburn tree this very morning. Died well, the broadsheet sellers cry. Gave praise to God and the Queen and did beg mercy of the Lord for his manifold sins.'

*

The constable tied Boltfoot's hands with a leash of rope and led him out into the streets of Southwark to the Clink prison, fifty yards away.

'Hold this man, Mr Keeper,' the constable said, pushing Boltfoot forward at the heavy gate. 'He says he is a good man and true, but I say he is a most desperate felon and horse-thief, nor is he to be trusted. Have him brought before the justice in the morning.'

'Have you got sixpence for his keep?'

'He can pay you himself or starve.' The constable handed over Boltfoot's weapons to the keeper. 'Or you may sell these on his behalf. But I say observe him well, for he is most dangerous and ungodly. I wish you good day, Mr Keeper.'

The turnkey's long, grey-flecked beard straggled down to his waist. He tugged at it as he watched the constable march off, then looked at Boltfoot with a morose, puzzled expression. His tongue lolled out like a dog's on a hot day.

'Mr Cooper?'

'Aye, it's me behind these bruises.'

'Trug's arse, Mr Cooper, I know that each honest parishioner must do his duty and serve a turn as constable, but that maggoty son of a whore Godfrey is too much. I say he should be strung up for having the wit of a haddock. A *dead* haddock. He is a night-soil man, to which I think him better suited. Now then, Mr Cooper, what have you done?'

'Nothing. And I need your help. Free me and you will have gold.'

'Sadly, I cannot do that, as you must know.'

'Then get word to Mr Shakespeare for me.'

The first thing Shakespeare saw was a pair of eyes, glowing like fire. Through the cloud of his semi-conscious brain, he tried to look closer and realised that it was nothing but a black mastiff, sitting on its haunches a few yards from him. The dog's ears were pricked and it was alert, watching him closely. The light in the animal's eyes was the flickering reflection of a candle-flame.

He tried to step forward, towards the dog, then realised he could not shift at all, not even his arms. He was tied to a chair. His arms were bound down the sides of the high back and his ankles were fastened to the chair legs. Another rope was wound tightly around his chest, holding him back into the chair. There was a fragrant smell of incense in the air as well as some other smoke. A few feet away stood a small table with three dishes and a cup. He shivered, and realised that he was naked from the waist up.

'The demon awakes.'

He twisted his head at the sound of the voice and a thundering pain made him groan. Now he recalled: he had been clubbed at the stables in Dowgate.

'Where am I?'

'Are you in pain, Mr Shakespeare? Perhaps you would like to take a drink. I will bring you water.'

He could not see her, but he recognised that strange, smoky voice. It was Beatrice Eastley, born Sorrow Gray. She moved across his field of vision. Now she was standing in front of him with her pipe in her mouth, belching forth smoke that seemed to him like the fumes of hell. She picked up the cup from the table and held it out to him. He clenched his jaw tight and averted his lips.

'Drink.' Roughly, she put it to his mouth. He tasted a sip, then drank greedily, but she took the cup away too soon. 'Not too much. Food?'

'No.'

She clutched her arms about her slender body. 'It is cold in here, is it not? And yet outside, the day is warm.'

Her manner of speaking was spindly and curt, very unlike her sister's in Wisbech. He studied her closely. At first sight, at the Countess of Kent's home in Barbican Street, there had been an impression of fresh, faraway innocence in her unblemished skin, yet now he saw a strange, troubling absence in her eyes. She was garbed in a simple dress of dark red, and wore her hair uncovered. She had cut it most unusually short, so that it fell about her face like a helmet. It was the unblinking eyes that unsettled him.

'Release me, Mistress Eastley. This is a treasonous act for which you will hang. Release me and I will protect you.'

She sucked at her pipe.

'In the name of God, you have fallen into a conspiracy that can only help England's enemies!'

'Do not call on God. Call on the serpent. You are his fellow and your body is a temple to his demons.'

'I demand of you, where am I? Why have you brought me here?'

He looked around him now, his foggy eyesight clearing, and saw that he was in some church. A thin light of reds and blues streamed through soaring stained-glass windows. At the end of the nave there was a high altar with an enormous crucifix. But this church did not hold the comfort and tranquillity of God's house.

'To cleanse your body and free your soul, Mr Shakespeare.'

'Is that what Regis Roag told you?'

The name had an instant impact. He saw it in her wide eyes and realised it was the reason he was still alive, the reason his throat had not been ripped open at the Dowgate stables. They needed to know what intelligence he had. Whatever it was they were planning, they needed to be sure it had not been detected.

'What do you know of him?'

'Everything. This conspiracy will fail. You will all go to your doom. Release me. Save yourself.'

There was a pulse in her smooth brow. Her eyes narrowed. Carefully, she put down the beaker of water on a small table near by. Shakespeare saw the glint in her hand as a sailmaker needle slid from her sleeve into her palm. She raised it up and, with a scream that seemed to last a full minute, she plunged it down into his shoulder. The triangular point tore through skin and flesh until it hit bone. Shakespeare gasped with pain and his head arched back. She pulled the needle out, then stabbed it once more into his other shoulder. He gasped again. Blood streamed down his upper arms, chest and back in rivulets, a delta of scarlet, flowing over him.

She breathed heavily. Smoke spewed from her mouth and nostrils as she held the blood-streaked needle in front of his eyes. Her hand was shaking but her eyes were everywhere, as though watching a swarm of butterflies.

'See how they fly, screaming from you? See how your demons fly at my tender touch? We shall cleanse you of your demons. They have claws, but we have God's needle. God is mightier than you, mightier than the demons. You will tell me the truth before you die.'

He was utterly at her mercy. She was raving. And yet his thoughts were with Frank Mills and the rope from which he had failed to save him.

'. . . with this needle I shall pluck them all out like lice. I shall rid you of all your lewd devils. I am God's instrument. At the end, when your body is free, you will thank us, for we will not have let you die in thrall to the beast.'

High in the church rafters, a dazzling phantasm swooped. Shakespeare caught its shadow in the periphery of his vision. Was it angel or demon? He looked up and saw that it was a trapped jay. It landed on a rafter, defecated, then shrieked.

Chapter 38

REGIS ROAG SAT at the front of the heavy draycart, whip in hand. His gaze seemed to be fixed straight ahead on the long dusty road, but he was watching constantly. He wore a cowl to conceal his face and ever-moving eyes, and to hide his fine head of hair. There was little chance of his being seen by anyone who could do him harm, but why take the risk?

The procession straggled for miles: horsemen and wagons as far as a man could see along the road south-west to the Palace of Nonsuch. Many of the wagons were the Queen's own, carrying her immense wardrobe and furnishings. Many more belonged to the hundreds of nobles and others who made up the royal court. Yet more were those of the hangers-on. Wherever the wealthy gathered, they attracted traders, beggars, jugglers and minstrels, just as meat left out will swarm with flies.

Roag's draycart was just one among many, trundling through the county of Surrey. It carried a striped pavilion tent and an array of playhouse costumes and props. His band of men either sat on the back or walked alongside the wagon. No one paid them any heed.

The journey here had been long and arduous, from a notion hatched in England, to the conspiratorial cloisters of southern Spain, and thence to the beaches of Cornwall. When Beatrice had entered his life, spouting her mad, half-formed ideas, he had not been slow to spot the potential.

'With one stroke, we could destroy them all,' she had said. 'Ten minutes of blood in God's name, and England will be saved.'

There was an elegant simplicity to her plan, but he had had to find the right men; he had had to find the right equipment. Her idea would not work without his exquisite attention to detail. Thanks to him, every obstacle had been bypassed or hurdled, every enemy removed. The recruitment of Ovid Sloth, with his terrifying debts and his contacts in England and Spain, had been the master stroke. It had been Sloth who had travelled to Toledo to commission the greatest of metal-workers to create the short, hard steel swords so neatly housed in their toy-like wooden frames.

All that was needed now was the extraction of a little information from a man named John Shakespeare and the way would be clear. Shakespeare was in good hands. The *best* of hands.

In nomine Patris, et Filii, et Spiritus Sancti . . .

The priest at the high altar intoned the words as he made the sign of the cross. He wore the long white gown known as an alb. Over this he wore a purple stole and then the chasuble, a sleeveless mantle.

John Shakespeare sat bound to the chair, unable to move more than his head. He closed his eyes and mouthed the Lord's Prayer, something he had not done for some time.

He could sense Beatrice Eastley behind him, and could smell the smoke of her burning tobacco. The dog's baleful eyes never left him.

Even before the priest turned, Shakespeare knew that it was Ovid Sloth. Englishman, Spaniard, merchant, traitor, priest: a man of many parts. He waddled slowly down the nave and stopped in front of the chair, gazing coldly at the captive.

'How do you know of Regis Roag?'

'He is the son of a king. How should I *not* know someone of such stature?'

'We are not here to make jest. Tell me how you know him. You mentioned such a man at St Michael's Mount, and then you knew him when you saw him. What do you know? How, too, did your man Cooper know where I would be this day?'

'Cooper? What do you know of Cooper?'

'What does he know of me? How did he find me?'

'We know everything about you. We all know of Roag, too, everyone who works for Sir Robert Cecil. Everyone in the office of the Earl of Essex. We knew he was coming to Cornwall. Do you think we would let such an enemy of the state enter the country unnoted?'

Since he had awoken in this malign place, Shakespeare had been thinking a great deal about the nature of Roag's entry into England. He was certain now that he had not come alone, that he had brought a band of mercenaries.

'We know exactly what he is about and whom he brought to England. We have spies aplenty in Seville and Sanlúcar.'

'Ah, yes, Robert Warner. A fine boy, by all accounts. Such a waste.'

'Warner? What are you saying?'

'Oh, I'm sure you know him. *Knew* him.'

'God damn you, Sloth. God damn you all. We know all about you. You will never walk free in England again.'

Sloth recoiled.

'He lies!' Beatrice's voice was a screech that echoed around the high vaulting walls of the old church.

'But he does know Roag. And that concerns me. *How* does he know him? How did Cooper find me?'

'It makes no difference. Regis can be anyone. You have seen him. He can transform himself. You know he can.'

Sloth ground his teeth so that the folds of his face quivered. 'Regis insists we must find out how this man knows his name. Well, we shall discover the truth. Satan cannot withstand the power of God.' He touched the corner of his purple stole to Shakespeare's bleeding shoulder. 'I do not like this man. I did not like him in Cornwall and I do not like him here. He is Satan's creature. He has serpents and clawed minions of the beast in his belly. They must be exorcised. Just as the devil inside the body of England must be cast down into fiery damnation. What are the signs, sister?'

'The chill air. He has no hunger. I see movement beneath the skin. Lesser demons have already flown. It is certain.'

Shakespeare struggled against the ropes. 'This is not about God. This is about temporal power. You are no man of God, Sloth – and you, Beatrice Eastley, are nothing but an assassin. You killed the old nun, Sister Michael. I had thought she was one of you. Did she not approve of your vile designs? Did you fear she would betray you?'

Sloth, who was clutching a crucifix, made the sign of the cross on his own breast, then on the breast, brow and lips of Shakespeare, who violently averted his face from the perverse ritual.

'*Oremus oratio . . .*'

Was this the way it had started for Loake and Trott and Friday? Did this woman and this man really believe in this gibberish, or was it some twisted entertainment, the way a child pulls off the wings of a fly, one by one?

'*Deus cui proprium est misereri semper et parcere: suscipe deprecationem nostram . . .* God who is ever merciful and forgiving, accept our prayer that this your servant, bound by the bonds of sin, may be granted pardon by your loving kindness.'

And so it went on. Verse after verse of the Latin rite of exorcism. Sloth called on God to crush the serpent, to cast him back down to hell where he belonged, having once fallen. He commanded Satan to be gone, to depart in fear with all his demons and servants, all this interspersed with flinging of holy water and signs of the cross.

All the while Beatrice watched Shakespeare intently, examining his torso and throat for signs of unholy creatures crawling within. Every so often, as if to keep him awake, she stabbed him with the needle in a different part of his body, whenever she believed she saw a clawed demon crawling beneath the skin. Even as he shuddered under the desperate and never-ending onslaught, Shakespeare could not help but think of the fishers in the fens, stabbing at the black water with their glaives in the hope of an eel. Like them, she was fishing . . .

As time wore on, Beatrice became more and more frantic and began foaming at the mouth. She made a guttural sound from her throat, her voice a growl, lower than a dog's, more disturbing than a wild beast's roar.

Suddenly a small cat appeared at the end of the nave, just inside the church door. Beatrice screamed, 'There it is! That is his kitling. Kill it, Sloth. Kill it!'

Looking about her, she saw a pile of wood lying close to the church wall. She picked up a long, crooked stick and began chasing the animal. Cornered, it bared its fangs and hissed at her. She lashed out at it, but the cat was too quick and dived for cover behind the lectern. The mastiff strained at its leash and barked.

'You see,' Shakespeare said to Sloth, 'she is insane. She is leading you all down to hell with this madness. Set me free and make your escape while there is still time. Make your way to Spain in safety.'

Sloth took a small box from beneath the folds of his gowns. He opened the lid and took out something brown and leathery. 'Light the brimstone, sister.'

Above them, the trapped jay flew about in panic, a flash of brilliance as it drove onwards from rafter to rafter, looking for its way out. Finally, as if summoning all its might, it flew for the light and collided with the ancient stained glass at speed. The impact must have stunned it, or broken its neck. It fell, spiralling black and grey and white, to the flagstone floor of the church and did not move.

Beatrice was on her knees stabbing at the cat, which was well concealed in the space beneath the lectern. Sloth's words broke her frenzy. She turned, still on hands and knees. Rising to her feet, she lit a taper from the altar candle and held it to one of the dishes on the table. After a while there was a sizzle and a burst of acrid smoke. Beatrice handed the dish to Sloth. He made the sign of the cross over it, then held it beneath Shakespeare's nose. Much as he wished to show no emotion, no physical distress or weakness to these people, the pungent fumes made him gag and choke. He gasped and coughed, using all his energy trying not to vomit.

'It is a demon in his throat, suffocating.' Ovid Sloth thrust forward the leathery brown object that he had taken from his box, pushing it into Shakespeare's mouth. Shakespeare gasped with shock. 'Oh, see how Father Sherwin's bone burns the beast. Oh, surely this relic is God's most potent weapon.'

Sherwin? Shakespeare recalled the name from many years ago. There had been a priest named Ralph Sherwin who died, butchered, on the scaffold along with Edmund Campion. Shakespeare could hold back no longer. He was sick, weakening fast, and knew he could not take much more before the blood loss made him slip into unconsciousness and death.

Beatrice thrust the sailmaker needle into Shakespeare's left leg. This time the surprise made him cry out.

'It is the devil that screams,' she shrieked. 'I hear the devil! He cannot last long. Baptise him, Mr Sloth, baptise the sinner, for that will burn the devil most wonderfully.'

Taking a pinch of salt from another dish, Sloth put it on to Shakespeare's tight-clenched lips and rubbed it in, as though coating a piece of meat. He wet his own fingers with the obscene dribble of his own mouth and smeared it on to his captive's eyes and lips. Then, from a little vial, he poured oil on Shakespeare's mouth and nose.

'*Vade retro satana*,' he intoned. '*Vade retro satana*. Begone, Satan. Return whence you came!' He held Shakespeare's head between his soft, grub-like hands and twisted it so that he spoke directly into his ear. 'Now tell me, John Shakespeare. Your life is ebbing. Tell me how you know of Roag. Do this and your family will live, though you die.'

The needle went in again, this time deep into his right thigh. Blood spat out on to the long white gown that Sloth wore beneath the chasuble and purple stole. Shakespeare did not even recoil this time. His body was growing colder, his life seeping from him like water through a colander. The surface of his body was now cloaked in blood. He had lost count of the times he had been stabbed. Soon, he knew, the mortal stroke would come: the needle through the jugular – if he survived that long.

Look after the little ones, O Lord.

He knew he could rely on Jane and Boltfoot, Ursula and Andrew, but he prayed that Sir Robert Cecil would watch over them, too. He closed his eyes. A vision came to him of his late wife, Catherine. Her dark waves of hair were tinged with a golden aureole, her eyes warm and serious, beckoning him, soothing him. The vision brought peace and acceptance, but faded like a sand picture under the incoming tide, only to be replaced by the carnal eyes of Lucia Trevail, beseeching him to live and join her in pleasure. But when he opened his eyes again they met the merciless gaze of Ovid Sloth and Beatrice Eastley, both staring at him with cold, deadly passion. They had no power over him.

Please God, he would be with Catherine soon.

Chapter 39

JANE COOPER AND Ursula Dancer hitched up their skirts and ran from the Cecil mansion in the Strand into the city streets. By the time they reached the bridge, Jane was out of breath and struggling to keep up. They both slowed to a brisk walk then began running again. They did not speak to one another as they manoeuvred their way through the late afternoon crowds down the lane between the houses that stood astride the great bridge. They did not notice the water rushing beneath.

At the south side of the bridge, they slowed to a walk again and caught their breath as they turned right, then began running once more, looking about them as they went.

Finally, they reached Clink Street and the dark oak door that held the gaol against escape or unwanted visitors. Both women leant against the wall, doubled over, exhausted by the two-mile race through waste-strewn streets, fighting their way past carts and traders.

'I thought my heart would pigging burst!'

Jane nodded at Ursula. Still gasping for breath, she banged on the door. From within, they heard slow footfalls and the clanking of keys. The turnkey pulled the door ajar a few inches and stared at them. Seeing two comely women, he opened it wider.

'How may I help you, fine ladies?'

He pulled back his shoulders, lifted his chin and smoothed his long bird's-nest beard as though that would somehow make him an attractive proposition. He licked his lips, leaving his tongue lolling out between his teeth.

'We want Boltfoot,' Jane said. 'Hand him over.'

'Boltfoot . . . Boltfoot?'

Jane was out of all patience. Mr Shakespeare was missing; their lives had been torn apart by the threat to the children, and the need to leave home and lodge in Sir Robert Cecil's house; and now Boltfoot was in gaol. Anger was barely known to her, but now it erupted like a blast of powder.

'Boltfoot Cooper. My cripple of a husband. Give him to me or you will suffer consequences the like of which you have never dreamt.'

The turnkey, taken aback by the sudden squall, shrank into the gaol, but Jane and Ursula were already inside before he could close the door on them.

'We have no one of that name.' He drew his short sword, which suddenly emboldened him. 'Think I'm frit of two drabs, do you?'

Ursula lunged at him and held him by the throat with one hand, while Jane pushed down on his sword arm. 'Where is he? Bring us to him or I'll have your balls for offal.'

Finding strength she did not know she had, Jane wrenched the sword from his grasp and held it out in front of her, pointing at him, its tip quivering. The turnkey tried to cry out but Ursula slammed her hand into his mouth.

'Can you read, Mr Keeper?' Jane said. 'We have with us a letter from Sir Robert Cecil, ordering the release of my husband. If he is not freed straightway into my custody, you will be brought before Star Chamber for impeaching the honour of Mr Cooper's person.'

She was not sure where the nonsensical words came from, nor the lie about the letter, but the keeper put up his hand.

'Very well, I will take you to him. But leave me be, ladies, I beg you.'

'Then take us to him. And if he's caught lice in this filthy place, I will make a bonfire of your stinking whiskers.'

Holding the sword at his back, they followed him through the cramped bowels of the ancient gaol. The other turnkeys stood back, trying to conceal their grins as their master passed them at the mercy of two women. The prisoners behind bars and in chains were not so restrained, openly laughing and jeering.

Boltfoot was standing with his arms folded in the centre of a small cell in which thirty men were crowded, some of them shackled and manacled. He had been here half a day or more, becoming more and more worried and frustrated as the hours passed. As soon as the cell door was opened, he stepped forward and removed the sword from Jane's hand.

'What is this, mistress? Why do you hold the keeper at swordpoint? Do you wish to be hanged?'

'He said you weren't here, Boltfoot. Anyway, he'll say nothing. The justice and jury would laugh so much that he was overpowered by women that he'd never be able to show his face in Southwark again.'

'He wanted garnish, that's all. It's how he lives, for no one else pays him for this dirty job he does.' Boltfoot handed the sword back to the keeper and apologised to him. 'You'll have your half a crown. Now hand me my cutlass and caliver and let me out of here.'

The tide was coming in, so they took the tilt-boat back to the Strand from St Mary Overy waterstairs. As they talked,

Boltfoot became increasingly alarmed to hear that there was no word from Mr Shakespeare.

'We have not seen him since you and he were together at Cecil House, which is more than twenty-four hours since,' Jane said. 'Sir Robert's steward sent messages to the palace at Greenwich, but now I am told they have all gone, headed for Nonsuch, so I don't know where he is.'

Boltfoot didn't like it. He badly needed to impart his new-discovered knowledge about Ovid Sloth and the playhouse costumes to his master. Should he ride for Nonsuch in Surrey or wait here? At least at Nonsuch he might be able to speak with Cecil or one of his assistants, even if Mr Shakespeare was not there.

In the event, the decision was made for him. As they arrived at Cecil's mansion, the door was opened by a servant who sighed with relief as he ushered them in. 'Thank the Lord you are here, Mr Cooper. You have a visitor.'

Boltfoot peered into the gloom of the hall beyond the door and saw a face from another place, from the watery wilderness of the Cambridgeshire fens. What in God's name was Paul Hooft doing here?

Pennants fluttered in the warm breeze of evening. Tents and pavilions of all shapes, sizes and patterns spread across the great park outside Nonsuch Palace. This was where many minor courtiers, administrators and other lesser mortals would spend their nights while the Queen and her favourites were in residence at the overcrowded palace. Even the city of tents had its hierarchy. The larger, grander pavilions were reserved for nobles and stood nearest the walls of the dazzling palace. Then came the senior officers of law, the bishops and government functionaries, followed by the gentry. And so it went on until, some quarter-mile from the palace, were to be found servants, cooks and the lower sort such as players and minstrels.

Hundreds of soldiers were in attendance, but they kept themselves apart. Many were stationed at the palace gates and inside its walls, for the Privy Council had ordered extreme security for this visit. The soldiers had their own camps, over-looking the city of tents, offering menace and protection at the same time.

The Ladies' Players were together in a large, striped pavilion that was in great need of repair, its canvas dirty and full of holes. Anyone stumbling into this tent in error would apolo-gise and stumble out again without a second thought. This was just another band of players, here by royal command.

Regis Roag held the book and directed his men. Suddenly he put up his hand. 'No! No! No! No! No!' He threatened to fling the pages to the ground, but thought better of it and smiled at his men like an indulgent father. His gaze alighted on Winnow. 'Have you lost all your wit, Dick?'

Winnow glared at him. Did these men know that Roag was leading them to certain death? He said nothing, merely turned his shoulder away.

Roag's voice did not betray his anger, only urgency. 'We are so close. This is about surprise and suddenness. If you do not convince, there will be no shock! Without it, we will fail.'

They all knew their parts, for they had been rehearsing since receiving the book. The Fitzgerald brothers, Hugh and Seamus, spoke with ease; they were natural players. Even the hirelings Ratbane and Paget, both of whom had non-speaking roles, were adequate. And what they lacked in style on stage, they more than made up for in their brutal skill with the short sword. But that was another rehearsal, one that had been perfected elsewhere.

Only the matters of John Shakespeare and Dick Winnow

caused Roag anxiety. No word had come yet from Beatrice. It was certain that Cecil's intelligencer knew his face from Cornwall – but how did he come by his name? They had never met, to his knowledge; and surely his brother William could not have made the connection. The case of Winnow was troubling, too. Until they sailed from Sanlúcar de Barrameda, he had seemed likely to be the strongest and most convincing member of the company. Since then, however, he had worried Roag; his heavy silences and truculence told of a man not to be trusted.

'When you enter, you fall to your knees in front of the Queen. Both knees, Dick, and you bow your head until your forelock almost touches the floor. This must be done with conviction. Is that clear?'

What was clear to Winnow was that he no longer wished to be part of this enterprise. It was not death that worried him, for it was in the cause of God. It was the thought of dying alongside Regis Roag that he could not stomach. He drew his short sword. It was housed in a slim wooden sheath that looked like a play-actor's prop sword. With cold anger, he thrust it into the ground and left it quivering there. Without a word, he strode from the tent out into the fresh air.

Roag cursed beneath his breath. Winnow was a danger to them all. With sun-bright clarity he realised he would have to do without Dick . . . and there *was* a way. He signalled to Ratbane and Paget, and spoke to them quietly.

'Go after Winnow. Take him to the river and send him downstream. I do not wish to see him again.'

He watched them go. Two sullen, brutish men, the sort who did the bidding of their masters with a will; the kind of men who in a past century would have slit the throats of Frenchmen bogged down in a muddy field at Agincourt without blinking. Slaughterhouse men. Just the men he needed. He would have dealt with Winnow himself, but he had other matters to attend to in an abandoned plague parish church a few miles north of this place.

Winnow ran for his life. He knew that Ratbane and Paget would be sent after him. He ran deep into the woods. At last he came to an area of dense bracken and sank into it, certain that he must be invisible. He turned on his back and looked up at the canopy of leaves, panting heavily, like a dog in summer. He would wait there all night, and survive.

Shakespeare was barely conscious. His head, the only part of him not coated in gore, was slumped on to his bloody chest. His breathing was shallow and rasping. His lips moved and he spoke a single word. *Live.* That was all. That was all he had left. *Live.* He had no idea whether the word was in his head or could be heard.

Sloth wrenched his head up by the hair. 'What do they know about Roag?'

'Everything,' Shakespeare said again, his voice faint and distant.

All he knew was that this man and this woman were all over him, crawling across him like clawed, frenzied reptiles, killing him bit by bit. Picking away at his body, scraping at his very soul.

'What, specifically? If you know the plot, explain it to me and I will finish you with a sword-thrust and your children will be saved.'

Somewhere, on a distant portion of his body, he felt the stabbing of a needle. He no longer even recoiled at the pain.

'He is full of demons, so full. They are without number.'

Beatrice was on the floor, on her knees, clutching at him with her long, narrow fingers, scratching the needle point along his skin until she thought she saw a demon, and then stabbing.

'He is alive with the creatures. I hear them talking to me.' She foamed and shrieked as she spoke. 'They cry out their names: Pippin, Maho, Modu and Soforce. These are the captains. They have under-demons each, numbering three hundred. I stab them and they growl and wriggle and laugh like girls. Except Soforce, which does not laugh. Why do they not flee? Even the lesser devils, Hilco, Smolkin, Hillio, Hiaclito, Frateretto, Hobberdidance and Tocobatto seem not afeared. Father Sloth, Father Sloth . . . give him more brimstone.'

Sloth was not listening. His face was so close to Shakespeare's that he was like a bear, open-mouthed, preparing to devour a piece of flesh from its prey.

'I will suck the truth from you. Speak, or be for ever cursed. Speak or your seed will die with you.'

Beatrice scratched her nails across the flagstone floor. 'Molkin, Wilkin, Lustie Dickie, Nurre, Killicocam and Helcmodon. But Maho is the tyrant. If we can burn Maho, then all will flee. And so I prick here . . .'

She stabbed again, in the sole of his foot.

Boltfoot Cooper stood inside the door to the little church with uncomprehending eyes. At his side was the slender young figure of Paul Hooft. Like Boltfoot, his blue eyes were wide in disbelief and horror.

'Have they killed him, Mr Cooper?'

Before them, in the centre of the nave, a blood-drenched figure sat, bound to a chair. It was impossible to tell who it was, or even if it was human. A large man, swathed in ecclesiastical robes, was almost on top of the figure, enveloping it. A woman had curled herself around his legs. The whole horrible tableau moved and squirmed like grubs in a fisherman's pot.

'I don't know, Mr Hooft. I pray he is alive. But I know this: it is time to put an end to this ungodly degradation.'

They had tethered their horses in the woods, then crept to the church. Pistols drawn and loaded, they had pushed open the door, unsure whom they would find, or how many. But there was no need for such caution. Beatrice Eastley and Ovid Sloth were too far gone in their lethal passion to notice the newcomers. Only the leashed dog saw them, wagging its tail and whimpering like a puppy.

Boltfoot limped forward and dragged Sloth off. He seemed surprised but did not resist. There was blood on his face, around his mouth. He looked at Boltfoot with recognition but no understanding. Boltfoot removed his weapons, then pushed him to the floor. Sloth tried to get up, but Boltfoot turned him over on to his front and placed a booted foot on his back.

Hooft pulled Beatrice away with surprising tenderness. She stood before him, shivering, full of loathing, but also triumphant. 'Fly, Maho, fly down to the depths. You are conquered! Go to your master in hell.'

'I am Paul. Do you not remember? You were to have been my wife.'

'Your devil's grease cloaks you in human form, Maho, but you do not deceive me. I escaped from you before. You will not snare me again. I am God's instrument now and I hold dominion over you and all your worms.'

Hooft gazed at her with a mixture of sadness and disgust, then turned to Boltfoot and raised his hands in a gesture of hopelessness. 'Look what the popish beasts have done to my bride, Mr Cooper.'

Boltfoot pulled her arm roughly and tried to wrench her down beside Sloth. 'Help me get her on the ground, Mr Hooft, then train the pistols on them.' He had a coil of cord slung around his body. He removed it and handed it to Hooft. 'Bind them tight. If they try to escape, shoot them. I must look to Mr Shakespeare.'

He took his dagger from his belt and began to cut the ropes that bound his master, all the time speaking to him, seeking some response.

'Can you hear me? All will be well now.'

He wiped the blood from Shakespeare's mouth and tried to give him a drink from his water bottle, but there was no response. He cupped his hand and poured a little water into it, then dripped some on to his master's lips.

He tried to decide what to do. They were four miles south-west of London, a third of the way to the Palace of Nonsuch. Mr Shakespeare was alive, but he was in a very bad way. He could not withstand a ride back to London, strapped across the back of a horse. This desolate ruin of a church stood in the middle of a field. The only other house they had seen in the vicinity was a farmhouse, half a mile away. That was their only hope.

'Are they bound, Mr Hooft?'

'Indeed.'

'Then bring the horses. We must get Mr Shakespeare away from this place. I will ride ahead and you can follow with these two fiends on leashes. We must trust there will be a barn where we can hold them.'

While Hooft went for their mounts, Boltfoot cut strips of cloth from Sloth's robes and, soaking them in water, cleaned as much blood as he could from Shakespeare's torso. Where the bleeding was not already clotting, he staunched the flow. There were so many needle wounds, so much blood.

Chapter 40

THE FARMWIFE WAS tall and strong, with power enough to restrain a struggling hog at gelding time. Though Shakespeare was six foot and well built, she took him in her arms and carried him like a child into the rambling old house, through to her own chamber. There she placed him on the large bed.

While Boltfoot and her children looked on, she began to tend to Shakespeare, cleaning and dressing the wounds with clean linen. After a while she turned to Boltfoot.

'Best thing you could do would be to fetch a physician, if you know one.'

'Is there one near here?'

'Not that you'd want to let loose on your master.'

Simon Forman was lying on his back, snoring and dreaming. He was always prone to vivid dreams, which he would recall and write down in the morning while he partook of his breakfast meat and milk. In this dream, Janey came to him with Alice Blague, the dean's lusty wife.

Both were wearing smocks of white linen and black shoes. About their hair, they had coronets of pearls. Both lifted their skirts and demanded he perform his duty as a man with them. Both wished to be first. They told him that if he chose correctly, something very good would occur; if he chose wrongly, then evil would befall him. As he looked from one to the other, trying to decide, their faces elongated like smithy's hammers and their white smocks turned black and became the handles. Giant fists seized them and began to pound him.

Suddenly he awoke. There *was* a hammering. Someone was beating at the front door of his house, in the middle of the night.

'Boy!' he shouted, but nothing would rouse apprentice Braddedge from his slumbers. Groaning, Forman slid from the bed and tripped downstairs in his nightgown.

'Who is there?' he called out through the heavily locked door.

'Boltfoot Cooper, Mr Shakespeare's servant.'

Cooper? Forman tensed at the name. Jane Cooper's husband. Had Cooper found out that his wife had been here? Did he plan violent retribution?

'What do you want, Mr Cooper? You have woken me. It is exceeding late at night, sir.'

'In God's name let me in and I will tell you!'

'Nothing untoward happened, I will swear as much on the Bible.'

'What? Open the door or I will break it down. My master is badly injured. He needs you.'

Forman scratched his balls and ran his fingers through his tangled hair, then, steeling himself for possible onslaught, opened the door. A squat, vaguely familiar man stood before him, speckled with blood and dust.

'Come in, Mr Cooper. You had better tell me what this is about.'

'I will tell you while you clothe yourself. There is no time to lose.'

*

They rode together through the night. A half-moon in a cloud-less sky lit their way along the well-worn track through the fields towards the wealthy parishes of Clapham and Tooting. Forman had explained to Cooper that he might not be the right man, that he had no experience of surgery or wounds.

'You're all there is, so you are coming with me,' Boltfoot had replied.

Forman accepted the order and carefully packed a bag of everything he believed he might need. In truth, he felt nervous, but excited. Usually people came to him with commonplace complaints like gout, difficult pregnancies, melancholia and afflictions of the skin. At the worst, they might consult him about the palsy. Often they begged charts to know the chances of a marriage succeeding or love philtres to help gain a suitor's interest. But no one had ever called him out to attend a badly injured man.

Dawn was still some way off by the time they arrived. The house was in darkness. That had been Boltfoot's suggestion. If anyone came looking for Sloth or the girl, they would head straight for a house where the lights burnt.

Boltfoot wondered, not for the first time, about Paul Hooft's part in all this. The Dutchman said he had come to London looking for John Shakespeare, to press his case once more for subsidies to drain the fens. He had gone to his house in Dowgate and had seen him being attacked. Unsure what to do, he had followed the assailants out into the countryside to an old church. Unarmed and unused to the area, he had returned to London to seek help and had found Boltfoot. He did not explain how.

The tale did not ring true, but that did not concern Boltfoot for the present. He had fetched weapons for Hooft and had ridden with him to the church. All discrepancies in the Dutchman's story would be a matter for Mr Shakespeare to investigate when he had recovered. For the moment, Boltfoot was simply glad that Hooft had come to him with the information concerning Mr Shakespeare's abduction.

'Come in, come in,' the farmer's wife said in a low voice to Boltfoot and Forman. 'I would beseech you to be as quiet as possible.'

'Is he still alive?'

She nodded with a sombre smile. 'His breathing is more regular. He has lost much blood and his pulse is weak. I have fed him sips of water as he would take them and I have bandaged him as well as I could. But I have never seen a man in such a state, sir.'

'Take me to him,' Forman said.

As the physician followed the woman, a widow, through to her chamber, Boltfoot hung back with Hooft. 'What of our captives?'

'I have bound them tight and gagged them so they do not cry out.'

'Has anyone been to the church, to your knowledge?'

Hooft lowered his voice. 'I heard a horse and went over in that direction, as silently as I could. I saw a lantern light so I did not go too close. Whoever it was did not stay long.'

'How many?'

'One horseman. He let the mastiff loose. I think he was hoping it would lead him to his confederates and I confess I was terrified it would come straight for me, but it ran off into the woods and did not return. The horseman tried to follow it, but then gave up and went back to the church. He waited there ten minutes or so and finally rode off. I have never held a pistol so tight, Mr Cooper, fearing he would come here.'

'Did you see his face?'

'No. He was too far away.'

'Which way did he go?'

'It seemed south, but I am not familiar with this land, so I could not say that for certain.' As if reading Boltfoot's thoughts, he added, 'The mistress of the house has put out beer and some food for us in the kitchen.'

Boltfoot smiled. Yes, beer would be most welcome.

As he followed Hooft through to the kitchen, he wondered again about Simon Forman. *Nothing untoward happened*, he had said. What did he mean by that? Well, it was of no import. Beer and a pipe of tobacco were the vital things right now. And then, when the sun came up, they would transport Sloth and Miss Eastley to Newgate. But what most concerned Boltfoot was the intelligence he needed to impart to Mr Shakespeare: the connection between Ovid Sloth and Mr Henslowe at the Rose playhouse. He needed to tell him what he had seen, and quickly.

In Regis Roag's head, the words of Richard of Gloucester spun around like the sails on a mill. *I can smile and murder while I smile*. What had happened? The church floor by the chair was coated in gore and yet there was no sign of them. Had Beatrice and Sloth been disturbed in their work? Had they fled with their captive? If so, where? Or worse, had they been discovered?

He was halfway to Nonsuch when he reined in his horse; he had to go back to the church. He should have looked close by. There must be a house or a barn in the vicinity. He wheeled the horse's head around and set off.

Helped by the bright half-moon, the ride took him an hour. Tethering the horse at the church, he took another look around and examined the ropes that had been left around the chair. The ends had been cut, not untied. Why would Beatrice or Sloth have done such a thing? And why had they not taken the dog? This had to be the work of someone else.

He walked out of the church and gazed into the silvery

gloom. In the distance he saw the outline of some buildings, probably a farmhouse and barns. When he was here before, he hadn't noticed them. But now, the roofs were visible against the sky.

Leaving the horse, he walked at a steady pace across the fields. As he drew near, he saw that the farmhouse was in darkness. He moved on, then stopped. Was that the flicker of a candle against a window? For a moment it was there, then it was gone. Had it been his imagination or some reflection on the leaded pane of the window? No, it was a candle.

He drew his pistol from his belt. It was loaded.

Boltfoot was on edge. He did not believe they were safe; the house was too exposed and too obvious. He should never have brought Mr Shakespeare here, but there had been no alternative. He struck a light with his tinderbox, put taper to his pipe and drew deeply of the fragrant New World tobacco. Instantly, he snuffed the taper. That had been a mistake. Anyone out there might have seen the light.

He glanced out of the window. All he saw was moon shadows. It could not be long now until dawn, when they could fetch assistance. He wondered again about Hooft and began to think he understood him; he was out at the barn, standing just outside the door, listening out for the breathing of the woman he still loved.

Roag saw the face at the window. He could not recognise it from this distance, but it confirmed that someone was there and awake. It was possible, of course, that the farmer or his wife was rising, but it was possible, too, that his quarry was there.

He moved forward, more stealthily now. If Beatrice and Sloth were in the house, they would not be alone and they might not be in control. He steeled himself.

Remember your heritage; you are the son of a king.

As he came within fifty yards of the house, he saw movement at the side and stopped to watch. A man was walking from the large byre towards the house. From the shade of a clump of trees, he peered into the gloom. It was no one he knew. Perhaps it was the farmer, starting his day's work, or maybe he had been up all night, calving.

When the man had gone into the house, Roag crouched down and ran across the open ground to the barn. A dog barked, but he ignored it and pushed on. If these were simple farm folk, they would have no defence against him; if they were his enemies, he had the advantage of surprise. Either way, he would blow them away.

The door to the barn was padlocked. From inside, he heard movement. He called out softly and heard a muffled grunt. He called again a little louder and the grunt came again, panicky. Someone was in there, unable to respond.

Crouching double, he crept around the barn, looking for some other way in, or an open window, but the barn was made of brick and was sealed solid. Pushing the pistol back into his belt, he slipped the sailmaker from the pocket inside his sleeve into his hand and worked it into the keyhole. This was a trick he had learnt years ago from one of his mother's seamsters, a man who had once been apprenticed to a locksmith. His fingers were steady. He stood still, moving the needle about, feeling for the way the padlock was made up. He smiled. It was simple. This lock was made by fools, for fools. A firm twist of the needle and the bolt sprang open.

Silently, he placed it on the ground, replaced the needle in his sleeve, then took out his pistol again and opened the door. Two shapes lay on the floor in front of him. He could sense their movement without seeing them. They were live bodies, bound.

Roag knelt and tore the gag from Beatrice's mouth. She gasped for air.

'What has happened here?'

'Unbind me, Regis, I beg you.'

'What did you discover from Shakespeare? How much do they know?'

'We discovered nothing. He would not speak. He is dead. There were too many demons.'

'Is it safe? Can we proceed?'

'I beg you, Regis, I do not know. His body was a very city to the devil's spawn.'

Roag stared at her. If Shakespeare was dead, they must still take their chance, even though it meant the death of them all. He had to do this. He was born with teeth, which plainly signified that he should snarl and bite and play the dog. And if the dog must be whipped, so be it. But there would be many others who would be bitten along the way. They would die, every one of them, all those who denied his royal blood.

His voice softened. 'Tell me what has happened, Beatrice. Who is in the house?'

The bedchamber where Shakespeare lay was at the back. The windows were shuttered to keep in the light of the single candle by which Dr Forman worked.

At last he arched his aching back and sighed.

'Well, Mr Shakespeare, you will live. You are most fortunate for, as far as I can tell, none of the wounds punctured a vital organ or artery.'

Forman was talking to himself. Shakespeare did not make a sound. His eyes were closed and his breathing was steady. His upper body and legs were bandaged, and Forman had dripped a vial of herb essence into his mouth to aid sleep, nothing more.

Boltfoot knocked at the door.

Forman nodded to him. 'All's well, Mr Cooper. Keep these wounds bandaged with clean linen. Ensure that water is boiled and allowed to cool before you wash him. Do you understand?'

'Aye. How long will he be like this?'

'With sleep, plenty of clean water to drink and nourishment, he will build up very soon, though he may be weak and in pain for a day or two.'

'But when can I talk to him? I have information that I must impart to him. Can he be woken now?'

'No. He must have rest.'

'How long, Dr Forman?'

'Eight hours, seven at best. Sit with him and see when he wakes. Do not expect too much, though. I will leave you now. Stay here until he is strong.'

'No, *you* stay here. I will need you if anything goes wrong.'

Forman laughed. 'Mr Cooper, I have work to do. People have appointments; they will be coming to see me.'

Perhaps even your wife.

Boltfoot put his hand on the hilt of his cutlass. 'Stay. You will be well paid. Whatever you would earn this day, we will double it.'

Forman had not survived to the age of forty or more by tangling with piratical men with calivers slung over their backs and glittering steel blades at their waists.

He nodded. 'Very well,' he said. 'But I, too, will need nourishment. If the farmwife is up, please ask her to bring me food and ale.'

As Roag took Beatrice in his arms, she sank on to his chest and clung to him as though he would suckle her. Her short hair was wild, as were the shivers of her body. He looked past her in the emerging light to the dark, squirming bulk of Ovid Sloth. They had the play, they had the costumes, they had the props, they had the way in. Sloth was nothing but a risk, too visible and too slow to carry away. How would he cope under torture in the Tower? Not well. Not well at all. He would tell everything he knew at the mere sight of the iron tools in the burning cresset. The sailmaker needle, Roag's most precious jewel, slid down once more from his sleeve.

He wrenched Beatrice away and pushed her sprawling into a heap of hay. She tried to crawl back to him, but he shook his head and put the needle to his lips to hush her. Her eyes widened and she shied away from him into the corner. She clutched her hands about her knees and watched as he descended on the whale-like bulk of Ovid Sloth, clothed in blood-stained tatters. Cradling the bulbous head in his left arm, he quested around the enormous throat with the right hand until he felt the pulsing throb of the jugular. Sloth struggled, but he was bound tight. Roag kissed his sweating bald pate, then jabbed with the sailmaker and gasped with pleasure as the blood seeped over his fingers. Such were the powers of a king. The power of life and death.

Ego sum rex. Ego sum Deus. The devil's words. *I am king. I am God.* He waited, holding the bucking body firm against his chest, while the blood drained into the earth.

He stood up and held out his hand to Beatrice. Her eyes glowed in the new light of dawn.

Chapter 41

THEY WERE ALL up and out by ten o'clock in the morning, meeting in the inner courtyard of Nonsuch Palace. The statue of the Queen's father, Henry, dazzled in the sunlight and the exquisite white plaster reliefs on the walls seemed to dance between rows of ornate red brickwork.

'Well met, sweetings,' said Lady Susan, the Countess of Kent, kissing the other three on the cheek. 'Let us venture out and visit our little troupe of players, to see that they are arrived safe and are well rehearsed.'

She took Lucia Trevail's arm, while Emilia Lanier linked arms with the Countess of Cumberland. As they walked forth, past the fountain and on to the outer court, and then through the majestic gatehouse to the parkland beyond, they knew that they cut a formidable dash. Four independent and proud women, the School of Day, in gowns of bright silk and worsted, their hair teased up and held with pins with diamond and pearl ornament, beneath small hats of felt. Each carried a fan and walked slowly so that all might gaze on them and admire them. Courtiers bowed low and swept their hats in great arcs by way of salute.

'Why, we might be a gaggle of girls on our way to the schoolroom,' Lucia Trevail said.

Emilia gazed at the array of armour and halberds on display

both inside and outside the palace walls. 'There are a great many soldiers about. Is there to be a tilt?'

'There is some scare, my dear,' the Countess of Cumberland said.

She might not have been as fetching as her three companions, but she was confident that her gown of cloth of gold and her long necklaces of rubies and pearls were a match for any of them.

'Not that I am complaining. You may send one or two handsome soldiers to *my* room tonight.'

'And what, may I ask, *is* this fright?' Lucia said. 'Why do they never tell us these things?'

Lady Susan glanced at Lucia with a questioning eyebrow and half a smile. 'They think such things beneath the feminine sex, which must bewilder Her Majesty, who is more learned than any man. But whatever it is, I would not be surprised if it involves the bold Mr Shakespeare in some way. What say you, Lucia? You know the delightful Mr Shakespeare well, I believe. Or is that mere tittle-tattle?'

Lucia tilted her chin and looked her straight in the eye. 'Do I detect a little envy, Susan?'

'What are you suggesting? I have a fine man-at-arms of my own. There is no want of a hard man in *my* bed. But one thing is certain. Mr Shakespeare is most keen to discover the whereabouts of our erstwhile companion Beatrice. I have received word that a squadron of men appeared at my house in Barbican Street late at night, wishing to apprehend her, but of course she was not there. Now, where is this grand pavilion? Where are our players? Let us see if they will do us proud. Mr Sloth has promised much. It is time to hold him to account.'

Roag spotted the four women approaching down an avenue of young oaks and grasped Beatrice by the arm.

'Slip away. Take off your vizard, go into the tent and put a coif about your hair. Then walk into the woods, keep your face down, and stay there, out of sight. Do not come back for an hour.' He pushed her in the back. 'Go . . .'

Without a word, she nodded and stepped into the tent.

As the women came closer, Roag pulled off his own golden mask and strode towards them, smiling broadly and extending his arms in welcome.

'Ah, the charming Mr Roag,' the Countess of Kent said as he bowed low before her and kissed her hand.

'Lady Susan, it is my pleasure to welcome you to our humble pavilion. And you, my Lady Trevail, Lady Cumberland and Mistress Lanier.' He kissed all their hands in turn. 'Might I offer you some refreshment? We have nothing but good English ale, I am afraid, but it is enough to quench a thirst.'

'I think we shall forgo the ale. We are here only to ensure that you are arrived as promised and that the masque is prepared for this evening's festivities, Mr Roag, nothing more. Is Mr Sloth not here? I had expected to see him, for he has done much work in preparing the entertainment.'

Roag affected a sigh. 'Poor Mr Sloth. He is indisposed with a summer sweat. And you are correct, Lady Trevail, we could not have done without him. However, all is now in place. I believe we are to perform when the hour strikes eight or thereabouts – sometime between the jesters and the banquet. I pledge that we shall produce a spectacle of great passion and vigour, one to be remembered for many a day.'

Lady Susan clapped her hands. 'Good. Play your heart out, sir, for if you do well, the Queen will wish to see you again . . . and again. And your star will surely ascend in the firmament.'

In her hand, she had a rolled document, which she handed to Roag.

'Here is your pass. You will be asked to produce it at the

gatehouse. It has been signed by the Earl of Essex and countersigned by Lord Chamberlain Hunsdon. You are expected.'

Roag took the pass and bowed. 'Thank you, my lady. You have no idea what an honour this will be for me.'

Margaret, Countess of Cumberland, a woman with a remarkable eye for detail and a dedication to the sciences, pointed to the sword at Roag's waist. 'I fear you will not be able to bring *that* into the palace, Mr Roag. No armaments of any kind within the presence of Her Majesty. It will not get past the outer wall.'

Roag laughed and drew his wooden sword from its scabbard. 'It is nothing but wood, my lady, and fragile, too. A child's plaything or toy. You would be hard-pressed to harm a mouse with it.' He waved it about, as though engaging in a mock sword-fight.

'And who else have you here, Mr Roag?' Emilia swept her arm around the gathering of players, all standing awkwardly about, still in their golden masks. 'Are there any players we might recognise?'

'You will see them when they take their bows, mistress. I pledge that the audience will gasp with amazement.'

The Countess of Cumberland looked upon the players, who certainly seemed a fine little group of men. 'I am sure you will all do very well, Mr Roag. It is always a pleasure to see you. I trust you have had time enough to prepare yourselves, for I know you have been absent from London some little time.'

'A death in the family, in the North, my lady. I had much to settle in the matter of probate.'

'Come, ladies,' Lucia Trevail said, 'let us leave poor Mr Roag to his labours. I do believe Her Majesty will soon have finished with Council business and will require us to join her for her morning volta and cards.'

*

Regis Roag watched them walk away and smiled with relief. God was with him, there could be no doubt. This was his destiny, this day. Would they have recognised Beatrice in man's attire, with the mask about her face? Probably not, but there was no point in taking chances before it became necessary.

In his hand he held the toy wooden sword. Slowly, he withdrew the true sword housed within. A thin, flat blade of finely crafted Toledo steel. This was no toy; this was an instrument perfectly devised and honed for one specific task: the killing of a Queen and her entire court.

John Shakespeare woke at six o'clock in the evening to find himself in a strange bed, in darkness. He lay still for a few moments, his eyes open, trying to make sense of his surroundings.

'Mr Shakespeare?'

He turned towards the voice and let out a low, involuntary scream of pain.

'Do not try to move, sir, you have suffered grievous injury to your body. Every movement will cause you great anguish.'

A face had appeared before his eyes. At first it was too close for him to focus on, then it moved back. It was a face he recognised. But in the name of God, what was Dr Simon Forman doing here – and where were they, anyway? This was not his own bedchamber, nor the one he had been assigned in the house of Sir Robert Cecil.

'Dr Forman, what is this? Where am I?'

'You are in a farmhouse. You were tormented almost to death by a woman who has been identified to me as Mistress Sorrow Gray and by a man, now dead, named Mr Ovid Sloth.'

'Boltfoot? Where is Boltfoot?'

'Close by. He brought me here to tend you. But I must insist that you lie quiet and still. You have lost a quart or more of blood. If you rest, you will regain your health; if not, then there is still danger. Here, let me give you some sips of water, sir.'

'Get Boltfoot.' In his mind he shouted the words, but in truth they were as faint as the illicit whisperings of a Cistercian. 'I must speak with him – alone.'

'Very well.'

Shakespeare's whole body was alive with pain. His torso and legs were bandaged as tightly as a corpse in its winding sheet. The slightest movement made him grimace. Even the simple act of breathing was agony.

Boltfoot came in and stood by the door. Forman stayed outside.

'Come closer, Boltfoot. I cannot move easily to see you.'

He limped over to the bed. 'I thank God you are alive, master.'

'Not God alone, I think.'

'Dr Forman has played his part, as has the goodwife whose farmhouse you are in. She has nursed you and fed us.'

'Us?'

'Dr Forman, myself and Mr Hooft.'

'Hooft is here? Why?'

'He discovered where they had taken you. You must talk to him when you have your strength back, but, in short, he says he came to London to find you, for he had hopes you might lead him to Sorrow Gray. I confess I am not certain of his story, but it is fortunate he followed you, for you were close to death when we found you.'

The events came back in a rush. The weird melding of exorcism and torture. But perhaps exorcism and torture were one and the same thing, both born of religious insanity. Beatrice had been there and Ovid Sloth, and then Boltfoot, wonderful Boltfoot with the astonishing tenderness of his callused hands.

'What of Sloth and the woman?'

Boltfoot ground his teeth and shut the door before returning to Shakespeare's bed.

'I confess I am not certain, master,' he said quietly. 'They were both bound and locked in the barn. But at first light when I went to them, Sloth was dead, his throat stuck through, and the woman was gone.'

'How? How did that happen?'

Boltfoot glanced back at the door. 'Mr Hooft was with them. I fear he might have freed her. It is all I can think. But he denies it, says he would never kill.'

Shakespeare was struggling to rise from the pillow, but fell back, breathing heavily.

'There was another matter, master. As commanded by you, I went in search of Mr Sloth. I found him at the Rose playhouse, with Mr Henslowe. He was buying or hiring costumes and certain props. It seems it was a long-standing agreement between the two men.'

'Why did you not take him then and there?'

'My caliver misfired and I was overpowered while Sloth made his escape. There was a young woman with him, pushing a handcart. Now that I have seen her, I believe it was Beatrice Eastley.'

'Have you no idea why they wanted these things?'

'Mr Henslowe said it was the practice of great men to put on plays for their friends, that is all. Whatever Sloth's part in all this, I think Henslowe an honest broker and innocent of crime.'

Shakespeare struggled to make sense of this new information. Sloth could not be staging a play; he had made himself a renegade. So why would he wish costumes and props?

The answer broke upon him like thunder from a darkening sky. Anthony Friday had been writing a play, though no one knew whom it was for. Of course, it was clear now: he was writing it for Sloth. This had always been about the Theatre and about players. Most of all, Roag. Regis Roag, the man who believed himself the son of a king and who had played Richard of Gloucester, a man who killed to be king. This was about a play – and it was suddenly clear whom the intended audience must be.

The words of his brother Will slid like an ice blade into his spine. *This golden ray, this English goddess, this nonsuch of our hearts . . .* The words he ascribed to Anthony Friday's play, the paean to Her Majesty. It was the word *nonsuch* that dealt the blow. The Palace of Nonsuch. That was the place. It would happen there. The Queen must be there by now.

'What is the date, Boltfoot?'

His man frowned and tried counting on his fingers. 'I believe it to be the twenty-third, master. August the twenty-third.'

The twenty-third. The number in the Wisbech letter. He had believed it referred to the landing of the Spanish galleys in Mount's Bay. That had been July the twenty-third. But that was not the vital date at all. *This* was the day. This was the day they would stage their play before the Queen.

But what bloody surprises were they preparing to unleash? The thought was too dreadful to think on; he had to act, whatever the pain.

'Boltfoot, get me out of this bed!'

Chapter 42

The captain of the guards put up his hand. Two halberdiers crossed their weapons, barring the way to the six players and their handcart. 'Hold fast. Who are you?'

Roag stopped and smiled. 'We are the Ladies' Players, Captain. We are to perform our humble entertainment before Her Royal Majesty.'

The guard had the hard look of a soldier who would not blink as he cleaved a skull in two. He ran the forefinger of his right hand down a list. 'I have you. Where is your pass?'

Roag handed over the paper. The captain studied it carefully, then looked up and stared hard into Roag's eyes. 'Have I seen you before? You look familiar.'

'I played with Lord Strange's Men before the Queen some time ago. It is possible you saw me then.'

The captain grunted. 'What's on the cart?'

'Our costumes and props.'

'I see you wear a sword at your belt. Take it off and leave it here.'

'It is a wooden sword, a prop for the play.'

'No weapons. Order of the Council.'

Roag laughed. 'But it is not a weapon.'

The captain held out a hand. 'Show me.'

Roag drew his wooden sword and handed it over. The

captain tested it and weighed it in his hands. It was light, for it was made of soft wood, and there was no hidden blade within, unlike all the others. The guard ran a finger down the thick, blunt blade, then handed it back.

'Are there other toy weapons?'

'Just what you see. A wooden sword for each of us. And there is also a white staff of office, the symbol of the Lord Treasurer, if you consider that to be a weapon. We need it because we are to represent the great men of the Queen's court, to pay tribute to her. Could you imagine Ralegh without his sword or Burghley without his white staff?'

The captain nodded to two of his men. 'Search the cart.'

'I beseech you to take care. Those costumes and masks are hired; they cost more gold than I could earn in a lifetime.'

The guards sifted through the costumes and masks but found nothing suspicious.

'Now search the players. Every inch of them.'

Roag looked at Beatrice. She wore doublet and hose and a velvet hat, but it seemed to him that she was shaking. She was the weak link in the chain. She was slim and her hips were narrow enough to pass for an effeminate youth, but a cursory examination would quickly detect her true sex. And even if, by some chance, they did not discover her secret, she was at the edge of her undoing. It would not take much to push her over.

'Captain, is this necessary? We have much preparation to do to set our scene.'

The guard stared at Roag again. Suddenly he nodded, then turned to a guard within the gatehouse. 'Take them through, Corporal.'

Roag breathed out and bowed his head to the guard in gratitude. He was nearly there now; he could almost taste the fear and the blood. He would likely die this day, but they would know who he was. *For yet I am not look'd on in the world.*

Oh, they would look on him. Never again would they deny his parentage, never shun him as though he were a scraping on their golden shoes.

He followed the corporal into the outer courtyard. Striding purposefully ahead of them, he caught sight of a small knot of courtiers, among them Essex. His former employer was looking in the other direction, but nonetheless Roag hurried by, head down, gaze averted.

There was a delightful intimacy about the inner courtyard of Nonsuch Palace, which made it perfect for the performing of entertainments on a warm summer's evening such as this.

A mighty noise of talking, laughter and music already filled the balmy air. The sun was low, and there were long shadows, but pitch torches and lanterns added lustre to the space. Scores of courtiers stood or sat or milled about, conversing and arguing. At the far end of the courtyard, beneath the windows of the Queen's Privy Chamber, a bank of seats had been erected for Her Majesty and her private party, protected from the weather by a large canopy of gold and green stripes. Directly opposite it, ranged behind the central fountain, was a low stage where a company of tumblers flipped their lithe and graceful bodies through the air.

The Queen was already in her place, seated on sumptuous cushions, idly sipping at a silver goblet of hippocras, watching the gymnasts and listening to some scandalous tittle-tattle that Henry, Lord Hunsdon, the Lord Chamberlain, dripped into her ear. Suddenly she laughed and struck him with the edge of her fan.

Essex sat on her right, his face imperiously sullen as he talked with Southampton. Cecil and his father, Lord Burghley, were seated near by, as were Heneage, Egerton and Puckering. Most of England's senior nobles and holders of the offices of state were here for the occasion. The entertainment did not interest them a great deal; their real purpose this evening was to jostle for favour and preferment while doing their rivals down.

From the window of their appointed tiring room, Roag looked out and noted the positions of these men who held England in their fists. Each of his players had his task; each knew whom he was to kill first. At the sign – the utterance of the word *Nonsuch* – he would lunge forward and strike Essex to the ground; Paget would kill Sir Robert Cecil, and Ratbane would see to frail Burghley. The Irishmen, Seamus and Hugh Fitzgerald, had orders to slaughter Southampton and Egerton, then turn on Puckering and Heneage. They would do the court in one by one, as many as God allowed.

And Beatrice? She would stab the Queen through the heart.

He spotted Richard Topcliffe, the white-haired torturer, crossing the courtyard, towards his Queen. Two guards appeared and shook their heads, turning him back. So Topcliffe was out of gaol; Roag laughed. He might be free, but it did not seem as though he was back in favour. It occurred to him, however, that Topcliffe could be dangerous. Despite his years, he was strong and deadly. Given the chance, he would delight in playing the man of action here. Well, Roag would not give him the chance. After Essex, he would attack the white dog.

In the second tier of seats, he saw his patrons, the four ladies. What would he have done without such useful, hapless fools? They had been his passport to this occasion; he doubted they would enjoy the evening.

John Shakespeare blacked out and slid from his horse two miles short of Nonsuch, crunching down on his shoulder. The pain shook him back to groggy consciousness. He rose to his hands and knees and tried to gather his thoughts.

Boltfoot dismounted instantly and knelt at his side. 'Master, you cannot go on.'

'I must.'

'I will go alone.' Boltfoot turned to Hooft, who had also reined in. 'Mr Hooft, stay here with Mr Shakespeare. If you can summon help, do so, but do not let him try to follow. I will return for you both when I can.'

Shakespeare nodded. 'You are right, I slow you down. Go, Boltfoot. Ride!'

Boltfoot remounted his horse and kicked on into a canter. The going was easy from here, lush countryside and parkland. He should be at Nonsuch within ten minutes, God willing.

They were ready. Every man primed: ready to kill and die. They were in their court costumes, each man attired as an English hero of Elizabeth's long reign. The words were well learnt; they would declaim in turn, and act out the great events of the past thirty-seven years, until the audience was lulled and unprepared, and the guards dozing. Roag was Burghley in his red velvet gown, his black, ermine-lined cape, his black velvet hat and his white staff of office. His *deadly* white staff.

The likeness of Drake was there, Essex and Hatton, too, Leicester and Sidney. And all with masks of gold and swords of finest Toledo steel hidden in their wooden toys. With hearts of iron, they walked from the tiring-house, through a series of passageways to the back of the stage. They waited until, at a signal from the Master of Revels, they strode out and took their bow. This was the beginning; they would say their lines of poetry, act out their parts, until the fell moment came that they would descend upon their enemies like wolves. Surprise would win them the day. In battle, surprise was everything.

Leading his companions, Regis Roag took his bow, then looked up, ready to embark on his great enterprise. But instead of an appreciative audience, agog with anticipation, he was faced with two solid lines of soldiers, separating them from their quarry. Two lines of men armed with swords, hagbuts and crossbows.

'You will drop your weapons!' a captain called, marching towards them. 'Drop them now, then fall to your knees with your hands above your heads.'

Roag looked about him at his five gold-masked companions, all staring at him through the eye-slits in their vizards, desperate for guidance. This was not how it was supposed to be. He drew his thin rapier from the white stick of office.

'Nonsuch!' he shouted. 'Attack!'

He drove forward, sword held out like a lance. Around him he heard the twang and whisper of a dozen crossbow bolts. Beatrice lunged forward at his side and crumpled with a dull gasp, a bolt embedded in her chest. Roag launched himself at the middle of the line of soldiers, roaring and snarling like a great cat of the Africas. The shock and ferocity of his charge tore the soldiers apart at their very heart, and he pushed through, stabbing at one with his rapier and ripping the short sword from his hand. And then he was there, facing his foe, the entire royal court of England, all now standing, looking at him in astonishment. He hesitated, suddenly overwhelmed with the power that lay in his hands.

Unsheathing their swords, the Queen's senior courtiers ran down the steps from the royal gallery to confront him. All of them – Essex, Southampton and the rest – were skilled swordsmen, having studied the art since early childhood. He had no hope against any of them. The soldiers at his back had already turned on him. He glanced this way and that, rapier in one hand, short sword in the other. He saw that his band – the Fitzgerald brothers, Paget, Ratbane, Beatrice – had all fallen, riddled with bolts or hacked down with swords. Roag was alone. His eyes fell upon the four women whose pass had gained him entrance to this place. They were but two paces away.

As a sword-thrust came at him from a soldier, he lurched sideways, dropped the rapier and grasped the wrist of the nearest woman, Lady Lucia Trevail.

A strong man with the rage of battle in him, he dragged her into the crook of his arm and thrust the short sword at her heart so that it slashed into her damson and gold gown and nicked her flesh. 'Stay back or she dies!'

They did hold back and he began to inch away from them. Roag's only hope now was escape, yet it was slender enough with a dozen or more soldiers and courtiers advancing on him.

Lucia struggled against him, but his arm was curled tight about her throat. He pulled her back into the outer courtyard, then increased his pace, wrenching her into a stumbling backward run towards the gatehouse.

As he came over the rise of a hill and steadied his mount, Boltfoot realised that something was amiss. A bugle was blaring and soldiers were streaming in through the main gatehouse. He dug his heels into the horse's flanks and urged it on towards the avenue of oaks that lined the approach.

Through the wind at his ears, he heard shouting, then two gunshots and screams from somewhere within the palace grounds.

Suddenly, there was movement at the gatehouse. A man in a golden mask and lavish robes emerged on foot, stumbling backwards like a stag at bay. He had his arm around a woman's neck, a short sword poised to strike her, holding a squadron of soldiers at arm's length.

Boltfoot slid down from his horse and drew his cutlass. He had no plan, but he saw a man with a sword to a woman's breast and knew he had to stop him. The man was not looking behind him, so he did not see Boltfoot loping towards him, dragging his club-foot along the soft grassy path.

Out of the corner of his eye, Boltfoot saw soldiers approaching from the left and right. They halted, uncertain what to do, but Boltfoot did not hesitate. As he came up behind the man and the woman, the man turned and rasped, 'Get away!'

Boltfoot slashed down with his cutlass on to the man's sword arm. The action dragged the swordpoint through the woman's gown, but the man had already lost his grip. The blade flew up into the air and spun away from him. The man screamed, his forearm shattered by Boltfoot's crushing blow.

The woman fell to one side, out of the man's grasp. Boltfoot was immediately on to him, wrestling him to the ground. 'Assist me!' he shouted to the soldiers.

As he struggled, Boltfoot saw the glint of a blade out of the corner of his eye. Suddenly the woman was on her knees beside him, a dagger in her hand. As Boltfoot held the assailant down, she lunged forward and thrust her dagger deep into the man's throat.

Chapter 43

SHAKESPEARE HAD HAD his fill of Newgate. It was a place of pain, the ante-room to slaughter. He had visited Father Robert Southwell there, and then Frank Mills. Each time the stench of death and ordure grew stronger. Yet now he was there again, to talk with the one called Dick Winnow, the only survivor of the band of assassins. He had been picked up five miles from Nonsuch and after initial denial had confessed all.

He lay in chains, his body broken by the rack. In the morning he would face the bloody passage to death known as hanging, drawing and quartering – godly butchery, as some would have it.

Shakespeare looked on him with pity and spoke softly. 'I believe you are a sea captain, Mr Winnow.'

'I was. Yes.'

'Tell me your story . . .'

Winnow's voice was faint but clear. 'My father was a fisher out of Yarmouth in Norfolk, but he and my mother held to the Catholic way, the true way, and were ever harangued by the parish priest and the justice with fines for recusancy. From an early age – from birth, almost – I was cut adrift from the society of my fellows. After my father was lost at sea, a mocking letter arrived, unsigned, that said his boat had been deliberately holed before he sailed. "*So drown all papists,*" it said.'

Shakespeare listened in silence. The tale had the ring of truth; many had been persecuted for their religion. His own family had suffered at the hands of Topcliffe and others. He nodded.

'I inherited money on my father's death, but I knew that I could stay no longer in Yarmouth without committing murder or being murdered, so I invested it all in a bark to take me away from Norfolk. I desired only to live in peace and hoped to earn my wealth trading between the coasts of England and the countries of Europe. But it was not easy, for my faith seemed to follow me like a slavering dog. Mariners did not like to serve with me, nor pilots. Then I heard tell that money was to be earned bringing sherry wines and tobacco from Andalusia, to break the embargo. But it was an ill wind that sent me there, for I was seized by the Inquisition and condemned as an English spy. That is, until Regis Roag and Ovid Sloth came to my aid. They said I could help them rid England of the Protestant tyranny.'

'What did Roag promise you?'

'He said that many thousands of lives would be saved by a simple act of justice. Good English men and women, now suffering under the yoke of a heretical dictator, would be set free. I knew what he meant, for I saw how my family had suffered. It was not spoken of, but I think I knew all along that my own survival was impossible. Yet it seemed a worthy use of my worthless life.'

'Who was behind the conspiracy?'

'I am not certain of its origins, but Roag was the leader and Sloth had the means. He was desperate for gold. He owed a great deal to Spanish moneylenders and was being threatened. The crafting of those swords of fine, sharp Toledo steel that we concealed within wooden toys: that was Sloth's doing. He also provided lodging, and assistance for us to perfect our skills as players and swordsmen. But authorisation had to come from the *casa de contratación*. A man may not fart on that coast without the house of trade's permission. The *casa* dithered and debated the matter for many weeks, but their decision never seemed to be in doubt and we departed at the allotted time. I suppose they reasoned that the death of Elizabeth could do nothing but enhance the claims of the Infanta Isabella to the throne of England.'

'Did the conspiracy begin in Spain?'

'No, here in England, that is all I know. I was told no more than I needed to know. None of us was.'

'Who were the others, the men who died at Nonsuch?'

'The Fitzgerald brothers, Hugh and Seamus. Ovid Sloth found them in the Irish College at Salamanca, where they were training for the priesthood. They were obedient and too stupid to know fear. They wanted nothing more than to fight and kill.'

'There were two more men . . .'

'Ratbane and Paget. They were lower than dogs, dredged up by the Spanish from the barrel of the renegade English regiment of the Low Countries. They would do what they were told and would not blink in the face of enemy fire. They spent their days fighting and their nights whoring and drinking. They are better dead.'

Winnow was in great pain. As well as the rack, he had been beaten without pity. He shifted position and groaned.

Shakespeare pressed on. 'Tell me about the College of St Gregory. Did you meet Persons? What of his assistant, Joseph Creswell? What was their part?'

'They came to me when I was held by the Inquisition. I could not swear what they knew of the plot, but I can tell you that Roag visited them often. He needed Father Persons's influence with the *casa*. But though Roag needed him, he did not trust him or anyone else at the college. He thought there were spies in their midst.'

'Was there talk of one particular spy?'

Winnow looked up at Shakespeare through a watery, blood-lined eye. 'I heard of one young man, caught writing a coded letter and taken to the Castillo de Triana. Was he yours?'

'What was his name?'

'I don't know.'

'What became of him?'

'You must know what the Inquisition does to heretics.'

Shakespeare felt sick at heart. Poor Robert Warner. A mere twenty-one years of age, he had been so courageous in agreeing to work under cover at St Gregory's. Revulsion welled up in Shakespeare at the thought of the Inquisition. It was a perversion of everything that Christ had stood for. And as for the traitor Persons, the Englishman who had blessed the Armada, he *must* have known everything. He had connived at cold murder – the killing of Loake, Trott, poor Ambrose Rowse, Anthony Friday, and the Queen of England herself.

'Mr Winnow, does the name Garrick Loake mean anything to you?'

'No.'

'Anthony Friday?'

'Yes, I was there at his death. It became clear to Roag that Friday had realised what we intended to do with the play he had written. He had to be silenced.'

'There was a paper there, one you left. It had three words on it: *They are cousins*. What does that mean?'

'I don't know.'

'What of Wisbech Castle and the priests imprisoned there? Men such as William Weston and Gavin Caldor? Do you know of them?'

As he asked the question, a sudden thought occurred to

Shakespeare. He would look more closely into Loake's family background . . .

'Again, no. I repeat, Mr Shakespeare, I know nothing of Wisbech nor the origins of the plan. All I know of this is what little I was told in Spain and what we did when we landed.'

'Ah, yes, the raid on the Cornish villages. What was the purpose of that?'

'We had to come into England as one and stay together. It was Roag's suggestion to attack Cornwall as a cover for our landing. The *casa* seized on the idea and provided a small fleet. I think it amused them to burn parts of the west country from where so many of their tormentors hailed – Drake, Hawkins, Grenville, Ralegh. They were astonished by the lack of defence put up against them. Why, we even said mass on the clifftop and the Spaniards promised to build an abbey there when they returned.'

Shakespeare shook his head. He would take this information to Cecil without delay; Cornwall must be reinforced.

'Who helped you in England?'

'Sloth again, but also the girl Beatrice. They had everything organised for us. We avoided inns and slept in the open air as we came to London.'

'Did you stay at a great house in Cornwall? Trevail Hall?'

Winnow shook his head. 'We had a tent. Sloth provided it for us and made us appear a genuine company of players. He had commissioned a play for us to say, and costumes and masks to wear. He used his influence with certain ladies to arrange our performance before the Queen.'

'Did you have any contact with Lady Trevail?'

'No. I know nothing of her.'

The suspicion was like an angry wasp in an enclosed room: impossible to ignore. Perhaps he had been taught too well by Mr Secretary Walsingham. Always looking for *the plot behind the plot*. Shakespeare could not get away from the doubts he harboured. Why did Lucia Trevail go down to Cornwall? Why did she go with Beatrice Eastley? And yet Lucia had been held by Roag at the point of a sword and was now the heroine of the day.

'What did you know of these ladies?'

Winnow was shackled by neck irons. He shook his head and his mouth opened in a rictus of pain. 'Nothing. I believe they knew Roag from his days at the Theatre, but we were to meet them only on the day of the performance.'

'Tell me more. Confess your crimes. Beg forgiveness of your maker before you meet him and hear his judgment. There were two more deaths . . .'

Winnow closed his eyes and grimaced with pain. 'I heard that a man and a woman were killed. Beatrice told the story to us. She said they were naked in bed together and she laughed. They had been Cecil's spies, she said. All his intelligencers were to be eliminated.'

'Their names?'

'She told us, but—'

'Mills? Was it Frank Mills and his wife?'

'Yes, that name sounds familiar. Mills. She told me Mills . . .'

Shakespeare sighed. Mills had indeed been innocent all along. The murders of his wife and her lover had been a matter of mistaken identity.

So much death and pain, and for what? Far from easing the lot of England's Catholics, these conspirators had probably made their lives much harder. Somehow they all needed to cross the divide, as he had once done, when he married Catherine. They had to realise they shared the same God and the same holy book; only the politics of vain, angry men divided them.

Chapter 44

THE BED IN Shakespeare's chamber was hot and damp with lust. Two bodies sprawled upon it, one tall and angular and adorned with bandages, the other slender and soft. Lucia Trevail turned over on to her front and exhaled deeply. Shakespeare sat up against the bedhead, catching his breath, all spent.

There was no tender dealing here. Their couplings were nothing but wanton greed and hunger. A brutal, desperate collision of bodies. There had been no time for small murmurings and fragrant kisses; they had merely pulled off each other's clothes in a frenzied tearing of stays and seams.

She reached out her slender arm and touched the bandages that still decorated his chest and shoulders. Her hand was light and warm.

'The wounds are healing well,' he said by way of conversation. 'I have my energy back.'

Food and plenty of water, along with herbal preparations from Dr Forman, had helped him recover more quickly than he might have dared hope.

'So I see.'

He laughed. She had been showered with diamonds by the Queen and fêted by courtiers. All had expressed awe and wonder at her courage when dragged away at swordpoint by a murderous savage.

'You know, Mr Shakespeare, you might have saved everyone a great deal of trouble and fear if you had allowed us ladies some intellect. Had you but entrusted us with information about your inquiries – your search for Mr Roag and Mr Sloth – we would have known straightway that there was something rotten about their plans to stage a masque for the Queen. But no, you would not have it, so how were we to know anything was amiss? None of you men will credit us with any wit.'

It seemed that her little group, her School of Day, as Lady Susan liked to call their intellectual gatherings, had been used most cynically by Ovid Sloth. And yet, at the end, it was this very same group that had proved the conspirators' undoing.

In particular, it had been the good sense of Margaret, the Countess of Cumberland, that had been decisive. There had been something about Roag that had roused her suspicions when they met him rehearsing at his pavilion in the park of Nonsuch.

'Instinct, sir,' she had told Shakespeare later when he called on the group at the house in Barbican Street. 'As a wild animal senses a hunter, I smelt it on him. He had the unholy stench of impending death. That, allied to the fear raised by the powerful military presence, alarmed me greatly.'

The intense feeling had stayed with the countess all day, but she had not acted on it. It was only as the evening drew on, and as fear gnawed at her, that she had confided in Emilia Lanier.

Emilia had known exactly what to do. She had gone straight to Lord Chamberlain Hunsdon and told him of the countess's fears. By this time, Roag and his group were inside the palace, closeted in the tiring room where they were putting the finishing touches to their costumes, donning masks of gold and checking their weapons in readiness for their blood-drenched performance.

Hunsdon did not waste a moment. He called out the

Queen's Lifeguard. The confrontation between the guards and the would-be assassins had been a moment of high drama: enjoyed immensely by Her Majesty but less so by her chief ministers, Burghley and Cecil.

In the fray that followed, a young Lifeguard had suffered a cut to the ribs from the assault by Roag, but his life was not in danger. The only other blood shed was that of Regis Roag's mercenaries. All had died on the stage. A hue and cry had immediately been set up for confederates and Winnow had been caught within the hour.

Shakespeare had asked Cecil in vain that he be spared the rack. 'He will die horribly, Sir Robert. Is it necessary to have Topcliffe break him first?'

'As squeamish as ever, John?'

'I would not treat the lowest creature on God's earth the way he treats his prisoners.'

'And yet *you* were tortured by this unholy band. For that was what your so-called exorcism amounted to, did it not?'

Shakespeare nodded.

'Fear not,' Cecil continued. 'Topcliffe might be out of gaol, but he is not back in favour. He will be consigned to his country estates where he can devote his energies to his peat and ironworks. Mr Winnow will face the rack, but it will not be Topcliffe who operates it.'

Shakespeare had his doubts. The thought of Topcliffe forgoing the pleasure of persecution was like a swift giving up the air: it would happen only at death.

Here in Shakespeare's chamber, however, such dark thoughts were very distant. He stretched and yawned. Lucia Trevail nestled closer to him and began to stroke him once again.

He gasped. 'You are a wanton, Lady Trevail.'

'Thank you, Mr Shakespeare.'

Again, he wondered about her. *You shoot at Spaniards and*

you stab a man to death with a dagger to the throat. Your skin is soft, but your heart is steel, mistress. What was he, John Shakespeare, to her?

'Am I nothing but a scratching post on which to pleasure yourself as the need takes you?' he asked her.

'You are indeed a fine post. Wood, strong and hard.'

He thought back to Cornwall. The way he had gone to Trevail House to spy her out. He thought of confessing the suspicions he still held, but decided against it. *Never reveal more than you need, John.* That had been one of Sir Francis Walsingham's first strictures.

Instead his hand went between her thighs and he pulled her to him once more.

In the evening, when Shakespeare woke, she was gone. There was no note. He smiled to himself. She was an uncommon woman.

With the sun slanting in from the west through the leaded pane, he rose from the bed, dressed at a leisurely pace and wandered downstairs. He longed for his family to come home from the Cecil mansion; yet the outcome of the conspiracy left many questions unanswered and he could not risk the girls' lives until all was settled.

The warning had been clear enough: little Grace and Mary would die if Shakespeare did not cease his inquiries. Who remained out there to exact revenge?

One question above all still troubled him: why had they killed the old nun, Sister Michael? He had put the matter to Dick Winnow in Newgate.

'We found her body at the same time as you did, Mr Shakespeare.'

'We?'

'Roag, Paget, Ratbane and me. The body was there, warm

and newly dead. Stabbed through the heart. Roag did not seem surprised; he merely laughed.'

'Did Beatrice do this?'

'Possibly. She was mad enough.'

And then there was the matter of Paul Hooft. Shakespeare wished to know more about his movements, but that could wait.

He drew a cup of ale from the keg in the kitchen and sipped it, then spat it out. It was stale and foul. It was time for Jane to come home and organise them all; brew some fresh ale and beer, and fetch good food from the market. He was longing to hear the chatter of Grace, Mary and Ursula, and once again turn this house back into a family home.

There was a knock at the door. He opened it, hoping to find Lucia again, but a young woman stood before him. She looked vaguely familiar.

'Yes?'

'I want to talk to you, Mr Shakespeare.'

'I know you, don't I?' he said, searching his memory.

'You should know every inch of me,' she said and gave him a look of brazen amusement.

Her audacious look brought back his memory. She had been Dr Forman's bedmate when he had called at the house in Fylpot Street before travelling to Cornwall.

'It's Janey, isn't it? May I ask what this is about?'

At Forman's house he had thought her rather plain, though full of sensual promise. Now, fully clothed and with her hair untangled and combed back from her face, he found her quite striking. As he looked at her, his eye was suddenly caught by a small mark above her right eyebrow. It was faint, but he would swear it was shaped like a new moon – a crescent moon.

Her hand went to the mark and she nodded. 'You know about that, I take it.'

Oh yes, he knew about the crescent moon.

He nodded. 'Yes, yes I do.'

'Then you must know that my name is not Janey, but Thomasyn.' She met his gaze, looking for his reaction. 'Thomasyn Jade. I believe you have been looking for me.'

Shakespeare smiled. 'I am very glad to make your acquaintance, mistress. I doubt you know how glad, for it enables me to fulfil a promise I made to a good man.'

'That fool Southwell—'

'Why do you call him a fool?'

'For getting himself killed for a childish superstition, that is why.'

'Perhaps he was misguided, but he was a good man for all that. And he wished well of you. Now, if you would care to repair to the Swan with me, I have a thirst that must be quenched and a hunger that must be satisfied. Step inside while I fetch my purse.'

The tavern was crowded with drinkers, but they pushed past some drunks and found a corner for themselves in a tiny partitioned booth.

'This place is so small it's like being locked away in a cupboard,' Thomasyn complained. 'And no one knows better than I what a cupboard is like, for they kept me prisoner for months, moved me from house to house, locked me in cupboards and cellars. Every day from dawn to dusk and beyond, they kept me tied to chairs and assailed me with their wicked rituals until I did come to believe I had demons within me.' She smiled ruefully. 'Buy me a gage of Mad Dog, Mr Shakespeare, for I have a desire to get as cup-shotten as a constable this evening.'

Summoning the potboy, he ordered a quart of spiced beer for Thomasyn and a flagon of Gascon wine for himself, as well as a trencher of cold beef pie, eggs and salad, for he had a mighty hunger.

'I trust you will excuse my ill manners in eating while you merely drink, mistress?'

'Fill your belly, Mr Shakespeare.'

'You have a story to tell, I think.'

She nodded. 'I do, if you wish to listen. But first I have an apology to make. You see, I have known for quite some time that you have been looking for me and I have done my best not to be found. I was worried that you had come to spy me out, so I tried to frighten you off.'

The potboy arrived with their beer and wine. Shakespeare watched her as she supped a deep draught of beer and waited for her to continue.

'It was me that left that note with the girl you keep, Ursula.'

Shakespeare frowned. 'What are you saying?'

'I wrote that letter that threatened you. I never meant it. I wouldn't harm a rat. Well, I would harm a rat, of course, but not a little girl . . .'

'You did that?'

'Yes.' She said the word very quietly.

Slowly, as the enormity of her words dawned, anger welled up within him.

'So that was you all along, the vile letter? We have all been scared out of mind for nothing?'

She nodded again and looked down into her beer.

'You even put their names, Grace and Mary, and all in the shape of a cross. In blood!'

'It was unforgivable.'

'But why?'

'Because I was scared myself. I thought you had sent your servant Jane Cooper to Simon's house to spy me out. I couldn't let you find me and I didn't want to run again.'

'But you threatened my children! In God's name, you sit here and drink beer with me, and tell me you sent a letter in blood threatening that my young girls would be harmed or even killed! Why would you do such a thing?'

She put a hand to her forehead and clenched it. Then she shook herself, took another sip of beer and placed her hands flat on the ale-sticky oak table. Taking a deep breath, she looked around as though they might be watched or overheard.

'Whatever it is, you *will* tell me.'

'Yes, I will. I say just this in my defence. I have known such fear and horror that I cannot bear to even think on it. I know you have done many brave things, Mr Shakespeare, but they were manly feats of arms. I know, too, from Simon Forman that you suffered one night at their wicked hands. But what I endured was the destruction of my soul, piece by piece over many months.'

'The exorcisms?'

'I thought you were sent by them to bring me back. I thought this time they would finish what was started and kill me.'

'But, Mistress Jade, your tormentors were all captured. Many were executed. Father Weston languishes in Wisbech Castle. Why would you think he could harm you from there? Indeed, why did you ever run from the safe harbour you had found in the home of Lady Susan, the Countess of Kent?'

'Because I saw her and knew I was in danger.'

Shakespeare's food arrived and he pushed it away irritably. 'Whom did you see? The old nun, Sister Michael?'

'Oh no, Mr Shakespeare, you do not understand at all. Sister Michael was my one friend in the world. She persuaded Father Southwell to intervene and put an end to the exorcisms. It was she who took me to safety in London and found me refuge. I could not have survived without her. Why do you think she hid away at Denham? Why do you think they killed her in your stables, Mr Shakespeare? Because they knew what she had done and she refused to tell them where I was. They wanted to get me because I was the only one that knew the truth. Poor Sister Michael was not the one I saw. The one I was fleeing was the one who ran it all, the one who was always there, urging them on, doing filthy things to me, stabbing me with needles, sticking bones and other disgusting things into me, forcing my legs apart and squirting strange liquids into me. And as soon as I saw her at Lady Susan's house, I ran.'

All Shakespeare's appetite had dissipated. He drank a goblet in one swallow. The horror unfolding was too much to hear.

'You know her name, Mr Shakespeare, for I saw her leaving your house this very day. I know all about her and her evil desires. The one I am still not sure of is *you*.'

Chapter 45

SHAKESPEARE WAS DISAPPOINTED and horrified, but not shocked; he had never lost his suspicions of her, even as she lay in his bed. He had not even persuaded himself that his suspicions were false; he had simply put them to one side.

So Thomasyn Jade fled from the sanctuary of Lady Susan's house because she saw Lucia Trevail.

Shakespeare was silent a few moments as he took in the story that Thomasyn Jade had told him.

'When you saw Lady Trevail at Lady Susan's gathering, why did you not simply report her if she was your tormentor?'

'To whom?' Thomasyn demanded. 'I was terrified.'

'To the other ladies in the group, the justice, the sheriff – even the Privy Council.'

'I didn't trust any of them. As far as I knew, the whole of England was of one mind. All bent on my destruction. You should have seen the gentlemen and nobles who crowded into the exorcisms. What power did I, Thomasyn Jade, the dirty common harlot from Denham, have against such men and women? Who would listen to me if I reported them? I was cornered like a bear at the baiting. Sister Michael was the only one who showed me kindness. She tried to persuade Weston and the other priests to be more gentle with me, but she had little influence with them. She was the only one I could trust and so I ran from London back to Denham, for I knew she would still be there and hoped she would shelter me.'

'What happened next?'

'Poor Sister Michael had no idea what to do for me, for I was close to madness. She needed a safe place for me – and she needed a healer. Eventually, she recalled hearing that Dean Blague had given refuge to another victim of exorcism – a girl servant much vexed with spirits – and approached him on my behalf. Blague is a good man and took me in without question. His wife knew Forman well and she took me to him. I went there many times.'

'How did he help you?'

'He cast my horoscope. He gave me soothing herbs – and he talked with me. Dr Forman brought me back to health. He may be a goat or a satyr, but he is a true healer of bodies and souls. Gradually I became well again. Simon Forman is a good man, though many speak ill of him.'

Shakespeare nodded. The doctor had helped save his life.

All London now knew of the deadly events at Nonsuch, but there was still one question that had to be asked.

'Do you believe Lucia Trevail was part of the conspiracy to assassinate the Queen and her courtiers?'

'I am certain of it, but that is for you to find out and prove, Mr Shakespeare. I also believe she killed Sister Michael – or ordered her killing – to silence her. I consider her capable of anything. Men testified that they saw demons running up my leg into my womanhood and others crawling, defeated, from my mouth. I saw but one demon in all the exorcisms I endured, and its name was Lady Trevail.'

Shakespeare froze. So at the end she had killed Roag not out of rage at being taken hostage, but to silence him, too; he was the one man who knew the truth about her. But he, Shakespeare, had suspected the truth, too – hadn't he?

I had my eye on her, and then I took it off. Now she is heading back to Nonsuch Palace, trusted by the highest in the land, with unfettered access to Gloriana herself. None would think to search her gowns for a long-bladed dagger or a wheel-lock pistol . . .

Nonsuch glowed in the night as he rode up to the gatehouse. The captain of the guard was in no mood to admit anyone without first scrutinising his letters of pass with meticulous care, and then checking them again.

'Who are you?'

'John Shakespeare, as it says on my pass. You have seen me a dozen times or more, Captain.'

'Why are you here? The palace is asleep.'

'I have urgent business with Sir Robert Cecil.'

'I will have to have these letters checked.'

'Captain, I believe you erred once before in admitting men with swords disguised as toys. I suggest you do not make another deadly error by barring me. Now let me in.'

The captain seemed put out. 'Very well, Mr Shakespeare, I will escort you in myself. But you must first hand me your sword and dagger.'

Shakespeare removed his weapons and held them, hilt first, across his palms.

The captain took them and handed them to one of his men. 'Look after these.' He nodded to Shakespeare. 'Come with me.'

They marched quickly through the outer courtyard and thence to the inner quad, which was ablaze with cressets of burning coals and lanterns by the walls. Three minor courtiers stood by the fountain, drinking themselves into oblivion. Otherwise, all was quiet.

'In here,' the captain said as they approached a door.

They entered a small ante-room where a steward immediately jumped up from his seat and stepped forward.

'This is John Shakespeare, assistant secretary to Sir Robert Cecil. He wishes to see him. Says it's urgent.'

The steward bowed to Shakespeare. 'Sir Robert is asleep, sir. Is this urgent enough to wake him?'

'Yes.'

'Then come with me, if you will.' He turned to the captain. 'That will be all.'

'Can you vouch for this man?'

'Yes, Captain, I know Mr Shakespeare well. Now return to your post.'

Cecil was not asleep. He was at the desk in his chamber, working on documents by the light of half a dozen candles. His eyes were dark with fatigue and his fingers were stained with ink.

'Come in, John.' He signalled to the steward. 'Fetch wine and some food for Mr Shakespeare. He looks as though he needs it.'

The steward bowed and departed.

'Now then, John, what is it?'

'It is Lady Lucia Trevail, Sir Robert. Is she in the Privy Chamber?'

'Why?'

'Because I have discovered reason to suspect that she was part of the conspiracy against the Queen's person.'

Cecil put down his quill. 'Well, she is not here. I know this because Her Royal Majesty was asking after her this evening. She wished to play some hands of primero with her. The Queen was exceeding displeased at her absence.'

'Thank the Lord . . .'

'John, sit down. I think you had better tell me exactly what you have discovered.'

Chapter 46

O N THE DAY of the homecoming, Jane immediately set to cleaning the house. Bustling about, she opened the windows, organised the laundry, dusted the floors and put down new rushes. Ursula forsook her stall for the day and helped her with the housework. Little John tagged along, trying to help but merely managing to be disruptive. Boltfoot, meanwhile, hid in the stables with his pipe, cleaning his caliver and oiling his cutlass.

Shakespeare spent some time with Grace and Mary, telling them about Andrew's new ship, the *Defiance*, with its figurehead shaped like a lion. He told them, too, of the day the Spanish had landed in Cornwall and how the brave Cornishmen had thrown them back into the sea whence they came. Finally, he tested them on the lessons they had learnt in Cecil's household and was pleased to discover they had been taught well.

He then told the girls to go and help Jane and Ursula, while he retired to his solar to catch up on reading intercepts and correspondence. More than anything, he longed to have word of young Robert Warner, the intelligencer he had sent incognito to the College of Gregory in Seville, but there was nothing. After a while there was a knock at the door.

'Come in.'

Jane stepped in with little John at her heels. Shakespeare noted how the boy was blossoming, as was she, back to her old, comely self. He found himself staring at her bosom, which seemed riper and fuller than he could recall in recent months. He looked up at her face. 'Forgive me . . .'

She smiled.

'Jane, are you—'

She nodded and her hand went instinctively to her belly, though there was nothing showing as yet.

'That is good news. I am delighted for you both.'

'I haven't told Boltfoot yet.'

'Well, I won't say a word.' Shakespeare turned back to his paperwork.

'I do believe that Dr Forman's potions have helped. He has made me believe the baby will come to term.'

Shakespeare had to laugh. 'I am sure Boltfoot had some part to play in your good fortune. In the meantime, I will pray for you.'

'But he also said that I would experience a death.'

'I think it the nature of astrologers that as many of their predictions are in error as correct. God alone is without fault.'

Jane hastily delved into her apron pocket. 'But it was not about me that I came to you, master. It was for this.'

He looked up and saw that she was holding a large needle.

'A sailmaker?'

'I found it while I was changing your bedding, master. It was beneath the cushions, pinned into the mattress.'

She put the needle down on the table in front of him.

He picked it up and turned it in his fingers. In the wrong hands it was a diabolical implement, as his perforated body testified. Had Lucia Trevail and Beatrice Eastley used this to kill Garrick Loake when they suspected he was about to betray their approach to him? Or perhaps it was another needle, just like it.

The thought of Beatrice and Lucia, killing together, both soaked in blood, sent a shiver to his heart. Poor Loake, deep in debt and a Catholic: he must have seemed a certain recruit to their cause. And, as Shakespeare now knew from his inquiries into Loake's family connections, he would have been recommended to the conspirators highly, for he had a cousin at Wisbech Castle: a young lay brother by the name of Gavin Caldor, connected to the Theatre just as Loake had been. The nervous young man who had pissed himself with fear at the thought of his own torture and death – surely that callow, terrified youth could not have had the diabolical brilliance to devise such a plot, unless he was a play-actor of uncommon gifts? Yet he was certainly involved.

That was what Anthony Friday had been trying to tell him with his scratched message: *They are cousins.*

'Does the needle mean something to you, master?'

'Yes,' he said.

Had Lucia meant to kill him before changing her mind? Was it a warning, or merely a little farewell gift?

'It is something I mislaid. A thing of no value. Thank you, Jane.'

He put it to one side.

There had been no word of Lucia Trevail. None of her friends from the School of Day had any idea where she might be, and all had been utterly shocked and bewildered by the secret side of her that they had never known.

'I simply cannot believe that Lucia had anything to do with those devilish people,' Lady Susan, the Countess of Kent, had told him.

'Which of you had the idea of putting on the masque for the Queen?'

The countess had thought for a moment. 'Why, yes, that was Lucia's notion.'

'And which of you commissioned Mr Sloth to organise it?'

'Well, I am sure that must have been Lucia, too.'

Shakespeare had sighed and said no more. Had Father Weston sent Beatrice to Lucia when she fled Wisbech? It seemed mighty probable. They had been partners in treason all along. Lucia had brought her into Lady Susan's circle, believing she would be protected from suspicion there; perhaps she had even introduced her to Regis Roag.

And then Lucia and Beatrice had travelled down to Cornwall together to await the arrival of Roag and his men, and to assist them in the initial stages of their mission. But something had happened to unsettle them before they reached Trevail Hall, and they had decided to part and meet again later. Perhaps someone got word to them that Shakespeare was on their trail with orders to apprehend Beatrice. Perhaps one of Lucia's servants had been watching him? Was it perhaps the same servant who told them later that Ovid Sloth was to be taken by sea to Falmouth? This was all surmise, but it made sense.

The ladies of the School of Day would come to their own conclusions about Lucia. Cecil had raised a hue and cry, ordering searchers and pursuivants to all her properties and any known haunts. The ports had been alerted. Word had been sent post-haste to Godolphin in Cornwall to seize her and bring her to London, should she arrive at Trevail Hall, but Shakespeare knew she would not be found.

He would never know the truth about Lucia and Roag. Something told him they had been lovers, but, again, this was nothing more than instinct and surmise.

*

Jane was leaving the room. He called her back.

'I will be away for a few days, but when I return, we will have a feast. There will be nine of us – ten including little John. This includes you, Jane. You are to commission the Swan Inn to provide food and servants – and then leave the work to them. *All* the work. You are to do nothing towards it, is that understood?'

'Yes, master.'

'I want good Gascon wine and fresh beer. There are to be three roasts – a sirloin of beef, a turkey cock and a leg of mutton. There will be salads, sweetmeats, fruit pies and sylla-bubs. If they can manage a subtlety of jelly, I would like that, too. In the shape of a lion as a tribute to Andrew and his ship. And, remember, their best potboys will serve us. Tell them they will be well paid, so take no disobedience from them. Is that clear?'

'Yes, master.'

He wasn't convinced. He knew Jane too well. She would never relax. The novelty of sitting at table, being waited on, would be simply too great.

'Send Boltfoot to me, if you please.'

'Sit down, Boltfoot,' Shakespeare said. 'Light your pipe.'

Boltfoot looked about him suspiciously, as though someone were trying to gull him.

'I want to thank you for saving me, and I want to ask you once again about Mr Hooft. What did he say when he came to you?'

Boltfoot limped to the settle and sat down.

'He said he had been following you, master. He had ven-tured to London, believing you might lead him to Sorrow Gray, the maid he was to have married. That is all he said.'

'Did you believe him?'

'I thought it mighty strange, but most welcome. Without him, I would never have found you.'

Paul Hooft, short-trimmed beard, fair and austere, smiled stiffly at Shakespeare as he welcomed him to his abbey farm home on the edge of fens. The waters had receded now, leaving dry land where once there had been a sea.

Shakespeare did not smile back.

'Can I offer you refreshment, sir?'

'No, I am not staying.'

'That is a great shame. I would welcome some company. We have much to talk about. Please, come through to my withdrawing room and sit awhile.'

'No. I will stand here. I owe much to you, Mr Hooft. Not only did you save Mr Cooper and me from the flooded fens, but you led Boltfoot to the place where I was lately held captive. So I thank you twice over.'

'It was my duty and pleasure, sir. For as I have said before, I owe my life and liberty to your great Queen and country.'

'And yet there is much that I find troubling and puzzling—'

'Mr Shakespeare, please, I am a simple soul. I was besotted with that woman and came to find her. I now know how wrong I was to follow you as I did. I should have come to you and told you my business straight. But I must thank the Lord that I was enabled to save your life.'

Shakespeare raised his hand. 'Let me speak. I have been thinking long and hard about the role you have played and it seems to me there is only one conclusion to be drawn.'

Hooft frowned. 'What are you saying, sir?'

'You know very well what I am saying. When first we met you on the road near Waterbeach, there was a suggestion that you had come from Cambridge, where we spotted you at the

Dolphin Inn. At the time we took you for a traveller, like us. Is that still your version of events?'

'Why, yes, I always stay at the Dolphin when I am in Cambridge. I was there for my trade.'

'Yes, you have told us of your business interests. You are a man of *many* interests. Farming, engineering, trading with the Low Countries.'

Hooft nodded.

'But, Mr Hooft, I suggest your journey did not start at Cambridge, but in London. What do you say to that?'

Hooft said nothing.

'I suggest not only that your journey started in London, but that you were following us all the time, and that was the sole purpose of your journey. I suggest, too, that you knew my name even before we met and that you knew where we were heading.'

'Why would I have followed you? I do not understand what you are suggesting. I am a farmer and a trader, nothing more—'

'But you have another interest: you are an intelligencer in the employ of the Dutch estates. You are engaged in espionage, sir. You may not be hostile, but you are still a spy. You are in the pay of a foreign power and have been trained in the role to a high degree. That is why I could never spot you, even though I knew I was being followed.'

Hooft shook his head, but it was a feeble, half-hearted denial.

'You have not merely engaged in observing and reporting back to your masters, but have actively fomented religious dissent here in the East of England. I say, Mr Hooft, that you have caused unrest in the fens among the more severe Calvinist and Puritan elements. You have stirred up rabble-rousing outside Wisbech Castle and you have undermined public order in the commonwealth. You may have saved my life, but you did so because it suited you.'

'Mr Shakespeare, everything I have done has been in the interests of England and Queen Bess.'

'No, it has been in the interests of the Dutch estates. It is mere coincidence that our requirements correspond with yours at the moment. Whose side would you take in a dispute between our two nations?'

Hooft rose from his seat, his back stiffened in a pose of defiance. 'This is preposterous. You come into my home and then accuse me of betraying you! Without me, you would be dead!'

'Betrayal. Yes, that is the word I was looking for. How do you think the Queen or Sir Robert Cecil would react if I told them about your double dealings?'

'They would thank me.'

Shakespeare snorted. 'You would be fortunate to be thrown out of the country with your life. Her Majesty likes Calvinists even less than she likes the Church of Rome. Her friendship for the Dutch estates is a mere convenience: two peoples joining forces against a mutual enemy, Spain. Least of all does she like strangers disturbing the peace of her realm.'

As he spoke, Shakespeare saw something in Hooft's face that he had not noted before – a sullen hardness. The soft features had been replaced by the ruthless, clever aspect of the assassin. Shakespeare had encountered many such men in his years as an intelligencer. Normally, he could spot the signs. Why, he had even seen them in Lucia Trevail. So why not in this man?

He stepped forward so that his face was a mere six inches from Hooft's.

'You are to leave England.'

Hooft did not back off. 'This country is my home—'

'No longer. You have two days to sort out your affairs and then you will be gone. I will come for you and accompany you to Tilbury, whence you will depart for the Low Countries aboard a vessel of my choosing.'

'No, sir, this is wrong! I am a friend to England. I can do you much good service. I have *already* done you good service. I am your friend—'

'Very well. If you are my friend, tell me the name of the man who ordered you to follow me.'

Hooft was silent. He bit hard at his lower lip.

'If you fight me on this, Mr Hooft, then I shall bring the full force of the law against you.'

The Dutchman was breathing heavily through his locked teeth, like a dog at bay. 'You do not know what you are doing, Shakespeare, nor who you are dealing with. I am God's vessel.'

Shakespeare had had quite enough of people believing they were God's instrument. His voice let slip his anger.

'I could have you incarcerated in the Tower and questioned under duress until you told me what I wished to know. But I will not because I remain indebted to you for my life.'

'*He* wanted you dead.' The words came out like the rasp of steel on flint. 'I thought you might have value alive. He was right; I was wrong.'

Shakespeare's body went rigid with anger. He might have many enemies, but only Richard Topcliffe, the Queen's own torturer, a man so severe in religion that he would drain the blood of every Roman Catholic in England – man, woman or child – wanted him dead with such slavering intensity of purpose. The white dog had sworn to destroy Shakespeare and his family. So even behind the dank walls of the Marshalsea, he had wielded power. And now he was out, and free to do his worst again.

Shakespeare raised his right hand and pointed his finger at Hooft.

'You are not God's vessel, but Topcliffe's.'

A fine pairing of zealots he and this hard-bitten Dutch intelligencer made.

'You said the name, not me. He wanted me to ensure you brought Weston back to the Tower and execution, but you could not stomach it. And he wanted me to be there when you hunted down the papist whore Sorrow Gray.' He snorted. 'Mr Topcliffe will kill you rather than lose my services.'

How had Topcliffe heard of Shakespeare's plan to go to Wisbech? It must, surely, have been someone from his own office: Mills, perhaps? Or even Cecil himself? It didn't matter now.

'And what did you plan to do with her when you found her? What would you have done had she not escaped?'

'What do you think? I would have taken her to Mr Topcliffe so that he could extract all her diabolical secrets and the names of every last papist traitor infecting this realm. I should have taken her straight to him – and left you to die.'

'You would have done this to the woman you claim to have loved?' Shakespeare did not wait for a reply, but strode towards the door, then turned briefly. 'Good day, Mr Hooft. I will come for you in two days' time. If you are not here, ready for me, you may consider yourself an outlaw and subject to the law of England.'

Thomasyn Jade stood alone beside the mound of earth in the churchyard of St Mary-at-Lambeth. The grave was beneath an old yew tree at the very edge of the field, well away from the tombs and vaults of the great men and women who were buried there. It was a peaceful, disregarded corner, set apart from the church and the archbishop's palace.

Dean Blague had secured permission for Sister Michael to be buried in this ground. He had not told the incumbent nor the archbishop the truth about her faith, merely saying she was a Christian friend who needed a final place of rest.

Thomasyn, too, had compromised on Sister Michael's behalf. She was well aware that, as a Catholic nun, she might not have liked the Protestant prayers that were said over her, but this was a holy place, whatever sect you belonged to. The church was named after the mother of Christ and it would have to do. Perhaps it might have amused the ragged old nun to lie so close to the graves of dukes and duchesses – even the grandmother of Queen Elizabeth. For herself, Thomasyn could not take seriously the doctrinal distinctions so beloved of the clergy. Did Protestants and Catholics not worship the same God and read from the same scripture?

The day was warm. In her purse, Thomasyn had a great deal of money, given her by John Shakespeare. He would say no more about it, other than that it had belonged to Sister Michael and had been impounded. Thomasyn could do with it what she wished, for he was certain the old nun would want her to have it. She had spent some of it on this funeral, and she had plans for the remainder. And should she need it, there was a promise of more to come, from the family of Father Southwell in Norfolk.

Bending down, she placed a posy of wildflowers at the head of the grave beside the little stone she had bought. She knelt awhile and said a prayer, knowing that Sister Michael would have liked that. It had been many years since Thomasyn had prayed. Back then, the ritual had been meaningless; her words and thoughts had merely wafted away into empty air, never to be heard. Now she expected no more, but she said the paternoster all the same.

The way from Waterbeach to Wisbech was a great deal easier than on Shakespeare's last visit. Now the floods had gone and the sky was clear. Gangs of parishioners were hard at work repairing the causeways and paths. It was a simple, gentle ride through a flat landscape. So this, he thought, is how it will look all year round if engineers such as Paul Hooft ever have their way and dig drainage channels to run off the floodwaters.

When he arrived at Wisbech Castle a little before dusk, he knew immediately that little had changed. From deep within the prison walls he heard shouting and banging: the seminary priests and the Jesuit faction were still at each other's throats.

'Mr Shakespeare,' keeper William Medley said, the surprise in his eyes evident. 'I had not expected the pleasure.'

'Is all in order?'

'Indeed, it is. The castle is now run with severe discipline and rigour, as befitting a prison for traitors. And it is a great deal more secure with the guards sent by Sir Robert.'

'What are those shouts I hear?'

'A minor disturbance, I am sure.'

'Well, we will talk of that in due course. For the moment, you will find me food and lodging, then bring Gavin Caldor to me in your rooms in an hour's time. Let him know he is to appear before me. I would like him to sweat awhile.'

Before this journey, Shakespeare had conversed again with Will about Caldor: Jesuit lay brother, builder of hiding holes and servant to Father Weston. His brother recalled him as an intense young man who spent more time trying to convert the players than he did on building sets.

It was clear that Caldor was the man with the connections at the Theatre. He was cousin to Garrick Loake and must have encountered both Lucia Trevail and Regis Roag. It was young Caldor who had given Beatrice papers of introduction to their furtive world of papist intrigue. But was the plan his? Was he the one with the simple idea of how to get a band of armed men into the presence of the Queen and her senior government officers by staging a play?

While Weston would never talk – and while Cecil insisted he be denied his martyrdom – Caldor most assuredly would. Fear would loosen his tongue.

Medley's face creased into a grimace. 'He is dead, Mr Shakespeare.'

'Dead? How?'

'Hanged himself a week ago.'

Shakespeare saw again the young man drenched in sweat, pissing himself with fear. He remembered how he had used that fear against Caldor – fear of the Tower, of the rack, of Topcliffe and his devilish irons, of the scaffold – and imagined how terrified he would have been when the news of the failure of the plot at Nonsuch reached him.

Shakespeare felt sick to his stomach. He very much wished to see Father Weston once more to tell him what he thought of him, but he was not certain he could stand to be in his presence again.

It was time to go home, to his family.

Chapter 47

Back in London, with Hooft duly sent on his way aboard a Dutch trading vessel, Shakespeare had a meeting with Sir Robert Cecil.

'Still no news of her, John?'

'Nothing. Not a single word.'

'Where do you think she is?'

Shakespeare gazed out of the window. The sun was full in the south. He supposed that she must be somewhere in that vague direction, certainly across the narrow sea. 'Spain, perhaps, or some nunnery.'

Cecil recoiled in disbelief. 'Lucia in a nunnery?'

Shakespeare laughed. 'Perhaps not.'

'Well, if she turns up at the Spanish court, we shall hear soon enough.'

'With every despatch that arrives, from Madrid, Seville, Valladolid, Paris, Rome, even Prague and the Germanies, I expect to hear of a sighting. Surely, she will grace some royal court with elegant tales of her clever plan to bring a band of assassins into the very presence of the Queen.'

'*Her* plan?'

Shakespeare had thought this over, time and again.

'I no longer believe this conspiracy was devised at Wisbech, Sir Robert. It began in the heart and mind of Lady Lucia

✝ 414 ✝

Trevail. As a lady of the Privy Chamber, she had intimate access to the body of Her Majesty. The power of life and death. But she had no desire to sacrifice her own life, so she devised a plan by which she would use her influence to allow half a dozen armed assassins to gain access to the Queen. I believe she took the idea to Wisbech, perhaps to Father Weston or others there . . .'

He thought again of the young man Gavin Caldor, hanging dead in his cell, and sensed a bitter taste in his mouth.

'I doubt she could have made that journey in secret, even under cover, John.'

'If not herself, then she sent a trusted minion. She knew she needed help and she knew of no better place to go than the Catholic seminary of Wisbech Castle. Maybe it was that other Jesuit in our midst, Henry Garnett, who went for her. And whom did they send back to assist Lucia, but Weston's own prize convert, his acolyte Sorrow Gray. You may think this is mere conjecture, but I believe it was all Lucia's doing. She played the part of the Protestant as well as any player at the Theatre.'

'But why did she do all this?'

'Like so many secret Catholics she felt helpless in the face of the religious settlement. I suspect that for years she attempted to subsume her feelings, but they could not be contained for ever and eventually burst forth like the lid on a kettle.'

Or perhaps it was simply the devil within her, a lust for pleasure and evil that could not be contained.

'So we were all taken for fools? The Queen and all her courtiers, the Countesses of Kent and Cumberland, and all their circle?'

'All of us. Myself included.'

'Do not be too hard on yourself, John. It was the work you had already done that alerted Margaret of Cumberland. It was your warning that made us ready.'

Shakespeare nodded graciously, then continued to unload his thoughts. 'Lucia kept up her façade perfectly, even reading to Her Majesty from that great Protestant tome Foxe's *Book of Martyrs* – without ever once disclosing that she considered the burning of heretics by Queen Mary to have been entirely laudable. Yes, we were all fooled. One day, I am certain, she will appear at the Escorial with a fan at her face, jesting at our expense to her new friend the Infanta.'

'Perhaps you are right. But, John, I hope not.' Cecil sat back in his chair and, for the first time in months, almost seemed relaxed. 'I like it the way it is. Utter silence. I think the fate of Lady Lucia should remain a mystery for all time. You know Her Royal Majesty feels betrayed and has no wish to hear of her again.'

Shakespeare looked hard at the young statesman. 'It would suit everyone, I suppose, if she had somehow met an accidental death, do you not think?'

'Such as falling from the back of a packet boat from Dover to Calais, you mean? Yes, you are right, that would be most convenient. But if such a thing had happened, none would ever know, would they?' He stood beside Shakespeare and together they gazed out of the leaded window at the empty sky. 'None but the seagulls and the fishes . . .'

John Shakespeare's table had never been so heavy laden. Almost every inch of the large, oak refectory board was covered with platters of fine food and flagons of wine and beer. He stood at the head and looked at his guests with warmth, satisfaction and a little impatience. One of them was late.

Grace and Mary sat side by side, giggling about the turkey,

which they said was the biggest chicken they had ever seen. The time at Cecil's house had been an adventure; they had been overawed by the size of the place and the dozens of servants who ran the household, but they were clearly happy to be home.

Next to them, Thomasyn Jade was talking to Ursula, who was just glad to have everyone back in the house. As soon as she heard they were returning, she had thrown over her swain because she had decided she really could not abide his mother.

Then there was Simon Forman, tousled and stocky, beaming at everyone through his bushy beard and holding his knife at the ready for when the eating began. His eyes swivelled from the food to the delectable Ursula and back to the food again. Why did Shakespeare not just say grace and get on with it? He had a mighty hunger on him, and his belly was rumbling in anticipation.

Beside him sat Jane with her promise of a swollen belly. She was plainly nervous of Forman's presence here, but Forman was playing his part, as was Thomasyn. They had shaken hands with Jane like strangers and were keeping up the pretence well.

Boltfoot stood awkwardly behind his chair, seemingly more bent and shrunken than ever. But for all that, the cares in his face had fallen away, now that they were home again and he no longer had to chase around England at his master's behest. Shakespeare wondered whether he suspected the good news that his wife had held back from him.

He wondered, too, whether it might not be time to start eating. The reason for the delay was the empty space at the other end of the table. Shakespeare did not wish to begin until the final guest arrived, but they could not wait for ever and he was just about to say grace when there was a knock at the door.

Jane stood up to answer it, but Shakespeare stayed her.

'Not tonight, Jane. You are no servant tonight. I will go.'

*

Francis Mills stood before Shakespeare like a ghost. His skin was grey, his eyes deep and his body gaunt; his clothes hung like long jute sacks from his thin shoulders. He brought to mind an ill-fed jackdaw.

'It is a fine thing to see you, Frank.'

'And you, John.'

'Welcome. We were about to start without you.'

They did not embrace, nor even clasp hands. Such gestures of affection would have seemed out of place to both men. But even at a distance, Shakespeare could tell that Mills had washed himself and returned to the world of the living. He had even trimmed his hair and beard. For the first time in many months, Shakespeare felt there was hope for him.

'Come in, come in.'

Mills stepped into the house; Shakespeare showed him to his seat and then said grace.

The two potboys from the Swan hovered behind the diners like mayflies, pouring wine, clearing platters and bringing more food as required. Soon, the strong drink and convivial atmosphere had everyone talking and laughing as though they were all old friends. Simon Forman held everyone's attention with his bawdy tales of patients and their problems.

'Enough,' Shakespeare said, banging the table and standing up as the laughter died away. 'I have asked you here this evening to celebrate our safe return home.' He looked down the table. 'First, it is my pleasure to welcome Mr Mills – Frank – back from the dead, as it seemed. He was an innocent man almost brought to the gallows for a heinous crime that we now know for certain he did not commit. Frank, you have suffered terribly. Your loss has been great and we must all pray that you can find a way to live again.'

Mills nodded, but said nothing.

'It seems that Her Royal Majesty could not sleep the night

before you were meant to hang. You were on her mind, because she knew your story – and she knew you to be a good and faithful servant. In the early hours, when the palace slept, she summoned Lord Chamberlain Hunsdon from his slumbers and ordered him, personally, to carry a royal pardon to Newgate. From what I am told, there were no more than a few minutes to spare . . .'

Mills nodded again.

Shakespeare turned and held his goblet up to Thomasyn. 'But more than anything, this evening is about this young lady, who has endured such horrors in the name of superstition that few could bear to imagine it. And so, I would ask you all to drink a toast. To life.'

Thomasyn smiled and looked around the group of friendly faces. In her hand she clasped a pearl, sent to her by the Queen of England. She raised her goblet, her demons all gone.

Acknowledgments

I am indebted to many people for their support and help. I would particularly like to thank Christine Clarke for giving me access to her scholarly work on the Wisbech 'stirs' – the infighting among Catholic priests held prisoner at Wisbech Castle in the late sixteenth century. As always, my heartfelt thanks go to my wife Naomi, editor Kate Parkin and agent Teresa Chris.

Books that have been especially helpful include: *The Medieval Fenland* by H. C. Darby; *Liable to Floods* by J. R. Ravensdale; *From Punt to Plough: A History of the Fens* by Rex Sly; *A History of Wisbech Castle* by George Amiss; *Ladies in Waiting* by Anne Somerset; *St Gregory's College, Seville, 1592–1767* by Martin Murphy; *The Spanish Inquisition, 1478–1614*, edited and translated by Lu Ann Homza; *The Spanish Inquisition: An Historical Revision* by Henry Kamen; *James Archer of Kilkenny* by Thomas Morrissey, SJ; *History of Penzance* by A. S. Poole; *Sex and Society in Shakespeare's Age* by A. L. Rowse; *The Elizabethan Renaissance* by A. L. Rowse; *Tudor Cornwall* by A. L. Rowse; *Eminent Elizabethans* by A. L. Rowse; *The Life of Robert Southwell* by Christopher Devlin; *William Weston: The Autobiography of an Elizabethan*, translated by Philip Caraman; *Popish Impostures* by Samuel Harsnett.

Historical Notes

Exorcisms at Denham

The sordid story of the exorcisms carried out by Father William Weston and other priests is still a matter of controversy more than four hundred years later.

That the rituals happened is not in doubt. Weston himself mentioned them with some pride in his autobiography, saying, 'out of many persons demons were cast . . . before my own eyes'.

What is in dispute is the nature of the exorcisms.

The chronicler and sceptic Samuel Harsnett documented evidence against a group of twelve priests who gathered at the houses of fervent Catholics around London and who, he claims, performed a series of disturbing and unsavoury rites.

The hub of all this activity in 1585–6 was the home of Sir George Peckham at Denham in Buckinghamshire. His son Edmund was the prime mover in allowing the priests to use the house.

Those present included the would-be assassins Father John Ballard, Anthony Babington, Sir Thomas Salisbury and Chidiock Tichborne. All four were executed later that year for conspiring to kill the Queen in the Babington plot.

The atmosphere at Denham was feverish. Harsnett names some of those who were exorcised over many months: these include three sisters – Sara, Alice and Frances Williams; and three men – Richard Mainy, Francis Marwood and a servant named Trayford.

There was much violent shrieking, banging of walls and ceilings, flinging of holy water and scratching the names of demons on the walls. The 'possessed' men and women were stuck with pins, forced to inhale burning sulphur and had relics applied to them.

On one occasion the priests were said to have applied a relic 'to the secret place' of a maid in the service of Lord Vaux when she was having menstrual problems. These relics were often the bones or clothes of martyrs.

Father Weston, a stern Jesuit, owned various relics of Edmund Campion, who had been executed at Tyburn in 1581. They included parts of his body, especially his thumb, which, said Weston, 'did wonderfully burn the devil'.

Sara Williams, who had become possessed in her mid-teens, was frequently bound to a chair and given potions, one of which consisted of rue, wine, oil and various other substances. Brimstone and feathers were burnt in a dish under her nose.

'At one time she was so extremely afflicted with the said drinks and smoke as that her senses went from her and she remained in a swoon. At her recovery, she remembers that the priest said that the devil did then go down in the lower parts of her body.

'Also, she remembers well, that at one time they thrust into her mouth a relic, being a piece of one of Campion's bones, which they did by force, she herself loathing the same.'

Harsnett says, too, that the priests 'caused a woman to squirt something by her privy parts' into Sara's body, 'which made her very sick'.

Sara's sister Frances claimed that the priests told them they needed to be baptised anew to be rid of devils. They were baptised this time with salt in the mouth, saliva on the eyes and oil on the lips.

Cats were seen as devilish creatures. Once, a group of priests whipped a cat around the room until it fled.

Father Richard Sherwood, who was later martyred, would pinch Frances until she was bruised all over and say it was done by the devil. He also thrust pins into her shoulders and legs, seemingly to stab and trap the devils that were supposed to crawl beneath the skin.

A young Catholic gentleman in the service of Lord Burghley testified that he saw the exorcisms and said, 'You could actually see the devils gliding and moving under the skin. There were immense numbers of them, and they looked like fishes, swimming here, there and everywhere.' This tale is related by Weston himself.

Dozens of demons were named. They included Modu (described as the dictator of the demons), Cliton, Bernon, Hilo, Motubizanto, Killico, Hob, Portirichio, Frateretto, Fliberdigibbet, Hobberdidance, Tocabatto, Lustie Jollie Jenkin, Lustie Dickie, Delicat, Nurre, Molkin, Wilkin, Helcmodson and Kellicocam.

But how much of Harsnett's account was a true reflection of events?

Weston's involvement is accepted as 'ill-judged' by Philip Caraman, a Jesuit priest who translated Weston's autobiography from Latin into English in 1955. He adds, however, that in the sixteenth century exorcism was 'considered a universal remedy for all cases that would now be classified as hysteria, mental derangement and obsession'. He describes Samuel Harsnett's book as 'worthless as historical evidence', used only to discredit the priests who had taken part, adding that 'the book contains charges of such gross immorality both against

Weston and the other participant priests that it must be rejected as Protestant propaganda'.

However, Father Caraman, writing in the introduction to his translation, fails to mention that Harsnett also attacked Protestants for carrying out exorcisms. Some Protestants did a roaring trade in the theatre of exorcism – and got equally short shrift from the disbelieving quill of Harsnett in an earlier volume, *The Fraudulent Practices of John Darrel* (a Puritan exorcist who attracted large crowds to his rituals), written in 1599.

Harsnett had sat on the commission that condemned Darrel for fraud. His volume exposing the Catholic priests, *Popish Impostures*, was written four years later in 1603 and was probably read by William Shakespeare, for he used the names of demons such as Hobberdidance and Flibbertigibbet in *King Lear*.

It should also be mentioned that some of the older priests in the company of Weston disapproved of the exorcisms. They had heard of similar goings-on in Europe and did not want them in England.

After his arrest, William Weston remained imprisoned in Wisbech Castle and the Tower of London until he was exiled during the reign of James I. He went to Spain where he wrote his autobiography.

Harsnett went on to become Master of Pembroke College, Cambridge, and later Archbishop of York.

The True Story Behind Sorrow Gray
The character in this book named Sorrow Gray was inspired by the true story of Ursula, the daughter of Thomas Gray, keeper of Wisbech Castle in Cambridgeshire when it was an internment camp to Catholic priests in the 1590s.

Ursula and her husband, already parents and expecting

another baby, were leading members of the Puritans, a strict Protestant movement considered heretical by the Catholics.

She was so zealous that she was considered almost a prophet among the Puritans of Wisbech and the surrounding fens of Cambridgeshire. She and her husband did their best to convert the Catholic priests to their religion.

Though the priests were held captive, they were allowed a degree of liberty and were permitted to argue with the Puritans who would flock to the castle to heckle them.

There was, too, infighting among the Catholic priests themselves. The inmates had split into two ill-tempered factions – the majority led by the unbending ascetic William Weston (who reveals the tale of Ursula Gray in his autobiography – see the Acknowledgments), the rest by his sworn enemy Dr Christopher Bagshawe, a seminary priest who despised the Jesuit order and resented Weston's assumption of power among the thirty or so priests held in the castle.

But it was the debates between the Catholics and the Puritans that enthralled Ursula. According to Weston, she was particularly struck by her husband's impotence in trying to refute the priests' arguments.

She converted in secret to Catholicism, the faith she had once loathed, and sometimes spoke out in favour of her new religion. Her father Thomas Gray, described as a 'vigorous Puritan', began to harbour suspicions.

As it became clear that she had converted, he became enraged and started to threaten her. 'Nothing was left him,' says Weston, 'except to show openly his implacable anger and hatred and his solid alliance with the devil.'

Her father and her husband joined forces against her. Though she was pregnant, they would not allow her the services of a midwife. Subsequently, she suffered a miscarriage, narrowly escaping with her life.

She left her husband and went home where she had to put up with daily barracking from her father. Even her mother, who still loved her, argued with her constantly.

When they tried to make her to go to the parish church, she refused and they attempted to drag her there by force.

Tempers boiled over and a public row ensued. Her father was heard to call her a 'base woman'. In a fury, he drew his dagger and ran at her. Ursula tried to flee but her father caught her. There was a struggle against a door in which she managed to wrest the knife from him. She ran off into the town but could find no refuge. The locals were terrified of her father. 'But an honourable and wealthy woman having pity on her took her in for the night,' wrote Weston. 'Then, with the help of Catholics, it was arranged for her to ride off on horseback as quickly as possible to a certain Catholic house.'

Not only did she leave behind her parents and husband, but also her own children. She is believed to have never seen her family again.

Though Ursula is long dead, it would be wrong to suggest that my character Sorrow Gray is based on her, nor would it be right to impugn her reputation in any way. It was merely the idea for Sorrow that came from the young woman's story.

The Deaths of Drake and Hawkins

In August 1595, the great mariners Sir Francis Drake and Sir John Hawkins set sail from Plymouth on what would prove to be their last voyage. They both died at sea while attempting to capture Panama from the Spaniards.

Hawkins, whose brilliant reputation as a seafarer and treasurer of the navy has been tarnished in recent times by his activities as a slave trader, died first, on 12 November of that year, after a two-week illness. He was sixty-three, and was buried at sea near Porto Rico. He was largely credited with having built the fast, nimble warships that defeated the Spanish Armada.

Drake followed two months later, dying, as he had lived, in a most dramatic fashion. The seemingly immortal admiral caught dysentery in January 1596 while refitting his ships at the island of Escudo.

He put to sea again, but his condition worsened and by 27 January, as they approached Porto Bello, it became clear he would die soon. An unseemly battle over his property and will then broke out between one of his captains named Jonas Bodenham and his brother Thomas Drake.

Sir Francis ordered the two men to shake hands to make up. In the early hours, sensing that death was close, he rose from his sick bed and had his servants dress him in his armour so that he might die as he had lived, as a warrior.

But he was too weak to remain on his feet and returned to his sickbed, where he died within the hour at 4 a.m. on 28 January, aged fifty-six. He had asked to be buried on land, but he was buried at sea in a lead coffin off Porto Bello.

His heroic place in history was guaranteed by his defeat of the Spanish Armada, but it was his circumnavigation of the globe – the first by a sea captain (Magellan died en route) – that was his greatest glory.

Three Early Feminists

Queen Elizabeth was not the only powerful and highly educated woman in England in the sixteenth century. Three of the very finest minds of the age appear as characters in this book . . .

Lady Susan Bertie, Countess of Kent (born 1554)

Susan Bertie spent her early years in exile in Poland with her parents Catherine Willoughby, Duchess of Suffolk, and Richard

Bertie. They were outspoken Protestant radicals who returned to England only when Elizabeth succeeded to the throne. Susan was educated to a high degree. Miles Coverdale, the translator of the Bible, has been named as her tutor. At sixteen, she married Reginald Grey, who was raised up as Earl of Kent, but she was widowed three years later, aged nineteen. Susan joined the court and was taken into Elizabeth's orbit. In 1582, she married the soldier Sir John Wingfield and went with him to the Low Countries where their son Peregrine was born in 1589.

Back in England, she became a patron of the arts and a mentor to the young Emilia Lanier, who was greatly influenced by Susan's Protestant humanist circle of friends. Lady Susan greatly valued and emphasised the importance of young girls receiving the same level of education as young men. Emilia Lanier called her 'The mistress of my youth, the noble guide of my ungoverned days'.

Emilia Lanier (1569–1645)

One of the first Englishwomen to be a published poet, Emilia has been suggested as the Dark Lady of William Shakespeare's sonnets. She was the daughter of Baptista Bassano, a court musician. On his death she entered the household of Susan Bertie, Countess of Kent, where she received a humanist education, learnt Latin and developed a love of poetry. She became the mistress of the great courtier and patron of the arts Henry Carey, Lord Hunsdon, who was forty-five years her senior and held senior office as Lord Chamberlain. When she became pregnant at twenty-three with his son Henry, Hunsdon paid her off and she married a musician named Alphonso Lanier.

She was clearly a beautiful woman and it is possible she met William Shakespeare about this time. The identification of her as his 'Dark Lady' – seemingly the object of the author's affection in his sonnets – was first suggested by the historian

A. L. Rowse. Much of what is known about her is revealed in the diary of Dr Simon Forman, who seems to have had a sexual interest in her but was rejected. He says she had several miscarriages and tells us much about her happy relationship with Lord Hunsdon and her subsequent unhappy marriage to Lanier. 'The old Lord Chamberlain kept her long,' says Forman. 'She was maintained in great pomp . . . she had £40 a year.' Not so with Mr Lanier. 'Her husband has dealt hardly with her and consumed her goods and she is now in debt.'

In 1611 her proto-feminist poem *Salve Deus Rex Judaeorum* was published with dedications to both Lady Susan Bertie and the Countess of Cumberland. It tells the story of Christ's passion almost entirely from the point of view of the women around him. Emilia makes a point of denying the subservience of women.

Margaret, Countess of Cumberland (1560–1616)

The countess was widely read with an inquiring mind that led her to embrace many subjects in the arts and sciences, including alchemy, medicine and mining. Born Margaret Russell, the daughter of the Earl of Bedford, she was given an extensive education – a benefit she would pass on to her own daughter, Lady Anne Clifford. At the age of seventeen, Margaret married George Clifford, the Earl of Cumberland, but eventually left him because of his continual adultery.

One of the talented women she helped was the poet Emilia Lanier, who had also been befriended and mentored by Lady Susan Bertie. In the early 1600s, Emilia spent some time at Margaret's home in Cookham, and in turn dedicated poetry to her. Margaret's daughter described her mother as having a 'very well favoured face with sweet and quick grey eyes and a comely personage'. She tended towards Puritanism and was deeply pious.

The Dean of Rochester's Wanton Wife

Alice Blague might be described, kindly, as a fun-loving girl. Married at fifteen to an ambitious clergyman named Thomas Blague, who was twice her age, she spent the rest of her life having affairs with other men and spending far too much money.

She doesn't appear in *The Heretics* as a character, but she is mentioned by other people. In truth she could easily be made the subject of a book in her own right.

Much of what is known about her comes from the secret diaries of Dr Simon Forman, who used the word 'halek' as code for having sex. He certainly *haleked* with Alice Blague on at least two occasions – in June and July 1593 – and earned a fortune from her by providing medical and astrological consultations for a wide range of conditions and personal problems.

Forman gives us a very clear description of her character and appearance: 'She had wit at will but was somewhat proud and wavering, given to lust and diversity of loves and men; and would many times overshoot herself, was an enemy to herself and stood much on her own conceit. And did, in lewd banqueting, gifts and apparel, consume her husband's wealth, to satisfy her own lust and pleasure, and on idle company. And was always in love with one or another. She loved one Cox, a gentleman on whom she spent much. After that, she loved Dean Wood, a Welshman, who cozened her of much: she consumed her husband for love of that man. She did much overrule her husband.

'She was of long visage, wide mouth, reddish hair, of good and comely stature; but would never garter her hose, and would go much slipshod. She had four boys, a maid and a shift [miscarriage]. She loved dancing, singing and good cheer. She kept company with base fellows of lewd conversation – and yet would seem as holy as a horse.'

Alice came from a well-to-do family, as did Blague, who had been schooled in the household of Lord Burghley, Queen Elizabeth's most senior minister.

Dr Blague, a Cambridge graduate, evidently believed he was destined for the very top of the church tree – for both he and his wife consulted Dr Forman about his chances of success when bishopric vacancies arose.

But perhaps it was his wife's activities that held him back. One of her lovers was, like her husband, a church dean. She was utterly infatuated with Dean Owen Wood, who was married to a wealthy widow, and she was desperate to know whether he was in love with her.

However, Dean Wood's eye was as roving as hers. We know this because a maid from his house consulted Forman (as did many great ladies and gentlemen of the court). This maid told Forman of the day she saw her master with another man's wife, having seen him 'occupy Wem's wife in her own house in the garret. He did occupy her against the bedside, her mistress being abed in Tottenham.'

Maybe Forman thought it wise not to pass on this bit of tittle-tattle to Alice Blague.

Alice gave Forman substantial amounts of money for her frequent consultations. For instance, she wanted to know whether her supposedly good friend Martha Webb (another patient that Forman took to bed) was having an affair with Dean Wood behind her back; she also wanted to know if she should have a child with Dean Wood. These two consultations cost her £1 3s 3d and she promised the huge sum of £5 if Forman would use magic to ensure that Wood would be hers alone.

Belief in magic and demonic possession were commonplace in the Elizabethan era. The Blagues knew all about supposed possession by devils, for one servant girl had been 'much vexed with spirits in her youth'.

Many of Alice's consultations concerned physical ailments. She and her husband were given expensive medicines for a whole host of illnesses and pains.

During the plague year of 1603, she became frantic with worry and went time and again to Forman. He said her only problem was that she was afflicted 'with melancholy, and much wind. It makes her heavy, sad, faint, unlusty and solitary; and will drive her into a melancholy passion'.

She survived the plague and continued her wanton way through life for many more years.

Did the Dean of Rochester know about his wife's philandering? He once asked Simon Forman 'whether she be enchanted by Dean Wood or no'. But the answer he got was evidently 'no', for Dr Blague never forsook her. On his deathbed in 1611, he made her executor of his will and praised 'her wisdome and fidelitie'. Little did he know. Or perhaps he simply turned a blind eye to her activities.

As for Alice, a mother of four, she went on to marry a prison keeper named Walter Meysey. They soon separated.

The sixth historical thriller featuring John Shakespeare,
available soon in hardback

The Queen's Man

RORY CLEMENTS

England is a Judas nest of conspiracy.

It is 1582, and the conflict between Protestant and Catholic
threatens to tear the country in two. While Queen Elizabeth I
holds the reins of power, there are those whose loyalty lies
with her imprisoned cousin, Mary Queen of Scots.

On his first major mission for Sir Francis Walsingham, the
young John Shakespeare is ordered to discover a conspiracy to
free the Stuart queen from Sheffield Castle.

All too soon, he realises that the tentacles of the plot reach
deep into his native Warwickshire and threaten his own
friends and family.

Now read on . . .

www.roryclements.com

Chapter 1

S HE WAS TWENTY-SIX; he was eighteen. They lay naked on a mattress made from hay with a covering of canvas that they had found on an old cart. Had *stolen* from a cart.

By their illicit bed stood a half-empty jug of cloudy cider. A light warm rain dripped through the rafters. Otherwise the only sound in this ancient ruin of a manor house was their breathing, growing softer with each moment.

The lovers had been coming to this place all summer long, believing that they were unlikely to be disturbed. It was known in the district as the Black House and fear kept people away, as it had done for more than two hundred years since the Black Death raged through its halls like the scythe of God. It was said that a family of ten had lived here with a dozen servants and retainers, and not a soul had survived. The building had been locked up and shunned ever since. Now it was overgrown and skeletal. A tall oak had grown in the middle of the great hall and much of the roof had crumbled, but the stone walls still survived, covered in a tangle of ivy and briar.

The house was largely forgotten. It stood three miles to the north of Stratford-upon-Avon; the park that once surrounded it was now dense woodland and the old walls were unseen, save by the occasional poacher or curious child.

The woman looked at her lover apprehensively. Initially, it had been his idea to come here, for he was not afraid of the place. He had told her that he first visited it seven years ago with another boy. His friend offered him a farthing to enter the ruin, so he had no option; he had to go in. He had won the coin from his friend and a badly gashed leg when a rotten board gave way beneath him. To his friend, the injury proved that the place was indeed accursed and haunted. But Will knew otherwise. He liked the house and had begun to go there alone, to read or think or merely to watch the sky.

And then, this spring past, he had brought her here. Together they had cleared a corner that offered enough shelter and a flat stone floor that would serve as a base for the straw mattress and that would not give way under their energetic couplings.

A drop of rain fell on his chest.

'Summer is done,' he said, looking up at the damp, grey September sky.

She kissed his face. She had a secret that she must tell and another that she would keep to herself. Tentatively, she took his hand down to her belly. Her flesh was warm, but she was nervous. She had been wondering how to tell him of her pregnancy. He had been besotted when this all started, exultant at having won the prize, the fairest young woman in the county, the one who had evaded the confines of marriage all these years. But how did he feel now, this boy, with summer gone and so much passion spent?

He allowed her to clasp his hand there beneath her own curling fingers, enjoying the quiet intimacy. At first he did not seem to comprehend the silent message she was trying to convey, but she held his hand to her soft mound all the harder and suddenly she sensed a tension. He turned to her and she met his gaze.

'Are you . . .?'

She nodded. There, it was out now. No going back.

'Is it certain?' he said, raising himself on his elbows.

The sharpness of his movement alarmed her. Was he angry? 'I believe so,' she said as evenly as she could. 'My flowers are three weeks late. Normally, they are as regular as the moon.'

He said nothing, his face a puzzle. She wished he would say something, not merely look at her. *Will. Oh, please say something.* Then he took her in his arms. Perhaps he had seen the desperation in her eyes. God in heaven, what would he say? Would he run from her? He had spoken often enough of leaving Stratford and Warwickshire. Now, he might think he had even more reason to leave. To *flee* . . .

They had both known the risk. She had been his teacher in love, and he the eager pupil. She had thought him grateful for such schooling. What man of eighteen would not? But now she noted the change in his demeanour. As though he were the master, and she the novice.

He pulled away from her and smiled, then kissed the tears from her cheeks. At last he picked up the fired-clay jar of cider, drank from it, then held it to her lips. He whispered in her ear words of love, the sorts of words that had wooed and won her; words that fell sweetly from his lips like honey from the comb.

The words and the cider warmed her heart, but they did not calm it. For there was still the other matter, the one she dared not confide in him. The secret that could kill her.

Chapter 2

Fʀᴀɴçᴏɪs Lᴇʟᴏᴜᴘ, ᴅᴏᴄᴛᴏʀ of medicine, and known this day as Seguin, walked beside the young Scot across the inner bailey or courtyard of Sheffield Castle. His journey from Normandy had been long and tiresome, riding a flea-bitten horse down pitted byways and peasant paths, all the time trying to avoid scrutiny. He felt dirty and unrested, despite a night's sleep at the local inn and a handsome dinner here within these ancient walls.

This castle was an abomination. The stench of an overflowing midden hung heavy and cloying in the air. With his one hand, he held a small silver pomander of musk and ambergris to his nose, but it did little to keep the smell from his wide nostrils. These English! How could they live like this?

Ahead of him, at the bottom of the steep flight of stone steps that must lead to the entrance of the castle keep where Mary was held, he saw half a dozen guards closing ranks. The guards were armed with ceremonial halberds, but the real weapons were at their belts: fighting short swords and loaded pistols. This was not merely for show. The Frenchman stopped and threw an inquiring glance at his young companion.

'They have to do this, monsieur.'

'Of course, Mr Ord.'

The Scotsman turned to the guard. 'This is the physician, Dr

Seguin.' He held out a paper. 'There, you will see the earl's mark. Monsieur Seguin is to be granted admittance to Her Majesty's presence.'

The guard thrust his pistol into his broad, hide belt then examined the paper carefully and slowly, occasionally looking at the Frenchman with an impassive face. He clearly knew the elegant Mr Buchan Ord, resplendent in his expensive black doublet studded with beads of jet and coral, but not his companion.

What the guard saw was a one-armed man in his late forties, perhaps even fifty, with dark, greying hair, a large nose and a sharp beard. He had a tanned skin and his slanting eyes seemed amused and clever. His attire was dark and sober.

'So this is the Frenchie is it, Mr Ord? Her Scottish Majesty not satisfied with her own physicians?'

'Be pleased to show some respect, Sergeant. Our visitor is a renowned doctor of medicine, held in high esteem throughout France. I believe the earl's steward has told you all you need to know. And you must recognise his lordship's mark and seal.'

'Yes, it's Shrewsbury's mark all right. I've seen it often enough.' The guard grinned and handed back the pass. 'That seems to be in order.'

'Then be so good as to let us enter, Sergeant.'

'Forgive me, Mr Ord, but first, as you must know, we are required to search you both. Don't want no dags or knives going near the Queen of Scots, do we? Don't want no nasty accidents.'

The Scotsman sighed and held out his arms, Christlike, to be patted down.

Still holding the silver ball of exotic perfumes in his hand, the Frenchman lifted his one arm with as little enthusiasm as he could muster. '*C'est vraiment nécessaire?*'

Ord looked at the newcomer apologetically. A body search

was, indeed, a tiresome condition of their entry. 'And we shall have to endure it all over again from her own men before entering the privy chamber. I am sorry.'

'It is nothing.' Leloup sighed and allowed a pair of guards to grope him intimately, all down his ribs and between his legs, their well-practised, insolent hands lingering at his balls. He found their attention quite pleasurable and wondered whether they understood the effect they were having. From their blank faces he guessed probably not; but this was a thing the English never did understand. At last the guards nodded to their sergeant, who stood back to allow Leloup to step forward and ascend the steps into the great hall of the keep.

The Frenchman laughed and leant towards Ord's ear. 'I am surprised they try so hard to keep her alive.'

'It is not such a mystery. They do not acknowledge her yet, but she *is* Queen of England. One day she will take the crown from the usurper, God willing, and these men will be her subjects. There will be many days of reckoning for those who scorned and mocked her and deprived her of liberty.'

'Vengeance . . .'

'. . . is golden. Like the sun after rain.' Ord looked sombre. There was a moment of silence, then he touched the French visitor on the shoulder. 'Before we go to her, Monsieur Seguin, I must warn you that she is in exceeding poor health. The black choler assails her.'

'Which is why she has summoned me, is it not?'

'Indeed, but I fear she will not wish to be seen, even by you.'

He had heard as much.

'Her hair is thin and patchy, her body is . . . a little stout. Her gut ails her with much farting and defluxions, and she goes days without sleep. I think that no woman, certainly no queen, would wish to be seen in her present humour. If you have a wife of your own, you must understand this. And, please, I beg you, speak softly in her presence.'

'I am a *médecin* of long standing, Mr Ord.' The Frenchman laughed again. 'I have faced many delicate situations over the years. You may place your faith in me.'

'Good. Once again, I crave your forgiveness if I seem a little too protective. But those of us who love Mary spend our whole lives safeguarding her from the slights and barbs of this infernal regimen – this imprisonment – to which she has been subjected these fourteen years.'

Leloup studied Ord. From his accent, he seemed Scottish, like his royal mistress, yet he was a very young man. Why would such a person devote his life to caring for this woman in her incarceration? He could have been no more than a child in 1568 when she came to England seeking refuge, and found only imprisonment. Had Ord been inspired by tales of her great beauty and saintliness from his Catholic parents? Inwardly, he shrugged; it was hardly worth speculating.

The presence chamber was lit by dozens of beeswax candles, and yet it somehow contrived to be funereal. A dozen people, both men and women, stood or sat in groups of two or three, stiff like mannequins that might crumble to dust if touched. They played cards or talked in low voices, their movements exaggeratedly slow. The scene was horribly cold, thought Leloup, like a badly wrought tableau. The retainers looked up at the two men as they entered, saluting Buchan Ord in slow acknowledgement.

At one end of the hall, against a high wall, a tall-backed chair rested on a dais. It was burnished with gold leaf so that it looked like a throne of solid gold. Above it hung Mary's cloth of state, in dazzling threads of scarlet and silver, with the words '*En ma fin est mon commencement*.' In my end is my beginning.

Leloup glanced at it and smiled. So she had taken the motto of her mother, Mary of Guise. Perhaps it was an omen.

Set into the opposite wall was a small doorway. Two liveried sentries stood to attention on either side of it.

'Those are Mary's own guards, monsieur,' Ord said. 'They are unarmed but as strong as wild cats and would fight like tigers to preserve Her Royal Majesty from harm.'

'Well, then I will not resist.'

The privy chamber where Mary, Queen of Scots lived and slept was lit by the glowing embers of a fire in the hearth. Leloup followed Ord's lead in going down on both knees by the large curtained bed, waiting for a word from the world enclosed within. He heard a snuffling noise, then the touch of something wet on his hand. A dog. No, three or four little dogs. They seemed to be everywhere, panting and sniffing and licking.

Gradually, as they waited in silence, Leloup's eyes grew accustomed to the desperate gloom and his hearing picked up the soft sounds of her breathing. Was she asleep?

'Mr Ord?'

The voice, when it came, was suprisingly firm and clear.

'Your Majesty.'

'Have you brought Le Docteur Leloup?'

'I have, ma'am. He is here with me. He is going by the name Seguin.'

An arm snaked from the curtain and a hand was held out, palm down and loose at the wrist. Buchan Ord took the hand in his and kissed it. He did not take it as a signal to rise from his genuflection.

'We bid you welcome to our humble prison, monsieur,' she said in French, instinctively moving her hand towards her visitor. 'Which name should I call you?'

'My real name while we are alone, Your Majesty,' he said.

'And may I say that it is to my eternal honour to be admitted to your presence.' He kissed the plump hand, which hovered a few moments before retreating behind the curtain.

'What news of our cousin Henri of Guise?'

'Monseigneur le Duc sends you his felicitations, ma'am.'

'I pray he has sent me more than that. Have you brought mithridate for my ailments? And horn of unicorn? Surely he has received my letter begging him for these precious elixirs.' An edge of frustration in the voice; so many of her letters to the great men and women of Europe had gone unanswered. Even her former mother-in-law, Catherine de Medici, ignored her missives and her pleas for succour.

'The duke has sent you something yet more valuable to him, his ring.'

'His ring?'

'As a token of his great love and as a pledge that he will do all in his power' – Leloup's voice lowered to a whisper – 'to free you from your present predicament and raise you up to your rightful place. He believes this will do more for your health than any potion, powder or tincture.'

The hand emerged yet again from the curtains. He already had the ring out. One of the little dogs leapt up to lick its mistress's hand. With the ring clenched in his fist, Leloup pushed the animal aside, a little too forcefully, so that it yelped. Now he uncurled his fingers and placed the ring in the Queen of Scotland's upturned palm. For a brief moment he looked at it in the glow of the fire. He had carried it for three weeks, secreted in a small pouch within his clothing, wrapped against his body, and all the time he was ready to kill any highway robber who might try to steal it. It was a broad gold band decorated with the cross of Anjou or Lorraine, part of the Guise crest. Mary's fingers closed around the ring and took it back into her tent of silk.

'Is it really his, Monsieur Leloup?'

'The duke placed it in my own hand. He wishes you to accept it as a token of his great goodwill – and as assurance that we will secure your freedom.'

'There is a candle by the bed, Mr Ord. Light it and give it to me.'

The Scotsman took the candle, housed in an ornate silver candlestick, to the hearth and lit it with a taper. Its long flame relieved the gloom and cast light along the delicate cream canopy and curtains that surrounded the enormous bed. 'Your Majesty.' He handed it into her and there was a gasp of pleasure from her as the bright gold shone.

'Oh, it *is* his. I know it well. Then I am not forgotten.'

'Indeed, you are most certainly not forgotten.'

'Monsieur Leloup, when I was a girl at the French court, the seer Michel de Nostredame came to me with foretellings. Queen Catherine had demanded he draw up my chart. He said I was to be Queen of France and also Queen of the isles. He said that I would live to a very great age and be known as a beloved sovereign to all the peoples of these islands. Is this still to come true as Monsieur de Nostredame foretold?'

'With God on our side, yes.'

'I have scarce dared hope it these long years.'

Leloup turned towards Ord. 'How freely may we talk here?'

'It is safe, but while Walsingham draws breath it is best to be circumspect. His spies are everywhere. Let us speak without specifics. No names. No details.'

'Could we be overheard?'

'No. We have searched every inch of this chamber, tapped at all the walls. One of our own stands outside the window alongside Shrewsbury's guards. Nothing can be heard, but still I do not trust them. If there is any way in heaven or on earth to do so, then Walsingham will listen.'

'Very well.' Leloup kept his voice low, then moved yet closer to the curtain of the bed and began speaking in French again. 'Your cousin has charged me with the holy office of bringing you away from this place. I concur with him that there can be no better medicine than this.'

'Then you are indeed a harbinger of good news, monsieur.'

'Mr Ord has discovered men and women of the true faith who will escort you from here to a place of safety and thence across the narrow sea to await the downfall of this heretical regime, which will not be long in coming.' He lowered his voice yet further. 'The invasion fleet is already under construction – at Le Havre, Fécamp and Honfleur.' And so, he thought, is the band of would-be assassins. *Englishmen trusted by the court of Elizabeth who will not hesitate to strike home the blade.* But he would not burden Mary with such knowledge. Not while there was any chance of a spy within earshot.

'Should you be saying all this, Dr Leloup?'

He laughed gently. 'I think it fair to say that they have always assumed you will try to escape. Hearing it will make no difference – so long as they do not know the method.'

'Mr Ord, can this be true that I am to have my freedom?'

'I believe it will happen, ma'am.'

'But why have you not told me this before?'

'I did not wish to raise your hopes, only to have them cruelly dashed as they have been so often in the past. Monsieur Leloup's arrival here changes everything. He brings gold for weapons and the great expense involved in concealing you as we carry you across England thence over the narrow sea to France. The plan is almost in place.'

'But how? How will this be effected?'

The light inside the tent seemed to blaze closer to the cream curtain and for a moment Leloup feared it would all go up in a burst of flames.

'Your Majesty, I beg you to ask no more. Not yet.'

'This is not good enough, monsieur! I must be sure. The she-cat knows I would escape if I could, so do her sharp-toothed minions, Burghley and Walsingham. They have the eyes and claws of rats, and there is an army of their guards around this castle. If your plan is attempted and fails, they will consign me to some dungeon like a common criminal. I cannot bear to have this fail, for I would become a worm, trapped deep within the earth.'

'Nothing will go wrong,' Leloup said. 'On the Bible and in the name of our Holy Mother of Christ I swear this.'

'The Holy Mother . . .'

From within the curtained bed, there was a gasp, then silence.

'Your Majesty . . .'

They heard a sob, which became a wail, deep and horrible.

Leloup felt Ord's breath in his ear. A whisper so quiet that Mary could not hear. '*Mother.* It is a word we must not use in her presence. She is a mother, too. Her son is fifteen years of age and never once has she heard his voice nor even had a letter from him. What torture is this for a mother?'

The Frenchman was silent a moment, then moved closer to the bed. 'Your Majesty, your ordeal will soon be at an end. I entreat you to trust us in this. I will send word to you with every detail when all is secured.'

The sobbing subsided.

'Madame?'

'You must come yourself.'

'That may not be possible. I doubt I will be trusted by the Earl of Shrewsbury again. But there is yet one favour that I must ask of you. Those who would help you in this noble enterprise require some sign from you – some article that will convince them that their work is indeed done in your name. I beg you to do this, for they will be risking their own lives.'

Mary's hand came once more from between the curtains. She held another ring in her hand. 'Take this. It was my mother's and bears the sign of the phoenix rising from the ashes. Her sign and now mine. Show it to our loyal people. And then, when I see it again, I will believe that all is prepared. As you have come from my beloved cousin Henri, so must I put my trust in you, Monsieur Leloup. Do not let me down.'

François Leloup took the ring. 'I pledge I will not fail you, ma'am.'

FOOTBALL'S COMING OUT

LIFE AS A GAY FAN AND PLAYER

By Neil Beasley
with Seth Burkett

Floodlit Dreams Ltd
www.floodlitdreams.com

Published by Floodlit Dreams Ltd, 2016.

A CIP catalogue record for this book is available from the British Library.

ISBN 9780992658564

Floodlit Dreams Ltd
5-6 George St
St Albans
Herts AL3 4ER.

www.floodlitdreams.com

Cover pictures by Alex Ridley
Cover designed by Josh Farley
Typeset by Peloton Publishing

COVENTRY CITY KID: Neil Beasley as a boy.

Contents

1

N-n-n-nineteen

She had a book but she wasn't reading. Her eyes were set on the page but the page wasn't turning. It had been five, 10 minutes. But still the page was the same.

It wasn't normal for Mum to be like this. She usually flicked through her books with great speed, quickly casting her eyes over a page before moving on to the next one. Antiques. They were always books about antiques. She had a house full of them, after all, and they were a great passion of hers. Yet now she was tense, her eyes fixated on the same spot of *Miller's Antiques: Professional Handbook Price Guide 2004*. They didn't even move to scan the page. I doubted that she'd reached a cliffhanger point but still I ignored her. Carried on watching the television. Sounds and visions going through my mind. It didn't matter what she was thinking about. She had her spot and I had mine: the screen.

"Neil..."

Her voice, though soft, pierced the room. She looked up slowly, away from that spot and up toward me. My face burned ever so slightly as I turned to face her. She was studying me, but not with that usual quiet admiration that mothers show their sons. This was different. Her eyes went beyond the surface. They saw right into me. She had my attention and now she was ready to pounce with whatever it was that was on her mind. The words came quickly, like she had wanted to ask them for a long time. Like she already knew, but feared the answer.

"Are you gay?"

Shit. Lie to her.

"No".

That was far too quick a 'No'. She'll see right through it. And what are you lying for anyway, Neil? Isn't this what you wanted? All this time you've been hiding it from your family. You're 19. An adult. A grown-up who should be free to live his life how he wants. Free from the pain and lies and deceit and fear and cowardice of the last few years. And she's still studying you anyway. She doesn't believe you. She knows you're a coward. She thinks you're too scared to admit it. What's the point of hiding it anymore? This is the easiest opportunity you'll ever get to come out.

"Yes," I added suddenly. Yes, Mum. Yes I am gay. I've been gay all my life. And now you know the truth and I couldn't be happier.

My response washed over her. It was as if she was unable to process it. Her eyes were still fixed on me. Her book was in the same place, her page still unread. It felt like minutes, hours before she spoke. Really it was only a matter of seconds, but when they came her words hit me hard, like waves crashing onto a rocky shore.

"Neil", she spoke calmly, her eyes still fixed on that same spot. "I just want you to know that it's a lonely life." And with that she sighed, forcing a short, pained, smile and returned to her unread book.

Mum, you couldn't have been more wrong.

2

Me and Michael Owen

Nobody learns to be gay. I'll never understand the line of thought that gays can be 'cured'. It's natural. I was born gay. I'm not saying that I waltzed out of my mum's womb in the August of 1985 dancing to *YMCA* by Village People. You'll find very few gays who do that anyway, to be honest. What I am saying is that these feelings are natural; they aren't nurtured. No matter what happens, I won't suddenly turn heterosexual overnight. You can't help your feelings and you certainly can't control them.

That said, there were times when I almost tried to 'grow out of it' myself. School can be a cruel place. It was only when I got to my local secondary school – The Cooper School in Bicester, Oxfordshire – that I figured my feelings weren't 'normal'. I put normal in quotation marks because, really, what is normal? A school is home to some of the strangest activities and traditions that are out there. But anyway, being gay certainly wasn't 'normal'. 'Normal' was kicking a panelled football around at lunchtimes, chasing after girls and trying not to look too keen in class.

At least I had the football part ticked off. I would soon become a football fanatic, Coventry City my religion of choice, the fiery Scot Gordon Strachan the chief architect in deciding our destiny each Saturday. It happened by accident – the Coventry City part, anyway. Dad is a big supporter of Liverpool FC and took me to a game at the end of the 1995/96 season.

He didn't fancy driving all the way to Liverpool, so we ended up going to Highfield Road, Coventry City's former stadium, to see his beloved side in action. Relegation-threatened Coventry ended up winning 1-0 against third-placed Liverpool. It was a brilliant game. Supporting the losing team would have put a downer on the whole day for my enthusiastic 10-year-old self, so from that moment on I became a Sky Blue, despite my Dad's best efforts. Was it Freud who said that a son spends his life rebelling against his father? Whatever the reason, it was definitely a case of short-term gain. If only I'd have known the long-term effect of such a disastrous decision. Hindsight is a wonderful thing.

Maybe my embrace of football was an extreme effort to fit in with what society expected of me. But I was only 10. It was more likely a case of wanting to make my Dad, a successful local footballer himself, proud. Football would go on to play a massive part of my life, both before and after coming out. No matter how hard I'd try over the years, football and sexuality just couldn't be separated.

At times the sport would confuse me – how could I be so 'normal' in one regard, yet so different in another? That wasn't the only emotion, though. Football would provide me with unbridled joy, sometimes it would push me to my lowest of lows, and at other times it would liberate me. And that was just through following Coventry City. Playing? That was something totally different. I played football regularly, though as I got older it would only confuse my sense of self. Even so, there's nothing quite like kicking that ball around a pitch.

Back at The Cooper School the only certainty I'd have got with coming out as gay would have been an avalanche of bullying sliding my way, trapping me helplessly under the barrage of abuse. It's enough for some kids to go under. After all, gay had been normalised as a derogatory piece of slang. Been told off by the teacher? She was gay. Been given an extra piece of home-work? That's gay. Had to run an extra lap of the field at cross country? So gay. Basically, anything that wasn't cool was gay and if you weren't cool then school was going to be a struggle.

I loved the naivety of the primary school I attended, Long-fields, also in my hometown of Bicester. Despite popular belief, there is in fact more to Bicester than the shopping village, a magnet for consumers and tourists and which sprouted up in 1992 whilst I was still a pupil at Longfields.

The school was a 10-minute walk from my house. Though it was relatively small in terms of pupils, the school grounds were big. The playing fields seemed to stretch for miles, though I'd unfortunately never get to grace them in the green and blue of the Longfields Primary School football team. Instead I seemed to spend much of my schooling in Portakabins, particularly the early years, despite the fact that there were only two of them and they were there to support the main school building. Though these structures were intended to be temporary, the only thing that ended up being temporary about them was the pupils. Indeed, the Portakabins were still there when I finished at the school.

In primary school you're too young to understand fully what is and what isn't normal. You don't know everyone else's thoughts and feelings and you don't know if your own thoughts and feelings are 'right' or 'wrong' or whatever. I always suspect-ed that I was gay from a pretty young age. It just got confirmed to me when I progressed to The Cooper School. Everyone would always talk about Kelly Brook and how good looking she was and I'd just stand there thinking: 'So what? Who cares'. I'd never had a girlfriend but all the other kids at school had. I wasn't interested in girls. All the other kids were. I was different, and no matter how much football I played at lunchtimes there was no changing that.

Being gay was immoral. That's what everyone told me anyway. It was all over the TV, then there were all of my friends
and everyone in school who taught me it was wrong. No wonder I kept quiet. I kept quiet in the hope that I would grow out
of it and become 'normal'.

It didn't work. No matter what anyone tells you, being quiet
doesn't turn you straight, and the only thing - or rather things -
I managed to grow out of were my shoes. In fact, if anything,
being quiet had the opposite effect. As I progressed into my
teenage years I began to develop an attraction towards my best
mate Paul. I'd known Paul since primary school. He came from
Cheshire and everyone loved him. In the playground he used
to think he was Robbie Fowler and because he seemed to be
from near Liverpool, everyone thought he was the real deal.
Everyone but me, that is. I thought Paul was a cocky so-and-so.
My opinion didn't really count for much, though, for he was the
most popular kid in school.

It was only when we got to secondary school that we began
to grow close. I learned that Paul was kind and caring – exactly
the opposite of what I had always perceived him to be – and
he became really special to me. We had a great laugh together. I
used to love his blonde hair. He liked me too, and we developed
a close friendship – just not as close as I would have wished. He
was interested in girls. I used to get so jealous when we would
sit together and he'd tell me about the latest girl he'd got together with. To this day I still wish I'd confided my sexuality to him.

Being gay was something that I always knew in the back
of my mind but by then it had certainly been brought into the
forefront. It was Michael Owen who did it. I was 14 and Owen
fever was gripping the nation. It was the World Cup of 1998
and the young Liverpool striker had the world at his feet. He
was our new English hope – the one who could finally propel
us to a first major title since 1966. As a football fanatic I too

was gripped, but the reasons for my obsession weren't so much to do with his skills on the pitch.

I'd only gone into my sister's room to get a PlayStation game. She kept them behind the door, and as I pulled the door toward me I got this glimpse of Michael Owen. He wasn't even in his football kit. It was one of those marketing calendars, filled with images of Owen in suits and fancy clothes that marketing people had probably paid him a lot of money to wear. I was transfixed. He was young, talented and a star. He had this amazing smile which just drew you in. I couldn't get over how down-to-earth he seemed. Over the next few weeks I kept on going into my sister's room and looking at that calendar, always with the alibi of fetching a new PlayStation game. I couldn't help myself.

The penny had dropped. I wasn't going to grow out of it. I am who I am and I was comfortable with that. The only trouble is that that 'who I am' couldn't deal with what could have happened to me had I come out at school. I saw how they treated the kids they suspected were gay. There were a few of them, though many more would come out later, and they were given a pretty rough time – ostracised, chewed up and spat out by the unforgiving social norms of a comprehensive.

Then there was my sister. She was also studying at my school. She wasn't in my year, but in school everyone knows everyone. I didn't want my actions to impact negatively on her. Later on in life people would tell me that my sister was there to protect me, and that if I had come out at school she would have done, that I shouldn't have worried about what would have happened to her. They're right. My sister would have protected me. I shouldn't have felt the need to protect her. And coming out earlier would have made my later years easier.

The lies and deceit grew as the days, months and years went by. I felt like I had consciously to alter my behaviour. I got a

girlfriend. To this day I'm ashamed of what I did. Ashamed I
used someone else's emotions to cover up my sexuality. Even
worse, I took her virginity. Is that not the most immoral thing
you've ever heard?

It almost happened by accident. We kind of fell into the
relationship. She was young and pretty and popular and the star
pupil. She was also the Head Girl. I liked her as a person. She
was chatty and we got on really well. We could talk for hours
and often we would. We got to know each other and then it
just happened. It was the perfect cover in every way possible.
School being a homophobic environment, her presence next
to me, along with the fact that I was playing football for a local
side in Heyford Athletic, meant that nobody suspected me.

Still, I couldn't wait to get out of the place and I left secondary school as soon as I could, at the age of 16. Academia and
I didn't click. You know that old joke about someone's exam
results spelling FUDGE? Well, I wasn't far off. I left The Cooper School without a single pass at GCSE. It was a case of me
never being able to concentrate in class, as well as the fact that
I'd decided my future lay with the British Army.

I didn't need qualifications. I was sure of it. I wouldn't be
doing some dead-end job holed up in an office. No, I'd be out
there fighting for my country. The great outdoors, the exercise,
the camaraderie was exactly what I felt I needed. I must admit
the hordes of sleek, muscular men I would come into contact
with didn't exactly put me off, especially since the Ministry of
Defence had recently overturned their ruling that homosexuals
were not allowed to serve in the army. Sure, it took more than
just one ruling for attitudes to change, and serving in the British Army as a gay man would be tough, even though I had no
intention of announcing my sexuality. Although I'd be continuing my life of lies and deceit, I knew that I'd still be having fun.
I'd enjoy it. I was in contact with a closeted gay man serving

with the Welsh Guards and he certainly enjoyed it. I was convinced that it was the life for me. Until I actually met with the people the army employed in their careers office, that is.

While building myself up for the army I'd forgotten that being in it meant that there was a good chance there would be people on the other side shooting at me. Trying to kill me. Then the people in the careers office pretty much told me that even so I wouldn't have to worry because I'd pretty much end up being a security guard. I didn't want to be a security guard but I didn't really want to be shot at either, so that was the end of that dream. Back to the drawing board then.

I pitched up at Tesco and stuck it out full time for a year or so. It was money, but I knew it wasn't a career, so when I saw that the local community college was running a National Vocational Qualification in football coaching, I jumped at the chance.

3

The Fashanu Factor

Studying on a football course would be an ideal cover to go alongside my girlfriend. Who knew of any gay footballers? Sure, there had been Justin Fashanu, but that was it. Football was working class, a 'proper' man's sport for 'proper' men who drank beer and liked women. Given the treatment that Nottingham Forest's million pound striker Fashanu received, and the attitudes to which he was subjected and which led to him hanging himself, I wanted to make sure I portrayed myself as one of those 'proper' men.

Fashanu's story is one of devastating sadness. Brian Clough is one of my heroes – I love the bloke – but he had a chance to help Fashanu and he didn't. What Clough did with his Nottingham Forest team was amazing. The nuggets he came out with that the press lapped up were amazing too. But his treatment of Fashanu wasn't. To be fair to Clough, in his autobiography he recognised that he could, and should, have done more to help Fashanu. It helps restore his legend, but it doesn't solve anything.

Justin Fashanu's plight took homosexual footballers back at least a decade in the fight for equality, and it wasn't as if we were close to being treated equally before that either. No wonder I felt like I needed to put on such a charade. Fashanu had tested the water of society, slipped in and drowned. Nobody had tried to pull him out. They'd just watched him sink.

The football course wasn't just a cover, though. I wasn't doing it purely as a means of trying to be the masculine male that society dictated I should be. No, football was an obsession. I loved the sport, though I couldn't be who I wanted to be on that football course. As expected, I'd walked into an environment that was extremely laddish. They'd have shot me down if I had shown that I was different. The tribal mentality was strong and so I went with the grain. I was at the height of my deceit.

I was actively seeing men at the same time as studying on the football course, but the separate circles I was moving in could never have met. There was no chance that the football course leader – a tough man named Ivor Gumm – would ever have asked why I kept going to 'that bloody poofs' club', as Clough had to Fashanu. He'd never have found out. There was, however, a chance that my parents would find out. Those were two circles I didn't exactly keep separate. The same men that I was seeing would occasionally stay the night at my parents' house under the illusion that they were merely friends of mine. It worked, and for the time that it worked I felt like a genius, like I was masterminding the whole scenario perfectly.

My relationship with my girlfriend was still going strong – in the eyes of society at least – and I carried the tag of being a 'hard man' on the football pitch. Doing stuff with guys wasn't anything new. I'd actually started a few years previously whilst still in secondary school, just after my long-term affair with the Michael Owen calendar.

There are a lot more gays than people make out. There's loads in fact, especially in the Air Cadets, which I joined at the age of 13 for the sole reason that Paul was a member. It was a chance to spend time with him, to try and impress him. I ended up staying in the Air Cadets for five years and though I didn't end up turning Paul in any way, I was able to meet a number of keen, young gay men. Given the similarities between the Air

Cadets and the army, such meetings didn't exactly put me off
my future career plans, especially as my success wasn't limited
just to gay men.

I actually had a lot of encounters with guys who were
straight. Supposedly, anyway. It wasn't anything too extreme.
With most of them it was just kissing when we were able to
isolate ourselves in private, though I went a bit further with
some and explored a bit with my hands, without ever going the
whole way.

I was with my girlfriend for a long time. Even though I was
seeing other men at the same time, I was still managing to see
her nearly every day. I wasn't necessarily sexually attracted to
her but there was still a spark. Whereas she'd have described
me as her boyfriend, I'd have described her as my best friend.

It was a difficult, confusing time, and I found solace through
the autobiographies of well-known gay men, such as Graham
Norton and Stephen Fry. I became addicted to Graham Norton's DVDs. It was comforting to see them both making people
laugh instead of hiding their sexuality. They were confronting
their audience with their sexuality, putting it in their faces and
not giving a damn how they reacted. I'd like to think that is how
I am now, but back then it certainly wasn't. I wished I could be
like them but I just couldn't. I was too scared to be outed in the
macho environment.

Whilst the whole charade was going on, I carried on working part-time at Tesco to get some money in. A few months
later, I decided to pursue another potential career path by joining the local police force as a Special Constable. Having just
turned 18, I was the youngest Special Constable they'd ever
had. It all came about at a family function.

After the disappointing meeting with the army, I didn't know
which way to turn. I'd pinned all of my hopes on living out my
life as an officer and had been thwarted by harsh reality. There

was something that really attracted me to the army: the camaraderie, the physical nature of the job, the outdoors, the feeling
that you were doing some good in the world – pretty much
everything that didn't come with stacking shelves at Tesco.

My family had told a few of their friends of my disappoint-
ment, and one day one came up to me and asked: 'Why don't
you try out with the police force? A Special Constable isn't too
dissimilar from being in the army.' He was right as well. I took
his advice and contacted Thames Valley Police that weekend.
I was given a voluntary role which, given my Tesco and college commitments, I decided to carry out mainly at weekends.
Finally, it was a role that could lead to something further down
the line. True, it wasn't the stereotypical career path for a homosexual, but why shouldn't it be? It was everything I wanted
and more, but in a way it made me feel so hypocritical. I mean,
here I was going after criminals whereas in reality I was the
criminal myself, always hiding the truth.

I needed to take a long hard look at myself. It was always
there, nagging at me. 'Come on, Neil. Are you going to be brave
or what?' Yet no matter how strong the urge to be brave, I just
couldn't do it. I was psyching myself up to get rid of my girlfriend and come out, but at the same time my little sister was
having problems at school. I didn't want to put even more on
her plate.

Then, one day, I got this text from my girlfriend: "We need
2 talk when u get home."

I froze. Shit. She's not pregnant is she? Hold on. This could
be good. She could be seeing someone else. Maybe she's already
slept with him. Please let it be that. That way I could finally get
rid of her. Ideally she'd do it herself. 'Oh Neil, I'm so sorry but
I can't stay with you. You've been wonderful'. If only she knew
how happy that would have made me.

But no. She wasn't pregnant. She hadn't cheated on me and

she was still in love with me, whatever 'love' is as a teenager. There was hope, however. She'd be going to university in Coventry from September. 'Oh, that's terrible,' I told her, all the while thinking that this must be it. Surely our relationship wouldn't survive her degree? She'd meet other boys and we'd drift apart naturally, each going our own separate ways.

She was upset but took heart from the fact that we'd still see each other now and again. I had a membership with the Sky Blues you see, even though the inevitable had finally happened and we'd been relegated to what is now the Championship two years previously. I'd be in the area every other Saturday. Damn. If only she went to a different university. She was the star pupil – surely she should have gone to Oxbridge? Better make that Cambridge, actually. If she was in Oxford she definitely wouldn't have been far away enough for us to drift apart naturally.

Still, it felt like a big weight off my shoulders. Mum and Dad were gutted. They loved her. Loved how she was always trying to save the world. Loved how kind and intelligent she was. They really wanted me to put the effort in to make the relationship work. They thought we were perfect together. If only they knew.

I went to see her a couple of times at university. I'd graduated from my football course and was now fully focused on my role in the police, with the job at Tesco giving me relative financial security, whilst she wallowed in the student lifestyle. It was all right seeing her. She'd had a hard time finding friends at first but was starting to settle in. She kept on saying that I wasn't coming to see her often enough. Of course I wasn't. That was the aim. But it was such a cowardly thing to do. I was making her split up with me. I was playing with her life and, yes, I was ashamed. Not enough to come out to everyone, although I had actually come out by this point to three people.

I didn't want to live my next 60 or 70 years as a lie. The only trouble was that I was still a bit of a coward, so I had to rely on alcohol to give me the courage – or stupidity – to come out. I've always said that drunk words are sober thoughts. Anyway, I was out on the town celebrating my birthday, and as always happens when drunk, I got a bit emotional.

I sent a text message to Joe, my best mate with whom I played for Heyford Athletic. He had convinced me to come along and sign for them. In the text I said that there was something I had to tell him as it was really bugging me. He asked what was up.

"Man, I'm gay", I told him, before adding, "You know, I don't know what to do about it. Sorry man if you're let down."

If you're let down. Even now I can't believe I wrote that.

Joe just responded with "I don't care." My reply was short: "Oh," it said.

"I couldn't care less," he continued. "You're my mate. Why does it matter?"

Then he asked if anyone else knew and I told him that two of my cousins, who also played on our team, probably had an inkling and he just said OK. So I told another of my mates. And he told me that he didn't really care either.

In a way I felt liberated, but then again I had psyched myself up so much for this: the agony, the betrayal, the deceit, and all for a reaction as tame as this? Did I really want a big drama, though? I had resigned myself to having to leave the team straight away. I thought that I'd never be accepted for being myself in such a macho environment. To be fair, I had picked two of the most understanding, liberal players on the team, but still...

A few weeks later I was out on the town again. And I was drunk again. And emotional. For some reason I was a bit tearful. I can't remember why, but there was someone I policed with who was on duty in town and he came up and asked me what was the matter. I told him. Straight up. He got me a lift home and everything seemed fine. Then the next day I woke up. Shit. That's all I could think. What had I done?

There was a deep-rooted attitude towards homosexuality in the police force. That may be unfair to the younger recruits, who by and large were very politically correct, but there were a lot of older people in the force who'd been there a while and held these backward attitudes which they'd never tried to change.

In one of my first shifts I remember an officer using Cockney rhyming slang in referring to a black man as an 'egg and spoon'. Then there was the guy who used to put his back to the wall when the one openly gay man in the unit was near him, insinuating that he needed to protect his arse. His colleagues loved it. This act always used to amuse them and they would actively encourage it.

"Watch it," they would whisper dramatically when the guy was near the gay man, attempting to set him off again. 'You idiots', I remember thinking, 'You absolute idiots. If the wrong person saw you now, you'd all be out of a job.' But then what's the point? If those people all got fired then new recruits would come in, many holding the same attitudes. Nothing would change.

If you asked any of them they would say it was just a joke, and it was just a joke. But the thing with these jokes – and we call it banter now – is that they always offend somebody. Shameless bullying can be masked as 'banter', and if you don't like it then you're not only perceived as strange, but you become a social outcast. There are policies in place to stop this kind of bullying, but that's all they are. Policies. What do they actually stop? In reality, it's just a tick in the box rather than people actually giving a shit. How can you really agree to treat everyone equally and with respect no matter their race, sexuality or gender when the guy who hands you the piece of paper refers to black people as egg and spoons?

At first I felt pride in being a Special Constable. Completing the training and working my way up to my new position was such an achievement. But then I saw how the force actually operated, not only when it came to racism and homophobia, but also with the lack of resources meaning that they could only ever respond. It wasn't like we were able to stop many crimes – a grand total of zero in my time with the police, in fact. It was like chasing your tail the whole time. Who was I actually helping?

I avoided going into the station for a good three or four weeks after accidentally telling my colleague on that fateful night. I feared the news would be everywhere, splashed all over the station. Wherever I'd look there would be officers backing into the walls, backing away from me, repelled by my sexuality. No, I couldn't deal with that. I couldn't even face it.

People were texting me. When was I next coming in? They hadn't seen me for a while, how was I getting on? I told them all I was away, and when I finally did come back in to the station, I made sure that it was at a time when the guy I told definitely wouldn't be in. Let me tell you, it took a hell of a lot of courage to go back in. On first inspection everything seemed to be fine, however. Nobody backed into the walls. Nothing was said. I repelled nobody. Indeed, I was treated as if I had never been away. Everything was normal. Nobody seemed to be any the wiser.

But I couldn't avoid *him* forever. A couple of weeks later I was allocated a different shift. I thought the guy I told wouldn't be in, but unfortunately we were very short-staffed and he got drafted in alongside me. My heart was racing and dread clouded my vision. Everything had gone so smoothly up until now. And that's how it would remain. He came up to me. I still remember it now, so vividly.

"Just so you know, thanks for telling me," he said. "I haven't told a soul. I never will and I'll take it to my grave. It is up to you what you do and I'll back you all the way. It was brave of you to tell me but it is not for me to do anything with that information other than support you if you need it." I made the decision then not to tell anyone else.

And that's how it stayed. Everything was going brilliantly. Until one day, when I was lying on the sofa watching television. It's strange how you can always remember the exact details of your life-defining moments.

I was watching *The Simpsons*. I love that programme. It can keep me entertained for hours. It was the episode where they build a monorail in Springfield, despite Marge Simpson's best protests. I remember there was a catchy song in it. Mum was the only other person in the room. We'd often come into the living room together after a meal. She was on the other sofa, a book in her hands. The pages were open but they weren't moving, her eyes fixed on the same spot.

4

The Bicester Kid

If I had a pound for every time someone recognised me as Mervyn Beasley's son then I'd be a rich man. I wouldn't exactly be a millionaire – unfortunately crowds at Bicester Town Football Club were never that big, and for some reason their games were never shown on *Match of the Day* – but I'd certainly be comfortable.

My Dad was the goalkeeper for Bicester in the Hellenic League. He played there for a long time and became something of a local hero. My Nan's house used to be plastered with newspaper clippings and photos of him in action. Though my Dad wasn't blessed with height – standing at around 5ft 7in, which is small for a keeper – he was strong and authoritative with lightning-fast reactions. He would talk to his defence all game, ordering them to push up or drop off, telling them if they had time to play or if there was a man closing them down. He was the kind of goalkeeper that defenders could rely on. If the ball went over them or in behind, they knew that he would come and claim it with welcoming arms. He had all the attributes to make it as a professional – all of them apart from height.

Given his love of the game, my Dad probably expected me to be a bit more excited when he bounded home one day to announce that he was due to start a new under-9s football team the following season. And I qualified for it. Football was all the rage at the time, even more so than usual. Rupert Murdoch would soon plough money into a newly-formed Premier

League and Gazza's tears at Italia 1990 had endeared many to the sport. Except me. I didn't really have much interest.

I was seven years old and preferred being a soldier. Pretending to be one, that is. Gunning down my friends was much more exciting than chasing a ball around a field. Gazza? I'd never heard of him. But my Dad was so enthusiastic and every young boy wants to make his father happy. I was no different. My Dad was my hero – still is, in fact – and buoyed by his enthusiasm I set about trying to copy his dives, only to realise that I didn't really like diving around a muddy field.

Not letting this put him off, Dad took me along to the first training session for his new team, due to be held on the playing fields at my primary school. Unfortunately for him it rained. And rained. And rained. I remember taking shelter under the roof of one of the temporary Portakabins, cold and shivering and fearing any venture out into the open to kick a few balls about. Getting even colder and wetter didn't seem like much fun and nor did learning a sport in which I had no interest and which had very little appeal. Fortunately my luck was in and the session was eventually cancelled. If only such luck had continued for the rest of the season.

It must be the same for all kids when they are pushed into doing something they aren't too bothered about. The automatic reaction is not to like whatever they are being forced to do, and that was the same with me, even though Dad bought me these really cool Paul Gascoigne boots. They had his signature on and everything.

I never really had the concentration or enthusiasm for football. Concentration, as my teachers will tell you, was not just an issue on the football pitch. Added to this, I didn't even have a team to support. I 'supported' Liverpool because Dad told me to support Liverpool. While that may be how it is for the vast majority of people, who then go on to embrace it, I didn't.

I hated the arrogance of the kids who played football in the playground. They were genuinely convinced they were the next big thing – especially that kid with the blonde hair who thought he was Robbie Fowler. I joined in with their game every now and again but I didn't really enjoy it. I just couldn't understand how my classmates would be in such awe at someone who could kick a ball between two jumpers, and my lack of understanding turned into jealousy toward those who were held in such high regard.

When I got to secondary school, I realised that all my classmates would talk about was football. That and Kelly Brook, of course. Fortunately for me by then, exposed to it so much, I had started to catch the bug.

It began when Dad took me to watch that Coventry v Liverpool game at the end of the 1995/96 season when I became a Sky Blue. Since that experience, I was itching to get to more live games, though I'd have to make do with the odd game here and there for the next season or so. Then my Grandfather came to the rescue.

He was a massive Nottingham Forest fan, but his health had deteriorated in recent years. He now had arthritis and couldn't commit to making the trip up to Nottingham for every home game – maybe he was bad luck, because the season he stopped watching them they won what was then the Nationwide League First Division, gaining promotion to the Premier League. For my grandfather the 12-mile trip to watch Oxford United, however, was much more feasible. And so, at the age of 12 and on the eve of the 1997/98 season, he asked me if I wanted to accompany him.

From that moment, our ritual began. Every other Saturday we would drive into Oxford and park outside this house in Headington that had a massive eight-metre long fibreglass shark poking out of the roof. It was quite a local landmark and we had no problem remembering where we had parked, which was always his concern. Then we would make the short walk to this rubbishy little stadium called The Manor Ground, located in the middle of a housing estate.

The first time I went I couldn't see any of the game. But then a man lifted me up on to this big railing, and suddenly I could see everything. It was amazing. It was actually thrilling. There were only about 7,000 people there but even that looked a strain for the dilapidated ground. There were a few people who had climbed up some of the trees in the right hand corner of the stadium to get a decent – and free – view of the match. They were definitely the smart ones.

My knowledge of Oxford United wasn't great. All I knew was that they were a bit of a laughing stock. Nobody at school supported them and why should they? Oxford were rubbish. They weren't even in the Premier League, and the league they were in – like Forest, Nationwide Division One – well, they were hardly troubling the top parts of the table. Little did I realise in later years when the club sank to the Conference that this was actually a high level.

Yet as the game started this popular myth began to unravel before my very eyes. Oxford weren't half bad. They were pretty good, in fact. They scored some goals and it was all very exciting. The raucous cheers which greeted their every goal were amazing and they got me hooked. I wanted more and more.

It wasn't just the football, either. In my fourth game at the Manor Ground, Oxford took on Swindon in the 'A420 derby'. To be honest, I didn't really understand the significance of local derbies at that stage. To me, Swindon Town were just another small Football League team that the boys in yellow would beat.

I'd seen the raw emotion, the passion and the cheers of the crowd in the three previous games, yet until that point I had never seen violence at a football game. Sure, I remembered the television images from Euro '96, though that was trouble, rather than violence – stuff like men on top of police cars. This was something totally different. In the second half the home fans, growing increasingly frustrated, began to throw coins at the Swindon goalkeeper. They were actually trying to hurt him. It was worse than the usual 'banter'. There was genuine anger and aggression.

It all got so bad that the referee blew the whistle and gathered all of the players into the centre circle, with an announcement coming over the tannoy that the game would be abandoned if the coin throwing didn't stop. The fans relented but I remember thinking how I'd seen this totally different side of football. I'd felt the adrenaline when my team scored a goal, yet now I saw how the sport could evoke other emotions. Anger, rather than elation, was the order of the day.

Instead of being upset at the idiots throwing coins I had this strange feeling. Maybe it was the tribal mentality of being a part of that crowd, but the violence gave me a buzz. It got the adrenaline flowing. Little did I know how that aggression of the football crowd would come to plague me further down the line, not only as I wrestled with coming out, but also in the form of a constant fear that it would be redirected at me because of who I was. How can you be a part of the tribe when you're different from the tribe?

In the end I guess Granddad didn't share my view that Oxford weren't half bad, because soon he started taking me to watch my beloved Sky Blues. Coventry were playing in the Premier League at this point and were proving competitive, occupying a respectable position in mid-table. It was a 50-minute drive, but for a chance to see some of the world's best players in action it was more than worth it.

Suddenly I was getting to see teams such as Liverpool, Arsenal and the all-conquering Manchester United side who had won the league four times in the previous five seasons. There were players such as Michael Owen, Dennis Bergkamp and David Beckham, though I'm not sure any of them came close to matching the on-pitch abilities of Coventry's star striker, the tall forward with the endearing name: Dion Dublin. Indeed, it was in part thanks to Dublin that we came away with a 3-2 home victory against Manchester United in one of my first few games at Highfield Road, and when we drew 2-2 with Arsenal – who would go on to win the title that season – three weeks later, our excitement levels started to peak.

I'd loved Oxford but I felt like I had a real connection to Coventry, and not only because of my magical first visit. The attendant for the car park outside the stadium always accepted our bribe and allowed us to park there. I soon discovered that this enabled us to park alongside all of the players and I came to meet the majority of them.

There was one time when Gary Breen spoke with me for at least five minutes. Now there was a player – a classic old school, no-nonsense centre half who was as safe as houses. I wouldn't want him dribbling out of defence and I'm not sure he could hit a barn door with a shot, but he wasn't half bad at getting that ball away from the danger zone. He'd just signed from Birmingham and ended up staying five years at Coventry. If I had my way he'd still be there now.

It wasn't just Gary Breen who stopped to give us his time, however. I remember similar chats with Colin Hendry and Mustafa Hadji, both of whom were true gentlemen. In fact, the players all took time to say hello and I remember thinking that they were great. They didn't distance themselves from us. It was like they were us. The fans and the players, all united as one. I was truly hooked, and this feeling only increased when we worked out where we needed to sit to be next to the players' tunnel. Suddenly I wasn't just meeting the stars of Coventry, but also the stars of the world, including the talented young striker who would stare out at me from the glossy pages of a calendar. A guy by the name of Michael Owen.

Highfield Road was better than Oxford United's ground, there was no doubting it. It was much bigger, the atmosphere even better and the smells even stronger, though one form of entertainment had been lost: there was no overhanging tree with onlookers clinging to it to distract me during the dull games. Fortunately those were few and far between.

As the season continued, the excitement grew and grew. That previous summer it had been unthinkable. Coventry had escaped relegation by the skin of their teeth. If Middlesbrough hadn't been handed a three-point penalty for calling off a fixture at short notice, Coventry City would have been slumming it with Oxford United in the Nationwide League. Fortunately they weren't, and fortunately in the season I started to watch them with Granddad they were flying. Qualification to the European competitions looked a real possibility, at least until a run of six draws from their final eight games meant they just fell short. Draws were something of a speciality for the Sky Blues: they managed 16 of them that season. If they'd turned just two of those into wins they'd have made the UEFA Cup.

Such excitement really gave me a passion for the sport, both on and off the pitch. In secondary school I realised the need to fit in or be cast out by the rules of the social hierarchy. If I wanted to make friends with the kids that didn't get bullied, I had to give my playing career another go. And so I did. I stepped on to the pitch once more, and it turned out that I was actually quite good. I no longer played in goal. Now I was a striker. Watching regular football had really helped me. Now I could imagine that I was Robbie Keane when I was playing, even though I was probably something closer to Gary Breen.

Most of all, I was good because I could actually head the

ball. Everyone else seemed pretty afraid when the ball was in the air, but not me. Whereas they would emit a sort of whimper as the ball hit their face, I'd meet it head on with a loud shout of "Neil's ball!" I wasn't afraid of anything on the pitch. I was a warrior, and not just when the ball was in the air. Slide tackles were my speciality. Hard but fair, that was my motto, though it was always best if you got both the man and the ball in the challenge. I wasn't just your stereotypical centre back, however. I mean, I did play up front after all and I did have a nice little finish on me. Shame that later on I wouldn't be able to score for love nor money.

I'd love to compare my style of play to Lionel Messi, but then I've never seen Messi win a crunching slide tackle. I guess Stuart Pearce is a better example, especially because he was something of an idol for me growing up. I thought the bloke was amazing, a tough tackler but fair. Any idiot can go around a pitch kicking people. My Mum could but it wouldn't make her good. Stuart Pearce would never cheat. I would like to think that I lead by example, just like him, with a proper professional attitude, but then I remember some of the things that I've said to referees over the years and I think maybe not.

Playing football has benefits which go far beyond the pitch. It's the best safety net in the world if you're gay. Sometimes I struggle to understand this supposed massive weight on your shoulders because of your sexuality. The pitch is egalitarian, and for me, playing was the best barrier in the world. I was putting myself in an area where no one could touch me, where no one thought twice. Nobody ever questioned anything when I was playing football. All I was judged on was my playing style. As the team's hard man it was the best protection ever.

Even so, I never got a look in with my school team. A place in the eleven was reserved for the really super cool kids. There was no chance that the team was selected by ability. All the kids

who played were in the same friendship group and although I
had avoided befriending the kids who were bullied, I had yet
to crack the super cool kids. We could have had a much better
side. There were quiet people who were far better than some
of the loudmouths who were selected, but I guess that's just
politics.

By now I was desperate to play regularly. I didn't even care
about the cold and the wet any more. Now I couldn't be happier at the prospect of a great big slide tackle in the mud. My
Dad had stopped running his team by now. He was never really
prepared for how much hard work it would be. It was all of the
hidden hours which threw him: the phone calls to poor Tim-
my's father who was unhappy at his son's lack of game time, the
hours of mind-numbing administration, sorting the equipment,
not to mention the amount of patience needed to deal with a
team of eight-year-olds where half of the players just wanted
to run around aimlessly and make daisy chains.

It was probably a good thing to play for a team other than
my Dad's. At the age of 12, I signed for a local Sunday league
team, Bardwell Boys. Dad would still come and watch me play,
but without his direct involvement it felt like it really was my
own decision to be on that pitch. I felt no pressure on his behalf. And there really was no pressure on me, because each week
when we turned up, the only question on everyone's lips was
whether we would lose by five or 10 this time round. We were
awful. Even worse than Swindon Town. And the worst thing
was that nobody seemed to care. It was like we had acquired all
of those eight-year-old daisy chain makers and dressed them
in matching kit and set them loose on the football pitch. They
might as well have put 10 garden gnomes out there. No matter
how much I'd yell at them they just wouldn't listen. Not even
Stuart Pearce could have whipped that bunch into shape.

The one positive with that team was that I was a very big

fish in a small pond, a shark, if you like – and a great big eight-metre long one at that. I liked that, but after a season I really felt like I had outgrown the pond. It was time to move on. I didn't want to get beaten every week. Stuart Pearce wouldn't have stood for it and neither would I.

Chesterton Boys was much more like it. They played in the small village of Chesterton, just outside Bicester, and used actual formations with actual tactics. The training sessions were prepared in advance and had a specific focus. Gary Brock was the manager. He was the brother of the former Oxford United and Newcastle United midfielder Kevin Brock, and Kevin's professionalism had really rubbed off on Gary. It was no longer about just turning up and playing.

I was proud to pull on the white and blue shirt of Chesterton. That badge had great meaning for me, even more so when I was made captain. By now my striking had let me down to the extent that I had been moved to play at right back. At least the move gave me a better view to yell my orders at everyone. And the best thing was that these players actually responded. They actually cared. They didn't want to see a bad result printed in the following week's local newspaper. I had high expectations of my teammates and by and large they met them.

Like all good things, however, Chesterton Boys had to come to an end. It was just a junior club and did not run sides aged older than 14 years. It created a void in my life. I missed football, missed yelling my orders and leading by example. Most of all I missed playing regularly with my mates.

I was in the football wilderness for a couple of years before I saw an advert in the local paper. You could say that it was by chance, but having left school with no real qualifications, then having my army dream shattered and deciding to work full time in Tesco, I was able to dedicate a lot of time to scanning newspapers. The tedium of my new life meant that I needed an escape, and in many ways that escape needed to come from playing on the pitch. There was only so much that watching the sport could give me.

To be honest, in the previous season watching had only made my emotions worse. Coventry finished the 2000/01 season in 19th place, meaning that they were relegated from the Premier League. Then there was poor old Oxford United, who were fulfilling their prophecy which echoed around my old school. As the years went by they were getting worse and worse, and the 2000/01 season saw them finish the Nationwide Second Division in 24th place, relegating them to the bottom tier of English professional football.

The advert, then, was timely, and it was for a team called Langford Village who were looking to recruit players for the new season. Perfect. They were an adult team in their first year, and having just turned 16 I was now eligible to play in adult football.

Named after a housing estate in Bicester, Langford played their home games in Merton, a small village five miles south of Bicester. Wembley it was not. I never actually saw him doing it, but it was very nice of the local farmer to plough the pitch before we used it each week. It wasn't just the pitch. Everything about Langford reeked of the fact that they were newly formed. I don't think any planning had actually gone into the team. It was almost like 11 friends just thought they could turn up and kick a ball about each week. There was next to no organisation and even less ability on show from our group of questionable recruits.

I stuck it out for a couple of seasons. The first season was pretty disastrous. The second saw a slight improvement, but not much. I managed to get my Dad in goal for one game. He made this amazing save, followed by a long clearance which I raced on to before finishing low past the keeper. That was one of my proudest moments in football, and after the final whistle the team all headed straight over to Dad to congratulate him on an outstanding showing.

What was strange about Langford was that though we were rubbish, our players thought they were world beaters. They knew it all. Nobody could tell them what to do. Of course they already knew. In their minds, if cruel fate hadn't conspired against them they'd be playing professionally. Maybe not for Liverpool, but certainly for Oxford because, come on, Oxford were rubbish. By the end of that second season I decided that I could no longer deal with these attitudes and losing all the time.

At Chesterton I had been playing alongside my best mate Joe Varney. Joe was a strange best mate in that I only really hung round with him at football. He lived over the other side of Bicester to me, in the area where they bred all the wrong 'uns, the kids who would beat you up for having the audacity to try hard in class or for going to a different school. None of this was true of course, but that's what I had been taught to believe by my peers.

When I met up with Joe I made sure I kept my phone hidden away and my Haribos in my bag. It wasn't necessary. Joe turned out to have a heart of gold. He was one of those people who would go out of their way to help you. The type of kid who made his parents extremely proud in the way he conducted himself. He was 100% committed to everything he did, both on and off the pitch.

Joe loved football. I've never met anyone who loves the game more, in fact. He was a defender, just like me (despite my insistence that I was a centre forward), and just like me he stood at around 5ft 7in. Neither of us was particularly athletic, though nor were we overweight. Joe was a good-looking lad, though it was his personality which really shone through. We clicked straight away, him on the left side of defence, me on the

right, working in unison to stop our wingers from getting their
crosses in. Having Joe in the team definitely made me feel more
confident that we would win.

There was one thing that really held Joe back, however: his
mouth. He may well have made his parents proud in the way
he conducted himself but it was fortunate for him they rarely
came to watch him play football. I've never heard Joe swear off
the pitch but how he could swear on it. The number of times
he told the poor referee to eff off must have been in the thousands. Sometimes I felt sorry for the referee: Joe giving him a
barrage from the left, me from the right. No matter which way
they turned, they'd be sure to be sworn at.

Joe hadn't followed me to Langford. Instead he had gone
to Heyford Athletic, where he'd had to make do with berating
referees by himself. When he learned that I was desperate for
a new challenge, however, he invited me over. I accepted, and
once again – much to the dismay of referees around Oxfordshire – we were reunited on the pitch.

Heyford was a beautiful little village. The green pitch that
Heyford Athletic played on had this lovely little canal running
down the bottom end – perfect for booting the ball into if we
were 1-0 up towards the end of the game. At the top end there
was the modern clubhouse. It was all very professional and the
club took great pride in their facilities. Even now that club has
a special place in my heart.

I joined Joe and a couple of my other mates in Heyford's
reserve team. It was brilliant, coming together each week for a
game of football before heading into the clubhouse for a drink.
My new teammates knew their limits. Unlike Langford they did
not think that we were world beaters, yet each and every one of
them would turn up each week and give 100%, showing pride
in the badge. I liked that attitude.

Unfortunately we were no good. We played in the third di-

vision of the Banbury District and Lord Jersey League. There
was no fourth division. We were the lowest of the low, and it
was just as well that we couldn't get relegated. When I joined
we were bottom. The season before that we had finished bottom. The season before that? You guessed it – we had finished
bottom. In the third division of the Banbury District and Lord
Jersey league everyone knew that as sure as the sun would rise
and set in a day, you could look at a league table and see Heyford Athletic reserves down at the bottom. I was still losing all
the time but it didn't matter so much now. I was playing well
and enjoying myself.

I had improved my game, there was no doubt about that, and
in an unlikely turn of events a large chunk of that was down to
working at Tesco. My boss there was a man named Mike – or
Mick, as he liked to be called – Keen. In his younger years Mick
had been quite a player, turning out for, and captaining, Queens
Park Rangers amongst others. He had also managed Watford,
Northampton Town and Wycombe Wanderers. By now he was
in his 60s but to this day for the life of me I don't know why he
was working in Tesco. Football's loss was my gain, as Mick was
truly one of the most inspirational people I have ever met. His
son Kevin was still involved in the game, though he was coming
to the end of his playing career with Macclesfield. Previously
he had played for West Ham, Wolverhampton Wanderers and
Stoke City, and once he hung his boots up he would go on
to coach at West Ham, Liverpool, West Bromwich Albion and
Reading.

Mick and I would talk for hours. In fact, most of my time at
work seemed to be spent talking to Mick. I would always listen
intently, captivated by his knowledge of football. Mick gave me
an insight into the professional game and he passed on tips that
I still cherish. At the time, the fact that I couldn't score for love
nor money really irritated me, especially as I really wanted to be

a centre forward. Mick told me to 'shoot before you should'.

Shoot before you should. What on earth did that mean? Mick explained how most people make it really obvious when they are going to shoot. If the opposing defender and goal-keeper know when you are going to shoot then they can act accordingly to prevent the ball from entering their goal. However, catching them off guard by shooting 'early' – before they have a chance to set themselves – gives you a greater chance of success. Your opponents cannot react so effectively. I took it all in and two weeks later I scored.

There was a lot more advice that Mick gave me, all of which I used to raise my playing standard. It ranged from the simple – "Don't think too much, Neil" – to the anecdotal – "Make sure you have a decent breakfast. One of my mates played the best game of his life after having a full English. He was told that he wasn't going to be playing, so he tucked in to a hearty breakfast, only to find out upon arrival at the ground that he was due to start the game. Guess what? He played the best game of his life." I never skipped breakfast again.

Mick didn't just help me with his advice. He always let me take time off when I had a game. He was great with switching around my shifts. He also allowed me time to watch football. I would speak at length about my appreciation of Newcastle United's Alan Shearer, a striker who in my eyes was the best in the country. I told Mick that it would be wonderful to see Shearer play. Mick agreed that he was a good player but didn't think that he had many years left in him at the very top level.

One day Mick turned up to work with a pair of West Ham tickets. By now his son had retired from playing and had taken up a coaching role with the Hammers. West Ham were due to play Newcastle that weekend and Mick, understanding just how much I wanted to see Shearer play, had got his son to sort my Grandfather and I tickets for the big game. It was a wonderful gesture which meant the world to me. Even though Alan Shearer ended up being injured, not even making the substitutes' bench, it was a great day out.

Mick motivated me to look into opportunities in football. The job at Tesco wasn't really going anywhere, and when my hours were cut – despite Mick's protests – it made my decision a lot easier. I returned to education, signing up for the NVQ in football coaching at Bicester Community College.

It turned out to be a rather faux macho environment. There were 20 of us on the course: 19 boys and one lone girl. None of us was exactly the brain of Britain. There must have been no more than 20 GCSEs between us. It may not have been an authentic macho environment, but it was certainly laddish.

Fair play to the lone girl on the course. We need more people like her in football: people willing to break boundaries, because without those people there would never be any change. If only I'd shown such willingness to break the traditional boundaries of football. The girl was a tough cookie who didn't lack in confidence and she flourished. The other 19 of us would tread carefully around her, being mindful of what was said. She was the only one who would receive such special treatment, however. For the rest of us the course was a good laugh so long as you didn't show any difference from the tribe. And I mean any difference, whether it was intentional or not. The slightest thing was picked up on and pounced upon by the bloodthirsty tribe.

There was one boy who dropped a tuna sandwich one day at lunch. As a result, he had to live with the nickname 'tuna' for the rest of the course. It started off light-hearted, as 'banter' usually does, but soon became a tool for winding him up. In the end he just relented and accepted that he was going to be called tuna for the rest of his days. On occasions the micky-taking got so bad that it would end in tears for the poor person who dared to be slightly different.

Ivor Gumm was our teacher. His personality suited his name. He was tough, someone you wouldn't cross in a hurry. He may not have been the biggest of people but boy could he shout. And the words that he did shout were certainly not suitable for youngsters. He was a fan of corporal punishment. Or at least he seemed to be. There was something about the way he looked every time he made us run laps of the field. This sinister smile would spread across his face as we struggled to maintain the speed that he demanded. It was like he enjoyed watching us suffer. Laps were his favourite form of punishment and because my classmates were an unruly bunch, we were forced into running laps pretty regularly.

Ivor was from the old school of football. He had played as a striker for Barnet and coached with Southampton, Swindon, Oxford and Bristol City. When he wasn't making us run laps and actually spent time teaching us, it was pretty obvious that he knew his stuff. Even though he was in his early 50s by now it was clear from the times he would join in with the practical sessions that he still had class on the pitch.

The two-year course wasn't short of practical sessions. It ran five days a week, and for three to four hours each day we would be out on the pitch or in the gym. I'd never been fitter in my life. My weight was down to 68kg and getting through 90 minutes was a breeze. There were only a few hours worth of classroom sessions a week and this suited my fellow classmates.

In a way it suited me too, because my football game was going from strength to strength and I'd never been able to concentrate much in the classroom. In an added bonus, I was now playing in the college football team. Not only was I playing; I was starting every game and was one of the most popular players in the team. It helped that I was a year or two older than everyone else, and being able to buy alcohol legally when nobody else could meant I had few enemies. My girlfriend, who I'd been with for three years, would bring a couple of her friends along to each game and they'd cheer for me and even make posters in support. It wasn't just my new fan group who would show appreciation of my playing style. The team hard man is often well liked and my solid slide tackles would always be received with gleeful cries from our support.

I was at the height of my deception. I had not only been accepted into the laddish tribal culture but had been championed by it. I was the poster boy. Their warrior. Nobody would ever have guessed that I was different to them. That I was hiding my big secret. That underneath the tough exterior I was conflicted. It was all an act, and an act that I had been playing to perfection.

But now things were about to change. For Mum was sitting on the other sofa, a book in her hands. The pages were open but they weren't moving. Her eyes fixed on the same spot. And then she uttered those words. Those four piercing words that would change my relationship with the beautiful game forever.

5

Joe's Story

My friendship with Joe Varney goes back a long way. In Bicester you don't really have much choice in the friends you make as everyone knows everyone. It's a small place. Our parents were friends and that friendship meant that Joe and I were made to go on play dates when we were toddlers. We progressed from play dates to training sessions and matches. We were on the same football team from a young age. Even when he lived over the 'wrong' side of town we remained friends, though admittedly it wasn't until we played together at Chesterton Boys that we became best friends. Over time I even trusted him not to nick my mobile phone if I got it out of my pocket. That trust would prove essential, because later on I would need to trust Joe on a whole different level.

Even now we play on the same football team. All these years and we're still holding defences firm. We deal in clean sheets. Clean sheets and yellow cards, that's our motto. We're still best mates, yet we still only really see each other at football. Joe continues to live in Bicester, happy to remain on the wrong side of town, though he's now working for a finance company. He's still a teenager in my mind.

Boy, how I've needed Joe over the years. He's calmed me down, put things into perspective and has generally put me at ease. That's just how it was with my coming out. If Joe hadn't reacted in the way that he did, everything would have been so much harder...

* * *

"*I* started to wonder about Neil's sexuality around the time that people our age began to drive. Liberated from the politeness of being escorted around by our parents, we were free spirits. Well, in theory, anyway. In reality all it meant was that we swore a bit more, made a couple more jokes and got to choose what played on the tape deck.

The rules of adolescence dictate that the person who rides shotgun is the one in control. Of course, the one behind the wheel is in literal control, but by definition he has to concentrate on the road. Though he can oversee what goes on in his car, the decisions behind directions to take, distribution of food and which music to play all lie with the person riding shotgun.

Except in Neil's car. In Neil's car I always rode shotgun, but in Neil's car it was always Neil who chose the music. Neil was one of the lads. He fitted right in and always made people laugh. He was bubbly, a really lively guy who always put others before himself. On the face of it, there was nothing unusual. His music selection, however… Well, that's what made me start to wonder if we were seeing the true Neil Beasley.

Foo Fighters were the sound of the time and my mates and I were all well into them. But in Neil's car he would insist on playing the latest Kylie Minogue song. I know he thinks that he hid his actions that would be classified as stereotypically homosexual, but he certainly didn't hide them all from me. Whenever Neil came to pick me up for football he'd always arrive with Kylie blasting out of the car stereo. He was even partial to a little sing-song.

It made me start to question things about him. I'm sure I wasn't the only one. You start to pick up on little things. It's a bit of a cliché that gay men love Kylie Minogue. There are plenty of straight men who like Kylie too but I guess that for as long as the cliché is there, questions will be asked. On the one hand Neil's sexuality was brought into question with his music choices, but on the other his persona on the pitch reinforced his status as a real man's man, taking him away from those questions about his sexuality.

If you ever made a mistake he'd be the first to let you know. I've certainly been on the receiving end of some infamous 'Beasley blastings' on the pitch over the years. It never mattered how close a friend you were – no matter who you were, you'd still get a blasting if you made a mistake.

It was always quite strange how aggressive Neil was on the pitch, because off it he's totally the opposite. Sure, he's my best mate so I'm a bit biased but he truly is kind and caring. I was surprised when he came out. Not shocked, but surprised. It didn't matter, though. Nothing mattered. I couldn't have been more proud of him. To hold something inside for so long and to just come out and say it to all your friends and family and colleagues, I can imagine it was so hard. It wasn't just hard. It was courageous. **"**

6

London Calling

The girlfriend was gone. Long gone, and so were my parents, although their disappearance was a lot more temporary. In fact, it was only for the weekend. But still, a weekend was a long time. Especially when the bright lights of London were calling.

The secret was out, my deceit unravelled. And it wasn't so bad. Despite my Mum's greatest fears, the world had not ended. Sure, it was pretty awkward. Dad still hadn't even mentioned it. Not a word. I was pleased that he didn't seem so upset but I at least wanted some acknowledgement.

Mum had definitely mentioned it. Coming out had caused no end of problems with her. Mum was worried about my sister, Rachel. How would she cope at school now her older brother had been outed as a homosexual? Maybe she'd be treated differently by the teachers. It certainly wouldn't reflect well on her. Wasn't it inconsiderate of Neil to inconvenience his sister like this – and just when Rachel had her exams.

All the while I was wondering when Mum was going to consider how I would now cope. A little support would have been nice. But no, it was all about my sister. None of that mattered now, though, because they were all gone. I was 19 years young and free for the whole weekend; I intended to make the most of it. London. I'd go to London. That dynamic, vibrant city. The bright lights, the big buildings, the energy, the atmosphere, the overwhelming feeling of insignificance in a city so vast and sprawling. London: a place where you can go wherever you want to go, do whatever you want to do and, most importantly, be whoever you want to be.

London could give me opportunities which just weren't there in either Bicester or Oxford. I'd been to gay clubs in Oxford before. Well, the one gay club that the city boasted, anyway, called Cloud 9. Located on the top floor of a shopping centre it wasn't a big club but it was always great fun.

Every time I went, it was a bit like one of the many television programmes I'd watched about the Serengeti. On the dance floor were the younger gays: the wild beasts. Observing from a raised position were the older, more experienced frequenters: the lions. All it took was for one of the younger gays to become separated from the herd and bam... a lion pounces with a wink and an offer of a free drink.

Venture into the toilets and there was your normal attendant who wants money off you for giving you a towel after you wash your hands. As in straight clubs, this same attendant would attempt to convince you that without a spray of his aftershave you would not get any sex – "No spray, no lay," he would say – and so you should also give him money for that. In Cloud 9, however, the attendant was always generous. No matter if you gave him money or not, along with everyone else who used the facilities you would be sprayed on the crotch with one of his arsenal of aftershaves as you left the bathroom. Though the 'no spray, no lay' concept is unlikely ever to be scientifically proven, in Cloud 9 it didn't seem to be a hindrance. Particularly when it was being sprayed on the wild beasts of the Serengeti.

I never had a bad night at Cloud 9. The music was cheesy, the drinks cheap and the company decent. Oxford is a small place, though. As decent as the company was, it was the same people in there each week. It was never that busy, either, so everyone could see what you were doing. You were pretty much always in vision. Added to that was the fact that I was still in

Oxford. It meant I always felt that I needed to be alert. It would only take one wrong turn to run into someone I knew and they'd be in there with every one of my steps evident under those bright lights.

It got me thinking. If I could have that much fun in a gay club in Oxford with the same lions preying on the same young gays each week, then why not broaden my horizons? Why not go to a place where I could truly let loose, where I could be who I wanted without a care in the world? That's why I'd been looking at G.A.Y for months.

G.A.Y is probably the biggest and most popular gay nightclub in England. Founded in London in 1976 it attracts a reported 6,000 clubbers through its doors each week. Imagine that... 6,000 people, and none of them judging me. I'd be able to hold hands with a man and nobody would bat an eyelid. I could kiss someone and it wouldn't be out of the ordinary. I doubt anyone would even look. And just think of all of those potential partners out on the dance floor.

I really wanted to go on a Friday night. That was when G.A.Y ran a night called 'camp attack', playing all of the camp pop music that I loved so – not that any of my former teammates knew. Or so I thought. Unintentionally, Joe was the only one who had any idea of my musical preference, it would turn out. Whereas I would have liked nothing more than to play Steps and Kylie before a big football game, I had to stick with the tribe and pretend I wanted Foo Fighters and Oasis and all of that house music they would insist on playing to get us pumped up. The only time I ever let my guard slip was when I was with Joe, and I always cursed myself for it.

To get to London on a Friday night in October I would need to go by bus, so I was straight onto the internet to check the price. It seemed manageable and everything was going to plan. Everything, apart from the fact that I had nobody to go with. So back I went onto the internet, where I'd been speaking with a guy called Charlie for a few months. I met him on a website called Face Party, one of those sites with a half naked man and half naked woman on the home page that asks you to 'join thousands of like-minded people, make friends and find love'. There was no hiding it. Though it masqueraded as a social network, there was certainly a heavy dating element. The majority of people joined with one of two things on their mind: a relationship or a one-night stand.

When I was matched with Charlie we clicked right away. Talking – or rather typing – to him was easy. We got on well and so when I asked him to come along to G.A.Y with me he agreed. He lived in Bromley in Kent so it wouldn't take him too long to get there. In those days, G.A.Y was at the Astoria at the top of the Charing Cross Road before it became a victim of the Crossrail development and moved to Old Compton Street.

Charlie agreed to meet me at around 8.30pm on Tottenham Court Road. He'd be with a friend and they knew a good pub in the area. Full of excitement at the prospect of finally living my life the way I wanted to, I finished my shift at Tesco early on the Friday and headed back home to don my favourite T-shirt and jeans. I had butterflies already, and they were multiplying at a ferocious and energetic rate, flying out of my stomach and all through my body. I hadn't felt like this for years.

The bus journey wasn't so bad. It was only two changes and I made it to Marble Arch in good time, giving myself half an hour to get to Tottenham Court Road. The energetic butterflies of excitement began to turn to nervous pangs as 8.30pm got closer and I realised that my knowledge of London was extremely limited. I was just a country mouse from Bicester, remember. To me Oxford used to seem big. And now I was in London. London.

There was a homeless man holding out his hand, limply

asking for money. Below him sat a beaten old hat with scarcely a handful of change scattered around the edges. A tired old dog accompanied him, faithfully sitting by his side. There's an old saying that dogs and owners come to look like each other and that was true in this case. Both were drained, yet united in their common struggle. And fortunately for them they'd just been stumbled upon by a sucker.

I'd zig-zagged my way from the bus stop to the homeless man and his dog, asking strangers for directions every minute. By and large they'd been friendly, helpful and wrong. But surely this homeless man would know London better than those I had previously asked? Obviously a taxi driver would have been the ideal person but those people don't come cheap, unfortunately, and I hadn't seen many sitting helpfully on the side of the street, not like this homeless man. So I went up to him. I put my hand in my pocket and produced a crumpled five pound note to place amongst the scattered change in his battered old hat, on the condition that the homeless man tell me how to get to Tottenham Court Road. He thought for only a second, then agreed to the deal. The crumpled note went into his hand, and then into his pocket. This one he couldn't risk leaving open to public viewing.

He looked up at me, content, and a warm feeling travelled through me. This was karma. I'd helped someone in need and I'd be rewarded with a good night out. It was definitely a sign.

"Tottenham Court Road, you said?" he asked. I nodded. "You're on it, mate", he said, smiling and giving his dog an affectionate pat on the head. They'd be eating tonight, and all thanks to that sucker in the T-shirt and jeans. For a second I considered asking for a refund, but if it was good karma to give him the fiver in the first place then it was definitely bad karma to wrestle it back from a homeless man. No, he could have his moment, and I could be happy that I was now in the right place.

It took me no more than a couple of minutes to get to Charlie and his friend. Unlike many people on the internet, Charlie looked just like his online pictures. He was on the short side, not unlike me, and had black hair which was styled in the fashion of the time, his long fringe swept over his forehead and the hair on top gelled up. Just like we had done online, we clicked immediately, Charlie's warm smile and bubbly persona making me feel at ease.

We decided to head to Soho – an obvious choice for the three of us. Charlie and his friend had picked a pub called Molly Moggs, which was just on the corner of Old Compton Street. From the outside it looked cheap and cheerful. The name of the pub was spelt out in gold lettering on a green frame, with the whole front of the pub painted in a strong green. Baskets of flowers hung from the corners, giving the place a homely appeal. Inside it was just as homely, with traditional décor and an even more traditional clientele. They must have been at least 50 years older than us, on average. In fact, I think we were the only people in the pub who didn't have grey hair. Other than the blonde barmaid who was paid to flirt gently with them, that is. It was like the three of us had stumbled onto the set of the film *Cocoon*.

We stayed for a swift drink and then left, not looking back once. The ice had been broken, though, so the three of us headed on to look around a few sex shops before visiting another couple of bars. The butterflies were still there but by now they were butterflies of excitement. I was having a great time. Everywhere I looked there were men holding hands and people just enjoying themselves, no matter their sexuality.

And I was beginning to form a chemistry with Charlie. We'd got on really well over the internet, but it's always hard to know what someone you've only met online will be like in person. They're two totally different personas. Interacting in real life is immediate and full of emotion. Online you can be calculated, deceptive and measured. Even so, Charlie was true to his online portrayal and was absolutely charming.

We went off to G.A.Y at 11pm and it was everything I had always imagined and more. It was youthful and buzzing with cheap drinks and an upbeat soundtrack inspired by Steps and Kylie. Everyone was having an amazing time and doing just what they wanted, whilst being exactly who they wanted to be. This had to be the most genuine place I'd ever been to.

We stayed until the club closed at 3am, drunkenly wandering the streets of London to take in some of the sights. The wander was great but borne out of necessity – none of us had realised that the tubes didn't run all night. It had seemed obvious that they would in the city that never sleeps. The bus station looked to be too far away and none of us had money for a cab (though later I would learn that the bus station was less than a mile from G.A.Y.). I was due in at the police station at 7am to start my shift. As 5am approached and the tube station remained closed I decided to do what all sensible, responsible workers in my position would have done: curl up in a ball and sleep.

The night had been far superior to anything I had ever experienced in Oxford. Cloud 9 was great and was the reason my football mates would always ask why I never came out in Bicester with them. Because it didn't have a gay club, obviously, but I couldn't say that. I told them it was because I always policed in Bicester so I wasn't comfortable going out and getting drunk there, whereas in reality I wasn't comfortable there for a whole other reason.

Compared to the bright lights of London, however, Cloud 9 was nothing. Just as my teammates never found out that I used to go to Cloud 9 instead of heading out with them, none of them found out about my visit to G.A.Y. Nobody at work found out. None of my family found out. There were no repercussions. Not even at work, where they barely noticed that I didn't turn up for my shift – though I'm sure it would have been different if I had been in a paid position. It didn't matter. I had been who I wanted to be and I had succeeded. I had learnt a valuable life lesson. And now I was closer to Charlie than ever before. We would meet up again and once again, I would be myself.

7
Changing Rooms…

Football hides so many problems. For 90 minutes you're surrounded by a load of people who all want the same thing: to win. At Coventry City the fans were often left disappointed, but at least the players tried hard. Everyone knows that God loves a trier. All problems disappeared when I was watching Coventry. Nobody thinks about the bills they have to pay or their dead-end job while watching the beautiful game. It sucks you in, grabs every ounce of your attention and evokes feelings you never knew were possible. Nobody ever knows true happiness until their team scores a last-minute winner in stoppage time after losing 1-0 for the majority of the match.

Football fans often get an unfair portrayal. It's the working class game, and because of that – along with the hooliganism of the 1970s – there is a widespread belief that football fans are merely thugs. What's that ridiculous saying? Football is a gentleman's game played by thugs; rugby is a thugs' game played by gentlemen. Fans, of course, are representative of players. All players were fans before they became the chosen ones, and all fans dream of being a player in their beloved team's colours. Outsiders enter a football stadium with this fear of hooliganism, and their fears are often compounded through the aggressive, hostile atmosphere at games. And when the outsider is gay? Well, they're definitely going to be pretty fearful of the hateful, often homophobic, attitude.

But not me. The hostility of a football crowd isn't really a problem. In fact, I couldn't think of anywhere safer than being amongst a loud, energetic home crowd. We all want the same thing. The shouting is just a release from having to work mind-numbing shifts throughout the week, a release from financial problems, a release from having to repress your homosexuality when you should have just told everyone about it. Just as I'm surrounded by like-minded people at G.A.Y, in a football crowd I'm also surrounded by like-minded people. I am welcome.

Playing on the pitch is just the same: a release. I'm with 10 like-minded people all working toward the same goal of over-coming the opposition. It doesn't matter if you're black, white, straight, gay, old, young, rich or poor, if you're good at getting that ball into the net then you're one of the team, all working together towards victory.

Even so, now that I was out, I'd resigned myself to the fact that I'd have to leave Heyford Athletic. I never thought a gay person would be accepted. Sure, the two 'safe' teammates I told had said that they 'didn't care', but there were a lot more in the team who portrayed themselves as the classic alpha male, thriving in the macho environment football encourages. Now my sexuality was common knowledge. I had come out to the world, and I fully expected the world – especially my corner of the football world – to spit it back in my face. You're either with the tribe or against it.

It would be a shame to leave football. First of all, the sport was one of the main loves of my life. Playing it regularly with my mates was amazing. It was a laugh, better than doing any-thing else. Keeping fit, running around, kicking a ball about with my best mates, carefree - there was nothing better. It was the purest, most beautiful form of escapism.

Then there was the fact that I was a gay guy and in an enclosed space with a load of men. Now I know that this is the fear of straight players. They fear that if they are in a changing room with a gay man, then the gay man will leer at them as they change, will follow them into the showers and then have their wicked way with them. No place would be safe.

Of course this is rubbish. Let's put the boot on the other foot. If it were a heterosexual girl in the changing room, how many of the men would she fall in love with, pin down and have her wicked way with? None. She may well look at them but so what? It's just a look. It's the same with gay men. Just because I'm a man, it doesn't mean that I'm going to want to jump into bed with every single naked man I see in a changing room. Gay people aren't attracted to every man they see, you know. I look, of course I look, but that's all it is. A look. I'm not going to suddenly make a move on a teammate and turn them gay. Being gay isn't exactly like leprosy. It's not contagious.

Whether gay or straight, the changing room is a great place to be. Not only for the aesthetics, but for the camaraderie. It's a laugh, isn't it? You have a joke and then you go about your work. Obviously you can't take yourself too seriously, but you're all in it together. At times the changing room was even a better place than being on the pitch. For starters, it felt like it was the only place where we actually had a plan. Then there was the fact that it was one of the only times we weren't all shouting and swearing at each other. It happened without fail every week. Even if we were winning, our players would still be shouting at each other with the plan long gone out the window. But in the changing room we actually got on. In the changing room we were more than just teammates.

The more I thought about it, the more I thought just one thing: fuck 'em. I wasn't going to leave the sport I loved just because I had announced myself to the world. Even though I'd come out it didn't mean that everyone knew. In fact, I'm pretty sure that only six or seven of my teammates knew, and that was only because three of my cousins played in the team. If it did get out to the rest of the team then so what? If they said anything then fuck 'em.

By now I was emotionally attached to Heyford Athletic Football Club. I cared how we did. I cared how much sponsorship we raised. I cared about my teammates. Football had become more than a passion and it actually helped to ease some of the tension. For as long as I can remember, my family would come and watch me play. There would usually be at least one person at my game each week, most often my Dad, though Mum also came fairly regularly. It brought us together, even in the hard times. Or at least it should have done. Come the final whistle my family would usually be ashamed at how they could have brought up someone who so frequently lambasted the poor referee.

I like to change people's opinions. Even now people always tell me that I'm not gay. What? You? No, there's no way that you're gay. It doesn't matter where I am – in town, on the pitch, at work – they never believe me. They just can't fathom that there are people who aren't camp but are still gay. At work I'm told about girls who fancy me and when I let the messenger know that I'm gay, they act surprised and say that they never knew. Do I have to wear a sign or something?

On the pitch my style of play got me so far away from people questioning my sexuality that it was unreal. All I had to do was kick a ball away from my goal and towards the other one. It was so simple. I guess it helped my decision to stay in the game. My teammates would watch me make another crunching challenge and think, 'No, he's not really gay. He's a man, just like us.' They wouldn't believe that I was different even if I had announced it. They'd think that I was really still a part of the tribe. And even if they didn't, I still had the back-up of being employed by the police. I guess any homophobic insults in my direction would have been ill advised.

I always wonder if my playing style was a subconscious effort to show my masculinity; whether I became this hyper masculine, hard-but-fair defender to get away from any allegations. People are ignorant. They see how I ride tackles and think, 'He's not rolling around like a fairy after that tackle so he can't be gay.' That must be it. All gay people are fairies, of course.

It used to play on my mind. As terrible as my team was at Heyford, we somehow managed to worm our way into the semi-finals of one of the league cups in my first season. It was great because I got to play on an actual pitch with a fence around it and everything – and even better when we beat our opponents, Barford United, 2-0 and I was awarded man of the match – but the most nervous part of the game was the bit before. I'll never forget it. As part of the whole event a programme was produced, and within that our manager was tasked with writing a couple of lines about each player. I was so nervous about what he would say about me. I don't even know why. When it came to it I opened up the programme to see 'Neil Beasley – tough tackling, no nonsense defender'. I couldn't have been happier.

I kept that programme and cherished those words. I might even get them written on my gravestone. But why did I cherish them so? Was it because I was a gay man playing in a straight team? Was it out of a desire to fit in despite being different? Was I trying to be deceptive through my playing style?

I used to think all of that, anyway. But now, here I am, a seasoned footballer comfortable with his sexuality, open to the world, and still an arsehole. A real hyper-masculine arsehole. I get booked all the time and my teammates are always coming over and reminding me that as captain I'm supposed to sort problems out, not start them. I suppose it's hard to get out of a style. Especially when it's borne out of fear, a way of pushing people further away from suggesting something, from making an allegation of criminality in the closed world of football.

Once you've got a style, there's nothing you can do about it. It's yours for your career. There was something I could do about playing at Heyford, however. Fuck 'em. That was going to be my attitude. They could talk. But I would keep on playing.

8

...And Changing Places

I moved out. Not a long way away but it didn't matter. I was still out. Far away enough to avoid the awkwardness and tension that I had come to detest. Not only did I move out of my family home – I moved in with a boy. And he wasn't just a friend.

I had been an official item with this boy, Chris, for a couple of weeks when I invited him to stay over at my house. As with Charlie, I had met Chris on the social networking site Face Party. At the time I was still chatting with Charlie, though we had agreed to be friends rather than anything more serious. Following that agreement, I clicked online and searched the depths of Face Party for a new companion. Up popped Chris, we matched, and we hit it off instantly. From staying up all night talking online we progressed to meeting offline, and when that proved successful we decided to become an item. My parents were aware that Chris was my boyfriend, though I'm not sure I ever told them explicitly, and I don't think they liked it. It had only been a short time since I hit them with the 'bombshell' that I was gay, and now I was bringing boys home.

Chris wasn't allowed to stay over. My parents defended their decision by pointing to the fact that my sister wasn't allowed to have boys stay over either. I'm not surprised. She was two years younger than me. I wouldn't let my kid have someone stay over when they were that age. My other argument was that it was just so much easier for Rachel. She could go into town and hold

hands with her boyfriend. She could kiss him in public. I could
do those things too but imagine the trouble it would cause, the
heads that would turn, those burning, searing eyes staring at us
with hatred. Being different. That's what they would see and
that's what would intimidate them, make them fearful, make
them hateful. Being in private was the only chance I had of
showing my affection to Chris and I wasn't even allowed that.
At the time it felt like my parents couldn't have made it any
harder for me.

It all kicked off when I risked letting Chris stay over.
Everyone knows those early stages of romance when everything blossoms... You want to be together all the time. You
want to show your affection for each other. You can barely take
your eyes off each other. It's beautiful and wonderful and tragic
at the same time.

I thought I was being clever. I was back to my old ways,
rooted in my deception, only this time I had an accomplice:
Chris. And it worked. We managed to get to sleep together
without any grief. Nobody found out. But I wasn't to come out
of it unscathed, because I was stupid.

If you are having someone over to stay without permission
what would be the main thing you would do to conceal their
presence? You'd probably keep them quiet. Well I managed to
do that. It wasn't a sound that gave Chris's presence away.

Your second priority? Hide all evidence of their presence,
starting from where they entered the house. Their shoes. The
most obvious sign of their presence. Why would anyone ever
leave their shoes at the front door unless they were inside the
house? A mother's eye is perceptive, especially in the home. It
notices when things aren't right. An extra pair of shoes on the
rack? Enough to arouse suspicion, especially when your son
has just come out and has a new boyfriend who isn't allowed to
stay over. The shoes themselves – they were scuffed. She knew

they weren't mine. If they were new and white and untouched I could have gotten away with it and said I'd just bought them that afternoon. But they were scuffed, and they weren't even my size anyway. Chris was a couple of sizes bigger than me. She guessed straight away.

I hate to say this, but Chris was obviously gay. He looked gay, he acted gay, and he just was gay. I could never imagine him dragging all of his family close together, having agonised over the decision to do so for months, years even, to tell them that he was gay, and for them to all be so surprised and shocked. You? No way. You're kidding...

No. That definitely never happened. I'm pretty sure Chris would have waltzed out of the womb and thanked the doctor for being just fabulous. A horrible stereotype, I know, but Chris was, and always has been, a truly flamboyant gay. His coming out would have perhaps been the least shocking thing his parents would ever have heard. He might as well have told them that the sky is blue and the Pope is Catholic.

I envied Chris, envied him for the confidence that he had in himself. He was everything that I was not. I've always been jealous of the fact that camp guys like Chris are so comfortable in themselves; that they act the way they do and don't care what the world thinks. Don't care how anyone reacts. Don't care that the world knows they are gay. Chris always wanted to hold my hand in public. I'd feel so guilty as I brushed him away. "Not now, Chris," I'd tell him, aware of the eyes on me. Let them look, I knew that was what Chris wanted to say, but he never did. I guess he understood.

I found it much harder to come out than Chris because guys who are camp never really need to come out. It isn't difficult for them. I've spoken with a load of gay men who are just like me – men who you wouldn't necessarily know are gay just from look-ing at them and speaking with them – and they all found the same problem. They were all attracted to camp guys but jealous of them at the same time. It comes down to this deep-rooted vision of homosexuality dictated by a homophobic society. Gay men are supposed to be feminine, gossip, love fashion, have tidy apartments and a passion for the theatre, especially musical theatre. They aren't supposed to like football and drink beer and not really care about their appearance, and because of this deep-rooted vision it made it seem unnatural that I was homosexual myself when of course it was entirely natural. I was uncomfortable in myself and I was attracted to a person who was completely comfortable and happy for everyone to know exactly who he was and what he stood for.

When I brushed Chris's hand away in public, I did so because I was fearful of how I would have reacted to the inevitable comments. A homosexual man becoming this alpha male, unleashing his anger on a hateful commenter who detests people being different – how confusing would that have been? It goes against all the conventions of a gay man living in a homophobic society. I'd have felt even less comfortable in my body. Who was I? What did I want?

Being with Chris was liberating. He encouraged me to be my true self. There was no need to deceive him. I could be natural. I could be open. There was no need to hide anything. Our relationship had flown quickly and sweetly. From that first click on his Face Party profile I was open to something deeper with Chris, and when we met up in Oxford for the first time, we hit it off just like that. It seemed inevitable that we would enter into a relationship.

My parents had disliked Chris at first, but after finding out that he'd stayed over that night, the dislike seemed to manifest into hatred. If they had made it hard when I came out then they were making it almost impossible now. It was obvious that Chris wasn't exactly welcome in the house. Our relationship was being stunted by our environment, held back from blossoming further into true love and happiness.

I was fortunate to have a good support network in place. Without it, and with the difficulties I was facing, it would have been hard to get by. It was another staff member at Tesco who helped me through it, an old boy who I worked closely with called Bob. Bob must have been in his 60s and was pretty flamboyantly gay. OK, he was really mega super flamboyantly gay. He was loud and camp and in-your-face and didn't care what anyone thought of him. The staff loved him; the management despised him. Never being afraid of what you say can make you dangerous.

Bob maintained that he always knew I was gay, even when I had my girlfriend. According to him, I was the kind of guy who would always go about doing stuff the wrong way, even though I'd often end up at the right place. Maybe that's why he loved flirting with me so much. No matter how many times I pointed out his shiny bald head and his old age – as well as his obvious similarities with Charles Hawtrey from the Carry On films – he would always come back with the same response: 'the older the piano the finer the tune'. The world needed more people like Bob. He was just so comfortable with who he was. In my eyes he was a true inspiration. He helped me so much by just being himself.

I talked regularly with Bob. At first we worked together on the lottery stand but management ended up moving him on to the tills. It was an enforced move. Bob was isolated on the tills and less able to spout his views. Still, I admired and trusted Bob. He had never let on about my secret and he was a good friend.

One day I was telling him all about Chris and how my parents reacted to him staying over. Bob listened carefully, then interrupted me with some words that have stayed with me to this day. "I'll give you some advice now," he said, pausing to make sure he had my attention. "Fuck everyone else. You have to live your own life. You have to go on and do it now and if you don't you will always look back with years of regret. Make decisions based on yourself, not anyone else." And that was that. Four simple sentences.

It was the easiest advice to give but the old man was right. I needed to start living my own life. Fuck everyone else. It was time to start putting myself first. I was part of a new generation, Bob continued. For me it was much easier to come out than it had been in his day. He couldn't understand why people my age found it so hard to come out. Not after what he'd been through, and because of this it was even more important that I started to live my own life.

Later that evening I logged on to Rightmove and rented myself a flat in Oxford that I could barely afford. It was time to stand on my own two feet, to learn about life the hard way. My parents seemed to be pretty cool with it when they found out. They couldn't have helped me any quicker. They weren't exactly pushing me out the door but nor did they hinder me. My coming out had nothing to do with it. The time was right. I was a grown man, at an age where I wanted independence, and my parents understood this. It was natural progression. My parents said that I could come back any time I wanted to and they meant it. It suited everyone for me to have more freedom.

My Dad still hadn't commented on my sexuality. To this day he hasn't. He just keeps quiet and ignores it. Is he ashamed? Disappointed? Does he refuse to accept it? Does he think that acknowledging it will make it real? I don't know. I've never challenged his non-reaction. I'll probably go to my grave wishing I'd said something at some point. I guess I'm scared of losing him. As the years have gone by we have got closer and closer. He's my best mate, but it makes it hard sometimes. Take one of

England's games that he and I went to, for example.

Dad and I started driving down to watch England's games in their qualification group for the 2014 World Cup in Brazil, and the game in question was the second or third we had been to in the campaign. There was something about the new Wembley that we loved – there must have been, anyway, because we'd only ever been to watch England once before that campaign – and the fact that the World Cup was going to be played in Brazil had really caught our excitement. I can't remember who it was against but the team we were playing were no good. Or they were supposed to be no good, anyway. You know what the England team is like – they just couldn't break their opponents down.

As the minutes went on, the fans became more and more restless, with one particularly vocal fan sitting directly behind me. Fans love a scapegoat, and this fan had picked out the Manchester United midfielder Tom Cleverley. The reason for Cleverley's underperformance was that he was a 'faggot', and the vocal fan carried on with a volley of aggressive homophobic abuse as the game continued. Inside I was seething. This idiot was trying to take us back to the Stone Age. What a prejudiced fool. I wanted to turn around to talk to him, to ask him what had gone so wrong in his life that he needed to scream abuse at others, maybe put an arm around him. Well, maybe a small part of me did. The rest of me wanted to thump him around that hyperactive mouth. Let him scream abuse then. I'd have probably ended up just turning around and asking him to be quiet because there were kids about, but I didn't. I was with my Dad. So I stayed quiet. Said nothing. Let him hurl his abuse while I sat back and shut him out.

Anyway, there wasn't much time between me renting the flat and actually moving out, maybe a week or two. It was so liberating being in my own flat with Chris. There was nobody to keep tabs on us. We could hold hands without disapproving eyes watching us. We could go into the bedroom and keep the door shut. I could go out when I wanted to. I could come back in when I wanted. I could even go to the toilet and leave the door open – sheer bliss. I didn't have to answer to anyone.

At first it was great. Our love continued to grow day by day. Chris was the first thing I'd see when I woke up and the last thing before I shut my eyes at night. I did everything with him. I even took him to watch the Sky Blues. OK, that was a waste of money. Chris had absolutely no interest in football, though he didn't look out of place in the crowd. Show me a Coventry fan who isn't depressed and uninterested after watching their team for just a short period of time and I'll show you a liar.

To be fair to Chris, he did make an effort. He asked me questions about the rules of the game and the players on show and commented on how attractive the Trinidad and Tobago winger Chris Birchall was. When Leon McKenzie scored late on, Chris bellowed out 'Twist and Shout' with the rest of the crowd. Fortunately for Chris, it wasn't anywhere near enough to get him hooked and he never came again.

Living away from home was kind of a middle finger to my parents. I was proving that I could cope alone. It's not like I'd cut them out of my life, though. I still went to visit them and they supported me throughout the move. Unfortunately I couldn't stick a middle finger up at my bank, who were pretty quick to remind me that I couldn't afford the flat I was now living in. I seemed to be getting some statement or other through each week, and no matter how much I added the figures up, income never exceeded outgoings. When I found out that Council Tax was a monthly cost, rather than a one-off payment, things really started to get desperate.

The police force offered me a paid role as a Community Support Officer. It wasn't the path I wanted to take within the force – especially considering my growing disillusionment with the force in general – but I felt I had no choice. Money was on offer. Tesco had been great but not only was it not leading anywhere, it didn't pay enough. It was the same with my role as a Special Constable. It was OK volunteering but the downside is that you don't get paid.

Borne out of necessity, I accepted the offer. Working as a CSO gave me a far better income than I'd had at Tesco whilst, to an extent, providing a potential career path. Still, it was intended to be more of a stop-gap, something to give me more money before I could move into a role as a police officer, though I also really fancied myself as a dog handler, mainly because that would get me into a different department within the force. Even at the time, I knew I'd made a mistake in accepting the offer, however.

Chris supported me just as much as ever but it was a hard time for us. Our honeymoon period in the flat was over. The strains and stresses of adult life were eating into me, corroding my youth and its lack of responsibility. I felt trapped. There were bills to pay. What would I do if I couldn't pay them? I didn't want to think about it. Just went to work each day and put all of my efforts into my job. Each night I'd come home exhausted. It's funny how quickly beauty can escape something wonderful.

9

Out On the Pitch

My heart was pounding. Sweat was pouring down my face. My stomach was doing backflips. I stuttered. I started. I stuttered. It was time. I could delay it no longer. It was something I knew that I had to do but I really didn't want to. I was terrified. Absolutely terrified of unravelling my deceit in the very area I'd been most afraid of being my true self.

Then I did it. I couldn't look them in the eye and I muffled my speech but I did it. I came out to my team and guess what? Nothing happened. Nothing changed. There was barely a murmur in the changing room. Nobody said anything. There were no snide comments. Everything remained the same. Nobody really seemed to care.

Five minutes later. Still nothing had changed. Nothing was any different to how it had been ten minutes previously. I began to calm down, my heart beat slowing and slowing and slowing until finally, finally, it approached a normal rate. Even so, no matter how much I tried to convince myself it was OK, I remained on edge. What if someone did say something? It's a feeling that never really goes away.

I didn't push my sexuality in anyone's face and I guess that helped. Maybe if I'd 'acted gay' – in the stereotypical sense – there might have been some difficulties, but I didn't. The only modification I made was to make a conscious effort to not look at my teammates when they got changed, though I never really had to because I was always in such a rush to get to the show-

ers. The quicker I got in, the quicker I could get out, and once
I was out I could start having some fun.

After every game I'd position myself next to the temperature tap and turn it to the extreme levels, either scolding or
freezing my poor teammates. If I didn't get there first then
someone else would, so I never really got the chance to either
look at, or be seen looking at, anyone else because I was always
in a race against time. Not that I'd have looked at them anyway
– I've seen more attractive animals in a zoo.

That's not to say it was an easy process. Even now I'm still
on edge whenever I enter into the football world, though it's a
feeling that's very much on the outer levels of my consciousness. It barely registers but it's still there, lingering.

The only time I saw any evidence of homophobia at Heyford was from the team manager, and that wasn't even directed
at me. The referee had made a decision which the manager
didn't agree with and because of that he was a 'mincer'. But that
was it. We still all got on. My teammates were more racist than
homophobic, anyway. Heyford was a proper village team out
in the sticks. We didn't have any black players and rarely came
across any in the Banbury District and Lord Jersey League. The
comments were always framed as banter but banter is often an
attempt to excuse ignorance, which was the case here.

We had the usual Neanderthals in our changing room.
Every football team has at least two or three. The further back
they are in their human development the more amusing they
seem to be, and we had a few who had barely evolved. There
were people from all walks of life, though. On the other end
of the spectrum we had the metrosexuals – the modern men.
These were the more 'macho' ones but 20 years ago, well,
they'd have had some pretty serious allegations thrown at them
regarding their sexuality. I guess David Beckham has a lot to
answer for. These guys fought for space in front of any mirror,

competed to see who could wear the most fashionable outfit and groomed themselves with immense care. Then there were the rest of them: the solicitors, the supermarket manager, the policeman, the student, the one on benefits, the one who was a genius, and the one who couldn't count. Some were extremely clever. Some were extremely stupid. There were different levels and personalities.

As far as I was concerned it was just a normal changing room, both before and after I came out. Probably a fair bit more varied than the changing room of a professional team, but a really normal grass roots changing room. Nothing changed once I came out and I don't think anyone even mentioned it to me. It's not like I suddenly had a flood of teammates race up to me to put their arms around my shoulder and tell me everything was OK and they were always here if I needed them. For that I am thankful.

In fact, their non-reaction was the best kind of support I could have had because really, did it matter that – in their eyes – I was now gay? I don't want to be patronised and told it's 'OK' to be gay. I know it's OK to be gay. I simply wanted to play football, and their non-reaction allowed me to do just that. It made me feel normal. After all, that's what it is all about. It's not about your sexuality. It's about your actions on the pitch, how you play the game and the mistakes you make – and by God did I make a lot of them.

Match days were always the same. Get into the changing room, have a laugh and then get changed. Sit down for the manager's team talk. A few loud claps and a couple of manly roars and then it was out on to the pitch, where all of the manager's words gleaned from listening to Sky Sports were wasted by a warm-up consisting of smashing balls as hard as we could at the poor goalkeeper. The game would then start, we'd then argue, the manager would helplessly shout some fancy instructions, and then we'd argue some more. Along the way we'd probably concede a few goals without scoring very many – if at all – and then it was back into the changing rooms.

The half time ritual – and I'll never understand this, because it was repeated at nearly every away game I played in – was to be welcomed with a tray of tea. Who on earth drinks a cup of tea at half time? It was always a lovely old lady who made it though and we never wanted to offend her. She'd probably been doing the job for years. As such, half time would always be spent politely pouring the cups of tea down the sink so she wouldn't get upset. We didn't have to drink it and the lovely tea lady would never get offended. Everyone was a winner. Well, until we got back out for the second half anyway, and by the time we'd been condemned to another defeat we would all be sick of arguing with each other anyway. So it was to the showers for a bit of a laugh.

And that's what it was: a laugh. Just a laugh, with 90 minutes of competition in the middle. It was like that before I came out. And it remained like that after I came out.

10
Giving It Up

In the grand scheme of things, it didn't take long for every-thing to go downhill with Chris. The initial honeymoon period, where it was all fun and new after we'd moved out of our homes, was great. Suddenly we could do whatever we wanted. We could stay up all night then lay in bed all day. And then the bills began to suffocate us. We had gone from living comfortably at our respective homes with a fair amount of spare money to no longer having any money because it was all tied up. That caused friction. It's not healthy.

Ultimately we both fell more in love with moving out of our family homes than with each other. When the freedom of moving out was restricted, things soured between us. It didn't help that we were leading totally different lives. I was work-ing a 24-hour shift pattern as a CSO. My days weren't regular. Sometimes I'd work in the day, sometimes at night. Often I'd work weekends. My days off each week varied. Chris worked a regular 9-5 from Monday to Friday. He was at the hospital, booking peoples' appointments. It was pretty basic and that was reflected in his pay. He earned quite a bit less than me and because of that I offered to contribute more to the cost of the flat. Our bills were well over £1,000 each month and I felt it would be right of me to offer that bit extra, given my higher salary.

That turned out to be a terrible suggestion. I began to resent Chris for paying less, even though the whole thing had been my idea. It didn't help that I couldn't really go out and have a good time at the weekend any more. Not regularly, anyway. Not like Chris. He'd be out every weekend, living it up and having a great time. And there I'd be, sat at work, earning the money, essentially to pay for his good time.

I was jealous of him. That was the simple fact of the matter. I was 20 years old and should also have been heading out on the town each weekend. It wasn't even a possessive jealousy, where I feared he might do something with another guy. I had complete trust that he'd stay faithful. The jealousy was purely down to wanting to be in his position. There is nothing more precious than your youth. I wanted to be the one having a good time. I wanted to be able to spend some money on myself. But no, Chris was out on the dance floor of nightclubs across Oxfordshire while I was trying to stop teenagers from painting graffiti on public property. It was two ends of the spectrum. Our worlds were moving further and further apart.

We hardly saw each other. If I was on a night shift then I'd spend most of the day sleeping. On the rare occasions when our days off matched up, we wouldn't have much money to go out and have fun. And then there was the football. Chris resented it. He really hated it. I'd always try and make one of my days off a Saturday. Instead of spending it with Chris, who'd want to watch box sets of *Sex and the City* on the sofa, I'd go off and get muddy for two hours. Chris never understood football. He didn't come and watch but I wouldn't really have wanted him to anyway.

I felt I had every right to play football. It was my money that was being spent on keeping the house and I wasn't getting much leisure time. Never join the public services. That's what my advice would be to young adults. It just takes over your life and eats away at everything you previously enjoyed.

It turned out Chris was pretty possessive. He wanted to

spend every minute of every day with me. I didn't with him. My football was important to me.

We had rushed into it but there was no turning back. Chris had previously committed the ultimate sin of moving out and then having to move back in with his parents. Nobody should do that. Once you're gone you're gone. He was desperate to move out and so was I. Neither of us ever thought it through properly. It would have taken us seconds to sit down and work out how much money we had saved up, our incomes, and how much it was all going to cost. But we let the situation take over. We never bothered to sit down because suddenly we were moving to the centre of the city and it was all new and exciting and it was the best thing ever. And then it wasn't.

We were very different people with little in common. It didn't take long for the cracks to appear. A few months at most. The contract was a year long, so we just had to grin and bear it. Money was the main problem. It used to annoy me when Chris would suggest that we get a new television or a new bed because I'd be the one who would have to pay for it. It wasn't really his fault. They were normal suggestions. It was just that the situation we were in took those suggestions and twisted them, forcing more cracks into an already eroding relationship.

The cracks led to arguments. We'd accuse each other of getting up to no good, of not staying faithful. It was all rubbish. I had no time for an affair and I'm not sure Chris did either, especially with his busy nightclub schedule. He knew that the only possible 'affair' I was having was with football but that didn't stop his accusations. It's always the first conclusion that anyone jumps to in a relationship. Any little problem and that's what you automatically conclude: they must be cheating. Everything's not as it was. You're so blinkered that you don't see all of the little problems building up into one big one. It's easy to fire off accusations. Are you seeing someone else? Why don't you ever have any money? Are you spending it on someone else? Of course not. We never have any money because we wasted it all on a lavish flat we couldn't afford. We never have any money because we shop in Marks & Spencers rather than Aldi. We just never have any money.

Something had to happen. We might have both fallen in love more with moving out than with each other, but that didn't mean that we weren't going to try and make our relationship work. Money was becoming tighter and tighter. Time was becoming less and less. Whereas once it had seemed endless, now it was limited, the hours and days turning into seconds and minutes. I guess this is what growing up is, but it didn't make it any easier. I had to make decisions. What was most important? What could I spare and what could I do without? And so I did something drastic. I quit football.

Chris always saw my football as valuable time we could have spent together. And now, with my decision, we could do just that. Suddenly I had time. Not a great deal of it, but time nonetheless. It wasn't exactly ideal but it was a start. A start towards better things. Towards our relationship developing and blossoming back to that time when everything was warm and exciting. When it felt like we truly loved each other.

My decision had nothing to do with my coming out to the team. We'd all just got on with it. But not everything was rosy on the pitch, though. Had it been, I suspect I may not have been so hasty to sacrifice everything for Chris. My decision to quit was confirmed after a bad game. The team had won but I hadn't played well, and I suppose the team winning actually annoyed me even more. Everyone was still effing and blinding at each other even though we came away with the three points. Added to the pressure I was getting from Chris, it ended up being too much. No, I wouldn't do it any more.

The thing about relationships is that they're supposed to be

about give and take. You each give and you each take. When
cracks start to appear, you may have to give a bit more to each
other. I understood this. Chris didn't. I gave up football. Chris,
who'd berated me so for spending 90 minutes away from him
on a Saturday afternoon, continued to go out each Saturday
evening without fail. Well, that didn't exactly help the cracks
disappear. Not only was I now subsidising his good time, as I
saw it, but I was unable to enjoy any personal leisure time. And
all because Chris wanted to see me more. The hypocrisy of it
was outrageous. Inside, my anger was building up.

My new look Saturday afternoons were boring. More boring than I ever could have imagined. Chris would take me out
shopping to places – and I hate shopping. I just don't see the
point in walking round all of those shops with their homog-
enous air-controlled temperature and their smiley overenthusi-
astic assistants and their in-your-face, you'll-never-believe-this
reductions. Just buy whatever and let's get out of here, that
was always my attitude. But no. Each week we'd pop into town
to walk around the same shops we'd walked around the week
before, looking at the same stuff as the week before and, ultimately, making the same decisions as the week before. We did
it because it was cheap and we had no money. What else was
there?

I desperately wanted to be playing football. I desperately
wanted to be watching football. But I had nobody to go with.
I'd grown apart from my mates because I'd given too much of
my time to Chris and even if I did have people to go with, I
couldn't. I'd made a commitment to my relationship with Chris.

It didn't stop me from missing it. Every Saturday afternoon
I'd be clock-watching. 1.15pm – they're just arriving in the
changing rooms. 1.45pm – I wonder how the warm-up is going
– how many balls have they lost by now? 2pm – kick-off. Why
aren't I at Heyford? Oh, look. It's because we're sitting here, the

two of us, doing the same thing we do every Saturday, getting more and more wound up in each other's presence. 2.45pm – half time. They're politely pouring the teas away. 3.45pm – it's over. And then the arguments would start.

You're a long time retired, that's what my Dad always said. If you don't play every week then you'll regret it when you stop playing altogether. That got to me. It hit me hard and seemed to boil to the surface each week at around 3pm. I knew I'd regret it and I came to associate Chris with that regret.

Come Saturday evening, I'd be on my own. I couldn't be bothered with Chris's mates and he never fought my refusal to come out with him and them. He never even fought me one night when I announced that I would be going out somewhere else. It seemed strange at the time for somebody so possessive. It still seems strange now. Every now and again I would go down to London to meet Charlie. We'd remained mates. I always loved how he had allowed me to just be myself that first time we'd met. I'd never felt so comfortable in my own skin. Of course, there was only one place we could go to in London. As far as I'm concerned there is only one place in London.

It was a good night in G.A.Y. It's always a good night in G.A.Y. The music, the atmosphere, the people - everything about that place is just incredible. It had only been a couple of months since I'd stopped playing football when I met Marcus. He was weaving his way in and out of the crowd when we literally bumped into each other. Unlike your normal nightclubs, everyone at G.A.Y. was there to have a good time, so we politely apologised to each other for our clumsiness. After that little ice breaker we got chatting and asked each other our interests and it turned out we both liked football. Not only did we both like football, but Marcus played for a team in London. London Titans, they were called, and they played in the National Gay Football League.

Now I'd never heard of a national gay football league.

Gay league? Gay football? I'd have been there years ago if I'd have known about it. I mean, just how much homophobia can you really get in a gay league?

If you're already playing for a gay team then you presume that everyone else knows that there's a gay league. Especially when you're in G.A.Y., speaking with gay guys. Marcus couldn't believe I didn't know about it. Surely I'd heard of Stonewall? No, I hadn't, and I wasn't sure many other people had.

It turns out Stonewall was not only the largest Lesbian, Gay, Bisexual and Transgender rights charity in Europe, campaigning for equality and progression, but they also ran Britain's first ever gay football team. The football team's success had been such that they were now the top ranking gay football team in Europe, and were so good they even played in the straight leagues as well as the gay league – fielding a side in the Middlesex County Football League Division One.

It all sounded amazing. Almost too good to be true. Marcus said that I should come down and see how I felt about London Titans. They trained in Richmond Park and played all over the country. He reckoned the standard was decent, telling me that he himself was a "quality player". If only I had £1 for every time I'd heard that. Still, Marcus was endearing, his passion, energy and humour making me feel welcome. I wasn't sure how right he was about being a "quality player", but the rest of what he said sounded bloody brilliant, and those were my exact words in response. Bloody brilliant.

I fully intended to take Marcus up on his offer. I got home and Googled the team and the league they played in and that's when I saw the list of all the teams who took part. There was Nottingham and Leicester and then two or three teams in London, as well as Birmingham and a couple of others.

Birmingham. That name just stood out for me. I'd never

been to Birmingham. London was about an hour away from Oxford. Maybe a bit more but it was easily doable. And then there was Birmingham. It was only about an hour in the other direction. Birmingham. If you've never been then why not? Why not try something new? That's all that I could think of. Logic had gone out of the window. I didn't think about the fact that I'd never been to Richmond Park either, that I'd never trained in an all-gay team, that I'd never played in a gay league, that I knew Marcus.

Birmingham Blaze, to give them their full name, had a website. I scrolled across to the contact section and found an email address for their secretary, a bloke named Joe. I sent him a message to register my interest and received a response pretty soon after. That started a little back and forth between us and it's going to sound really strange because it was only over email, but we had a really good connection. It was like we just clicked straight away. Like we were on the same wavelength.

After that there was only one team I was going to sign for. All I could think of was Birmingham Blaze. The nerves, the excitement, the newness of it all; it captured my imagination. There was just one problem. Chris.

Sure, we'd argued. Since I'd quit football we'd argued more regularly than ever before, in fact. Despite the arguments, though, Chris had grown used to having me with him on Saturday afternoons. He wasn't going to let me leave him be without a fight, no matter how many times I told him that Blaze actually played their games on a Sunday.

That wasn't all. Chris had this real misconception that every single one of Blaze's players was going to be really good looking with muscular, sculpted bodies. Airbrushed athletes, that's what he envisaged. He thought that because they'd all be batting for the same side as me, I was likely to run off with one. In the end, it turned out he was right.

The first few times I sort of welcomed Chris's intervention. I'd arranged with Blaze's secretary to go up to Birmingham to train with the team. When it comes to meeting new people, however, I'm a bit of a wimp, and I was almost hoping to be given a reason not to go. That reason arrived as Chris launched into his attack. You're not really going, are you? Why are you doing this? What about me? Chris was worried because he was possessive but in the end that possessiveness was what pushed me away even further.

It was pointless arguing with him. It was like arguing with Vicky Pollard. Yeah but, no but, yeah but. I just couldn't get a word in edgeways, which, I must admit, for myself is very frustrating. The arguments themselves weren't aggressive. They were shouty but not aggressive. Even so, they made me resent Chris even more because I just couldn't win.

And so the pattern continued. I'd arrange to train with Blaze. Chris would start an argument with me over something pointless. I'd argue back. Chris would win the argument. I'd wimp out of training. Another crack would appear. And then one Sunday morning I just woke up and thought: 'Be brave'. That was the very first thing that came into my head. Be brave. Let Chris come at me. Let him come with his arguments and his anger and his desperation. I wouldn't let him make me wimp out. Not today.

11
Blazing the Trail

I don't really like driving to places I've never been to before. It makes me nervous, and driving up to Birmingham was pretty nerve-wracking. Not at first though, because all I could think about was how I had overcome Chris. He'd tried to put me off and he had failed. I was actually going. Going to train with an all-gay team who played in an all-gay league. The adrenaline was flowing.

I arrived pretty early to find an empty car park. Joe had told me that Birmingham Blaze were holding an intra-club tournament so it would be an ideal starting point – a good chance to meet everyone. There would be three or four five-a-side teams with the majority of the 50 or so members of the club in attendance. I sent Joe a message letting him know I'd made it and then sat back and waited for him to come and meet me and introduce me to everyone, trying with all my might to prevent my nerves from getting the better of me.

As time went by, players started arriving in dribs and drabs. The first few came in to the car park, one of them was swigging a can of lager and I just remember panicking. It seemed like everything I had been trying to get away from. No. I needed to calm myself. I needed to approach the day with an open mind. Joe would sort out the rest.

As it turned out, the whole experience wasn't anything like what I thought it was going to be. It was fun – a really good laugh. The players were all so much like me. We clicked straight away. It was like having a new family. Better than a family, even. They were all just so nice and welcoming. And it helped that the standard of the tournament was low. It made me look like a great player, that's for sure.

I was hooked from the off. It wasn't just on the pitch either. Blaze placed big emphasis on socialising and would head out on the town every weekend. Considering that our games were always on a Sunday, it probably wasn't the best of preparations, though in fairness we did try and go out on Friday nights rather than Saturdays. Suddenly I was spending more and more of my time up in Birmingham. Chris was fading into the distance. No matter how hard he pulled, he'd always end up pushing.

Blaze was markedly different to Heyford. An outsider would easily have been able to tell that they were a gay team, and not only because they had some pretty camp players. In the changing room it was just innuendo after innuendo after innuendo. A constant flow of manipulated words and meanings, all to the delight of the audience. I certainly had to be careful with what I said to gee up the lads before the game. No longer could I urge my teammates to stick one up 'em and expect to be met with a serious response. Playing in the hole? Forget it.

At Heyford it was all about taking the piss out of each other. At Blaze it was so much more. A lot of it revolved around how people were dressed. At Heyford the players couldn't have given two hoots about what I wore, but Blaze was different. It was pretty bitchy actually. If we were all together in the park it wouldn't be uncommon for a player to look over at a family with a daughter and come out with something like, 'Who the fuck has dressed her like that?' The only thing missing was the sassy finger clicks.

Bitchiness formed an integral part of the changing room culture. It wasn't horrible bitchiness, like you often get in straight teams; it was more to keep spirits high. Sexual partners were always a hot topic of conversation. There was the running joke that when some players went to the clinic and had to list their sexual partners, their file would have to be brought in on a trolley. It didn't help that often, if a player had slept with a few opponents or teammates, you could usually claim that by association they'd slept with the whole league.

The young, gay, promiscuous man is a common stereotype, and though there were players in the changing room who could certainly be categorised as such, there were more who couldn't. It wasn't like a straight changing room, where there's a common consensus that the more girls you sleep with, the more manly and therefore the more respected you are. At Birmingham Blaze it depended which side you were on. Those who had slept with lots of different partners saw their promiscuity as the ideal, a target that should be aimed at by all, and those who hadn't believed that their ways were best.

The football itself was pretty relaxed. It was slower. You could make a mistake without getting called some obscenity, which was just as well because there were a lot of mistakes. Everyone laughed instead. At Heyford, players rarely laughed once they crossed that white line.

That's not to paint Blaze as some kind of utopia, however. The bitchiness from the changing room often spilled onto the pitch. It was very much an atmosphere of bitchy competitiveness without ever boiling over into violence. There was a lot of gobbing off at opponents from 15 metres away, which was always quickly curtailed if that same opponent got within five metres of the player gobbing off. It was definitely a case of the players having all bark and no bite.

I'd come to learn that calling opponents 'queens' was a favourite insult, and if a geographical reference could be incorporated, all the better. 'Fuck off back to Birmingham, it's a shit hole,' is never a good insult to make when the person gobbing off is standing knee deep in dog poo in Richmond Park. Sometimes it proved hard not to direct that anger at teammates. Try as I might it couldn't go as far as me not shouting at them because at times it was frustrating. It was for all of the better players. Some of our teammates were really poor. They could barely kick a ball in a straight line. Weighing it all up though, I had to admit that the whole situation was amazing.

I had five or six training sessions with Blaze before being included in the squad for a friendly match against Bournemouth. It was to be played at Blaze's home venue at Moor Lane in Upper Witton, Birmingham – a short distance from Aston Villa's Villa Park.

The home ground of Birmingham University's football sides, Moor Lane was pretty much the Midlands' answer to Hackney Marshes. The pitches weren't great – even though the groundsman had an annoying habit of calling off all games at the first sign of a drop of rain – but there were loads of them, and a large number of teams were based there. The changing facilities were better. There was a large pavilion in the corner of the complex which couldn't have been more than 15 years old. It was one of those bland, uninspiring modern buildings but at least it was clean and spacious.

I'd been scoring goals in training – which was just as well, because I'd done my usual trick of telling my new team that I play up front – and was generally feeling good about myself. Even so, it didn't stop the nerves coming as I put the Blaze match kit on for the first time. The red and black striped shirt, with all that it represented, suddenly made everything seem real. In training I had felt like one of the better players, but the shirt somehow felt weighted, as if it held the expectation from all of the other players in its thin nylon. They let me wear my favourite No. 17 shirt, my hero Gary Breen's number at Coventry City.

By now I was integrated into the team dynamic. I had literally been welcomed with open arms and a kiss on the cheek, as is the way in gay football. Now I was keen to impress. I would, however, have to wait until the second half as I was selected to start on the bench. Fair enough. I was new – I'd have to earn my place like anyone else. It didn't matter. I'd prove myself to them. At least that's what I thought.

There were about 25 minutes remaining when I got my chance. I went on up front, somewhat of a throw of the dice with us 2-0 down. I started OK: I won quite a few headers and flicked on some bits and pieces. Nothing spectacular but enough to impress quietly. Maybe it made me a bit complacent and put me off my game, because within 10 minutes my opportunity came. Now was my chance, the chance to prove my skill to all of my teammates, to make my mark on the team, to bring the scoreline back in our favour...

The ball was floated across the box. I saw it coming to me in slow motion. Everything was in slow motion. The players, the keeper, the sounds; everything just stopped. For a few seconds it was just me and the ball and nothing else mattered. I looked and all I could see was the empty net. That and the slowly rotating ball, its panels worn by time. I was no more than three yards out. Three yards. To this day I still don't know how I missed that chance. I didn't even hit the target. I connected with the ball but all I could manage to do was put it wide of the goal. It would have been easier to score.

The ball ended up in some bushes. That's how horrific my attempt was. I'd been overcome with shock long before the ball came to rest. I was a fraud. My shirt was so heavy. At least there'd be no expectations now. Fifteen minutes later, and with the score still at 2-0 to Bournemouth, I only came to regret the miss more as the final whistle sounded.

I think a lot of people were surprised by that miss. It was no shock that I was swiftly moved back into my normal defensive position the very next game against London Titans, which was the first in the league. As with most gay clubs, Birmingham Blaze played in the Gay Football Supporters Network League, to give it its full title. Blaze were in the third division of three, but were positive about their chances of promotion to the second tier – especially, modesty eluding me, now they'd made their star signing of the summer.

The Gay Football Supporters Network had initially been set up in 1989 to provide a place for gay football supporters to meet and share their views and watch games together. It provided safety in what could occasionally be a hostile matchday environment. They later discovered that some people would rather play football than watch it, however, and so they organised a five-a-side tournament, to take place at the annual GFSN summer get-together.

The success of these tournaments, and the desire for more regular competition from those who took part, led to the formation of the national 11-a-side GFSN League in 2002, with four clubs involved: Bristol Panthers, London Leftfooters, Leicester Wildcats and Yorkshire Terriers. It was – and still is – the only league of its kind. There is no other nation in the world which has its own LGBT football league.

It seems strange because the GFSN league has grown and grown, to the point where there are now three leagues with six teams in each. Each league is national so there's quite a bit of travelling – fair play to Saltire Thistle FC, based in Glasgow and up against teams as far south as London Falcons FC. The league itself is committed to tackling homophobia, biphobia and transphobia in football.

Inclusivity is the watchword of the league, with the aim being the creation of a safe and tolerant environment for all with each matchday. That's the main reason a lot of the teams can't play in the straight leagues. Transgender players kind of blur the Football Association's boundaries, seeing as they don't allow female players to play in adult male leagues. That's not the case in the GFSN. All are welcome: gay, straight, black white, rich, poor. We don't want to isolate ourselves. We don't want to hide away from the world and create an environment where it's only gay people and nobody else is allowed in. That's the beauty of the GFSN League.

There are a number of straight people who play. Sure, a few of the clubs moan because the straight players that some teams bring in tend to be better than their gay players, leading to accusations of them being ringers, but they only moan out of jealousy. Everyone wants the best players. At Blaze, there were a couple of straight players when I joined. Straight was a bit of a loose term for them, really. They said they were straight but they had definitely experimented at some point in their life. There was always one man they'd had 'an experience' with.

I guess you can maybe mention one of our players, Lucas, in the same breath because he claimed he was bisexual, though nobody had ever seen him so much as talk to a woman, a pattern that continues to this very day. How long are you something before inactivity defines you as something else? If you stop going to a school you're no longer a pupil. Maybe it's best to ask Lucas that one.

With the straight players you tend to find this attitude where they think that they're going to be the best player on the pitch because of their sexuality. A lot of straight players join because they believe in the cause of the GFSN, and a lot more join because they've got mates who play in teams, but still the attitude of being a big fish in a small pond is quite prevalent.

To be honest, there was a little bit of me that arrived at Birmingham Blaze with that attitude. I thought that I was going to be the best player and that everyone would be awestruck by my ability, a myth which was destroyed in about 10 minutes. There are some pretty amazing players in the GFSN. There are also quite a few awful ones, but the amazing ones would stand out in straight leagues as well.

Harry was one straight player we had at Blaze who certainly had the attitude that he was better than everyone else. He enjoyed believing that he was the best, whereas in reality he was pretty average. A lot of straight players find it frustrating when they join that they're not the best player, but Harry seemed to be happy with living his own self-made myth in his head. We didn't mind too much. He was very much a part of the team, though he was often the butt of the jokes because of how straight he was. Still, Harry got involved, and he even enjoyed taking part in the bitchiness every now and again. Personally, I didn't see eye to eye with him. I thought that I was better than him, so it was inevitable that we would clash.

Anyway, my change in position turned out to be a blessing in disguise, and even more so when Harry was left on the bench for the game against Titans. The match itself wasn't anything to write home about, but we still came away with a victory. I even made up for my horror miss the week before by opening my account with a looping header from a free-kick to put us 2-0 up.

As I wheeled away in celebration I had to contend with a sulking Lucas, who moaned that if I hadn't headed the ball he could have chested it down and volleyed it into the net. I didn't take it too much to heart. Lucas is the kind of guy who'd hide the presents at Christmas, and there was no way I was passing up an opportunity to score my first goal in the GFSN.

Instead of finding a comeback to aim at Lucas's downbeat face, I ran to the taker of the free-kick, Fiona, the one transgender player on our team. Fiona is the only transgender person I've ever played with. She was a good laugh – a strong character both on and off the pitch who led by example. Her reliability on the pitch and good nature in the changing room made her well respected throughout the team. Nobody ever said anything spiteful to her, and to be honest, if they did then they would have probably been in for a beating. She was well protected by our team, and not only because she took great free-kicks.

Fiona was one of a number of transgender players who played in our league. And transgender players were the main reason for clubs not affiliating with the Football Association. It's not as if the FA hasn't tried to get us to affiliate. They're always contacting clubs in the GFSN to invite them to affiliate so they can take part in FA competitions. Yet there still persists in gay football the myth that the FA, and county FAs, don't want anything to do with gay football. It seems to just be a get-out.

Maybe in the past FAs weren't interested, but their regular invitations in the modern era suggest otherwise. It comes down to people in the GFSN having this fear where they believe that if they play against a straight team they're going to encounter homophobia. I can understand that but I always tell them not to worry, just to focus on marking their opponent and not letting them score. My advice usually falls on deaf ears. It'd be nice to affiliate with the FA, but not allowing transgender players a chance to play would undermine what the GFSN stands for. And with Fiona producing assists like that for me, I couldn't afford to lose her. Anyone who can help me score is a valuable player to have.

Fiona went on to produce a couple more moments of magic in that game. Even though she probably deserved it, I was awarded man of the match for my performance at centre back. We'd won the game 4-1 and the award, along with my goal, really got the ball rolling for me at Blaze. From that game on, I was in.

Whilst things were going great with Blaze they were going terribly with Chris. There was a direct correlation between the two. More than anything, I think he was lonely. He just wanted to be in the house with someone. By now there were so many cracks that the full break seemed inevitable. We'd barely been seeing each other. We would just work away and then go to bed. I'd be up in Birmingham with my time off; Chris would be out on the town. He was still just as possessive. He wanted me all to himself and he feared that I was running away from him. I guess he was right.

We'd argue and then make up for a day. And then argue some more. It seemed pointless and I told Chris that. I wanted it to be over. And then it was. We broke up, just like that. That wasn't a mistake. To this day I can certainly say that breaking up with Chris was not a mistake. What was a mistake, however, was not moving out. We shouldn't have stayed under the same roof. Once you separate you should separate. It should be a physical and an emotional separation. Ours was only emotional, though in reality we had been emotionally separated for some time. We'd merely confirmed what we both already knew.

I tried moving out for a little bit. I stayed at a friend's place in her spare room but I didn't really like it. It wasn't home. It was temporary; a life lived out of bags. And so I returned to my overpriced flat in Oxford. There seemed to be no other option. We had a contract to fulfill. Neither of us wanted to go back home to our parents. I felt like I couldn't go back and Chris made me feel sorry for him, making out that he was the victim in all of this.

Unsurprisingly we no longer stayed in the same room. I moved across the hallway but we would still always be bumping into each other. It seemed like we saw each other more when we broke up than when we were still together. It would always be awkward. Neither of us wanted to be there and neither of us was much good at small talk. There was a fake politeness about everything. We were both living a lie. Did we want to be polite

to each other? Not a chance, but it seemed the best way to deal
with the situation.

And so we tried to get on, we really did. But when you've
broken up, every little thing becomes an issue, even more so
than when the cracks were nearing breaking point. It was as
if everything that Chris did was to spite me, even though that
wasn't really the case at all. I'm sure the feeling was mutual.

Even though the break-up was inevitable, I was happier
about it than Chris was. Once we were separate, Chris did
things to try and make me jealous. He was out a lot, shoving his
freedom in my face. He wanted to make me think that he was
out hunting for a new man – someone better than me – so that
I'd want him back. I couldn't have cared less. I wasn't some little
kid who had had his favourite toy taken away from him.

Nearly all of my spare time was being spent in Birmingham.
Joe the secretary put me up. He was one of my first good mates
up there. About 10 years my senior, he guided me into my new
lifestyle. Away from Blaze he was just a regular guy. An average
Joe, if you like. He was around six feet tall and a bit chubby
around the edges, but there was nothing really to set him apart
from the crowd. I guess you could just say that he was really
normal.

Without him things wouldn't have been easy, and down in
Oxford things certainly weren't easy. There, I had no friend, no
Joe. I had only my bitter ex-boyfriend. Even though we were
no longer together, Chris would still get upset at my absence.
He'd always make a great deal of moaning how he 'hadn't seen
me for weeks' whenever I'd return from the Midlands. He had
a point, I suppose. I mean, at one stage it got so bad that I had
to go out and buy a load of extra clothes so that I could stay
up there for an extra few days. Birmingham was my utopia –
and I'm not sure that's something that has been uttered much
before.

I never went to Birmingham with the intention of finding a new boyfriend. For me it was all about enjoying myself – which I wasn't doing at home under all of the tension and fakeness and deceit – and playing football. In Birmingham I was having fun with my mates and it was a laugh. Birmingham was my life. Blaze was my life. I had found myself. I could be the true Neil Beasley. And I liked it.

12
Team Dynamics

Adam. Now that was a strange relationship, and one that would eventually return me to the footballing scrapheap. We started off as rivals. Before I arrived at Blaze he was the top dog. He was the one they all adored. He could take on seven players and make them look silly. He could do loads of kick-ups and balance the ball on his neck and everything. To many of the Blaze players Adam was the real deal.

And then I turned up. Suddenly there was another good player in the ranks. Sure, I couldn't do all of Adam's fancy skills and I didn't look the part, but I could see through all of his flash. Maybe Adam felt intimidated. Whatever it was, it became evident that there was a rivalry between us from almost my first touch on the training pitch.

Adam was one of the few people I didn't really take to at Blaze. Considering there were more than 50 members of the club I'd say that's pretty impressive. Those I didn't take to were a bit gobby and had a lot to say for themselves – kind of like me – so there was a bit of a personality clash. If only they could have seen that I was always right. Too bad they always thought that they were right themselves, so friction was pretty much inevitable. Adam was different. He wasn't really gobby. He was pretty quiet in the changing room in fact; he just let his feet do the talking on the pitch.

It was pretty surprising that Adam was quiet in the changing room because he was so outgoing. He loved life and life loved him. So did everyone else. Adam was a good-looking bloke. He had it all: the six pack, the pecs, the muscles, the haircut, the smile. Everyone fancied him – in our own team and in those we played – even though he looked like he should still be at school.

On the pitch he played in the number 10 role, just behind the main striker. He was our creativity and our attacking force. To him, this meant licence to try and take on everyone in the opposing team. Now, because a lot of our players at Blaze weren't really too knowledgeable about the game, they were pretty impressed by this. Oh, Adam, he's like the gay Maradona, they would swoon. I was a little more pragmatic. If he's taken on and beaten seven opposing players then that means that seven of our players are probably free, I'd tell them. Why then, I would ask, does he try and beat an eighth player when he could just pass it to one of his teammates so they can have a chance at glory? Why could he never just create an opportunity without taking someone on?

My pragmatism was merely dismissed as jealousy. The effective stuff – the stuff that actually makes you win games – was secondary to them, no matter how many times I reminded them that you only get points as a result of sticking the ball in the net, not for taking on players. Yes he could do all the flicks and tricks but how many goals are actually awarded for that stuff? It's wonderful to watch but it doesn't win you matches. Pah, jealousy.

It was always frustrating to see my teammates lauding Adam as he cantered along with his show. With such support it was no wonder that Adam backed himself. He held a high opinion of himself – though it was more a case of confidence than arrogance. Me? I was probably equally confident and arrogant. Adam was always quicker than me and more athletic but I'd just tell my teammates that it was the ball that had to move. Sure, he was more skilful, but I was better at the basics. There really wasn't much in it and we both wanted to be top dog.

We'd never really spoken and had no reason to. Other than playing on the same team, of course, but at the time that just seemed trivial. I didn't think he was as good as other people said and Adam knew this. He resented it. He probably thought the same about me. It was common knowledge that we didn't really think much of each other. At least I thought it was, anyway. Because of this, whenever someone asked me about Adam, I'd always try and be diplomatic.

One Sunday we'd played together in a league game. Afterwards I decided to go back to Oxford to chill out. I had work the next day and wanted to get through it OK. I was in the bath when I got a text from our manager, Craig. Now, I got on really well with Craig and classified him as a close friend. Tall and athletic with a Yorkshire accent, Craig was a good laugh and an all round nice bloke. He was quiet – pensive, if you like – but shouted when he needed to. He had taken up the managerial role in addition to his status as a player. Coaching was his full-time job and he didn't half know his stuff.

That said, there were times when I knew that he didn't really want to be the manager, that he wanted to just focus on being a player. It must have been frustrating for him, being from a footballing background and such a good player himself, to have some players who were unable to understand and then carry out his instructions. Still, he never shouted at us. He was a thoughtful person who not only had our full respect, but the respect of the gay community in general. Everyone in gay football knows of Craig Simpson, and he's widely regarded as one of the best gay players there is. He's a good player, and not just by gay standards.

Craig would only ever bring himself on when he was needed. He wasn't one of these 'me, me, me' guys who has to do everything. I don't think he's ever played at a good standard, but he springs to mind as one of these players who could have played at a high standard if he wasn't gay. Maybe I'm wrong but he strikes me as the kind of person who wouldn't put himself forward for trials because his sexuality held him back. There are loads of gay players like that. They hold themselves back because their sexuality is clear and they're afraid of the reaction. You can certainly tell that Craig is gay before even speaking to him.

Craig used to message me quite regularly. We got on well. He made me his captain pretty early on and used to send me messages like 'I'd give you a ten-year contract if I could.' No wonder I got on with him so well. Anyway, the fact that he'd messaged me after the game wasn't really surprising given our friendship. 'Can I ask u something.' Straightforward, to the point, I thought. Of course you can Craig. 'What do u think of Adam', he asked. Do. That was a strange word. The present, even though our game was in the past. Do. I went down the diplomatic route. Craig was the manager after all and I didn't want to upset the team dynamic. 'I thought he played ok 2day.' And he had – he'd only tried to take on six players at a time rather than his usual seven. The response was immediate. 'Not like that.'

Do. He really had meant do. Well, this was strange. That was all I could think at first, then I became cynical. It had to be a joke. People knew that we didn't get on. But then why was the manager in on it? The manager – the leader of the team dynamic – the unifying force. Surely he wouldn't be having a laugh at my expense? Again, I went down the diplomatic route. 'I've never really entertained the idea,' I replied and it was the truth – I really had never thought of Adam in that manner. Again the response was almost immediate. 'Well Adam wants to hang out with u.'

Now I thought that he was taking the micky out of me. Why

would he do that? Why would the manager, who had so much of my trust, do this to me? I couldn't accuse him though – he was the manager. So I asked him where he'd heard the story from. And just why wasn't Adam messaging me this if what Craig was saying was actually true? Maybe Craig had got the wrong end of the stick, misheard something from somewhere. But no, Adam was just too shy apparently. Too shy? The guy was built like a gladiator. Too shy my foot. It was definitely a wind-up.

But it wasn't. Adam truly was attracted to me. The signs had apparently been there but I'd missed them all. For example, there was this night when we were in a pub and Adam was sitting there with his cousin, both of them drunk. For some reason – probably alcohol – we were actually chatting and he just leaned over and gave me a kiss. He was complaining that when another of our teammates, Dan, arrived I'd got up to give him a hug and kiss – pretty much the bog standard gay welcome; we're very continental you know – and I hadn't greeted him in the same manner. So he gave me that kiss and it wasn't just on the cheek. Our lips touched. Just for a second. It was really quick and I hadn't thought anything of it, but to Adam it had obviously meant something. Drunk actions are often sober intentions.

Craig said that Adam wanted to go for a drink with me the following Saturday. At that point I was still sceptical but I played along anyway. Sure, I told him, but Adam would really need to text me to confirm. Then, around half an hour later I received a text from an unknown number. 'See u Saturday.' And that was it. No name, no emotion, no nothing. It confirmed nothing, making me even more suspicious of being on the end of a wind-up. Craig had probably just got another of the players who was in on the joke to message me.

I didn't go to training that week. I didn't want to be laughed at. To be treated as a joke by my manager and my teammates. I didn't go for the drink, either, but I did send a text to the mystery number. 'Why don't you come down to Oxford,' I asked. Chris was out – of course he was, it was a Saturday night – so it seemed like ideal timing. The mystery number agreed and down he came.

Now, I didn't know what to expect. I didn't know whether it actually would be Adam who would arrive on my doorstep or a whole group of Blaze players ready to laugh at me. When it came to the day I was nervous. Really nervous. The butterflies were back and my whole inside had been turned upside down. My heart was looping. Did I really want it to be Adam at my door? I didn't know, but it would be exciting. And if it was the group of Blaze players then at least the whole thing would be over.

When I feel nerves I often approach the situation in a cool, calm, collected manner. Being sensible is essential. And so it was in this situation, which is probably the reason that I drank half a bottle of Jack Daniels. It's how I've always approached problems. Usually it solves them, and so it did in this case, because when Adam turned up on my doorstep I'd lost all inhibitions. I dragged him in by the hand, sat him down on the sofa and just went and kissed him. Not even in the bog standard gay way. In an emotional way. Well, an alcohol-induced one. After that it wasn't awkward. Not on my part anyway. For Adam it probably was. I was really drunk and it's safe to say that Adam, having driven two hours down the motorway, probably wasn't. It didn't matter though; I was too drunk to care.

I'd promised the mystery number that we could hop on the bus and head down to G.A.Y. It wouldn't be too intense – just a good, friendly introduction to each other. Now that I'd introduced myself to Adam in the comfort of my living room, we both headed off to the bus station for further bonding. It was

a good night in G.A.Y – it always is – and I even met up with
Charlie again to see how things were. Adam had a great time.
I'm not sure he had ever been to G.A.Y before. Of course we
danced together and got close and kissed a few times, then we
came back and things got a little close but then that was it.
Nothing. Nothing at all and it was the weirdest thing ever.

We had been close but now we were just as distant as ever.
We went off to play football and it was like nothing had ever
happened, as if we had never even known each other in the first
place. I think it was a case of neither of us knowing how to
handle the situation. We didn't know what to do and so we did
nothing at all. There were no words exchanged between us. No
conversations, no contact. It was all purely on the pitch, where
a rivalry of sorts remained. There had been text messages but
even they were strange.

After our night together I wanted something to happen.
I wanted to be Adam's boyfriend. I didn't know what Adam
wanted. If anything, I thought he wasn't so keen on me. Why
would he be? With his looks he could have had pretty much any
man he wanted. Maybe he wasn't very good at giving off signs
or maybe I'm just not very good at reading them, because it
turned out that Adam wanted just the same as me.

Anyway, after a short period we started to message each
other again and decided we should see each other a bit more
regularly. At first it was the odd date and then we'd start to go
round to each other's houses. It wasn't easy to get much time to
ourselves though. First there was the distance. Then there was
the workload. Then the fact that if I was in Birmingham we'd
usually be with the rest of the team. We'd still see each other
but it wasn't the same. Fortunately the chairman of Blaze, a
kindly man named John, had got wind of the fact that we were
struggling. He was one of the few people who knew the situation between myself and Adam, and so he invited us to stay at

his house one night. We did and we had a great time: relaxed, fun and intimate. It did our relationship the world of good.

After that night word got round the changing room. We'd wanted to keep it a secret but I guess it was inevitable. Like I said, everyone wanted to be with Adam – he was the golden boy of Blaze. Our now public relationship actually ended up making things easier. We no longer had to sneak around behind everyone's backs. I'd done enough hiding in my life. Now I was out in the open and I couldn't have been happier. I was so far from the deception, the fraud, everything that had plagued my formative years. I was myself.

Once we became a public item, we were able to see each other relatively often. The distance was a bit of a problem but my shift pattern had changed and I was able to see Adam a fair amount in the week. Sometimes I'd work three days a week, sometimes four. Adam was a Monday to Friday worker. I never really understood what he did. He'd go off to a load of fields with his dad and see how big they were. Maybe there's a science to it that I don't really understand.

Chris took my relationship with Adam surprisingly well. He'd take the mick out of Adam's Brummy accent, but other than that, he didn't say much about the whole thing. Adam had been round a few times by now and Chris was always perfectly amiable. I don't know if he was just putting it on or not but it seemed genuine. He was less possessive these days but I still tried to keep out of his way when Adam was about. I felt it would be disrespectful to shove Adam in his face.

By and large our teammates at Blaze took the relationship well. At first, anyway. Before mine and Adam's relationship there had been a few other relationships within the team, and one or two were still active. The main trouble with being in a relationship in the changing room was the involvement of everyone. It was always done with the best of intentions but it wasn't half frustrating. Everyone would chip in. They all liked to get involved and give their advice, even though I was never particularly interested in it and didn't even ask for it in the first place. It ranged from the infuriating to the downright ridiculous.

"Relationships are like working in a shop," one particular teammate informed me, "you've got to keep working at them." Right.

Added to all of the 'advice' was the fact that we were no longer individuals. Neil and Adam. Adam and Neil. We were always the collective. People would never refer to just Neil. At first you feel pride in it, then after a while that slowly turns to frustration and finally annoyance. There were a few snide comments in the changing room. Adam was the golden boy of Blaze, remember, and there were certainly a few people who were jealous of my privileged position.

"Oh, what a surprise," came one remark, "the two best players getting together." What on earth was that supposed to mean? What a stupid comment. There were more to come: "Well, you two will always get in the team now." We always got in the team before. And the half-wit who came out with the ridiculous comment was always on the bench, which would still have been the case whether Adam and I were together or not. A lot of people still fancied Adam and that's where some of the malice came from.

Adam wasn't bothered by any of it, even when one half of another couple in the team approached me. It was the stronger one in the relationship and he asked if we could trade partners for the night. He'd get Adam and I'd get his partner. No. Of course not. Well, I wasn't that blunt but what on earth was the bloke thinking? I trod the diplomatic path again. "I'm not sure Adam would be up for that," I remember saying.

The comments weren't just confined to our team either. A lot of players we came up against would have a thing for Adam.

There was a time when we were playing a team from London and one of their players, who was young and confident, went over to Adam before the game and started putting his arm around him and being a bit too friendly.

Adam nodded in my direction and told him: "You know that's my boyfriend over there," to which he replied: "Oh yeah, he won't mind." Won't mind? Won't mind? "I'm going to break you in half. Once that whistle blows you're going to regret you ever met me."

On reflection I probably should have just thought that. I shouldn't have said it out loud, and I definitely shouldn't have said it in such an aggressive manner when I was standing next to Craig Simpson. It was no surprise when he benched me for the game. He didn't even bring me on to the pitch and I don't blame him. I'd have been a walking red card. To this day I stand by the belief that I'd have broken him in half. For just one game I'd have let my hard but fair approach slip.

Once again, Adam wasn't fazed by it. In fact, the only thing that bothered him about our now public relationship when we were at football was that I didn't pass to him very much. So he thought, anyway, because I was the first to point out that as a centre back, most of my passes either went to the opponent or off the pitch. He wouldn't listen and maintained that I should pass the ball to him more often, just like I had never done before.

As time wore on the comments from our teammates continued. It was mainly little things but each one just built and built on the previous ones. Then there were things like the Secret Santa. Whoever it was bought me a packet of nappies because Adam looked like he was still a kid. We all had a laugh about it but the whole time I was wondering just how malicious it was. Was it banter or 'banter'? Everyone just kept on chipping in with their thoughts and opinions. Nobody would leave us alone. It wasn't just Neil. It wasn't just Adam. It wasn't even just Neil and Adam. The whole time it was Neil and Adam featuring Birmingham Blaze and anyone else who wanted to give their two penn'orth.

We'd still go out with the rest of team. Everything was still the same. But it shouldn't have been. We should have focused on us more, because ultimately the involvement of everyone else would end our relationship. I had strong feelings for Adam. Was it love? I don't know. Love is a big word. He was special though. Maybe I felt a bit of pressure because I knew that everyone else was after him. I wasn't as happy as Adam was in the relationship. I should have been but I just couldn't shut out all of the noise. It haunted me. I was in a pantomime. Me and Adam, acting out our relationship to the captivated audience. Adam barely even noticed. He seemed oblivious to what everyone else said. He was probably used to it. When you're that good looking you become aware that people talk about you.

In the end I dealt with all the little annoyance in a bad way. I had a fling with another team member. There was alcohol involved and I was frustrated, but I shouldn't have done it. I really hadn't meant to, either. I'd approached the team member with the best of intentions, wanting merely to put an arm around him and cheer him up after his mistake had cost us the game we'd been playing in. As we got talking and the alcohol got flowing we got closer and closer and before I knew it I'd done something terrible.

Even then, if I'd have just let it be a one-off I could have smoothed it over with Adam. But I didn't. We met up a few more times and when the team member realised that I wasn't going to give him what he wanted he blabbed. Our secret got out and obviously after that my relationship with Adam couldn't continue. I was so ashamed of my actions, but in a way I also felt liberated.

Now the comments would stop. I hadn't been happy. That was why I had done it. If I was happy with everything then there's no way in a million years that I'd have cheated on Adam. I should have just ended it. I shouldn't have cheated. Adam remained special to me. If it wasn't for all of the pressure from my teammates and the feeling that we were just part of a pantomime, I'd have happily been with Adam and just Adam. I was young, immature and stupid.

When it ended, everyone took Adam's side, and rightly so. How could I blame them for that? It meant that I lost a lot of friends though. I'd lost most of my friends down in Oxford through my relationship with Chris and now I'd lost all of my friends in the Midlands because of another relationship. I had barely anyone left and it was all my own doing. My own stupid doing. I couldn't have felt lower. Everything was over.

13
Into Management

We tried to get back together but it didn't work. Adam wasn't happy and neither was I. We needed to be apart. I needed to give him some time to himself. Things weren't the same at Blaze. I no longer felt particularly welcome up in the Midlands. It caused me to sit down and add everything up, leading to an inevitable conclusion: I had to leave Blaze. Had to leave Adam behind and get on with everything, away from all of the mess.

I broke the news to my teammates at Blaze and many of them encouraged my decision. 'Oh yeah, just have a little break and give it a while. Everything will all work out' was the response of some. Later on, I would find out that the same people who ushered me away from the club had a vested interest in me being away from Adam. After I left, a number of them tried it on with him. Craig was keen for me to leave. He was a close friend but ultimately he was the manager and he couldn't risk breaking up the team dynamic. Either Adam or myself would have had to go to preserve the team chemistry and Adam wasn't in the wrong. It made sense.

And so I returned to the rented flat in Oxford that I could barely afford with an ex-boyfriend I had barely seen since the whole fiasco began. I never wanted to go back to Blaze. As the weeks went by there were a few people who tried to persuade me to come back but that was it. Chris was as good as gold. He wasn't gloating at all when it all soured with Adam. It was like he had transformed into a different person; the person I had first fallen for all those months ago – as good as gold, kind, caring and understanding. He listened to everything I had to say and gave me a shoulder to cry on. He still went out, I still worked for the police but things between us had changed.

I might have quit Blaze but I hadn't quit football. As gutted as I was to leave behind the gay league, I still had Heyford. I'd actually started back playing for them again a couple of months before finishing with Adam. Being myself and living my life and feeling free at Blaze had really given me a taste for football again, so much so that I'd rejoined Heyford's reserve team, playing for them on a Saturday and Blaze on a Sunday. My passion for the game had been ignited and now the fire was roaring. I'd have played on every night of the week if I could.

When we were still together, Adam would even come and watch the odd game down in Oxfordshire before then trekking back up to the Midlands with me the day after for our game with Blaze. Now I was just playing on a Saturday but that was fine; Heyford reserves was the only team I wanted to be a part of. It was exactly as before I left. Attitudes toward me remained the same. I was once again welcomed with open arms – though unlike at Blaze, not with a kiss on cheek. I was the prodigal son.

We ended up having a good season by our own standards, which basically meant that we didn't finish bottom. Things were on the up. There had been some new players joining who weren't all that bad, and that filtered out some of our more atrocious players. It got me thinking. If the team had been run a bit more smoothly, had paid a bit more attention to tactics, had played a bit more football, then well, they could have even done a bit better. If everything was done right the following season, with the potential in the new-look squad, we could even be looking at a mid-table finish... Such optimism was a far cry from the bad old days

By now you will have discerned what I'm like. I'm confident in my own ability and as far as I was concerned, I was the man to take the reserves at Heyford forward. The guy who had been managing the team the previous season was the same guy who had been managing it for the past 14 seasons before that. He'd done a great job and his commitment was unquestionable, but you always need to shake things up to keep them fresh.

I knew that he carried out his duty grudgingly. He was the chairman at Heyford and each year he'd ask if anyone else fancied taking up the role of reserve team manager. For 15 seasons nobody had. With this in mind, I headed to the club's AGM at the end of the season. By now I was confident that not only was a mid-table finish a certainty, but a promotion push was on the cards – if I was allowed to take the role. I could bring in a few more decent players – my cousins for a start – and introduce stuff that most good football teams do. Like tactics and stuff.

When it came to the point in the evening where the chairman stood up and sighed that he'd manage the reserve team again if nobody else would, I jumped at the invitation. I literally jumped up and spouted out: "I want to be the manager." And immediately I was. It was that simple.

I was on the phone straight away. My first recruits were my cousins and a couple of their mates. All of them were straight. As soon as some of my closer mates from Blaze found out, they were on at me to sign them up but I didn't want to and said no. I didn't want to deal with all the hassle of having more gay players in the changing room.

I was accepted because I'd been about for years but I didn't know if other gay players would have been. I felt that their presence could have caused a bit of tension. 'Oh, he's only picking them because they're gay like him', that kind of thing. I didn't want my sexuality to become an issue. I was probably totally wrong. I'm pretty sure that it would have been fine, but at the time that's just what I thought, rightly or wrongly.

Anyway, the players I did bring in were pretty handy. My cousin Mark from my Mum's side of the family was a decent goal scorer. That helped because suddenly we had goals in the team, though he came with a bit of baggage, mainly in the form of a steady number of bookings throughout the season. He was a couple of years younger than me and was studying at Oxford Brookes University.

Then there was Wesley, a cousin from my Dad's side, though in a fortunate turn of events he was best mates with the cousins on my Mum's side. He was a talented player who was previously on the books at both Oxford United and Northampton Town as a kid. Wesley could do stuff with the ball that most people just couldn't. It was a shame that he didn't have the mentality to make it in the professional game. He was a real hothead, even more so than Mark.

As a player you can be as amazing as you want but you can't score a goal if you're serving a three-match ban. Inevitably, Wesley would end up spending half of the season suspended - but it was worth it for the minutes that I would get out of him. To be fair to him, I'm not sure he had the easiest of upbringings. His mum and dad split up when he was in school, and he was also really close to our Gran, who died when he was younger. Both those incidents happened in a short space of time and they hit him hard. It was no wonder he went a bit off the rails, though by this point he was helping others get back on track with their lives as a prison support officer at Bullingdon prison.

Joining Wesley and Mark was a third cousin, Ryan, who was Mark's older brother. He remained local to the area, working on the line in a nearby BMW factory. He wasn't as good as the other two but he made up the numbers and was still a fair bit better than a lot of the players we had. Though Ryan didn't add too much to us on the pitch, he gave a lot in the dressing room. He was a really nice, down-to-earth guy, and one of the only people to support Manchester City before Thaksin Shinawatra's 2007 takeover, despite living nowhere near Manchester.

The three of them then had other decent mates and before I knew it I had a good squad on my hands. Ryan got a couple of people from the factory involved, Mark brought along some fellow students, and fortunately Wesley didn't get any of the inmates from Bullingdon nick to come down.

Even with the new additions, there was still a whole culture that needed changing. And so I changed it. I introduced tactics, brought in a few more people, started doing warm-ups – and not just the warm-up they were used to, of blasting balls at a goalkeeper with the substitute going to get their wayward shots out of the bush; but warm-ups including stretching, changes of direction and technical possession drills. I was barely out of my teenage years but everyone gave me their full respect.

All of a sudden life was good again. Adam was merely a fling long past – a mistake from which I had learned and moved on. Football had taken me far away from him. Now I would come back from work and plan my training session for the week. I'd agonise over team selection. Should I play three at the back or stick with the rigid 4-4-2 that is so successful in the grass roots game? How could I possibly implement a possession-based game when most of the pitches we played on were little more than ploughed fields? Most importantly, could I finally get away with playing myself as a striker when everyone else had always put me in defence?

Nearly all of my time was being taken up by football. When I wasn't working I was at football. When I was at work I was thinking about football. And when I was at football there was nothing else. I didn't have time to think about Adam. I didn't have time to linger in the past. It was time to move forward.

Which makes Chris's revitalisation all the more strange. Chris had totally changed his persona. He was now kind and caring, interested without being intrusive. At the time it was exactly what I needed.

As Chris and I warmed to each other once more, the inevitable happened. We decided to give it another go and get back together. The fact we were living together proved to be something of a catalyst. Even so, he'd been there for me, my shoulder to cry on. I suppose it just made sense for us to give it one more try. And so it was. I was moving forward whilst moving backward. And it felt good.

14
Connor's Story

Sometimes when life gets tough, you need a bit of inspiration from somewhere. Inspiration, though, can be hard to find. I had my Graham Norton DVDs and a whole host of teammates, but you're always looking for something new. That's how I found Connor Natella.

I first learned of Connor's story on social media. Social media is great. You get the trolls and the keyboard warriors and the people intent on abusing others, but in general social media makes it so much easier to find people who are going through what you are. In Connor's story I found inspiration and hope. Here was someone achieving his dreams in football as a gay man. I had to contact him, had to find out the secret behind his success. I sent Connor a message through Twitter. He soon responded and our friendship grew from there.

Still just 22 years of age, Connor was living in Southampton, coaching at New Milton Town FC of the Wessex League and scouting for a couple of Premier League teams. It was the New Milton Town part of that which had first led me to him. Connor became a media sensation – in the gay football world at least – when he was featured in the newspapers for being an openly gay coach at the semi-professional club. For Connor, it was just another step on his journey to coaching full-time in professional football. It was a journey that had begun at the age of 17, when he moved from his native Folkestone to Bournemouth in search of his dream...

* * *

"*I only 'came out' to myself when I was 18. Deep down I'd always known but I was unable to bring myself to accept it. I was in an inner turmoil: whenever I thought about it I felt a sense of dread. What would happen if people found out? Would I be strong enough? Would I be able to shut out all the words and phrases and malicious comments? Would I enjoy being myself in a world that isn't yet equal?*

Playing football as a kid was a difficult period for me. So was getting into coaching when still at a young age. I ran before I could walk in almost every situation. At 15 I was in charge of a local youth side. By the age of 16 I was coaching a senior Sunday league team. I was severely out of my depth. What better way to learn?

I learned the hard way. The Sunday league team ended in a mess. It was nothing to do with my sexuality as nobody knew at that point, not even me. I was trying to manage players twice my age and the players twice my age didn't take too kindly to being ordered around by someone who could easily have been their own kid. Trying to get them to drop deep to receive possession on the half turn or to run a couple of shuttles at training was near impossible. All they wanted to do was boot the ball at the goal. They weren't having me in that regard and I found myself being shown the door before too long. That was fine. Setbacks make me hungrier. Sometimes you have to fail to achieve.

Back then I was young, naïve and inexperienced. To top it all off I didn't really know what I was doing. Fast forward to now. I took charge as the manager of a semi-professional team. They knew I was gay. It's no secret anymore. I've accepted it and those around me have accepted it. Why fight it? It's natural. The support from the club and the players was incredible. They gave me the confidence to enjoy my life as much as ever. I feel proud of what I am doing, and it's all a result of a life-changing decision, a decision made around my 20th birthday, two years after I first knew, when I uttered those dreaded words. "Oh yeah, I've got a boyfriend."

Now, when most people say those words it is liberating, pulsating and terrifying. It was for me too. However, most people don't have to see their words the very next day on the back page of the newspaper. I'd uttered those words to a journalist, you see, and he put my confession on the back page of the local paper. Confession. It makes it sound like a crime, doesn't it? And people say homophobia isn't ingrained in society.

That interview sparked further media interest. First of all, though, I had to face my team. The anxiety was unreal as I made my way to football training on the evening of the article. I was supposed to be these players' leader; I needed their respect. I'd received an unreal amount of support since the paper had come out, but even so I was unsure of how my team would take it. I felt physically sick as I walked the short distance to the training ground. At every step I wanted to turn and run.

The first person I came across was Ross, the team captain and a good personal friend. If there's one person I'd have wanted to encounter it would have been Ross. The team captain is your right-hand man. He's the example for all of his teammates: exemplary professionalism, full commitment and a can-do attitude, leading by example both on and off the pitch. Well, the first thing that Ross did was take the piss out of me. Off he went, railing off joke after joke about my newfound 'fame'. I'm not even sure he mentioned my sexuality. It was all about me making the back page.

Banter is currency in football. If you're not able to take it, don't give it. People are ruthless. They'll give banter to anyone when sometimes they shouldn't. Footballers aren't the most sensitive of people. Nobody is immune from being the subject of a joke or two. A number of non-football people have tried to convince me that Ross's remarks were offensive. Rubbish. I just can't see them in that way. What Ross was doing – and the rest of the team all followed his example – by teasing me about the interview was telling me that he accepted it. He accepted it enough to make it funny. It was his, and the team's, way of saying "it doesn't matter". Later on in the season, once everyone was openly comfortable and everything was accepted, they started to tease me gently about my sexuality – nothing malicious and always quite funny. I'll never forget Ross, during his end-of-season speech describing me as the 'Non-League Graham Norton', trying

*and failing to hide his massive grin. I can't say how much their acceptance
helped to remove my anxieties. Football made me feel so comfortable in my
own skin.*

*How did I manage to get so far in my coaching journey, I hear you ask.
It's a valid point. After all, at the age of 16 my prospects were looking
pretty hopeless, even though I remained certain that one day I was going to
achieve. Everything changed when I was around the age of 18. I managed
to wangle myself a job at AFC Bournemouth, just when their dramatic
rise up the leagues was about to be kick-started. In the professional environment that AFC Bournemouth provided I learned a huge amount, both
about the sport and about myself as a person. Working under experienced,
full-time coaches gave me new focus and introduced me to different ways of
thinking and doing. Suddenly I was walking, but I was walking quicker
and quicker, ready to break into a run. And there was still no less ambition on my part, especially now I had a much clearer route of progression.*

*It was that focus, however, that made me keep my secret a secret. I
wanted a future in the sport and I didn't want to do anything that would
impact that future. In my opinion I'd never be able to come out in football.
If you want that, they can't know that. It was all I could think, over and
over in my mind. If you want that, they can't know that.*

*It took two years for those thoughts to go away. Two years to develop
the confidence to be true to myself and those around me. I am what I am.
Though I must admit, the confidence to come out to everyone was also borne
out of an increasing demotivation with everything to do with coaching. It
was a time when I was feeling it was less and less likely that I'd achieve my
ambitions. What was the point? My progression was slowing. I was going
nowhere. If I was going nowhere when I was working in a professional club
then what chance did I have? Looking back it was stupid, but I guess you
can't help that youthful enthusiasm. Indeed, it made everything work out
for the best, because without my motivation dwindling I'd never be in such
a happy, comfortable position as I am now.*

*I needed a new challenge. That much was obvious. With Callum
Brooks I found one. Now, before you jump to conclusions, Callum wasn't*

my boyfriend. He's heterosexual, but it was my meeting with him that changed everything. My boyfriend at the time was actually called Ben. I'd met him in a nightclub and we began seeing each other not long after. Soon one thing led to another and then a lot of people started to cotton on – a lot of people from outside the football world, anyway.

I'd always assumed that coming out would be like tearing off a plaster. There'd be that moment where I just came out and then bang, my life would be changed forever. It turned out it was nothing at all like that. You can't just assemble everyone you've ever met into a great big room, stand up at the front and scream out "I'm seeing a guy". I wish you could but alas, you can't. So instead I was tactical in my approach. I told the office loudmouth and urged him to keep it secret. Of course, it was less than four days before everyone in the office knew. Problem solved. Partially, anyway, because the office wasn't AFC Bournemouth's. The work I was doing at Bournemouth was only part-time, and there was no overlap between my work life and my football life.

Ever since I had admitted to myself that I wanted to find a new challenge away from the rigid structure and power struggles that come with attempting to work your way up in a professional football club, I was wondering whether I'd tell the football world about Ben. Why not? Not telling them about him had hardly catapulted me along my journey to becoming the next Jose Mourinho.

I'd known Callum for a while. We first met in the Slug and Lettuce to discuss our season ahead with the AFC Bournemouth academy. Ever since then we've had a running joke that when we win the Champions League together, we'll say how it all started in the Slug and Lettuce. We've still got some way to go, but at least our target has become a bit closer since that initial meeting. Anyway, Callum had left Bournemouth the previous season. He'd been appointed as the manager of New Milton Town FC in the first division of the Wessex League and went on to guide them to an 11th-placed finish in his first season in charge.

I met Callum to discuss a new venture. We're similar people, Callum and I. In the discussion we shared a mutual frustration at the lack of autonomy available to young coaches getting into the game. It was the reason that Callum left AFC Bournemouth for New Milton Town, and it was the reason that I was being pushed away. As our meeting went on, and it did for some time, the elephant in the room became more and more apparent. I was talking freely. It was kind of like the situation with the office loudmouth. Not that Callum's a loudmouth, but deep down I think I wanted him to know. I wanted to test the water with my football life, to see how the news went down. We sidestepped the issue a few times throughout our discussion, but we couldn't push it to the side forever. Eventually Callum stopped and asked the question. "Connor, are you gay?" I'd love to say I thought about the answer, considered all of the ramifications of a yes and a no, how to make sure a yes would have the right effect and all that. But I didn't. The question was direct and so my answer was direct. Instinctive, even. "Yes".

From that moment Callum's support has been invaluable to me. As far as I'm concerned our environment shapes us; the people you surround yourself with have to be the right ones if you want to achieve. Oh, and by the way, he gave me a job.

I spent that first season learning as I went on in my new role as assistant manager of New Milton Town FC. Unfortunately being an assistant manager of a Wessex League team doesn't pay the bills, so I got myself a teaching job at a local secondary school. The bills started to get paid and the hours allowed me to dedicate a great deal of time to coaching. It helped that the students were incredible. They were welcoming, accepting and usually hilarious, which was exactly what I needed because that year I broke up with Ben. I needed all the cheering up I could get.

At the end of the season Callum left New Milton Town FC. He'd received a pretty decent offer from Conference-bound Poole Town FC. They wanted him in a coaching role and he'd have been a fool to turn it down. That gave me a tough decision: I could go for the vacant manager's job or I could just walk away from it. It took a great deal of thought. It's always hard for a number two to step into the big boss's shoes. As a number two you're supposed to be the nice guy, the one the players can have a laugh with. Sometimes it's hard to get the respect from the players if you make the transition to being the big boss. The day after Callum broke the news I received a call from the chairman. We spoke at length and by the time I put the phone down I had taken the job – my arm had been twisted.

Life as a Non-League manager was a bit of a rollercoaster. To put it one way, I needed to carry my phone charger at all times. When I wasn't chasing players to train I was speaking to journalists and trying to keep a personal life. We drew our first game at home. It wasn't a bad result and, after all, the football season is a marathon and not a sprint. As the games came thick and fast, I grew further into the role. I'd never had more conversations about football in my life. It was exhausting but exhilarating. Which made having to leave all the more agonising.

Becoming the manager turned the focus from coaching to logistics. It was good to have the power over everything, but at that stage of my career I needed to be developing my coaching. Added to that, there was no money for the manager at New Milton Town. I was having to rely on my day job, and when I got a better offer from back home it seemed a no-brainer. Callum had an opportunity for me at Poole Town – a coaching one – and so I took it.

That's not to put a negative on my experience at New Milton Town. Throughout my three months in charge, not one person mentioned my sexuality. My boyfriend even openly came to several of our games and he had no trouble at all. A couple of people seemed to distance themselves from me when they found out, but those people were few and far between. By and large, nobody had an issue with it. The chairman showed faith in me. Every single player pledged to stay on to play under me. Journalists didn't say anything, fans didn't say anything, nobody really said anything.

I can literally count the number of people who have had an issue over the years on one hand, and they're the type of people who take issue with anything anyway so it's not exactly something to lose sleep over. As far as I'm concerned, in my experience of football, my sexuality is a non-issue. Maybe it's different because I was a manager and not a player, so there's a different hierarchy of respect, but I'm not sure that's the case.

I was quoted in my 'coming out' article as wanting to be "judged on my merits as a football coach, nothing more". It felt as if I was. There may well have been conversations going on that I don't know about but that's not important. What was important was that I was able to pursue my passion with the same ambition I had when I first picked up a rack of cones at the age of 14.

So far I've had eight years of coaching experience. If I coach until I'm 60 I'll have had my eight years of learning more than five times over. I can't tell you how glad I am that I'm able to look ahead at the challenge I face as a professional one and not a personal one. There's a lot that I want to achieve in this sport.

Each day I sit down and remind myself that life isn't linear; it isn't how it looks on a CV. There are twists and turns, peaks and troughs, and being aware of that is the only way to survive on what can be a very lonely pathway. I'm doing all right so far. **"**

15
Missing the Action

My time as a football manager began well and suddenly Heyford Athletic Reserves were winning more than they lost. The sun still rose and set each day, but when the good people of Oxfordshire studied the Banbury District and Lord Jersey third division of three, they no longer saw Heyford helplessly rooted to the bottom. We were a team on the rise.

I didn't play much myself. I was always scared of leaving players out of the team. It was much easier to make the decision to not play myself. On the rare occasions that I did start, I would always make sure to substitute myself off before the final whistle. I guess I learned a lot from Craig in that regard, and in every other regard to be honest. A lot of the stuff that I was doing as a manager came directly from Craig. I always tried to be calm and collected just like him. It was all about sitting back and adjusting the team as the situation saw fit. A game plan was essential, as was having a back-up plan in case anything went wrong.

The control over everything was good. I'm so competitive – I love winning – and suddenly everything I did directly affected the three points on offer. As we started to rack up the points I got a bit carried away. In the end I was probably a bit too full of my own hype.

I might have been careful enough to manage my game time but when I did step out on to that pitch I made sure to maximise every opportunity I got. I put myself on penalties. I know,

I know. I'm not proud of it but I let the situation get the better of me.

There was even one time where we were playing against our close rivals, Heyford United. One of our players was brought down and the referee pointed to the spot. The player who was brought down wanted to take the penalty and nobody could blame him. He had earned it. But I didn't let him. I simply overruled him, picking up the ball and planting it on the spot myself. And then I went and missed the bloody target.

That Heyford United game made me start to question everything. The missed penalty wasn't all that happened. That was only small fry. There was a big punch-up in the same game and one of the other team smacked one of my cousins in the face so I started laying into him. My watching Mum and Dad were just stood on the touchline gobsmacked. At least they stayed there. My Granddad was trying to get on the pitch to give the culprit his own two penn'orth and then Mum started crying and everything all got a bit out of hand. If only Wesley had been there. He'd have been able to do all of the laying in to people for me. But he wasn't. He was suspended.

Heyford United apart, things went so well that Heyford Athletic Reserves enjoyed their most successful season ever, finishing fourth in a division of 13 teams. Promotion was even on the cards for a while. Everyone thought me staying on as manager for the following season was a given. But I didn't. I quit at the end of the season.

When you put in all of your time and effort to make something go well, other people think that they can do your job better than you. They don't see all of the hard work that goes on behind the scenes. They don't understand that you've already done all of the hard stuff which allows the team to thrive. They just see all the success on the pitch. A part of me feels sorry for people who do good jobs because it makes

everyone think that it's easy. That's because the person's hard
work has made it look so easy. Maybe I wanted more credit for
what I had created at Heyford reserves. Probably, however, I
just wanted to leave on the crest of the wave.

I was enjoying playing and managing but it's always better to
go when things are going well; much better than when they're
not. Tainted memories and all that. I'd done the job for a year
and I wanted to be remembered for my successes.

The circumstances of my personal life had changed over
the course of that season and that ended up influencing my
decision. Chris and I had barely got back together before everything fizzled out. Nothing had changed, other than the fact that
I was perhaps more vulnerable after what had happened with
Adam. If I'd wanted to leave the relationship with Chris on the
crest of the wave then I should have packed my bags the moment that we made it official. All of the old problems were still
there. The same reasons we split up in the first place came back;
Chris's persona reverted almost overnight. Suddenly he was the
possessive, jealous boyfriend that I had tried to distance myself
from. It was never going to last.

After a couple of months of it not working we decided to
end the relationship. I moved out as I didn't want to have to go
through everything again. I had had enough and didn't want to
make it the same as the last time. A wise man once said that a
mistake is only a mistake if you don't learn from it. So I phoned
the landlord and gave him a choice. "Look, we've split up," I
said. "Do you want two unhappy tenants or do you want me
to pay you the rest of the month and leave? It's your decision."
Fortunately, he chose the latter and I was off, away from the
past and forward once more.

With Chris out of the picture I was moving forward in all
aspects of my life. History was history, never to be repeated, a
fact that I emphasised to my Heyford players as they hurtled

up the table. There was no way we'd be finishing bottom again. History would not be repeated. There was still around three quarters of the season left when me and Chris broke up and the free time I now had on my hands was dedicated even more to football, though my life was unfortunately unable to revolve totally around the beautiful game. I had a new job and had also to pay enough attention to that to ensure that I could pay each month's bills.

Despite my frustrations with our inability to get much done, I'd enjoyed working for the police. The trouble was that the job associated itself with my previous life and all of the lies. It reminded me of what I was trying to repress. I guess it didn't help that Chris and I had had a massive argument in the house one day, so bad that the police had ended up coming round to settle things down. It was hard going into work after that. Looking for a new job was a way of cleansing myself and starting afresh.

I didn't want a drastic change, though, so when I saw an advert in the newspaper for work with the ambulance service I jumped at the chance. As with the police, I'd be providing a public service with a pattern of shift work and, of course, a uniform. Who doesn't love a uniform? I'd gone to the interview and done well enough to be offered the position.

From my first day in the job I enjoyed it. It was exciting. I was helping people and felt like my job was an important one. Based in the operations department, my main role was to process 999 calls before dispatching the emergency ambulance to the patients. Every day was different and I was getting to meet a whole load of new people, the vast majority of whom were friendly and fun. Two of them I got on so well with that I ended up moving in to the spare room in their house.

My two new housemates from the ambulance service were both gay. They weren't necessarily camp but they were pretty stereotypical, the kind of people whose sexuality is evident even before you first speak to them. One was called Dion. He was tall, standing at around 6ft 2in, though that's where the comparisons with his namesake, Dion Dublin, ended. This Dion was really thin. He was one of the managers at work, which meant I'd have to do my best not to annoy him too much.

The other was Mark. Around 6ft tall, he was slightly more camp than Dion and worked on the road as an ambulance technician. We got on well, going out in Oxford all of the time, especially on Saturday nights, and enjoying the good life. We got a bit of a name for ourselves around the town. People must have thought we were alcoholics. It was always a good laugh. Neither of the other two had boyfriends so most of the nights would be quite flirtatious. Mark and Dion suited the stereotype in every way, meaning they were both relatively promiscuous in their dealings.

It also meant that they didn't really like or understand football. They thought it was weird that I was so into football. To them 4-4-2 and 4-3-3 were but arbitrary numbers used to convey meaningless points. Yeah, but the whole aim of the game is to kick the ball into the goal, right? I'd try and explain to them how different formations were needed to break down opponents and give my team a greater chance of scoring a goal. I'd never get more than a blank expression in return, save for a look of relative disgust. Each to their own, I suppose.

If anything, moving out of the house with Chris and in with Dion and Mark had a positive impact on my football. Even though I'd come out to all the players at Heyford, I still held this fear of suffering homophobia from opponents, so I continued to attempt to repress my true feelings. It was a strange situation. With Chris out of the picture everything seemed a bit more secure. Without a boyfriend I reasoned it was less likely opponents would find out about my sexuality. Well, so long as they didn't frequent Cloud 9 in Oxford. It meant that I could focus purely on football, now that I was single.

Football is an amazing vehicle to take you to a better place. All of my worries and fears and concerns, everything was swallowed up by the beautiful game. All that mattered were the three points. Being back in football was being back in my comfort zone after a couple of disastrous relationships, and by the end of my season as Heyford Reserves manager, Chris and Adam were mere specks on the horizon. I was in a much better place where I had no worries. Football had purified everything.

And then football went. Sure, it was a case of me leaving on the crest of the wave, but by this point everything was going so smoothly in my life that I didn't necessarily need football so much. There were other things that I wanted to try my hand at. Now that my life was much more stable I wanted to start enjoying my free time a bit more, and as a manager I had barely any free time to enjoy. Even in those rare instances when I did get a moment to myself, I'd still be considering tactics and what drills to do at training the next week. I'll never know how Sir Alex Ferguson managed it for so long.

Work was a factor. Once again my day job was taking up more and more of my life. I'd work all day in the office and then come back and speak about work with my two house-mates/colleagues. It made my decision easier. Part of me was disappointed about quitting football – and I was quitting football; the option of joining another team barely even crossed my mind. I didn't want to start all over again with everything, with the same questions, the same hassle and the same gay thing again.

At Heyford the people were all fine, they were decent people, whereas at another team I'm not so sure. People may have had issues. There was another part of me that held an air of arrogance. Whichever way you looked at it, I had done a really good job as manager. This way I'd remember it as having been a job well done, and that was the main incentive for walking away. I didn't know how I could better what I had achieved. At the time it felt like I was making the right decision.

And for a couple of months I stood by that. Then a new football season started and I realised that I'd made a terrible mistake. Who was I kidding? I missed the game and, more than anything, the competition. I could turn the most mundane activity into a contest. It's lucky that I prefer the competition to the victory, because the majority of teams I've played in over the years haven't won much. I think I've had more relegations than drinks from G.A.Y. And I love G.A.Y.

I also missed the team spirit. You can't beat the changing room environment, especially on the day of a match. It's the same up and down the country, from kids' football to the Premier League. I may not have missed the management side of things – the logistical side anyway, because that was a real pain – but I certainly missed the atmosphere. I always did wonder whether I was a bit young to be giving up my involvement in football but I did it anyway, probably because I'm so stubborn.

The alternative proved not to be very appealing. My weekends consisted of a mixture of work, watching football, going out drinking and dossing around. The more I did it the more I realised that quitting was a really bad idea. My life had needed a change but to give up football was kind of stupid. Work took my mind off things but it's work. It's not like it was an enjoyable alternative. Not like football was.

Sure, I still got to watch football, but it was pretty much limited to the odd Coventry game and the weekly screening of Match of the Day. I suppose I did manage to get the odd Soccer Saturday in but it just wasn't the same watching it with a load of stereotypical gay people in the house who hated the game. They must have felt like I did when they tried to make me watch the Eurovision Song Contest. I couldn't have cared less. I might as well have watched paint dry. It'd probably sound better, too, though my housemates all went mad for it.

I stuck it out for a bit longer, putting on a brave face. At least going out drinking was still fun, but it had been when I was playing football; it was no real consolation. It was the same with dossing about. Eventually I decided that I could stay away no longer. It had got to mid-October and enough was enough. My cousin Mark had taken over the management of the reserve team at Heyford but I couldn't go back there. Well, I could, I just didn't want to. You should never go back to your past – I'd learnt that much from Chris. Then there was the fact that Mark was building on the foundations I had laid. The reserves had a decent team and were going from strength to strength both on and off the pitch. I didn't want to upset their dynamic.

That didn't mean there weren't opportunities at Heyford Athletic, however. As one team got better, the other got worse. The first team were really struggling. At that point they had a worse side than the reserves. It sounds strange but I knew that I'd get more playing time in the first team than the reserves. Plus they had my best mate Joe playing for them.

So, come the first week in November I played my first game for the first team. And with it began the next chapter in my story, this one featuring a Neanderthal manager with little awareness and even less decency.

16
Bruised and Beaten

Heyford Athletic's first team manager got it all wrong. I'm not saying that because I'd enjoyed a good season as a manager with a fair bit of success and everything fitting into place. No, that didn't mean that I had some superior insight into the game, but whichever way you looked at it, his management style was a shambles.

Thick set with short, cropped hair and eyebrows permanently scowling, the manager reminded me of Neil Ruddock. Well, an unfunny and unkind version of Neil Ruddock who was permanently angry. He seemed to think he could win games purely by shouting and when we didn't, there had to be a public execution of somebody. It always had to be someone's fault because of course, how could his team lose a game? I didn't think it was worth pointing out that if you want something you need to work for it, not shout at it. It wouldn't have mattered, because he was one of these coaches who think of themselves as some sort of prophet. You know how it is – any old bloke who has kicked a ball in his life thinks that he's an expert.

Now this guy was a real expert. A sofa expert, if you like, because as soon as you got him up off his sofa, it turned out he was clueless. That and the fact that he was trying to apply his football philosophy to a bunch of players with about as much collective ability as Wayne Rooney's broken metatarsal. 3-5-2? High press? Some of our players could barely kick a ball in a straight line.

We needed to go 4-4-2. Classic English style. It might not necessarily work in the Premier League any more but at grass roots it remains a solid formation. Plus everyone knows how to play it, especially if you keep it simple. We were a village team and we wanted to play like a village team. You wouldn't dress mutton as lamb so why try and make a team at the foot of the Banbury District and Lord Jersey League play this fancy kind of football?

Even on the rare occasions we were winning there was abuse. The manager had assembled a squad of players who, by and large, shared his Neanderthal qualities. They were motivated by his screams. They fed off aggression. Everything was so serious to them and they were world beaters. They may have been playing two divisions higher than the reserve team in a better standard but they themselves certainly weren't better than the reserves.

Nobody in the first team knew that I was gay. Joe did and that was it. There was a real disconnect between Heyford's two teams. They weren't just two separate teams – it was like two separate clubs, joined only by name. The best players weren't necessarily in the first team and the weaker ones weren't necessarily in the reserves. I wouldn't have dared come out in that first team environment, even though there had been nothing bad said when I had come out in the reserves. I was frightened into repressing it by the dictatorial manager. It was his team and it was a team that fed off fear. I just couldn't be bothered with all of the drama.

I didn't actively hide it but subconsciously I did. I'm sure of it. And I hated it. Why should I have to feel like that? Why should I have to hide who I am? Why should I feel fear? I don't regret not coming out to that team, even to this day. I stand by my belief that they'd have taken it badly.

Homophobia wasn't uncommon in the team and a referee

who was pretty camp had already been on the receiving end. I'm not sure if the referee was gay but whatever, he was camp. The manager wasn't exactly nice to him. It wasn't the referee's fault that we played terribly. Very rarely is it the referee's fault. Blaming the referee reeks of desperation. Even so, our manager hammered him. The bloke had even brought his kids along – his own kids... What kind of example was he supposed to be setting when he screamed, "That fucking little poof has lost us this game", gesturing toward the man in black. No, he didn't. You did. How on earth could I come out in that environment?

It wasn't even all the homophobia and rage and shouting that annoyed me the most. It was having to play at left back because, come on, everyone knows the type of player who has to play at left back. It's the position reserved for the player who can't get into any other position – particularly at grass roots – the player who deserves to be 'left back' in the changing rooms, so the old saying goes.

Joe was actually able to play at left back. Much more ably than I can, I'd like to add. Unlike myself, he'd spent a number of seasons in the position, which I regularly pointed out to our manager. It didn't matter; he kept his position at right back and I was forced to left back. I was quite clearly no good. I had to do what you shouldn't and let my winger cut inside just so I could try and tackle him, which is pointless and, quite frankly, dangerous.

Worse still, I was playing alongside the Neanderthal manager at the back. I was literally next to him. When you're playing as a manager you need to be careful when you're having a go at other people. On the sideline you've got a bit more leeway when criticising, but when you're playing you have to be absolutely perfect before you criticise someone else or you'll lose all respect. If only the manager understood. He knew everything. Thought he was God's gift. Thought he was it.

In essence, he was a typical hard man centre back who thinks that being hard outweighs ability and that being hard is an ability in itself. In fact, to him, being hard was the only ability. I didn't want to mention to him that he maybe should have measured his performances on different metrics. They didn't even have to be complex; maybe he could just consider his passing, tackling and heading. It'd be nothing to trouble Prozone but at least it would be a start. After all, that's pretty much what centre backs have to be able to do.

Intimidating other players is one thing but intimidating your own? Nobody plays well when they're scared. There was one game where I was getting loads of stick from the manager. Granted, I wasn't having the best of games but a little encouragement wouldn't have gone amiss. I committed some heinous crime like not winning a header and the manager slaughtered me. We were winning 3-1 at the time and went on to get the three points, yet afterwards the manager just wouldn't let it go that I didn't win that header.

It made me realise that I'd had enough of being called a wanker. We'd won the game and we were playing in the Banbury and District League – it was rubbish, we were rubbish, everyone we played against was rubbish. Not only that, but to top it all off, we were adults. Grown men. As much as I love football I just didn't need the hassle, and I didn't need the hassle of joining a different team either. So sod it, I quit.

I lasted just under six months in the first team. A lot of people hated playing under that manager – even Joe, and he's the nicest guy ever. That was the only thing I've ever known Joe to hate. Well, that and referees I suppose. But anyway, now I was away from the manager and away from Joe and away from pretty much everyone. All I had left were my two housemates. I was back to that life I'd tried to escape where I sat around with my stereotypical gay housemates who didn't like football and didn't understand why I loved the game.

There was no point in fighting it anymore. I felt like I had nowhere else to go. If you can't beat 'em, join 'em. Maybe box-sets of *Sex and the City* weren't so bad. I don't really like starting new things but at least it'd mean I wouldn't have to meet new people and go through the whole charade again, plus I'd kind of already experienced all that with Chris anyway. It'd be like being back with Chris, only without all of the questions and the possessiveness.

Look at what the fear of homophobia does. It makes you pander to their stereotypes. That oppressive, Neanderthal man-ager had scared me into the passive, almost effeminate person-ality which he associated with homosexuality. He'd scared me away from what I loved and scared me into what I feared. Con-formity. Stereotypes. I was bruised and beaten. What was the point of playing up to masculinity when people like him would never consider me as a man? What was I? Who was I? I was liv-ing a lie again and there was no answer. Nothing. So I sat back and let my new life take me away.

It worked for about a year. Then I started to get restless. There were voices. There had been since the first time I'd left. No, no, I'd tell them. Never go back - that's what I'd learned from my second relationship with Chris. No matter how many ghosts you feel you need to exorcise, never go back. No matter how many unproven points you feel you have to make, never go back. No matter how badly it ended and how much you want to repair it, never go back. New beginnings are always better than old endings. Even if you're gay.

But I can resist everything except temptation. It only took one training session to get me hooked again.

17
European Football

People at Birmingham Blaze had been trying to get me to come back to the club for a while. Even when Adam was still playing for Blaze they would try and persuade me back. Then, the season after I left the club, Adam left too, moving up to Manchester for work. He quickly became a distant memory at Blaze and nobody ever really heard from him. After Adam's departure the requests pretty much doubled in both their frequency and intensity. With time, I began to listen. All things considered, I had been away from football for a year. Struggling with all the restlessness that that involved, I decided it was safe to return.

Once back, I would never want to leave again. I had returned to the fold of the family; come home as the prodigal son with a point to prove. I wanted to win trophies and my first crack at that would be a remarkable experience.

It came at the 2012 European Games. No, not Euro 2012 in Poland and Ukraine. Unfortunately my football ability had not improved so drastically that I had been called into Fabio Capello's England side, and nor did that England side now consist solely of homosexual men. Instead this was in Budapest in Hungary, and Blaze were taking part in the European Gay and Lesbian Sport Federation's EuroGames.

The tournament comprised teams from all across Europe. It sounds prestigious but it wasn't really. We were hardly one of the premier gay teams in England but we still got invited. And there aren't very strict entry requirements. You don't have to be gay to be invited – or any good at sport – and they even allow teams from outside of Europe to play.

The Budapest EuroGames were the 14th held by the EG-LSF. Founded as a means of creating a competitive sporting environment without any prejudice or discrimination, the EuroGames seek to bring together gay, lesbian, straight and mixed sport teams in a celebration of equality. Inspired by the Gay Games in San Francisco, the first EuroGames were held in the Netherlands in 1992. Around 300 people from five different countries participated, with competitions across four sports. Within three years the number of participants had grown to 2,000 with 13 countries represented at Frankfurt's EuroGames. The numbers continued to grow and 40 countries were represented at Barcelona's 2008 EuroGames, with well over 5,000 participants across 25 sports. Homosexuality in sport was becoming less and less of a taboo.

The numbers had grown once again in Budapest. There were more participants, countries and sports than ever before. My teammates and I weren't just there to make up the numbers, however. We were there to win. We meant business. The football component of the EuroGames was split into two separate competitions. Division One featured the top teams and Division Two, which we had opted for, was for the teams who weren't quite as good but still fancied a shot at glory. It suited us down to the ground.

This was to be my first experience of European football. All of my mates back home were so impressed that I was off to represent England, and I certainly didn't keep it quiet. They must have thought that I was some player, travelling all that way to represent my country in a European tournament. If only they knew.

The man tasked with navigating us through Budapest knew

even less than my friends back home. To him we were just a football team looking to enjoy Euro 2012 in a city of cheap alcohol and wild nights. He didn't feel unsafe with the 12 of us on his beer bike – a vehicle navigated by one sober person at the front while guests drink at a small bar behind, pedalling at the same time.

"There are many people out protesting," he informed us. "We have to go a different way to the one we would usually."

Then we saw them. I didn't know what they were saying but I knew they were angry. Livid, in fact. All of them, more than 50, pushed up against the towering urban jungle: the caged beast, pegged back by their reluctant keeper. Forward they would surge, their cries piercing the darkening air. The human barrier kept them at bay, their taunts cutting through our skin but nothing else.

They didn't know that we were the object of their hatred. They just knew that they hated homosexuality and so they yelled and screamed and raged. All around their rage echoed, their ammunition reverberating off the soulless grey blocks of concrete that protruded up toward the sky. The caged beast must have been there for some time – maybe even their whole lifetime – and yet still it persisted with the same energy that can only be expressed through hatred. They wanted to break past their keeper, to rage against the inexplicable terrors let loose in their city, their area, their territory. But they couldn't. Their keeper was armed. Hundreds of guns stood in their way. And so all of their conviction was put into their cries.

Usually, our navigator told us, we would have gone that way, but because of the blockade we would have to go a different way. He was a man of the city. He had seen this kind of hatred before. To a degree they were his people. He had been raised among them. Did he share their views? Probably not. He was our protector. For this one night, that was his job. To protect us.

A police car surged past us to provide some reinforcement for the zoo keepers on the front line.

"We have to leave this place. It's not safe. We have to go," our guide continued, his voice quickening, his eyes constantly flashing to assess the scene. "We have to go because there's a load of gays around in town."

Jason, oh Jason. Big, rugged, good-looking Jason. I'm sure he meant well. He came mincing straight up to our protector, caught his eye and proudly proclaimed: "Yeah, that's us." The guy took it in his stride. Just batted it off but you could tell he wasn't overly happy. Now he had reason to feel unsafe, and amongst his own people as well.

But he ushered my Birmingham Blaze teammates and I onwards, down the darkened streets of Budapest and toward safety, as we fled from the caged beast as fast as we could, which was about four miles per hour. It had been a long day and our legs were drained, after all.

After leaving the shameful scene behind, the drinks once again began to flow and we regained our confidence, soon taking over our protector's stereo system and using it to pump camp pop tunes out into the same night sky that had previously been filled with the hateful cries. It was defiance. Loud and proud. Either that or inebriation. Having thought about it, it was probably more of the latter.

I had been in danger, we all had. But I was still glad to be once again among my Blaze teammates.

I had come in to the tournament not really knowing what to expect from my team. We had a side that was patched together. Just 12 of us made the trip over, and even then we had to bring in three ringers. Unfortunately the 12 included our full complement of strikers, so I remained confined to the defence. Usually when you get ringers they're no good, but apparently we had brought in three of the best in the business. I say apparently because I had only seen one of them in action.

Craig Simpson was our old manager at Blaze, the one who had sparked mine and Adam's relationship, and a legend of the GFSN leagues. I'd go as far as saying he's the best player I've ever played with. Craig wasn't just amazing on the pitch, either. With his kind, softly spoken manner he's exactly the type of person you just want to go up to and cuddle. It's not even a gay thing. You'd want to cuddle him, no matter your sexuality. Since being with Blaze he'd moved on to Nottingham, but we were definitely pushing to bring him back on board with us.

Joining Craig were Murray and Ritchie, two unknown quantities as far as I was concerned. Murray was playing for Cardiff and was every bit the Welshman. I was told he was a traditional no-nonsense centre half who brought confidence into any defence. Ritchie had played for every team going because Ritchie had upset every team going. More clubs than Tiger Woods, so the saying goes. Despite this, I was assured that he was by far the best player who played in our league. Comfortable across any position on the pitch, he was a player of real class. Apparently.

All that considered, we supposedly had a decent team. A decent spine of the team, anyway, because some of the other players we took with us could barely kick a ball in a straight line. There are only so many positions you can hide a player in on the pitch, especially when that player is truly useless. We managed to fill in the gaps with them, if not the large gap on the substitutes' bench.

The tournament itself was played on an artificial surface in sweltering conditions. Games may have only lasted for two halves of 25 minutes but when you were carrying as much timber as some of our team, in such hot conditions, they might as well have lasted for 125. As with the regular European Championships, the competition started with a group phase before progressing to knockouts and, ultimately, a final. Unlike the European Championships, however, all of the games were to be played over three days. The two teams who made up the final would play seven games in total. It was going to be demanding, especially for a squad of just 12.

We were in a group of four alongside Village Manchester, London Falcons and a team from the Czech Republic. We were familiar with Village Manchester and London Falcons but the team from the Czech Republic were an unknown quantity and we found ourselves up against them first.

As the game approached the temperature was touching 36 degrees Centigrade. We weren't exactly at the height of physical fitness, remember, and the conditions were playing on a few of our players' minds. Although I was buzzing to play in my first game in Europe, I remained sceptical about two of our three ringers. Were they actually any good? They had better be, because two of them were playing in defence. That put me out a bit. I'd been playing at right back all season but I really fancied myself at centre half for the tournament.

The rest of the team were incredibly excited. Buoyed by the inclusion of our ringers, they appeared to be ready to run through brick walls to try and win the ball back. It was one of those games where you don't really need a team talk. Everyone was already so psyched up before the whistle went. So was I, but even so I didn't think that we were going to win. I just didn't want to lose in an embarrassing manner.

Our opponents didn't look like your stereotypical gay men. They were big and rugged. All of them bar one had a beard. They looked like the type of people you wouldn't mess with. Just before the kick-off they joined together, huddling in and talking in deep, masculine voices. Now I didn't like that. I hate it when I don't know what people are saying and they were talking in a language I couldn't understand. Were they talking tactics, set plays? What? It intimidated me.

And then they did it.

They broke from their huddle and set up in two lines, staring us down across the halfway line. They were trying to get inside our heads. To intimidate us further. The captain started the movement off and then all at once they were moving. It was like a Haka, that war dance performed before games by the New Zealand Rugby Union team. The Czechs were trying to intimidate us by carrying out this bewildering, slow, choreographed piece of movement. Within 30 seconds it was over.

Then they all came together, hugged and screamed out: "Homosexual!" Finally, they were speaking my language.

It didn't take long to see that my teammates were correct in their evaluations of our ringers. They really were top footballers. I'd been expecting to lose so I was blown away when we recorded a 5-0 victory in that opening game. Despite their best efforts, our opponents hadn't intimidated us. In fact, they'd probably done the opposite. It focused us even more, motivated us really to go for the win. Our opponents weren't even that bad. We just clicked as a team and took them apart like Terry Venables's England team took apart Holland back in 1996. I wasn't the only one who was shocked. None of my teammates could believe it.

There was a bit of handbags in the game. There was always likely to be. We were competing to be European champions and for all of the pride and glory that comes with such an accolade. There was a lot at stake. The very title of 'European Games' suggests such prestige that a lot of people – myself included – get carried away with the seeming importance and give everything to win. Even more so than usual.

The Czechs were no different. A couple of them had got in my face and tried to gob off at me. I'd probably scythed down one of their poor wingers. Anyway, me being me I probably stoked them up further by reacting and gobbing back off at them. I never know when to keep quiet when I'm on a football pitch. The game would set the tone for the entire tournament. It was really aggressive. A lot of tackles went in and there were a lot of confrontations. It was exactly what people think gay football isn't.

All of a sudden it looked like we could actually get out of the group. We had three points and we knew we could probably scrape through with four. It called for a celebration and that night we headed out into the town. The 5-0 ended up being a bit of a false dawn, however. On reflection it probably wasn't best to have our rehab session in the pub. I'm not sure beer is that isotonic and there certainly wasn't an ice bath in sight.

There were a few stiff players the next morning for our game against London Falcons and it showed. We were really lethargic. We went behind early on and suddenly everyone went from thinking we'd already qualified to: 'Shit, we're going to lose this'. It was my fault as well. I didn't get close enough to my man and he volleyed it in. Wouldn't have happened if I was playing at centre back.

With five minutes to go, they should have sealed the game but their striker rounded our keeper and somehow shot wide. It was a turning point. They suddenly fell apart, which was just as well because it allowed us to draw level and snatch a point - with Ritchie grabbing a last-minute goal. I swear to this day that he levitated. He was at least a foot above any of his markers as the corner came over and he seemed to hang there, waiting for the ball to meet his head so he could direct it into the top corner.

So we now had four points and were all but through. The celebrations were something else. We knew that only a disaster would prevent us from progressing and this was the bulk of the team talk for our third and final game, played later that day, which would be against Village Manchester.

By the time the game came round, the temperature had risen to 38 degrees Centigrade. It always feels so much hotter when you're playing on an artificial pitch. The surface is unforgiving. It's hard on the joints and seems to store up all of the sun's heat before unleashing it on those who dare to tread on it. After our first game of the day we had had to take our boots off and run our feet under cold water. Some players had even done that at half time, though maybe they'd also used the cold water to try and shake off their hangovers.

There was an air of complacency in the camp. I didn't like it. The team talk shouldn't have focused on how only disaster could prevent us from progressing. We should have been geed up to go on and win the group.

Village Manchester were the best team in our group, probably in the whole tournament. It wasn't going to be easy, and as soon as you start framing the game as: 'Oh it's all right, we won't lose this game by THAT much so we're already through', that's when you start to lose people. We had to avoid defeat by 5-0 to go through. It seemed a lot before kick-off but it wasn't really. We'd lost by more than that in the past.

The alarm bells were ringing when we found ourselves three goals down in the opening 10 minutes. Nerves were really setting in and people were panicking. The best players started booting the ball away, the OK players suddenly couldn't kick the ball in a straight line and the bad players, well, I think we'd have been better off without them to be honest. We couldn't really lose 5-0. Could we? We certainly could because that was what we trailed by come half time. The game didn't even matter to Village Manchester, who were already through after their first two games.

We needed to score. That was the simple matter of it. Score and not concede, which judging by the first half was going to be somewhat of a challenge. The team talk had been all wrong. We should have concentrated on the fact that we had a chance to win the group. Now the manager had a real task on his hands in trying to rally his shell-shocked troops. For him, though, it was a shot at redemption, a chance to change attitudes.

Five goals is a lot to concede in a half. Especially when the half is only 25 minutes long. Even by my standards that is a lot. Fortunately the half time team talk worked. That or Village Manchester got a bit bored with scoring. We managed to keep a clean sheet and even scored three goals of our own to bring the score back to 5-3. It was enough to see us through. We'd done it. Done it with just one sub and a few of the team carrying injuries in our third game in two days. Now we'd be going into a quarter final clash with Trowbridge.

That was the night of the beer bike. We hadn't learnt from our previous evening's festivities and the resulting sluggish performances. Lightning couldn't strike twice, could it, so we headed out into the town for another rest and recovery session on the beers.

We'd been aware of a certain level of hostility among some of the local population before the beer bike incident. It had all started at the airport where we'd first encountered the many police assigned to 'protect' us. Then there was the venue itself, where there was also a heavy police presence. Ridiculously heavy. It was a big complex but even so, everywhere you looked there were police.

I heard that the European Gay and Lesbian Sport Federation went half a million pounds over their budget just because of the police. It was so bad they even ended up asking each of the participants for extra money at the end of the tournament. I'm not sure such a heavy presence was quite so necessary, but then the organisers would point to the fact that our games were advertised. Homophobes and bigots knew where to target us.

Rather than make us feel safe, the police presence had the opposite effect. It made us feel like we were prisoners. Like we were confined to the football complex, being hemmed in so we couldn't escape and spread our gay ideology over Budapest. The police who guarded us were armed. Some walked around with big German shepherd dogs. It seemed like they were only one small step away from erecting a watchtower and fencing us in with barbed wire. They'd even check our bags every morning when we first got to the complex and look under our transportation for bombs. It was all just so unnecessary. Did they really think anyone was going to blow us up?

You have to go through less hassle to get on to an RAF base. Not only would we have to go through all of these checks, but the police would confiscate any alcohol we had. They'd get really funny with us when we asked them why. Was it because they wanted to maintain control over us? Did they think that if we were drunk we would start to shove our sexuality in their face? Who was the prisoner? Who was the victim? Were they protecting us or the people of Budapest? At times it certainly felt like the latter. They didn't want our homosexuality to spread from our confined, controlled area.

The night of the beer bike was the only time we saw people actively protesting against our presence. It was on the outskirts of the centre, not really that near where everything was going on. It didn't look like the best area. It wasn't residential as such but all of the buildings were just so grey and non-descript. That joyless, classic communist style.

It seemed a strange place to stage a protest. We had been assigned a specific bar in Budapest where all those taking part in the tournament were meant to congregate each night. We only made it there on the last night, preferring to go off and do our own thing on the first few nights. It turned out to be pretty good, an opportunity to mix with people of different nationalities and backgrounds. The protest was taking place a good few miles from that bar. You'd have thought they might have done it a bit closer to us but then I guess there was barely a brain cell between them. Either that or they were so clouded by their ignorance that they were unable to think straight.

When we saw them I couldn't get over how angry they were. It always baffles me how someone can be angry with you before they've even met you. Never judge a book by its cover and all that. We weren't exactly dressed in a stereotypically gay way. A couple of people were wearing vests but nowadays that is pretty normal, normal enough for our protector to presume we were a 'normal' football team. The protestors wouldn't have known that we were the objects of their ire but it was still a terrifying experience, one which really brought home the animosity towards us from some quarters. It really made me aware of myself and being different. It made me feel even more unsafe. And that despite the UN style checkpoint which separated us from Budapest society.

I doubt the protestors would have been able to tell that we were gay from the way we played football, either. Maybe if they had come to watch it would have changed their opinions. I know exactly what they would have expected. They'd have expected us all to be effeminate and scared to go into tackles. They'd have thought we could barely kick the ball straight and definitely without any power. I bet they'd have expected us to jump out of the way screaming if a ball was fired near us. Homophobes always expect the same things. They think that we can't wait to get into the showers after the game for a bit of fun, that the game itself is just an excuse to get hot and sweaty. There's barely a brain cell between them.

The protest put only a slight dampener on the night. I mean, what better way to stick a big fat middle finger up to them than riding around their city belting out our camp pop tunes while dancing around and getting drunk? It was the most passive-aggressive playing of Kylie Minogue that I've ever been involved in. A show of pride. We weren't going to let them get us down. Most of us had been bullied for our sexuality at some point in our lives. I guess you could say that to an extent we were used to it.

We awoke the next morning raring to go. We were just three games away from being crowned champions of Europe. We needed three big performances, and it seemed that our recovery session on the beer bike had done the job. There were no injuries in the camp. Soreness was at a minimum. Adrenaline masked everything. It ran through us, urging us to get on that pitch and put in a performance. For our egos, if nothing else. A victory would, in essence, put us into the top four in Europe. That's what we would tell our friends, anyway.

Our opponents Trowbridge were an interesting team – a predominantly straight team (around 80% of their players were straight) from Wiltshire who played in the gay league to show solidarity. They were well known for being strong at home but tended to be weak away. Straight players never seem to travel well in the GFSN. It's a different dynamic when you have a girlfriend. Most gay players bring their boyfriend along to games. Their boyfriend is involved in the whole event, including the drinks that follow the game. Girlfriends stay away, however. They barely ever come to watch games and when they do they don't stay for the festivities afterwards.

Away games in a national league are a big commitment. It takes up your whole day. Even so, boyfriends often come along to those, too. Players with girlfriends get pressure on them. Their girlfriends don't want them to be away for the whole day and so you get this situation where a lot of straight players only play in the home games and the closer away ones.

The EuroGames was a whole different kettle of fish, however. This was for the European Championship, and away from the clutches of their girlfriends we expected Trowbridge to have a strong side, especially after they had got through their group with relative ease.

I must admit, it was hard to take Trowbridge seriously as they ran out onto that pitch. They wore the tightest shorts. Honestly, they were worse than rugby shorts. They played from head to toe in orange and as they were Trowbridge Tigers they'd even made up their own song to run out to. Well, made up is a bit of an exaggeration. It was that song from the third Rocky film – *Eye of the Tiger* – but they'd changed the lyrics to Trowbridge Tigers. Over and over again they'd just sing: "And it's the, Trowbridge Tiii-gers", the players joining in with the ridiculous music booming from the stereo. And people think it's the gay football teams who pander to the gay stereotype.

If that temporarily eased our nerves then the early stages brought them back. Passes went astray and players generally looked uneasy. Gradually, we got into our stride, if never really being on top of our game, and the match finished 1-1. It would go to penalties.

Still we weren't convincing. Ritchie got us off to a good start by scoring, then Ben and Jason both missed. Fortunately Trowbridge were missing their penalties as well, so it came down to me…

The keeper saved the ball enough with his initial dive to slow it down, then dived back to the ball as it flirted with crossing the line, yanking it towards safety. I'm not sure if all of it was over the all-important white line but I made sure to celebrate like crazy and I think that convinced the ref to award the goal. Trowbridge went on to score their fourth penalty too, so everything ended up riding on the last ones. We scored; they missed. We were through.

In the EuroGames there is no rest for the wicked. Or the

good. Or anyone in fact. We were only afforded a couple of hours rest before our semi final against an Italian team.

The quarter final hadn't been without its complications. There are always casualties in war. We'd not only picked up an injury, but one of our players must have been so traumatised that he didn't turn up for the semi final. Well, a combination of trauma and the effects of the previous night's beer, anyway, because he'd struggled to see straight in the quarter final. It meant we had to borrow a player from another team. Imagine seeing that in the proper European Championships – Germany borrowing Wayne Rooney because Miroslav Klose couldn't be bothered to turn up. Maybe we're just paving the way for the football of the future.

We picked a pretty good player as well, a lad called Ian who played for London Falcons. It didn't go down well. We had other teams moaning that we couldn't just go and pick the best player in the whole GFSN to play for us, which was a bit of an exaggeration. Anger often clouds logic. One team even lodged an official complaint to the organisers. Ian was good, to be fair, I have to give him credit. He was a central midfielder, a real ball player, though he was also one of the most booked and sent-off players in the entire league. Ian wasn't short of aggression, and he was a rare example of a player in the GFSN who was talk and action. His dismissals included a couple of red cards for fighting.

Even with our reinforcement, however, we were up against it. By this stage it had begun to dawn on us that maybe the beer bike wasn't such an effective method of recovery. We could barely move. We weren't exactly athletes in our physical prime, remember. Fortunately the Italians were in a pretty similar condition to us. The game we played out was an embarrassment to football. It was barely played at walking pace.

We drew 0-0. Of course we did – we were playing against

Italians, and this particular bunch of Italians had absolutely no interest in winning. They just wanted to draw. I don't think they even set up to counter attack. They just set up to not concede. Italians certainly know how to keep a clean sheet. And when they weren't doing their best to keep a clean sheet, they were doing their best to fight us. Even though neither team had much energy, our opponents made sure it was still a pretty feisty affair. Once again I probably stirred it up. I can't help myself. I just love gobbing off.

The referee must have realised that sending us off would actually be less of a punishment than keeping us on the pitch. That way we'd get a rest. We would no longer be subjected to the bitter pain of movement in the oppressive heat. And so he kept us all on the pitch. There were a few bookings, yes, but that was it. No red cards.

This meant that both teams had a full quota of penalty takers. Fortunately there was no extra time. It just went straight to penalties. We really should have been confident, given our previous success, but we weren't. There should have been no excuses.

Now, looking at it logically, nobody should miss from 12 yards. It really should be very easy to score, even for a bunch of amateurs. I blame Ritchie. Everyone had him down as a certain to score our opening penalty. When he missed, it really gave everyone the jitters. Suddenly the pressure was on, and what pressure it was, especially because I was next up. My penalty in the last game hadn't been convincing and it must have been playing on my mind. I got my run up totally wrong, didn't connect with the ball where I wanted to and didn't even manage to hit the target. I missed the goal. That massive white thing 12 yards in front me. Talk about bottling it. I'd wimped out a treat, and all because Ritchie had missed that first penalty.

My miss then put the pressure on our next penalty taker,

who missed, which put even more pressure on our fourth penalty taker, who also missed. So then we were out. Four penalties – four misses. Thanks for coming.

I think we were secretly rather grateful that we lost. There was little chance we'd have been able to play another game. Manchester ended up playing the Italian team and annihilated them. It was only 2-0 but the gap between the teams was huge. Manchester had a squad of 20 and all of their players were still relatively fresh. They were chasing after lost causes, making 50/50s into 80/20s and winning their second balls. The Italians kept their Italian tactics of playing for the draw and not conceding, which really didn't work well once Manchester scored their opener.

What made it even worse was that the final took place on the showcase pitch. It was massive, much bigger than the pitches we had been playing on previously, with space everywhere. For some reason the final was two halves of 45 minutes, almost twice as long as we had been playing. It would have been a slow and painful death for us if we had scraped past that Italian team. I mean, Manchester scored five goals against us in a half of 25 minutes – imagine how brutal it would have been in a half of 45. The only way we'd have made it through the full 90 would have been by wearing oxygen masks.

So Manchester won the Division Two title, with Stonewall claiming the accolade in Division One. Still, we were delighted with how we'd done. Before the tournament we hadn't expected to get out of the group. We just didn't want to get embarrassed. Our threadbare squad of 12 had performed admirably in difficult conditions. We were all hugely proud of what we had achieved, even if we could barely walk near the end of the tournament. And I guess we could kind of say that we were the third best team in Europe. The other semi final had been decided in 50 minutes whereas we had gone to penalties. That

must mean that we were the stronger of the losing semi final-
ists. That's what we'd tell everyone. The fact that we were only
in the second tier of the competition wouldn't be mentioned.

It had been a great tournament. Within the complex, the
EuroGames organisers created a utopic, equal and joyous environment where teams could thrive. But the scenes outside of
it really put a reality check on this utopia. In our own world we
were safe, but out in the big bad world it was made clear that
being different was still seen as taboo. We were made to feel like
prisoners by the overwhelming police force. They never wanted
to be there.

To a man, the police weren't chatty. They didn't smile; they
were just uncomfortable. Too busy looking macho and intimidating. They didn't want to feel comfortable in our culture.
They wanted to distance themselves as much as possible. No
wonder they always used to patrol the football complex on the
outside, rather than the inside. They were always on the outside,
looking in.

The atmosphere was probably best summed up by an experience on the first day. Ecstatic after our opening victory, we
had ordered a taxi from the sizeable rank outside the football
complex to take us back to our hotel, a drive of five minutes, if
that. We knew because we had done it that very morning.

The taxi driver looked pretty mean. His face looked like he
was permanently scowling and he had these really thick set eyebrows. As we got into his cab, he didn't smile. Barely said a
word. Just drove. And drove. And drove. He knew about us
being different.. How couldn't he have? He'd been sitting outside our complex, waiting for a fare. Throughout that time he'd
have been subjected to our joyous whoops and celebrations as
the balls hit the back of the net. Was he abducting us? Was he
taking us to an isolated place where a gang of homophobes
would be waiting? We didn't know, and we didn't like it. We

were longer than half an hour in that car, and even then we were nowhere near our hotel. With nerves running high and a number of worried glances, we screamed at him to stop. Eventually he relented and out we got, right in the middle of some random Budapest street.

It was yet another reminder of how, out in the open, we were not safe. There were people who hated us being different, and no matter what the EuroGames organisers did to create that utopia inside the football complex, they couldn't shield us from those poisonous attitudes on the outside.

Sometimes I sit back and think that it really was a minority who hated us. Granted, we'd see this hatred in some form or other each day, no matter how small. But it was hardly on the scale we saw on the night of the beer bike, and even then there wasn't exactly a group of thousands of people. It was far less than 1% of the people we came across – not nearly enough to justify such a heavy police presence throughout the tournament. Maybe that's why there was such scaremongering.

But then there's another part of me who remembers how I never felt safe throughout my whole time in Budapest. Half of me thinks that I may have overstated the hatred and animosity. The other half acknowledges that I was actually in a pretty dangerous place. As a gay man I spend a great portion of my life brushing things off, minimising the damage, and that may have been the case in Budapest.

I brushed off all the negativity and focused on the football. Or at least I tried to, because all the homophobic stuff, along with what happened on the pitch, well, that was only half the drama.

18

Down and Out in Budapest

It was the evening after the night before. Less than 24 hours previously there had been such celebratory scenes, with everyone on a high following a wonderful tournament and a top four finish. The drinks were flowing, the dancing was energetic and the camp music was playing loud and proud. And now here I was, laid across three airport chairs, sobbing my eyes out into a Richard Branson book. I didn't care who saw me. I didn't care what they thought. Everything was broken.

David. David. The name just rolls off the tongue. He was different. Not like the others. Those eyes, they just drew me in. His smile, faint yet warming, the small gap in his teeth an imperfect perfection. Genuine, kind-hearted and caring, Dave was everything I wanted. But now he was the source of my tears.

He hadn't been there the first time round. Dave had joined Blaze a few months before I rejoined, and by then he had become an established member of the team. It was no surprise because he was the star man. He had come from a straight football team who had apparently given him a hard time after coming out. In fact, they had made it impossible for him to carry on. No wonder he joined a gay team after that.

I remember seeing him play at Goals – the five-a-side place – early on after joining Blaze for the second time. I don't know about love at first sight – that's probably a bit strong – but I do remember thinking, 'Yeah, best of a bad bunch'. It was a while before I bonded with him. After that first sighting I carried on admiring him from afar. Not exactly lusting, just admiring.

The moment came when we were playing a game against Devon Lions. It was in October, so still fairly early on in the season, and I was playing at right back. Once again I'd come into a club and told them I was a striker, only to be shifted back into defence. Dave was playing in the centre of midfield. I'd still never really had a conversation with him.

Devon had this pretty tricky winger. Now, in such a situation my philosophy is distinctly Argentinian: either the man gets past me or the ball gets past me. Never both. There was one point in the match where my philosophy failed me, however. I thought I'd tackled him but this tricky winger managed to squirm past me with the ball still in his possession. And then, out of nowhere, Dave came flying in on the cover. It was like something out of *Karate Kid*. One high-pitched scream away from a Jackie Chan movie. Essentially, Dave kung-fu kicked this poor winger in mid-air, leaving him in a heap on the floor. A man after my own heart. If he'd have done that on the street he'd have been arrested. It was at that moment that I thought, 'Yeah, respect'.

We went on to win the game 3-1. I gave away the free-kick from which they scored. Our manager had a bit of a go at me in the changing room afterwards but what was I supposed to have done – just let the winger run past me? If I'd let him do that he'd have turned me inside out all game. Fortunately, it would soon be forgotten as I started at right back the next game. There was one memory that would never be forgotten though. That powerful yet elegant kung-fu kick was ingrained in my memory. It had become a fantasy.

After that we started speaking to each other. Nothing too personal. It was usually just in the pub after games. By this stage I really fancied him. He wasn't only an attractive man who liked to kick people, he turned out to also be a really nice guy. I always felt he was just like me, and there were few gay people I had met who had given off that impression. Little did I know that he was already seeing someone else on the team, but even if I was aware I'm not sure I could have done things so very differently. Love knows no boundaries.

I always think of that Rihanna song when I remember the moment that Dave and I first started to get together. We found love in a hopeless place. For there's no doubting that Wolverhampton is a hopeless place.

We were there for a Christmas football tournament at the back end of 2011. It wasn't anything too serious. Just a five-a-side tournament played in Santa hats. Myself and Dave had been put on different teams for the tournament. When my team weren't playing I made my best effort to watch Dave in action. It must have been in his second or third game that he came off the pitch to get a quick rest as sub.

I was on the side, and as he came off I put my arm around him and said, "Oh, you're really hot."

Shit. That could easily have been misconstrued. Better correct yourself fast, Neil, you don't want to seem too flirtatious.

"Not in a sexy way," I quickly gabbled. "In a temperature way."

Shit. What if he thinks you're not interested at all? You've really screwed it now, Neil. You're in too deep. Just come out and say it. You've barely even given him time to think. You can still rescue this.

"But actually you're really hot like that anyway, but we'll discuss that later," I added.

In my memory, I then winked at him and played it real cool. *Greased Lightning* style. In reality I probably turned an extremely vibrant shade of red and started to sweat profusely. I'd made a right idiot of myself.

There was a chance to make it up, however. Once the tournament ended, the attention turned to the night out that had been planned. All of my Blaze teammates were heading out on the town. I didn't have a hotel room booked, but in a spur of the moment decision I opted to try and rescue things with Dave. Either that or, in the best case scenario, I'd be able to take things further with Dave now that he knew how I felt. I jumped in with some of the other guys and off I went out into the hopeless place of Wolverhampton.

Our first stop was a local bar. All of the gay teams were there and there was a big competition taking place on the stage. I was forced to sign up for it – any chance to impress Dave, I guessed – without really knowing what I'd let myself in for. It turned out that the competition was to see who had the hairiest legs. A drag queen was up on stage and it was his job to judge the legs of each competitor by caressing his hands up and down them. Three of us, each from different teams, had been put forward, and competition rules stipulated that we had to strip down to our underwear for the judging. The prize? A load of free drinks.

I had to win and so when the drag queen got to me I just took his hand and stuck it right on my crotch. The audience loved it. The drag queen loved it. And the free drinks were mine.

I got a choice of drinks. From my frequent post-match pub visits I knew that Dave didn't drink beer. He only really drank vodka, so I just ordered a load of vodkas. I didn't want it to look too obvious so I made sure I shared the vodkas out around the team. That really kicked the night off, and from the first bar we moved on to the main nightclub and by that time we were really drunk. It wasn't long before I'd isolated Dave. He was pretty drunk too and soon we were dancing together, and then kissing. It was everything I had imagined and more.

Our feelings were out in the open. We both knew that it was on. But what was 'it'? We had danced and kissed but nothing else. Dave walked me back to my hotel and we had a good talk. Then that was it. We said goodbye and my heart fluttered knowing our success together.

Fortunately it was on. The next day we were messaging each other and it grew from there. We met up soon after to eat at Nando's and do some Christmas shopping. My idea of Christmas shopping, anyway, which pretty much involves me buying stuff for myself. The whole thing wasn't anything too formal. Just a casual get-together, two guys getting to know each other better. And we certainly did, especially after the next few dates, which led us to spending Boxing Day together. It was a great Christmas that year, and it only got better when I drove up to Dave's that day to eat pizza and watch DVDs.

Although everything may sound all rosy and joyful, it wasn't. The distance was really tough. I was by now working in Wokingham and Dave was up in Birmingham. That's a big distance.

I had left my job in the control room in Bicester to work at Wexham Park Hospital in Slough as an ambulance liaison officer, only to find out that I didn't really enjoy doing that. I wanted my old job back but it had already been taken. It took six months of working in Slough before I was able to get a job in a control room, this time in Wokingham. It was only available because they were going to be closing it down in the near future. I didn't care, I just wanted to get back into the control room.

It was a case of my professional life and personal life clashing. I couldn't exactly just pop round Dave's if he felt lonely or if we wanted to eat dinner together. If we wanted just to talk. It's just not the same on the phone. You need that physical presence, that reassurance. Even so, it was exciting with Dave. He was just so normal and that, paradoxically, was what made it exciting. His normality was different. It's what made him stand out in comparison to all of my previous relationships. It was a situation I'd never been in before, and I liked it.

The distance between us meant that we had an on-off relationship for around six months. It was a weird time. I was so overwhelmed by Dave, so excited, yet also so scared. Maybe that's a bit extreme, but there was always this little voice in the back of my mind asking why I'd suddenly fallen for this person who acted relatively straight. I became even more confused. Just what did I want? What was right for me?

Our relationship was almost perfect, yet at the same time it couldn't have been further away from being perfect because of the logistics of it all. Then there was the niggling voice in the back of my head. Who are you Neil? What do you want?

It got even tougher when our teammates at Blaze started to find out. At first there were whispers, then accusations, before it finally became common knowledge. Neil and Dave. Dave and Neil. Our right back and our central midfielder. We had tried to keep it quiet – we didn't want to damage the team's dynamic, and then there was Adam and all of my experiences with him – but keeping it quiet can only work for so long.

Some of the other players were jealous, I'm sure of it. Dave is a good-looking bloke and there were definitely a couple of players in the team with an eye or two on him. Then there was the fact that he had been in a relationship with one of the other players. Nothing spiteful was said, however. Our teammates were supportive and it would only cause an issue if we let it.

People have a real misconception when it comes to gay teams. Even reading that last paragraph you'll probably have started to form the same common misconception: players in a gay team are all in relationships with each other. It's a different man every night and we're only there for a good time.

It's rubbish, of course. We're a football team like others.

First and foremost we are there to win matches. For 90 minutes we give our all. Then we celebrate – if we have something to celebrate – and that's it. It's the same as every football team up and down the country. There really aren't many relationships within teams, though there are probably more among players who play for different teams. In the same team, it is far rarer than people would have you believe.

If you saw our team you'd understand. Someone once had the idea that we should do a naked calendar. Well, that idea was scotched pretty quickly. We wanted to sell calendars, not scare people. There really weren't very many lookers. That's not to say there isn't any flirting that goes on. We like to have a laugh and sometimes players will flirt to get that laugh, but it's often nothing serious. On rare occasions their flirting will lead to more, but usually it's all done for show. For a laugh. Unless there is alcohol involved. Then teammates may begin to do stuff together, once they're out of that match day environment, but it's usually just because the alcohol has broken down the barrier. One night stands between teammates are, to be honest, not too uncommon.

The changing room environment isn't really that different in a gay team compared to that of a straight team. If anything, it's more reserved in a gay team. From my experiences, and even when there are alpha male Neanderthals involved, it's the straight team who often act more gay. People think that in gay teams we're all chasing each other around in the nude whilst in the changing room, whipping each other with towels and giggling, prancing around in the showers, gawping at each other. In actual fact, it's the straight teams who do that. Gay teams? Not a chance.

It's because the players in the straight teams are more comfortable. There's no reason to suspect that anybody is 'checking you out'. In a gay team everyone is a lot more self-conscious.

We're all batting for the same side but that side is men and all
of a sudden we're all in the same room together, conscious that
even to be seen looking at each other might suggest that we're
flaunting our sexuality. It's just not what people think.

Anyway, back to Budapest...

Dave and I flew out to Hungary together along with the rest
of the team. We weren't officially an item at this point. We were
still just 'seeing' each other. From the outset it didn't look like
it was going to be an easy trip. One of Dave's exes was playing
on our team and I shouldn't have been wary or jealous but I
was. I couldn't help myself. I guess it's human nature. It didn't
take me long to get upset at something pathetic. We hadn't even
boarded the plane to Budapest when I objected to Dave's ex
telling him that his boxer shorts looked cool. Playing the ultra
over-protective boyfriend I did a great job of getting into a
strop with Dave, his ex and the world in general. My toys were
out of the pram and the trip was barely a minute old. The signs
weren't good.

Even so, I managed to make it through most of the tournament relatively strop-free. Off the pitch, that is, because on the
pitch there's nothing I like more than a little strop. It all kicked
off again, though, when it came to the final night, thanks to a
classic Neil Beasley strop.

After the end-of-tournament awards, we all went to this gay
nightclub that was underground. All of the teams were there
and it was a really good vibe. But then Dave's ex went and
ruined everything. We were all dancing in a big group when he
got with a guy from a French team. The French guy had been
with us for a while and we had got to know him fairly well. It
wasn't unnatural for him to ask Dave if he had a boyfriend but
it still made me jealous, and when Dave replied that no he didn't
I saw red.

I stormed off. Dave could see I had lost it. Everyone could

see I had lost it. Dave kept on coming up to me but I couldn't face him. I kept on walking off each time he'd try to speak to me. Dave doesn't give up easily, however, and he eventually managed to pin me down. "What am I?" he asked. "What am I? You're not my boyfriend. You can't keep stringing me along. If this is how you act then I'll have to move on."

Dave's words hit me hard. They were just words but they were so forceful, weighted destructively. It all shattered. My heart was broken glass. "You're not my boyfriend..." The words just replayed over and over.

He was right. I wasn't his boyfriend. But I should have been, if the circumstances allowed. It had always seemed like it would be an inevitability. Move on? Surely he couldn't. Wouldn't. But his words. They just seemed so real. So purposeful. Dave wasn't a man to give empty threats. He was a man of action. My man of action, who I'd strung along.

I'd ruined everything. It was all my fault. It took me less than a minute to realise but by that time Dave was gone. His words had left me broken but I'd still reacted with anger. "Go on then... fuck you... you can move on," my shattered heart told me and my mouth opened and said those words right to his face.

Why was I so stupid? Off he had fucked. Right off, away from my despairing, broken love. My mouth had barely closed when I realised how much I regretted those idiotic, aggressive words. Dave had nothing to do with it. It was all my fault. And now he was gone. Probably to find someone else. Someone who wouldn't string him along but who would make him happy instead. It couldn't have been further from the truth but that was all that I could think of.

I awoke from my word-induced coma and set about tracking him down, though not before a couple of idiots had stepped in to give me 'relationship advice'. It was so condescending and patronising and I didn't need it. Not at that time. I was in no state to listen to anyone but Dave.

It didn't take long to find him. Not after shaking off the idiots, anyway. We talked it through. I was gushing in my words, my actions and my emotions. I let them all pour out. The more they poured out, the more hopeful I became, and they must have worked. To an extent, anyway, because we slept in the same bed that night. It was the first time in the whole tournament that we slept in the same bed.

Matters had been complicated by the tournament organisers deciding to put our whole team in the same room with six bunk beds. Dave's bunk bed was on the opposite side of the room to mine. He had the top bunk in one corner, I was on the top bunk in the other. Bunk beds. What kind of establishment makes grown-ups sleep in bunk beds? I wonder if that's what Fabio Capello had his England side doing at that year's European Championships. If not, maybe he should start. I mean, at least we got past a quarter final, and we even won a penalty shoot-out on the way.

We slept in Dave's bed that night. If people didn't know that we were together then they certainly did after that night. Dave got up early the next morning and everyone was wondering where I was. They couldn't see me in my own bed and so they were asking where I was. They only had to look across the room to see me in Dave's bed but upon waking up, in the cold light of day, I wondered what it all meant. I had, after all, allowed my emotions to take hold of me once more.

It took a while for my feelings to manifest themselves. That morning was our last in Budapest and we spent it in a local shopping centre. About half of the team went. After the first couple of shops the weirdest feeling swept over me. Everything was broken. It was all wrong with Dave. I'd ruined it.

He was going to Bratislava the next day. The whole team

was. Everyone except me. I had to go back to England to work while they headed out to Slovakia to let their hair down on a lads' holiday. Dave would remember what I'd done and I wouldn't be able to salvage the situation. Even so, it wasn't right. I wasn't right. Things just weren't right. The previous night kept on flashing back into my memory. Each time I'd shudder. It hurt me to think of how childishly I'd reacted. I'd messed everything up.

I could barely bring myself to say goodbye to Dave when the moment came. It was early afternoon and everyone else would be flying on to Slovakia the next day, so they didn't come along to the airport with me. I went by myself. Isolation never helps when you're emotional. I was alone with my thoughts and they were becoming more and more self-destructive with every moment that passed. I'd messed up the best thing that had ever happened to me. I'd never do any better. Nothing could bring Dave back.

It didn't take long for the tears to start. They were just trickles at first, small droplets sticking to my cheeks. They made me think of Dave and that just made me think of how much I had messed up and that just made it even worse. It was inescapable and by the time I'd made it to the British Airways desk I was bawling. To make matters even worse my flight wasn't until quite late that evening. I couldn't wait that long. Not in the state that I was in. I had to get back to England as quickly as possible but British Airways only had one earlier flight and it would cost an arm and a leg to change. Not even my tears earned me any sympathy. I would have to wait.

That's why I was laid across the three airport chairs, a Richard Branson book absorbing my tears while my life seemed to be spiralling out of control. No matter what happened the tears just wouldn't stop. I was crying and crying and crying. Every time I tried to think of something else Dave just kept on creeping back into my memory. Love was torturing me. No matter what I did, he was there. I even went and got myself a massage in the airport. It didn't work. I just laid on the massage bed, my head poking through that hole whilst my tears bucketed through onto the carpeted floor. When I think back to it now, I always wonder just what was going through the masseuse's mind as she sought out the knots in my back.

I ended up being in that miserable airport for nine hours. I felt like I was in that Tom Hanks movie, *The Terminal*, only this was a sadder version. I wasn't the only person from the Euro-Games at the airport. Village Manchester were there along with a couple of other teams. I didn't care. Their thoughts wouldn't bring back my happy relationship with Dave, whatever that was. The other teams were all pleased with themselves. They'd had a great tournament and an even better time. Then there was me. I'd never felt so bad. It felt like a part of me had died.

If only I'd known how happy Dave was at that moment in time. He was under the impression that we were going to get back together as soon as we were reunited in England. We were going to be an item. In his eyes, at least. As soon as I was through security I worked up the courage to text him. It didn't take him long to reply and tell me that everything was fine and that we'd sort it all out when we got back.

I was too much of an emotional wreck to believe him. His digital words barely reached me. I needed them said. Then they'd be real. Just like those sentences he had spoken the previous night that felt so real: "You're not my boyfriend. I'll have to move on."

19

Dave's Story

No two people have the same story. That's true in any sphere, no matter what race, class or gender. When you consider gay football players, however, it rings especially true. Nearly everyone has fear when they come out. They fear that everything is going to change for the worse; that they're going to be ostracised and cast away from society. Yet it's something they know they have to do. Nobody can live their whole life as a lie.

It would take me a while to understand David Yates's background. He was quiet and unassuming, preferring to listen rather than talk. Like countless other gay men in football, he had attempted to repress certain memories. Coming out is painful. It's better to forget than to remember, yet forgetting is in itself a battle. It doesn't come easy.

Dave was blessed with an enjoyable childhood. Growing up in Great Barr, a pleasant suburban area of Birmingham in the North West of the city, allowed him to have a pretty settled upbringing.

He could count on the love of two doting parents and was rarely without friends. But as the years went by, and Dave's realisation of his sexuality came to the forefront of his mind, things became complicated.

Dave has had his fair share of struggles. He's battled them, beaten them and come out of them better for the experiences. It's best if I let him tell you all about it…

* * *

'*I started playing football as a means of fitting in. Maybe that's a bit extreme, but as a young six or seven-year-old I must admit that football wasn't really a passion. I just did it because everyone else at my school in Great Barr did. Who really wants to be by themselves in the playground, trudging around with their grubby hands in their pockets, talking to the teacher on duty who doesn't really want to be there and is barely listening to you anyway? Not me, that was for sure, so I got myself doing what everyone else was doing. From those early days playground football became a key part of my lunch hour.*

I wasn't much of a follower of football till the age of 12, when I went to Great Barr Comprehensive School. Before then I didn't support a team and didn't watch the sport on the telly; I just played. Yet every Monday morning, the weekend's football matches would be the talk of the school. With more than 2,400 pupils there, it wasn't just a small matter and the more it happened, the more I wanted to get involved. Fortunately for me, I would soon find my first love.

Everything changed with Liverpool FC. It was the 1994/95 season, around the time that Robbie Fowler was starting to become really influential. They had a good team, with John Barnes and Ian Rush key performers. I would say that they inspired me to get out there and grace the hallowed turf, but for some reason there was this inverse relationship between playing and watching. As I began to watch the game more and more, I played the game less and less.

Maybe it was because I was at that age where your interests start to change. Girls came onto the scene. Again, I just did what everyone else did. I really enjoyed school and had some great mates there, but school doesn't really encourage individuality. At school you just do what your mates do. My mates were starting to get girlfriends so I joined them. It was weird though. I had these girlfriends but there were these feelings that I was having, deep down, that girls weren't really for me. Call them gay sensations if you will. There was just something that was different. I tried to fight them, these feelings, tried to stop what was natural. It was a strange time. I did like girls but even so there was just something that was different. I liked boys too.

I guess a lot of boys are confused around that age. Their bodies go through a lot of changes. All of these hormones start coming into play. Now when I look back, I can see that being gay was something I always knew. It was just quite deep down inside me. As I got older I was able to deal with it better and so I started letting it gradually come to the fore.

At first it was unconscious. I didn't necessarily ignore it, but I felt like I should have been with girls, so I tried to reject the natural thoughts that I was having. Society conditioned me to believe that I needed to be with girls. Imagine how confused these natural thoughts made me. Of course I tried to hide them. I'd been conditioned to believe that these natural thoughts were unnatural, that I had to be in a relationship with a girl, that I had to love girls, that I had to find them attractive.

And, to be honest, I did find girls attractive. I'd look at certain girls on the street and think, 'Yeah, she's nice'. To be honest, even now I look at girls and think that. I'm comfortable with my sexuality and who I am and yet I still have those thoughts, so just imagine how confusing it must have been for my 14-year-old self going through puberty.

The problem at that time was that I was going through exactly the same process with boys. I'd see a lad and think, 'Yeah, he looks good'. I didn't necessarily fancy them. It was more of an appreciation. I bet straight lads have those thoughts as well. You can get your feelings mixed up, especially as a teenager.

It wasn't until the age of 16 that I began to push my sexuality into my consciousness. I realised who I was. There was no point in repressing it anymore. Until then I'd not necessarily ignored the urges, but it was more a case of the pressures of society making me think that I should be with girls even when deep down there'd be a voice screaming 'BOYS, Dave, you like boys!'. Even so, I still got myself into a couple of relationships with girls. I was still in denial. The thoughts were in my consciousness but at the same time I was thinking, 'I'm supposed to be attracted to girls'.

I came out at the age of 18. The Millennium had come and gone, we'd survived Y2K and people were looking to the future. Progress was being made. It was around the time that the Labour government allowed homosexuals to join the army by scrapping a policy that had been in place for hundreds of years. The Conservatives opposed the move. They seemed to fear that allowing homosexuals into the army would not only affect morale, but lead to an outright collapse of Britain's famed military might. Discipline would go out of the window, rules wouldn't be followed and our forces would be a laughing stock. Who elects these people?

A few months previously, I'd got my first proper job working as the assistant manager of a pub in Perry Barr. I'm not sure how I got the role of assistant manager without any previous experience but I wasn't complaining. Despite my inexperience, I took to the role quickly. I enjoyed the conversations with both customers and co-workers, and soon met a group of five or six straight lads who I became close with.

When I first got the job, I had a girlfriend but I knew something wasn't right. It's weird trying to explain it. Even now it seems weird. This girl was funny and beautiful with an incredible personality – she really was amazing. I'd been friends with her since we started secondary school and we had got together after leaving that same school. Yet still she wasn't doing it for me. It was like a sudden epiphany. I just thought, 'You know what, if this beautiful girl isn't doing it for me anymore and I've got these feelings for men, then I need to be true to myself.'

So I was. I came out of the relationship. Confessed to her. Emphasised how amazing she was. It wasn't her fault. It was just that I had always liked men. She didn't react well at first. I don't know if she felt betrayed in any way or if she thought it was her fault or whether it was all just too much to take in. For a minute or two she couldn't speak, then the tears came. They rolled down her cheeks, she sobbed, and I didn't know what to do. I didn't know whether to hug her or to just run. A couple of minutes later my decision was made easier. She left. For a week I couldn't get through to her. It was like I'd been blanked off the face of the Earth. And then, finally, a text message. We agreed to meet up, she apologised and was really supportive of me. It just took her time to get her head around the whole situation.

After that whole episode I realised that I couldn't live like this anymore. I had to be true to myself, and everyone had to know who the true me was. I came out to my friends. Everyone was fine. Eventually I got round to telling my family. I was a lot more nervous about that, which is why I delayed it. When I got my first boyfriend I felt like I could delay the inevitable no more, however. I had to tell them. I couldn't just pass my boyfriend off as some friend. It would be unfair to everyone involved.

Coming out to my family was, and still is, the biggest thing I've ever had to do in my life. And in the end it was an anti-climax. I brought my boyfriend Gary into the room and just came out with it – "Mum, I'm gay and this bloke here, Gary, he's my boyfriend." Mum barely flinched. Without doubt, Gary's presence was a calming influence. It wasn't like my family could go crazy in front of him. But then Mum came out and said she already knew anyway. Both my grandmothers said the same thing. They already knew. To them it wasn't really a surprise.

My Dad was a bit funny about it at first and so was one of my brothers – though the other was fine – but once they got their heads around it they were really supportive. All my friends were great. The group of straight lads from work loved having a token gay guy around. We'd go out on the town most Thursday and Saturday nights. It just worked, our group dynamic, especially when I'd go up to girls on the dance floor and give it the big one on behalf of the others. I guess my mates thought that because I was gay I could help them break the ice with girls who took their fancy. Either way, it never worked.

Hanging around with that group of lads got me into playing football again. Every Sunday we'd stumble out of bed, horribly hungover, and head over to the park to play football. There'd be nine or ten of us each week and we'd have a right little kickabout. Then one of my mates, Dean, moved jobs and his new boss was also the manager of a local football team called Yardley, based near the airport in East Birmingham. Yardley were looking for new players as they embarked on another season in the second division of the Birmingham Festival League so Dean invited all of us along to join him.

Five of us – Chris, Mark, Jim, myself, and Dean – went along to that first session. We had a great laugh. There was already an established squad of around 12 players, most of whom also worked for the manager. They worked together and they played together and because of this there was a great team spirit. Rather than upset that spirit, our presence only served to further the chemistry. We were immediately made welcome.

We would train each week and play on a Saturday. It was only a local league so there wasn't much travelling or anything involved. I told the coach that I played in central midfield and that was all I told him. Nothing else. I didn't tell him about my sexuality. Why should it be important? Even so I told my mates not to say anything because, you know, just in case. Gays could now officially serve in the army but large parts of the population still didn't like the idea. The belief that 'embracing' homosexuality would destroy the army was yet to ring true, but people still held on to it. If elected MPs could spout such rubbish then what was stopping your average Joe who played for Yardley FC?

So I played in central midfield and we had some good results and I did well. I was being picked in the number 8 role week in week out. I'm a bit quiet but I'll get my foot stuck in. The manager liked that. He liked how I'd slide tackle, head the ball, be the first one there if there was ever a dispute. I've never had the skill – I've never been one of the show ponies or anything like that. I've always been the simple one. Just get the ball down and play. My style of play bought me some time. I was willing to do all of the dirty work and people just don't perceive gay footballers as doing that. It took the gay factor away. For a bit.

One week we were in the pub after a game having a few beers. It was our post-match ritual. Everything was fine and as usual we were all getting on well. Then Dean let it slip. He didn't do it on purpose. It wasn't malicious. He was actually trying to protect me, which is pretty ironic because he ended up doing the exact opposite.

One of our teammates was joking about me not having a girlfriend.

Well, that's because he's not into girls, Dean had said. As soon as those words came out, I knew it was game over. I froze like a rabbit in headlights. My heart stopped. Everything went quiet. There were a few funny looks but then it just carried on as normal.

OK, I thought, that wasn't so bad. Maybe I should have been true to myself all this time. Maybe I should have been honest. I hadn't been because I was enjoying the football side of things and enjoying the general laddishness and didn't want to ruin it. I hadn't been sure how the others would be if they knew the truth.

They used all the homophobic language that's so deeply ingrained in football culture. 'Oh, he's a poof.' 'Don't be a fairy.' All that jazz. I didn't even take offence at it because what's the point? It's so deeply ingrained that there was no point in taking offence. It would have changed nothing and merely alienated me. Yet it was that homophobic language which had held me back so much because I didn't know how they'd react and didn't really want to know anyway.

Even though the initial reaction had been OK I still didn't go to training the next week. My mates tried to drag me out but I refused. I don't really know what stopped me going because I absolutely loved it. I really did. I guess it's because after Dean's words, everything to do with football just seemed to be a weight on my shoulders.

They managed to drag me back to Yardley for the next home game. With a considerable weight still on my shoulders, I turned up to find that I would not be starting in my favoured central midfield role. No, I'd be playing at left back. That raised suspicions. I'm not great on my left foot and I'm not great at full back. To top it off, the regular left back was even there in the starting eleven. At least I had made the team. That's what I told myself. It's not ideal but it could be worse. I hadn't been dropped or anything.

So I just carried on. In the changing room I didn't feel as free as before. I didn't feel like I could have the laughs I had had in previous weeks. I was much more guarded. My teammates weren't speaking to me as freely as they had been before. It was nothing horrible. It was just like there was an invisible barrier or something. Then, after two or three weeks, the inevitable happened. I turned up to a game to find out I'd been dropped. Not just dropped from the starting eleven, but dropped from the squad altogether.

I went and found the manager, told him that I thought I'd done OK at left back. Yeah, he told me, you did. You're just not playing today. That was it. The extent of his explanation for my total exclusion from the matchday squad. You're just not playing today.

Anyway, they lost the game that day and I can't say that made me too unhappy. Even though I'd been dropped and was obviously frustrated, I still couldn't get away from the fact that the eleven players who had started the game were my mates, especially Dean, Chris, Mark and Jim. I went in after the final whistle to have a word and see if there were any plans for after the game. Obviously I hadn't played so I was fully clothed. Well, as soon as I walked in the cat was out of the bag... "Backs against the walls lads, look who it is."

That was it. For the first time in three weeks it was out in the open. I was gay. I knew, they knew, and they didn't like it. I hadn't been comfortable since Dean let it slip and now there were no secrets. A couple of other unfunny jokes came off the back of that first one. "Careful in the showers, lads. Watch the soap..." all that kind of shit.

Dean, Chris, Mark and Jim backed me up. They told the others that they were pathetic. Mark just walked out. He wasn't having it at all. It was so disrespectful. Me? I just stayed there, unable to move, their words thudding into me. Deep down I knew it would be like this. I knew they wouldn't accept me for who I was. Sure, it was only a select few who were giving me grief, but they were the jokers, the 'laddy' ones who had most say in the team. You know the type: the ones with all the bravado – the show ponies.

At first it hurt but later I'd realise it was them who had all of the problems. They were so uncomfortable in their own skin, with all of their own deficiencies, that they had to pick on someone else. They had to make someone appear weaker than themselves so they could feel better about their own shortcomings. In their eyes, that's what made them a man. They're not happy, not with themselves.

What hurt me the most was the manager, Steve. I thought that I had a good relationship with him. We talked regularly and I classed him as a friend. After everything kicked off, he didn't send me one message of support. He didn't ask why I hadn't come to training. He didn't do anything. The bloke just distanced himself from me. He never directed anything at me, never made out he had an issue with my sexuality, but he also never stopped the other players from their snipes and never consoled me after suffering their abuse. I'd like to think that he was just pressured and poorly influenced. I don't think he was homophobic. Even so, how hard is it just to say, 'Come on, lads, let it go'?

At the end of the day it was probably a case of the many outweighing the few. Steve recognised he had a team to run. I was one person and there was more than one person who took offence at my sexuality. And so he sided with the many, which again is ironic, because after all of that Dean, Chris, Mark and Jim left. They really were good mates and were sickened by how I had been treated. If only there were more people like them in football.

After Yardley I took time out from the game. I couldn't be dealing with it all any more. I didn't want to have to go through the whole charade of revealing my true self again, only to be trampled over. The whole episode made me realise that you can have football mates, but they're just that. Deep down I always knew how they'd react. My worst fears were proven. And so that was that.

Football is art. It should be about expression and liberation, both on the pitch and off it. There should be no confines, no boundaries. It always makes me sad that my last experience of straight football was pretty much of me not being myself.

* * *

Here's a lesson for all you homophobes out there. Without Budapest, Neil and I would probably not have got together. Until then our relationship had been on and off. In my opinion it was dying a death. I wanted to give it

*a go but Neil was wary. In all fairness to him I think the ghost of Adam
haunted him a bit. He'd had prior experience with a relationship with a
teammate and it hadn't worked out well for him. Me? Well, I'd only been
playing gay football for around nine months. I'd had a kind of relationship
with a teammate but it only lasted for three weeks so I'm not counting it.*

*If it wasn't for another relationship, I wouldn't have even been play-
ing football. Still devastated by everything that had gone on at Yardley, I
remained retired from football for four years. It took a chance sighting of
a small poster to get me back on the pitch.*

*I remember the night of the poster well. I'd just finished with Gary,
my boyfriend of five years, and was pretty messed up about everything. A
load of my girl friends had persuaded me to come out with them to try and
take my mind off everything. We went to this bar and I was drinking my
vodka thinking maybe there's more fish in the sea when I saw this small
poster in the corner of the room. BIRMINGHAM BLAZE. I looked
and looked at it. Gay football? It sounded amazing. Perfect, in fact. How
had I never heard of it before?*

*I copied the contact details down and that same night I sent an intro-
ductory message. Within a few days, following several more messages, I'd
arranged to train with the team.*

*I arrived expecting to find a load of footballers who were scared of the
ball, who'd all be singing and dancing in the showers and slapping each
other with towels. I thought they'd all be pansies prancing around a field.
I couldn't have been more wrong. The standard of play was decent. Not
quite Saturday straight league level but not far off. At that point in my life
it was a perfect standard for me. I was pleasantly surprised and it really
got my hunger back for the game, especially after the first competitive match
I played for them.*

*I was playing with people I felt comfortable with. There were no invis-
ible barriers, no weight on my shoulders. Most importantly, I felt that I
could be myself. I was back playing in central midfield and I was surrounded by people who were comfortable with themselves, playing against
teams who knew what we were and respected us for it. There was no hiding,*

no deception. Everything was out in the open.

It seems almost ridiculous that I had never heard of Birmingham Blaze. The gay scene in Birmingham is pretty small. It's the same faces in the same places each week. Yet I'd never heard of a gay football team and had never met any of the players who played at Blaze, even though there must have been hundreds over the years as the club had been going for more than ten years.

Four months later Neil joined the club, just as I'd started my three-week relationship with a teammate. It was nothing serious. To be honest it was a simple case of us misjudging each other. He thought I was something that I'm not and vice versa. There was nothing malicious about it. We just went back to being friends.

With Neil it was different. It was one of those situations where you know from almost as soon as you meet them. The first thing you notice is looks. It's horrible that that's how it works but that's just the way things are. Fortunately for me, Neil was properly my type – he was really nice looking, a bit shorter than I'd usually go for but that didn't really matter. I guess you can't have it all. His personality was amazing. He was so easy to talk to and, credit where credit's due, he's funny. Everyone likes to laugh and I'm no different. He had me laughing from the very start.

It wasn't really that awkward when we were getting together. We kept it quiet. I didn't feel any need to publicise it and Neil still felt that his teammates had been the downfall of his relationship with Adam. It made him quite conscious about how he's perceived with someone in the dressing room. He didn't want anyone to get involved and ruin something good for him. I didn't mind that. I had to be understanding. It didn't bother me either way, though. I tend just to put stuff out there. I don't mind what people think. I am what I am. Obviously I don't let others get in the way but even if they do it rarely bothers me.

The first few months were really good but then there were complications. Mainly, it was the distance. It was hard to progress in our relationship because we were so far away from each other and we both had to work, which meant we didn't see each other as much as we'd have liked to. We were in this strange situation where we were together but we weren't. For me, Budapest seemed like the perfect opportunity to revive our relationship and move on to the next step so that we were together, rather than apart.

At first, Neil wasn't coming. Fortunately I can be quite persuasive when I want to. I didn't manage to get him along to Bratislava – which is where we were all heading for a few days after the tournament – but I did get him to book enough time off work to come along to Budapest.

We shared a dormitory in Budapest. It's a shame we had to share it with our 10 teammates as well, Neil in one corner, me in the other. It wasn't as intimate as it first sounded. We couldn't have been further apart. It didn't help the strange feeling that had been between us previously, and which continued throughout the whole tournament. We had a really good time and it didn't feel like we were just friends, but it didn't feel like we were in a relationship either. Maybe we were just trying to make too much of a conscious effort to keep it quiet. Until the last night, that is.

In the end, Budapest made us stronger. It nearly broke us, but in the end it worked out for the best. What doesn't kill you makes you stronger. It all happened on the last night. There was alcohol involved and that's never a good sign when you're trying to keep something quiet.

We went to a few bars and got a bit loose and then there was this guy who was flirting a bit with me and I wasn't necessarily shutting him off, though of course I wasn't leading him on, and he asked if I had a boyfriend and I replied honestly that no I hadn't, I was single. We were keeping it quiet after all. Well that set Neil off. He was all over the place and so I gave him an ultimatum: "You don't want to be my boyfriend so what do you want? You can't have the best of both."

That hit him hard. Budapest in general hit him hard, I think. But those two sentences hit him hardest. They had the exact impact I wanted, though not necessarily first off. Sure, Neil ended up in my bed that night and people started to latch on to what was happening, though in reality they'd suspected it for ages. It meant that few people were surprised and actually, by and large, they were supportive. There was no awkwardness at all because we were all friends anyway in that team.

Isolation didn't help Neil. When he gets emotional he shouldn't be left alone with his thoughts. He's prone to overthinking. So whilst we were all off to Bratislava and the lads were asking me what was going on with Neil, he was alone. He had nobody to talk it over with. Maybe he didn't think the previous night had been real, that it was just an illusion. We'd gone our separate ways so quickly the next morning that bad thoughts had started to creep into his mind. All he could fixate on were those words I had uttered: "You're not my boyfriend." Then there was the fact I was off to a foreign city with a load of mates to have a good time. The silence was louder than all of the noise from the interrogation I was under on that train to Bratislava.

He thought he had lost me. I thought he was finally mine. It really was a ridiculous situation. We texted each other regularly for the few days that I was in Bratislava. It was only when I arrived there that I found out about his mini-breakdown in the airport. I managed to calm him down and we agreed to just take it nice and slow and to give it a go when we were home. None of our teammates had been shocked by it and they were all comfortable with us being together. It made him realise that it was for the best, and it meant that I enjoyed my few days in Bratislava knowing that we'd started something, finally.

As soon as I got home from Bratislava, I got Neil to come round. Of course, we'd agreed to give it a go via text but I wanted to say it to him face-to-face as well. What are digital words? I wanted it actually to mean something and I wanted to do it as soon as possible. It was very much a case of getting rid of all of his worries and making it – us – real.

It really is ironic that in the homophobic environment of Budapest our homosexual relationship truly began. We'd had six months in England where we were able to be as free as we liked, yet it wasn't until we were placed into this homophobic environment where we were watched over by a military patrol, where being different was thrown back in our face 24/7, that it all came out and we properly decided to give it a go.

Cheers, homophobia. I guess you're not all bad. **"**

20

Mr. Chairman

It turned out that Dave was right all along. His impression that we'd get back together as soon as we were reunited in England was right, and thank goodness for that. The first thing I did when we came face-to-face was to apologise for being an idiot. He seemed confused because a lot of my ridiculous behaviour went straight over his head. He must have been having too much of a good time in Bratislava because he'd barely even registered my desperation.

Even though we'd already agreed to give it a go via text, I still headed to Dave's that day expecting to leave just as a friend. My glass was half empty and it had been for weeks. Dave filled it right up. We hit it off again straight away. It was like all of the damage and desperation of the previous few days had been undone; forgotten, even. And then we decided to make it real. There'd be no grey areas in the relationship. I'd be Dave's boyfriend and Dave would be my boyfriend. I couldn't have been happier.

It set the tone for a busy few weeks. The Blaze Annual General Meeting was approaching and I decided to stand for the role of chairman. I knew that the chairman who'd done it the previous season wanted to stand down, and I felt that with the boost we'd had from our performance in the EuroGames I could continue our upward ascent as a team and a club. It was like the situation at Heyford all over again, and again there was initially nobody else who wanted the role. It was the only reason the poor bloke had been the chairman for so long. No-one could be bothered with all of the extra work.

I had a conversation with Jason, the manager of the first team at the time. I asked if he could envisage us working together if I became chairman and he said that yes, of course he could. Talk about shooting yourself in the foot, because I really didn't think that Jason was the right man for the job – not that I told him that. I'd need his support and besides, being the manager was the same as being the chairman – nobody else wanted to do it so you just supported the poor bloke who got lumbered with the role.

Jason did put a spanner in the works, though. He said he knew of not one but two other people who were putting themselves up for chairman. Imagine that... Three people all going for a position that nobody wanted. In a bid to increase my chances I made a pact with Jonny. He was one of the others going for the role and we had a long conversation about it at the Birmingham Pride event, deciding to put in a joint application. It would be a case of two for the price of one, if you like. It would certainly raise our chances of success at the AGM. Jonny even had previous experience in the role, having been the chairman when I first joined Blaze. That was the main reason for him coming back...

A few months previously he had come along to watch a Blaze game. He was asked to play as the side was short and was shocked. Jonny had left the club in a healthy state and couldn't believe that things had got so bad. But they had. Disappointed, he vowed to return to Blaze to rectify the situation and then push them on. I had similar ambitions and so we agreed that I'd focus on the football side of things and he'd deal with everything off the pitch. We knew we'd work well together.

I thought I could turn things round, just like I had done at Heyford. Though things at Blaze weren't as desperate as there, improvements had to be made and I was the man to make them. My first task would be to convince everyone that we had been failing. Other clubs could never understand how we weren't successful, always finishing near the bottom despite our resources. Being based in as big a city as Birmingham meant we had a good number of players at our fingertips, yet we didn't utilise them. It had annoyed me for years. Birmingham Blaze should have been one of the top gay clubs. I wanted to prove all of the other clubs right. And I wanted to prove wrong all those who said I couldn't.

There was only one thing holding me back and that was Dave. He was then the club captain. If I was the chairman as well, then people would always be mindful of what they'd say in front of us. It wouldn't be natural. Would it put him off? Would it disrupt everything? Would it put a strain on our relationship?

I weighed everything up and decided to go for it. As with everything I did, I'd go for broke. I had a point to prove, after all. I still wasn't fully over the Adam situation and the subsequent enforced resignation from Blaze. I wanted to prove my importance to the club, that they shouldn't have let me go so readily before.

The AGM arrived and I was duly voted in along with Jonny – comfortably, I was told. The applause had barely died down before it was time to get to work, but there was an immediate friction. I wanted to set about a load of changes straight away. Jonny didn't. He wanted an easy transition and he also thought he knew best. He had done the job before and he thought that' the club had been perfect when he was calling the shots.

In a way, Jonny was exactly what I was fighting against. He always valued the off-pitch side of the club over the football side. If we lost, he'd conclude that, 'It's only a game. Just a laugh, isn't it?'. Even so, I did manage to make some changes as I tried to make us more professional. If you improve the attitude, make people proud to wear the club badge, introduce respect, then you can go a long way.

Planning became essential. We wanted the committee members to plan how to maintain funds, the manager to plan his sessions in advance, to have all the logistics in order. The players had to act smart and look smart. No longer were they allowed to smoke at training sessions. In fact, they weren't even allowed to smoke when they were wearing anything with the club badge on. If you're representing Blaze then you'd better represent them as a role model.

The new guidelines were fair. I didn't want to task the team with getting promoted. The changes should have brought an improvement in performances and results but telling the manager he had to get promoted felt a bit too Football Manager for my liking. How could I tell the manager he needed to get promoted when I was playing in the team, especially when it could be my mistake costing us the three points? It was my job to keep the ball out the net, after all.

The players all agreed with me. From now on they'd be more professional. No longer would they look like a shambles, all mix-and-match with a beer in one hand and cigarette in the other. It was time to get serious. It was time to show the league what we were made of.

It lasted about a month. The manager lasted a bit longer but only just. Cracks appeared pretty early with him and a few committee members began to voice concerns. Our main sponsor – a local pub – was not thrilled with some of his behaviour and their money was our lifeblood. Sure, they liked the fact that he drank beer, but the fact that he drank beer whilst on the sideline wasn't necessarily seen as a positive, especially when it started to take effect. Our location and standing in the community meant that we were in a place where everyone knew everything, and the pub's association with a club managed by a guy not conducting himself properly wasn't doing them any favours. On top of that we weren't getting the numbers at training sessions and players generally weren't happy. It seemed like a no-brainer and Jonny agreed: Jason had to go.

Jason's departure had been a committee decision but when we then appointed Dave as the temporary manager, fingers were pointed at me. The thinking seemed to be that it had been my plan all along to get rid of the manager and replace him with my other half. It wasn't true. Dave was the club captain and the obvious man for the job, especially seeing as it was only on a temporary basis. That was the initial plan, but then Dave got off to a decent start, drawing his first game in charge – and at that point anything other than a defeat was a positive. Nobody wants to lose their first game and as a club we had been losing too often.

In a way I'd done what I set out to do. I'd committed to approaching the task like the proverbial bull in a china shop and the china had certainly been scattered. We had a new manager, a new philosophy and now a big challenge. Even with the point from Dave's first game in charge we were rooted to the bottom of the league. Considering we were in the third league of three that wasn't a great statistic.

The season ended up being a struggle both on and off the pitch. Not only that, but Dave's and my relationship struggled. The dynamic of me as chairman and him as manager put a strain on things, especially because I was desperate for him to succeed in a position that I had almost forced him to take. Results weren't going his way.

There was one game we played against Nottingham where we were 2-0 up. Nottingham pulled a goal back and as soon as the ball hit the net, we all knew what was coming next. Once you get into the habit of losing it's really hard to get out of it. Sure enough, the equaliser followed soon after. A few minutes later their manager stepped up and slotted a free-kick into the top corner of the net. 3-2 and Nottingham weren't done. There were only around 10 minutes left when they took a corner and the ball fell awkwardly and bounced around a bundle of bodies. Dave tried to take control of the situation and clear his lines but all he could do was pass the ball straight to an opponent, who gleefully accepted the gift and rifled the ball into the roof of the net.

I was manic after that, ready to burst. I managed to hold it in until we got in the car. That was when I told Dave that we were better off under the previous manager. Dave thought that was unfair. I didn't need any encouragement. "Their manager scores a goal today and our manager gives one away," I ranted. It was a horrible thing to say because Dave knew how bad his mistake had been. Everyone knew. They'd all seen it. I was just trying to push buttons because I was angry. It's how I work. Rant, rant, rant, then I apologise. Dave's different. He's calm and collected. Sometimes I wish he'd just react. I wish he'd rise to my bait, call me a dickhead, but he never does. He just acts like an adult.

I was attacking Dave because I wanted him to succeed at what he was doing. I was more bothered about his reputation than mine, but I was doing neither of us any favours. In the end, I probably became the worst person for him. Over that whole season I said some pretty horrible things in the heat of battle. At times it was bad between us but we never came close to splitting up. Football would have gone long before it ever came to that. Sure, we both loved the sport; it's just that our relationship was more important.

My relationship with Jonny was also strained. Having joint chairmen never works. The same goes for joint anything really. We weren't pulling in the same direction and I was being a bit of a weak leader. There were so many times when I needed

Jonny there with me but he was nowhere to be seen.

Ex-manager Jason joined Wolverhampton and when we played them in a league fixture, Jonny was again missing, leaving me to issue the smiles and fake politeness when I knew that he probably wanted to thump me. In fact, nearly every incident where we needed to manage people was left to me, which was something I hated because I cannot stand confrontation. If only we'd just sat down and had a discussion and he'd realised that I was right. Jonny even stopped me carrying out my on-pitch duties as had been agreed.

As the season went from bad to worse Jonny just simply stopped turning up. You only find out someone's true character in hard times. 'If you can't handle me at my worst then you sure as hell don't deserve me at my best.' That was my attitude with Jonny. I'm not sure Marilyn Monroe intended her quote to be meant in that context but there you go. Jonny must have realised. He didn't stick around to see me at my best because at the end of the season he left. Everyone had seen it coming.

The big surprise was that he actually turned up to the AGM at the end of the season. I was expecting a pretty rough ride because we'd finished bottom of the league, which had surpassed everything Blaze had ever done before. I'd taken the club, focused on their on-field performance and made them even worse. It was literally impossible for them to finish any lower in the gay league. We were officially the worst gay team in the whole of Britain. Yet Jonny defended me. He did such a good job that I got off lightly.

Everyone could see that we'd finished bottom. It was beyond personal failure. Birmingham Blaze played such an important part in my life. I had to put things right. And so I made a decision: I would go through the tears, arguments, fall-outs and fights, all over again. It was time to take the role as chairman once more but this time take it on by myself.

21

"We're Getting a Bit Straight"

"Neil…" he said. I didn't like the way he said it or the way he was looking at me. He was small, and flustered. His red face had beads of sweat trickling down. This was a man looking for an argument. Well, let him come at me. I'd dealt with people like him before, and now there was no Jonny to hold me back.

"Neil," he repeated, only this time trying to place more authority on the word, a ridiculous attempt to seize power. "I don't like what's happening with Blaze. We're getting a bit straight."

Believe it or not, this wasn't an isolated incident. It was a sentiment echoed by a few. Even one of my closest allies warned me that we were 'getting a bit straight'. What on earth does that mean? 'A bit straight'. Who cared? Why should we limit the number of straight people allowed in the team? It's all about inclusion and acceptance. That and getting the three points.

The second season had started well. Jonny's departure gave me free reign as chairman. It was a move which initially left me nervous that I wouldn't be able to cope alone, but as it unfolded, it proved a big relief. I was being held accountable for my own actions and not someone else's. It made me the responsible person that I needed to be in the first place.

I had imagined the previous season that changes would be implemented with results coming immediately but actually, coming rock bottom in that first season was the best thing that could have happened. After the shock and humiliation, I came back focused and motivated anew. Whatever happened in that second season, I knew that things couldn't get worse.

Fortunately, I had some good people round me and while they didn't let me mess up, they gave me enough autonomy to get things done. For a new era, I wanted a new kit and we were now in one that Dave and I had chosen. The red and black stripes were replaced by a bespoke black shirt with a pink stripe. It looked really smart and everybody liked it. New players came in, a number of them – as the small flustered man who stood in front of me pointed out – straight.

There's a weird dynamic with straight players in the gay leagues, and their numbers have increased as the league has gone on. At first we didn't have many at Blaze and there were only a handful in the whole league. We rarely played against straight teams, or predominantly straight teams, when I first joined. You could mention it to the players and they'd all fearfully whisper that, 'Oh no, we'll all get beaten up'.

Attitudes have begun to change but even so, when I joined the second time round and we played against a straight team, or a gay team with a number of straight players, then our players would approach the game expecting to lose. Worse still, it was deemed acceptable. Losing to anyone is not acceptable. It doesn't matter if they're gay or straight. In fact, it annoys me more when we lose to a straight team because until we gay players are good at football we are never going to change anyone's opinion. If you lose 10-0 to a straight team then what have you proved? You've only reinforced the stereotype that gay men can't play football because they're 'not macho'. If you compete with them, let them know they've been in a game, that's when you start to change perceptions.

I've got my theories as to why straight players want to play in the GFSN league. Sure, they're sympathetic to the gay cause and in no way are they homophobic, but that's not the only reason they play. I was guilty of it when I first joined gay football. 'This is brilliant,' I remember thinking, 'I'm going to be the best player here by miles.' And that is the case for quite a few of the straight players.

They come with all of these pre-conceptions that gay players aren't going to be the greatest of footballers and reckon that they'll be the biggest of big fish in a small, homosexual pond. They turn up young, straight and full of confidence, dragging their girlfriend along because they're a bit unsure and they feel they need to prove to everyone that they're straight. Then they realise that some gay people actually can play and that they're not the best player on the pitch. Worse than that, they realise that their opponents aren't afraid to kick the shit out of them.

Not all of our straight players were like that. By the middle of my second season as chairman we weren't far off being 50/50 with gay and straight players in the team. The straight players felt totally comfortable playing in the same team as gay players. For some reason that was seen as a negative. I didn't understand why. Surely having a load of straight players in the team is the ultimate aim? Because the last thing you want is a gay league and gay teams. Then you're segregating yourselves from the mainstream, whereas really what you want is to be incorporated.

We had to set up our own league because we weren't accepted, and now that we're beginning to be accepted some people resent it. They don't like winning the war because then what have they got left to complain about? The fight's almost won. On pretty much every front other than football the fight is won. Some people like to be the victim, though, and how can they be the victim if everything suddenly becomes fine?

Indeed, how could I have enforced a ban on straight players

at Blaze? How ironic would that be? We can't start excluding people because of their sexuality. I was pretty mindful of asking people their sexuality anyway, not only because I had no right to, but also because how could I have known whether they were telling the truth?

I don't understand what people want sometimes. They wanted an organisation that protected them and allowed them to play in a safe environment. They got that. They were able to play a sport in which the mainstream leagues had isolated them and kicked them away. Now the mainstream leagues are welcoming them back and everyone is being integrated and they don't like it. There's so many ironies here. I've always said that being the chairman of Birmingham Blaze is essentially overseeing all of these ironies.

To put it bluntly, I have to preside over a number of people who want equality and to be treated equally but do not want that enforced inside their own club. They're happy in their own little world in the GFSN. Gay football for gay footballers.

As a concept, the GFSN league that we were a part of worked. It started off as a social league with the emphasis on the night out that took place either before or after the game – usually before. It was meant as a way of like-minded people meeting each other, though in reality it ended up being a way for players from the two teams to hook up with each other.

The league itself was founded at a time when gay football fans often had to conceal their sexuality. Straight football was never the safest of environments, so the league offered a safe, inclusive place where people could be whoever they wanted whilst playing a sport they loved. Times change. Whereas mainstream football became more and more accepting, the GFSN league stayed the same. It was still a social league where like-minded people could meet and have a laugh. It remained fun whilst not necessarily catering for those of us with ambition.

Although the standard has improved over the years, the more serious players have to make do with a handful of GFSN games and the irregular EuroGames.

It explains why teams have started to leave the GFSN leagues. Stonewall, for example, play in the Middlesex County Football League Division One. Their reserve side play in the London West End AFA Sunday League, and it is only their third team who play in the gay football leagues, competing in the London Unity League. They've had no issues at all, and now other teams such as Village Manchester are taking their lead.

In that regard, it can be said that we're all ultimately working toward our own demise. It seems strange, doesn't it? Our ultimate goal is acceptance, yet once we're fully accepted we'll no longer need gay teams.

Teams leaving the GFSN in search of better, more regular competition can cause problems internally. In-fighting is not uncommon. Clubs like ours that aren't quite big enough to have two teams, yet are too big to have just one, are torn. In an ideal world we'd have a first team competing in a straight league, aiming to get as high up the pyramid as possible, and a reserve team in the GFSN league. One would take their football seriously; the other would take their football socially.

As soon as someone voices that we should take things seriously and enter the straight leagues, however, the dissenters always gather around them. 'If you want to go and take it seriously, go and join a straight team,' they get told. It annoys me. Why can't you be gay and take it seriously and have pride in your team? It doesn't make any sense at all, but it's the kind of attitude that the structure of the GFSN breeds.

There is currently no registration for players. You can play who you want, when you want. It's a ringer's paradise. Nobody is tied to a team. If you play for Stonewall one week you can go and play for Birmingham Blaze the next. Everything is focused on inclusion. The league has been left behind, because as the teams and players have become more professional, the league itself hasn't.

It's not just the competitive element forcing teams into straight leagues. Clubs are becoming more and more influential in their communities, and as time goes by they want to make a greater difference. To be honest, I'm not helping anybody in the West Midlands if I spend my Sunday heading off to London to play a game of football. Playing nationally and keeping ourselves to ourselves and only playing against other gay teams is not furthering the cause. If I play in a local league, however, I can make a positive difference in my local community.

I suppose there is some kudos in playing in a national gay league. The very fact that it's played nationally gives it credibility, and it also gives clubs publicity, which can lead to exceptional opportunities. You can actually feel privileged just for being a gay man who likes football. How times have changed. I've been invited to play at Villa Park twice, I've met with Birmingham City's top players and I've been wined and dined by any number of marketing executives from professional clubs. None of that would have happened if I played in a regular Sunday league team.

Why do the professional clubs do it? Do they really care? Probably not. It's usually done to tick boxes. All we do is serve a purpose. The professional club goes back to the FA and can boast about championing equality and the FA says well done and gives them an award, perhaps even a grant. The club is thus rewarded for acting how any half decent human being should. We shouldn't be celebrating this kind of behaviour – it should just be the norm. Acceptance should be widespread.

Some people in the gay football world believe the breakthrough for us was when these opportunities started to come.

They think that being invited into the hospitality suites to watch Birmingham City on their Football vs. Homophobia Day, that playing at Villa Park, meant we'd finally been accepted. I didn't see it like that.

In my opinion, the main reason we were invited to play at Villa Park was so that Aston Villa could put it on their website. It was exactly the same reason that Birmingham City invited us, though at least they were up front about it. "To be honest," we were told, "your presence here benefits us more than it does you."

Being given privileges isn't the breakthrough because we don't want to be treated differently. The aim is to be treated the same as everybody else. Our sexuality shouldn't matter. It all goes back to competing. To change perceptions, we have to compete regularly with straight teams on the pitch and prove that gay people can play and are just as good as anyone else at a sport as physical as football.

Times are changing, and for the better. Though the GFSN league is bigger than ever before, it's also becoming more and more unnecessary. The people who organise the league will probably be the first to admit that in 10 years it won't exist. There will just be no need.

That being likely, we had to make the most of our time in the GFSN and of the resources available to us at Birmingham Blaze. That's why we decided to start picking players regardless of their sexuality. Unsurprisingly, being able to select from a pool of gay and straight players made us stronger. And the straight players we brought in were the catalyst behind our improved performance as we only brought in straight players better than what we already had, to complement a decent foundation of gay players. We had to let a few players go which I didn't like doing, but if you want to be the best you have to make a few sacrifices and sentiment takes second place.

In *Cristiano Ronaldo: The Biography*, Guillem Balague tells how Ronaldo was tested by his teammates and almost bullied when he first joined Manchester United. He had to deal with snide remarks, people saying he was only keeping David Beckham's number seven shirt warm while Beckham was in Madrid, negative comments about his fashion sense and, humiliatingly, being placed in the weakest group for rondos – a ball drill with players in a circle passing it around a piggy in the middle – where he was often intentionally stitched up. Players would fire balls at him at knee height knowing that he was only allowed one touch to deal with it. Giving the ball away would make him look like a weak player. It would mean he'd have to go in the middle of the circle and take his turn chasing the ball, trying to win it back.

Ronaldo was truly tested and came out of it to become the player that he is today. It's refreshing to know there are similarities between straight football and gay football. When straight players come into a gay team they get tested, just not in the same way as Ronaldo did. We're not bullies – and we certainly wouldn't be bullies if Ronaldo turned up to train with us.

It's no secret that he's a beautiful man. There are some in the gay community who believe that he may be gay, but more likely it's a case of them hoping he is. Unfortunately Ronaldo hasn't yet turned up, so instead we test the straight players we do get along with relentless flirting. What makes the flirting even more fun is the trend for straight players to seem more attractive, though that's probably a case of forbidden fruit. We know they're off limits.

Even so, we love to watch them squirm in their skin with every passing line we throw their way. Almost all of them take it in good spirit – and some even take it in their stride and flirt back – but the vast majority of them are uncomfortable with it. We want to see just how comfortable they get so we push them to their limits, seeing if they break. They rarely do.

Despite our flirting, the new recruits at Blaze conducted themselves admirably and it helped that results were improving. None of them ever turned if they were kicked. Even at their most aggressive they never started spouting homophobic rubbish. We were in it together.

The referees never seemed to think that way. Even though – or perhaps because – the referees themselves tended to be straight, it seemed to be that more straight players than gay ones got sent off, and they'd only ever get sent off for gobbing off at the referee. There was certainly no equality when it came to the referee's interpretation of the rules. Gay players seem to have this invisible force field protecting them from going into the referee's book, though I'm not going to complain too much about that form of positive discrimination. Imagine how many red cards I'd have suffered if things were equal...

Still, the gobbing off was quite rare, and referees in the GFSN usually have a pretty relaxed job. There aren't many easier ways to pick up £30 for 90 minutes' work. We only had one incident with a straight player, this one sparked by a referee.

The straight player had been sent off and obviously hadn't agreed with the decision. Back in the changing room he was angry. He sat there, focused intently on the concrete floor, his brow furrowed and his kit still wet with mud. We went in there and tried to console him, but he just couldn't tone down his anger. He hadn't deserved it, he reckoned. That ref was a faggot, that's what he was.

I let it go at the time. Emotions were running high and it just wasn't worth it. There was no point in making it into a big thing. I knew the straight player in question. He wasn't malicious. He wasn't homophobic. Later on, when he was calm and having a drink in the clubhouse, I approached him.

"What do you think I want to talk about?" I asked him. I felt like a school teacher, him the naughty school boy, too shy to look me in the eye. It must be the red card, he concluded, taking a bitter sip of his drink.

"Nope, nothing to do with your red card," I told him. That surprised him. What then? "It's what you said about the referee after the game."

Now he was confused. He hadn't said anything about the referee had he? Certainly not anything out of order, anyway. So I mentioned the faggot word and he physically recoiled. He hadn't a clue what he had said. It had been in the heat of the moment and he wasn't thinking. He was just saying words, angry aggressive words and he didn't know where they came from. He apologised profusely and said he hadn't meant it.

Not for a second did I ever believe that he had done. It all comes back to the playground though, that attitude of, 'Oh, this is gay, that's gay'. Gay used as a word with negative connotations. People take it on subconsciously, programmed to think that way. It's ingrained in their psyche.

They may be only words but the player in question had to understand the effect such language had on those around him. It had only been an hour or two between his outburst and my clubhouse chat with him and already two club members had asked me to expel him from Birmingham Blaze FC. He immediately made a verbal apology and the next day I got this lengthy written apology totalling two sides of A4. The club members calling for his head relented. He stayed and would play a sizeable part in what would be a successful season.

The reaction to his comment was justified, but it was also ironic considering how the gay players can be pretty homophobic themselves. I'm guilty of it too. To explain...

There are players with whom I've got into arguments and I've just come out with something like, "Fuck off you old queen." I'm not condoning it but you get drawn in by the culture. When you consider that, the way straight players keep their cool becomes even more admirable. Loads of gay players call each other queens and mincers and names that are, shall we say, more colourful.

In fact, gay footballers can be vicious to each other. Often they have a sharp tongue because of all they have had to deal with in their lives. They become automatically defensive, and when you add in the competitive element of football to make their emotions run high, you've got a pretty aggressive concoction on your hands. That doesn't make it OK. There's no excuse for homophobic language from anyone, gay or straight. Because we're gay we think we can use these words. Every time I call someone a mincing old queen I should get held to account. Both straight and gay should get castigated for such remarks. It's not right, yet it's so prevalent in gay football. Sometimes we're our own worst enemy.

The whole homophobic slip of the tongue was one of only two real issues we had in an otherwise smooth season. I agreed to be a player when I pulled on the Birmingham Blaze match shirt and a player only. No longer would I try and be a chairman from right back (and despite my best persuasive techniques, Dave had still refused to play me up front).

At the start of the season we had also agreed to be a bit less hands on. It was time to relinquish some of the power. Dave had been both manager and captain but now we decided to give the captaincy to someone else. There were a few obvious candidates, but I wanted to make more of a left-field appointment and Dave agreed.

I wanted to appoint someone unpopular in the hope that it would change him from the confrontational character with whom I often clashed – perhaps because of our similarity, some pointed out. Instead, the armband went to his head and it became the second issue of the season.

In the end we took the captaincy off him but left it too

long, almost half a season. He angered his teammates as he thought everyone should be perfect and was intolerant of people's weaknesses while overlooking what they did well. At our level all players are different, yet he just couldn't fathom that. Now, I like a good argument now and then, but his regular rows became a distraction. Our original decision to make him captain had been all about catching people off guard and showing them that we weren't scared to do something different. It backfired. Lesson learned.

Despite that hiccup, Blaze were motoring along quite nicely. With our reinforced side – a little 'straighter' than usual, apparently – we ended up finishing second in the league, guaranteeing us promotion the following season. Not only that, but we won the local league: the Midlands Unity league. The one blot on an otherwise perfect season, excluding the whole captaincy issue and the homophobic slip of the tongue, of course, was our swift exit from the cup competition that the GFSN holds annually. Ever since their foundation, Birmingham Blaze had never got past the first round of that cup. That's 10 whole seasons, 10 failed attempts to get just one win, and it's a tradition we managed to uphold despite our other successes.

We could have done with some cup games. The GFSN leagues don't really provide you with enough for a full season. The three divisions that make up the GFSN are national, remember, meaning that there's a lot of travelling for all of the clubs taking part. It's not cheap, which is why there's only five teams in each division. Teams play each other home and away to make up eight games in the whole season. Teams then supplement this by creating and entering leagues locally. The gay London teams were the first to do it. They all joined together to create the London Unity League, and such was its success that the practice grew throughout the UK. Along with Nottingham Ball Bois, Leicester Wildcats and Wolverhampton Warriors, we founded the Midlands Unity league, which gave us an extra six games in the season.

The Midlands Unity League was a laugh and we wanted to win, but the GFSN League was our main focus. Joining us in the Third Division were Cardiff, London Leftfooters, London Romans and London Titans. Three trips to London gave us another reason for wanting to get out of that league. The first time you play in London it's great because of the bright lights and the big city and the fact that G.A.Y is just around the corner, but the novelty soon wears off. It's not long before you realise that an away trip to London takes up your whole day, and when you're playing the same teams each season it becomes that extra bit dull.

Thank goodness we managed to escape that. That was our initial reaction, anyway, because not more than two weeks after our promotion was confirmed, the people in charge of the GFSN League decided to condense the three leagues into two. It was a sensible move. Though travelling costs would go up, the extra games would add more of a competitive element. We'd be going one step further away from the 'let's turn up and have a kickabout' mentality.

We soon found out that with the restructure we'd be placed in the bottom of the two leagues, thus rendering our promotion pointless so were less enamoured of the new arrangements. We'd pushed so hard to escape those London teams and now we were due to be thrown back into the depths of the GFSN with them. We weren't exactly over the moon at the prospect.

We lodged an official complaint. It was the first time that Birmingham Blaze had ever been promoted and we weren't going to let the men in charge take that away from us. It seems we weren't the only club to do so because the GFSN soon changed their tune. Instead of putting the highest ranked eight teams into the First Division and the bottom seven into the Second, as had first been proposed, the GFSN were instead going to honour any promotion from the previous season. That meant that the top two teams from the Second and Third Division would join the teams who finished in the top four in the first division.

Neither situation was ideal. We wanted our promotion to count for something but we'd essentially be going up two leagues, which seemed to be too big a step. We had a group of players who were now used to winning and that was probably going to end. I was now against taking promotion but the players were up for it. They wanted their chance to show they could compete with the best. I couldn't fault their attitude. They'd come a long way from being social players.

We informed the league that we'd accept their proposal of placing us in the top league. It'd be tough but we'd be heading into the elite of gay football with a mixed team of gay and straight players. In hindsight, it was just what the club needed.

Under Birmingham Blaze's new philosophy, it wouldn't matter if a player was gay or straight. Sexuality would, and should, never enter into the equation. Ability was the criterion. Everyone should be treated equally, and under Blaze's new direction, they would.

After all, we weren't building fences. We were building something that enabled everyone to take part in something they loved, to mix freely and not to hide away in fear. If we could all take part together then surely that would make the activity just that bit more fun. Everyone feels happier when they're accepted. Bit by bit, Birmingham Blaze were getting to that stage, both on and off the pitch.

22

A Non-League Player's Story

Football culture is strange. You'd think it was just 22 players, a ball and two goals. It's not. It's much more than that: a whole set of unwritten rules and politics and attitudes. When you're growing up you don't really understand it all. You're young and innocent; you think that football is purely what happens on the pitch. If only that was the case.

Over the last couple of years I've come to know the person whose story appears in this chapter. He was part of the academy system at his local professional club, until the system chewed him up and spat him out. He represents a majority. He was in that system from the age of eight, one year after Howard Wilkinson first unveiled his new academy vision to bring the World Cup back to English soil.

He stayed there until the age of 16, growing up and learning the game, and football culture, from a number of teachers, many of whom were steeped in the old school way of doing things. It didn't help. Hardly any players make it in the game, even when they have all that contact time with professional clubs, and he was no exception.

Upon his release he dropped into Non-League football. He's still young, a mere 24 years of age, and is hoping to fight his way into full-time football. He knows it's not just the on-pitch stuff that will get him there. There's a whole set of un-written rules and attitudes to master. The tribal mentality is strong. Racism, sexism, and just plain bullying – he's seen it all.

This is football culture, through his eyes...

* * *

"*Football is gay. Think about it for a minute. The bonds between the players, between supporters, between opponents. Think about the reaction when a player scores a goal. There's the elation in the stands and the elation on the pitch. You get grown men running up to each other, sharing in the moment. They're hugging each other and maybe sometimes even kissing. Human contact. Men touching men. Maybe that's why football is homophobic. It's so gay that people need to be homophobic to prove their sexuality.*

It's not just the things you see on a matchday that stand out as being gay. It's all of those things behind closed doors. The football culture is drilled into players as soon as they enter a club. For me, it began at eight years of age when I joined the academy of my local professional side. In one of the first few weeks, I vividly remember being told in no uncertain terms that we would have to shower naked, just like 'proper men'. After each training session the players used to play this game where we would urinate on each other in the showers. Rather than stop it, the coach encouraged it as a form of bonding.

While that was going on, the football culture that we were being catapulted into was also schooling us in machismo. Tackle like a poof and you'd get yelled at. Players couldn't fanny about on the ball. Nothing but hyper masculinity would do – and this for a team of eight-year-olds. It's weird that football culture brings you up to hate homosexuality. As I grew older, players who were considered to be gay – and over the years there were a few – would be ostracised from the group. It's every footballer's worst nightmare to be accused of being gay.

There was one time when a 15-year-old boy decided he would shower in his boxer shorts. He was new to the system and didn't know how everything worked. He was made an example of. Everyone's got a penis, he was told by the coach. I remember such-and-such a player, who is now an international, the coach went on, and he had the smallest cock I've ever seen when he was your age. Just get on with it. The boy never made that mistake again.

I didn't make it in the Academy system. I wasn't good enough. At the age of 16 I had to leave that lifestyle behind and join a Non-League team. Now I was with seasoned adult players, many of whom had experienced football at a professional level. The double standards football culture applies to homophobia only increased in such an environment. I was just a kid and lacked the strength to seriously compete at the level. I was called a poof for not going into tackles strongly enough. It wasn't just confined to the pitch, though. Off the pitch I didn't have a girlfriend. I hadn't ever really had a proper girlfriend. I didn't drink alcohol. For some people it all added up.

Homophobia was certainly evident in that changing room, which is strange because it really was a pretty gay environment in there. Well, what people consider to be gay, anyway. The players, for example, had this habit of sticking their fingers up each other's rectums...

It started in training. We'd always run laps of the pitch before working with the ball and without fail there would be a couple of people lurking behind you, trying to stick their finger up your arse. Then there was our star winger. He was pretty well endowed. The tripod, they called him. Looking well endowed in the showers was taken seriously. After games players would disappear to 'get blood' into their penis before going into the shower. Either that or they'd do it openly, just standing there in the changing room flicking their penis up and down.

My teammates had great fun with our well-endowed star winger. The assistant manager of our team, a former pro himself, would always wear a suit and tie to matches. The players couldn't believe it and so they created this elaborate routine. After games they'd get our star winger to strip so that he was totally naked. They would then tighten the assistant manager's tie around his penis, with the other end taken by a player. This player would then parade the star winger around the changing room, the tie acting as a leash, much to the amusement of the onlookers.

It wasn't just the overtly homosexual acts, either. There was a great deal of what would traditionally be labelled as 'femininity' in the changing room. Players would boast about how long they had spent on the sunbed each week. After games there were a handful of players who put on women's deodorant because it 'smells nicer'. It wasn't just the players, either. The manager would get waxed in certain areas each week. Apparently the term is sugaring. He'd give out business cards for the company who did it, and many of the players would end up using that company to get their own waxing done.

All of which makes any form of homophobia seem truly strange in a football environment. But it was there. Always. I was 'accused' of being gay a number of times. For my weak tackles, for not drinking, for not having a girlfriend, for not going to the gym, for not being able to do 100 push-ups. It wasn't necessarily malicious. Usually it was in good spirits. But it was still an accusation.

I'm not sure I've ever played with someone who actually is gay. Football culture is one which teaches you that being gay is wrong. Nobody wants to be a 'fucking poof'. Even so, I'd like to think that there would be no problem at all with having a gay player in the changing room. I genuinely think that the players would be fine with him.

They just need to create a culture where you aren't a poof if you don't tackle hard enough. Where a lack of traditional alpha male masculinity doesn't mean that you're a homosexual. Where players don't fear being labelled as homosexual. Football culture needs to open its arms and expand its mind. Then, and only then, will the beautiful game, our beautiful game, be propelled into the 21st Century. **"**

23

Out At the Top

With every victory on the pitch we earn a small victory over homophobia. We can't rely solely on us players at grass roots to overcome homophobia, however. Kids need role models. For me it was Graham Norton and Kenneth Williams. I read their books and understood what they had been through. It made me feel that I wasn't alone in my struggle against society's norms.

Nowadays there are loads of positive role models, both in and out of the sporting world. You've got people like the Welsh rugby player Gareth Thomas and the Olympic diver Tom Daley who have come out and helped to change attitudes. It's made it easier for this new generation – you don't get much more macho and myth shattering than Gareth Thomas – though I'll be the first to admit that it's easy for me to say that. Every older generation thinks that it's easier for the younger one.

Coming out was agony for me. The fact that I waited so long, wrapping myself in such deceit, made it incredibly hard. But how could I have come out in such a homophobic environment? That's what I always ask myself. We were talking about a time when Section 28, a bill that precluded the so-called promotion of homosexuality among children, had just been introduced. In fact, 1988, the year that the infamous ruling was introduced to schools up and down the country, was one year before I started primary school at the age of four. Throughout my entire schooling, the authorities made sure that homosexuality was not allowed to be portrayed in a positive light.

Section 28 is long gone now. Schools are much more understanding, the media is much more understanding and that affects the wider population. Kids tend to come out earlier now. I was recently in London, walking out of a busy underground station, and there were two teenagers to the right of me. As the crowd bustled past they stood still, trapped in time. They couldn't have been more than 14 years of age. Slowly, slowly, they leant forward and kissed each other goodbye. It was a kiss of passion, emotion and longing. It was a kiss that said the receiver was the most important person in the world and the kisser didn't care who knew. They were proud of their other half. It was the most wonderful thing I've seen in a long time. Guess what? They were both male.

In many areas of life it seems sexuality is not much of an issue. I guess that's an endorsement of our society. Even though it seems not to be an issue, the Home Office revealed that there were still 5,597 homophobic crimes in England and Wales in 2014/15 – and those were just the ones reported to the police. Still, we believe that to be progress.

The football world seems as cruel as ever, though. Maybe that's an exaggeration. When I was coming to terms with my sexuality, I had Justin Fashanu to look up to. Born in Hackney, Justin started his career at Norwich City before becoming Britain's first black £1 million footballer when Brian Clough signed him for Nottingham Forest. That was when the problems started. Clough didn't take kindly to Fashanu's visits to "that bloody poofs' club".

It wasn't until 1990, nine years after Fashanu first signed for Nottingham Forest, that he publicly came out. By then his career was on the slide, limited to appearances for semi-professional teams such as Southall and Leatherhead. Still, he hauled himself back into the full-time game with Torquay United, and even ended up as their assistant manager for a short time.

From there, Fashanu became somewhat of a journeyman. Though he claimed that the majority of his teammates accepted his sexuality – despite it being the subject of many malicious jokes – he had to deal with constant crowd abuse. The worst vultures, however, were closest to Justin. His brother John, also a professional footballer, with Wimbledon, disowned him after he came out, having previously offered Justin £75,000 to keep his sexuality a secret. "I begged him, I threatened him, I did everything I could possibly do to try and stop him coming out," he later said. Justin's coming out was "an embarrassment" for him and his family. John Fashanu would later say that he regretted his words, but the damage was done.

As the years went by, Justin began to take his career global. Spells in Scotland were followed by a season in Sweden and, finally, the United States of America with Atlanta Ruckus and Miramar Rangers. It was in the USA that the beginning of the end arrived.

In the March of 1998 an allegation was made that Justin had sexually assaulted a 17-year-old. With homosexual acts illegal in the state of Maryland, where Justin found himself, he was taken in by police for questioning. Two months later he was found dead, hanged in a garage in London. Justin had fled the USA under the presumption that he was to be arrested, that he wouldn't receive a fair trial in the USA because of his sexuality. Justin, his brother concluded, had never been accepted by the world as a black homosexual football player, and that left him devastated.

The Justin Fashanu episode took the issue of homosexuality in football back 10 or 15 years. All other areas of life were becoming more tolerant, but the tragedy of Justin returned football to the Dark Ages. I was 13 at the time and just coming to terms with my own feelings of being different. I'm not sure how aware of Justin's situation I was, but the repercussions from his tragedy would have a big effect on my subsequent unease to reveal my true self to the world.

Had Justin's coming out been a success, and had he gone on to live a happy and fulfilling life, it probably would have helped me come to terms with myself. Having a Premier League footballer to look up to would have been a positive. Your main influences will always be your family, though. No matter how many gay Premier League footballers there are, you'll always be guided in your actions by the tolerance of your family. Everyone wants to make their parents proud.

My parents were the main reason I took so long to come out. The whole Section 28 debacle along with the Justin Fashanu tragedy and the widespread negative attitudes toward homosexuality in the media all had an effect on my decision, yes, but most of that decision was down to my parents. It's one of my biggest regrets. Had I come out at the age of 14 or 15, the next five years of lies and deceit wouldn't have existed. I would have just been my true self. But I couldn't do it then.

Parents are more liberal these days. Everyone is a lot more educated about homosexuality. It's not necessarily seen as a threat any more, so everyone tends to be pretty politically correct. It hasn't always been that way. One of my most vivid memories as a kid is watching the TV soap Emmerdale with my parents. There was this scene where one of the characters announced that she was a lesbian, and I just remember so vividly how my Dad tutted. It was a tut of disapproval.

That wasn't the only incident. There was another occasion when my parents took me shopping in Milton Keynes. We walked past two men holding hands and that didn't go down well with my parents. They're little moments that lasted no longer than a few seconds, but which stuck with me forever. My parents' reactions had such a huge impact on my future actions.

You know how it is: everyone thinks that having someone else's kid who's gay is the best thing ever but when it's their own, well, that's another matter altogether. It makes it hard for parents to support their kids when they come out. Instead the support network tends to be aunties, uncles and nans. Parents eventually come to terms with it, and my parents have grown to become really supportive of me, but at first it can knock them for six. That was the case for me and for a lot of people I've spoken with.

A Premier League star coming out as gay wouldn't necessarily make it easier for a young footballer to come out, but it would help with football's general understanding of, and attitude toward, homosexuality. Prejudices will live on unless challenged.

David Beckham has already done a lot of good, and for nothing more than doing his hair, having a wash and looking smart. He didn't really care who was offended by what he did. He just presented himself as he was and that was that. I'm sure he was aware that he had a pretty big gay following but it didn't bother him. He helped a lot of people. He changed football's attitude, taking it away from this sport where you had to be perceived as macho. Sure, people still think you have to be macho to play football, and they still think that gay people can't be macho, but these beliefs aren't as widespread or as strong as before Beckham, whose influence went far beyond the pitch.

The closest we have to a positive role model in football is Robbie Rogers. Robbie is an American midfielder, born in California and moulded in Major League Soccer with Columbus Crew. From there he was signed by Leeds United, for whom he could never quite replicate his MLS form. At the age of 25 he was released by the Yorkshire club. He subsequently announced that he was retiring from the game and that oh, by the way, he was gay.

Now, Robbie Rogers has been painted as an absolute hero. Why? Why did he feel that he needed to quit football before he could announce his sexuality? Not only that, but he quit football and ran off to the other side of the world after he'd announced his sexuality. Who was he helping by doing that? Once he touched back down in America he realised that actually people were fine with him being gay. Of course they were. Football in the US is different to football in England.

Over here it's traditionally the working man's sport, over there much of the development has taken place due to the womens' game, where the US are world leaders. In England it's not uncommon for women who play football to be considered lesbian. Football is dismissed as a sport merely for 'butch' girls, though attitudes are thankfully changing. In the US, women playing football is normal. Indeed, it's one of the most popular women's sports in the US. Football over there just doesn't have the same association with masculinity. The masculine sports are American football, basketball, baseball and ice hockey. Football, or 'soccer', is way down the list.

So Robbie went back to football. It had been three months after his original decision to quit, a decision he had made to "avoid the pressure and scrutiny from the press and fans – the circus." His mind was changed during a speech he made to a 500-strong crowd at an LGBT event in Portland, Oregon. As he looked out at the sea of faces he realised that he was being a coward, that he had the ability to act as a role model, his football providing a platform to give him a voice. And so he signed for LA Galaxy, making him the only openly gay professional footballer to play in the top league in America.

Good on him for realising that he had made a mistake. We all make mistakes in life, and Robbie Rogers's decision to go back to professional football has gone some way to rectifying his original decision. That said, his feeling the need to run off to a different continent after making his announcement will have only scared people more.

And why did he only feel the need to come out afterwards? The same goes for Thomas Hitzelsperger, the German midfield player who had a spell with Aston Villa. They were both courageous in coming out, but why did they wait? I don't see the point.

Coming out is an extremely personal thing. It should always be done for yourself, not for anybody else, but it is a pity that these players felt they couldn't do it sooner. It's something that has to be done, and these people are grown adults. Nobody can live their whole life as a lie. Think how many people they could have helped if they had come out earlier, while they were still playing in England.

I understand their way of thinking. You only have to look at what happened with Matt Jarvis. The West Ham winger, who is straight, appeared on the front cover of the gay magazine *Attitude*. It was brilliant, a real act of forward thinking, yet what happened? He got a load of abuse. He couldn't go anywhere without people asking if he was gay. He's got a wife, family, yet people still make these assumptions. All he did was appear on the front of a magazine and a few pages in the middle.

The media is not the enemy for a footballer if he comes out. I believe there would be nothing but support in that regard. The fans, however – I'm not so sure. Being a football fan goes beyond attending the match. In England they're the 12th man, an organic part of the game, who consider themselves to be active contributors to the spectacle. The tribal mentality is strong. It only takes a couple of loudmouths to push the limits of acceptability, which are often forgotten in favour of the spectacle.

Football fans aren't necessarily homophobic, but if they can put an opposition player off his game by shouting something, then they may well do it. If the something that they shout is homophobic, and it visibly frustrates the player, then they aren't likely to stop. In such situations you lose your inhibitions. Sport is all about exploiting weakness in your opponent and if your opponent was homosexual it would be too good an opportunity for some fans to miss. That doesn't necessarily mean that they'd be homophobic, however. In the heat of the moment all some people can focus on is helping their team to win.

If they're your own fans and you're playing well then everything is great and there's no criticism, but if you're not doing the business each week, that's when people turn on you. It's a problem that's worse in the lower reaches of professional football. Down in League One and League Two, where the stadiums are older and fans tend to be closer to the pitch, that's where you can hear every bit of abuse aimed at you. It's football, but less sanitised than the polished global giant that is Premier League football. Prices are less prohibitive as well.

The prawn sandwich brigade rule Premier League football. The working class have been priced out from going regularly, so you get a crowd that tends to be more middle class. They're more reserved and on the surface more accepting. They tend to have had a better education, and the Neanderthals are fewer and farther between than 25 years ago, before the Premier League. The atmosphere is less hostile.

The GFSN, in association with the Brighton & Hove Albion Supporters' Club, spent a season going around the country with the football club, which represents a town with a large gay community, analysing the abuse that their fans receive at both home and away matches. Their findings don't make for pretty reading.

Brighton's fans, the subject of the infamous 'We can see you holding hands' chant, received homophobic abuse in at least 70% of their away games and around 57% of all matches. The abuse ranged from the moderate – 'Does your boyfriend know you're here?' – to the more malicious – 'You're just a town full of faggots.'

Nottingham Forest's fans gave Brighton the whole repertoire. The GFSN reported that they heard the two less malicious chants above as well as: 'You only sing when you're bumming', 'Have you ever shagged a girl?', as well as sporadic shouts of 'faggots', 'gay' and 'nonce', with a number of limp-wristed gestures from a certain section of the crowd.

The abuse wasn't even limited to fans. In an early season encounter with Hull City, a Hull player rubbed his hands up and down his buttocks while standing with his back to the Brighton fans. It was a move that was meant to antagonise, and it did.

What did the Football Association do about it? What did the police do about it? They reassured the GSFN and the Brighton & Hove Albion Supporters' Club that there was a zero-tolerance approach to homophobia in place. Then they took no action. None of the clubs were fined. No points were docked. The player in question got off scot-free. That inaction needs to be changed. Manchester City's fans booed the UEFA Champions League anthem ahead of their game and their club was fined for it. The GFSN present all of their findings and nothing happens. Does that make booing a song worse than abusive chants which dramatically impact peoples' lives? I guess it does.

The vast majority of the abuse reported was aimed at Brighton's supporters. It makes you wonder what would happen if the sets of supporters dishing out the abuse had to cheer on a homosexual player wearing their team's colours? I'd be inclined to think that they'd support him as long as everything was going well and he was playing well. Then he'd be tolerated, maybe even championed by his own fans.

We've seen it before with racism. As recently as 2003, a section of fans sang: 'We all agree, our coons are better than your coons' at a Premier League game. Fortunately, attitudes have moved on from that mode of thinking, yet applied to ho-mophobia, we're not even at that level of acceptance – if you can call it that – yet.

Homophobia, directed from supporters toward their own players, already goes on to some extent, and that's without any players being out. If a player doesn't go in for a tackle you can often hear a stray 'get stuck in you faggot'; if a player wears gloves to play in then he's labelled a 'poof'. You always get these football fans who get offended as soon as their traditional notion of masculinity is challenged by what they see on the pitch. If they suddenly had to cheer on a player who openly challenged their masculine ideal, who contradicted their beliefs and didn't care what they thought, and then had the audacity to go through a bad spell on the pitch then, well, I'm not sure he'd have a positive experience.

What is needed is for homophobia to start being treated the same as racism. At the moment, there's no way the two prob-lems are treated anywhere near the same. Where we are with homophobia is where we were with racism in the 1990s. That's not to say that racism in football is a problem that has been totally eradicated – particularly in countries such as Russia – but it's thankfully come a long way since the days of monkey chants and banana skins being thrown at players.

Back in those days, racism wasn't necessarily seen as a prob-lem, and it's only been in recent years that homophobia has begun to be seen as an issue. Now, racism in English football is rarely seen, despite the fact that we live in a society that is still racist. The fall-out from the European Union referendum, with tensions over migration leading to the rise of far-right political groups, has shown that racism and xenophobia are still alive. Yet in the football stands racism is not far from being non-existent.

It's unrealistic to expect homophobia to be purged from

our society in the near future, yet the fact that football has gone some way to tackling racism should be used as a blueprint for homophobia. Of course, there are obvious differences between the two. For starters, it's pretty easy to spot a black player, whereas spotting a homosexual player is impossible unless he is out. It makes it easier for black players to dispel prejudices. It is prejudice that unites us, however. Black people didn't choose to be black and homosexuals didn't choose to be homosexual. We can't help what is natural.

There have been a number of fantastic initiatives to rid football of racism. Homophobia, on the other hand? We have our designated Football vs. Homophobia Day where everyone is all cheery and happy. But what actually happens? If I went to a referee and said: 'This player has just called me gay', what's going to happen? If I go to the same referee, however, and tell him that the player in question has called me a coon, then what's going to happen? A sending off, straight off, no questions and a lengthy report to the Football Association.

It makes no sense. We seem to have forgotten all about the individual. People are so busy ticking boxes and wanting to look good so they can get their diversity awards, they forget that these are individual lives at stake. Yet because of the awards and the boxes there's no real will to change anything. Someone has committed suicide over the issue and still the penny hasn't actually dropped at how this toxic atmosphere can affect peoples' lives.

Maybe it's that people are fearful of being 'accused' of being homosexual. It figures. Homosexuality is seen as not 'macho'. Questioning a man's masculinity is a big faux-pas. Men don't want to be seen as 'not macho'. Even straight guys with nothing to worry about can fear this labelling. It's easier with racism. You wear your skin colour on your outside. You can't be accused of not being white if you report racism. Sexuality though? That's far more complex, and maybe it holds some people back.

You have to start making examples of people. Start fining individuals, start docking clubs points, start sacking people. It begins with the FA themselves. There are so many old-school coaches who spout this racist, homophobic dialogue.

I recently completed an FA coaching course and the tutor certainly wasn't doing much for race relations. There was a Chinese man on the course, and the tutor spent the whole week referring to him as Jackie Chan and making kung-fu noises whenever the ball went near him. Of course, the black man on the course was referred to as Denzel for the entire week. They both played along and everything was done in good humour but was it really? This is an FA course run by FA people for goodness sake... How is this acceptable?

I compare that to my police training. There was another person training alongside me who kept on using 'gay' in a derogatory way. Oh, this is gay, that's gay. Eventually I got fed up and reported him. Just like that, he was kicked off the training. Yet in football it's totally acceptable and that needs to change. You only ever effect change when something is made law. Make homophobic abuse a bookable offence, for example. We're happy enough to reward people for minor change, or for saying they've changed, because, to be honest, anyone can be a saint when there's money or some FA certificate involved. We're not happy to bring in rulings which would have a major effect, however.

You wonder what happens in the academies at professional football clubs. Each club must have hundreds of young players on their books. How many of them are going to be gay? There's bound to be some, but how many of them are not going to progress because they think it's not necessarily a safe environment for them?

Attitudes filter down eventually. If a current Premier League star came out as gay, I'm sure they'd be well supported and I'm sure it would help to change the football culture. It'd be interesting to see if a player plying his trade in League One or Two would get similar support. I suspect not, and to be honest it's unlikely. Players at that level are effectively self-employed. They don't have the luxury of a long, lucrative contract. Coming out as gay without such luxury would be a hell of a risk. That's why it will probably have to be a player from the top end of the game.

It was reported during the 2015/16 season that two Premier League stars were toying with the idea of coming out publicly as gay. Good on them. The time is right. Every time a story like that emerges I always log on to Twitter to see the reaction. Every other comment is always 'Well, who cares. It doesn't matter'. But it does matter. It matters so much to the person involved. It is literally a life-changing moment. To them, it matters more than anything.

I don't know whether it will happen any time soon. Football seems still a long way away from something like that taking place. It is strange, though, because at Birmingham City quite a few of the support staff are gay. It's the same at Aston Villa and why wouldn't they be? Football clubs have a lot of staff members. It's the same in the newsrooms, the media centres, the television networks, the offices, so to say that football as a whole is homophobic simply isn't true. It just seems to be on the pitch, the training ground and in the stands that this homophobia lingers. As soon as the setting changes something clicks and everything is different.

The breakthrough will come once we truly reach all on the pitch, the training ground and in the stands. That's when clubs won't need to get rewarded for their 'anti-homophobia' stance. That's when being accepting of homosexuals will be the norm, rather than simply paying lip service.

I don't necessarily think that we have a problem with homophobia at grass roots level. That's not to say that the game there is free of homophobia, but it's just at a more personal level. It's individuals who have prejudice, and when they meet a gay footballer they soon change their tune. All it takes is for them to get to know such a player.

There's still a lot of casual homophobia, mind, and that needs to change. People don't even think when they spout it, and it's rarely done maliciously. Unfortunately, that is precisely the issue. These people aren't aware of what they're saying even though they're actually having a massive effect on others. It's how they've been brought up, to expose others subconsciously for any weakness. That's why you get this straight, muscular, Caucasian male ideal that is put on a pedestal. Everything else is inferior.

In my experience, if someone who is gay performs the same task to the same standard as a straight person, it'll always be perceived that the straight person has done the task better. Gay people are always perceived to be weaker and less macho, even when they've proved that's just not the case.

Physically, most of us gay footballers will compete with anyone on the pitch. We'll happily fight all day long for our team. People don't expect it when they come to watch. They go away saying 'I can't believe you're gay'. If that's the case then how many other people must they speak to in their normal day-to-day life who they didn't know were gay? Probably quite a few, yet it only becomes an issue once the person finds out. The truth doesn't benefit the straight, muscular, Caucasian male, so these lies get spread. Gays are weaker. Gays can't play football. Gays aren't aggressive enough. The result? The straight, muscular, Caucasian male holds on to their fictional macho powers. It's only a matter of time though. We're living in a world where the boundaries are forever shifting.

The true breakthrough is getting closer. Through our efforts on the pitch we're challenging outdated misconceptions of masculinity. Society is getting ever more liberal. I don't blame my parents for their reactions toward homophobia when I was younger. They were merely the reactions of a wider society. Now that society is more liberal, parents are more accepting. It makes the potential impact that role models can have on young people unsure of their sexuality all the more profound.

If a top footballer came out it could be a game changer. If the Football Association started to take homophobia seriously it could have an impact beyond measure. Soon a book like this won't need to be written. A person's sexuality will not be an issue in football. We'll be a million miles away from the tragedy of Justin Fashanu. It may take another year or five years; it may take 25. All I know for certain is that it will happen. Personally, I can't wait for that beautiful day to come.

24

A Premier League Player's Story

The world of professional football is different to any other. People say footballers at the top are sheltered, that they don't understand the life of your average bloke who lets out his emotions on a Saturday afternoon after a week of nine-to-fives. If that's the case then they definitely wouldn't understand the struggle that those of us have faced with coming out. Would they accept a gay player in their team? Would they put on one face for the cameras and another for the dressing room banter? I'd like to think not, but I had to find out.

I asked some people, who asked some other people, who asked some further people, and eventually I tracked down a professional footballer. You'll have heard of him, I'm sure you will have, but he wants to remain anonymous. It's the sad fact of the matter. He's got a family, he's got a wife, yet if he declares his support for gay footballers there's a chance he'll be stigmatised. People might ask questions. It's not a risk he's willing to take. Not yet, anyway...

* * *

'I just want to play football. That's all I want to do. Getting out there on that pitch in front of thousands of fans who are all cheering you on – there's no better feeling. I've had a good career. When I retire I can sit back and reflect with a smile. I've played in the Premier League. I've played for my country. I've scored a lot of goals, won a lot of medals and

lived the dream of millions of people all over the world.

Until recently, I'd never played with an openly gay player. Nor had any of my teammates.

It made for a strange feeling in the changing room when we knew we were going to sign an openly gay player. Not a bad kind of strange, more a 'don't know what to expect' kind of strange.

It turned out not to be a problem. Not in the slightest. I've had a pretty liberal upbringing so I was always OK with it, and I'm pretty sure everyone else in the team was too. All we cared about was how he played in our team.

I didn't feel uncomfortable showering with him around and I didn't feel uncomfortable getting changed. The only thing that mattered was what happened on the pitch. Maybe there'd have been some attraction but it's only natural. You can look at any woman on the street and fancy her. You can't stop the thoughts but what are you going to do? It's just a feeling. It doesn't hurt anyone. You look but you don't do anything. He'd have been the same. His thoughts are only natural. As long as he didn't hurt or intimidate anyone – which he never did – then it was fine.

He didn't want any of us to tip-toe around him. He is who he is and he didn't want to hide that. We have bits of banter with him and he encourages it. He just laughs it off and comes back with something else. To be honest, I never would have known that he was gay if he hadn't come out.

It makes me wonder if I have played with other players who are gay. I must have. I really do feel for them if they ever felt too scared to come out. If they're gay or bi-sexual or whatever they should be allowed to express themselves. They shouldn't have to live a lie. They shouldn't feel like they have to go out with girls and look this way or that way or whatever.

In my opinion it is 100% OK for a gay player to come out. They should be allowed to. That being said, I understand why they don't. I respect my teammate for making his decision. It must have been an incredibly tough one to make. He was so brave and he's been rewarded with an overwhelmingly positive reaction. In the changing rooms he's well accepted. He's one of our best players. He has a partner but we have normal conversations about our personal lives. It's just normal. I act the same around him as I would around anyone else. My other teammates feel the same way.

There have been no negative comments thrown in his direction from the fans either. It helps that we're not in England. Think about all the chants you hear over there. 'He's gay, he's bent, his ass is up for rent.' Then there was that period when fans used to sing 'eggy bum' at Fernando Torres to insinuate that he was gay.

There are differences in the changing rooms too. In English changing rooms there are players who would say that they wouldn't play with a gay player. I've heard players tell how they'd be devastated if their son or brother was gay. I've even heard players say they'd disown them for such a heinous crime.

The Premier League gets players from all over the world, which is brilliant. But some of the places they come from are very conservative and very much influenced by religious beliefs. I know for a fact that in the leagues that these players have played in before, players would get disowned if they came out. Former teammates have told me that there'd be no chance for them. It's wrong, they'd tell me, it's in the Holy Book. They'd carry on: 'I don't like gays. It's wrong. That's it.' Short, sharp and to the point, their minds closing and closing.

Over here it's just not like that. This is a pretty bold statement, but I'd go as far as saying there is no homophobia in football. In England there is. It is much more ingrained in the football culture. There's so much stigma attached to being gay. It's in the language: You're a faggot. That's gay. Don't be a poof. Tackle him. Then there's the view that gays aren't as tough. That they're 'fairies'. How idiotic can you get?

In England there's still stigma attached toward actively supporting homosexuality. You only have to make one move and people will instantly start to question you. Because of this, footballers are often scared to show their support. Think back to Matt Jarvis, when he did the cover for Attitude. He got a lot of abuse for that. People coming up to his wife and asking her about him. People 'accusing' him of being gay. All he did was have his picture taken!

Things are getting better in England. It's not as bad as it once was. In *society in general there has been less homophobia and greater strides toward equality, and this is reflected to an extent in the stands. The courses that organisations like the FA are running, coupled with campaigns such as Stonewall's Rainbow Laces, are improving peoples' awareness and understanding.*

There's good work that's being done. We're getting closer. Now it's time for the final push. More needs to be done. **"**

25

Reader, I Married Him

With Birmingham Blaze, Dave and I were having success on the pitch. It wasn't going too bad off it, either. We'd got over the potential banana skin posed by Budapest and were going from strength to strength, despite the distance and my shift pattern limiting the time we could see each other. To try and maximise the time we did have, we'd make the days we spent together the same days that we had training. It was a way of killing two birds with one stone, though it meant that everything we did revolved around football.

Still, I spent pretty much every single day off I had with Dave. Because of football we were mainly around Birmingham, and together we must have visited every zoo and aircraft museum in the country. Admittedly, they were two passions of mine, but who doesn't love looking at animals? Aircrafts are a bit more of a specialist interest, and though Dave never complained I'm not sure he quite realised just how many there were. It all meant that I more or less ended up moving to Birmingham. I'd take this big bag up to Dave's house and live out of it for as long as possible. At one stage it got so bad that I ended up shopping for a whole new wardrobe to keep at Dave's.

Dave would occasionally come to stay at mine down in Oxford for a few days. It made much more sense for me to be closer to him though. Our relationship moved on to the next stage when we decided to get a cat together. To this day, I still don't know what was going through our minds when we made that decision. The cat initially stayed at mine in Oxford, only for us to realise that I was rarely there. When you factored in my hours spent at work and added in the time spent at football and at Dave's, you really were talking about a minimal amount of time. So we relocated the cat to Dave's house, which the cat wasn't very happy about, particularly because Dave had a great big dog in the house.

Moving in was the next step. It was logical. Dave thought that it was going to take a long conversation. He knew all about the bad experience I'd had in moving in with Chris and he understood any caution on my part. Without my knowledge, he began to research jobs down south so that he could make the move in with me. If he came to Oxford, where I was comfortable, he believed that it would be easier to make the next logical step. What Dave didn't know was that I couldn't wait to escape Oxford. I had a whole former life to cleanse. All of those bad memories, those lies, the constant reminders of the struggle I'd had – I wanted to be away from them and suddenly I had an opportunity to do just that. It was time to begin a new chapter.

Those bad memories ended up making everything take a bit longer than it should have done. I was walking down a well trodden path, only this time it truly seemed different. We'd officially been together for a number of months and the relationship still hadn't grown stale. Every time I saw Dave I got that excitement. I genuinely loved him from the bottom of my heart. Unlike with some of the others, the attraction never got old. It felt different and it felt right.

In the end, the conversation was much easier than either of us thought it would be and we agreed a date for me to move to Birmingham – July 4th – our own Independence Day, timed perfectly with the contract on my house in Oxford running out and Dave's female housemate, whom I had never particularly got on with, moving out. It just made sense, and not only because my rent would be less than half of what it was in Oxford. I'd continue with my job as an ambulance dispatcher down in Oxford. The hours in the job were long but the days weren't frequent. A typical week would see me do three shifts of 12 hours, so it was perfectly feasible to make the 90-minute journey down south.

Finally, I was moving away from everything that I'd tried but failed to move away from for years. It'd be so much easier to block out everything that had happened. A new life was on offer, and it was a new life with a man for whom I had special feelings.

After what seemed like an eternity, the day came. I hired a removal van and lugged all my stuff up to Birmingham where an anxious Dave greeted me. I couldn't work out why he was acting so strangely. It was supposed to be our special day. He greeted me with a brief hug and a peck on the cheek, then spent the next 10 minutes pacing about. He couldn't string a sentence together. Was he having second thoughts? It was like Budapest all over again. My reliably pessimistic mind jumped to the worst of conclusions. He wasn't ready. But my boxes were all over his house. My whole life was unravelling with my possessions barely out of the van. I had nowhere else to go. I didn't want to go back to Oxford. I wanted a new chapter. A new life.

And then he was on one knee. The bastard was on one knee and there was a gigantic ring in his hand. He looked at me and I looked at him. Time stopped. All I could feel was the beat of my heart. Bump. Bump. Bump. A trickle of sweat ran down my forehead. My goodness, if you want to shut me up just propose to me. It's the only known way of making me quiet for at least a couple of seconds. And then the words came out. Slowly but surely, they came.

"Will you marry me?"

Four softly spoken words, just like my Mum's all those years ago. As her four words had done back then, Dave's hit me hard. It was like the wave on the shore all over again, only this shore wasn't rocky. It was anything but. It was a beach. A wave against a smooth beach of pure, white sand, stretching into the distance. Into eternity. I looked at Dave. I really looked at him. Those eyes, they were fixed on me, his emotion washing through me. It was different. It was real. Everything was real. Everything was clear. It was true.

And do you know what happened? Reader, I married him.

But only after I'd said no. That damned defence mechanism I'd perfected in my days of deceit. It was the exact same mechanism that had been triggered when my Mum asked if I was gay. A lifetime of inner torment and you're always on the defensive.

Dave popped the question and my instant reply was "No". He stopped. I stopped. Everything stopped. For seconds, minutes, hours. Why on earth had I said No? I couldn't work it out. And so I said "Yes". Dave, who looked deflated, moved his eyes up to me slowly. Yes. I said it again. His mind was racing, the words entering his brain without being fully processed. Yes. Yes. Yes. Over and over again I said it. Slowly, so slowly, he smiled and embraced me.

Just like my Mum, Dave always knew.

26
Championing the Cause

My sexuality and football are both equally as important in my life. They define me. It's just a shame that the two can't often be intertwined. Literally speaking they can, of course, but it evokes a lot of conflict. Sometimes it feels like I go from one conflict to another in a series of never ending issues.

Life would have been easier without football. There's no doubting that. I'd have probably had another hobby, something like stamp collecting, and there's not much homophobia in collecting stamps. Then there's school. Looking back now I can see how torn I was – a young male coming to terms with his sexuality, yet infatuated with a traditionally 'macho' sport. How could I have fitted in with the 'macho' sport when gay people are the antithesis of 'macho'? Over and over in my head there was a little voice which repeated 'you play football, you can't be gay'.

I didn't know what I was. Without football, school would have been a lot easier. There'd have been less need to pretend to be someone I wasn't, less confusion about my true identity. I'm not saying that I would have definitely come out during my school days if I hadn't been involved in football, but it certainly would have been more likely. For starters I'd have been more likely to accept my natural feelings toward men, rather than mask them with a number of caring yet ultimately meaningless girlfriends. There'd have been nothing to hide – other than from my family.

There's the flip side. Football bonds fathers and sons, and more and more it is bonding mothers and sons. Subconsciously it probably made it easier for my Dad to accept my sexuality. He's a football man, after all, born from a generation who saw homosexuality as a disease. The fact that I not only liked, but played football, would have made it easier.

As a father you always see your son as an embodiment of yourself. You want them to be masculine; you want to be proud of them. The revelation that I was gay was almost counterbalanced by my love of football. What masculinity I'd been seen as having lost – even if he subconsciously thought so – would have been put against the fact that I not only played a masculine sport, but led by example on the pitch. My style of play was, and still is, built on the traditionally masculine concepts of strength, controlled aggression and fearlessness.

When I was wrapped in my deceit, such masculinity was a comfort blanket. I prided myself on how I conformed to those masculine ideals. I don't know why. That same sense of masculinity has plagued me all of my life. It's confused me, eroded me. The first rule of masculinity is that you don't talk about it. It meant that I built up all of this confusion, all of these emotions, and felt that I couldn't express them. I couldn't go against the conventional notion of masculinity.

But what is masculinity? Mostly just a load of bullshit. It's a set of expectations that society dictates for males, using these expectations as a stick to beat them with when they don't match the opinion of whoever is judging them on something. We made it up. A social construct. Yet if you don't conform then you get outcast.

Now that I'm in my 30s and fully at ease with my sexuality, I can claim that things are better nowadays. Of course they'll seem that way. I've been through all of the trauma and the lies and the deceit. But the statistics say that they aren't.

As recently as 2012, Stonewall conducted a 'School Report' study, which found that 16% of gay and bisexual boys and 29% of lesbian and bisexual girls have attempted suicide. 57% had contemplated taking their own life. That's more than half. If you're gay you're more likely than not to think about taking your own life. These figures are backed up by the Lesbian and Gay Foundation, which states that the suicide rate for gay youngsters is up to three times higher than for heterosexuals of the same age.

And for what? For failing to live up to this arbitrary set of values dictated by society? It breaks me, it really does. Why does so much come down to 'masculinity'? It's a totally outdated concept, used in a bygone era when men had to hunt for their food. Nowadays you just go to Tesco and buy it.

It makes the link between football and masculinity all the more ridiculous. Football is for everyone and thankfully, down to people like David Beckham blurring the boundaries, it's becoming more and more that way. You can play football if you don't go out and hunt for your food every day. You can play football if you're a woman. And you can play football if you're homosexual.

We aren't half proving that at Birmingham Blaze. Our promotion season was followed by another shot at European glory, this time at the EuroGames in Stockholm. What was more, we'd be able to do it whilst purely focused on football. Unlike in Budapest, we couldn't have been made to feel more welcome in Sweden. The reception was incredible. There were no protestors at all, quite the opposite in fact. The Swedes embraced the EuroGames. It actually seemed to be a pretty big event for the city. When we checked into our hotel and they asked the purpose of our stay, we replied that we were in Stockholm for a football tournament.

"The EuroGames?" the man on reception asked, smiling.

They were honoured to have us to stay.

With Dave, now my fiancé, as manager, and a squad of 15 to choose from, I was feeling the pressure to make an improvement on our performance in Budapest. We made it out of the group stage of the Division Two tournament with relative ease, facing London Leftfooters in the quarter final. A 7-1 win in that match got us all dreaming. We suddenly believed we could go all the way.

The result led to a tasty match in the semi final against Hot Scots, Scotland's first LGBT friendly team. The England-Scotland rivalry is fierce in gay football. Games are a matter of national pride and the intensity is always ramped up; except when two tired teams meet in the semi final, that is.

As much as both teams tried, the game was played at a speed barely above walking pace. The fixture schedule was just as crammed as it had been in Budapest, and both teams were playing their fifth game in three days. With proper preparation we could have given the neutrals a good game, but both teams' recovery methods from the previous day had been, questionable, shall we say. Despite all of society's scientific advancements, there's yet to be a beer created which is 'isotonic'. I guess the alcohol content doesn't really aid recovery either. It certainly didn't for us, anyway.

Both teams limped to half time, content to keep each other out and not lose the match. They were tiring faster than us, though, and that was proved when we made the breakthrough with 10 minutes remaining. For me to outpace someone, there's got to be something wrong. OK, my opponent was in his fifties but that's not the point. I still outpaced him before nonchalantly knocking it past the keeper and into the net. The celebrations were as crazy as can be expected of a shattered team.

I celebrated like mad, only to turn round and realise that most of my teammates were just standing there, choosing to applaud me from their position on the pitch. I didn't care; I was on a high, so much so that five minutes later lightning struck twice. For me to score twice in five minutes, well, something must have been seriously wrong. The Hot Scots definitely weren't on the isotonic beers the night before, let's put it that way.

We held out for the 2-0 win, which put us into the final against Stonewall FC. We couldn't have had a better opponent. Everybody wants to beat Stonewall because everyone in gay football dislikes Stonewall's football side. The dislike doesn't stem from all the work they've done in advancing our cause, because it's been truly fantastic. They've made a real difference and have had a positive impact on so many people's lives.

No, the dislike is there because Stonewall always win everything. They're like the Manchester United of gay football. If that wasn't enough motivation, Stonewall FC's official Twitter account had tweeted just before the game 'Today is the day we become double European champions'. Not on my watch.

As we lined up to face Stonewall the butterflies were really going. It's ridiculous. I still get butterflies before every game, even if it's only a friendly. Our opponents were Stonewall's second team. Their first team had been placed into the top tier competition and had also made it through to the final, hence their double European champions tweet. It was still set to be a tough match. I suppose you don't really get easy matches in the final of a European Championship.

As with the previous game, the final was played at a low intensity. It was a case of both teams shutting up shop and playing to not lose the game rather than really going for it. I had a half chance when there was a great pass played through, but as I couldn't run it meant that the ball just evaded my outstretched leg.

That small sniff was about as exciting as the game got. It

dragged on and on until just before penalties, when players from both teams began to get mysterious injuries. 'Don't-want-to-take-a-penalty-itis' is the medical term, I believe. The inevitable happened and the referee blew his whistle and though I hadn't suffered a mystery injury, I really didn't want to take a penalty either. Through sheer politeness – 'Oh, go on mate, you have it...you can do it' – I managed to make myself the sixth penalty taker. I just needed the boys to do the business.

As I looked over at Steve, I knew I'd made a mistake. He was due to take the fifth penalty and he was pacing up and down, his cheeks puffed out.

"I'm going to score, Neil, I'm going to score," he said over and over again. As the penalties started getting dispatched, he increased the intensity. "I'm going to score."

As soon as I saw that I knew that he wasn't going to. Up he stepped and up the ball went, right over the crossbar. There's a chance NASA have got an image of where the ball ended up. It meant that it was all down to our keeper, Josh, to keep us in it.

Fortunately I had complete faith in Josh. He'd been on the books of Tottenham Hotspur as a kid, and if he'd bothered to maintain any form of fitness he could have been a hell of a player. He was our safe pair of hands and now we needed him more than ever.

Their player placed the ball on the spot, took aim and fired. Josh guessed right, springing to his left and deflecting the ball round the post. Relief, pure relief, flooded over us, at least until I realised that it was me up next. But what was Josh doing? He was going crazy. He was sprinting toward us, arms raised, yelling at the top of his voice. Then the referee put his whistle to his lips and blew up. It was over. We'd won.

It was the strangest feeling ever. A true anti-climax. Other than Josh, none of us really knew what had happened. I'd miscounted the number of penalties we had taken and because I was trying to motivate our players after each penalty, they'd all thought I knew what was going on. They'd followed my lead and were also waiting for the next penalty.

Stonewall, on the other hand, had realised that they had been defeated. There they stood, their heads bowed, their fallen taker looking to the gods. I'm not sure they were too used to losing. Fortunately for us, our non-celebration came across as rather dignified. I should have been happy, ecstatic even, but I wasn't. I was bewildered. Absolutely bewildered. It didn't matter, though, because guess what? I was also a European champion.

I'll never get tired of telling people that I'm a European champion. It's the proudest moment of my life by far and not one I'm going to forget in a hurry. It makes a nice change. So much of my life has been about forgetting. You always want to forget the bad and remember the good, and over my life there's been a lot of bad. Living a lie, refusing to come out, the trauma that I put my 'girlfriend' through, taking her virginity, cheating on Adam – they're memories that make me shudder. All of the pressure that I felt from the society in which I lived resulted in some bad life choices. I wasn't thinking straight. I wasn't me. I wasn't allowed to be me.

As a result of these memories, I always think things are going to be worse than they end up being. Life is a series of disasters waiting to happen, especially when you're a gay man in a straight world. Things are changing, though.

Recently my life has had far more good than bad, none more so than the European Championship win. Getting engaged to Dave, then marrying him in the August of 2016, wasn't bad, either. It's strange how life improves as you become more comfortable in your own skin.

Football has gone a long way toward making that improvement. I've never felt more at ease on a football pitch than I do at the moment. It's still a form of escapism, but the fewer worries I have away from the pitch mean that I can channel more of my energy into actually enjoying the experience.

Writing this book wasn't easy. I've spent a lot of my life trying to run from the memories written on these pages. They were buried deep, deep in my mind; muddled, half forgotten but always lingering. Putting them on paper with my co-writer Seth Burkett has been a form of liberation. It's allowed me to stop running. It's allowed me to accept these memories for what they are, to accept myself for who I was and, most importantly, for who I am.

I'm Neil Beasley. I'm gay. And I'm a football fan, a football player and a football club chairman.

Acknowledgements

When I first started out as Blaze chairman I had no idea what I was doing and didn't know where I could go to for help. I found myself in Waterstones in Birmingham looking through the football section, where I found a book called *Floodlit Dreams* which was by Ian Ridley, who had become chairman of the club he supported, Weymouth FC, and tried his best to turn the club around.

I found this book totally enthralling and could not put it down. Having enjoyed the book so much, I went out and brought another of Ian's books called *There's A Golden Sky*, which looked at the effect the first 20 years of the Premier League had had on football. Appreciating how much Ian's books had helped pass the time during nightshifts, I tweeted Ian the pictures of his books and stated how much I had enjoyed them, asking if he would sign them for me. He obliged after sending me his address via Twitter.

Several weeks later, after many months of wondering if it were viable, I messaged Ian and asked if he thought anyone would be interested in publishing my story about my life as a gay football supporter and player. He asked me to write a chapter and send it to him. Though this thought thoroughly scared me, I gave it a go.

Ian must have liked the story because he suggested that I work with a young guy called Seth Burkett, who was himself a published author. I had already read Seth's book *The Boy In*

Brazil, in which he talked about his time playing football professionally in Brazil. I owe so much to Ian and Seth. Ian gave me
the opportunity and supported me throughout. Seth and I have
become good friends and I value him highly. He's had to put
up with my awful memory, poor time-keeping and constantly
changing my mind. He's made me laugh and smile whilst also
asking deep and probing questions. Some more welcome than
others... I will remain friends with these two forever and will
never forget what they have done for me.

I must also thank my soulmate, rock and husband David,
without whom none of this would have been possible. Everything we have achieved at Birmingham Blaze is down to David's passion and enthusiasm. He helped me with this book by
allowing his own difficult story to be told and helped me recall
events and moments that we shared together. I also need to
apologise to David for my constant moaning and complaining,
for making his job as Blaze manager more difficult and for leaving my clothes all over the place. I am not easy to live with...

I am also grateful to my family who have always stood by
me. I appreciate that I haven't always been easy but which son
is? Their continued support in recent years, particularly every
time there is a problem with my car or when I can't even afford
food, has been very much appreciated. My Dad came to watch
Blaze play recently to support me even though my sister was
in labour. It seems there are very few things that are more important than football. I would also like to mention my nephew
Zachary. Even looking at pictures of him smiling gives me endless joy.

I have been welcomed by my new family members from
David's side – his Dad Robert, Mum Julie and brothers Joseph
and Luke, and their partners Emma and Kate respectively. Not
forgetting the family dog Molly, whose hair I am forever trying
to get off my clothes.

There is also someone not quite a family member but whom in recent years I have become very fond of, and that is my Godmother's son, Josh. We've had some good laughs over text when I've been working nights and he's been out drinking. His love life has given me hours of entertainment and will no doubt turn him grey before long.

Then there are all the people who have made Birmingham Blaze the force it is, starting with Joe S, Anthony and Ben, without whose tireless efforts behind the scenes all the success on the field would not have been possible. In addition, my thanks go to Joe Varney, with whom I have played for a long time, and Josh Holt, who is the best goalkeeper I've played with. Time and time again, Josh has bailed out our many mistakes at the back and his handling is second to none. His many penalty saves are legendary. Well, within Blaze anyway.

Thanks, too, to close friends in the team Steve Atkinson, Craig Simpson, Matt Hall and Kiahno Dhillion. The one player that made me realise what was possible was Luke Yates, whose legs at times appear to be telescopic. Adam Fox, Joe Yates, Matt Matthews, Tom Rose, JP, Craig Underdown and Taz have between them provided many stunning goals and laughs. Andy (Daddy) King has sponsored the club and become a great friend, as have many others at The Fox, and Max Woodhouse from my new team Castlecroft Rangers has been supportive and given me an opportunity to manage and coach with him.

There have been so many people who deserve a thank you over the years. Blaze has been like a family and the memories will stay with me forever. Everyone who has been a part of it knows what I mean.

Neil Beasley
Birmingham, July 2016

ABOUT THE CO-AUTHOR

Seth Burkett was born in 1991 and grew up in Stamford, Lincolnshire. On leaving school he received an offer to play professional football in Brazil. His first solo book, *The Boy in Brazil*, details his experiences and was shortlisted for Football Book of the Year at the 2015 British Sport Book Awards. Seth has a degree in English from Loughborough University, where he also played futsal, representing England B.
He now lives and works in London.

ALSO BY SETH BURKETT

THE BOY IN BRAZIL
Living Learning and Loving
in the Land of Football

DEVELOPING THE MODERN
FOOTBALLER THROUGH FUTSAL
With Michael Skubala

THE YEAR OF THE HOBBY
With Molly Burkett

ALSO BY FLOODLIT DREAMS

ADDED TIME
Surviving Cancer, Death Threats and the Premier League
Mark Halsey with Ian Ridley

THE BOY IN BRAZIL
Living, Learning and Loving in the Land of Football
By Seth Burkett

A DAZZLING DARKNESS
The Darren Barker Story
Darren Barker with Ian Ridley

THE SOCCER SYNDROME
English Football's Golden Age
By John Moynihan
(Foreword by Patrick Barclay)

THE HITLER TROPHY
Golf and the Olympic Games
By Alan Fraser

READER, I MARRIED HIM: Dave and Neil.